International Music
Journals

Historical Guides to the World's Periodicals and Newspapers

This series provides historically focused narrative and analytical profiles of periodicals and newspapers with accompanying bibliographical data.

Children's Periodicals of the United States
R. Gordon Kelly, editor

International Film, Radio, and Television Journals
Anthony Slide, editor

Science Fiction, Fantasy, and Weird Fiction Magazines
Marshall B. Tymn and Mike Ashley, editors

American Indian and Alaska Native Newspapers and Periodicals, 1925–1970
Daniel F. Littlefield, Jr., and James W. Parins, editors

Magazines of the American South
Sam G. Riley

Religious Periodicals of the United States: Academic and Scholarly Journals
Charles H. Lippy, editor

British Literary Magazines: The Modern Age, 1914–1984
Alvin Sullivan, editor

American Indian and Alaska Native Newspapers and Periodicals, 1971–1985
Daniel F. Littlefield, Jr., and James W. Parins, editors

Index to Southern Periodicals
Sam G. Riley

American Literary Magazines: The Eighteenth and Nineteenth Centuries
Edward E. Chielens, editor

American Humor Magazines and Comic Periodicals
David E. E. Sloane, editor

Index to City and Regional Magazines of the United States
Sam G. Riley and Gary W. Selnow, compilers

INTERNATIONAL MUSIC JOURNALS

Edited by
Linda M. Fidler
and
Richard S. James

Historical Guides to the World's Periodicals and Newspapers

Greenwood Press
New York • Westport, Connecticut • London

Library of Congress Cataloging-in-Publication Data

International music journals / edited by Linda M. Fidler and Richard
    S. James.
        p.   cm.—(Historical guides to the world's periodicals and
    newspapers, ISSN 0742-5538)
        Bibliography: p.
        Includes index.
        ISBN 0-313-25004-9 (lib. bdg. : alk. paper)
        1. Music—Periodicals—Bibliography.   2. Music—Periodicals—
    History.   I. Fidler, Linda M.   II. James, Richard S.   III. Series.
    ML128.P24I6   1990
    016.78′05—dc20   89-11842

British Library Cataloguing in Publication Data is available.

Library of Congress Catalog Card Number: 89-11842
ISBN: 0-313-25004-9
ISSN: 0742-5538

First published in 1990

Greenwood Press, Inc.
88 Post Road West, Westport, Connecticut 06881

Printed in the United States of America

The paper used in this book complies with the
Permanent Paper Standard issued by the National
Information Standards Organization (Z39.48-1984).

10 9 8 7 6 5 4 3 2 1

Contents

Acknowledgments   vii

Introduction by Richard S. James   ix

Profiles of International Music Journals   1

Appendix A: New Journals of the 1980s   458

Appendix B: Music Periodical Indexes   471

Appendix C: Chronological Listing of Periodicals by Title   482

Appendix D: Geographical Listing of Periodicals by Title   487

Appendix E: Subject Listing of Periodicals by Title   493

Selected Bibliography   501

Index   503

Contributors   539

Acknowledgments

An undertaking such as this one owes its success not only to the consultants and contributors, but to the people whose assistance frequently goes unacknowledged. We would like to offer our thanks to the following people whose help and support have seen us through this project: to our graduate assistants Patricia Hodges, Aletha Johnson, Julie Kemp, Jolene Parker, and Suzanne Thierry, for their diligence in seeking out missing details; to the librarians and staff at the music libraries of the University of Michigan, Oberlin College Conservatory of Music, the University of Arizona, the University of North Carolina at Chapel Hill, the Library of Congress and New York Public Library—Lincoln Center, for assistance in locating materials; to Michelle Koth and Michael Fling at Indiana University, for verifying bibliographic information; to the Bowling Green State University Faculty Research Committee for financial support in the indexing of the manuscript; to Lee Norden for his computer expertise and assistance in the indexing; to Robin Lamprecht, who entered the contributions onto computer; and to our families—Gloria Pfeif and Flo and Jim Fidler—for the encouragement to complete the project.

Introduction

While Germany can rightly claim chronological primacy in the field of music periodicals, the word *journal* comes from the French—*journée,* day; *journalier,* daily—where its secondary meanings include diary, newspaper, day-book, and, by the eighteenth century, any periodical publication. It was gradually supplemented, in the French lexicon, by such terms as *echo, chronique, revue, gazette, album, courrier, moniteur,* and *presse.* Parallel German terminology ranges from *Wochenblatt, Nachrichten, Beiträge, Zeitung, Briefe,* and *Magazin,* to *Blatt, Archiv, Rundschau,* and, of course, *Zeitschrift,* while the English-speaking countries adopted magazine, review, register, gazette, record, circular, guide, herald, times, reporter, and news. Compound terms such as monthly journal/*journal mensuel*/*Monatschrift* added further terminological precision.

Traditionally, periodicals have served to disseminate a wide variety of information which, due to its topical or ephemeral nature, modest scale, or intended audience, does not readily lend itself to the medium of the monograph. Contents generally include some combination of the following: studies of less than monographic size, essays, critiques or reviews, editorials, reports, reader input, and news items pertaining to current musical events or the life of an institution or organization. This is often supplemented by pertinent advertising and illustrative material. The nearly universal emphasis on some sort of contemporary relevance or timeliness results in interesting declines and changes in audience and content. A final distinguishing feature of periodicals is, of course, their serial nature: they appear at more or less regular intervals, and bear some sort of sequential numbering.

The following overview summarizes the central issues, developments, trends, and types represented in the periodical literature of music. Examples will be drawn almost exclusively from the major German, French, and English-language periodicals, since these provide the central core of music periodical literature, illustrate the necessary points well, and are most readily accessible to the majority of the expected readership of this volume. To stray into the fascinating, broader world of the other Western and the many non-Western journals is simply beyond the scope of this book. The reader is advised to consult the bibliography, particularly Imogene Fellinger's *Grove* article and the many regional periodical bibliographies appearing in *Notes* for more specialized information.

The periodical devoted exclusively to musical topics is the culmination of a number of relatively autonomous pre-eighteenth-century developments in the history of periodical literature. Articles and information on musical topics were initially placed in journals of a more general nature such as *Mercure galant, Monatliche Unterredungen,* and *The Gentleman's Journal.* This practice continues to the present day and remains, in some countries, a major source of musical commentary and scholarship. The exclusion of such publications from this volume is unfortunate but, again, necessitated by space limitations.

The earliest serial publications devoted exclusively to music—appearing at the end of the seventeenth century—were not compilations of articles and information, however, but contained relatively brief musical compositions, especially songs and piano pieces. The inclusion of complete musical works continued in subsequent journals whose content was divided between text and music. More commonly, text journals often included musical supplements or inserts, a practice that has not been abandoned entirely even today.

Gradually music periodicals of an exclusively or predominantly literary nature became common. Early examples were offshoots of two existing strains in the general periodical literature: encyclopedic journals of a scholarly nature, and didactic journals intended for educational and/or moral improvement. The former may be viewed as manifestations of the waning rationalism and exclusivity of the eighteenth century. The latter, as well as the newsier general music periodicals of later in the same century, were a response to the needs and interests of the growing European middle class.

It is only appropriate to begin a survey of these early literary music journals in eighteenth-century Germany where most of the initial steps were taken. Johann Mattheson's *Critica musica . . .* (1722–25) is widely considered the first music journal. The title and lengthy subtitle of Mattheson's innovation bear translation: *Musical Criticism, that is, searching critiques and assessments of the many opinions, arguments and objections, whether preconceived or spontaneous, that are to be found in old and new, printed or handwritten, papers on music. Designed to eradicate so far as possible all vulgar error and to promote a freer growth in the pure science of harmony. Arranged in several parts and issued separately.* In seeking to develop and share a critical approach to the music of his day, Mattheson made literary history by seeking a periodical venue. Though *Critica Musica* was relatively short-lived, Mattheson's satisfication with the concept was further illustrated in his contribution to the more didactic, moralizing type of music periodicals: *Der musicalische Patriot* (1728), a series of forty-three discourses designed to defend music against decadence and outdatedness.

Mattheson's successors included Lorenz Mizler's *Neu eröffnete musikalische*

Bibliothek, oder Gründlich Nachricht nebst unpartheyischem Urtheil von mu-sikalischen Schifften und Büchern (1736/8–54) and J. A. Scheibe's *Critischer Musicus* (1737/8–39/40) (the latter actually more a parallel to *Der musicalische Patriot*). F. W. Marpurg also edited a number of both scholarly and moralizing music journals, the most important of which was the scholarly *Historisch-kritische Beyträge zur Aufnahme der Musik* (1754/5–78).

The late-eighteenth-century development of a periodical aimed at current musical events and topics of interest to the amateur was first seen in J. A. Hiller's *Wöchentliche Nachrichten und Anmerkungen die Musik betreffend* (1766/7–70). J. N. Forkel combined Hiller's content innovations with theoretical and historical items in his *Musikalisch-kritische Bibliothek* (1778–79).

From the late eighteenth century through World War I, the dominant type of music journal, both in Germany and elsewhere, followed Forkel's lead, integrating current events coverage with moderately scholarly essays of topical, theoretical, and historical interest. While a certain amount of national or regional bias was commonplace, the goal was to provide broad international coverage. Following a few clear but short-lived predecessors, this type of journal was firmly and successfully established with the *Allgemeine musikalische Zeitung* (1798/9–48). Much of the credit for both the quality and scope of the journal's subject matter and contributorship must go to its first editor, Friedrich Rochlitz (ed., 1798–1818). Even its format, dividing entries between biography, essays, reviews of books and music, descriptions of instruments, news items, letters and miscellany, became the model for many future periodicals, including *Le Ménestrel* (1833/4–1940) and *The Musical Times* (1844/5–   ). Arguably the most famous journal of this type is *Neue Zeitschrift für Musik* (1834–   ), created as a forum for the creative artist rather than the scholar. Robert Schumann, and co-editors Friedrich Wieck, Ludwig Schunke, and Julius Knorr, hoped it would militate for Romanticism and reverse the decline of (German) music after the deaths of Ludwig van Beethoven, Franz Schubert, and Carl Maria von Weber. Subsequent editors have not always been so idealistic, and partisanship has frequently reigned; yet, the journal has survived over a century of editorial and cultural vicissitudes and remains a highly regarded publication.

Finally, a new generation of these general publications, developing from the 1870s, contained less opinion and more fact. These journals were largely concerned with practical musical issues and musical life, for example, *Musikalisches Wochenblatt* (1870–1910), *Allgemeine (deutsche) Musik-Zeitung* (1874–1943), the *Neue Musik-Zeitung* (1880–1928), and *Die Musik* (1901/2–42/3).

Neighboring Austria, particularly Vienna, was also the birthplace of a wealth of early music periodicals. Most lasted only a few years; yet, many of the important aesthetic and musical debates among leading composers and critics of the day were waged in the pages of these journals, some of which were formed expressly to promote the views of certain factions. The more international, general type of periodical was also well represented, and exists even today in the form of *Oesterreichische Musikzeitung* (1946–   ).

The earliest French music journal dates from 1756 (*Sentiment d'un harmon iephile sur differents ouvrages de musique*), but the first title of note was *La Revue musicale* (1827–35). Founded by the famous scholar F. J. Fétis, *La Revue* offered both scholarly contributions and critical evaluation of Paris musical life. It was combined with *Gazette musicale de Paris* in 1934 to create *Revue et gazette musicale de Paris* (1835–80), and included material authored by such composers as Franz Liszt and Hector Berlioz. The previously mentioned *Le Ménestrel* (1833/4–1940) started in a similar vein and became gradually but moderately more scholarly.

England's first contributions of substance to the field of music periodicals were *The Quarterly Musical Magazine and Review* (1818–28) and *The Harmonicon* (1823–33). Of greater impact, however, was *The Musical World* (1836–91), a more international publication patterned to some extent on French and German predecessors and containing, in addition to historical articles, news and critiques from throughout Europe. Another early milestone was *The Musical Times*, first appearing as *The Musical Times and Singing Class Circular* in 1844. Founded by J. A. Novello, *The Musical Times* exists today as the oldest continuously published music periodical. First intended as part of the singing revival, it soon expanded to cover all aspects of music and musical life.

The United States comes somewhat later to the field of music periodicals, beginning with the *Euterpeiad* (1820/21–23), a collection of essays, notes on musical life of Boston, biographical sketches, anecdotes, and reviews. A more sustained effort, with more international content, was *Dwight's Journal of Music* (1852–81), succeeded to some extent by *Musical America* (1898–   ).

Italy also entered the music periodical arena in the early nineteenth century with a variety of titles, mostly short-lived and devoted to theater and opera. Perhaps the most significant of these was the *Gazzetta musicale di Milano* (1842–1912), which focused on Italian opera in Italy and abroad, but also included biographical, historical, and bibliographic material and current events. A more lasting, high-quality general music periodical with noted contributors and international coverage was *Rivista musicale italiana* (1894–1955), continued in 1967 as the *Nuova rivista musicale italiana*. *La rassegna musicale* (1928–62) also deserves mention as a significant, general periodical.

In contrast to the majority of general periodicals, which balance some degree of international coverage with a clear national or regional orientation, some publications have been truly international. A leading exponent here has been the International Music Society, formed originally as a reaction to the ardor of late nineteenth-century nationalism. Its publications have embodied that sentiment: *Zeitschrift der Internationalen Musik-Gesellschaft* (a news publication, 1899–1914), *Sammelbände der Internationalen Musik-Gesellschaft* (the *Zeitschrift*'s scholarly counterpart, 1899–1914), and *Acta musicologica* (1928–   ). Other international periodicals, though of narrower focus, include the *Journal of the International Folk Music Council* (1949–68), *Review of the Aesthetics and Sociology of Music* (1970–   ), and *Fontis artis musicae* (1954–   ).

By the middle of the nineteenth century, a new phase in music journals was evident. Contrary to the quasi-international, general periodicals mentioned so far, these titles were devoted to specific topics and specialties: single repertoires such as chamber music or choral music, instrument making, education and pedagogy, religious music, single composers, musicology, and specific instruments. This trend has only intensified since World War I with journals focused upon certain schools, publishers, narrower repertoires such as film music and specific types of popular music, methodologies, new technologies such as recordings or electronic music, librarianship, and entertainment. Furthermore, scholarly and nonscholarly materials have become, on the whole, more thoroughly segregated; organizations with a scholarly orientation have increasingly relegated their nonscholarly communications to a separate bulletin. Along with this larger trend, advertising and commercial interests become increasingly evident.

While tracing the rise of each type of specialized journal is well beyond the intent of this essay, the advent of the musicology journal, with a wider scope and more general nature than many a specialized journal, would seem a worthy illustration of the type. As with music periodical literature in general, the musicology journal first appears in Germany. *Caecilia* (1824–48) can be seen as a bridge between the more scholarly general periodicals and a true musicological publication, the latter featuring a broader range of historical topics and distinguished contributors. *Caecilia* became the model for Chrysander's *Jahrbücher für musikalische Wissenschaft* (1863–67) and *Allgemeine musikalische Zeitung* (1863–82), and Robert Eitner's *Monatshefte für Musikgeschichte* (1869–1905). Together these journals foreshadowed the *Vierteljahrsschrift für Musikgeschichte* (1885–94), the first mature musicological journal. With the end of World War I, a number of similar publications sprang into existence: *Archiv für Musikwissenschaft* (1918/9–   ), *Zeitschrift für Musikwissenschaft* (1918/9–35), and the *Zeitschrift*'s successor, *Archiv für Musikforschung* (1936–43). In the aftermath of World War II a similar rebirth of musicological publishing is evident: *Die Musikforschung* (1948–   ), the revival of *Archiv für Musikwissenschaft* (1952–   ), the *Deutsches Jahrbuch der Musikwissenschaft* (1957–   ), and the *Beiträge zur Musikwissenschaft* (1959–   ).

In France, the earliest musicology journal was *Revue d'histoire et de critique musicales* (1901–12), which was amalgamated with the *S.I.M. Revue musicale mensuelle* until their joint demise in 1914. Their postwar successor *Revue de musicologie* (1917/19–   ) quickly achieved a fine reputation. It was soon joined by *La Revue musicale* (1920–   ), which established itself as a major modern music forum. A more recent entry here is the impressive *Annales musicologiques* (1953–79).

The Netherlands have, for over a century, provided the noteworthy *Tijdschrift van de Vereniging voor Nederlandse Muziekgeschiedenis* (1882/5–   ). English musicology founded the *Proceedings of the (Royal) Musical Association* in 1874/5 and followed with *Music and Letters* in 1920. Both still in print, these periodicals have been joined by *The Music Review* (1940–   ). The United States has offset its somewhat later start in the field of musicology with a wealth of fine titles: *The Musical Quarterly* (1915–), *Musica disciplina* (1946–), Journal of the American Musicological Society (1948-), *Journal of Musicology* (1982–), *Nineteenth-Century Music* (1977–), and *American Music* (1983–). Italian musicology has also been highly visible since World War II with *Quaderni della rassegna musicale* (1964–72) (continuing *La rassegna musicale* [1928–62]), *Rivista italiana di musicologia* (1966–), and *Chigiana: Rassegna annuale di studi musicologici* (1964–).

The twentieth century has also seen the rise of a number of journals specializing in contemporary music. Most of these have a specific national slant or even champion a particular school's or publisher's music. Distinguished examples include the German *Melos* (1920–), Austria's *Musikblätter des Anbruch* (1919–37), the aforementioned *La Revue musicale*, the American *Modern Music* (1924–46), and *Perspectives of New Music* (1962–), *The Chesterian* (1915–19, ns. 1919–61), and *Tempo* (1939–) in England, and, from the Netherlands, *Sonorum speculum* (1958–74), which was continued as *Key Notes* (1975–), and *Interface: Journal of New Music Research* (1972–).

The combined impact of the Great Depression and World War II destroyed or transformed a huge number of journalistic ventures and was especially hard on those journals already struggling to keep abreast of the changing times. Others were merged and reborn under different names. Yet music periodicals as a whole rebounded vigorously, and numerous vital new titles appeared. In addition to some of the musicological ventures mentioned above, one might note England's *Music and Musicians* (1952–) and *Early Music* (1973–), *The Black Perspective in Music* (1973–), and *The Journal of Music Theory* (1957–) from the United States, the Dutch *Mens en melodie* (1946–), Germany's *Zeitschrift für Musiktheorie* (1970–78) and *Musique en jeu* (1970–) from France.

There are several fine guides to periodical literature in music, a selective list of which appears in the bibliography. Most of these delimit their contents along geographical or linguistic lines and attempt to be all-inclusive within these boundaries. As a result, they take the form of checklists, usually with extended bibliographic information and/or some sort of brief annotation.

The present volume, by contrast, attempts no such comprehensiveness. Instead, the editors have sought considerably more in-depth characterization and evaluation of the leading journals throughout the many musical professions. It was conceived as a thoroughly international and cross-disciplinary guide, and includes titles of historical as well as contemporary significance. In addition to journals representing the traditional fields of music scholarship (musicology, ethnomusicology, theory, therapy, education, and their subcategories), publications important in performance, composition, popular music, discography, and librarianship are included.

The selection of journals for inclusion was based on several criteria: length of run, quality of content, historical importance, nature of contents, impact on the discipline or subdiscipline, uniqueness of coverage or approach, and regional importance. Journals also needed to be reasonably likely of inclusion in the collections of at least the major Western research libraries, for example, accessible to the expected readership of this volume. Beginning with Imogene Fellinger's massive catalog of music periodicals in *The New Grove Dictionary of Music and Musicians,* we initially narrowed the list to 350. This list was then sent to an international group of nine consultants—major figures from the United States and Europe in a variety of musical disciplines as well as library science— who were asked to add any titles they felt deserved mention and suggest what they would remove from the list to achieve our goal of 150 to 175 items. Collation of their responses and the final selection of titles were the work of the editors.

The length assigned to each entry was likewise governed by the type of coverage, content, quality, impact, and longevity of the journal. No completely objective formula proved satisfactory, however; various more subjective factors also were taken into account. For instance, a current events journal with a colorful, thirty-year history comprised of numerous significant changes of editorial policy, coverage, and format might necessitate more space than a leading scholarly journal that has been very consistent over a sixty-year run and could thus be concisely summarized.

Contributors to *International Music Journals* were asked to address five general aspects of each journal: (1) physical properties: size, typical number of pages, design, layout, and languages; (2) historical issues: origin and circumstances of founding, founding individuals or institutions, title(s) and any title changes, stated aims and purposes, editors and editorial policies, contributorship, frequency and regularity, publishers and their role, and reason(s) for cessation (if applicable); (3) content profile: subject area(s) and time period(s) covered; number, length, and depth of articles and reviews; geographical scope; editorial content; regular features and departments; special issues and supplements; internal indexes; and advertising; (4) critical assessement: social, political, economic, cultural, artistic, and ideological issues affecting the journal; level and quality of material; significant viewpoints or positions; influence of the journal; role and impact of individual contributors, editors, organizations, or advertisers; outstanding issues and articles; innovations; degree to which stated aims and purposes were fulfilled; the role of advertising; reactions to the journal; and relation to other journals in the same or related fields; and (5) bibliography: reviews, histories, and external indexing.

Finally, journal essays are arranged alphabetically by journal titles in this volume. These titles have, of course, frequently changed, merged, or been absorbed, as catalogued in each essay. Generally, journals appear under their most recent or present title, but exceptions were made for journals best known or longest published under earlier titles (for example, Schumann's famous journal will be found under *Neue Zeitschrift für Musik,* not *NZ Neue Zeitschrift für Musik*).

Richard S. James

International Music
Journals

Profiles of
International Music
Journals

A

ACTA MUSICOLOGICA

Begun in 1928 as a publication strictly for members of the International Musicological Society (IMS) and containing little more than general membership information, *Mitteilungen der Internationalen Gesellschaft für Musikwissenschaft* became a scholarly journal with v. 3. The publishers signaled this change with a new title, *Acta musicologica*, and the announcement of its first editor, Knud Jeppesen. By v. 5, the quarterly numbers regularly consisted of four scholarly articles, three to four short book reviews, a list of new publications in the field, and society news.

The articles, four to sixteen pages in length, demonstrate the international and catholic nature of the organization. Topics were typically historical, often consisting of archival studies and manuscript inventories; ethnomusicological articles appeared as well. The society's continuing interest in discussing the nature of musicology, musicological research and scholarship, and the state of the discipline in various countries was also evident. The IMS was founded in Basel in 1927 to replace the prewar International Musikgesellschaft. In keeping with the international nature of its parent organization, the journal printed society information in German and French, the contributorship was truly international, and articles were published in the language of the contributing scholar. Today, the official languages of the society are English, French, German, Italian, and Spanish; the current editorial board is composed of noted scholars representing Eastern and Western Europe, Great Britain, and North America.

The political turmoil of the late 1930s and 1940s severely hampered the international aims of the organization and thus its journal. The number of issues dropped from four per volume to two, and then one, with vs. 16 and 17 (1944 and 1945) published as a single combined issue. Likewise, issues often consisted of less than one hundred pages, with as few as three contributions. Book reviews were sometimes dropped, though the list of new publications in the field continued.

In the 1950s, *Acta musicologica* returned to issuing four numbers per year, though some numbers were combined. While book reviews were discontinued permanently, postwar editors reaffirmed most of the other founding editorial policies: an international scope, attention to the current state of musicology, and providing a forum for both the discipline and individual scholarship. Examples of articles on the discipline include Edith Gerson-Kiwi's "Musicology in Israel" (30.1/2:17–26), Lloyd Hilbert's "Musicology Reconsidered" (31.1:25–31), and, more recently, Claude Palisca's "Report on the Musicological Year 1974 in the United States" (47.2:283–289). The latter was the first of a continuing series of yearly reports on the state of musicology in various countries, reports in which new publications, activities of national societies, and specific university programs were showcased. Reports of society meetings as well as international conferences appear frequently. Of particular interest is a report entitled "The Fourth Congress of the International Musicological Society" (21.1:1–7) which offers insight into the general impact of the war on musicology, a topic very much in the air at the first IMS meeting held after the thirteen-year wartime hiatus.

The earliest issues of the *Mitteilungen* were typically sixteen pages in length in a 5⅞" by 8⅞" physical format. With the change to *Acta musicologica* in v. 3, issues increased to forty-eight to fifty pages in length and an expanded 6⅜" by 9⁷⁄₁₆" physical format. During the years it was published in Copenhagen (1936–53), the physical format changed slightly to 6½" by 9½". With the resumption of a stable political climate and the move to Bärenreiter, issues expanded to eighty-four to ninety pages in length in a 6¹¹⁄₁₆" by 9⅝" physical format. In 1972 the journal adopted a semiannual publication schedule wherein each issue, approximately 150 pages in length, contained an average of seven articles plus communications in a 6¹¹⁄₁₆" by 9½" physical format. Currently the journal runs over 300 pages per issue in a 7⅛" by 9⅞" physical format.

Occasional photographs and musical examples are printed as well as several pages of advertisements, again reflecting the journal's international scope. V. 25 contains an index for the first twenty-five years of the journal; a yearly index of names did not appear consistently until v. 9.

Information Sources

BIBLIOGRAPHY

Pruett, James W. "Annotated Listing of Selected Musical Periodicals." In *Research Guide to Musicology*, edited by James W. Pruett and Thomas P. Slavens, pp. 141–46. Chicago: American Library Association, 1985.

INDEXES

Internal: vs. 1–25 in v. 25.

External: Music Index, 1954–   . RILM, 1967–   . Bibliographie des Musikschrifttums, 1937, 1939, 1950–   . Arts and Humanities Citation Index, 1976–   .

REPRINT EDITIONS

Paper: Johnson Reprint.

Microfilm: Research Microfilm Pub. Dakota Graphics.

LOCATION SOURCES
Widely available.

Publication History

TITLE AND TITLE CHANGES
Mitteilungen der Internationalen Gesellschaft für Musikwissenschaft, 1928–30.
Acta musicologica, 1931– .
VOLUME AND ISSUE DATA
Volumes 1– , 1928– .
FREQUENCY OF PUBLICATION
Quarterly to 1971. Semiannual, 1972– .
PUBLISHERS
Breitkopf und Härtel, 1928–35. Levin and Ejnar Munksgaard, 1936–53. Bären-
reiter, 1954– .
PLACE OF PUBLICATION
Leipzig, 1928–33. Copenhagen, 1936–53. Kassel, 1954– .
EDITORS
Knud Jeppesen, 1930–53. Albert van der Linden, 1954–55. Arnold Geering, 1956.
Hans Albrecht and Arnold Geering, 1957–58. Hans Albrecht, 1959–61. Hellmut
Federhofer, 1962– .

Susan C. Cook

AFRICAN MUSIC JOURNAL

The *African Music Journal* is the African Music Society's official organ. Dr.
Winifred Hoernlé founded the society in 1947 and published its first newsletter.
Hugh Tracey initiated the journal in 1954 and became its first editor. In addition
to the journal, Tracey also founded the International Library of African Music
(ILAM), which houses recordings of African music that he began making in the
early 1930s. The society recognized a growing interest in African music among
both Europeans and Africans and wanted "to ensure that pitfalls were avoided
and that opportunities were grasped" (1.1:6). The stated purpose of the journal
was "to present disciplines and foundations of African artistry upon which future
generations can build" (1.1:7). After a quarter century of publication the editors
asserted that the journal had "become one of the best-known and most-consulted
sources of African music" (6.2:3).

Africa, for the journal's purposes, is tacitly defined as sub-Saharan Africa.
For most articles the geographic center of gravity lies somewhat farther south:
regions bordering on the Sahara (the traditional "Sudan") and those of the Horn
receive relatively little attention. The nature of the articles is also narrower than
the declared scope of the journal. Articles concentrate chiefly on music (theoretical and practical considerations), with a preference for that of traditional
"tribal" culture. An interesting exception to this tendency is "church music."

The bulk of contributors are ethnomusicologists, anthropologists, and other researchers and lecturers, as well as missionaries. Regular features include articles, reviews (book and sound recordings), a column from the editor, letters to the editor, biographical notes on contributors, miscellaneous news and comments, and a map (back cover) showing the geographic focus of each article.

The frequent editorial messages reflect some revealing attitudes about the society and the history of African countries. In 1956 (1.3:5) the editor requests missionaries to revise their attitudes and amend their hymnbooks. At the same time he praises those who (apparently) had already moved in that direction. At times the editor's political notions mingle with his ideas on music. In a 1958 editorial he asserts that songs constitute the true vocation of African people and "function better than politics... (particularly) politicians seeking swift self-advancement" (2.1:5). Africans should make music and stay away from the unwieldy world of politics. Again, in 1961, the editor states that Africans' music and art clearly reveal the meaning of their life and "their Negrohood." He continues, "it [is] essential to emphasize that all men [sic] are created special. We suggest that a cultural statement of this kind holds far more promise for future recognition of individual talent in a highly competitive world than the egalitarian shibboleths of pop politics" (2.3:5).

The political unrest in African countries and the vicissitudes of modern times also inspire some editorials. In 1963 (3.2:5) the editor reports that insufficient original research is available for publication owing to the political situation. In 1973–74, he reprimands contributors for what he perceives as a "concentration on GIMMICKRY and GADGETRY without being able to deal with political and technical changes in society" (5.3:5).

A significant change occurred between 1976 and 1980 (vs. 5 and 6). An editorial in the latter volume apologized for the four-year hiatus in publication and explained the details: ILAM was to become the official publisher. ILAM was supported by the Chamber of Mines of South Africa, its long-standing patron. The Chamber of Mines agreed to fund the journal for three years provided ILAM became affiliated with the Institute of Social and Economic Research at Rhodes University (Grahamstown, South Africa). The editor assured the readers that with this change there would be no loss of independence or change in "raison d'être." Yet, the history of the journal's publication since 1980 is characterized by uncertainty and dissatisfaction. For instance, a well-known writer gave up publishing usable music transcriptions on the grounds that he did not want "partially informed people playing them both incorrectly and without reference to their originators" (6.2:3). The editor criticizes the reading audience for their use of the journal's contents: "Now that you have access to this 'knowledge object,' what are you thinking of doing with it?" (6.2:3).

The publication schedule of the journal is somewhat irregular. It appears to have been conceived as an annual, with four yearly issues comprising one volume. It began in 1954, but 1.4 (1957) may not have been published. Vs. 4.1, 5.3, and 5.4 each cover a two-year period, and there is a four-year gap between

5.4 and 6.1. Since the mid–1960s, the typical issue has featured eight articles, each about fifteen pages in length.

From the beginning, the journal has used a 6" x 9" format with a white gloss paper cover and the title in black print. The English title is in bold print, while the French title appears underneath in smaller print. Centered on the front cover is a different *object d'art* (e.g., a musical instrument, design, or mask) for each issue. The articles are in English, with only an occasional review or letter in French.

Information Sources

INDEXES
> External: Music Index, 1968– (retrospective to 1954). RILM, 1967– . Bibliographie des Musikschrifttums, 1962– . Arts and Humanities Citation Index, 1976– .

LOCATION SOURCES
> Widely available.

Publication History

TITLE AND TITLE CHANGES
> *African Music Journal.*

VOLUME AND ISSUE DATA
> Volumes 1– , 1954– .

FREQUENCY OF PUBLICATION
> Annual (with irregularities).

PUBLISHERS
> African Music Society, 1954–80. African Music Society with International Library of African Music and Institute of Social and Economic Research, 1980– .

PLACE OF PUBLICATION
> Johannesburg, South Africa, 1954–80. Grahamstown, South Africa, 1980– .

EDITORS
> Hugh Tracey, Esq., 1954–70. Andrew Tracey, 1971– .

L. JaFran Jones

ALLGEMEINE DEUTSCHE MUSIK-ZEITUNG. See ALLGEMEINE MUSIK-ZEITUNG

ALLGEMEINE MUSIKALISCHE ZEITUNG

The *Allgemeine musikalische Zeitung (AmZ)* ushered in a new age of music journalism when its first issue appeared on 3 October 1798. Foremost in the minds of the publisher, Gottfried Christoph Härtel, and editor, Johann Friedrich Rochlitz, was to provide a music journal that would educate the sizable new audience of musical amateurs as well as professionals on all aspects of current musical life. Because of its didactic aim, the *AmZ* set new standards for musical criticism by which other journals were later judged. When the journal folded, after fifty years, the editors claimed there "was no further place for a general *allgemeine*] music journal." But by then, the *AmZ* was also having difficulty competing with more innovative and specialized journals such as the *Neue Zeitschrift für Musik* (q.v.). Two subsequent attempts to revive the *AmZ* were unsuccessful.

G. C. Härtel, the publisher and second editor of *AmZ*, joined the Breitkopf music publishing firm in 1795 and bought it the following year. Härtel proved to be a farsighted publisher (he was the first to adapt the technique of lithography to music publishing), and one of his goals upon buying the firm was to start a music journal. Rochlitz was just twenty-nine when he became the editor of the new journal, but he was an established writer, and his German translation of Wolfgang Amadeus Mozart's *Don Giovanni* was highly regarded. Härtel exerted a great control over the journal, and the two worked together to insure that the writing and criticism published in the *AmZ* would be of the highest quality.

Rochlitz and Härtel sought to provide their readers with the broadest possible coverage of musical life, as indicated by the inclusion of "allgemeine" in the title. To do so, they enlisted the aid of many contributors. Within its first decade, 130 different individuals wrote articles and reviews for the journal, and all major European cities had correspondents who regularly wrote on the musical life of their region. Coverage was not limited to Europe; reports on concert life in the United States, particularly New York City, appeared with some frequency by the mid-nineteenth century.

The journal is most remembered for its musical criticism, specifically new music and performance reviews which reflected the rational, objective spirit of the age. The *AmZ* reported on virtually all composers and performers active in the first half of the nineteenth century. One of the best-known contributors and critics during the early days of the *AmZ* was E.T.A. Hoffmann, who wrote for the journal until 1815. Hoffmann was recognized, in particular, for his reviews of Ludwig van Beethoven.

Joseph Haydn and Mozart received special attention in the journal, and Breitkopf and Härtel undertook to publish their complete works. Härtel later befriended the young Beethoven, whose works the firm would also publish. Though Beethoven was later well covered in the journal, the reviews which appeared in the first issues of the journal betray Rochlitz's musical conservatism. After 1800, the *AmZ* came to support Beethoven, and Rochlitz then acknowledged him as the leading figure in new German music.

Within its weekly eight-page issue, the *AmZ* contained reviews of one to three pages and shorter reviews of a paragraph; two- to three-page essays on historical and aesthetic topics or abstracts from recent theoretical works; half-page notices about musical events or other matters of musical interest; and correspondence. A regular topic covered in the short essays, which had been announced in the journal's prospectus, was the invention of and improvements to musical instruments.

Every two or three weeks the *AmZ* published a two-page "Intelligenz Blätter," which contained paid advertisements and lists of works either not deemed worthy of receiving full reviews or to be reviewed later. Musical supplements of one to four pages appeared on the average of six times a year during the first twenty-five years, then less frequently before being discontinued during the last decade of the first series. These supplements included piano works, folksongs, partsongs, opera arias, and church music by composers such as Beethoven, Haydn, Mozart, Giovanni Palestrina, and lesser-known composers popular at the time. Beginning in the first volume, with its vignette of J. S. Bach, the *AmZ* regularly published engraved portraits of composers, performers, its editors, and other contributors.

In 1818, Rochlitz, who was by then a director of the Leipzig Gewandhaus, stepped down as editor, and Härtel assumed complete control. Härtel remained editor until his death in 1829. Rochlitz continued to contribute articles to the journal until 1835. Härtel was succeeded by Gottfried Wilhelm Fink, who had been a major contributor since 1808. Fink put his own distinctive stamp on the journal with articles providing an historical perspective on music, as well as reviews which voiced his distrust for current musical trends. After accepting Robert Schumann's review of Frédéric Chopin for the 7 December 1831 issue, Fink refused subsequent reviews by Robert Schumann, allowed no further mention of Schumann's works or writings, and voiced opposition to Chopin as well. Schumann's *Neue Zeitschrift für Musik* was started largely in opposition to the conservative views of Fink as expressed in the *AmZ*. After Fink's departure in 1841 to assume a position at the Leipzig Hochschule für Musik, the journal suffered from a lack of editorial control, and it is often difficult to determine editors as they appear and disappear from the masthead or served for less than a year. The last official editor was J. C. Lobe, a composer, who continued to edit and write for music journals after the demise of the *AmZ*.

In 1863, the Viennese critic Selmar Bagge tried to revive the journal in a new series. Although he engaged a distinguished circle of contributors, including Eduard Hanslick and Otto Jahn, Bagge was unable to make the journal a success. He tried again in 1866 using a new title, the *Leipziger allgemeine musikalische Zeitung*. The great pioneer of German musicology, Friedrich Chrysander, subsequently became the editor of this third series, which returned to the original title in 1869. Chrysander retained almost complete editorial control until the journal folded in 1882. Even under Chrysander's guidance and with contributors such as Guido Adler and Phillip Spitta, the new journal never regained the glory of its first three decades with Rochlitz and Härtel.

The first series maintained a consistent physical format of 8¼″ by 9⅜″. Issues were eight pages long, with an occasional ten or twelve-page issue during the later years. Musical examples and illustrations were frequent and often as long as a half page. After the suspension of the "Intelligenz-Blätter," the journal published a half page to a full page of advertisements. The two subsequent series published by Bagge were in a physical format of 7½″ by 9¹¹⁄₁₆″ and were typically eight pages in length, occasionally running to twelve pages. Both retained the weekly schedule of the first series but had a separate numbering sequence. Detailed yearly indices appeared for each volume of the original series as well as the later two series. The first series also published three cumulative indices for years 1798–1818, 1819–28, and 1829–48.

Information Sources

BIBLIOGRAPHY

Barbour, J. Murray. "*Allgemeine musikalische Zeitung*: Prototype of Contemporary Musical Journalism." *Notes* 5 (1947–48): 325–37.

Bruckner-Bigenwald, Martha. *Die Anfänge der Leipziger "Allgemeinen musikalischen Zeitung.*" Hilversun: Frits A. Knuf, 1965.

Mueller-Blattau, Joseph. "Friedrich Rochlitz und die Musikgeschichte." In *Hans Albrecht in Memoriam*, edited by Wilfried Brennecke and Hans Haase, pp. 192–99. Kassel: Bärenreiter, 1962.

Ehinger, Hans. "Die Rolle der Schweiz in der *Allgemeinen musikalischen Zeitung* 1798–1848." In *Festschrift Karl Nef zum 60. Geburtstag*, edited by Edgar Refardt, Hans Ehinger, and Wilhelm Menan, pp. 19–47. Zurich: Komissions-Verlag, 1933.

———. *Friedrich Rochlitz als Musikschriftsteller*, 1929. Reprint. Neudelin, Liechtenstein: Kraus, 1976.

Fellinger, Imogen. "Das Brahms-Bild der *Allgemeinen musikalischen Zeitung* (1863 bis 1882)." In *Beiträge zur Geschichte der Musikkritik*, edited by Heinz Becker, pp. 27–64. Regensburg: Gustav Bosse, 1965.

Gleich, Clemens Christoph von. *Die Bedeutung der "Allgemeinen musikalischen Zeitung" 1798–1848 und 1865–1882*. Amsterdam: Frits Knuf, 1969.

Hase, Oskar von. " 'Allgemeine musikalische Zeitung.'" In *Breitkopf und Härtel Gedenkschrift und Arbeitsbericht*, v. 1, 149–51; v. 2, 31–37. 2 vol. Leipzig: Breitkopf und Härtel, 1917, 1919.

———. "Gottfried Christoph Härtel." In *Breitkopf und Härtel Gedenkschrift und Arbeitsbericht*, 2 vols., v. 1, 135–254. Leipzig: Breitkopf und Härtel, 1917, 1919.

Jorgenson, Dale. *Moritz Hauptmann of Leipzig*. Lewiston, N.Y.: Edwin Mellon, 1986.

van der Linden, A. "La Place de la Hollande dans L' 'Allgemeine musikalische Zeitung' (1798–1848)," In *International Musicological Society Compte Rendu, Utrecht, 1952*, pp. 293–95. Amsterdam: Vereniging voor Nederlandse Muziekgeschiedenis, 1953.

Schmitt-Thomas, Reinhold. *Die Entwicklung der deutschen Konzertkritik im Spiegel der Leipziger "Allgemeine musikalische Zeitung" (1798–1848)*. Frankfurt am Main: Kettenhoff, 1969.

INDEXES

Internal: 1798–1818; 1819–28; 1829–45.

REPRINT EDITIONS

Microform: Library of Congress. Schnase. Datamics. (complete). Sibley Music Library, Eastman School of Music (1798–1848). University Music Editions Paper: (1798–1848).

Paper: Fritz Knuf (1798–1848)

LOCATION SOURCES

Widely available.

Publication History

TITLE AND TITLE CHANGES

Allgemeine musikalische Zeitung, 1798–1848, 1863–65. *Leipziger allgemeine musikalische Zeitung*, 1866–68. *Allgemeine musikalische Zeitung*, 1869–82.

VOLUME AND ISSUE DATA

Volumes 1–50, 1798–48. New series, volumes 1–3, 1863–65. Third series, volumes 1–17, 1866–82.

FREQUENCY OF PUBLICATION

Weekly.

PUBLISHERS

Breitkopf und Härtel, 1798–1848; 1863–65. J. Rieter-Biedermann, 1866–82.

PLACE OF PUBLICATION

Leipzig.

EDITORS

Friedrich Rochlitz, 1798–1818. Gottfried Härtel, 1818–27. G. W. Fink, 1827–41. C. F. Becker, 1842. Moritz Hauptmann, 1843. C. F. Becker, intermittently 1844–46 along with publisher. J. C. Lobe, 1847–48. Selmar Bagge, 1863–65; 1866–68. Friedrich Chrysander, 1868–71. Joseph Mueller, 1871–72. Friedrich Chrysander, 1874–82.

Susan C. Cook

ALLGEMEINE MUSIK-ZEITUNG

Founded in 1874, the *Allgemeine Musik-Zeitung,* or the *Allgemeine deutsche Musik-Zeitung* as it was called for the first eight volumes, described itself as a "weekly publication for the complete musical life of the time." It was one of a number of nineteenth-century German periodicals which provided general musical information and reported on contemporary concert life for an audience of both music professionals and serious amateurs in the style of the earlier *Allgemeine musikalische Zeitung* (q.v.) (Leipzig, 1798–1848). The *Allgmeine Musik-Zeitung* typically contained one or two main articles of two to five pages in length, a number of one-page concert and opera reviews, shorter reviews of new books and music publications, lists of other new publications, plus brief notices of upcoming events, new items, obituaries, and letters from readers.

Wilhelm Tappert, who succeeded founding editor O. Reinsdorf in 1876 (v. 3), published on Richard Wagner and was a recognized authority on lute music and tablature. His interest in historical and scholarly topics set the tone for the journal's main articles. Subsequent editors followed his lead: articles typically dealt with Medieval, Renaissance, and Baroque topics or covered nineteenth-century masters such as Richard Wagner, Johannes Brahms, and Franz Liszt, and popular performers in a scholarly, if abbreviated, fashion. Coverage was frequently, although not exclusively, limited to German and Austrian music history and individuals. In the twentieth century, theoretical, aesthetic, and psychological topics appeared, as well as some coverage of twentieth-century figures: for example, Paul Riesenfeld's "Aesthetische Ammerkungen zu Arnold Schoenberg's 'Pierrot Lunaire' " (40.1:1–3). In some cases articles were serialized over three to four issues. The *Allgemeine Musik-Zeitung* claimed to publish the essays of the most notable writers and critics throughout its seventy-year history. In fact, contributors included such notables as Hans von Bulow, Oscar Bie, Hugo Riemann, Felix Weingartner, Paul Bekker, Hugo Leichtentritt, Wilhelm Altmann, and Walter Abendroth.

In 1899 a change in the *Allgemeine Musik-Zeitung*'s masthead proclaimed it a forum for the "reform of contemporary musical life." And until 1904 its title page fittingly carried an illustration of St. George slaying the dragon. (In 1904 the cover illustration changed to an art deco depiction of St. Cecilia at the organ.) This reformist claim is difficult to discern from the journal's contents except in their conservative tone and their continuing appeal to an audience of music professionals and interested nonprofessionals. The journal's own publishing imprint, which began in v. 8, published a number of practical books on music history and theory before World War I as part of this overall aim to bring music to a larger audience. In 1925, the masthead dropped its claim to reform and returned to read "a weekly publication for musical life of the time." Throughout its existence the most important feature of the journal was its detailed and consistent coverage of Berlin concert life (after the journal moved its publishing headquarters there in v. 3). It regularly reviewed activities in other German cities as well as publishing occasional reviews of events in New York, London, and Paris. In the first two decades of this century the journal also provided extensive coverage of the various national and international festivals and conferences common during that time, such as the Handel Festivals and the Donaueschingen and Baden-Baden Chamber Music Festivals of the 1920s. Often an entire issue was devoted to such an event. Issues also contained from three to nine pages of advertisements for businesses and performers either available for hire and/or lessons, or announcing their Berlin appearances. These advertisements—often a full page in length and with photographs—provide further documentation of Berlin's active musical life.

Paul Schwers, the fourth editor, wrote many of the reviews during his thirty-two-year tenure, reviews that reveal him to have been an outspoken opponent of all modern trends. During the late 1920s and into the 1930s, Schwers became increasingly vitriolic toward new music, both German and non-German, and his criticism echoes the rhetoric of the growing National Socialist movement in its nationalistic tone and anti-Semitism.

In 1920–21 (vs. 47–48) the journal functioned as the official organ of the Organization of German Music Teachers (ODM) and during this time it published organizational news. In 1932 (v. 59), the journal, most likely in response to the worsening economic situation of the Weimar Republic, published together with the *Rheinische-Westfälische Musikzeitung* and the *Süddeutscher Musik-Kurier*. The coverage remained largely the same except for the increased number of reviews from cities other than Berlin; reviews, in general, became shorter in length. Issues were also devoted to particular topics such as "Musikwissenschaft and Musikpflege" (65.5) or "Wagner" (65.6). Midway through 1943 (v. 70) the journal merged with *Die Musik* (q.v.), *Neues Musikblatt* and *Zeitschrift für Musik* (q.v. *Neue Zeitschrift für Musik*) to form the National Socialist music periodical *Musik im Kriege* (q.v.), "united for the duration of the war" and dedicated to reporting on "practical" musical life. Herbert Gerigk acted as the general editor, and each journal retained its own volume numbering.

Issues of the *Allgemeine Musik-Zeitung* typically ran twenty pages in length, although during World War I, individual numbers decreased to twelve pages. After the war the previous length returned, and in the mid–1920s expanded to as many as thirty pages per issue, finally reducing in the 1930s to sixteen pages before its merger into *Musik im Kriege*. Pagination was consecutive through a volume. The physical format changed often throughout the run; the initial 9¼" by 12⅛" format which changed in 1899 to 9" by 13¼", in 1905 to 11¼" by 15¾", in 1911 to 10¼" by 13⅞", and finally in 1939 to 9¾" by 13⁹⁄₁₆". Each volume carried an in-depth yearly index. Musical examples were common as were photographs of performers, composers, and conductors published within the body of issues and on covers.

Information Sources

INDEXES
>Internal: each volume indexed
>External: Bibliographie des Musikschrifttums, 1937, 1939.

REPRINT EDITIONS
>Microfilm: Schnase. Library of Congress. Datamics Inc. (complete). New York Public Library (incomplete).

LOCATION SOURCES
>Newberry Library (most complete run). Library of Congress (partial). University of Arizona (partial). New York Public Library (partial). University of Illinois (partial). Public Library of Cincinnati (partial).

Publication History

TITLE AND TITLE CHANGES
>*Allgemeine deutsche Musik-Zeitung*, 1874–81. *Allgemeine Musik-Zeitung*, 1882–1924. *Allgemeine Musikzeitung*, 1925–43. *Musik im Kriege*, 1943–44.

VOLUME AND ISSUE DATA
>Volume 1–70.6, 1874–1943.

FREQUENCY OF PUBLICATION
>Weekly.

PUBLISHERS
>Breitkopf und Härtel, 1874–75. Luckhardt, 1876–80. Paul Lehrsten (Verlag und Expedition der "Allgemeine Musik-Zeitung"), 1881–1943. Neuen Musikblatts, 1943–44.

PLACES OF PUBLICATION
>Kassel, 1874–75. Berlin, 1876–80. Berlin (Charlottenburg), 1881–1935. Berlin/Leipzig/Cologne/Munich, 1935–43. Berlin, 1943–44.

EDITORS
O. Reinsdorf, 1874–76. Wilhelm Tappert, 1876–81. Otto Lessmann, 1882–1907.
Paul Schwers, 1907–37. Paul Schwers, Richard Petzoldt, and Elly Schumacher,
1938. Paul Schwers, Richard Petzoldt, and Ernst Henninger, 1939–43. Herbert
Gerigk, 1943–44.

Susan C. Cook

AMERICAN CHORAL REVIEW

The *American Choral Review* is the quarterly publication and the official
journal of the American Choral Foundation, an organization founded in New
York City by Margaret Hillis in the late 1950s. The objectives of the American
Choral Foundation are to further the education of choral conductors and to foster
the development of choral groups in the United States. Toward these ends, two
publications are produced by the foundation: (1) the *American Choral Review*,
a journal containing features on the history and performance practice of choral
music; reviews of choral books, concerts, records, and scores; and other regular
departments; and (2) the supplementary *Research Memorandum Series*, listings
of choral music classified according to historical period, specific occasion, or
individual composer. As of September 1985, 139 titles had been published in
this rich and useful supplementary series.

The scholarly essays found in regular issues of the *American Choral Review*
speak to varied and intriguing topics. These include textual considerations, such as
"The English Canzonet: Introductory Notes on Poetry and Music" by James
McCray (16.1:11–14); early music, like Linda Horowitz's "Jewish Choral Tradition in Antiquity"(22.4:11-17); choral composition, such as "Writing for the Amateur Chorus: A Chance and a Challenge" by Randall Thompson (22.2:5–15);
twentieth-century concerns, such as Carol Longsworth's "Women Composers of
Choral Music"(26.7:17-25); and lesser known topics, such as Edith White
Mann's "Armin Knab: A Timeless Master" (20.2:21–25) or "On the Repertory
for Chorus and Band: Introductory Notes" by David Whitwell (7.3:12).

In addition to musicological essays, the *Review* offers interviews with choral
conductors and composers, profiles of successful choral groups, and reviews of
choral concerts, books, records, and scores. The reviews of choral concerts are
especially thorough, describing events in the United States and throughout the
world, with an emphasis on Europe and the Northeast and Midwest in America.
Other regular features, listed from least to most frequent, are: "School Music,"
"Music in the Curriculum," "Choral Music in the Liturgy," and the "Choral
Conductors Forum." Also, *In Memoriam* tributes are paid to persons, such as
Archibald Davison and Zoltán Kodály for their outstanding contributions in
choral music.

Beginning with v. 11, special issues make up 50 percent of those published,
thereby constituting a substantial literary contribution in a professional journal.

Sample subjects include: "The Symphonic Mass" by Paul Henry Lang (18.2:7–21) and "The Madrigal in the Romantic Era" from the pen of Percy M. Young (19.4). Alfred Durr, Elliot Forbes, and Jens Peter Larsen are also among the distinguished contributors. V. 13 represents a different kind of contribution: an entire English translation, co-authored by Alfred Mann, of *The Choral Conductor* by Kurt Thomas.

The *American Choral Review* assumed its current title beginning with v. 4, when the present editor, Alfred Mann, took over the position in October 1961. The physical design and layout of the *American Choral Review* have undergone only one format change since the journal's inception in 1958. The *American Choral Review* began as a bulletin of three to eight pages with the text in columns on a 7⅞" by 10⅝" pages. Then, with v. 9.2, the *Review* became a small scholarly booklet, 6¾" by 9⅞", averaging thirty-five pages in length. Fine holograph musical examples are interspersed with the text. The resulting appearance is that of a clear and readable page. Pictures are excluded, and the minimal advertising is mostly membership information for the American Choral Foundation and a related organization, the American Choral Directors Association.

Vs. 1 and 3–8 are indexed by volume, whereas following v. 13 is an index covering 1958–71. Since 1985 the contents of the back issues for both the *American Choral Review* and the *Research Memorandum Series* have been listed and annotated in a computer data base according to author, title, subject, and period in a joint project of Temple University and the American Choral Foundation.

In a recent interview, long-time editor Alfred Mann spoke of his constant efforts to obtain articles that are clearly written with solid content so that they can be available for the self-education of choral conductors throughout their careers. In this he has succeeded. The *American Choral Review* combines fine quality and captivating material with clear prose. The historical and literature aspects of the journal are the strongest with a great variety of authors, including musicologists, critics, conductors, and composers. Of the historical periods, articles concerning the Renaissance, Baroque, and twentieth century are the most frequent. Some of these have been reproduced in other journals, such as *Journal of Music Theory* (q.v.) and *Early Music* (q.v.).

Information Sources

BIBLIOGRAPHY
Interview with Alfred Mann, editor, Eastman School of Music, Rochester, New York, October 4, 1985.
INDEXES
Internal: each volume indexed (vs. 1, 3–8); vs. 1–13 in v. 13.
External: RILM, 1967– . Music Index, 1962– . Music Article Guide, 1967– . Arts and Humanities Citation Index, 1976– .
LOCATION SOURCES
Widely available.

Publication History

TITLE AND TITLE CHANGES

> *Bulletin of the American Concert Choir and the Choral Foundation, Inc.*, 1958.
> *Bulletin of the American Choral Foundation, Inc.*, 1958–60. *American Choral*,
> 1961–   .

VOLUME AND ISSUE DATA

> Volumes 1–   , 1958–   .

FREQUENCY OF PUBLICATION

> Quarterly.

PUBLISHERS

> American Choral Foundation; 1958–66. University of Missouri Press, 1967–68.
> American Choral Foundation, 1969–85. Association of Professional Vocal En-
> sembles, 1 February 1985–   .

PLACES OF PUBLICATION

> New York, 1958–66. Columbia, Missouri, 1967–68. New York, 1969–1 February
> 1985. Philadelphia, 1 February 1985–   .

EDITORS

> No editor given for vs. 1 and 2, Milton Goldin listed as administrative director.
> Milton Goldin, 1960. Alfred Mann, 1961–   .

Rosalind Knowles

AMERICAN HARP JOURNAL, THE (HARP NEWS)

The American Harp Journal began publication under the editorship of Samuel Milligan in 1967, four years after the founding of its parent organization, the American Harp Society. The direct impetus for the journal was the demise of *Harp News*, a publication established sixteen years earlier by the Northern California Harpists Association to improve communications among harpists. Although a modest publication in pamphlet format, *Harp News* (principal editor: Grace Follet) set certain standards, which were appreciated by its audience—in addition to news about harpists and events, activity and topics relating to the instrument were treated in articles and features, while advertising by teachers, publishers, and manufacturers served an educational as well as financial purpose. When the journal was dissolved in 1966, its physical properties were turned over to the American Harp Society and its editorial policies served as a model for its successor.

The new journal was larger—7″ by 8½″; it had a glossy cover, more extensive advertising, and broader coverage of current and historically important events. It was addressed to "all parts of the harpistic community: students, professionals, teachers, historians, devoted amateurs, and friends of the harp" (1.1:4). The first issue offered nearly fifty pages of biographical, historical, and pedagogical articles, analysis, a tribute to American Harp Society founder Marcel Grandjany, and reminiscences of Claude Debussy by French harpist

Pierre Jamet. In addition, it included lists of European and national harp events, chapter and national conference news, a "People and Places" column, and a Teacher's Directory.

The publication rapidly gained recognition as the major journal for harpists around the world. While its principal focus remained American, the list of contributors and society members showed an increasing international influence. During the 1970s, the *Journal* expanded to an average of seventy-five pages and began to include more extensive reports of major European and national events. Articles, anywhere from two to five pages in length, are contributed primarily by harpists and an occasional guest scholar. Illustrative material is modest. Reviews of new music and recordings also appear.

When Dr. Jane Weidensaul assumed editorship in 1979, she polled the readers before establishing new directions. As a result, communications from the society were streamlined and chapter newsletters were developed to disseminate information of local interest. The *Journal* recognized its role as "the most important repository of harp lore in the world," and stated that this responsibility must be fulfilled with "taste, refinement, discrimination and *usefulness*" (Winter 1979 editorial). To this end new standards of scholarship were determined; perhaps the most ambitious result of these to date was the comprehensive Carlos Salzedo commemorative issue (Summer 1985).

Information Sources

INDEXES
    External: Music Index, 1950–66 (Harp News). Music Article Guide, 1965– .
LOCATION SOURCES
    Widely available.

Publication History

TITLE AND TITLE CHANGES
    Harp News (Harp News of the West), 1950–66. *The American Harp Journal*, 1967– .
VOLUME AND ISSUE DATA
    Volumes 1– , 1967– .
FREQUENCY OF PUBLICATION
    Semiannual.
PUBLISHER
    American Harp Society.
PLACES OF PUBLICATION
    New York, 1967–73. Hollywood, California, 1974. Lubbock, Texas, 1975–78. Beaumont, Texas, 1978–79. Teaneck, New Jersey, 1979– .
EDITORS
    Grace Follet, 1950–66. Samuel Milligan, 1967–71. Gail Barber, 1971–79. Jane Weidensaul, 1979– .

Ruth K. Inglefield

AMERICAN MUSIC LOVER, THE. See AMERICAN RECORD GUIDE

AMERICAN MUSIC TEACHER

American Music Teacher is the official journal of the Music Teachers National Association (MTNA), which describes itself as a "nonprofit organization, representing music teachers in studios, conservatories, music schools, public schools, private schools, and institutions of higher learning" (36.1:2). In practice, the MTNA differs from another music teacher's association, the Music Educators National Conference, in that the membership of the former is primarily studio music teachers, while the latter attracts primarily classroom music teachers and school ensemble directors.

The MTNA, which was founded in 1876, began publication of its first journal, the *Music Teachers National Association Bulletin*, in 1939. This small journal (5" x 7") provided news of MTNA meetings and activities to its members and was edited by Theodore M. Finney. It was published semiannually, and somewhat irregularly, until 1950. In 1951 MTNA completely revised the format, content, and title of its official journal. The first unnumbered issue of *American Music Teacher* was published in July 1951. V.1.1 appeared as the September–October 1951 issue.

To accommodate the interests of its diverse audience, the journal's articles, screened by an equally diverse editorial board, cover a broad range of topics. The articles can be grouped into two broad subject-matter categories: music and music teaching. Music articles include analysis and discussion of composers, genres, pieces, aesthetics, and interpretation. Those on music teaching present approaches for teaching voice and a wide variety of instruments. Articles are short, generally no more than two pages in length. Approximately eight articles appear in each issue.

Regular features focus primarily on MTNA news and include the following: (1) reports from the MTNA president, (2) reports from representatives of various MTNA committees (e.g., Local Associations and Student Chapters, National Certification, Independent Music Teachers Forum, Development Commission), (3) news of national and state conventions, (4) announcements of MTNA-sponsored competitions, contests, awards, and scholarships, (5) letters to the editor, and (6) short reviews of published music and books of interest to music teachers and performers. Beginning in 1974 an annual list of MTNA-approved, nationally certified teachers has been printed in the September–October issue.

In the earlier issues there was more emphasis on the MTNA's organizational agenda, with much space devoted to information on meetings, officers, conventions, and membership drives. As the organization grew, the emphasis shifted, and currently there is a more equal balance between MTNA news and articles on music and music teaching. Articles in current issues are also more sophisticated than in earlier issues. This is particularly true of the music teaching articles. Earlier articles on teaching methods were mostly anecdotal, typically describing one teacher's solution to a teaching problem. Today's articles often refer to learning theories and research results. Contributors of these later articles are primarily applied music college faculty and independent music teachers.

The editorial content of the journal has been an important means of articulating the goals of the MTNA. During the 1950s their goals were to increase membership and to bring greater professionalism to studio music teaching. Editorials of the time focused on the value of the MTNA to the music teaching profession and on means of establishing accreditation standards for private music teachers. Editorial influence grew, and in the mid–1960s editorials were replaced by a regular feature, "From the President." Under Homer Ulrich, "From the Editor" was reinstituted as an irregular feature. One measure of the success of the editorials was the establishment of procedures for music teachers to achieve Associate, Professional, and Master Teaching Certificates. Robert Elias succeeded Ulrich as editor in January 1988, announcing "a new editorial emphasis on matters affecting—and affected by—the professional music teaching community" (37.3:2). The most readily apparent changes were the addition of several new columns: "Items of Interest," "Industry News," "Letters," "Studio Tips," "You and Your Finances," and various news briefs from local, state and even individual members.

American Music Teacher is useful as a source of information on the activities of MTNA and as a resource for studio music teaching methods. Its articles are generally not scholarly, nor are they meant to be; their brevity does not allow for much depth. Although MTNA's *American Music Teacher* and the Music Educators National Conference's *Music Educators Journal* (q.v.) serve similar functions for their respective memberships, *Music Educators Journal* seems to be better written and has a slicker, more professional look than does *American Music Teacher*. However, any critical assessment of *American Music Teacher* cannot ignore the journal's contributions to the studio music teaching profession. The membership of MTNA has grown dramatically since the inception of *American Music Teacher*, and the journal has offered these teachers a means to share their musical and educational ideas, and has helped to raise standards for the music teaching profession.

For its first ten years, the journal was published regularly five times per year (September–October, November–December, January–February, March–April, and May–June). In 1961 (v. 11) a July–August issue was added. In 1965–66 (v. 15) the publication schedule was changed slightly with the six issues appearing as September–October, November–December, January, February–March, April–May, and June–July. No internal indexing of the articles is available.

The physical format of *American Music Teacher* has undergone several changes since the journal's inception. Early issues were 8″ by 12″ and contained twenty-four to twenty-eight pages. Through the 1950s and early 1960s the number of pages per issue increased to about forty-four. Beginning with the September–October 1963 issue the size shrank to 8″ by 11″, though the number of pages per issue continued to increase. The journal was changed to standard magazine size (8½″ by 11″) as of the September–October 1981 issue. Each issue currently contains approximately sixty pages. Production quality has also changed over time, although the change has been gradual. For many years a two-color process was used for the covers, and illustrations for articles were black and white or two-color. Not until 1973 did full color photographs begin to appear on the covers. Currently the illustrations for articles are still black and white or two-color.

American Music Teacher is financially supported by the MTNA and through advertising. Current circulation is over 23,000. Approximately twenty pages per issue contain advertising from such sources as music publishers, instrument manufacturers, and music schools.

Information Sources

BIBLIOGRAPHY

Ulrich, Homer. *A Centennial History of the Music Teachers National Association.* Cincinnati, Ohio : Music Teachers National Association, 1977.

INDEXES

    External: Music Index, 1951– . Music Article Guide, 1965– . Bibliographie des Musikschrifttums, 1974– . Education Index, 1959– .

REPRINT EDITIONS

    Microform: UMI.

LOCATION SOURCES

    Widely available.

Publication History

TITLE AND TITLE CHANGES

    Music Teachers National Association Bulletin, 1939–50. *American Music Teacher,* 1951– .

VOLUME AND ISSUE DATA

    Volumes 1– , 1951– .

FREQUENCY OF PUBLICATION

    5/year, to 1960. Bimonthly, 1961– .

PUBLISHER

    Music Teachers National Association.

PLACES OF PUBLICATION

    New York, July 1951–March/April 1953. Baldwin, New York, May/June 1953–July/August 1963. Cincinnati, September/October 1963– .

EDITORS

    Theodore M. Finney, July 1951. S. Turner Jones, September/October 1951–July/August 1961. Frank S. Stillings, September/October 1961–June/July 1972. Albert

Huetteman, September/October 1972–November/December 1972. Homer Ulrich, January 1973–December 1987. Robert Elias, January 1988–   .

John K. Kratus

AMERICAN MUSICOLOGICAL SOCIETY, JOURNAL/ NEWSLETTER OF

The first issue of the American Musicological Society's *Journal (JAMS)*, edited by Oliver Strunk, appeared in the spring of 1948, some fourteen years after the founding of the society itself. It was intended to replace three earlier publications: the *Bulletin of the AMS (BAMS)*, *Papers of the AMS (PAMS)*, and the society *Newsletter (NAMS)*. BAMS (vs. 1–13; 1936–48) contained abstracts of papers read at chapter meetings and official business carried out at national meetings. *PAMS* (1936–38; 1940–41) published papers read at annual meetings, while miscellaneous items of interest to society members were announced in the typewritten and mimeographed *NAMS* (January 1944–June 1947). The *Journal* thus became the central source of information about the society. Its success was immediate: by 1949, *JAMS* was recognized as the foremost American musicological periodical (*Notes*, 6:240).

The editorial policy, while never explicitly defined, has remained strikingly homogeneous over the years. Strunk refused to state one, considering it inappropriate "to impose a particular view of musicology upon the *Journal* and thus upon the Society" (*JAMS*, 1:3). He placed the responsibility for the quality of the *Journal* in the hands of the membership. Donald Grout, the journal's second editor, reinforced the emphasis on quality and selectivity: "The value of a periodical such as the *Journal*, of course, is determined simply by the quality of the articles it contains. It is the hope of the Editorial Board that the *Journal* will continue to attract, and in increasing measure, the best products of American musicological scholarship" (*JAMS*, 4:71). The clearest policy statement was given, in 1978, by then new editor Nicholas Temperley.

An "appropriate" article for this *Journal* in my view, is one which is essentially an essay, and which aims to establish facts or theories about music in human life, by means of verifiable evidence and reasoned argument. Articles that are mainly lists, tables, or collections of uninterpreted data lie outside the scope of the *Journal*; so do articles which analyze individual pieces of music merely as abstract patterns of notes or sounds, without reference to their cultural context.

In judging "quality" . . . I may take into account factors such as style, length, originality of goals or methods, and breadth of issues addressed. (*JAMS*, 31:1–2)

The bulk of each issue is given over to between three and six articles that are, with few exceptions, models of scholarly inquiry. Each is a lengthy, detailed, thoroughly documented exposition of a particular historical point. Although there is no stated limitation on topic, articles dealing with the Renaissance clearly predominate (30 percent). Next in order of frequency are articles concerned with the Middle Ages and the Baroque and Classical periods (all with approximately equal shares of 50 percent). The remaining 20 percent of the journal's space is shared by ancient and non-Western music (6 percent), the nineteenth century (4 percent), the twentieth century (2 percent), and various systematic topics (8 percent). The emphasis on Western art music before 1800 no doubt reflects the interests of the society's members as a whole, but it has probably forced scholars in "neglected" fields to find other avenues of publication. Two special issues deserve notice: an eightieth birthday offering to Otto Kinkeldey (13.1–3) and a "Beethoven Bicentennial Issue" (23.3).

In Spring 1962 another department, "Studies and Abstracts," was instituted; in 1975 it was retitled "Studies and Reports." This section is devoted to shorter articles, although the same standards of scholarship are applied. Period emphasis parallels that found in the full-length articles.

Book reviews have always played a major role in the *Journal*, and very few issues have been without them. Written by subject specialists, they can be as long as the articles, and often contain lists of errata and/or supplementary information. In a few cases, the objectivity of the review is questionable, especially when the reviewer is known to disagree strongly with the author. (One of the most infamous instances was Lawrence Gushee's review of Frank Tirro's *Jazz: A History* [*JAMS*, 31:535–40; 32:367–68, 594–98.]) But all reviews are informative and represent the current state of knowledge. Music and recordings are not reviewed in the *Journal*.

The only other department to appear regularly since publication began is entitled "Communications." During Nicholas Temperley's tenure as editor it was renamed "Comments and Issues," but returned to its former title immediately afterward. At first the department was reserved for smaller contributions, communications other than letters to the editor, and news items other than those concerned with the society or its chapters. Almost immediately, however, it became a forum for reader's comments on published articles, and it remains so to the present.

In 1954 the *Journal* began to provide a list of "Publications Received," including both books and music. This department appeared irregularly until 1966, when it became a feature of each issue. Three other sections appeared regularly until 1972. "Notices" (or "Announcements") contained items of interest to society members, including deadlines of various sorts, projected publications, and detailed programs for annual meetings. "Reports" included minutes of annual meetings for the preceding year. Finally from 1948 to 1971 the *Journal* published abstracts (later lists) of papers read at chapter meetings. Since 1972, all this information is now found in the semiannual *AMS Newsletter*, distributed to all members.

Before 1970, certain issues of the *Journal* contained "Lists of Members," the constitution and by laws of the society, and its organization. The "Organization of the Society," including the Board of Directors, publication editors, and Council members, still appears in the Spring issue of each volume, but it is also published, along with the list of members and the society by laws, in the annual *Directory of Members and Subscribers*.

For the first sixteen years of publication, the position of editor-in-chief was held by a variety of people at irregular intervals. Oliver Strunk was editor-in-chief for the first two issues (Spring and Summer 1948). By Fall of 1948 he was listed as consulting editor, while the responsibilities were carried out by acting editor-in-chief Donald J. Grout. Grout assumed full editorial responsibilities in Spring 1949, and continued in that position until Fall 1959, although Charles Warren Fox held the position of editor-in-chief for most of the period from Summer 1952 until Spring 1959. In addition, some issues were directed by temporary editors: Spring 1952 (Otto Kinkeldey and Curt Sachs), Spring and Fall 1957 (Gustave Reese) and Summer/Fall 1958 (William S. Newman). A similar situation exists for the period Summer/Fall 1959 to Summer 1963. David G. Hughes served as editor-in-chief for all of the issues except 13.1–3, the Kinkeldey *Festschrift*, which was edited by Charles Seeger. Since the Fall of 1963 the job of editing the *Journal* has been passed on in a more regular fashion. Each editor serves for a three-year period and is responsible for eight or nine issues. Only one change is to be noted. In 1972 the transferral of power was brought into line with the calendar year.

No general index of the *Journal* has ever been prepared. Rather, the Fall issue of each volume contains an annual index for that year. Articles and studies are listed by author and title; reviews and communications are indexed by author. In addition, there is an index of illustrations. A modest quantity of advertisements and announcements for various publication is a regular feature. The size of the volumes has increased from 200–300 pages to approximately 600 6⅛" by 9" pages.

Information Sources

BIBLIOGRAPHY

Campbell, Frank, Gladys Eppink, and Jessica Fredricks. "Music Magazines of Britain and the United States." *Notes* 6 (March 1949): 239–62.

Crawford, Richard. *The American Musicological Society: 1934–1984*. Philadelphia: The American Musicological Society, 1984.

Dahlhaus, Carl. "Besprechungen." *Die Musikforschung* 17 (1964): 78–81.

Grout, Donald J. "Reports on the Journal." *Journal of the American Musicological Society* 4 (Spring 1951): 71.

Holoman, D. Kern, Joseph Kerman, and Robert Winter. "Comment and Chronicle." *Nineteenth Century Music* 1 (1977): 187.

New York Times, 19 September 1948, sec. 2, p. 7, col. 6.

Spivacke, Harold. "Book Reviews." *Notes* 19 (1961): 57–59.

Strunk, Oliver. "An Editorial." *Journal of the American Musicological Society* 1 (Spring 1948): 3.

Temperley, Nicholas. "Editorial." *Journal of the American Musicological Society* 31 (Spring 1978): 1–2.

Westrup, Jack A. "Review." *Music and Letters* 42 (1961): 281–83.

Zaslaw, Neal. "Editorial." *Current Musicology* 7 (1968): 77–80.

INDEXES
> Internal: each volume indexed.
> External: Music Index, 1949– . RILM, 1967– . Arts and Humanities Citation Index, 1974– . International Index to Periodicals, 1949–63. Humanities and Social Sciences Index, 1964–73. Humanities Index, 1974– . Bibliographie des Musikschrifttums, 1937, 1950– . Music Article Guide, 1965– .

LOCATION SOURCES
> Widely available.

Publication History

TITLE AND TITLE CHANGES
Journal of the American Musicological Society.
VOLUME AND ISSUE DATA
> Volumes 1– , 1948– .

FREQUENCY OF PUBLICATION
> 3/year.

PUBLISHER
> American Musicological Society, Inc.

PLACE OF PUBLICATION
> William Byrd Press, 2901 Byrdhill Road, Richmond, Virginia 23228

EDITORS
> Oliver Strunk, 1948 (1.1, 2). Donald J. Grout, 1948–51 (1.3–4.3). Otto Kinkeldey and Curt Sachs, 1952 (5.1). Charles Warren Fox, 1952–56, 1957 (5.2–9.3,10.2), 1958 (11.1), 1959 (12.1). Gustave Reese, 1957 (10.1,3). William S. Newman, 1958 (11.2,3). David G. Hughes, 1959 (12.2,3), 1961–63 (14.1–16.2). Charles Seeger, 1960 (13). Lewis Lockwood, 1963–66 (16.3–19.1). James Haar, 1966–69 (19.2–22.1). Martin Picker, 1969–71 (22.2–24). Don M. Randel, 1972–74. Lawrence F. Bernstein, 1975–77. Nicholas Temperley, 1978–80. Ellen Rosand, 1981–83. John W. Hill, 1984–86. Anthony Newccomb, 1987– .

Vincent J. Corrigan

AMERICAN ORGANIST

With the establishment of the journal *Music: The A.G.O. Magazine,* in October 1967, the American Guild of Organists ended an association, dating back to 1935, with *The Diapason.* The guild's decision to abandon *The Diapason* and establish its first in-house publication seems to have been motivated primarily by economic reasons. Despite a steady increase in membership throughout the 1960s, the guild faced mounting debts. Its only previous publishing venture, a scholarly pamphlet called *The American Guild of Organists Quarterly*, had been a financial liability since its inception in January 1956. The governing body of the guild felt that financial solvency could be achieved through income from advertisements in a new self-owned journal. Moreover, *Music: The A.G.O. Magazine* served to consolidate the guild's publication aspirations; in it, the news service provided by *The Diapason* was merged with the scholarly pursuits of the *AGO Quarterly*. By October 1968 (2.10), the guild decided to co-publish *Music* with the Royal Canadian College of Organists (also formerly with *The Diapason*). Hereafter, *Music* would bear the subtitle, *The A.G.O. and R.C.C.O. Magazine*.

In naming the journal, the founders chose "Music" to indicate that matters more general than the specialties of organists and choirmasters were to be covered. Seeking a readership unexplored by *The Diapason*, they wanted to produce a journal with general newsstand appeal. Deviating from *The Diapason's* dated newspaper-like format, *Music* is more compact (8½″ by 11″) with a colorful, eye-catching cover, numerous black and white photographs sprinkled throughout the articles, and a slick layout. The overall length of the journal approximates *The Diapason* with an average of forty to sixty pages.

Charles N. Henderson, editor for vs. 7.9 through 16.7, acknowledged in a retrospective editorial in v. 11.10 (November 1977) that the original aims of the founders of *Music* have been sacrificed in order to give full coverage to A.G.O. and R.C.C.O. affairs. Though more accessible to the average reader than *The Diapason* and more general in its coverage, the monthly *Music* has, from the beginning, been preoccupied with keeping the guild membership informed, with regular departments such as the "Classified" advertising, "Recital Programs," "Chapter News," "Letters to the Editor," and "Calendar of Events" (the latter listing recitals, chapter meetings, and special events of interest to A.G.O. members). Early issues included a "President's Page" in which the guild's chief executive passed on a personal, albeit *pro forma*, message. *Music* has further cultivated a specialized profile with regular departments such as the "Organists Directory," "Positions Available," "Guild Student Groups," "Appointments," and "Chapter of the Month." The numerous advertisements also target the organist: publishers, artists, artist managements, instrument builders and repair experts, and record companies. Likewise, many of the feature articles cover A.G.O. and R.C.C.O. conventions as well as various organ conclaves and festivals. Topics that could appeal to a broad musical audience are usually confined to brief, cursory articles of two to three pages. Finally, in January 1979 (13.1), the guild moved to portray the journal's content more accurately by changing its name to *The American Organist*, appropriating the name of a journal that had ceased publication in 1970.[1]

Over the years, *Music* has demonstrated a sincere devotion to improving the lot of the working church musician. Many issues contain articles on how to get a church position, how to keep that job, or how to do it more efficiently. Through *Music*, the A.G.O. has promoted educational programs for choirmasters and organists leading to certificates through thorough examinations. Furthermore, the monthly "Reviews" column has acquainted the readership with some recently published books, music, and recordings. Detailed organological information is provided in monthly columns devoted to the harpsichord and to the installation of new organs. In 1977, *Music* also became the official magazine of the Associated Pipe Organ Builders of America, who have ever since been represented in a regular column.

Although few would consider *Music* a truly academic journal, it has, over the years, included contributions by some well-respected scholars: Paul Henry Lang, Denis Stevens, Gilbert Chase, and Franklin Zimmerman. Famous performers such as E. Power Biggs and John Obetz, composer Virgil Thompson, and organ builder Fritz Noack have also appeared in its pages. However, most contributors are lesser luminaries who, not infrequently, belong to the upper echelon of guild hierarchy. In more recent volumes, a trend toward longer historical articles is evident. Despite the limited value *Music* may hold for the academic community, the editors have treated it as an important reference source by providing yearly indexes and an impressive ten-year index in v. 11.11 (November 1977).

Music, now *The American Organist*, has achieved many of the aims of its founders. First and foremost, it has been a faithful communications link for members and chapters of A.G.O. and R.C.C.O. It has also been a successful commercial venture for A.G.O. Through the sale of copious amounts of advertisements in each issue, the guild has remained financially sound.

Note

1. *The American Organist* began publication under the auspices of the A.G.O. in January 1918 and remained the official A.G.O. journal until August 1922. After *Music* appeared in 1967, it rapidly lost subscribers and financial support.

Information Sources

BIBLIOGRAPHY
Milligan, Stuart. "Music and Other Performing Arts Serials Available in Microform and Reprint Editions." *Notes* 37 (December 1980): 239–307.
INDEXES
Internal: each volume indexed; vs. 1–10 in v. 11.
External: Music Index, 1973– . Music Article Guide, 1965–   .
LOCATION SOURCES
Widely available.

Publication History

TITLE AND TITLE CHANGES
Music: The A.G.O. Magazine, October 1967–September 1968. *Music: The A.G.O. and R.C.C.O. Magazine*, October 1968–December 1978. *The American Organist*, 1979–   .
VOLUME AND ISSUE DATA
Volumes 1–   , 1967–   .

FREQUENCY OF PUBLICATION
    Monthly.
PUBLISHER
    The American Guild of Organists.
PLACE OF PUBLICATION
    630 Fifth Avenue, New York, NY 10020.
EDITORS
    Clifford G. Richter, 1967 (v. 1). David Coleman, 1968 (2.1–9). Peter J. Basch
    (1968–73, 2.1–7.5); Leon Carson, 1968–73 (2.1–7.6). William Bossert, 1973–
    74, (7.7–8). Charles N. Henderson and Anthony Baglivi (asst.), 1973–82 (7.9–
    16.7). Baglivi and Arthur Lawrence (asst.), 1982–   (16:8–   ).

Matthew Steel

AMERICAN RECORD GUIDE

With the initial commerical success of the phonograph recording industry in
the late 1910s, budding audiophiles were quick to perceive a need for a source
of information on and reviews of recordings that was independent of the major
recording, publishing, and retailing companies. The pioneering *Phonograph
Monthly Review (PMR)* had been just such a strong independent voice from 1926
until it folded in March 1932. Beginning in September of that year, Rob Darrell,
who had been largely responsible for the quality of the *PMR*, established *The
Music Lover's Guide*. It was to be published by the New York Band Instrument
Company, a firm that dealt in imported as well as domestic recordings, and
which employed, at various times, much of the new journal's staff, including
Peter Hugh Reed, the future editor of the *American Record Guide*.

The *Music Lover's Guide* lasted only two issues, but was replaced shortly
thereafter (1935) by *The American Music Lover (AML)*. The editors of *AML*
made the conscious decision to found a magazine that would deal with reproduced
music—an answer to the recordings versus radio controversy of the late 1920s.
It was intended to serve as a literal "record guide," primarily for the serious
music lover, the person who could truly be classified as a "Listener." To be
sure, not much "serious music" was coming from the American recording
studios; most of the best of what the magazine reviewed was imported, at least
until World War II. The magazine considered itself an adjunct to music appreciation education in America and embodied a belief that one should read about
music and musicians as well as listen to them.The subtitle "A Musical Connoisseur's Magazine" was added in 1935 to reflect this intended audience as
well as the rising sophistication of recorded sound audiences.

In September 1944, *The American Music Lover* staff decided to change the
title to *The Listener's Record Guide*, and then, only a month later, to the present
American Record Guide (the final change largely a product of wartime nationalism).

James Lyons, who assumed editorship of the *Guide* in 1957, made it one of the most respected publications devoted to music and musical activity in the country. His devotion to furthering the interests of good music, primarily though not exclusively through recordings, remained the guiding editorial principle. After a brief dormant period following Lyons' untimely death in 1973, the *Guide* resumed publication with the November 1976 issue and has carried on the standards and ideals of Lyons' tenure. Many of the writers long associated with the *Guide* continue to lend their expertise to its pages. Contributors cover the gamut of the musically interested performers, teachers, composers, collectors, and critics. Issue size has increased several fold and now averages fifty to sixty pages in a 5½" by 9" format. Recording and audio equipment manufacturers contribute a modest amount of advertising.

Thus, the ongoing aim after the revitalization was to review the latest in classical recordings as accurately and impartially as possible. Attention continued to be paid to live performances of opera and ballet, to newer and upcoming artists, and to the contributions of small or obscure record companies. Since 1976, the *Guide* has also endeavored to deal in greater length with American musical theatre and the music of film and dance. Rock and other more inherently pop musical forms continue to be more or less ignored.

Each issue has reviews of well over a hundred recordings. They are for the most part carefully written with a scrutinizing eye for detail, but with a touch of liveliness and not infrequent barbs. Each review contains a discussion of the work and the performance, a comparison with other recordings of the same piece, an assessment of the technical quality of the recording, a designation of the recording formats available, and complete contents, reference, and price information.

Although "serious" music has been the *Guide*'s focus, it has also, as a matter of policy, reviewed children's recordings, documentaries, folk music, musicals, film music, and some jazz music ("Swing Music Note" was a popular column in the mid–1940s). Beginning with the September 1957 issue, it started including reviews of prerecorded tapes as well.

Throughout its fifty-year history the *Guide* and its predecessors included pertinent, informative articles within its covers, particularly those of a biographical or historical nature. Some of the current special feature articles include John W. Barker's "The Nuclear Brahms" (47.5:2–17), Louis Blois's "The Symphonies of Edward Rubbra—A Perspective" (47.4:3–8), Gerald S. Fox's "Resurgence of Mahler" (48.2:3–9), and Teri Noel Towe's "*Messiah* Review" (47.2:21–28).

During the late 1930s and early 1940s, the magazine featured a regular "Radio Notes" column as well. Other valuable features currently include "The Monophile"—Peter J. Rabinowitz reviews prestereo recordings and rereleases of historic performance, reviews of lesser-known but important labels (CRI, Spectrum, Owl, Opus One), and "Soundwise"—trends in sound reproduction.

Information Sources

BIBLIOGRAPHY

Caine, Milton A. "Statement of Intent from the Editor: The Same But Different."
    American Record Guide 40 (November 1976): 3.

Cooper, Matt. "In Retrospect (Tracing the History and Development of *American Record
    Guide* from Its Beginnings up to the Present)." *American Record Guide* 41 (1978):
    6–7; (1978): 16–17.

"From the Majority (Return to Smaller Format)." *American Record Guide* 23 (August
    1957): 166.

Miller, Phillip L. "And an Update (Antecedents of the ARG)." *American Record Guide*
    40 (1976): 9.

"Music Periodicals." *Notes* 15 (1958): 385–86.

INDEXES

    External: Music Article Guide, 1965–   . Music Index, 1949–   . Readers' Guide,
    1961–   . Popular Music Periodicals Index, 1973–76. Magazine Index, 1977–   .

LOCATION SOURCES

    Library of Congress, Boston Public Library, Brooklyn College, New York Public
    Library, St. Paul Public Library.

Publication History

TITLE AND TITLE CHANGES

    The American Music Lover, 1935–44. *Listener's Record Guide*, September 1944.
    American Record Guide, October 1944–   .

VOLUME AND ISSUE DATA

    Volumes 1–   , 1935–   .

FREQUENCY OF PUBLICATION

    Monthly, 1935–80. 10/year, 1981–82. 6/year, 1982–   .

PUBLISHERS

    The American Music Lover, 1935–44. Listener's Record Guide, 1944. ARG
    American Record Guide Publishing, 1944–81. Helen Dwight Reed Educational
    Foundation, 1981–85. Salem Research, 1985–October 1987. Record Guide Pro-
    ductions, December 1987–   .

PLACES OF PUBLICATION

    Pelham, New York, 1935–71. Melville, New York, 1976–81. Washington, D.C.,
    1981–85. Millbrook, 1985–October, 1987. Cincinnati, Ohio, December 1987–   .

EDITORS

    Peter Hugh Reed, 1935–57. James Lyons, 1957–72. Milton A. Caine, 1976–81.
    John Cronin, 1981–83. Doris Chalfin, Managing Editor, 1983–85. Grace Wolf,
    Managing Editor, 1985–87. Donald R. Vroon, 1987–   .

William L. Schurk

AMERICAN STRING TEACHER

In 1951, Paul Rolland, *American String Teacher's* first editor, convinced the
officers of the American String Teachers Association that a journal promoting
quality string teaching was needed if string education was to survive in the public

school. The aims of the journal were to encourage quality string teaching and playing; promote excellence in performance of solo, ensemble, and orchestra repertoire at all levels; and to establish the highest artistic and pedagogical standards in string teaching.

American String Teacher (AST) is the official journal of the American String Teachers Association and is a nonprofit publication. It serves as a liaison between its membership and the Music Educators National Conference, the Music Teachers National Association, the Music Industry Council and other similar groups. *AST* 's scope is international, and it is the only publication for all kinds of string performers and teachers.

The format is approximately one-third organizational and information, one-third feature articles, and one-third forums and reviews. The feature articles, averaging 1,500 words, are submitted for the exclusive use of the journal, but may be reprinted in other sources if they are used to promote string education. Contributors range from recognized leaders in string pedagogy and noted performers, to private teachers with the time and interest to share their insights. Articles cover a variety of topics, for example, biographies about past and present artists and pedagogs, research pieces on historical and current teaching methods and practices, and reports on the status of strings in education. A representative sampling of feature articles includes "Teacher's Teacher: A Panoramic View of Sam Applebaum, Fiddler and Teacher to All" by Ishaq Arazi (19.2:12–18), "The Viola D'Amore Yesterday and Today" by Robert Dolejsi (20.2:13–18), "Analysis of Locke's D Minor Suite" by Daniel Chazanoff (25.2:38–39), and "Fingerings: Is the Expert Always Right?" by Marya H. Giesy (32.2:46–49).

Of particular note are the forums. Now nine, forums include one each for violin, viola, cello, double bass, guitar, harp, chamber music, the private teacher, and the school teacher. Each has its own editor, appointed for a two-year term. The forums present information from experts in that field, and guest writers are urged to participate. Most forums appear in every issue and average 2,500 words.

Of equal value and importance are the book review, album review, and new music review departments. An average of fifteen 250-word reviews appear in each issue. Also included are convention and clinic reports, letters to the editor, and memorials. One issue per year (Spring) identifies string institutes and workshops, including fifteen to twenty co-sponsored by a state ASTA organization, for association members to consider for summer study.

Several special issues have revolved around themes, such as the Bach Tricentennial or one of the journal's anniversaries. One issue (Summer 1984) was printed partially in Spanish and distributed throughout Latin America. The *American String Teacher* has also made significant contributions to the acceptance of new music. Another activity of the journal is the publicizing of ASTA's biannual solo competition for young artists.

The journal is critically acclaimed by musicians and educators for providing a source of highly informative articles about the study and teaching of all stringed instruments. It also provides space for members to communicate within their areas of specialization.

The journal is issued quarterly and has maintained a standard 8½″ by 11″ size since its inception. An average size in the last decade is eighty pages per issue, with a color cover since 1972. The first four-color cover appeared in 1982 and has been standard since. Photographs, along with illustrations, average some fifty per issue; musical examples are used where applicable. The first issue contained twelve pages with four advertisements and had a press run of 3,000. In the entire history of the journal, the longest issue had ninety-six pages and a press run of more than 7,000 with ninety-six advertisements. As a nonprofit journal, *American String Teacher* relies heavily on advertisers, particularly universities, violin shops, and publishers.

Information Sources

INDEXES
    External: Music Index, 1957– . Music Article Guide, 1966– .
LOCATION SOURCES
    Widely available.

Publication History.

TITLE AND TITLE CHANGES
    American String Teacher.
VOLUME AND ISSUE DATA
    Volumes 1– , 1951– .
FREQUENCY OF PUBLICATION
    Quarterly.
PUBLISHER.
    American String Teacher Association.
PLACE OF PUBLICATION
    Key Biscayne, Florida.
EDITORS
    Paul Rolland, 1951–60. Howard Van Sickle, 1960–66. Paul Askegaard, 1966–69. Anthony Messina, 1969–72. John Zurfluh, 1972–76. G. Jean Smith, 1976–81. Nancy Cluck, 1981–83. Jody Atwood, 1983– .

Victor Ellsworth

ANBRUCH

In the first part of the twentieth century the Viennese music publishing house Universal Edition, under the direction of Emil Herztka, established its distinguished record of commitment to the publication of new music. It is not surprising then that its in-house organ, *Anbruch*, founded in 1919, became the leading voice for the German-speaking musical avant-garde between the World Wars. Other journals that might have rivaled it, such as *Melos* (q.v.) and the Czech journal *Auftakt*, could not compete with *Anbruch*'s stable of special contributors, drawn from the ranks of composers published by Universal.

Anbruch advertised itself, from the outset, as a journal for everyone interested in music with the intention of being a forum for all serious discussions of modern music—at least German modern music—rather than limiting itself to certain schools, trends, or viewpoints. *Anbruch*'s first statement of purpose went on to echo a common concern in post–World War I Germany and Austria: the need to rebuild cultural life. Rather than recreating prewar models, *Anbruch* sought to foster new relationships between society and modern culture.

Because of its tie to Universal Edition, *Anbruch* excelled in publishing articles by composers on aspects of their own works. Of particular interest were the lengthy articles by composers that preceded premieres of their works. Composers who received frequent exposure in the pages of *Anbruch* included Arnold Schönberg and his students, Ernst Krenek, Kurt Weill, Béla Bartók, Franz Schreker, George Antheil, and Egon Wellesz. Composers also frequently wrote on the works of other composers. Critics such as Oscar Bie, Paul Bekker, Paul Pisk, Hanns Gutman, and H. H. Stuckenschmidt contributed commentaries on all other aspects of modern musical life including aesthetics, philosophy, and psychology; discussions of performers and conductors; and large-scale reviews of modern music festivals.

From the beginning an issue consisted of six to eight articles of two to six pages each plus other regular features such as a number of short music reviews, lists of new music publications, announcements, and letters to the editor. The works of Universal Edition composers, new Universal publications, and Universal business received primary though not exclusive attention. Musical appendices consisting of a single movement of a newly published work were also occasionally included.

Issues were frequently devoted to a single topic or individual, and could run as long as ninety pages. Notable special issue topics included Gustav Mahler and his legacy (2.⅞), Arnold Schönberg in honor of his fiftieth birthday (6.⅞), and ones on such pertinent topics of the time as jazz (7.4), machine music (8.⅘), and modern opera (9.½). The latter was the subject of many *Anbruch* articles and reviews.

Like all journals in the early 1930s, *Anbruch* suffered from the worsening financial and political situation. In 1930 another Universal Edition publication, *Pult und Taktstock*, was combined with *Anbruch*, without visible impact on the latter. By 1935, two years after Adolf Hitler had become chancellor of Germany, Universal Edition succumbed to criticism from the conservative German musical press for its support of ''cultural Bolshevism'' and ceased publishing *Anbruch*. Picked up by Vorwaert Press, *Anbruch* subsequently announced a change in its subtitle to *Österreichische Zeitschrift für Musik*, dropping any reference to ''modern music,'' and published on less controversial topics during the last two years of its existence.

The first four volumes of *Anbruch* were issued once every two months, with publication suspended during the months of July and August. Vs. 1–3 were in a 7³⁄₁₆″ by 9¹³⁄₁₆″ physical format and of thirty-six to forty pages in length per number. V. 4 was reduced to 7¹⁄₁₆″ by 9⁷⁄₁₆″ format. In v. 5 the journal began offering monthly issues of thirty-five pages, and the length increased in several years to fifty pages per issue. V. 7 contained eleven numbers, and with v. 8 the journal stabilized at ten numbers per year, again skipping the summer months. In the last years of the journal's existence, issues dropped to as low as thirty pages in length. Occasional illustrations and photographs were published, and the unusual cover graphics (sometimes quite abstract) and lettering changed frequently to reflect the nature of the special issues. Musical examples and larger excerpts appeared in appendices and occasionally within the body of the text. A yearly index was published for each volume.

Information Sources

BIBLIOGRAPHY
Stefan, Paul. "Rechenschaft und Programm." *Anbruch* 17 (1935): 1–5.
INDEXES
    Internal: each volume indexed.
REPRINT EDITIONS
    Microform: Schnase Microform Service. Library of Congress. Datamics, Inc.
LOCATION SOURCES
    Widely available, though often partial.

Publication History

TITLE AND TITLE CHANGES
    Musikblätter des Anbruch, 1919–28. *Anbruch*, 1929–34. *Anbruch Österreichishe Zeitschrift für Musik*, 1935–37.
VOLUME AND ISSUE DATA
    Volumes 1–19, 1919–37.
FREQUENCY OF PUBLICATION
    Semiannual, to 1922. Monthly (with irregularities), 1923–1925. 10/year, 1926–1937.
PUBLISHERS
    Universal Edition, 1919–34. Vorwaerts Press, 1935–37.
PLACE OF PUBLICATION
    Vienna.
EDITORS
    Otto Schneider, 1919–22. Paul Stefan, 1922–37.

Susan C. Cook

ANNALES MUSICOLOGIQUES

Les Annales musicologiques (moyen-age et renaissance) was a publication of the Société de Musique d'Autrefois. The Société was founded in 1926 "to research, publish and make heard works of early music" (1:7). Their aspiration to publish a review dedicated to Medieval and Renaissance music was finally achieved when the first volume of *Les Annales* appeared in 1953.

The journal was conceived as a joint Franco-American production. The editors of volume 1 were François Lesure in France and Leo Schrade of the United States. Manfred Bukofzer and Genevieve Thibault joined these two on the editorial board. With this editorial staff it comes as no surprise that *Les Annales* embodies excellent, fastidious research that has received wide acclaim. Their self-stated goals, printed in the first volume, assert that:

> This periodical . . . will gather in-depth studies chosen either for their doc-
> umentary interest (bibliographies, analysis of manuscripts, general research
> materials), or for their interesting approach, articles which revise or alter
> the direction of a subject . . . the domain of *Les Annales* from the Middle
> Ages to the Renaissance will cover equally all facets of intellectual and
> artistic thought relevant to comparative musicology. The editors hope never
> to lose sight of the fact that the history of music is a part of the history
> of civilization.

Individual volumes run 300 to 400 7⅛″ by 9″ pages in length and contain seven or eight articles. The selections are more or less chronological from the twelfth through the sixteenth centuries. The eight articles in v. 1, five in English and three in French, represent four different types of articles; three contributions deal with a specific manuscript, one is a bibliography of music, two articles discuss actual compositions, and two essays relate music to outside fields. The articles are all of the highest quality; the impressive standard and breadth established in v. 1 is not diminished in successive numbers.

It is difficult to single out specific articles when so many are written by such established and well-respected musicologists as Kenneth Levy, Oliver Strunk, Claudio Sartori, and others. Articles that have received special acclaim and continue to serve as important reference sources for their field deserve some mention. In v. 1, F. Lesure and G. Thibault present their "Bibliographie des editions musicales publiées par Nicolas du Chemin (1549–1576)" (1:269), a treasure of new music sources that brings to light many important works previously overlooked. A history of the printer and his relationship to his principal composers precedes a presentation of previously unpublished dedications. The majority of the titles are exactly reprinted with three type fonts, giving complete title, location, table of contents, and useful comments. Facsimiles of title pages are frequently included and three indices permit quick access to the material. Dragan Plamenac's study of the Riccordiana chansonnier, Cod. 2356, appeared in the 1954 issue (2:105). This article, embued with Plamenac's traditional high standard of thoroughness and accuracy, has been called a standard reference source for historians of fifteenth-century music.

Minor criticisms have been voiced. Occasionally, for example, articles are considered to be outside the stated subject of the journal. "Dramatic Religious Processions in Paris in the late Sixteenth Century" by Francis Yates (2:215) was judged perhaps insufficiently musicological, while an article on Trichet's *Le Traité des instruments de musique* (c. 1640) is, strictly speaking, a bit outside the stated chronological boundaries. But in neither of these cases is there anything but praise for the articles themselves. The journal was intended to appear annually, but did so only between 1953 and 1957. Two subsequent volumes were completed: the first appeared in 1964, the second in 1977. The last, a special issue, was dedicated to Thibault (d. 1975) who was a founding member of both the Société de Musique d'Autrefois and *Les Annales'* editorial board. The third of the original four editors to die, her passing seems also to have marked that of the journal.

Beginning with the third volume, *Les Annales* received financial support from the French government through the Centre National de la Recherche Scientifique (CNRS). The CNRS is France's most prestigious source of research funding. Its signature alone is a clue that *Les Annales* is a serious journal devoted to rigorous music research of the highest quality.

There are no advertisements, reviews, or editorial features in *Les Annales*. For the sake of accuracy the articles are never translated. Corrections and addenda appear at the end of each volume. The table of contents and table of illustrations are also to be found at the end.

Information Sources

BIBLIOGRAPHY

Albrecht, Hans. "Französische Sammelpublikationen zur Geschichte der Kunste in der Renaissance und zur älteren Musikgeschichte." *Musikforschung* 11 (1958): 342–347, 498–502.

Clercx, Suzanne. "Annales musicologiques." *Revue belge de musicologie* 9 (1955): 169–71.

Husmann, Heinrich. "Annales musicologiques: Ein neues internationales wissenschaftliches Jahrbuch." *Musikforschung* 9 (1956): 202–6

Kenney, Sylvia W. "Annales musicologiques. Tomo 2." *Journal of the American Musicological Society* 10 (1957): 124–28.

"A New Periodical." *Musica disciplina* 8 (1954): 4–5.

Reese, Gustave. "Annales musicologiques, moyen-age et renaissance." *Renaissance News* 7 (Autumn 1954): 102–4.

INDEXES

External: Music Index, 1953–77. RILM, 1967–77. Bibliographie des Musikschrifttums, 1952–63.

LOCATION SOURCES

Widely available.

Publication History

TITLE AND TITLE CHANGES

Les Annales musicologiques.

VOLUME AND ISSUE DATA

Volumes 1–7, 1953–77.

FREQUENCY OF PUBLICATION
   Annual, 1953–57. Two additional issues: 1964, 1977.
PUBLISHER
   Société de Musique d'Autrefois.
PLACE OF PUBLICATION
   Neuilly-sur-Seine, France.
EDITORS
   François Lesure and Leo Schrade, 1953– . Manfred Brukofzer and Genevieve
   Thibault, 1954– .

Lyn Hubler

ANNUAL REVIEW OF JAZZ STUDIES. See JOURNAL OF JAZZ
STUDIES

ANUARIO MUSICAL

   The *Anuario musical* is a major scholarly yearbook devoted mainly to the
history of Spanish music before the nineteenth century. Begun in 1946 as the
official organ of the Instituto Español de Musicología (under the aegis of the
Consejo Superior de Investigaciones Científicas), it was edited for over two
decades by Msgr. Higinio Anglés (1888–1969), whose work on Cristóbal Mo-
rales and Tomás Luis de Victoria (in the series, *Monumentos de la Música
Española*, which he founded in 1941), Medieval topics (for example, Las Huelgas
MS, cantigas of Alfonso el Sabio), and early Spanish keyboard music attracted
international attention. Such musicologists as José Subirá, Nicolás A. Solar
Quintes, José M. Madurell, Santiago Kastner, José López Calo, and Miguel
Querol Gavaldá were frequent contributors during the years of his editorship.
   The journal is a very rich source for the history of cathedral music in Spain
from the period of Mozarabic chant (that is, before 1085) until about the second
half of the eighteenth century. (A few articles on music of the nineteenth and
early twentieth centuries do appear.) Particular emphasis has been placed on
archival documents and detailed inventory lists of archival holdings. Historic
cathedral organs (such as those at Lérida, Burgos, and Barcelona) have been
described at length. José Marís Madurell has edited a series of articles providing
the exact working of early documents: "Documentos para la Historia de músicos,
maestros de danza, instrumentos y libros de música (siglos xiv–xviii)." Ethnic
and folkloric subjects—*la música popular*—have not been eschewed; scholars
such as Marius Schneider, José A. de Donastia, M. García Matos, and José
Romeu Figueras have made notable contributions along these lines, and Anglés
himself provided an article on the troubador music of the Provençal area (15:
3–20). World music subjects are treated occasionally, for example, Marius
Schneider, "La relation entre la mélodie et la langage dans la musique chinoise"
(5:62–77).

The *Anuario musical* is an indispensible source for the scholarly study of Spanish music from the Medieval era to the eighteenth century. For the Baroque period especially, a substantial amount of basic bibliographical and biographical data can be found; among the important composers of this period, Sebastian Durón (1660–1716) has been the subject of several path-breaking articles.

Individual volumes, averaging about 250 5″ by 9¾″ pages, are separately indexed. Each features from seven to as many as fourteen, twenty- to twenty-five-page articles (some continued in the following volume). Rather thorough documentation is the rule, and many articles are illustrated with musical examples (sometimes complete works), song texts, and facsimiles; photographs, tables, and charts are included occasionally. Early issues (2–10) include a regular feature, entitled "Crónica," on the activities of the Instituto Español de Musicología. Reviews ("Bibliografía") are provided in issues 5–10. Necrologies appear sporadically (for example, 11, 33/34/35). Most articles are in Spanish, but an increasing number have been appearing in German, English, French, and Italian. Non-Spanish authors (Hans Spanke, Paul Collaer, and Robert Stevenson) and non-Spanish topics (such as Voya Toncitch, "Aperçu sur l'Esthétique de Chopin") have likewise become somewhat more common. Commemorative or dedicatory volumes for Cristóbal Morales (8), Juan Cabanilles (17), Antonio de Cabeźon (21), Anglés (24), Felipe Pedrell (27), and Manuel Querol Gavaldá (36) have been issued. Double volumes appeared for 1973–74 (28/29) and 1976–77 (31/32); a triple volume appeared for 1978–80 (33/34/35).

Information Sources

INDEXES
> Internal: each volume indexed.
> External: Music Index, 1956– . RILM, 1973– . Bibliographie des Musikschrifttums, 1950–[1967–73]– .

LOCATION SOURCES
> Widely available.

Publication History

TITLE AND TITLE CHANGES
> *Anuario musical.*

VOLUME AND ISSUE DATA
> Volumes 1– , 1946– .

FREQUENCY OF PUBLICATION
> Annual (with some irregularities).

PUBLISHERS
> Consejo Superior de Investigaciones Científicas, Instituto Español de Musicología.

PLACE OF PUBLICATION
> Barcelona, Spain.

EDITORS
Higinio Anglés, 1946–69. Interim, 1970–71. Miguel Querol Gavaldó, 1972–80.
José M. Llorens, 1981– .

John E. Druesedow

ARCHIV FÜR MUSIKFORSCHUNG

The *Archiv für Musikforschung* (*AfM*) was published between 1936 and 1943
in Leipzig. According to the preface to the first issue, the periodical was to
assume the tasks of the *Zeitschrift für Musikwissenschaft* (q.v.) as the "German
musicological trade journal published by the Deutsche Gesellschaft für Musikwissenschaft, supported by the Staatliches Institut für deutsche Musikforschung." The first three volumes list both the *Gesellschaft* and the *Institut* on
the title page, but the former was dropped beginning with v. 4. Like all publications from this period in Germany, the journal was under firm control of the
Nazi regime and therefore has a somewhat dubious reputation in the field of
musical scholarship.

Some of the editors of and contributors to *AfM*, like Heinrich Besseler, Willy
Hess, Arnold Schering, and Leo Schrade (to name only a few), are among the
most prominent in the field. Most were associated with German or Swiss universities, with the occasional exception of a foreign scholar writing about music
in his own country, for example, Denes Bartha and Higinio Anglés.

Despite the prominence of the scholars involved, Nazi collaboration, while
not permeating every page, does run like a thread through the journal. Propoganda
Minister Goebbels demanded cooperation from the field of musicology in achiev-
ing the goals of the state, and, according to the report on one conference in
1939, "a large number . . . thankfully heeded the call to assist appropriately in
the necessary task by means of presentations on topical themes, especially on
the questions of race, the state, the people (das Volk) and music" (3:381).

In fact, many of the articles in the *Archiv* are devoted to folk music (of all countries), German *Kleinmeister*, and the cultural history of German cities—all in line
with Goebbels' directive, but also favorite topics in German musicology long before the rise of the National Socialists. Most of these articles could appear in almost any musicologically oriented publication without seeming unusual. Some,
however, make a special, often exaggerated, attempt to link their subject to the
quest for German culture and folk spirit. One disturbing example is the report of a
conference on Wolfgang Amadeus Mozart, where many of the papers were devoted to an exaltation of Mozart's Germanic roots. Perhaps such viewpoints would
be innocuous in a different context, but in these circumstances they become a sin-
ister reminder of how subtly scholarship can be manipulated. Most blatant are the
few articles and conference reports dealing with the distasteful subject of music
and race. In a disconcertingly pseudo-scientific article (v. 2), Siegfried Gunther
outlines the differences in musical talent among the races, concluding with a quo-

tation from one of Adolf Hitler's speeches to the Reichstag. Later (v. 7), Hans Engel refines Gunther's theories in a discussion of individual composers, an example of the ultimate distortion of scholarly thought.

No perceptible change occurred in the content or slant of the articles as the war progressed, but the decline of Germany's fortunes can be seen in other aspects of the journal. Most obvious is the gradual decrease in the size of the volumes, from around 500 pages each year in the first three to 125 in the last. Later issues carried fewer and fewer reports of conferences, which obviously became increasingly difficult to hold, and more and more reports of scholars called away to the army and even being killed in action. The last editor, Hans Thierstappen, was actually "Im Felde" with the *Wehrmacht* during his entire tenure. Though v. 8 carried a notice that the journal had to be reduced by half that year but would resume full publication the next, no further issues appeared.

In outward format *AfM* differs little from standard scholarly publications before and after. It was issued quarterly with consecutive pagination; pages measure 7" by 11". The articles, six to eight in early issues and about half that number later, range from brief reports of five to six pages to in-depth studies of fifty to sixty, with some extending over several issues. Most make use of the standard scholarly apparatus, including extensive musical examples, charts, and verbatim presentations of archival material. Likewise standard are the book reviews, which take up an increasingly large proportion of each issue in the later volumes. Special features show the journal's close ties to German universities and musicological societies: Each volume contains a catalogue of music courses offered at various universities in Germany, Austria, and Switzerland, joined in v. 3 by a list of musicology dissertations accepted at those institutions. In addition, reports on activities of the Deutsche Gesellschaft für Musikwissenschaft and the Staatliches Institut appear at the end of each issue, along with personal notes about members of the organizations (birthdays, promotions, deaths, and the like). The last few pages were traditionally given over to Breitkopf und Härtel advertising.

Information Sources

BIBLIOGRAPHY
Hill, Richard S. "German Wartime Music Periodicals." *Notes* 5 (1948): 199–206.
The New Grove Dictionary of Music and Musicians. S.v. "Periodicals," by Imogen Fellinger.
INDEXES
Internal: each volume indexed.
External: Bibliographie des Musikschrifttums, 1936, 1937, 1939.
REPRINT EDITIONS
Microform: Dakota Graphics.
LOCATION SOURCES
Widely available.

Publication History

TITLE AND TITLE CHANGES
Archiv für Musikforschung.

VOLUME AND ISSUE DATA
   Volumes 1–8.2/4, 1936–43.
FREQUENCY OF PUBLICATION
   Quarterly.
PUBLISHER
   Breitkopf und Härtel.
PLACE OF PUBLICATION
   Leipzig, Germany.
EDITORS
   Rudolph Steglich with Heinrich Besseler, Max Schneider, and Georg Schuneman,
   1936–39. Rudolph Steglich, 1939–40. Hans Joachim Thierstappen, 1939–43.

Mary Sue Morrow

ARCHIV FÜR MUSIKWISSENSCHAFT

One of the world's premier musicological journals, the *Archiv für Musikwis-senschaft* (*AMw*) has, since its founding in 1918, served as a forum for many of the most important products of German music scholarship in the twentieth century. Though its publication has not been chronologically continuous, what with a lengthy hiatus between 1926 and 1952, the journal's continuity in title, purpose, and general character has been remarkable. It remains today, as it was originally conceived, a compendium of the most serious music scholarship, primarily by Germans, edited by and featuring the work of some of the greater luminaries in the German-speaking musicological community.

The first eight *Jahrgänge* of the *AMw*, which have been reprinted by Georg Ohms Verlagsbuchhandlung, provide a fascinating perspective on the years when musicology was first gaining a foothold as an established discipline. The team of three editors reflected early musicology's preoccupation with music of the Baroque and earlier, and each member was a student of one of the great pioneers in the study of early music: Max Seiffert (Baroque, Phillip Spitta), Johannes Wolf (Medieval and Renaissance, Spitta), and Max Schneider (Baroque, Hugo Riemann). The editors' introduction to the first *Jahrgang* (1918/19) constitutes an important document in the history of musicology:

The far-sighted generosity of a German Prince (Adolf of Bückeburg) has made for musicology, in the *Fürstliche Forschungsinstitut* at Bückeburg, a place which, even in peacetime hardly imagined by the boldest fantasy and now amidst and in spite of the distress of the terrible world war come to reality, offers the young discipline, having struggled with limited success but steadfastly for a century now, the possibility of free, unrestrained and secure development of its strength.

With the *AMw* the *Fürstliche Institut* opens its series of publications. . . .

Musicology is less independent than the other humanistic disciplines, being closely bound by necessity to Theology, Philosophy, Psychology,

Aesthetics, Mathematics, Natural Science, History, Linguistics, even Physiology and the Visual Arts . . . .

The nature of the new *AMw* is similar to that of the *Sammelbände der Internationalen Musik-Gesellschaft*, disbanded during the war, but more specifically devoted to German music, though not to the exclusion of everything foreign. German music has always (in earlier centuries even more than now) had close connections with music of other countries. (1.1:1–2)

The contents of the first *Jahrgang* seem fully in accord with the editors' view of their purpose. In an imposing total of 640 pages, forty-one substantial articles are presented. The volume contains no advertisements nor any short reports other than those on a single page of *Nachträge*. In early issues, an index (*Inhalt*), compiled with typical German thoroughness, stands at the head of the issue and lists all signed articles, with their page numbers, alphabetically by the author's name. More recently the *Inhalt* is arranged by page number as in a conventional table of contents. Contributors include, besides the editors, such important musicological personages as Curt Sachs, Egon Wellesz, and Arnold Schering. Topics range from specialized studies of (usually early) music or music-related materials—for example, "Die Tänze des Mittelalters. Eine Untersuching des Wesens der ältesten Instrumentalmusik" by Johannes Wolf (1.1:10–42) (with a twenty-four-page musical supplement), "Ein Breslauer Mensuraltraktat des 15. Jahrhunderts" by Johannes Wolf (1.1:329–345), and "Die alte Chorbibliothek der Thomasschule in Leipzig" by Arnold Schering (1.1:275–288)—to studies of a meta-musicological or interdisciplinary nature—the foundations of music-historical research, art-historical paths to musicology, iconographical evidence for instrumental accompaniment of the vocal works on the sixteenth century. Worthy of special note is the inclusion of several articles that would today be considered examples of ethnomusicology, such as one on Chinese musical notation and one on folk music of the Volga region. On the other hand Western art music of the nineteenth century is almost completely ignored, and there is not a single article dealing with early twentieth-century music.

The next seven *Jahrgänge* are slightly less massive, each covering a single year rather than overlapping two as did the first. They are, however, no less weighty in the nature of their contents. The editorship remained constant, and so did editorial policy. The only notable changes were the addition, as of the third *Jahrgang* (1921), of several pages listing publications received, and, as of the sixth (1924), of a short section containing "Brief Communications."

In 1927 the *Fürstliches Institut* was dissolved and the *AMw* discontinued. Perhaps the competition with the *Zeitschrift für Musikwissenschaft* (q.v.), published from 1918 through 1936, had ultimately proved too severe. In 1952, however, thanks to the establishment of the Ernst Hohner Stiftung in Trossingen, the *AMw* was resurrected. According to the new editors, in their preface to the ninth *Jahrgang* (1952), the *Archiv für Musikforschung* (q.v.) (1936–43) had taken over the role of both the *Zeitschift für Musikwissenschaft* and the *AMw*. However, *Die Musikforschung*, established in 1948, did *not* cover both roles, but rather left room for a journal devoted exclusively to major essays as the earlier *AMw* had been. Hence the resurrection.

In format and subject matter the revived journal was remarkably similar to its earlier incarnation. Each *Jahrgang*, however, was now divided into several different issues (three for 1952, four for most subsequent years), and the total pagination in each *Jahrgang* was somewhat less than before, averaging about 300. As earlier, the articles were all in German and almost exclusively by German-speaking authors, but topics were not limited to German music. Studies in methodology, acoustics, aesthetics, and other topics were included with some frequency. The nineteenth century was still largely avoided. The only differences seem to be that the ethnomusicological articles that appeared in the early volumes were now (temporarily) excluded, their place apparently being taken by occasional studies of twentieth-century music.

Changes in the journal's character since 1952 have been minimal. The eleventh *Jahrgang* introduced the practice of providing short biographies of the contributors. In 1964 the listing of "books received" was reinstated (having been omitted from 1952 to 1963). The most important trend since 1970 has been toward the inclusion of more articles on twentieth-century music, particularily that of the Second Viennese School, which now receives conspicuous attention.

The editorial staff has remained remarkably constant since 1952. Hans Heinrich Eggebrecht, who shared the chief editorship with Wilibald Gurlitt in 1952, took control after the latter's death in 1963. Membership on the editorial board, consisting at any given point in time of several German musicologists, has changed over the years but only very gradually. The best-known figures among the current membership are probably Carl Dahlhaus (since 1973) and Kurt von Fischer (since 1965).

As of 1985 the journal is issued quarterly, averaging seventy-five pages per issue or 300 per *Jahrgang*, and measuring 6⅝″ by 9⅝″. Each issue typically contains four articles. A thorough index for each *Jahrgang* is issued at the end of the year. Advertisements for publications of musicological nature are now included, but very sparingly. The most recent issues show a revival of interest in ethnomusicological studies, but otherwise the nature of topics treated remains as outlined above.

Since 1966 the *AMw* has issued an important series of *Beihefte* averaging about 150 pages each and appearing as a rule once per year. The first volume was a collection of essays by Wilibald Gurlitt, but most others have been monographs on a particular topic (corresponding in range to the topics treated in the journal). Many of the volumes are publications of doctoral dissertations.

Information Sources

INDEXES

    Internal: each volume indexed.

    External: Music Index, 1954–   . RILM, 1967–   . Bibliographie des Musikschrifttums, 1952–   . Arts and Humanities Citation Index, 1984–   .

REPRINT EDITIONS
  Microfilm: Library of Congress (1918–27). Dakota Graphics (1918–27).
  InterDocumentation (1918–27).
LOCATION SOURCES
  Widely available.

Publication History

MAGAZINE TITLE AND TITLE CHANGES
  Archiv für Musikwissenschaft.
VOLUME AND ISSUE DATA
  Volumes 1–8, 1918–27. Volumes 9– , 1952– .
FREQUENCY OF PUBLICATION
  Annual, 1918–27. Quarterly (somewhat irregular), 1952– .
PUBLISHERS
  Breitkopf und Härtel, 1918/19–27. Verlag Archiv für Musikwissenshaft, 1952–
  61. Franz Steiner Verlag, 1962– .
PLACES OF PUBLICATION
  Leipzig, 1918/19–27. Trossingen, 1952–61. Wiesbaden, 1962– .
EDITORS
  Max Seiffert, 1918/19–27. Wilibald Gurlitt and Hans Heinrich Eggebrecht, 1952–
  61. Hans Heinrich Eggebrecht, 1962/63– .

David R. Beveridge

ASIAN MUSIC

Asian Music, journal of the Society for Asian Music, welcomes articles on
all aspects of music in Asia, including dance and drama, and addresses a reading
public of cultivated amateurs as well as those who desire to deepen their knowledge and enjoy the many musics of Asia. The professional musician, the scholar
with specialties in Asian music, the informed layperson, and the Asian specialist
all will find value in the journal.

Articles encompass a variety of topics: ethnomusicology, sociology, anthro-
pology, and cognate fields. All regions of Asia are covered. The editor notes
that v. 11.1 is the most geographically diverse issue with contents ranging from
France through North Africa, the Middle East and India, to Java and China.
Most issues, of course, do not attempt such an encyclopedic span. Contributors
to the first volume (1968) represent a blend of interests and personalities that
set the pace for the journal's subsequent course: the late Jon Higgins, the late
Robert Graves, John Cage, Chou Wen-Chung, Fredric Lieberman, and Harold
Schramm. Special issues have been frequent. While some are issue oriented—
Symposium on the Ethnomusicology of Cultural Change in Asia (7.2)—most
focus on a specific country or region: Near East-Turkestan (4.1), Southeast Asia
(7.1), Afghanistan (8.1), Korea (9.2), and Tibet (10.2). Of these, the one on
the music of Afghanistan is particularly well regarded.

Each issue contains approximately five articles of fifteen to forty pages each. The first issue was only forty pages long; by 1977 (v. 8) the size had grown to one hundred. Reviews of books and records first appeared in 2.1, and ethnomusicological film reviews were introduced in 3.2. Membership lists and discographies are published periodically. Photos, maps, drawings, and both Western and traditional musical notation amply illustrate the volumes. Glossaries, bibliographies, and other collections of data are frequently appended to articles. In 17.1 (1985) the editor began a public service feature at the end of each issue: notices, not to exceed one page, for nonprofit events, endeavors, or publications that center on Asian music and Asian ethnomusicology. English is used throughout.

The journal is published semiannually by the Society of Asian Music. Willard Rhodes (also a charter member of the Society for Ethnomusicology) was founding president of the society, and an editorial board was responsible for the publication of the first two volumes (1968/9 and 1971). In 1972 (v. 3), Mark Slobin became editor. Both v. 6 and 7.1 were issued in 1975. Since then the first issue of the volume appears in fall while the second issue appears in the spring of the following year. The covers are color-coded: the fall issues are green, while spring issues are yellow.

V. 1.1 was 9" x 5½". The following issue assumed the current fomat of 9" x 6". Until 1983 the journal used photo-reproduction of typewritten sheets. From 15.1 (1983) some articles began to appear in reduced photocopy of computer printout, an editorial experiment to computerize formatting and printing. Once a final decision has been reached, the editors anticipate faster, more accurate publication. Articles may now be submitted on floppy disk, compatible with IBM PC.

Information Sources

INDEXES
>External: Music Index, 1975–   (retrospective to 1969). RILM, 1976–   . Music Article Guide, 1974–   . Arts and Humanities Citation Index, 1976–   .

LOCATION SOURCES
>Widely available.

Publication History

TITLE AND TITLE CHANGES
>*Asian Music.*

VOLUME AND ISSUE DATA
>Volumes 1–   , 1968–   .

FREQUENCY OF PUBLICATION
>Semiannual.

PUBLISHER
>Society for Asian Music.

PLACE OF PUBLICATION
>New York.

EDITORS
> Editorial Board, 1968–71. Mark Slobin, 1972–84. Martin Hatch and Mark Slobin, 1984– .

L. JaFran Jones

ASSOCIATION OF RECORDED SOUND COLLECTIONS BULLETIN.
See ASSOCIATION OF RECORDED SOUND COLLECTIONS JOURNAL

ASSOCIATION FOR RECORDED SOUND COLLECTIONS JOURNAL

The Henry Ford Museum in Dearborn, Michigan, was the site chosen for the first exploratory meeting in July 1965 by a group of scholars, historians, writers, archivists, and collectors to gather and set down the organizational structure of what was to become the Association for Recorded Sound Collections (ARSC). This was, in many ways, the outgrowth of such events as the founding of the Rodgers and Hammerstein Archives of Recorded Sound at the Library and Museum of the Performing Arts at Lincoln Center in the mid–1960s, and the recognition of other thriving historical sound archives already established in other parts of the United States, notably at Yale, Stanford, Syracuse, and Michigan State universities. Such archives were springing up in many places, sometimes with no more than local notice. Some included unique and irreplaceable recorded material that was in many cases purposely being shielded from wide public usage.

The early issues of the association's *Journal* were meant to chronicle the group's annual meetings by printing its proceedings, business reports, and summaries of the papers presented there. Early on, the *Journal* also served as a clearinghouse for record sales and want lists, information sought by collectors, and reports on research projects by its members. Most of these housekeeping features were subsequently relegated to the association's *Bulletin* and *Newsletter*.

A Table of Contents first appeared in v. 4 (1972), now delineating a more structured editorial organization. From then on the journal would conform to the following content format: first a series of articles, followed by a discography, then a special report, and finally the book and record review section.

By the fifth issue of the *Journal* (3.1; Winter 1970–71), articles based upon historical research began appearing. Until this time there were few forums for such scholarly endeavors. This issue featured Daniel W. Patterson's insightful "Hunting for the American White Spiritual: A Survey of Scholarship, with Discography" and Walter Darrell Haden's "Vernon Dalhart: His Rural Roots and the Beginnings of Commercial Country Music." Book reviews were also included in this issue for the first time. This scholarly tone was reinforced in the next issue with the entire journal devoted to the untiring Edison record research of Ray Wile. Since then the *Journal*, a publication created by discographers for discographers, has incorporated only the most exacting research and attention to detail, making it a unique and valuable source of information.

Even though an historical perspective for discographical research has been the primary focus of the *Journal*, informational articles related to copyright laws, sound reproduction, and descriptions of new or existing archives are also common. A regular column, which made its appearance with the very first issue, was Paul T. Jackson's "Bits and Pieces," a forum in which new publications, special articles, dealer announcements, and currently available recordings were noted. This column was assumed by Michael Biel in 9.2–3 (1977) and retitled "For the Record."

A partial list of artist discographies includes those for Edgar Varèse, Leonard Bernstein as composer, Elliott Carter, William Shuman, Karl Muck, and Richard Strauss. To date there have been no popular music discographies. Discographies of specific subjects include the "World's Greatest Music" and "World's Greatest Opera" series; pre-LP recordings of RCA on 33⅓ rpm, 1931–34; phonograph recordings used in the practice of medicine; and the "Goon Show."

Beginning with v. 6.2 (1974), Michael Gray and Gerald Gibson began publishing, on a periodic basis, comprehensive bibliographies of discographies. They called upon experts with strong discographic reputations in their respective subject fields to work with them to produce this long overdue reference service. Subjects included country, folk, ethnic, blues, gospel, spoken and documentary, jazz, classical, and later, pop, rock, and soul. Each discography is evaluated on the basis of the types and quality of information included.

Almost every issue of the *Journal* features at least one article concerning record archiving, preservation, or record classification. Important examples include Gordon Stevenson's 1975 article on "Collectors, Catalogs and Libraries" (7.1/2:21–32) and Tim Brooks's "The Artifacts of Recording History: Creators, Users, Losers, Keepers" (11.1:18–28). John Swan, a librarian like Stevenson, wrote in 1980 of "Sound Archive: The Role of the Collector and the Library" (12.1:8–17), and Tim Brooks made another important contribution in 1984 with "A Survey of Record Collectors' Societies" (16.3:17–36).

Individual volumes of the *Journal* are comprised of three issues, each of which averages 100 to 150 pages in a 5½" by 9" format. A variety of line drawings, diagrams, and musical examples make an occasional appearance, though photographs are rare. Advertisements, found only in later issues, are likewise sparse and emphasize publications and electronic equipment. The intent of the *Journal* is clearly scholarly, and the various articles, bibliographies, discographies, and technical reports chart a high standard.

The ARSC *Newsletter* began publishing in April 1977. Its main purpose is to keep the association members informed of recent events, upcoming meetings, items wanted and for sale, and recent publications. With a more flexible publication schedule than that of the *Journal*, the *Newsletter* can disseminate information to members more quickly. Its contents are similar in scope to what Paul Jackson had envisioned for his column ''Bits and Pieces.''

The ARSC *Bulletin* also serves an important function that at one time had been envisioned for the *Journal* itself. Issue number one, published following the second annual ARSC conference at the University of California at Los Angeles, November 21–23, 1968, included the minutes of the business meeting. Each successive annual issue includes not only the minutes but also other pertinent official documents and proceedings of interest to members, such as the bylaws, committee reports, charter changes, the president's report, membership roster, and conference reports and programs. The membership roster of the association has grown to such an extent that it is now published separately.

Information Sources

BIBLIOGRAPHY
''ARSC *Journal* Highlights, 1968–1983.'' *Association for Recorded Sound Collections Journal* 16 (1984): 100–103.
INDEXES
External: Music Index, 1969– . RILM, 1978– . Music Article Guide, 1971– .
LOCATION SOURCES
Widely available.

Publication History

TITLE AND TITLE CHANGES
Journal, 1967– . *Newsletter*, 1977– . *Bulletin*, 1968– .
VOLUME AND ISSUE DATA
Volumes 1– , 1967– .
FREQUENCY OF PUBLICATION
3/year.
PUBLISHER
Association for Recorded Sound Collections. New York City, 1967–71. Silver Springs, Maryland, 1972–76. Manassas, Virginia, 1976–82. Linden, New Jersey, 1983. Washington, D.C., 1984. Silver Springs, Maryland, 1985– .
EDITORS
David Hall, 1967–71. Gerald Gibson, 1972–76. Michael Gray, 1976–82. Sam Brylawski, 1983. Mort Frank, 1983–84. John W.N. Francis, 1984–85. Richard Perry, 1986– .

William L. Schurk

ASSOCIATION OF RECORDED SOUND COLLECTIONS NEWSLETTER. See ASSOCIATION OF RECORDED SOUND COLLECTIONS JOURNAL

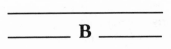

B

BASS WORLD. See INTERNATIONAL SOCIETY OF BASSISTS JOURNAL

BEITRÄGE ZUR MUSIKWISSENSCHAFT

The *Beiträge zur Musikwissenschaft* is an East German scholarly periodical published by the "Verband deutscher Komponisten und Musikwissenschaftler." Though the society claims both composers and musicologists as members, the journal focuses mainly on the concerns of the latter. The scope and tone of the publication are colored by the Marxist orientation of members of the editorial board and many contributors, an orientation reflected in both the type and content of the articles presented. For the reader unacquainted with the Marxist musical perspective, Alfred Brockhaus's article "Georg Kneplers Konzeption der musikalischen Historiographie" (9.2:81–90) provides a good introduction.

Knepler served on the editorial board of the first volume (1959) and as editor-in-chief for the next twenty-three years. His interest in interpreting music in terms of society and social progress and his belief in the significance of folk music and the music of countries outside the mainstream of Western musical culture help explain the seemingly eclectic collection of topics addressed in the journal. Most of the articles are devoted to studies of eighteenth-and nineteenth-century German musicians, but a considerable number deal with historiography, aesthetics, music of the Near and Far East, folksongs of various Eastern European countries, music education and songs of the working class (*Arbeiterlieder*). While much recent musicological research in the West has focused on archival and manuscript studies, that trend does not surface in the *Beiträge*, where the emphasis appears to be on analysis and interpretation. Few citations to any recent Western research are found, even in articles where they would seem indicated.

While this last characteristic in particular might limit the usefulness and reliability of some of the articles, many are excellent and often provide thought-provoking viewpoints.

The publication is headed by an editorial board drawn chiefly from the universities of East Berlin and Leipzig and the Zentral Institut für Musikforschung. Three of the current board members have been with the journal since its inception, a circumstance that explains its stability and relative consistency of outlook. Most of the contributors are associated with the same institutions, though scholars from other parts of Europe and the United States do publish there occasionally. Frequent contributors include: Harry Goldschmidt, Georg Knepler, Doris Stockman, and Jurgen Mainka.

The journal is issued quarterly, with a typical volume running to 300 or 350 pages, in a 6¾″ by 9½″ format. Beginning with the fourth volume, pagination is consecutive, and a yearly table of contents is provided. Most issues contain five or six articles, which can vary in length from three to thirty pages. In recent volumes, citations are placed at the end of each article, a practice that, coupled with the small print, poor quality paper, and unattractively presented musical examples, makes the journal somewhat tiring to read. It is fortunate, however, especially for the non-German reader, that most of the writing (which is exclusively in German) manages to avoid the impossible thickets of modifiers, qualifiers, and disappearing verbs that bedevil much academic prose in that language.

In addition, the journal regularly provides a section of book reviews and conference reports. As might be expected, most of the publications and conferences discussed are Eastern European and German, and those selected for discussion tend to reflect the interests of the editorial board. For example, a recent year saw reviews of two books on historiography, two on music of the various social classes, and one each on the mass media, folk music, Stravinsky, and the fugue. The journal also has issued a series of *Beihefte* containing bibliographies of post–World War II musicological literature in East Bloc countries (*Musikwissenschaftliche Literatur sozialistischer Länder*), which can be useful in identifing otherwise hard-to-locate publications. Included in the early volumes was a list of courses offered at various East German universities, but that feature has been dropped.

Information Sources

BIBLIOGRAPHY
Blum, Fred. "East German Music Journals: A Checklist." *Notes* 19 (1962): 399–410.
INDEXES
> External: Music Index, 1967– . RILM, 1967– . Bibliographie des Musikschrifttums, 1958– .
LOCATION SOURCES
> Widely available.

Publication History

TITLE AND TITLE CHANGES
> *Beiträge zur Musikwissenschaft.*

VOLUME AND ISSUE DATA
   Volumes 1–   , 1959–   .
FREQUENCY OF PUBLICATION
   Quarterly.
PUBLISHER
   Verlag Neue Musik for the Verband deutscher Komponisten und Musikwissen-
   schaftler.
PLACE OF PUBLICATION
   East Berlin.
EDITORS
   Editorial board of various East German scholars, 1959. Georg Knepler (Editor-
   in-Chief), 1960–82. Konrad Niemann, 1983–   .

                                                            Mary Sue Morrow

**BERIGTEN/VEREENIGING VOOR NEDERLANDSE MUZIEKGES-
CHIEDENIS.** See TIJDSCHRIFT VAN DE VERENIGING VOOR NEDER-
LANDSE MUZIEKGESCHIEDENIS

BILLBOARD

The best information available indicates that *Billboard* was founded in Weil-
ert's Saloon on Vine Street in Cincinnati over two glasses of beer, shared by
William H. Donaldson and James F. Hennegan. The idea for the journal originated with Donaldson, who theorized that those in the entertainment promotion
industries, many of whom traveled constantly, would appreciate a magazine that
would enable them to keep in touch with one another. The cover of the first
issue of what was originally called *Billboard Advertising* carried the following
slogan: "A monthly resume of all that is new, bright and interesting on the
boards." Donaldson, its first editor, explained that the publication would be
"devoted to the interests of the advertisers, poster printers, billposters, advertising agents, and secretaries of fairs" (1.1:1).

In its first issue, *Billboard Advertising* declared the following editorial policy:
"We will carefully canvass the field we have entered, ascertain its needs and
requirements, and ground ourselves thoroughly in the principles of a policy that
will enable us to best achieve our aim." This same first issue contained eight
pages in a simple, four-column page layout. There was one page of display
advertising and a page of classified advertisements.

Two months after its founding *Billboard Advertising* published its first
special—a New Year's issue. Special editions have, in fact, appeared regularly
throughout the history of *Billboard*, with issues devoted to various genres of the
recording industry (new recording concepts, distributorship, packaging), specific
record labels, geographic artistic emphasis, salutes to industry personalities, and
trade conventions. In addition, especially from the 1960s through the early 1980s,

Billboard published separate special annual supplements aimed at specific segments of its readership: "The World of Country Music," "World of Religious Music," "Billboard Campus Attractions," and "Billboard International Directory of Recording Studios." Initially these supplements appeared as part two of a weekly issue and were usually 8″ by 11″ in size (as compared to the larger 11″ by 14″ regular issue). Later they were issued at the same size as the regular issue and bound within. By 1 June 1896, the publication was enlarged to include an agricultural fair department, and a year later, sensing expanding horizons, the name was changed to *The Billboard* (since 1961, merely *Billboard*).

Toward the end of the century, Donaldson and Hennegan disagreed over a question of an editorial, and for a period of time Donaldson took no active part in the publication. By 1900 *Billboard* was virtually bankrupt. That same year Donaldson bought Hennegan's interest in the company, assumed the publication's liabilities, and converted it from a monthly to a weekly. The first weekly edition of *The Billboard* appeared dated 5 May 1900, thus inaugurating ninety years of uninterrupted weekly publication. During 1901 Donaldson reshaped the publication. Editorials were bold, imaginative, and unrestrained. In March he published a street fair number. By October of the same year he assigned columns or departments for carnivals, street fairs, stock and repertoire, music and opera, parks, minstrels, vaudeville, and burlesque. The company had opened offices in New York and Chicago and, in 1906, had added a music column for the publishers in New York. In 1907 a department called "World of Moving Pictures" began, and in June 1913 the periodical issued its first full-color cover.

From its very first issue, *Billboard* placed heavy emphasis on industry news briefs. To strengthen this area, Donaldson, in 1913, took steps to make the magazine truly timely by equipping his offices with a telegraphic news service. Within months *Billboard* was publishing reviews and accounts of events which took place a mere four to five days prior to the issue appearing on the newsstands.

Billboard has frequently taken note of new types of entertainment industry technology. An important example is coin-operated entertainment devices. Beginning in 1899, *Billboard* carried advertisements and sketchy news of these devises. Then, in March 1932, the magazine launched its "Amusement Machines" department. This department kept *Billboard* in business during the trying years leading up to World War II. An important element of the coin-operated entertainment industry was the jukebox. To assist jukebox operators in determining which records they should place on their machines, *Billboard* began a "Record Buying Guide" in its 7 January 1939 issue. Record company advertisements started appearing for the first time.

On 4 November 1950, *Billboard* abandoned its magazine format in favor of a five-column tabloid newspaper format. *Billboard* was thus able to get the news to its readers more quickly and to present the news in a more interesting, exciting style. These changes were important factors in establishing the publication as the communications nucleus of a fast-moving, dynamic music/record industry. To improve the look of *Billboard*, the editors went to printing on coated paper with the 5 January 1963 edition. This also provided the editors the opportunity to take the paper into the field of photojournalism and shortly thereafter into four-color halftones.

Charting has been a mainstay of *Billboard*, whose record popularity charts today are the industry's measurement of performance. They reflect the consumer's taste, sales over the counter, amount of radio exposure, and relative strength of individual records versus competition. They are a marketing tool to stimulate additional sales and airplay as well as to reflect success.

Billboard actually printed its first chart, "Tunes Most Heard in Vaudeville Last Week," in the early 1900s. When recordings started to make inroads, charts were prepared weekly for *Billboard* by the major labels and printed individually, for example, the Top Ten of RCA Victor. As the recording industry expanded, *Billboard* began compiling national charts with all recordings and labels combined. The types and number of charts grew after World War II, fueled by the rising number of jukebox locations, new phonograph equipment, the introduction of the LP in the late 1940s, and the "battle of the speeds." "The Honor Roll of Hits" chart, for instance, was introduced because a top tune would frequently be recorded by a succession of artists, with several versions surfacing in the charts simultaneously. For "The Honor Roll of Hits," all versions were combined to determine its final position for the week. Sheet music sales were also a factor and a separate chart was printed for "Best Selling Sheet Music." There were charts for "folk music" (now called country) and for race music, which became rhythm and blues, then soul music, and finally black music. Classical record charts were important in the late 1940s as were children's records. At that time, most of the charts only ran ten or fifteen positions. The charts were gradually expanded to the listing of the Top 30 "Best Selling Records," the Top 30 "Most Played on Radio," and the Top 30 "Most Played on Jukebox" charts. Album charts were also expanded. In early 1950, *Billboard* also included monthly charts for other categories such as jazz, folk, international, semiclassical, the perennial "Honor Roll of Hits" chart as well as "Best Selling Sheet Music" charts for the United States and a separate sheet music chart for the United Kingdom.

As the 1950s progressed, industry changes led to the combining of the three individual singles charts (sales, radio play, and jukebox play) and the introduction of "Country and Western" and "R & B" album charts. The most important chart in the early and mid–1950s was the "Best Selling Pop Singles in Stores" chart. "Breakout" singles and LP charts were expanded far beyond fifty positions each week. Extended country and soul singles and LP charts, better year-end charts, and many additional, special topic charts compiled for special issues appeared. The late 1960s saw the introduction of the "Best Selling Tapes" chart, and the "Best Selling Folios" chart.

As of 1987, *Billboard* carries eight LP album charts ("Black," "Compact Discs," "Country," "Hits of the World," "Latin," "Rock Tracks," "Spiritual," and "Pop"), ten hot singles charts ("Adult Contemporary," "Black,"

"Black Singles Action," "Country," "Country Singles Action," "Dance/ Disco," "Hits of the World," "Hot 100," "Hot 100 Singles Action," and "Latin 50") and four video charts ("Business and Education," "Health and Fitness," "Videocassette Sales," and "Videodiscs"). The "Action" charts are divided into two sections, "Radio Most Added" and "Retail Breakouts." "Radio Most Added" is a weekly national compilation of the five records most added to the playlists of the radio stations reporting to *Billboard*.

Sound recordings are, of course, not the only thing covered in *Billboard*. As various forms of entertainment emerged or declined in popularity, their current status with the public was reflected in the pages of the journal. Live entertainment departments have included coverage of the circus, fairs, theatre buildings, minstrel shows, films, burlesque, wild west shows, skating rinks, stock and repertory theatre, magicians, Lyceum and Chautauqua, piers, beaches, musical comedy, medicine shows, rodeos, and zoos. Strictly music-oriented content has included departments for song, sheet music, radio, concerts, and, of course, sound and more recently video recordings. Short-lived departments have abounded throughout the years of *Billboard*'s existence, catering to the sporadic popularity of America's pastimes.

Billboard has its own staff of writers who contribute the major portion of its feature, signed articles, and of course the weekly departmental columns. Other articles are written by knowledgeable persons within the trade. The merits of newly released singles, albums, and tapes are invariably presented in descriptive, one- or two-line, unsigned notices.

The history of the music and recording industries is perhaps most accurately and methodically chronicled in the pages of *Billboard*. From sheet music, the invention of the phonograph, radio, and the "battle of the speeds," to stereo, open reel, cassette, and eight-track tapes and compact discs, *Billboard* has covered it all. Genres from vaudeville, musicals, jazz, and dance bands, to rock and roll, the "British Invasion," disco, punk rock, and new age music have been thoroughly documented. The regularly appearing columns and departments (roughly 40 percent of the content), feature articles (50 percent), and "charts" (5 percent) are only part of the news *Billboard* imparts to its readers. The advertisements, taking up the remaining 5 percent of the seventy- to eighty-page issues, are both brilliant examples of sales methodology and a demonstration of distinctive graphic art.

Information Sources

BIBLIOGRAPHY
"*Billboard* to Change Publication Format." *Billboard* 72 (1960): 1.
"*Billboard* 75." *Billboard* 81 (1969, section two): entire issue.
Littleford, Roger S. "The Man Who Loved Show Business: A Special Remembrance."
    Billboard 91 (1979): 4, 14.
INDEXES
    External: Music Index, 1894–   (retrospective). Popular Magazine Review. Business Index. Trade & Industry Index.

REPRINT EDITIONS
    Microform: Krauss International, 1894– . UMI, 1970– .
LOCATION SOURCES
    Milwaukee Public Library, Nashville Public Library, Cleveland Public Library
    (early issues). Widely available (later issues).

Publication History

TITLE AND TITLE CHANGES
    Billboard Advertising, 1894–97. *The Billboard*, 1897–1961. *Billboard*, 1961– .
VOLUME AND ISSUE DATA
    Volumes 1– . 1894– .
FREQUENCY OF PUBLICATION
    Monthly, 1894–1900. Weekly, 5 May 1900– .
PUBLISHERS
    Billboard Advertising Co., 1894–1 March 1897. Billboard Publishing Co., 1 April
    1897– .
PLACES OF PUBLICATION
    Cincinnati, 1894–1960. New York, 1961– .
EDITORS
    James H. Hennigan, 1894-early 1900s. D. C. Gillette, 1926–1930. W. J. Riley,
    1930–31. A. C. Hartmann and Elias E. Sugarman, 1931–41. R. S. Littleford,
    1941–56. Sam Chase, 1961–63. Lee Zhito, 1963–80. Gerry Wood, 1981–83.
    Lee Zhito, 1983. Adam White, 1983–85. Sam Holdsworth, 1985–88. Ken
    Schlager, 1988– .

William L. Schurk

BILLBOARD ADVERTISING. See BILLBOARD

BLACK MUSIC RESEARCH JOURNAL

Black Music Research Journal began publication in 1980 under the editorial
leadership of Samuel A. Floyd, Jr., the founding director of the Fisk University
Institute for Research in Black American Music in Nashville, Tennessee. An
annual publication at its inception, the journal's purpose was to encourage and
promote research in all aspects of black American music. Articles discussing
black music from the seventeenth century to the present, from Africa to Europe
and the Western Hemisphere, and from sacred to folk and concert music were
to be included. The focus of the articles, which were solicited, was to be primarily
philosophy, aesthetics, and criticism.

In the early years, each issue averaged between five and nine articles, usually
between fifteen and thirty pages in length. Topics ranged from black gospel
groups in Burt Feintuch's "A Noncommercial Black Gospel Group in Context:
We Live the Life We Sing About" (1:37–50) and rhythm and blues with Arnold
Shaw's "Researching Rhythm and Blues" (1:71–79) to the philosophy of black

music scholarship with Samuel A. Floyd's "Toward a Philosophy of Black Music Scholarship" (2:72–93).

In 1983 Floyd resigned his position at Fisk to become the director of Columbia College's Center for Black Music Research in Chicago. At this time the journal became a joint publication of Columbia College and Fisk University; however, by 1985, Fisk University no longer appeared either in the copyright statement of the journal or in the masthead of its sister publication *Black Music Research Newsletter*. The journal continued to publish substantive articles on black music as well as bibliographic essays and concordances of scores and recordings of black music. Papers given at the National Conference on Black Music Research were included in the 1986 (v. 6) issue while papers from the "This Little Light of Mine Project" appeared in the next year (v. 7). In 1988 *Black Music Research Journal* announced a change in its publication schedule, from annually to twice a year, in fall and spring.

The physical format of the journal has been a consistent 6½″ by 9″ with issues averaging 100 to 120 pages. Musical examples and illustrations appear as needed. Later issues conclude with two to three pages of publishers' advertisements. A single index for vs. 6–8 appears in v. 8.2.

The *Black Music Research Newsletter*, which Floyd began in 1977 while at Southern Illinois University, consists of brief articles that report preliminary research as well as columns of noteworthy news from the Institutes of Black Music. It also serves as a means of disseminating current and future events affecting black music research. Early newsletters were four pages in length, later issues eight pages. Frequency of publication changed from twice to three times annually. In 1988 the title changed to *Black Music Research Bulletin*, and a new publication, *CBMR Digest*, began publication. With this change, the *Bulletin* will publish shorter articles of research. The *CBMR Digest* will disseminate, free, news items and other short articles of interest.

Information Sources

BIBLIOGRAPHY

Paul, Angus. "New Research Center in Chicago Strives to Preserve and Promote the Legacy of Black Music." *Chronicle of Higher Education,* January 28, 1987, pp. 6, 7, 10.

Reich, Howard. "Black Music Ensemble Makes Founder's Dream Come True." *Chicago Tribune*, March 28, 1988, Sec. 5, p. 4.

INDEXES

Internal: vs. 6–8 in 8.2.

External: RILM, 1981– . Jazz Index, 1981–83. Musical Article Guide, 1981– . Arts and Humanities Citation Index, 1986– . Music Index, 1988– .

LOCATION SOURCES

Widely available.

Publication History

TITLE AND TITLE CHANGES
  Black Music Research Journal, 1980– . *Black Music Research Newsletter*, 1977–
  88. *Black Music Research Bulletin*, 1988– . *CBMR Digest*, 1988– .
VOLUME AND ISSUE DATA
  Volume 1– , 1980– (*Journal*). Volume 1–10, 1977–88 (*Newsletter*). Volume
  1– (*Bulletin*). Volume 1– , 1988– (*Digest*).
FREQUENCY OF PUBLICATION
  Annual 1980–87, Semiannual, 1988– (*Journal*). Twice a year, 1977– (*News-
  letter*). Twice a year, 1988– (*Bulletin*). Twice a year, 1988– (*Digest*).
PUBLISHERS
  Floyd, 1977–79. Fisk University, 1980–84. Columbia College, 1984– .
PLACES OF PUBLICATION
  Edwardsville, Illinois, 1977–79. Nashville, Tennessee, 1980–83. Chicago, Illi-
  nois, 1984– .
EDITORS
  Samuel A. Floyd, Jr. 1980– . Marsha J. Reisser, 1988– (*Digest*).

                                                            Linda M. Fidler

BLACK PERSPECTIVE IN MUSIC

In the past two decades the number of publications dealing with black music
has mushroomed, but most have concentrated on the areas of jazz or popular
music. One that differs from the norm is the *Black Perspective in Music*. In her
inaugural editorial, its founder and editor Eileen Southern stated:

> The *Black Perspective in Music* is committed to the publication of news
> from all over the world about musicians and their music. . . . It seeks to
> become a source of current history of Afro-American music and to provide
> information periodically about the past of this music. . . . There will be
> published lists of music, reviews of music and recordings, and lists of
> relevant books. Finally the journal seeks to serve as a clearing house for
> persons engaged in research who have important (or not so important)
> things to say about black musicians and their music.
>
> The *Black Perspective in Music* is concerned about all kinds of music
> and writings produced by black musicians whether in the so-called black
> tradition or in other traditions and styles. It is concerned about all types
> of musicians: composers, performers, and writers. (1:1)

A slightly modified and abbreviated statement of the aims was included in a
1983 subscription advertisement:

> The primary purpose of the journal is to provide an opportunity for the
> free expression of ideas and opinions by persons interested in Black-

American and African performing arts, particularly from a creative point of view.

The "perspectives" in the journal have not only been those from black writers; Southern welcomes all comers. Some effort has also been made to solicit non-American contributions. Articles by British and German authors, as well as African, have appeared from time to time. The range and quality of the articles vary; some are simple two to three page reports, others are ambitious analyses or historical articles exceeding twenty pages. The average length of articles is ten to fifteen pages, and there are three to five per issue.

In the selection of articles Southern seems to try to strike a balance among historical subjects, the work of living musicians, and material concerned with African as well as Afro-American music systems. Discussions range from the ethnomusicological to the theoretical to the anecdotal. The writing styles of the journal contributors avoid both the highly esoteric and the excessively informal. *Black Perspective in Music* maintains, however, a clear historical/analytical bent, reflecting the training and concerns of its editor, a Harvard professor of music and Afro-American studies. The emphasis is on individual musicians and their works, and on musical genres, rather than on aesthetic theory, editorial statement, methodology, or politics.

Two special issues have been brought out: a 1976 Bicentennial Issue devoted to nineteenth-century black musical activities (co-edited by Southern and Josephine Wright), and a 1983 multiple index, including five different alphabetical lists of citations from the journal to that date: (1) author, title, subject, department, miscellaneous, (2) reviews and reviewers, (3) illustrations, (4) musical examples, and (5) obituaries.

Regular features include "Conversations," interviews with composers and performers; "In Retrospect," brief sketches of historical figures or reprints of articles, programs, old photographs, and music facsimiles; and book, record, and music lists and reviews. A "Commentary" section is devoted to news about black musicians—awards, honors, premieres, debuts, festivals, competitions, donations to research archives, new periodicals, and miscellaneous information of note. A series of brief obituaries appears annually in the Spring issue. Occasionally a page or two is given to letters from readers.

Joseph Southern, the editor's husband, is managing editor, but the journal is more than a family organ. Its advisory board has included J. H. Kwabena Nketia, John Terrence Riley, Christopher White, Rene-Dominique de Lerma, Doris McGinty, Samuel A. Floyd, D. Antoinette Handy Miller, and Mezi Nzewi. Josephine Wright (music lists), Lewis Porter (jazz and record reviews), and George Starks (jazz and blues records and music reviews), along with Southern and Floyd, have been regular, major contributors.

Under Southern's guidance, the journal has appeared semiannually (Spring and Fall) since 1973, supported by subscriptions, and published by the Foundation for Research in the Afro-American Creative Arts, Inc. It carries no regular advertising. The number of pages (sized 5⅞" by 8¾") varies from 100 to 250 per issue. A brief index is included at the end of each volume.

Information Sources

INDEXES
Internal: each volume indexed. Vs.1–10 in v. 10.
External: Music Index, 1973– . Music Article Guide, 1973– . Jazz Index, 1973– . RILM, 1973– . Bibliographie des Musikschrifttums, 1974– . Arts and Humanities Citation Index, 1976– .
REPRINT EDITIONS
Microform: UMI, 1973– .
LOCATION SOURCES
Widely available.

Publication History

TITLE AND TITLE CHANGES
Black Perspective in Music.
VOLUME AND ISSUE DATA
Volumes 1– , 1973– .
FREQUENCY OF PUBLICATION
Semiannual.
PUBLISHER
The Foundation for Research in the Afro-American Creative Arts, Inc.
PLACE OF PUBLICATION
Cambria Heights, New York.
EDITOR
Eileen Southern.

Thomas L. Riis

BOUWSTEENEN: EERSTE/TWEEDE/DERDE JAARBOEK DER VER-EENIGING VOOR NOORD-NEDERLANDSCHE MUZIEKGESCHIE-DENIS. See TIJDSCHRIFT VAN DE VERENIGING VOOR NEDERLANDSE MUZIEKGESCHIEDENIS

BRAINARD'S MUSICAL WORLD

In 1834 Nathan Brainard brought his family of seven to Cleveland, Ohio, from Lempster, New Hampshire. The family soon opened a music store and, in January 1864, began publication of its monthly house organ, first known as *Western Musical World/A Journal of Music, Art, and Literature.* The journal was to be devoted to "the cause of Music and Fine Arts in the 'Great West.' "The "Introductory" proposed that each issue include from two to four pages of good popular music, vocal and instrumental, which alone will be worth the subscription price—fifty cents a year. Choice musical sketches and miscellaneous items of interest, shall fill our columns, together with a record of musical events as they may occur from time to time. (1.1:2)

In short, the fledgling magazine sought to appeal to a wide public of diverse musical backgrounds.

From this rather inauspicious start *Musical World* grew to become important on the national scene during the nineteenth century. It continued without a break in publication for the unusually long time of thirty years and achieved a remarkably wide circulation. The initial eight-page monthly issues grew to sixteen (1865), twenty (1870), and thereafter up to forty-eight pages, always 8½″ by 12″. In 1895, a few years after its parent company relocated in Chicago, it was finally merged with *Etude* (q.v.), a piano magazine begun by Theodore Presser some twelve years earlier. For a brief time the merged publication was known as *Etude and Musical World*. Although the name *Musical World* soon disappeared, its impact may be seen to live on through *Etude* until the demise of that journal in 1957.

The journal saw itself as an important contributing force to musical development in the Great West. From its Cleveland headquarters it looked for musical leadership to Boston, which it called "the first city in this country, which advanced in the right direction" (14.159:38). Its horizon encompassed national issues, as indeed its large parent company, in its heyday, had business branches in Chicago (its ultimate headquarters), Louisville, and New York City. *World*'s essays touch on the saengerfests, the state of church music, music in the schools, musical conventions, the founding of our important conservatories, music libraries in the United States, the Boston Peace Jubilees of 1869 and 1872, the artists of the day—Patrick S. Gilmore, Theodore Thomas, and many others— and on music celebrating our nation's Centennial ("We shall know better the next time!"—13.155:164). Of particular interest is the series of some 144 biographies of American musicians. Along with a host of lesser names we find articles on such figures as Dudley Buck, Leopold and Walter Damrosch, Arthur Foote, and Louis Gottschalk. The articles, rarely more than a few columns in length, were supplemented by a variety of shorter reports, increasingly organized into departments, such as the "Cincinnati Department" and the "Home Department." Also interesting are the many advertisements for instruments, schools, teachers, and even nonmusical commodities, as well as music and music texts.

The music carried in *Musical World*, some 1,580 pieces in all, was of the parlor variety, so popular in nineteenth-century America. Much of it was aimed at home consumption, particularly by women. Piano music predominated. Compositions for solo voice and piano were also numerous. Many of the earlier songs contained refrains, some scored in the earlier American way for TASB. Changing trends in popular taste were reflected in the mix of pieces published as, for example, we find a number of works for cabinet organ during the mid–1860s and for guitar during the latter 1880s. The piano pieces were often dances. The songs sometimes treated contemporary issues, such as political campaigns and temperance. Although there were occasional pieces of European provenance, works by J. S. Bach, Frédéric Chopin, or Franz Schubert, or transcriptions from European opera, the focus was clearly American.

Although its underlying purpose was clearly commercial, with the music it published on sale also at Brainard's store, it nonetheless developed a respectably wide musical perspective. The editorial writing managed to remain largely free of commercial considerations. A contributing factor to editorial independence was undoubtedly the fact that the main editor of *World*, Karl Merz, was never otherwise tied to the company, nor did he live in Cleveland.

In its thirty-year retrospective (January 1894) the editor of *World* wrote:

If art depends upon the people for support, then it must make itself friends among the people, and artists should labor hard to gain for it friends.

The present is a most important period of our musical history, a period of development and progress. Journals, lecturers, schools, teachers and musical books are all throwing out light. The *Musical World* will continue to do what it can to popularize art, and to teach the people that music has always aided them, in its development and growth and is worthy of support. We believe there is great hope for our musical future. (31.361:5)

Brainard's Musical World clearly fulfilled its commercial purpose of bringing the wares of its parent company to the attention of a wide public. But it achieved much more than that as, over a long period of time, it reached a large audience on behalf of music.

Information Sources

BIBLIOGRAPHY

Alexander, J. Heywood. "Brainard's (Western) Musical World." *Notes* 36/3 (1980): 601–14.

————. *It Must Be Heard: The Musical Life of Cleveland, 1836–1918*. Cleveland: Western Reserve Historical Society, 1981.

Davison, Mary Veronica. "American Music Periodicals, 1853–1899." Ph.D. diss., University of Minnesota, 1973.

Osburn, Mary Hubbell. *Ohio Composers and Musical Authors*. Columbus: F. J. Heer, 1942.

REPRINT EDITIONS

Microform: New York Public Library (incomplete).

LOCATION SOURCES

Twenty-five libraries are known to the author as holding *Musical World,* most of them with scattered issues only. The Western Reserve Historical Society in Cleveland, however, possesses a nearly completed run.

Publication History

TITLE AND TITLE CHANGES
   Western Musical World, 1864–68. *Brainard's Musical World,* 1869–95.
VOLUME AND ISSUE DATA
   Volumes 1–32, 1864–95.
FREQUENCY OF PUBLICATION
   Monthly.
PUBLISHER
   S. Brainard's Sons.
PLACES OF PUBLICATION
   Cleveland, 1864–March 1889. Chicago, April 1889–95.
EDITORS
   None listed (Charles S. Brainard), January 1864–March 1871. C. S. Brainard
   (Editor), Karl Merz (Associate Editor), April 1871–December 1871. Horace E.
   Kimball (Editor), Karl Merz (Associate Editor), January 1872–April 1873. None
   listed, May 1873. Karl Merz, June 1873–March 1890. A. J. Goodrich, April
   1890–December 1890. None listed, January 1891–October 1895.

J. Heywood Alexander

BRASS AND WOODWIND QUARTERLY. See BRASS QUARTERLY

BRASS BULLETIN

   Jean-Pierre Mathez of Switzerland began *Brass Bulletin* in 1971 and has been
its sole editor to date. In his prefatory comments to the first issue, he stated that
his intent is "to offer brass players a centralized source of information and the
opportunity to exchange ideas." This "clearinghouse" aspect of *Brass Bulletin*
is achieved quite successfully through the letters, articles, and reviews provided
largely by the journal's impressively international readership.
   Brass Bulletin has consistently maintained a format that features editorials,
most of which are written by editor Mathez; articles, one to five pages in length;
a calendar of major events (Chronicle); a listing of new publications received;
concise reviews up to one page long of brass literature, records, books, and
articles; and letters. The articles, written by a well-rounded roster of international
performers and teachers, often demonstrate a definite historical and even scholarly bent. Mathez's own six-part biography of the nineteenth-century French
trumpet pedagogue and artist Jean Baptiste Arban (beginning with 9:11) is but
one of the highlights of the magazine's past. Other noted authors, including
Edward Tarr, Francis Orval, and Thomas Stevens, have written on performance
practice and pedagogical viewpoints, provided interviews with performers and
composers, and commented on festivals and brass symposiums. *Brass Bulletin*
has also displayed an admirable history of publishing old photographs, early
woodcuts, and original brass compositions in their entirety.

Brass Bulletin has established itself as one of the major resources for brass players worldwide because it is one of the few such journals that is published in Europe, offers an international viewpoint, and is multilingual. Most of the rest are written, sponsored, and published by American-based organizations or are concerned primarily with local events or ensembles, such as British brass bands.

The periodical first appeared in an 5½" by 8½" format which was expanded to 8½" by 11" in 1976. The frequency of the early volumes (each issue has a separate volume number) was somewhat erratic. Starting with but one volume in 1971, the number of issues increased steadily until the *Brass Bulletin's* current format of four regular, sixty- to one-hundred-page volumes per year was established in 1976. Full or partial page advertisements for music publications, records, instruments, and brass-related specialty items are included. All material except the advertisements is printed in three languages: French, German, and English.

Information Sources

INDEXES
> External: Music Index, 1974–   (retrospective to 1972). Bibliographie des Musikschrifttums, 1977–   .

LOCATION SOURCES
> Widely available.

Publication History

TITLE AND TITLE CHANGES
> *Brass Bulletin.*

VOLUME AND ISSUE DATA
> Volumes 1–   , 1971–   .

FREQUENCY OF PUBLICATION
> Irregular to 1975. Quarterly, 1976–   .

PUBLISHER
> Jean-Pierre Mathez.

PLACES OF PUBLICATION
> Moudon, Switzerland, 1971–78. Bulle, Switzerland, 1979–   .

EDITOR
> Jean-Pierre Mathez.

Paul B. Hunt

BRASS QUARTERLY/BRASS AND WOODWIND QUARTERLY

The *Brass Quarterly/Brass and Woodwind Quarterly (BWQ)* was "devoted to articles, research studies, bibliographies, and reviews concerning brass instruments." Printed in Milford, New Hampshire, it began a rather short-lived publishing history in September 1957. Its existence is well characterized in a passage from a "Notice to Our Subscribers" (*BWQ* 1.1/2:48):

> *Brass and Woodwind Quarterly* is probably unique among musicological periodicals (and indeed almost unique among "scholarly" journals in any field) in being privately financed by its editor. It receives no institutional nor foundation support whatsoever, and subsists solely on the fees of its subscribers (and, from time to time, out of the pocket of its editor, who receives no remuneration for her services). In other words, *Brass and Woodwind Quarterly* is nothing more than the rather expensive hobby of its stubborn and dyspeptic editor.

Mary Rasmussen, the editor of both *Brass Quarterly* and *Brass and Woodwind Quarterly*, intended those articles which appeared in her journal to be of a sound musicological nature; the majority were, in fact, written by Rasmussen herself. Other contributors, mostly historians and performers with a bent for musicological research in brass, include Egon F. Kenton, Denis Arnold, Robert Gray, T. Donley Thomas, and Keith Polk. Their topics were almost exclusively historical, particularly the use of brass instruments throughout history, for example, the use of brass in the music of the Gabrielis, a listing of choral music with horn ensemble accompaniment, the trombone in chamber music, sources of early music suitable for transcription and performance. Especially worthy of mention is a recurring feature in which the editor gradually compiled a reasonably comprehensive brass bibliography for most of the years preceding the periodical's demise, still a highly valuable resource.

The reviews especially can be noted for their negative, almost condescending tone. A comment from Rasmussen, which unfortunately appears in the last issue published (*BWQ* 2.1/2:101), gives credence to this observation:

> We sometimes feel the *Brass and Woodwind Quarterly's* ever-grumpy review columns fail to make a very positive contribution to the quality of published music for wind instruments. Therefore, we present in each issue our quarterly free advertisement—on the house—for music, books, or records which the editor personally feels worthy of special commendation.

The publication history of these periodicals is somewhat convoluted: the *Brass Quarterly* appeared in September 1957 and, with an issuance schedule parallel to the academic calendar, was published in a quarterly format through 1962–63. The v. 7 issues (1963–64) were delayed in their publication, and v. 8 never did appear. The *Quarterly* was instead superseded by the *Brass and Woodwind Quarterly* in the winter of 1966–67. The second and last volume of *Brass and Woodwind Quarterly* appeared as 2.1/2 Spring/Summer 1969.

The format under these two titles was essentially consistent. The average issue, consisting of roughly sixty pages, included two or three ten- to fifteen-page articles, five to ten pages of brief reviews of music, books, and records, and approximately fifteen pages of information on current publications. More often than not, three to five pages of bibliographic citations on articles and books appeared as well. The later issues were frequently "double," averaged one hundred pages, and were usually expanded primarily by additional articles.

The publications, which were professionally typeset throughout their history, appeared in a 5½" by 8½" physical format. They displayed some musical examples and, on occasion, reprinted pictures. The pagination is continuous throughout a volume. Very few advertisements appeared and were almost always relegated to the back of the issue. Indexing for vs. 1–5 appears in 5.4 indexing for vs. 6 and 7 appears separately in the fourth number of its pertaining year.

Information sources

BIBLIOGRAPHY
LaRue, Jan. Review of "Brass Quarterly." *Notes* 25 (1968): 35–37.
INDEXES
 Internal: vs. 1–5 in v. 5; v. 6 and v. 7 separately.
 External: Music Index, 1957–69. RILM, 1967–69. Bibliographie des Musiksch-
 rifttums, 1956–68. Music Article Guide, 1965– .
LOCATION SOURCES
 New York Public Library, University of Cincinnati, Colorado State University,
 Los Angeles Public Library (partial).

Publication History

TITLE AND TITLE CHANGES
 Brass Quarterly, 1957–65. *Brass and Woodwind Quarterly*, 1966–69.
VOLUME AND ISSUE DATA
 Volumes 1–7.4, 1957–64. Volumes 1–2.1/2, 1966/67–69.
FREQUENCY OF PUBLICATION
 Quarterly.
PUBLISHER
 The Cabinet Press, Inc.
PLACE OF PUBLICATION
 Milford, New Hampshire.
EDITOR
 Mary Rasmussen.

Paul B. Hunt

BRIO

In 1963, ten years after the United Kingdom branch of the International Association of Music Libraries, Archives, and Documentation Centres—or IAML (UK)—was founded, its members voted to publish a journal entitled *Brio* (1.1:3). Published twice a year since the first issue appeared in spring 1964, *Brio* is both a vehicle of communication for the branch (with contributors mainly from its membership) and a source of timely information of various kinds helpful to music librarians. More than either *Notes* (q.v.) or *Fontes artis musicae* (q.v.), *Brio* serves the practical needs of its organization's members.

During its first decade *Brio* was ably edited by Ruzena Wood, and every issue contained an index to current British music periodicals compiled by Christel Wallbaum. Articles from that period included several descriptions of music libraries in the United Kingdom, a survey of national music libraries, practical articles on various phases of librarianship from technical processes to training for the profession, and serious bibliographical studies. There were also a few book reviews and some brief reports of the organization's meetings, as well as news items on members and descriptions of contributors.

In 1973, when both Wood and Wallbaum tendered their resignations, *Brio* nearly perished through a lack of human and financial resources, as well as a lack of publishable material (10.2:20). But two younger members of the association, Clifford Bartlett and Malcolm Jones, were persuaded to try editing *Brio* for a year. Their instructions were to concentrate on topics more closely related to library activities than to scholarly research and to find a less costly way to produce the journal (Ibid.). Furthermore, it was decided that the advent of *RILM* and better coverage in the *British Humanities Index* had made the periodical index which had been the core of the "old" *Brio* unnecessary. Thus, the first issue under the new editors (11.1, Spring 1974) was no longer typeset but reproduced from typescript, and devoted a large portion of its space to a description of activities at IAML(UK)'s annual conference. *Brio* survived, and Bartlett and Jones served as co-editors through v. 17 (1980) with Bartlett continuing as sole editor until v. 22 (1985), when he was replaced by Ian Ledsham.

The editors of *Brio* from 1974 on found various ways to make the journal increasingly useful to its primary audience: British music librarians. There was expanded coverage of IAML activities and of major changes in the library world (e.g., changes to cataloguing rules). There were also articles on other timely topics such as interlibrary loan and copyright of music materials. Bibliographies began to appear frequently, including ones on Honegger (vs. 14–15), and magazines for fans of popular music (v. 18). Book reviews came to be more numerous, along with other features to help librarians in selecting material. An annotated list of "Books Received," begun in v. 15 (1978), was transformed the following year into "In Brief," an extensive list of new books with evaluative and descriptive paragraphs written mainly by Bartlett. Reviews of scores and recordings have appeared irregularly. By the mid–1980s these sections highlighting new publications frequently made up over half of each issue.

The size of *Brio* has been 6½″ by 9″ since its inception. It was reproduced from typescript for six volumes (vs. 11–16), until increased revenue from advertisements allowed a return to the more pleasing typeset format. *Brio* averaged twenty-two to twenty-four pages per issue for its first twelve volumes (to 1975), but grew until issues were often double that size in the early 1980s. Advertisements, mainly from publishers, appear in each issue while illustrations have been very rare. An index to vs. 1–12 (1964–75) was compiled by David M. Baker in 1977.

Information Sources

INDEXES
>   Internal: vs. 1–12.
>   External: Music Index, 1966–   . RILM, 1967–   . Bibliographie des Musikschrifttums, 1964–   .

REPRINT EDITIONS
>   Microform: UMI, 1974–   .

LOCATION SOURCES
>   Widely available.

Publication History

TITLE AND TITLE CHANGES
>   *Brio*.

VOLUME AND ISSUE DATA
>   Volumes 1–   , 1964–   .

FREQUENCY OF PUBLICATION
>   Semiannual.

PUBLISHER
>   United Kingdom Branch of the International Association of Music Libraries, Archives, and Documentation Centres.

PLACES OF PUBLICATION
>   Edinburgh, Spring 1964–73. London, 1974–Spring 1985. Birmingham, Winter 1985–   .

EDITORS
>   Ruzena Wood, 1964–73. Clifford Bartlett (Co-editor, 1974–1980; Editor, 1981–85). Malcolm Jones (Co-editor, 1974–80). Ian Ledsham, 1985–   .

Peggy E. Daub

BULLETIN DE LES SOCIÉTÉ FRANÇAISE DE MUSICOLOGIE. See REVUE DE MUSICOLOGIE

BULLETIN DU HOT CLUB DE FRANCE, LE. See JAZZ-HOT

BULLETIN OF THE AMERICAN CHORAL FOUNDATION, INC. See AMERICAN CHORAL REVIEW

**BULLETIN OF THE AMERICAN CONCERT CHOIR AND THE CHO-
RAL FOUNDATION, INC.** See AMERICAN CHORAL REVIEW

BULLETIN OF THE METROPOLITAN OPERA GUILD. See OPERA
NEWS

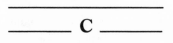

C

CÄCILIA. See CAECILIA (1824–1848)

CAECILIA (1824–1848)

Caecilia, one of several nineteenth-century German periodicals to bear the name of the patron saint of music, was founded and first edited by Jacob Gottfried Weber (1779–1839), composer and music theorist. Published from 1824 until 1848, the journal is an important source for information on musical life and thought in Germany during the early Romantic era.

Caecilia marked a new trend in music journalism in Germany, as Weber himself announced in the first issue. He used the word newspaper (*Zeitung*) to describe other music journals and the word magazine (*Zeitschrift*) to characterize *Caecilia.* Weber contended that while other music periodicals of the early nineteenth century related events generally of dated interest, *Caecilia* would offer readers a ''collection of interesting, entertaining, and informative articles, essays, and other inventions of enduring interest'' (1:1).

Caecilia did in fact contain informative articles that continue to be of interest today. One example was a sixty-three-page article on the state of music in Italy in the early nineteenth century. The journal also went beyond the realms of Western Europe. There were, for example, discussions of the music of Mexico (7:199–222), Russia (11:15–24), Egypt (15:179–183), and ancient Greece (20:73–91). Musicological history was made within the pages of the journal when Weber wrote an article questioning the authenticity of certain parts of Mozart's *Requiem,* basing his argument on a letter from Franz Xaver Süssmayer to Breitkopf und Härtel (3:205–232).

In addition to scholarly articles, the journal included reviews, two to four pages in length, of recently published music, both classical and popular. Fifteen- to twenty-page reports on music festivals and the musical life in important

European cities, such as Rome, Vienna, and Paris, were a popular feature, and, on the lighter side, there were anecdotes and poems. A supplement to each volume was the *Intelligenzblatt*, a folio with up to eighty-eight pages of advertisements that still retain considerable archival value. Most were publisher's announcements, but there were also advertisements for musical instruments and job openings. Weber edited the journal until his death in 1839, when Sigfried Wilhelm Dehn (1799–1858) took over the job. Dehn edited the journal until its demise in 1848, redirecting it toward a more scholarly emphasis.[1] *Caecilia* was published in twenty-seven volumes between 1824 and 1848, in an 5″ by 8½″ format. Usually one volume appeared each year, but there were some exceptions. No volumes were published in 1838, 1840, and 1841. Two volumes appeared in 1825, 1826, and 1829, and there were three volumes in 1828. Each volume contained four sixty- to seventy-page issues and an index for the entire volume. A cumulative index was published in the tenth volume.

Caecilia, produced by connoisseurs of art for the "educated," appears to have met its goals. Its approach to subject matter and the high standards of the contributors offered its readers informative articles that are of "enduring interest," even over a century later. The journal was successful from the start; reprints were required even during the inaugural year of publication (1:345). Among *Caecilia*'s famous readers was Johann Wolfgang von Goethe.[2] The journal survived when other periodicals of its type folded (15:1). *Caecilia* eventually ceased publication only due to the uncertain political situation. It had, however, made a lasting impact on musical scholarship, for it was after *Caecilia* that Friedrich Chrysander modeled his *Jahrbücher für musikalische Wissenschaft*.[3]

Notes

1. Albert Fleury, "Die Musikzeitschrift 'Cäcilia.' " (Diss., Frankfurt am Main, 1952/53), p. 104.

2. Wilhelm Bode, *Die Tonkunst in Goethes Leben,* 2 vols. (Berlin, 1912), 2:314ff.

3. *The New Grove Dictionary of Music and Musicians*, s.v. "Periodicals," by Imogen Fellinger.

Information Sources

BIBLIOGRAPHY

Bode, Wilhelm. *Die Tonkunst in Goethes Leben.* 2 vols. Berlin, 1912.

Fleury, Albert. "Die Musikzeitschrift 'Cäcilia.' " Diss., Frankfurt am Main, 1952/53.

The New Grove Dictionary of Music and Musicians. s.v. "Periodicals," by Imogen Fellinger.

The New Grove Dictionary of Music and Musicians. s.v. "Weber, (Jacob Gottfried)," by Mark Hoffmann.

Rohlfs, Eckart. *Die deutschsprachigen Musikperiodica 1945–1957: Versuch einer strukturellen Gesamtdarstellung als Beitrag zur Geschichte der musikalischen Fachpresse.* Regensburg, 1961.

Schaal, Richard. "Die Musikzeitschrift 'Cäcilia' und ihr Inhalt." In *Das Antiquariat: Halbmonatsschrift für alle Fachgebiete des Buch-und Kunstantiquariats,* 7th Jahrgang, Vienna, November–December 1951.

INDEXES
Internal: vs. 1–10 in v. 10.
REPRINT EDITIONS
Microform: Datamics, Inc. George Olms Verlag. Library of Congress. New York Public Library. Krauss International.
LOCATION SOURCES
Widely available.

Publication History

TITLE AND TITLE CHANGES
Cäcilia, 1824–25. *Caecilia*, 1826–48.
VOLUME AND ISSUE DATA
Volumes 1–27, 1824–48.
FREQUENCY OF PUBLICATION
Quarterly (with some irregularities).
PUBLISHER
Schott-Verlag.
PLACES OF PUBLICATION
Mainz, Brussels, and Antwerp
EDITORS
Jacob Gottfried Weber, 1824–39. Sigfried Wilhelm Dehn, 1839–1848.

Diane McMullen

CAECILIA (1844–1944)

After the establishment of an independent Netherlands in 1839, Utrecht publisher L. E. Bosch en Zoon perceived the need for a journal devoted to the nation's music and musical life. On 15 August of that year Bosch released the first issue of the *Nederlandsch Muzikaal Tijdschrift (NMT) (Netherlands Music Journal)*. On four pages, and soon after eight to twelve pages, editor A. P. F. de Seijff summarized musical events in the Netherlands and in other European countries during the past fortnight. The newsletter also contained information on new books and music. Bosch's enterprise, under the title *Caecilia* and a variety of publishers and editors, lasted over one hundred years, ending only in 1944 as a result of the German occupation of the Netherlands in World War II.

In 1841 A. P. F. de Seijff was first joined, then succeeded by F. C. Kist, and after three years broke with the journal's publisher. While L. E. Bosch en Zoon continued the *NMT* as a monthly with another editor until 1848, F. C. Kist started a new journal with the publishing firm Kemink & Zoon, also in Utrecht.

Under the title *Caecilia*, but with the same policies and formats as the *NMT*, Kist built the most important general music journal in the Netherlands. Published twice a month, it contained a chronicle of musical life, contributed by many correspondents from at home and abroad. F. C. Kist himself contributed interesting brief essays on historical subjects of all kinds. Articles had an average length of two to three pages, but some longer contributions appeared in successive issues, continued in three to over ten installments.

With Kist's death in 1863, the publication of the journal was taken over and maintained by Van Baalen in Rotterdam. In May 1871 *Caecilia* was taken over in turn and revitalized by the publisher Martinus Nijhoff in The Hague. The new editor, W. F. G. Nicolaï, promoted, among other things, the music of Richard Wagner in his contributions to *Caecilia*.

After the death of Nicolaï in 1896, another Wagnerite by the name of Henri Viotta succeeded him. In the following years great changes in the editorial policy of *Caecilia* took place. Since concert reviews were by that time readily found in the daily papers, Viotta no longer listed full concert programs. From October 1902 on, *Caecilia* became a monthly publication, featuring an overall survey of the musical life during the past month in the larger cities in the Netherlands and abroad. The yearly volumes of *Caecilia*, prior to 1902, had a length of about 200 to 250 pages. As a monthly it was expanded to about 500 to 600 pages by including larger articles (ten to fifteen pages) on musical subjects of all kinds.

Early in this century, *Caecilia* absorbed two competing journals: the *Weekblad voor Muziek* (*Weekly for Music*; a Wagner-oriented publication) in 1909 and *Het Muziekcollege* (*The Music Lecture*; a more Frankophilic publication) in 1917. In that year, Henri Viotta was succeeded by *Het Muziekcollege* editor Willem Landré who, until the end of *Caecilia's* existence, remained its primary editor, in most years joined by one or more co-editors. The absorbing of one journal by the other was made recognizable by the title *Caecilia en Het Muziekcollege*, and by double numbering of the yearly volumes through 1931 (v. 88/18).

The physical format of *Caecilia*, which until 1909 (v. 66) had always been about 8" by 10⅝" was then enlarged to about 10" by 13". From November 1917 (v. 75) on, however, it was reduced again to the former format size, and the length of the yearly volumes was reduced to between 250 and 300 pages.

In a final merger, *De Muziek*, published separately by the Federatie van Nederlandsche Toonkunstenaars-Vereenigingen (Federation of Dutch Societies of Musicians) since October 1926 joined *Caecilia* in November 1933. As when *Caecilia* absorbed *Het Muziekcollege*, so the combination of *Caecilia* and *De Muziek*, was made recognizable by the double title *Caecilia en De Muziek* and by double numbering of the yearly volumes. The fascinating articles on all kinds of musical subjects which until September 1933 were contained in *De Muziek*, then became the important feature of *Caecilia en De Muziek*, where they ranged from five to twelve pages in length. Earlier written by learned amateurs (like Kist) and schoolteachers (Viotta), articles were now lent a more scholarly tone by a new generation of musicologists.

During the last several decades of its existence, Caecilia was adopted as the official organ of several important Dutch music societies, each of which inserted its own newsletter. The German occupation of the Netherlands during World War II caused a paper shortage and greatly affected the contents of *Caecilia* as well. No communications or articles that were unfriendly or undesirable in the eyes of the German authorities were permitted. Until June 1943 (100.6) *Caecilia* still appeared monthly, but thence only every other month, and the length of the issues was reduced to sixteen pages each. After August 1944 the publication ceased entirely.

Information Sources

LOCATION SOURCES

New York Public Library. Yale University, 1844–88. Library of Congress, 1844–1937. Newberry Library (Chicago), 1934–44. Koninklijke Bibliotheek, Gemeentemuseum at The Hague, University of Utrecht, University of Amsterdam, University of Groningen.

Publication History

TITLE AND TITLE CHANGES

Nederlandsch Muzikaal (or: *Muzijkaal*) *Tijdschrift*, Vol. 1 #1–9, 15 August–15 December 1839; Vol. 2–10, 1840–48; *Caecilia: Algemeen Muzikaal Tijdschrift van Nederland*, Vol. #1–9, 15 August–15 December 1844; Vol. 2–19, 1845–62; *Caecilia: Algemeen Muziekaal Tijdschrift van Nederland*, Vol. 20–28 #8, 1863–15 April 1871; *Caecilia: Algemeen Muzikaal Tijdschrift van Nederland*, Vol. 28 #9–59 #17, 1 May 1871–September 1902; *Caecilia: Maandblade voor Muziek*, Vol. 60, October 1902–December 1903, Vol. 61–74 #10; 1904–October 1917; *De Vereenigde Tijdschriften Caecilia en Het Muziekcollege: Algemeen Toonkunstblad voor Groot-Nederland*, Vol. 75/5–76/6 #15, November 1917–August 1919; *De Vereenigde Tijdschriften Caecilia, Maandblad voor Muziek, en Het Muziekcollege: Algemeen Onafhankelijk Toonkunstblad voor Groot Nederland*, Vol. 76/6 #16-88/18, September 1919–October 1931; *Het Muziekcollege Caecilia*, Vol. 89–90, November 1931–October 1933; *Caecilia en De Muziek*, Vol. 91/8–93/10, November 1933–October 1936; Vol. 94/11, March 1937–February 1938; Vol. 95/12, March–December 1938; Vol. 96/13–98/15, 1939–1941; Vol. 99–101 #4, 1942–August 1944.

Maandblad voor Muziek, tevens Orgaan der Wagner-Vereeniging te Amsterdam, Vol. 1, October 1888–September 1889; Vol. 2, November 1889–October 1890; Vol. 3–5, January 1891–December 1893, succeeded by:

Weekblad voor Muziek, Vol. 1–16, 3 February 1894–28 December 1909.

Het Muziekcollege: Halfmaandelijksch Tijdschrift voor Muziekvrienden en-beoefenaars, Vol. 1–4, 1 November 1913–16 October 1917.

De Muziek: Tijdschrift, tevens Officieel Orgaan van de Federatie van Nederlandsche Toonkunstenaars-Vereenigingen, Vol. 1–7, October 1926–September 1933, succeeded partly by:

Orgaan der Federatie van Nederlandsche Toonkunstenaars-Vereenigingen, (tijdelijke uitgave without nr., October 1933–September 1934; Vol. 1–2, October 1934–September 1936; *De Muziekwereld: Orgaan der Federatie van Nederlandsche Tookunstenaars-Vereenigingen*, Vol. 3 #1, October 1936; *De Wereld der Muziek: Orgaan der Federatie van Nederlandsche Toonkunstenaars-Vereenigingen*, Vol. 3 #2–9, November 1936–September 1943; *De Wereld der Muziek: Orgaan van het Muziekgilde der Nederlandsche Kultuurkamer*, Vol. 10, October 1943–September 1944.

VOLUME AND ISSUE DATA
Volumes 1–101.4, 1844–1944.
FREQUENCY OF PUBLICATION
Semimonthly, to 1901. Monthly, 1902–1944.
PUBLISHERS
Nederlandsch Muzikaal Tijdschrift: L. E. Bosch en Zoon
Caecilia: Kemink & Zoon, 1844–62. J. van Baalen & Zonen, 1863–15 April 1871.
Martinus Nijhoff, 1 May 1871–1906. van Holkema & Warendorf, 1907–09. Loman & Schut, 1910. Uitgeversmaatschappij Caecilia, 1911–October 1917, Emil
Wegelin, November 1917–June 1918. Emil Wegelin, July 1918–September 1920.
Emil Wegelin, October 1920–October 1936. J. J. Lispet, March 1937–August
1944.
Maandblad voor Muziek and *Weekblad voor Muziek:* Amsterdam: de Erven H. van
Munster & Zoon
Het Muziekcollege: Haarlem: Emil Wegelin
De Muziek: Amsterdam: N. V. Seyffardt's Boek-en Muziekhandel
Orgaan . . . , De Muziekwereld . . . , and *De Wereld der Muziek . . .* were published by
the Federatie van Nederlandsche Toonkunstenaars-Vereenigingen
PLACES OF PUBLICATION
Nederlandsch Muzikaal Tijdschrift: Utrecht.
Caecilia: Utrecht, 1844–62. Rotterdam, 1863–15 April 1871. 's Gravenhage, 1 May
1871–1906. Amsterdam, 1907–October 1917. Haarlem, November 1917–June
1918. Amersfoort, July 1918–September 1920. Bussum, October 1920–October
1936. Hilversum, March 1937–1944.
Maandblad voor Muziek and Weekblad voor Muziek: Amsterdam.
Het Muziekcollege: Haarlem.
De Muziek: Amsterdam.
Orgaan der Federatie . . . , De Muziekwereld, and *De Wereld der Muziek:* Amsterdam,
October 1933–April 1941. 's Gravenhage, May 1941–September 1944.
EDITORS
Nederlandsch Muzikaal Tijdschrift: A. P. F. de Seijff, 15 August 1839–1840. A. P. F.
de Seijff and F. C. Kist, 1 January–1 September 1841. F. C. Kist, 15 September
1841–15 August 1844. Ernest van Wachten (pen name of W. J. F. Nieuwenhuysen), November 1845–December 1848.
Caecilia: F. C. Kist, 15 August 1844–15 March 1863. W. F. Thooft, 15 May 1870–15
April 1871. W. F. G. Nicolaï, 1 May 1871–15 April 1896. Henri Viotta, 1 July
1896–September 1902. Henri Viotta and Simon van Milligen, October 1902–
1910. Henri Viotta, Simon van Milligen and A. D. Loman, Jr., 1911–October
1917. Willem Landré, Piet de Waardt, and P. A. van Westrheene, November
1917–October 1921. A varying group of six to seven editors, November 1921–
October 1930. Willem Landré and Herman Rutters, November 1930–October
1933. Herman Rutters and Eduard Reeser, November 1933–1938. Willem Landré,
1939–1941. Willem Landré and E. Elsenaar, 1942–June 1944. E. Elsenaar, August
1944.
Maandblad voor Muziek: Henri Viotta
Weekblad voor Muziek: Hugo Nolthenius and Simon van Milligen, 1894. Hugo Nolthenius, 1895–1909.
Het Muziekcollege: Willem Landré, Piet de Waardt, and P. A. van Westrheene.

De Muziek: Paul F. Sanders and Willem Pijper.

Orgaan der Federatie . . . , *De Muziekwereld*, and *De Wereld der Muziek*: An editorial committee, of which the secretary was K. Veldkamp, October 1933–September 1934. K. Ph. Bernet Kempers, October 1934–April 1941. Toon Verhey and Frans Vink, May–September 1941. Frans Vink, October 1941–September 1944.

Alfons Annegarn

CAECILIA EN DE MUZIEK. See CAECILIA (1844–1944)

CAHIERS CANADIENS DE MUSIQUE, LES. See CANADIAN MUSIC BOOK

CANADA MUSIC BOOK/LES CAHIERS CANADIENS DE MUSIQUE

In v. 1, Gilles Potvin, the journal's first and only editor, announced that "The *Canada Music Book* would endeavor to offer the professional musician and the music lover as well a series of major articles on various subjects, reviews of new recordings, books on music, music and scores, plus a series of reports from all parts of Canada" (1:9). Material, he added, would be printed in English or French without translation, though second-language summaries of major pieces were common. Appearing semiannually from 1970 through 1976, *Canada Music Book* followed Potvin's description closely. Each volume, measuring 5¾" by 9", contains some dozen articles from four to twenty-five pages in length; a report of up to one page from each province under the heading "Canadian Chronicles/Chroniques canadiennes"; a section supplemented from v. 7 on by a "Chronique de Paris"; numerous one- to five-page reviews, usually quite substantive; and sometimes a few pages on pedagogy and dance.

The journal's editor and editorial board and their basic editorial policies remained largely unchanged during the seven years of publication. Some of the articles, especially in later issues, are quite scholarly, for example, one on linguistics as an analytical tool in music theory. But these are the exception; *Canada Music Book* rarely taxes the sophistication of a devoted amateur music lover. The diversity of articles is suggested by the inclusion, in v. 9, of articles of "Composing Computers for Kids," "Musique et vie quotidienne en Tunisie," and an International Society for Contemporary Music (ISCM) report. In each issue, one or two composers—usually among those active within the past century—are singled out for feature coverage. If living, the composer generally had considerable input in the form of an essay, interview, or considerable quotation. Once a year, *Canada Music Book* allotted considerable space to a report on that year's Canadian Music Council national conference. Keynote addresses were reprinted, and both the schedule and important presentations summarized. Other major topics and special issues include "Première semaine mondiale de la musique au Canada" and the twentieth anniversary of the Canadian League of Composers. The contributors were mostly Canadian composers, journalists, radio hosts, educators, and scholars, heavily drawn from Quebec and Ontario. The noted Canadian composer R. Murray Schafer contributed regularly.

Canada Music Book (CMB) was founded and supported by the Canadian Music Council, an umbrella organization for Canadian musicians and music organizations. It succeeds, in a sense, an earlier journal publishing effort of the council: the *Canadian Music Journal* (1956–61). Edited by Geoffrey B. Payzant, this publication also contained articles, provincial reports, and many reviews. Though initially more general in nature than the *CMB*, it became gradually more scholarly. The *Journal* was also published almost solely in English and reflects a somewhat more overt Canadian as well as English-speaking Canadian bias.

Like the *Canadian Music Journal*, the *Canada Music Book* appears to have had difficulty maintaining a sufficient subscribership. Vs. 11 and 12 appear as a double issue, which contains a notice that *Canada Music Book* would henceforth appear yearly. V. 13 never appeared. The last issue also notes that the council would initiate a new, quarterly publication entitled *MUSICANADA*, which they would initially provide free to all *Canada Music Book* subscribers. This new item, essentially the council's bilingual newsletter, did indeed survive the demise of the *Canada Music Book* and contains information on artists, events, festivals, and the cultural climate in general.

Information Sources

BIBLIOGRAPHY
Potvin, G. "Editorial." *Canada Music Book/Les Cahiers canadiens de musique* 1 (1970): 9–10.
McMorrow, K., and C. Lindahl. "Music Periodicals: Canadian Music Periodicals." *Notes* 36 (1980): 907.
INDEXES
    External: Music Index, 1972–76. RILM, 1967–76.
LOCATION SOURCES
    Widely available.

Publication History

TITLE AND TITLE CHANGES
    Canada Music Book/Les Cahiers canadiens de musique.
VOLUME AND ISSUE DATA
    Volumes 1–12, 1970–76.
FREQUENCY OF PUBLICATION
    Semiannual.
PUBLISHER
    Canadian Music Council.

PLACE OF PUBLICATION
    Quebec.
EDITOR
    Gilles Potvin.

Richard S. James

CANADIAN COMPOSER, THE

The Canadian Composer/Le Compositeur canadien appeared under the aegis of the Composers Authors and Publishers Association of Canada (CAPAC) in May 1965. The journal's founder and first editor, Senator Allister Grosart, cited the following needs in an early editorial: better communication among CAPAC's members; adequate recognition for the music of Canadian composers at home and abroad; a place to publicize news and information on Canadian composers; and clarification of misunderstandings about performing rights.

The Canadian Composer has, over the years, devoted a considerable amount of space to aspects of copyright, for example, reports from France, Spain, and the United States in n. 13, the "International Copyright Issue" and the "Special Copyright Issue" (n. 34) with articles reflecting "some of this new determination to obtain a square deal from Parliament for Canadian creative efforts" (34:2).

In dealing with factors that affect the musical scene, it was stated in the Fifth Anniversary Issue (n. 40) that more attention would be devoted to popular music. Since that time, an ever-increasing amount of space has been given to commercial musicians (the main membership of CAPAC), almost to the exclusion of the classical tradition.

By 1984 the journal had established several regular departments: "Profile," "Feature Composer," and "Moving Up" (articles of various lengths on Canadian composers); "Music Business" (the financial side of the profession); "Composer's Workshop" (new technology); "CAPAC Reports"; "New Records by CAPAC Members"; "CAPAC Members in the News"; "New CAPAC Members"; "New CAPAC Publishers"; "Letters"; and "Quotes." An editorial ("Starting Point") appears in each issue and is usually written by the journal's editor. Most editorials focus on the pressing concerns of composers—performing and publication rights being chief among them. Until 1983 when signed articles became the norm, it was difficult to determine who was responsible for the various features (and even the editorial) that appeared. According to the current editor, Richard Flohil, most unsigned articles were written by the editors and/ or staff members in the journal's employ. Photos of prominent Canadian composers from every phase of the profession grace front and back covers and are usually featured in extensive articles within. Sir Ernest MacMillan, Norma Beecroft, Oskar Morawetz, François Dompierre, Harry Freedman, Eddie Eastman, Kelsey Jones, and Jacques Faubert are among the over 400 composers who have been so honored.

Aside from some early inconsistencies in the frequency of publication, *The Canadian Composer* has appeared regularly, ten times a year; all issues are numbered consecutively and are forty-eight pages long. The journal is entirely bilingual (English and French) and has received high praise for consistently maintaining this policy (n. 5). Very slight format changes (typography and layout) were seen throughout the years, but the size has remained 8" by 11". Each issue contains many photos (largely of composers and performers); musical examples appear as needed but are quite infrequent. Advertisements are not included.

Information Sources

INDEXES
> External: Music Index, 1972– . Canadian Periodical Index, 1969– . Point de Repere. Popular Music Periodicals Index, 1973–76. Magazine Index, 1983– .

REPRINT EDITIONS
> Microform: Micromedia, Ltd.

LOCATION SOURCES
> Toronto Public Library (complete). Partial holdings widely held.

Publication History

TITLE AND TITLE CHANGES
> *The Canadian Composer/Le Compositeur canadien.*

VOLUME AND ISSUE DATA
> Volume 1– , 1965– .

FREQUENCY OF PUBLICATION
> 10/year.

PUBLISHER
> Creative Arts Company.

PLACE OF PUBLICATION
> 1240 Bay Street, Suite 303, Toronto, Ontario M5R 2A7.

EDITORS
> Senator Allister Grosart, ns. 1–25. Donald Schrank, ns. 26–35. Ronald Hambleton, ns. 38–51. Richard Flohil, ns. 52– . No editor can be identified for ns. 36–37; it is assumed that during this time the journal was assembled by its publisher.

Marilyn Shrude

CASH BOX

Cash Box has undergone three distinct phases of development since it began publication in 1941. During World War II it existed as a mimeographed tip sheet of two or three pages catering to distributors of coin-operated music and game machines. The publication's primary purpose was to inform and advise route owners and operators about the trends relating to jukeboxes, pinball games, slot machines, and pool halls.

Following World War II, *Cash Box* played a pioneering role in the integration of the hardware end of the music business with sound recordings. Jukebox operators accounted for over 90 percent of all record purchases throughout the 1930s and 1940s; *Cash Box* endeavored to reflect this state of affairs in its record reviews and sales charts. News about nonmusic vending machines, however, continued to occupy a prominent position in the magazine.

The third phase of *Cash Box*'s history coincided with the substantial impact made by consumer buying habits upon the record industry, beginning in the early 1950s. In response, *Cash Box* redirected the bulk of its energies and news space to private sector impact points such as retail outlets and the mass media (radio, television, and motion pictures). The magazine now considers its main audience to be record company executives, booking agents, artists and musicians, talent agents and managers, music publishers, and music industry unions and organizations. It employs a standard trade weekly format, incorporating feature stories (devoted to major people and events in the music business world), news briefs divided by various genre headings (such as mainstream pop, country, black contemporary, jazz, inspirational/gospel) and software formats (for example, video cassettes and discs, compact discs, video games), record reviews, concert reviews, directories (of artists, talent agents, record companies, music publishers, and so on), specialized columns (such as cover act profiles, new artists), and advertisements and classifieds (primarily record companies and hardware firms). George Albert, president and publisher of *Cash Box*, considers the magazine's primary purpose to be one of "serving the music business at large by offering a commercial gauge of noteworthy contemporary trends" (private communication).

Charts hold a prominent place in the fifty to one hundred pages forming each issue, and *Cash Box* has long been recognized as possessing perhaps the best-defined and accurate charts in the business. The magazine places an emphasis upon sales in determining chart positions; radio play is noted either by separate lists or via symbols on the charts.

Cash Box's editorial policy consists of promoting the industry's overall interests through a combination of the spokesperson and advocacy approaches. The magazine strives for honesty and open access to information, while employing a "criticism-within-limits" stance. Unlike consumer publications, *Cash Box* chooses to eschew blatantly negative forms of analysis with respect to record and concert reviews. However, the magazine frequently chooses to provide a philosophical position on various issues of a controversial nature, such as racism, the rise of rock and roll, payola, quadraphonic sound, video games, the blank tape tax proposal submitted to the federal legislature, and censorship in its myriad manifestations.

Cash Box is credited within the music industry for a number of key innovations. In addition to the aforementioned interfacing of vending machine and record industry coverage, the magazine led other trade weeklies in opening up international markets for American music. After establishing branch offices in key

U.S. music centers such as Nashville and Los Angeles in the late 1940s, *Cash Box* opened foreign departments in London, Mexico, and Canada in 1957, followed by Germany, Italy, Sweden, France, Holland, Brazil, Argentina, Japan, and Australia in the late 1950s and early 1960s. These offices employed local people well versed in the indigenous music of their respective countries. Beginning in the late 1950s, *Cash Box* offered regular international features and chart compilations.

In addition to owner George Albert—whose contributions to the music industry as a songwriter, arranger, record company entrepreneur, and journalist span more than fifty years—notable writers and editors for the publication have included Marty Ostrow, Irv Lichtman, record executive Marv Schlacter and the late Neil Bogart. Dick Clark has used the *Cash Box* charts for many years as the basis of his syndicated radio and television hit parade programs.

Since adopting a tabloid newsprint format following World War II, the magazine has outstripped all trade weekly competitors in the area of graphics design and layout. *Cash Box* has used glossy stock paper exclusively since the early 1960s and features a color cover portrait of a selected music act each issue which is highly sought within the industry. The magazine has recently adopted a slightly downsized, albeit more manageable, 10″ by 13½″ format.

Information Sources

INDEXES
>   External: Music Index, 1962–65.

LOCATION SOURCES
>   Postwar issues widely available.

Publication History

TITLE AND TITLE CHANGES
>   *Cash Box: Coin Operated Machines, Vending Machines*, 1941–64. *Cash Box: Records, Music, Coin Operated Machines Vending Machines*, 1965–76. *Cash Box: The International Music Record Weekly*, 1977–   .

VOLUME AND ISSUE DATA
>   Volumes 1– , 1941– .

FREQUENCY OF PUBLICATION
>   Weekly.

PUBLISHERS
>   Joe Orleck and William Gersh, 1941–46?. Joe Orleck, William Gersh, and George Albert, 1946?–62. Joe Orleck and George Albert, 1963–66. George Albert, 1967–   .

PLACES OF PUBLICATION
>   Chicago, 1941–46?. New York, 1946?–71. Hollywood, 1971–   .

EDITORS
>   Joe Orleck and William Gersh, 1941–50. Martin Ostrow, 1950?–66. Irv Lichtman, 1967–76. Julian Shapiro, 1977–78. Dave Fulton, 1979–80. Alan Sutton, 1981–84. David Adelson, 1984–86. Stephen Padgett, 1987. Lee Jeske, 1988–   .

Frank W. Hoffman

CHIGIANA

Chigiana is an Italian serial published under the auspices of the Accademia Musicale Chigiana in Siena on the occasion of the coincident music festival Settimana Musicale Senese. The academy, reviving the spirit of academies that flourished in Siena in earlier centuries, has presented these music festivals under the patronage of Count Guido Chigi Saracini since 1939. A serial publication has accompanied the festivals since the beginning. The academy's earlier, untitled monographic series ran to twenty volumes (1939–63, excepting the war years), generally related to the respective themes of the various festivals. Monographs in this old series addressed such topics as individual composers (for example, Antonio Vivaldi, Giovanni Pergolesi, and Giuseppe Verdi) or more broadly conceived topics like "Exotic Images in Italian Music."

The "new series" under the fixed title *Chigiana* began publication in 1964. The periodical has since embraced various aims and formats. Overtly "musicological," the first issues address the international scholarly community. These early volumes reveal a tripartite organization: "celebrations" (scholarly essays on composers to commemorate the anniversary of their birth or death), "studies" (historical-critical investigations of significant scholarly issues), and appendices (also "anniversary" essays, here concerned with extra-musical figures—Galileo and Michelangelo, for example—and their relationship to music). Appendices of this nature, harbingers of expanding musicological vision, sadly disappeared after the first two volumes. In the double issue of 1969–70 (ns. 6–7), under different editorship, new aims became clear, principally an editorial intent to nurture a closer unity between the academy, the festival, and the publication *Chigiana*. Accordingly, in subsequent years, volumes have characteristically presented proceedings of congresses sponsored by the academy in collaboration with the University of Siena, transcriptions of composition seminars held at the academy, and excerpts from the program notes of the Settimana Musicale Senese (ranging from extended discussions to brief annotations). *Chigiana* has emerged then a strong manifestation of the rich Sienese musical life.

The scope of subjects considered is broad. In the first seven volumes, taken as a whole, there is a balance between *seicento*, *settecento*, nineteenth (international), and twentieth-century (international) topics. Pre-Baroque, French Baroque, and eighteenth-century German topics are represented, but to a lesser degree. Later volumes have presented studies devoted to twentieth-century Italians (Giannotto Bastianelli, Alfredo Casella, and Don Lorenzo Perosi), and composition seminars by Goffredo Petrassi and Sylvano Bussotti. The Sienese congresses whose proceedings are reported in these volumes addressed broadly based topics, which include Christoph Gluck and Italian culture in Vienna, Italian musical and theatrical culture in Paris during the Enlightenment, and the musical avant-garde of the 1920s.

Contributors to *Chigiana* number musicologists, scholar-performers, and composers. Frequent articles by Mario Fabbri and Luciano Alberti attest not only to their scholarly commitment, but also to their roles as artistic directors of the academy (Fabbri was the first editor of the serial as well). Sergio Martinotti, Francesco Degrada, and Giovanni Carli Ballola are also regular contributors. Scholar-performers have included, in addition to Degrada, Jean-François Paillard, René Clemencic, and Newell Jenkins. Jenkins's article "Geminiani's 'The Enchanted Forest' " (4:167–179) is a particularly felicitous confluence of interests, as he gave the first modern performance of Geminiani's work at the Settimana Musicale Senese in 1967.

In many cases, ample musical examples accompany the texts. One instance of editorial generosity in this regard would be the inclusion of a nineteen-page facsimile from Giuseppe Paolucci's treatise *Arte pratica di Contrappunto*—a motet by Caldara with Paolucci's commentary—in a study devoted to Caldara (6/7:223–430; facsimiles: 395–413). Illustrations (black and white) are also liberally included in earlier volumes.

Volumes appeared annually through 1968; double issues combining two years and a less regular schedule have characterized subsequent volumes. The length of each of the first ten volumes averages 300 pages (6″ by 9″); later volumes have been closer to 400 pages. *Chigiana* publishes in four languages: Italian, German, French, and English. However, the overwhelming majority of its texts, like its contributors, are Italian. A cumulative index of nos. 1–5 and 6–10 (subject and author) facilitates research.

Information Sources

INDEXES
    Internal: vs.1–5, vs.6–10.
    External: RILM, 1968– . Bibliographie des Musikschrifttums, 1961– .
LOCATION SOURCES
    Widely available.

Publication History

TITLE AND TITLE CHANGES
    Chigiana.
VOLUME AND ISSUE DATA
    Volumes 1– , 1964– .
FREQUENCY OF PUBLICATION
    Yearly, 1964–68. Irregular, 1968– .
PUBLISHER
    Leo S. Olschki, 1964– .
PLACE OF PUBLICATION
    Florence, 1964– .

EDITORS

Mario Fabbri, 1964–68. Cesare Orselli, 1969–84. Guido Burchu, 1985–   .

Steven Plank

CHORAL JOURNAL, THE

The first issue of *The Choral Journal* appeared in May 1959 and announced the foundation of a new association, the American Choral Directors Association, (ACDA), whose purpose would be to foster and promote choral music in America. The founders of the association felt that it was imperative to have a publication, and affiliation with established journals had been rejected in favor of its own organizational bulletin. While early issues served mainly as a newsletter for members, the journal ultimately developed, under R. Wayne Hugoboom, managing editor from 1959–77, into a periodical of international scope.

From the outset, *The Choral Journal* was designed "to disseminate professional news and information about choral music" to the members of the ACDA. In addition to serving as the primary means of communication for the business and professional affairs of the association, *The Choral Journal* also includes brief reviews, two- to six-page articles of high quality, announcements of important events and activities of the choral profession, and other news and information. Subject areas for articles published in the *Journal* have included historical research into choral music, practical choral methods and techniques, analytical studies of choral works, as well as profiles of excellent choral teachers and interviews with choral personalities. Written primarily by members of the ACDA, these articles and features lend a more serious, scholarly tone to the journal than is common among choral journals.

Regular features and departments have been a part of the *The Choral Journal* since its inception. While some have come and gone, personal columns written by the current president and the executive secretary of ACDA are always included. Equally regular and very important is the "Choral Reviews" section. The association has always felt that the discovery of quality choral literature is vital, and emphasis has been placed on this aspect of the profession in the *Journal*. Selected members of the association regularly review choral releases from the various publishers and provide information about their quality and usefulness in different choral situations. Other departments, more irregular or short-lived, include "From the Editor," "Book Reviews," "Record Reviews," Popular Choral Corner," "Children's Choral Column," "The Editor's Notebook," "Literature Forum," "Conductor's Commentary," "Research Report," and "DaCapo" (reprints from other periodicals and excerpts from previously published literature about choral music).

One of the major functions of the ACDA at the national level is the planning and execution of national conventions. In the beginning stages of the organization these conventions were held under the aegis of the national Music Educators National Conference (MENC), and *The Choral Journal* played an important role in announcing and promoting these meetings. As the association grew and became more independent, so did the conventions. The *Journal* became the major means of promoting these conventions. Special convention issues appeared prior to the national and divisional meetings; normally including a detailed schedule of events and information about the performing choirs and guest clinicians.

In addition to the convention issues, other special issues have been devoted to "Swedish Choral Music" (12.6), "Church Music" (14.4), "The Adjudicator and Critic" (14.6), "Contemporary Purview of the Arts" (14.7), "Community Outreach" (14.8), and most recently an issue honoring Robert Shaw, "Celebrating Seventy Years" (26.9). Tributes to famous choral personalities and profiles of well-known choral conductors and teachers have also been included in various issues throughout the history of the *Journal*.

The physical format of the *Journal* has remained basically the same, after the initial growth years. The first seven issues (May 1959–May 1961) comprise v. 1 and were essentially four to eight-page newsletters. Beginning with v. 2 (September 1961–May 1962) a standard 8½" by 11" magazine format was established, and the final, thirty-two-page issue of this volume was indicative of its new size and scope. By v. 4, the content format was fairly well solidified, and the *Journal* was being published on a schedule of six issues a year, each containing between twenty-four and thirty-two pages. This schedule has continued to increase to the current ten issues yearly, published from August to May. Photography, illustrations, and musical examples are abundant. A substantial amount of advertising, anywhere from fifty to one hundred items, has been included in the format since the September/October 1963 issue (v. 6), and ranges from university and college notices, music publishers, and travel services, to position and workshop announcements. An index of advertisers is included at the end of every issue.

Information Sources

INDEXES
External: Music Index, 1967– . Music Article Guide, 1965– . RILM, 1976– . Also, published by ACDA, *The Choral Journal: An Index To Volumes 1–18*, by Gordon Paine (covers 1959–78).
REPRINT EDITIONS
Microform: UMI. AMS Film Service (vs. 1–10).
LOCATION SOURCES
Widely available.

Publication History

TITLE AND TITLE CHANGES
The Choral Journal.
VOLUME AND ISSUE DATA
Volumes 1– , 1959– .
FREQUENCY OF PUBLICATION
6/year, 1959–69. 9/year, 1969–83. 10/year, 1983– .

PUBLISHER
    American Choral Directors Association.
PLACE OF PUBLICATION
    Lawton, Oklahoma.
EDITORS
    R. Wayne Hugoboom, 1959–77. H. Judson Troop, 1977–81. Mark Dalton, 1981–
    82. Ronnie Shaw (Managing Editor), 1982–   . James McCray, 1982–   . Lynn
    Whitten, 1983–85. Wesley Coffman, 1985–   .

Terry E. Eder

CLARINET, THE. See WOODWIND WORLD

CLAVIER

When *Clavier* published its premier issue in April 1962 as a "magazine for pianists and organists," it joined the ranks of the ten-year-old *Piano Quarterly* (q.v.) and the short-lived *Piano Teacher* (subsequently absorbed by *Clavier*) as one of the principal journals devoted to the support and encouragement of the continually growing number of private piano teachers in this country. The fact that two such enterprises with an almost inevitable overlap of goals can continue to publish successfully today—they are to be found side in by side the studios of many teachers and in public and academic music libraries alike—proves that the need for specialized information from experienced practitioners and authors on the topics of piano pedagogy, new publications, profiles of master artists and teachers, and current events, is indeed great and not likely to be adequately met by generalized music periodicals which aim for the broadest possible readership. In Ruth Watanabe's study, "Current Periodicals for Music Libraries," the then-young *Clavier* was aptly characterized as a combination of "learned journal" ("directed to the professional and the specialist rather than the layman") and a "journal of performing media" (with "articles on instruments and the forms of music used by them").[1] The description is still suitable today in *Clavier's* third decade of publication.

Clavier was founded by, and continues to be published by, The Instrumentalist Company, publishers of the long-established *The Instrumentalist* (q.v.). Unlike the *Piano Quarterly* with its modest beginnings, *Clavier* was immediately established on an impressive scale with a large production staff and a board of advisors who comprised some of the best-known and most highly respected artists and teachers in this country. In the inaugural issue, the editors stated: "We are dedicated to supporting keyboard teachers in the increasingly important and influential role they must fill in our developing future. We seek to give inspiration and practical guidance. We seek to improve the status of the performer and the music teacher in the community. We seek to explore the wonders of keyboard music and spread them before our readers'' (1.1:4).

Articles span a variety of topics in essay or interview formats, by or about leading pianists, piano teachers or other educators, and are concerned with all levels of piano teaching, study, and interpretation (master lessons with artist teachers on the traditional literature or on special problems). Each issue contains six to eight such articles, each between four and six pages in length. The inclusion of piano pieces, *Clavier* commissions, or little-known brief works with background information and suggestions for performance and further study, has been a hallmark of *Clavier*.

Regular features include current events (news about forthcoming piano competitions or an announcement of recent competition winners, new appointments, news from foundations, and so on); ''New Music Reviews'' by a panel of leading teachers or authors; selective book reviews; and occasional features designed to appeal to young readers. Organ music was accorded similar treatment until recent issues. Worthy of special mention is the ''Question and Answer'' column by master teacher Frances Clark, which serves as a forum for teachers' unique problems and general pedagogical concerns. In recent volumes, additional features include an annual directory of summer music camps and other opportunities for seasonal study; a ''Classified'' section; and a brief, selective listing of professional openings for teachers.

Clavier, while perhaps less scholarly than *Piano Quarterly*, is notable for a consistently attractive format, which reaches out to the teacher who works exclusively with young beginners through high school, college, and university-level teachers, and pedagogy specialists, as well as pianists who would establish for themselves careers as performers, in all, a readership of over 24,000 subscribers. The original 8" by 11" size and physical appearance have remained practically unchanged since the first issues. Under the guidance of Dorothy Packard, who served as editor for the first sixteen years, issues were and continue to be forty-eight pages in length and occasionally longer. The journal appears ten times a year and contains advertising from a variety of publishers, instrument manufacturers, and educational institutions.

The editorial of the twenty-fifth anniversary issue summarizes the success of *Clavier*: ''Over the past years it has been *Clavier's* good fortune to have a publisher with the courage to give the magazine life; an illustrious board of advisors to lend it counsel; and a host of talented editors, associate editors, editorial assistants, art directors, typesetters, and advertising managers . . . it has had thousands of articulate keyboard performers and teachers who have spent free moments and vacations writing practical and inspiring articles. Consulting editors have spent long hours searching for covers, seeking out composers to write new teaching pieces, and interviewing major concert artists who have taken the time to let *Clavier's* readers get to know them better. All the while, the loyalty of its advertisers has kept *Clavier* viable'' (25.1:2).

Note

1. Ruth Watanabe, "Current Music Periodicals for Libraries," *Notes* 23 (1966): 225–29.

Information Sources

BIBLIOGRAPHY

Enoch, Yvonne, and James Lyke. *Creative Piano Teaching*. Champaign, Ill.: Stripes Publishing Co., 1977.

Katz, Bill, and Linda Sternberg Katz. *Magazines for Libraries*. 5th ed. New York: R.R. Bowker, 1986.

Watanable, Ruth. "Current Music Periodicals for Libraries." *Notes* 23 (1966): 225–29.

INDEX

    Eternal: Music Index, 1962– . RILM, 1967– . Arts and Humanities Citation Index, 1976– . Music Article Guide, 1965– .

LOCATION SOURCES

    Widely available.

Publication History

TITLE AND TITLE CHANGES

    Clavier.

VOLUME AND ISSUE DATA

    Volumes 1– , 1962– .

FREQUENCY AND PUBLICATION

    10/year.

PUBLISHER

    The Instrumentalist Publishing Co.

PLACE OF PUBLICATION

    Northfield, Illinois.

EDITORS

    Dorothy Packard, 1962–77. Beverly McGahey, 1977–78. Christine A. Nagy, Lee Yost, 1978–89. Lee Prater Yost, 1981–83. Barbara Kreader, 1983–88. Olivia Wu, 1988. Carol Montparker, 1989– .

David Knapp

CODA

The history of *Coda* is fundamentally linked with John Norris, the man who founded the magazine in Toronto in May 1958. Norris, still the co-publisher of *Coda*, has been its major writer, and it is due to his perseverance—and that of the magazine's numerous supporters—that *Coda* has survived, despite not becoming a profitable publishing venture. A thirteen-page mimeographed newsletter at its inception, *Coda* had progressed to printed magazine format by mid–1959, though type was set by typewriter for about a decade longer, and picture reproduction was uneven in quality. Substantial improvements in printing and reproduction quality were made after 1963. Excellent cover pictures on improved paper stock have characterized *Coda* since 1973.

Norris reported that the initial guiding policy was to cover "strictly traditional jazz," but that after a year it "became obvious that it would be impossible to fulfill the magazine's purposes and ideals by concentrating entirely on one aspect of jazz" (*Record Research*, 81.3:3). While traditionalists still receive substantial coverage, modern jazz artists are the subjects of more than two-thirds of the magazine's content today. The emphasis is revealed in their annual choices for the top ten record albums by *Coda* reviewers and writers. The annual poll began in 1981, and only five of twenty-four of the 1984 poll participants favored traditional jazz albums in their choices.

From its beginning, *Coda* has published well-written and researched features (two to four pages long) on leading jazz artists, some using a lightly edited question-and-answer format and others using interviews to build on a central theme. In addition to Norris, David Lee and Bill Smith also have been primary contributors and editors at various times in the past decade. Smith, who began contributing photography in 1966, became co-publisher in 1970 and has been editor since 1978. Pictures were provided in the early years by Jack Bradley, a well-known jazz photographer. The value of the excellent photography used in *Coda* has been somewhat diminished by the failure to use captions in earlier issues and to provide sufficient ones even today.

Notable coverage in *Coda* includes its "Around the World" section, which spans the globe with the assistance of a network of contributors. It profiles people, concerts, clubs, bands, and anything else pertinent to jazz. Substantial coverage is given to artists and events in the United States and Canada, the latter country being frequently ignored by most other publications in the field. Reviews of records and jazz literature are extensive, and concerts are covered in the "Heard and Seen" sections. Each issue contains up to ten pages of these reviews, most of which are two to six paragraphs in length.

Its most celebrated special issue, on pianist Fats Waller (5.10), has become a collector's item. Other special issues included fifty-two pages of comprehensive written and photographic memories of Louis Armstrong's career (11.2) in 1973 and an issue featuring saxophonist Charlie Parker in n. 181. A sampling of other jazz performers covered in major features includes Lester Young, Jim Galloway, Cannonball Adderley, Milt Jackson, Art Blakey, Red Allen, Stephane Grappelli, Milt Buckner, Mose Allison, George Lewis, Anthony Braxton, Dexter Gordon, Warne Marsh, and Gene Krupa. Authorities in the field, such as Bill Russell and Charles Delaunay, also have been featured.

Norris has been both an advocate and a critic in his writing. While reporting favorably on articles in the first issue of the *Journal of Jazz Studies* (q.v.) in 1973, Barry Tepperman was dubious about the need for "a high-priced journal" for a relatively limited scholarly audience (11.4:24). Norris praised jazz music as "uplifting and cleansing" and the creative expression of "talented human beings who overcame adversity and produced beautiful music from within an often hostile environment" (199:10).

In a one paragraph assessment in *Coda*'s twentieth anniversary issue, Norris commented that "we have managed to exist without pandering in any way to popular taste" (161:30). "The magazine has always been an avocation of people who love jazz," he reported (*Record Research*, 81:3), and his vision, ideas, and knowledge have enabled *Coda* to contribute significantly to the literature of jazz for some twenty-eight years.

The frequency of the magazine has varied, and publication was suspended from December 1961 to April 1962. *Coda* was published monthly until changing to bimonthly in late 1963. It offered ten issues a year from early 1974 until late 1976, then switched back to bimonthly frequency. Furthermore, volume numbering gave way to issue numbering within v. 12—the August 1975 issue of v. 12 bore the issue number 140; thereafter only the issue number appears. Current issues average forty pages and contain considerable advertising, primarily of sound recordings.

Assistance in publishing the magazine has come from the Canada Council and the Ontario Arts Council, as noted in its masthead since 1977. Additional support came from the magazine, book, and record business that Norris and co-publisher Bill Smith operated as the Jazz & Blues Centre in Toronto between 1970 and 1983. A mail order service is still promoted in connection with the magazine. Smith and Norris also are principals of Sackville Records.

Coda was additionally identified on the cover as "Canada's Jazz Magazine" for nearly two decades, then adopted "The Jazz Magazine" as a subtitle in 1977. Dates and volume numbers were used for the first fifteen years, but since then the issues have been numbered consecutively, with n. 200 appearing in February 1985.

Information Sources

INDEXES
> External: Music Index, 1971– . Popular Music Periodicals Index, 1973–76. Canadian Periodicals Index.

REPRINT EDITIONS
> Microform: UMI. Micromedia, Ltd.

LOCATION SOURCES
> Later issues widely available.

Publication History

TITLE AND TITLE CHANGES
> *Coda, Canada's Jazz Magazine*, 1958–76. *Coda, The Jazz Magazine*, 1977– .

VOLUME AND ISSUE DATA
> Volumes 1–12, 1958–74. Numbers 1– , 1975– .

FREQUENCY OF PUBLICATION
> Monthly, 1958–63. Bimonthly, 1963–73. 10/year, 1974–76. Bimonthly, 1976– .

PUBLISHER
  John Norris, May 1958. Bill Smith, co-publisher since 1978.
PLACE OF PUBLICATION
  Toronto, Ontario.
EDITORS
  John Norris, 1958–78. Bill Smith, 1978–   .

Robert Byler

COLLEGE MUSIC SYMPOSIUM

College Music Symposium is the official organ of the College Music Society (CMS), an association for teachers of music in higher education. The society was established in 1958 with the merger of two faculty organizations: the College Music Association (founded in 1947) and the Society for Music in the Liberal Arts College (founded in 1949). According to the first CMS constitution, the purpose of the organization was "to gather, consider, and disseminate ideas on the philosophy and practice of music as a part of liberal education in colleges and universities" (17.2:154). This was amended in 1965 to " . . . as an integral part of higher education" (18.2:113).

For the first two years of CMS's existence, the organization published the *CMS Newsletter* and the *CMS Proceedings*, the latter, edited by George Hauptfuerer, describing details of the annual meetings. In 1959 William Mitchell, chairman of the Publications Committee, proposed a journal distinct from the *Proceedings* and *Newsletter*, but then-president of CMS, G. Wallace Woodworth, postponed the idea until the financial condition of the organization improved.

Membership in CMS grew as did the organization's finances, and in 1961 the first volume of *College Music Symposium* was published with Donald M. McCorkle as editor. *CMS Proceedings* then ceased to exist as a separate publication and instead became a regular feature in the *Symposium* until 1985.

In the first volume of the *Symposium*, editor McCorkle wrote that the purpose of the journal was "to cut across lines of specialization, to be a literary forum for discussing ideas and problems relating to college music, whether this be in the liberal arts college or the professional music school, and whether the musician concerned be musicologist or composer, theorist or conductor, pianist or singer, music educator or administrator" (1:11).

The first volume (Fall 1961) was almost entirely devoted to papers presented at the 1960 CMS meeting in Berkeley. The two topics addressed in these articles were "The Lag of Theory Behind Practice" and "A Re-examination of Teacher Training in Music." The section of "CMS Proceedings" included a presidential report, a CMS resolution on college bands, and the bylaws of the CMS. Later issues relied less on papers from CMS annual meetings. In v. 2 (Fall 1962), only one-half of the articles were originally papers delivered at the 1961 CMS meeting.

The contents of the *Symposium* are grouped under various section headings. In the early issues these included: "Prelude" (editorial); "Symposium" (articles on a single topic related to music in higher education, such as the doctorate in composition, performance as a humanistic study, the crisis in theory teaching); "Campus Focus" (highlighting activities, programs, ensembles, and innovations at various college campuses); "Music and Liberal Education"; "Book Reviews"; "CMS Proceedings" (Presidential Report, reports on annual meetings, reports of various ad hoc committees, lists of officers and members); and "Coda" (information about contributors).

The content and the focus of the *Symposium* has changed somewhat under each new editor. Beginning in v. 15 (1975), a section entitled "New Approaches to Analysis" was added, featuring articles of particular interest to music theorists. Articles in this section typically present the analysis of a particular work or a discussion of methods for analysis. Since 1975, this section has had various titles and is currently called "Traditional and Fresh Approaches to Analysis." Also added in 1975 was "Aspects of the Profession," which includes articles about college music teaching (for example, the role of arts in the core curriculum, faculty accountability).

In v. 16 (1976) a new section, "Views and Viewpoints," debuted, presenting articles on music in a wider context (for example, music in contemporary society, music and youth culture, aesthetics). In later issues the focus of "Views and Viewpoints" changed to include views of composers, musical works, and performance practices (for examples, melodic contour in Burmese music, Sir Arthur Sullivan's music).

The "Campus Focus" section exists in current issues, but the focus has changed somewhat. An earlier focus on the programs and activities on individual college campuses has given way to broader concerns, such as computer-assisted instruction and music in community colleges. The section entitled "Book Reviews" was changed to "Sources and Resources" in v. 10 (1970). Unlike reviews of single books, the articles in "Sources and Resources" review groups of related musical resources, such as resources for opera workshop, psychology of music books, and archive holdings. In recent issues, the definition of "resource" has been broadened to include musical works (such as Beethoven piano cadenzas).

The *Symposium* has published two special series of note. Under editor Philip Nelson (1967–69) a series of articles on comprehensive musicianship was published. V. 7 (1967) described the Institutes for the Contemporary Music Project for Creativity in Music Education (CMP), v. 8 (1968) presented a CMP Progress Report, and v. 9 (1969) reported on a CMP workshop held at the Eastman School of Music. Another special set of articles was a five-part series on the history of the College Music Society by Henry Woodward in vs. 17–19 (Spring 1977– Spring 1979).

In the late 1960s and 1970s in particular, the journal contributed greatly to the debate on curricular change in college music. Issues contained articles on such topics as program development, comprehensive musicianship, and the role of college ensembles. In the early 1980s, however, the editorial policy of the journal showed a distinct shift away from the discussion of college music teaching concerns toward a policy of publishing specialized musicological studies. By doing so, the *Symposium* deviated from its original purpose of cutting "across the lines of specialization" to become more like many other specialized academic music journals. An illustrative issue, for example, included such articles as "A New Look at Palestrina's *Missa Papae Marcelli*" (23.1:22–49), "Harmony in the Solo Piano Works of Olivier Messiaen: The First Twenty Years" (23.1:65–80), and "Four Songs by Margaret McClure Stitt" (23.1:124–142). While these articles were all scholarly and well written, it was clear that the *College Music Symposium*'s primary purpose was no longer seen as a unique forum for sharing the professional concerns of all college music teachers. It is reassuring to note that more recent issues suggest a return to the *Symposium*'s original focus.

The first fourteen volumes of *College Music Symposium* were published annually each fall. In 1975 and 1976 (vs. 15 and 16) the publishing time was changed from fall to spring. Between 1977 and 1984 (vs. 17–24), two issues per year were published (Spring and Fall). In 1985 (v. 25), the College Music Society, citing financial considerations and the need to redeploy resources to other areas as reasons, returned to the publication of a single issue per year. As a part of the 1985 change, "CMS Proceedings" were taken from the *Symposium* and published separately. The only internal index published thus far is the "Cumulative Index to CMS Proceedings and Symposium: for 1958–1972" in v. 12 (Fall 1972).

The physical appearance of the journal has not changed dramatically since its inception. The size of the first volume is 7¼″ by 9¼″, while currently the journal is 7″ by 9½″. Present volumes contain approximately 200 pages per issue, including an average of eighteen pages of advertising. *College Music Symposium* is a handsome journal with wide margins and large type. Its content and appearance has been enhanced by occasional poems (including two by William Carlos Williams in v. 1), photographs, and drawings.

Information Sources

BIBLIOGRAPHY

Woodward, Henry. "Annals of the College Music Society, I, II, III, IV." *College Music Symposium* 17 (Spring 1977): 121–34; 17 (Fall 1977): 144–60; 18 (Spring 1978): 173–86; 18 (Fall 1978): 110–23.

INDEXES

Internal: vs. 1–12 in v. 12.

External: Music Index, 1962– . Music Article Guide, 1966– . RILM, 1967– . Arts and Humanities Citation Index, 1983– .

LOCATION SOURCES

Widely available.

Publication History

TITLE AND TITLE CHANGES
   College Music Symposium.
VOLUME AND ISSUE DATA
   Volumes 1– , 1961– .
FREQUENCY OF PUBLICATION
   Annual, to 1976. Semiannual, 1977–84. Annual, 1985– .
PUBLISHER
   The College Music Society, Inc.
PLACES OF PUBLICATION
   Kingsport, Tennessee, 1961–69. Geneva, New York, 1970–74. Madison, Wisconsin, 1975– .
EDITORS
   Donald M. McCorkle, 1961–62. Henry W. Kaufmann, 1963–66. Philip F. Nelson, 1967–69. Donald M. McCorkle, 1970. George J. Buelow, 1971. Henry Woodward, 1972. Chappell White, 1973–75. Carolyn Raney, 1976–Spring 1979. Charles M. Carroll, Fall 1979–Spring 1983. Theodore Albrecht, Fall 1983–85. Jan Herlinger, 1986– .

John K. Kratus

COMPOSER (LONDON)

Composer was founded in the late 1950s by the committee of the Composers' Guild of Great Britain, whose chairman at the time was Malcolm Arnold. The first editor was Richard Arnell, who was assisted by the Australian journalist John Thomson. The journal's chief aim was not only to publicize the work of British composers, but also to feature articles that proposed to raise aesthetic and artistic awareness. The magazine itself was preceded by *The Bulletin* (twenty to thirty duplicated pages, which were distributed to guild members only) under the editorship of Norman Demuth. Upon his retirement in 1958, *The Bulletin* became *The Composer*. The new printed format, which followed several issues later (n. 10), occasioned the title change to the present single word (n. 28). Regular features now include several articles (averaging ten to twelve pages) on twentieth-century composers and their music, "BMIC (British Music Information Center) News," "Letters," "Book Reviews," "Concert and Radio Analysis," "Regional Reports," and "Lists of First Performances and Commissions."

The journal has no regular contributors but relies on the expertise of any qualified professionals (largely British) who are willing to donate their services. Among the many contributors have been Richard Arnell, Lesley Bray, Francis Routh, Peter Dickinson, Susan Bradshaw, Peter Racine Fricker, and Buxton Orr, many of whom have been on the editorial staff as well. The editorial staff works in an advisory, voluntary capacity; assistants are employed only for specific features, such as "First Performances." The journal "as

sumes musical literacy, and some sophistication on the part of the reader"
(Routh correspondence). The articles, though of interest primarily to professional composers, are written in a manner that would interest other musically
astute readers also.

Though not specifically designated as "special or landmark" issues, the contents of the journal will periodically focus on one particular subject. These issues
usually contain articles by three or more authors of diverse backgrounds, thus
giving varied perspectives to a single topic. Issues of special note have included
"Music and Education in the Commonwealth" (n. 19); "Technical Advances
and the Modern Composer" (n. 66); "The Composer-Publisher Relationship"
(n. 67); "Tippett at 75—A Tribute" (n. 70); "Learning to Compose" (n. 71);
and "Performers' Platform" (n. 76/77). Periodically articles will appear as
reprints—these have included Jonathan Harvey's "Electronics in Music: A New
Aesthetic?" (85:8–15) from the *Journal of the Royal Society of Arts*; Robert
Palmer's "Which Way Contemporary Music?" (75:6–12) from the *Cornell University Music Review*; and "How Shall We Deal with Composers?" by Donald
Henahan (83:6–8) from the *New York Times* (May 1984).

The opinion of current editor, Francis Routh, is that *Composer* is often the
only source of information about the work of living British composers, other
than the house journals of Boosey and Hawkes (*Tempo* [q.v.]) and Novello
(*Musical Times* [q.v.]). While the latter periodicals tend to represent the composers whose works they publish, *Composer* does not favor any particular individuals. Although a statement by the editor does not exist as a regular
feature, the present editorial policy (according to Routh) is "to draw attention
to the shortcomings in today's musical environment in England (which means
basically the large centralised bureaucracies, such as the BBC)" (Routh, correspondence of 11 February 1986). "Concert Analysis," which appears with
some regularity, presents an objective summary of performances in the United
Kingdom, for example, the literature performed by every full and chamber orchestra during the 1977/78 concert season with a per hour ratio of the works
by British composers, by living composers of other nations, and by composers
of other historical eras. *Composer* has yet to become seriously involved in the
world of commercial music, although articles have occasionally appeared on
jazz (Ken Rattenbury's extensive and analytical piece, "Blues Chromati-
cism"—84:1–14, Spring 1985) and music in media ("Today's Music on Television"—82:1–15).

The current size, 6½" by 9¼", has been the same since the journal's inception.
Each issue, consecutively numbered, averages thirty-six to forty pages with
illustrations and musical examples as warranted by the articles. Internal indices
exist for issues 1962–72 and 1978–85. Advertisements are of a professional
nature, for example, Mendelssohn Scholarship Foundation, Arts Council of Great
Britain, and Musicians Benevolent Fund. The Composers' Guild provides the
financial base through subscriptions from its members and contributions from
various organizations.

Information Sources

INDEXES
>   Internal: vs. 5–15, vs. 21–28.
>   External: Music Index, 1967– . RILM, 1981– . British Humanities Index,
>   1968– . Arts and Humanities Citation Index, 1976– . Music Article Guide,
>   1969– .

LOCATION SOURCES
>   Widely available.

Publication History

TITLE AND TITLE CHANGES
>   *The Composer: The Journal of the Composers Guild of Great Britain*, 1958–65.
>   *Composer*, 1966– .

VOLUME AND ISSUE DATA
>   Volumes 1– , 1958– .

FREQUENCY OF PUBLICATION
>   Quarterly, 1958–74. 3/year, 1974–87. Suspended publication Winter 1987.

PUBLISHER
>   The Composers' Guild of Great Britain.

PLACE OF PUBLICATION
>   British Music Information Centre, 10 Stratford Place, London W1N 9AE.

EDITORS
>   Richard Arnell, 1959–64. Stephen Dodgson, 1965–69. Richard Stoker, 1970–79.
>   Francis Routh, 1980– .

Marilyn Shrude

COMPOSITEUR CANADIEN, LE. See CANADIAN COMPOSER, THE

COMPUTER MUSIC JOURNAL

Computer Music Journal is "devoted to high-quality musical applications of digital electronics" (1.1: cover). Founded in September 1976 as an "offshoot" of People's Computer Company, the goals of the first editor, John Snell, were as follows: "to publish the results of computer music research (mostly university-based at the time), and to publish articles by composers who were making interesting use of computers" (10.1:13). Subsequent editors have included Curtis Abbott and, with v. 2.3, Curtis Roads.

Since *Computer Music Journal* began publication, the scholarly, progressive thrust has been evident and impressive. According to Roads, the journal has always tried to be on the "leading-edge." Articles have consistently originated in the most prestigious research centers (Center for Computer Research in Music and Acoustics, Institut de recherche et de coordination acoustique musique, Massachusetts Institute of Technology), and the journal's primary contributors have been individuals maintaining a high profile in computer music: Joel Chadabe, John M. Chowning, Lejaren Hiller, Otto E. Laske, D. Gareth Loy, F. Richard Moore, James A. Moorer, Dexter Morrill, Jean-Claude Risset, Julius O. Smith, and Barry Truax.

Many articles have dealt with technical aspects of the profession—"The Synthesis of Complex Audio Spectra by Means of Frequency Modulation" by John M. Chowning (1.2:46–54) and "A General Model for Spatial Processing of Sounds" by F. Richard Moore (7.3:6–15). However, attention has been given to the compositional and performance-oriented sides of computer music as well—"Computer Improvisation" by Christopher Fry (4.3:48–58), "Composing with Computers: A Progress Report" by Lejaren Hiller (5.4:7–21), and "Live and in Concert: Composer/Performer Views of Real-Time Performance Systems" by Jon Appleton (8.1:48–51). Several articles have served as guides to technical material usually found in a typical issue—"A Tutorial on Non-Linear Distortion or Waveshaping Synthesis" by Curtis Roads (3.2:29–34) and "An Analysis/ Synthesis Tutorial" by Richard Cann (3.3:6–11; 3.4:9–13; 4.1:36–42). Of historical value have been the comprehensive conference reports and the candid interviews with such notables as Gottfried Michael Koenig (2.3:11–15), Harold Cohen (3.4:50–57), Marvin Minsky (4.3:25–39), Max Mathews (4.4:15–22), James A. Moorer (6.4:10–21) by Curtis Roads; Clarence Barlow (9.1:9–28) by Stephan Kaske; and Robert Moog (9.4:62–65) by Henning Lohner.

Though not specifically designated as such, several issues/articles can be described as "landmarks." Of recent note is 10.1, Spring 1986, the Tenth Anniversary Issue, with a complete index of contents by issue and author for vs. 1–9 by Nicola Bernardini (10.1:17–36, 37–39) and a short history of the journal by Curtis Roads and John Snell, as assisted by Curtis Abbott and John Strawn (10.1:13–16). Bernardini continues in 10.2 with an index by subject for vs. 1–9. Also important are the issues on artificial intelligence (4.2), composition (5.4), and computer music in France (8.3). Articles that merit special attention have been those by D. Gareth Loy, "Notes on the Implementation of MUSBOX: a Compiler for the System Concepts Digital Synthesizer" (5.1:34–50) and "Musicians Make a Standard: The MIDI Phenomenon" (9.4:8–26), and F. Richard Moore's "An Introduction to the Mathematics of Digital Signal Processing. Part I: Algebra, Trigonometry, and the Most Beautiful Formula in Mathematics" (2.1:38–47) and "Part II: Sampling, Transforms, and Digital Filtering" (2.2:38–60). As a special project, "Soundsheets" (floppy plastic records) were included in 5.4 and 8.3, representing the works of composers such as Jean-Baptiste Barriere, Jonathan Harvey, Michael McNabb, Gary Kendall, Xavier Rodet, and Iannis Xenakis.

Aside from some inconsistencies in the early volumes, *Computer Music Journal* has maintained several regular departments. Current issues begin with several pages of editorial information, as well as "Editor's Notes," "Letters," "News," and "Announcements" (the latter two dealing with symposia, special workshops, individual accomplishments, touring ensembles, and similar news). About sixty pages of articles follow, each averaging ten pages in length. The journal has consistently reviewed new books and records (about ten pages per issue) and has provided the reader with a valuable overview of the latest products in the field (''Products of Interest''). About ten pages of commercial advertising appear at the end of each issue. Of special note is the ''Machine Tongues'' column, introduced by Curtis Abbott in 2.1 (July 1978) and appearing at least once a year since then. ''Devoted to capsule descriptions of programming languages and techniques'' (10.1:14), it has provided an overview of LISP, Pascal, ADA, and Prolog, to mention a few examples.

The original intention, to publish six issues a year, was abandoned upon reaching 1.4, and to date the journal is published quarterly with a circulation of about 3,400 paid subscriptions. Early issues averaged sixty-four pages and were printed on inexpensive paper; after sponsorship was assumed by MIT Press (4.1), the journal took on a very sophisticated look and was printed on glossy paper with a colorful heavy-weight cover. Issues have since averaged one hundred pages and have remained 8½″ by 11″. Photos and illustrations are frequent; musical examples appear as necessitated by an article's content. With v. 4.2, an international editorial board was formed, consisting of such experts as Curtis Abbott, M. Battier, Pierre Boulez, William Buxton, Herbert Brün, Max V. Mathews, F. R. Moore, J. A. Moorer, and Barry Vercoe.

Information Sources

BIBLIOGRAPHY
Several books have been published as part of a project to revise and update papers from
　　　Volumes 1–3 of the journal, as well as to provide new articles on related subjects.
Moore, F. R. ''Review of the Journal.'' *Journal of Music Theory* 27 (1983): 127–35.
Roads, Curtis, ed. *Composers and the Computer*. Los Altos, Calif: William Kaufman,
　　　1985.
Roads, Curtis, and John Strawn, eds. *Foundations of Computer Music*. Boston: MIT
　　　Press, 1985.
Strawn, John, ed. *Digital Audio Engineering: An Anthology*. Los Altos, Calif.: William
　　　Kaufmann, 1985.
Strawn, John, ed. *Digital Audio Signal Processing: An Anthology*. Los Altos, Calif.
　　　William Kaufmann, 1985.
Wuorinen, Charles. ''Review of the Journal.'' *Musical Quarterly* 68 (1982): 424–27.
INDEXES
　　　Internal: vs. 1–9 in v. 10.
　　　External: Music Index, 1978–　. RILM, 1978–　. Arts and Humanities Citation
　　　Index, 1983–　. Bibliographie des Musikschrifttums, 1977–78. INSPEC (online
　　　file from *Computer Music Journal),* December 1978–　.
REPRINT EDITIONS
　　　Microform: UMI.
LOCATION SOURCES
　　　MIT (Complete). Partial holdings widely available.

Publication History

TITLE AND TITLE CHANGES
   Computer Music Journal.
VOLUME AND ISSUE DATA
   Volumes, 1– , 1977– .
FREQUENCY OF PUBLICATION
   Quarterly.
PUBLISHERS
   People's Computer Company, 1977–79. MIT Press, 1980– .
PLACE OF PUBLICATION
   Cambridge, Massachusetts.
EDITORS
   John Snell, 1977. Curtis Abbott, 1978. Curtis Roads 1978–88. Stephen Travis
   Pope, 1989– .

Marilyn Shrude

CONTRIBUTIONS TO MUSIC EDUCATION

Contributions to Music Education is an annual publication of the Research
Committee of the Ohio Music Education Association (OMEA). It was created
in 1972 to "support scholarly work in Music Education conducted in Ohio
primarily and in the field of Music Education as a whole secondarily" (1:3).
Contributions was intended to present research reports, speculations about research, and discussions of music education and research techniques in music
education. All forms of scholarly research were encouraged: descriptive, experimental, historical, and philosophical.

The format of *Contributions* primarily features research articles, with each
issue including about eight articles averaging ten pages in length. The incor-
poration of several two-page book reviews became standard in n. 4 (1976) and
a Speculative Comment section appeared as a regular feature from ns. 6–9 (1978–
82). The content includes presentations based on recent graduate work, usually
completed at Ohio institutions, and university faculty research reports. While
most contributions were submitted by students and faculty from Ohio State
University, other Ohio institutions, such as Case Western Reserve University
and Kent State University, are frequently represented. Articles also appear from
non-Ohio institutions: University of Michigan, University of Iowa, University
of Texas, Catholic University, Florida State University, and others.

Feature articles cover topics related to musical perception and memory, the
history of music education, creativity, musical competitions, affective response,
tests and measurements, personality, music reading and learning, motivation,
and research techniques. The Speculative Comment section addresses such topics
as statistical procedures, historical research, sociology of music education, music
reading, competency-based music education, and the perceived gap between

music education research and music teaching. N. 3 (1974) contained a special collection of four articles on international concerns in music education: "World Music in American Education: 1916–1970" by William M. Anderson (3:23–42) and Henry L. Cady's "Music in English Education" (3:43–71). N. 8 (1980) featured an article by Terry Lee Kuhn on the measurement of music attitudes, including an extensive bibliography on the subject (8:16–38). The contents of ns. 10–12 clearly suggest that a more national representation is the policy of the current editor.

Originally, the journal was distributed free to active research members in MENC (Music Educators National Conference) who are also members of OMEA, members of the MENC Executive Committee, members of the Music Educators Research Committee of MENC, libraries of four-year colleges and universities of Ohio, and individuals by request. In n. 2 (1973), the distribution list was increased to include libraries of national doctoral degree granting institutions. In n. 4 (1976) this was further increased to include libraries of national institutions granting master's degrees in music education. In 1980, subscription rates were announced for institutions and individuals.

Contributions to Music Education is managed by an editor and an editorial board. The board began with ten members representative of the major graduate music education degree programs in Ohio. Over the years, the board has expanded to thirteen members and includes a representative of the general OMEA membership.

The journal appears in a 6″ by 9″ format, without photographs or musical reproductions, with issues averaging ninety pages in length. Typesetting began with n. 10 (1983). There is one issue annually; a double-year issue (1981/1982) is incorrectly labeled n. 5; it is actually n. 9. An index to ns. 1–5 (5: 84–91) is organized by author and title and also includes a keyword index. The comparable index to ns. 6–10 (10:49–51) includes only the author and title index.

Information Sources

INDEXES
> Internal: ns. 1–5 in n. 5; ns. 6–10 in n. 10.
> External: Music Index, 1976– . Music Article Guide, 1972– .
LOCATION SOURCES
> Widely available.

Publication History

TITLE AND TITLE CHANGES
> *Contributions to Music Education.*
VOLUME AND ISSUE DATA
> Volumes 1– , 1972– .
FREQUENCY OF PUBLICATION
> Annual.
PUBLISHER
> Ohio Music Educators Association.

PLACE OF PUBLICATION

Ohio State University, Columbus, Ohio, 1972–1974. Kent State University, Kent, Ohio, 1975–77. Case Western Reserve University, Cleveland, Ohio, 1978–1982. Kent State University, Kent, Ohio, 1983–85. Youngstown State University, Youngstown, Ohio, 1986–88. Case Western Reserve University, Cleveland, Ohio, 1989–   .

EDITORS

Henry L. Cady, 1972–74. Melvin C. Platt, 1975–77. Peter R. Webster, 1978–1982. Terry Lee Kuhn, 1983–85. Duane Sample, 1986–88. John Kratus, 1989–   .

Richard P. Kennell

COUNCIL FOR RESEARCH IN MUSIC EDUCATION BULLETIN, THE

Research in music education was gaining increased prominence in the United States during the 1950s and early 1960s. However, with the exception of the *Journal of Research in Music Education* (q.v.), first published by the Music Educators National Conference in 1953, there was no national forum in which music education researchers could report the results of their inquiries on a regular basis. Discussion of this situation at the state meeting of the Illinois Music Education Association and at the North Central Music Educators Conference in the spring of 1963 led to the founding of the Council for Research in Music Education (CRME) under the direction of Richard J. Colwell at the University of Illinois. The council immediately embarked upon a CRME *Bulletin* designed: (1) to stimulate interest and provide guidance for would-be researchers, and (2) to disseminate information about recent research.

The first issue of the *Bulletin of the Council for Research in Music Education* was dated simply 1963 and established a format based on two sections: "Articles" and "Critiques on Research." More specifically, the sixty-seven-page issue contained five articles (three of which suggested research methodologies and directions for music education research) and six critiques of research. In more recent years, there have been three major sections in each issue: "Feature Articles," "Articles of Interest," and "Critiques." Other alterations and expansions have included editorials, book reviews, lists of books received, rebuttals, and critiques of dissertations.

Several feature articles in recent years have focused on music education research in general, as well as philosophy, aesthetics, and creativity in music education. For example, a lengthy article on research in music education was accompanied by three responses from other authors and a reply by the original author (n. 83, Summer 1985). An earlier issue (n. 49) presented an extensive overview of research in music education in several major areas, for example, music teaching, learning, perception, and performance. Two reviews of recent research findings (one for creativity research in music education, the other for aesthetic education in theory and practice) appeared in the Spring 1983 *Bulletin* (n. 74). Several special issues of the *Bulletin* have been published since its inception, for example, papers presented at the Second International Seminar on Research in Music Education held in Stockholm, Sweden, 2–6 July 1970 (n. 22), the fifteenth anniversary of the Yale Seminar (n. 60), and "Early and Middle Childhood Research in Music Education" (n. 86). Articles are solicited in but not limited to the following areas: technology in music education including computer-assisted instruction, allied arts, research in other fields with implications for music educators, and experimental studies with implications for the profession. In addition, starting with n. 33 (Summer 1973), feature articles periodically summarized the status of research in a particular field within music education, such as instrumental music (33:8–20) or elementary music education (34:23–40).

As a service to readers, the *Bulletin* began publishing the tables of contents of other music education journals in the early 1980s. Those for *Psychology of Music* (q.v.) first appeared in the *Bulletin* in ns. 66/67 (Spring/Summer 1981), *Journal of Research in Education* in n. 69 (Winter 1982), and *Psychomusicology* (q.v.) in n. 77 (Winter 1984). Recent issues have also included lists of books received as well as book reviews.

Several editorial policy changes have recently been made in the *Bulletin*. In n. 75 (Summer 1983) it was announced that, due to a paucity of philosophical research, the editorial board would endeavor to include more philosophical articles, hoping that such entries would stimulate the thinking of the research community. In the following issue (n. 76) it was announced that the Council for Research in Music Education supports the position adopted by many similar organizations that authors should not simultaneously submit the same manuscript for consideration by two or more journals. The Fall 1983 issue also indicated that the *Bulletin's* review process was being expanded to include periodicals and other documents pertinent to the music education profession.

The Summer 1984 (n. 79) issue contained an unusually lengthy editorial that focused on academic dialogue as exemplified by the rebuttal–reply model common to many other academic disciplines. Though rebuttals to critiques had been published before in the *Bulletin*, especially in recent years, there was no formal opportunity for a reply by the reviewer. This policy was consequently altered as of n. 79 to allow reviewers the chance to continue the published dialogue by replying to rebuttals.

A length of sixty pages became the norm after issue n. 10 with occasional expansion to seventy-six or ninety-two pages for subsequent regular issues. Special or double issues (e.g., ns. 66–67, Spring/Summer 1981) have been as long as 184 pages. Ns. 1–9 of the *Bulletin* (1963–Spring 1967) were published on 8″ by 10½″ paper. However, a smaller size (6″ by 9″) was introduced with the tenth issue (Summer 1967) and remains to the present. The *Bulletin* is published quarterly without advertisements.

Information Sources

BIBLIOGRAPHY

Standley, Jayne M. "Productivity and Eminence in Music Research." *Journal of Research in Music Education* 32 (1984): 149–57.

INDEXES

Internal: vs. 1–12 in v. 13; vs. 13–26 in v. 27; vs. 27–38 in v. 39; vs. 38–53 in v. 54.

External: Music Article Guide, 1966– . Music Index, 1963– . RILM, 1969– . Education Index, 1977– . Music Psychology Index, v. 2, 1978, and v. 3, 1984. Music Therapy Index, v. 1, 1976.

Mark, Michael L. *Contemporary Music Education.* 2nd edition. New York: Schirmer, 1986. Indexes ns. 1–78 on pp. 298–309.

LOCATION SOURCES

Widely available.

Publication History

TITLE AND TITLE CHANGES

Bulletin of the Council for Research in Music Education.

VOLUME AND ISSUE DATA

Volumes 1– , 1963– .

FREQUENCY OF PUBLICATION

Quarterly.

PUBLISHERS

College of Education, School of Music at University of Illinois, and Office of the Superintendent of Public Instruction, 1963–Summer 1972. University of Illinois School of Music, Division of University Extension College of Education, Fall 1972–Winter 1972. Council for Research in Music Education, School of Music at University of Illinois, Spring 1973– .

PLACE OF PUBLICATION

Urbana, Illinois.

EDITORS

Richard J. Colwell, 1963–Summer 1975. Jere Forsythe, Fall 1975–Summer 1976. Richard J. Colwell, Fall 1976– .

Vincent J. Kantorski

COUNTRY MUSIC FOUNDATION NEWSLETTER. See JOURNAL OF COUNTRY MUSIC

CRAWDADDY

Before *Crawdaddy* there was no publication that took rock and roll seriously. The more mature fans of the new, mid-1960s rock sought a forum better suited to their interests and intelligence than the teen-oriented fan magazines and the business-oriented trade publications. In February 1966, seventeen-year-old Paul Williams (not the pop singer) founded *Crawdaddy*, and the professional rock press was born.

The first issues of *Crawdaddy* were a few mimeographed pages stapled together and were mostly the work of Williams alone. It was a typical example of a "fanzine": an amateur publication by and for fans. By 1967 Williams was attracting material from other like-minded rock fans—Jon Landau, Robert Somma, Sandy Pearlman, and Richard Meltzer—who were to contribute to the founding of rock criticism. By the time *Rolling Stone* (q.v.) was founded in November 1967, *Crawdaddy* had published eleven issues, grown to fifty-two pages, and become a professional magazine; its now slick cover could already be found on newsstands.

Each issue of *Crawdaddy* was a wondrous revelation for its readers. In its pages could be found the very personal reaction of Williams to the music of the Beatles or the Beachboys, the absurd and convoluted arguments of Meltzer, the often nearly as convoluted intellectual exegeses of Pearlman, and the level-headed criticism of Landau. Much of what appeared in Williams's *Crawdaddy* has become classics of rock criticism.

In late 1968 a disillusioned Williams left the magazine he founded, and Chester Anderson, a former Haight-Ashbury activist and pamphleteer, took over the editorship. Most of the familiar names left as well, and after four issues, in June 1969, the original incarnation of *Crawdaddy* ceased publication. An era of rock journalism passed with it, for Williams's *Crawdaddy* helped create and define rock criticism, even if, in retrospect, much of what appeared there may now seem pretentious. Examples of the writing found in the groundbreaking, early, and now rare, issues of *Crawdaddy* can be found in Williams's *Outlaw Blues* (Dutton, 1969).

In March 1970 *Crawdaddy* was revived under the editorship of Peter Stafford in a tabloid format similar to *Rolling Stone*. The new subtitle, "Rock Culture Newspaper," reflected its intent. Contributors included Vince Aletti, Bud Scoppa, and Peter Stampfel. This was *Crawdaddy* in name only, bearing little resemblance to its predecessor.

After a period of inability to pay contributors, this incarnation of *Crawdaddy* folded in November 1970 (5.1) having published only fourteen issues. It was resurrected once again, still as a tabloid, in May 1971 under the editorship of Reanne Rubinstein. In December 1971 publication was assumed by the Crawdaddy Publishing Company, and Peter Knobler was promoted to editor in September 1972. Publication reverted to monthly in July 1972 (n. 14), and in October 1972 (n. 17) an eighty- to one-hundred-page, 8½" by 11" magazine format was adopted. The Knobler *Crawdaddy* continually decreased its music coverage in favor of general interest items, attempting to reflect the cultural interests of its audience. Its title was changed to *Feature* in January 1979, but publication ceased after only five issues.

Information Sources

BIBLIOGRAPHY

Bauerlein, Charles Robert. "Origins of the Popular Music Press in America." Master's thesis, Pennsylvania State University, 1979.

"Crawdaddy." *Newsweek*, 11 December 1967, p. 114.

"Face to Face With the Editor of a Rock and Roll Magazine."*Seventeen*, April 1967, p. 159.

Flippo, Chester W. "Rock Journalism and Rolling Stone." Master's thesis, University of Texas at Austin, 1974.

Ginsburg, David D. "Rock Is a Way of Life: The World of Rock 'n' Roll Fanzines and Fandom." *Serials Review* 5 (January/March 1979): 29–46.

Proctor, David Paul. "A Critical History of American Rock Journalism in Popular Magazines: 1955–1976." Master's thesis, University of Utah, 1981.

Swenson, John. "Rock Dreams/Schemes: The History of Crawdaddy(!)." *Crawdaddy*, March 1976, pp. 67–69.

INDEXES

External: Music Index, 1968–79. Annual Index To Popular Music Record Reviews, 1972–77. Popular Music Periodicals Index, 1973–76. Popular Periodicals Index, 1973–79. Access, 1975–79. Magazine Index, 1977–79. Reader's Guide, 1978–79.

REPRINT EDITIONS

Microfilm: UMI, 1966–74 (incomplete), 1975–79.

LOCATION SOURCES

Indiana University (no. 1–23, 1966–69; v. 4:7–4:8, 1970). The following libraries have partial holdings of the first twenty-three issues: Bowling Green State University, Los Angeles Public Library, Detroit Public Library, Flint Public Library, Rochester Public Library, University of Illinois at Urbana, University of Mississippi, University of Utah, Cornell University, Library of Congress. Many libraries hold later volumes.

Publication History

TITLE AND TITLE CHANGES

Crawdaddy!: The Magazine of Rock 'n' Roll, February 1966–January 1967. *Crawdaddy!: The Magazine of Rock*, March 1967–June 1968. *Crawdaddy: The Magazine of Rock*, August–September 1968. *Crawdaddy: The Magazine of Roll*, October 1968–June 1969. *Crawdaddy: The Rock Culture Newspaper*, 1970–November 1971. *Crawdaddy*, December 1971–December 1978. *Feature*, January–May 1979.

VOLUME AND ISSUE DATA

Volumes 1–5.1; February 1966–June 1969, March 1970–November 1970. Five issues, May 1971–May 1979.

FREQUENCY OF PUBLICATION

Monthly, irregular.

PUBLISHERS

Crawdaddy Enterprises, 1966–67. Crawdaddy Magazine, 1967–69. New Crawdaddy Ventures, 1970. Randolph Publishing, Inc., 1970. Superstar Productions,

1971. Beulah Publishing Co., 1971. Crawdaddy Publishing Co., 1971–78. Feature
Publishing Co., 1979.
PLACES OF PUBLICATION
Swarthmore, Pennsylvania, February–March 1966. Cambridge, Massachussetts,
August–November 1966. New York, January 1967–May 1979.
EDITORS
Paul Williams, February 1966–October 1968. Chester Anderson, October 1968–
June 1969. Peter Stafford, March 1970–May 1971. Reanne Rubinstein, June 1971–
August 1972. Peter Knobler, July 1972–May 1979.

David D. Ginsburg

CREEM

Founded by Barry Kramer in March 1969, the early tabloid issues of *Creem*
covered an eclectic blend of revolutionary politics, avant-garde jazz, and the
high energy rock and roll for which Detroit was becoming famous. *Creem* at
this time had more in common with the political and countercultural underground
newspapers than it did with other music publications; gradually, however, the
politics and jazz were shed, while hard rock remained *Creem*'s mainstay.

V. 1 consisted of five undated issues, while v. 2 ran to eighteen. Circulation
initially was local, but after four issues it was picked up for national "head
shop" distribution, and in August 1971 the Curtis Circulation Company put it
on the general newsstands. The tabloid format was replaced by an 8½" by 11"
magazine format in March 1971 (3.1), and both a glossy color cover and a
monthly publication schedule were adopted in September 1971 (3.4). Issues
came to average some seventy pages, with articles of three to five pages. Other
regular features included "Rock 'n' Roll News," "Eleganza," and a variety of
reviews.

While there was no official editor until 1975, Dave Marsh did function in this
role until his departure in 1973. This period marked the editorial peak of *Creem*.
Many leading rock critics were attracted to its pages: Greil Marcus, Lester Bangs,
Robert Christgau, Simon Frith, Ed Ward, Richard Meltzer, Greg Shaw, and
Vince Aleti, some of whom were disenchanted with the regressive *Rolling Stone*
(q.v.).

A highlight from this period was Greil Marcus's "Rock-A-Hula Clarified:
The Sound of the City as the Sound of the City" (3.3:36–52), a lengthy sociopolitical analysis of the rock phenomenon. That same issue also featured the
inimitable Lester Bangs on "Psychotic Reactions and Carburetor Dung" (3.3:56–
63), an early and fanciful appreciation of 1960s garage-band punk. Other highlights include Dave Marsh on the MC5 (3.5:36–46), the Stooges (2.13:1, 29–
33), and Bob Seger (3.12:46–51, 78–79), as well as his editorial column, "Loo-
ney Tunes"; an early appearance of poetry by Patti Smith (3.4:26–29); Robert
Christgau's "Consumer Guide" column (beginning July 1972 and still in ex

istence); and Lester Bangs on the Velvet Underground (3.2:44–49, 64–67). Lester Bangs perhaps best epitomizes the *Creem* spirit in the depth of his perception and the extent of his knowledge, as well as in his gross irreverence.

While perhaps not "America's only rock 'n' roll magazine," as its cover has proudly proclaimed since 1972, *Creem* has stuck to rock. It has not diluted its coverage with nonmusic features, and more importantly, it has kept its finger on the pulse of rock and roll and has never deserted its younger readers, as upward publications such as *Rolling Stone* have done. Creem became "the journal of a large disenfranchised segment of America's youth, a segment that has not been served by any other publication."[1] But at the same time, it has never descended to the teeny-bopper fan magazine level either. Coupled with this is *Creem*'s famous irreverent attitude, which is perhaps nowhere better seen than in its letters column.

Creem's strength as a youth-oriented publication may also be its weakness. Championing Grand Funk and Black Sabbath in the 1970s led to a critical dead end. *Creem* began to lose its edge in the mid–1970s and became more predictable. Coverage increasingly leaned toward mainstream hard rock and heavy metal bands.

Upon Barry Kramer's death in 1981, his wife Connie took over publication of the magazine. Experiencing financial difficulties, publication was suspended in October 1985. Kramer sold the magazine to Cambray Publishing, and publication was resumed with the February 1986 issue, albeit in a toned-down vein.

Note

1. Chet Flippo, "The History of *Rolling Stone:* Part II." *Popular Music and Society* 3 (1974): 264.

Information Sources

BIBLIOGRAPHY
Flippo, Chet. "The History of *Rolling Stone:* Part II." *Popular Music and Society* 3 (1974): 258–80.
INDEXES
    External: Annual Index to Popular Music Record Reviews, 1972–77. Popular Music Periodicals Index, 1973–76. Music Index, 1974– . Access, 1975– .
REPRINT EDITIONS
    Microform: Oxford Microfilm Publications, 1976–85. UMI, 1976– .
LOCATION SOURCES
    Bowling Green State University and University of Pittsburgh (full run). Widely available (partial runs).

Publication History

TITLE AND TITLE CHANGES
    Creem, 1969–July 1972. *Cream—America's Only Rock 'n' Roll Magazine*, August 1972– .

VOLUME AND ISSUE DATA
    Volumes 1– , 1969– .
FREQUENCY OF PUBLICATION
    Irregular, 1969–August 1971. Monthly, September 1971– .
PUBLISHERS
    Creem Magazine, Inc., 1969–October 1985. Cambray Publishing, Inc., February
    1986– .
PLACES OF PUBLICATION
    Detroit, Michigan, 1969–September 1971. Walled Lake, Michigan, October
    1971–September 1973. Birmingham, Michigan, October 1973– .
EDITORS
    Collective staff, 1969–1975. Wayne Robins, August–December 1975. Lester
    Bangs, January–September 1976. Bill Gubbins, October 1976–March 1977. Susan
    Whitall, April 1973–April 1983. Dave De Martino, May 1983– . JK and Bill
    Holdship, ?–1987. John Korolosh, 1988– .

David D. Ginsburg

CURRENT MUSICOLOGY

Current Musicology is a journal organized, edited, and published by the graduate musicology students of Columbia University. Founded in 1965, the journal expressed goals unique among scholarly journals, striving to be

a semiannual review that would primarily serve the needs of musicologists who are about to undertake, are presently engaged in, or have recently completed their graduate studies. It would contain detailed discussions of the materials, procedures, and results of research seminars, and descriptions of lecture courses and other relevant activities at the graduate musicology departments of colleges and universities in North America. It would review doctoral dissertations (both foreign and domestic) that otherwise go unnoticed in the periodical literature but that contain much of the significant research done today. It would establish communications with centers of musical studies in foreign lands and list their dissertations whether recently published, recently completed, or still in progress. It would present other aids and information of value to scholars such as bibliographies, and lists of scholarships and fellowships. It would publish short articles of research, criticism, and opinion predominantly by younger authors. (1:42)

The intentions expressed in this policy statement are borne out by the contents of subsequent issues. Its standard categories of "Articles," "Bibliographies," "Announcements," and "Reports" are regularly augmented with studies (or entire volumes) dedicated to exploring topics of general interest. Musicology as a field has been broadly defined, and contributions have included studies in aesthetics, ethnomusicology, performance, pedagogy, and bibliography, as well as in traditional historical musicology.

Of particular note are the many issues devoted entirely to a particular topic or issue. N. 5 (1967), for example, offered a forum for a discussion of aesthetics: "Musicology and the Musical Composition." It presented two essays, the first by Richard L. Crocker entitled "Some Reflections on the Shape of Music" (5:50–56) and the second by Patricia Carpenter, "The Musical Object" (5:56–87). Responses were offered by Leo Treitler, Rudolf Arnheim, Ruth Halle Rowen, Edward T. Cone, Bernard Stambler, and David Burrows. N. 6 added five more responses, as well as replies by the original authors.

Several issues addressed the concerns of graduate students, particularly the status and approaches of other graduate schools. A series of articles on "Musical Literacy and the Teaching of Music in School, College, and University" may be found in n. 4 (1966). N. 21 (1976) contained a list of grants then available to musicology students. N. 11:7–54 reported on the contents of preliminary qualifying exams in musicology departments around the country.

Issues addressing methodology also appear. N. 19 (1975), for example, contains the research papers prepared for a seminar given by Christoph Wolff at Columbia University on Johann Sebastian Bach's *Art of Fugue*. Position statements on the direction of music research are offered by Alfred Mann (n. 1, 1965) and by Alan P. Merriam and Bruno Nettl (n. 20, 1975). The journal's interest in theses and dissertations is evident in its many dissertation reviews (particularly in the earlier numbers) and in a partial listing of master's theses, published in n. 12 (1971) and n. 17 (1974).

The emphasis on information concerning other graduate programs is particularly stressed in the "Reports" section, which generally opens each issue. Here a network of about one hundred "Corresponding Editors," each representing a different university from around the world, report on activities, seminars, library acquisitions, and the like. N. 7 (1968), for example, printed twenty-seven reports, including a notice of the revised graduate musicology curriculum at Boston University, a report on a local American Musicological Society meeting at City University of New York, an explanation of the then new series entitled "Harvard Publications in Musicology," and a commentary on a "Seminar in Contemporary Musical Materials" given at the State University of New York at Buffalo, as well as several reports from universities overseas.

Current Musicology has also maintained a long-held interest in the relationship between musicology and performance. N. 15 (1973) contained the results of a survey of the "Relationship between Musicology and Performance in the Music Departments of Thirty-Nine North American Graduate Schools"; this project was continued in n. 16. N. 22 (1976) added a companion study on the interests and activities of Collegium Musicum groups in thirty-two American universities. N. 26 (1978) contains articles grouped under the general heading of "Opera: Performance and Musicology." Contributors included both performers and musicologists (Sarah Caldwell, Martin Chusid, Robert Darling, Philip Gossett, and others). Perhaps the journal's best-known contribution to performance, however, is its "Performance Practice Bibliography," scattered over three issues (8: 17–96, 1969; 10: 144–72, 1970; and 12: 129–49, 1971). This project, which originated as a seminar guided by William S. Newman, subsequently swelled to great length. The items in ns. 8 and 10 were published separately by Norton (1971), edited by Mary Vinquist and Neal Zaslaw.

Other bibliographies are found as well. The inaugural issue included "Articles Concerning Music in Non-Music Journals, 1949–64" (1:121–27). N. 31 (pp. 65–70) discussed access to nineteenth-century English-language periodicals. Among the many other bibliographies are lists of sources concerning Mieczyslaw Kolinski (3:100–103), Ernest Bloch (6:142–46), Arnold Bax and a list of free music periodicals (10:124–43), Pierre Boulez (13:135–50), "The Renaissance of Early American Keyboard Music" (18:127–32), and early organum (21:29–45). Of particular interest is the list of "Important Library Holdings at Forty-One North American Universities," found in the Reports section of n. 17 (pp. 7–68).

Current Musicology is directed by a student editor-in-chief who manages an editorial board usually consisting of about ten senior graduate students, who are responsible for the majority of the editing tasks and who make decisions concerning the acceptance of articles. Also assisting is an editorial staff of graduate students, who are involved in editing and other managerial duties. A faculty advisor oversees the journal. The contributorship ranges from major scholars to graduate students at lesser-known colleges, giving *Current Musicology* an irregular but reasonably high level of scholarliness.

The journal appears twice a year, although it is usually behind in its publishing schedule, with each issue separately numbered and paginated. In 1967 and again in 1970 only a single issue was published. It is produced in soft cover in a 6″ by 9″ format with about 120 to 200 pages on average. Content varies widely, though between four and seven articles with an equal number of reports, a few announcements, and perhaps one or two bibliographies is the current norm. Music examples and iconographic illustrations are frequent. The typeface is clear, margins are ample, and the general design and layout are pleasant and easy to follow. Articles appear only in English (foreign articles appear in English translation). A page at the back of each issue describes each of the contributors.

Information Sources

INDEXES
> External: Music Index, 1967– . RILM, 1967– . Bibliographie des Musikschrifttums, 1966– . Music Article Guide, 1967– . Humanities Index, 1982– . Arts and Humanities Citation Index, 1977– .

REPRINT EDITIONS
> Microform: UMI, 1978– .

LOCATION SOURCES
> Widely available.

Publication History

TITLE AND TITLE CHANGES
  Current Musicology.
VOLUME AND ISSUE DATA
  Volumes 1–   , 1965–   .
FREQUENCY OF PUBLICATION
  Semiannual but irregular.
PUBLISHER
  Columbia Department of Music.
PLACE OF PUBLICATION
  New York
EDITORS
  Austin Clarkson, 1965, 1966–67. Jamie Croy, 1965–66. Neal Zaslaw, 1968–70. L. Michael Griffel, 1971–73. Margaret Ross Griffel, 1972–74. Richard Koprowski, 1975–77. Douglass Seaton, 1977–79. Douglas A. Stumpf, 1979. Dale E. Monson, 1979–80. Jeanne Ryder, 1980–83. Murray Dineen, 1984–85. Brian Seirup, 1986–   .

Dale E. Monson

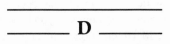

D

DANSK MUSIKTIDSSKRIFT

Dansk musiktidsskrift (*DMT*) was established in 1925 by the Young Musician's Society (Det unge Tonekunstnerselskab—DUT). This society, founded in 1920 and modeled on Arnold Schönberg's Society for Private Performances in Vienna (1918–21), was to be a forum for the exchange of ideas and the discussion and performance of new music from abroad. In the first five years, the emphasis on the private nature of the society's activities was converted to one more open to the public, and *DMT* was a part of this outreach. Its present position as the oldest, most vital, and most widely circulated music periodical in Denmark can be credited to the ability of the successive editors to maintain a healthy balance between the concept of the journal as a forum for active musicians and the conviction that such exchange should be carried out openly, the better to benefit from the participation of the public.

In the inaugural issue the editors announced their plan to include features by foreign and Danish authors, biographical essays about older and younger Danish musicians, short news items, and announcements of interest to members of DUT. To encourage open debate, readers' views would be aired in a special section, "Forum" (1:1). Although political and economic exigencies have altered Danish society in the past sixty years, the editors have generally retained the original formula and consequent diversity.

The two dominant groups of contributors have been composers and music educators. The two overlap, since composers in Danish music culture tradition-ally function as professionals in a variety of musical fields; they have contributed to *DMT* most often in their capacity as critics, theorists, historians, music ad-ministrators, or educators. Thus *DMT* consistently reflects the composers' interest in topical and current subjects or issues, for example, compositional techniques, folk music research, new music, discoveries in historical or modern performance practices, in-depth presentations of known or unknown composers, and the effect of repressive political regimes on musical culture. The educators for their part have embraced practical, theoretical, and political issues in music education—primarily, though not exclusively, in Denmark. Historically *DMT* has served unofficially and officially as one of the principal channels for information concerning the Music Teacher's Association (MTA), a relationship that was interrupted (1942–47) when the MTA published its own journal, *Levende Musik*.

The appearance and outlook of the journal is Danish and its main interest remains Danish music, musicians, and culture, but it has exerted persistent effort to overcome cultural insulation. The result has been a gradual broadening of scope and an increased interest in cultures beyond those of the traditional European leaders. While ISCM (International Society for Contemporary Music) activities were always reported, general coverage of the European scene was typically uneven. In the first volumes attention was focused on Igor Stravinsky, Paul Hindemith, and Arnold Schönberg. Music in Russia was a subject of continuing interest. Conspicuous attention was paid to jazz from the very beginning because of its innovative character and its influence in Denmark, but news about the rest of American musical activity was absent. As late as 1950 a report titled "American Music in Salzburg" (25:157–58) was limited to music composed in America by European emigrants who fled political repression in the 1930s. When American composers began to exert greater influence in musical circles in the late 1950s, *DMT* followed the development with articles.

In spite of the editors' efforts, *DMT* suffered from lack of contact with foreign cultures during the military occupation in World War II and the economically oppressive postwar period. Following the recovery, efforts to overcome the enforced isolation led to the quarterly publication of *Nordisk Musikkultur*, under the banner of *DMT* (1952–63). While laudable, the publication never attained the depth of coverage achieved increasingly by *DMT*.

By 1949 *DMT* had found its role in the belief that "True democracy does not aim at giving the people the bad music they want to hear at the expense of the valuable music . . . but endeavors to contribute to the opportunity for everyone to partake of the genuine riches of culture" (20:30, quoted from English abstract of article, pp. 12–17). Subsequent expansion of interest in areas beyond Europe along with heightened critical thought gained momentum and erupted in the strong anticonservative statement of 1963: "The journal shall be *contemporaneous*. . . . That mandates the consideration of contemporary music, its problems and circumstances in musical life from the pedagogical, scientific and social points of view" (38:249). This determination resulted in the use of "theme" issues to cover areas otherwise neglected in *DMT*: opera, 29.4, 45.5/6; ballet, 33:1, 39:6/7, 45:8; "Avant-garde" in music, 38.7; folk music, 32.3, 36.3;

electronic music, 56.2; dodecophony church music, 39.8; and beat music and rock and roll, 41.4, 56.1.

The most significant changes in the journal reflect the growth of music journalism both in the area of reporting and in technology. This is evident notably in the reviews and analyses, which began as short accounts and evaluations of live and recorded performances and became more sophisticated and detailed. The influence of strong writers and editors played a major role, as in the decidedly critical writing introduced by the composer Vagn Holmboe in the late 1930s and the highly objective analytical work of the composer/musicologist Jan Maegaard beginning in the 1950s.

Musicologists and historians Finn Viderø, Knud Jeppesen, Mogens Wøldike, Jens Peter Larsen, and especially Poul Hamburger also left their mark on the journal with critical writing and historical studies drawn from their scholarly research. Poul Rovsing Olsen, Morten Levy, and Vagn Holmboe are among those who contributed to the growth of interest in folk music. Articles by performing musicians were very rare until recently; nonmusicians contribute even less often. Mention should be made of composers whose influence has been particularly important: Finn Høffding and Vagn Holmboe in the early years and, more recently, Per Nørgaard.

The text is primarily in Danish, occasionally in Swedish and Norwegian. English-language summaries were published for a short period (vs. 22–24). Direct impact from foreigners on the journal has been felt through extensive and generously illustrated interviews conducted by well-informed Danes, a procedure that avoids problems inherent in translations and brings immediacy to the contribution. It is also germane to mention the sense of humor that threads its way through sixty years of publication, for example, sarcastic commentaries, signed "Pepper Bird," in the late 1930s, graphic illustrations since the late 1950s, and long meandering reviews of Mahler-related publications by the fictional Baron Alphonse Grisemarc-Fougère in the 1970s.

For the first twenty years (1925–45), *DMT* appeared ten times a year. Between 1946 and 1959 (vs. 21–33), the number of issues varied, but publication stabilized at eight issues a year in vs. 34–39, and at six since v. 52 (1977). The number of pages per volume has gradually increased from an early average of 230 to the current 318, while the average number of pages per issue increased from between twenty and twenty-five to fifty. Vs. 1–47 were approximately 6½″ by 9″; in 1973 the A4 format was adopted with 7½″ by 10¼″ dimensions. Typically an issue has four articles of varying length; the lead articles are usually ten to twelve pages long. In addition, contents comprise criticism of live, recorded, and broadcast performances, lists of accomplishments in Danish music and Danish musicians, book reviews, debate, and editorials. Work lists of Danish and leading international composers have been published since v. 7. Advertising is music-related. Graphic design, musical examples, and photographs have been used extensively for illustrations.

Information Sources

INDEXES
  Internal: vs. 1–10; vs.1–60, forthcoming.
  External: Music Index, 1949– . RILM, 1967– . Bibliographie des Musiksch-
  rifttums, 1950–[1964–69]– .
LOCATION SOURCES
  Widely available.

Publication History

TITLE AND TITLE CHANGES
  Dansk musiktidsskrift, 1925– . From 1952–63, four additional issues each year
  had the title *Nordisk Musikkultur. DMT, Dansk musiktidsskrift,* 1966– .
VOLUME AND ISSUE DATA
  Volumes 1– , 1926– .
FREQUENCY OF PUBLICATION
  10/year, 1926–44. Irregular, 1945–59. 8/year, 1960–76. Bimonthly, 1977– .
PUBLISHER
  Young Musician's Society (Det unge Tonekunstnerselskab).
PLACE OF PUBLICATION
  Valkendorfsgade 3, 1151 Copenhagen K, Denmark.
CHEIF EDITORS
  Helge Bonnen, 1925–28. Gunnar Heerup, 1929–42. Jens Schrøder, 1942. Nils
  Schiørring, 1943–45. Sverre Forchhammer, 1946. Søren Sørensen, 1947. Sigurd
  Berg, 1947–65. Hans Jørgen Nielsen, 1966. Poul Nielsen, 1967–71, 1974–76.
  Svend Erik Werner, 1972–75. Bo Holten, 1976–80. Anne Kristine Nielsen, 1980–
  85. Ivan Hansen, 1985–86. Jesper Brinkmann, 1986– . Important coeditors:
  Vagn Jensen, 1952–61. Gregers Dircknick-Holmfeld, 1962–64. Jens Brincker,
  1965. Hans Gefors, 1980–85. Jesper Brinkmann, 1985–86.

Jean Christensen

DIALOGUE IN INSTRUMENTAL MUSIC EDUCATION

Dialogue in Instrumental Music Education has an intentionally limited audience. It is aimed at members of the music education profession who are involved
with the preparation of instrumental music teachers. Founded by Gerald B. Olson
of the University of Wisconsin–Madison, in 1977, *Dialogue in Instrumental
Music Education (DIME)* pursues the following goals: (1) to aid in improving
instruction and the preparation of instrumental music teachers, (2) to prepare for
change in music education, (3) to identify innovative programs, (4) to present
a forum for philosophical discourse and debate, (5) to report pertinent research,
and (6) to review appropriate books and materials (1.1: inside cover.)
  Published twice each year in the spring and fall, it reflects the personal interests
of its founder and editor who introduce each issue with an informative editorial.

A five-year index covering 1977–81 (5.2:66–74) pinpoints Olson's interests: In-service Growth (9 articles), Performance Problems (6), Teacher Preparation (7), program Innovations (4), Philosophical (6). The journal encourages all those involved with teacher training to use *DIME* as a forum. Contributors are mainly college/university faculty members, although a few graduate students and public school personnel are represented. To date, contributors and subscribers, however, are mainly music education specialists.

With the Spring 1982 issue Olson announced the formation of a distinguished council of advisors which "alters the structure of *DIME* to enable it to become a refereed journal" (6.1:3). Advisory Council members include Hal Abeles, Eugene Corporon, A. Peter Costanza, Roy E. Ernst, Paul Haack, Steven Hedden, Michael Mark, David Nelson, David Peters, and Melanie Stuart.

The Spring 1983 (7.1) issue was dedicated to "Technology and Teaching" and included articles on the use of microcomputers in music education. The editors also reprinted *A Nation at Risk* (National Council on Excellence in Education, 1983) (7.2:33–54; 8.1:5–20) as an attempt to draw teachers of music teachers into the national debate on education. In the Spring 1985 issue, David J. Nelson became editor of the journal and Gerald Olson became consulting editor. This issue included a reprint of "An Address Presented to the Symposium on Teacher Education, Madison, Wisconsin, October 24, 1984" by Dr. Charles Leonard (9.1:1–13) and an informative bibliography by Thompson Brandt of materials relating to teacher training (9.1:22–48). The Spring 1986 issue (10.1) includes two papers from a symposium on teacher training sponsored by Arizona State University in February 1985: "Teaching Music in the 1990s" by Paul R. Lehman (10:3–18) and "A Process for Improvement of Undergraduate Teacher Training Programs" by Eunice Boardman Meske (10:19–37).

Regular features of *Dialogue in Instrumental Music Education* include "Annotations"—reviews of books and materials, "Citations"—announcements of new materials related to the journal's interests, "Letters to the Editors" which appears irregularly, and "Contributors"—biographical sketches of contributors and reviewers. *DIME* is neither a technical journal nor a popular one. It holds the middle ground, attempting to report recent research that holds promise for instrumental music teachers.

While the publication history of *DIME* is brief, it has become a useful journal to a small but active group of subscribers. Over 50 percent of the approximately 300 subscriptions are libraries. The remaining individual subscriptions are held mainly by music education faculty members in the United States and Canada. The journal is completely self-sustaining through subscription and is not associated with any institutional sponsor. There is no advertising. The page size has remained a consistent 5¼" by 8¼". The first typeset issue was 8.2. Photographs and illustrations appear infrequently. Each volume has an annual index at the end of the Fall issue.

Information Sources

INDEXES
    Internal: vs.1–5 in v. 5.
    External: Music Index, 1977– . RILM, 1982– .
LOCATION SOURCES
    Widely available.

Publication History

TITLE AND TITLE CHANGES
    Dialogue in Instrumental Music Education.
VOLUME AND ISSUE DATA
    Volumes 1– , 1977– .
FREQUENCY OF PUBLICATION
    Semiannual.
PUBLISHER
    Editor, School of Music, University of Wisconsin—Madison.
PLACE OF PUBLICATION
    Madison, Wisconsin.
EDITORS
    Gerald B. Olson, 1977–84. David J. Nelson, 1985– .

Richard P. Kennell

DMT, DANSK MUSIKTIDSSKRIFT. See DANSK MUSIKTIDSSKRIFT

DOWN BEAT

When *down beat* began in July 1934, it specified the intended audience by identifying itself as "the musicians' newspaper." By the mid-1960s its editors felt they had effected a "changeover from a trade journal to a consumer [music] magazine" (41.13:6). In reality, however, it adopted both audiences. A readership survey in 1974 revealed that more than 96 percent of its readers were active instrumental musicians, averaging twenty-three years old (41.21:6). Another 1974 analysis by the magazine, however, showed that more than half of the readers were high school and college players. The 40 percent classified as "professional" included those who earned a living from "a changing combination of playing, writing, teaching, and participation in the various businesses of music" (41.6:6). It was estimated that only about 5 percent of the nation's union musicians earned a living as full-time performers, and *down beat's* coverage has focused primarily on that elite group. The claim of a "consumer" thrust may be partly justified in that most of the remaining musicians/readers also are fans of the highly visible performing professionals and the targets of instrument makers' advertising.

down beat's content has been modified to reflect changing preferences for jazz and popular music by youthful audiences over the decades. At the outset, it quickly developed broad coverage of the swing and dance bands, jobbing and theatre musicians, and national radio music programs of the 1930s. Emphasis switched from traditional jazz to more modern forms during the 1940s and 1950s, then focused increasingly on the jazz-related rock and roll fusion music of the 1960s and 1970s. By the early 1970s, the cover line, a good barometer of its coverage, read "jazz-blues-rock." That changed to "contemporary music magazine" on its fortieth anniversary in July 1974, and by the early 1980s, specified that the magazine was "for contemporary musicians."

An influential and perennially anticipated feature has been the report on the annual Readers Poll choices of most popular bands and musicians. It was first published in 1937 (for 1936) and ranked top musicians on their respective instruments and "swing bands," "sweet bands," and "corn bands." The complexity of classifying types of music is reflected in the frequent changes in the poll categories. For example, changes for the 1983 poll were to subdivide the former "blues/rock" category into "pop/rock" and "soul/rhythm & blues" categories, and the "jazz" category for bands into "acoustic jazz" and "electric jazz." No category is offered for traditional/dixieland/ragtime music, and fans of those styles have largely turned to other publications for coverage. Many traditional musicians have been honored, however, partly because of the longevity of their renown, in the *down beat* Hall of Fame. Created in 1952 in connection with their other polls, it now lists more than sixty famed musicians.

For many years, readers learned who would be playing where through city-by-city listings of performance dates in *down beat*. These listings are no longer used, but reviews of notable performances still are published. Record reviews have been an important part of the content. Musicians' views about music and other musicians have consistently been a major element of *down beat*'s coverage, and many early articles were written by noted musicians. In its intriguing "Blindfold Tests," a musician listens to five or six tunes on an instrument or in an idiom similar to his, then tries to identify the players and critiques the quality of the performance by awarding up to five "stars" for a top-rated effort.

down beat coverage has included in-depth interviews with leading players of each era, and the cover usually pictures the subject of the lead article. These interviews, as well as the feature articles, have become longer (now three to five pages) and more prominent within the journal. The Readers Poll idea was expanded to include a Critics Poll in 1961, and a category of "talent deserving wider recognition" was added to help promote the careers of younger or relatively unknown musicians.

The journal has consistently been an advocate of musicians' interests and has not hesitated to be critical. Early editorials often criticized the American Federation of Musicians for restricting rather than widening its members' freedom to perform. In July 1937, the editors stated that they had particularly encouraged "the bands who favored good musicianship rather than commerciality, and who made an effort to be original'' (4.1:22). Any bias against commerciality disappeared in later decades as the magazine's content followed popular interest.

down beat began as an eight-page tabloid and was edited by saxophone players Glenn Burrs and Carl Cons until they sold it in 1946 to John Maher. Charles Suber published the journal from 1955 to 1962 and was brought back when Maher's son assumed control in 1968. Many noted journalists have served as editors. By early 1936, the format had changed to a sixteen- to twenty-page folded magapaper with extensive use of pictures on the separately printed cover sheet. That format served for nearly three decades, until it became a standard magazine in 1964. The monthly frequency was changed to biweekly in late 1939, and after forty years, it reverted back to monthly in October 1979. It then expanded to about seventy-six pages per issue, from the average forty-eight pages of the previous biweekly issues. Reviews and interviews/features each make up roughly 40 percent of an issue with the remaining 20 percent divided between polls and items of a more instructional nature. Advertisement are dominated by instrument makers with additional space given over to the promotion of books, recordings, clinics, concerts and arrangements.

Early circulation growth was rapid. From the 3,000 copies of the first issue in July 1934, circulation grew to about 35,000 in 1937, to 70,000 in 1944, and to 90,000 in the mid–1980s, with a reported readership in more than 140 countries. It took *down beat*'s founders a scant three years to exceed "all its rivals in circulation gains, advertising growth and reader interest." After half a century, the magazine is still the most widely read popular music publication in the world.

Information Sources

INDEXES
> External: Music Index, 1949– . Music Article Guide, 1965– . Reader's Guide, 1978– . Popular Music Periodicals Index, 1973–76. Arts and Humanities Citation Index, 1976– . RILM, 1978– .

REPRINT EDITION
> Microform: UMI, 1937– .

LOCATION SOURCES
> Library of Congress. Institute for Jazz Studies at Rutgers (complete). Widely available (v.5–).

Publication History

TITLE AND TITLE CHANGES
> *down beat*. A trade publication, *Up Beat*, was published in connection with *down beat* in the 1940s, incorporated as the music education section of the magazine in the 1950s, then published separately again in the 1970s.

VOLUME AND ISSUE DATA
> Volumes 1– , 1934– .

FREQUENCY OF PUBLICATION
    Monthly, 1934–38. Bimonthly, 1939–79. Monthly, 1979–   .
PUBLISHERS
    Albert Lipschultz, 1934. Glenn Burrs and Carl Cons, late 1934–46. John Maher,
    Sr., 1946–52. Norman Weiser, 1952–55. Charles Suber, 1955–62. Various per-
    sons, including Martin Gally, under Maher's direction, 1962–68. Charles Suber,
    1968–82. Maher Publications, 1982–   .
PLACE OF PUBLICATION
    Chicago.
EDITORS
    Glenn Burrs and Carl Cons, 1934–42. Ned Williams, 1942–51. Jack Tracy, 1952–
    56. Don Gold, 1956–59. Gene Lees, 1959–61. Don DeMichael, 1961–67. Dan
    Morgenstern, 1967–70. John Maher, Jr., as executive editor with various man-
    aging editors, 1970–84. Art Lange, 1984–88. John Ephland, 1988–   .

Robert Byler

DWIGHT'S JOURNAL OF MUSIC

John Sullivan Dwight (1813–93) was America's first significant music critic.
His great accomplishment, as Edward Waters has noted, was nothing short of
"the [establishment] of a method of criticism where none had been before"
(Musical Quarterly 21:69). Although neither a scholar nor a virtuoso, Dwight's
passion for music was no less strong for his lack of advanced training. With the
financial backing of his friends and the Harvard Musical Association, which he
had helped to found, he announced his plan for a journal in a sales circular in
February 1852:

The tone to be impartial, independent, catholic, conciliatory aloof from
musical clique and controversy, cordial to all good things, but not eager
to chime in with any powerful private interest of publisher, professor,
concert-giver, manager, society or party. . . . It will insist much on the
claims of classical music and point out its beauties and meanings, not with
a pedantic partiality, but because the *enduring* needs always to be held up
in contrast to the ephemeral. But it will also aim to recognize what good
there is in styles more simple, popular, or modern, will give him who is
Italian in his tastes an equal hearing with the German, and will even print
the articles of those opposed to the partialities of the editor, provided only
they be written briefly, decently, and to the point.[1]

A "prospectus" published on the first page of his first issue foretold a wide-
ranging journal: critical reviews, analyses, biographical sketches, notices of new
publications, correspondence, essays (original and reprinted, American and European) on any and all musical topics, notices concerning the other arts, poems,

short tales, anecdotes, and relevant advertising. As ambitious as this plan sounds, Dwight more or less fulfilled his stated goals in a journal issued "fortnightly" from 10 April 1852 to 3 September 1881.

The articles (one or two per issue) and features concentrate on the history and analysis of eighteenth- and nineteenth-century music with an especially large number of items devoted to early nineteenth-century Germans. Dwight also printed or reprinted the writings of the most knowledgeable commentators about music in America: A. W. Thayer, W.S.B. Mathews, W. F. Apthorp, and F. L. Ritter, among others. Regular features of the journal included "Fine Arts," descriptions of art exhibitions (usually in Boston); "Musical Chit-Chat," concert announcements, obituaries and the like; and "Musical Correspondence" and "Music Abroad," both of which consist of a range of short critiques and reports. Virtually all items were generated by Dwight, either solicited by him or, more often, culled from his voluminous reading of foreign and American newspapers and books, translated or reprinted from sources that he found stimulating. He wrote the local reviews and excerpted the material of others carefully.

The format of the journal varied only slightly through its history. Dwight invariably issued eight 9¼" by 12¼" pages, three columns per page. A regular supplement of four pages of sheet music was added to each issue beginning in 1858. In that year Oliver Ditson took over as publisher, relieving Dwight of the heavy costs and all duties related only to the business end of the journal, and encouraging Dwight to add the music supplement. For this supplement Dwight chose music by recognized European masters spanning the era from Johann Sebastian Bach to Robert Schumann. Indexes appeared for every two volumes.

Dwight's firmly established tastes did not change with the times, and as Romanticism reached America in full flower, he did not deviate from what was seen increasingly as a stodgy and old-fashioned editorial posture. Disagreements with Ditson led to a break and a change of publisher in 1879. He finally ceased writing the journal altogether in 1881, explaining that "the paper does not pay but actually entails a loss upon the editor, . . . [and that there] never has been any adequate demand or support for a musical journal of the highest tone and character" (41:122). He frankly admitted to being out of sympathy with the "new music," the likes of Richard Wagner and Franz Liszt, in which he heard only chaos or superficiality. And the aesthetic outlook of the day he viewed as both vulgar and pompous. He refused to adopt the apparent formula for successful journalistic competition: more sensational copy and increased advertising. Dwight retired gracefully, never compromising his high standards or his opinion of art and music as lofty subjects, worthy of concentrated endeavor, spiritual disciplines which at their best elevated human minds and souls.

As the first major arbiter of cultivated taste in America, John Sullivan Dwight and his journal possess a self-evident historical significance. Although the circulation of the journal seems to have been small, it clearly had an impact beyond its subscribers (*Musical Quarterly*, 21:79). Dwight's was a temperate voice in an age of enthusiasm, and his detailed and considered comments—even about music which he detested—are models that reflect careful listening, all the more remarkable for his relative lack of musical training, especially in theory, harmony, and composition. *Dwight's Journal* has been and will continue to be mined by historians for precise and trenchant aesthetic perspectives of the period in which it was published.

Notes

1. As quoted in George Willis Cooke, *John Sullivan Dwight: Brookfarmer, Editor and Critic of Music* (1898; reprint ed., New York: Da Capo Press, 1969), p. 147.

Information Sources

BIBLIOGRAPHY

Cooke, George Willis. *John Sullivan Dwight: Brookfarmer, Editor and Critic of Music.* 1898. Reprint: New York: DaCapo Press, 1969.

Dwight, John Sullivan. "The Intellectual Influence of Music." *Atlantic Monthly* 26 (1870): 614–25.

Lebow, Marcia Wilson. "A Systematic Examination of the 'Journal of Music and Art' Edited by John Sullivan Dwight: 1852–1881, Boston, Massachusetts." Ph.D. diss., University of California at Los Angeles, 1969.

Waters, Edward N. "John Sullivan Dwight, First American Critic of Music." *Musical Quarterly* 21 (1935): 69–88.

INDEXES

Internal: two years in every other volume.

REPRINT EDITIONS

Paper: Arno Press. The musical supplements were not included, but an introductory essay, a reprint of the Waters article (see Bibliography above), appears in the first volume.

Microform: AMS Film Service.

LOCATION SOURCES

Trinity College (Connecticut), Newberry Library, Boston Public Library, Wellesley College, New York Public Library, Columbia University. Several other libraries have incomplete runs; many own the reprint edition.

Publication History

TITLE AND TITLE CHANGES

Dwight's Journal of Music, A Paper of Art and Literature.

VOLUME AND ISSUE DATA

Volumes 1–41, 1852–81.

FREQUENCY OF PUBLICATION

Biweekly.

PUBLISHERS

Edward L. Balch, 1852–57. Oliver Ditson and Company, 1858–78. Houghton, Osgood, 1879–81.

PLACE OF PUBLICATION

Boston.

EDITOR

John Sullivan Dwight.

Thomas L. Riis

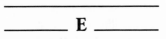

E

EARLY MUSIC

Since the late 1960s there has been a dramatic increase in the interest in and performance of what is loosely called "early music"—music written before the Classical period. A *collegium musicum* is now an assumed feature of any satisfactory undergraduate program, and specialized graduate degrees in performance practice have been instituted. Highly skilled performers on early instruments and ensembles devoted exclusively to early music abound and have thriving concert and recording calendars. Instrument builders do a lucrative business with both the professional and nonprofessional musical community. "Early music" is big business, and its audience is vast.

Early Music, first published in January 1973, was founded in the hopes of becoming "an international forum where diverse issues and interests can be debated and discussed . . . a link between the finest scholarship of our day and the amateur and professional listener and performer" (1:1). Its founder, John M. Thomson, was also its first editor. In April 1983 he was succeeded by Nicholas Kenyon. The journal is published quarterly by the Oxford University Press, and measures 7¼" by 9½". Early issues averaged eighty pages in length, but the size has now increased to approximately 150 pages.

The journal's intended audience encompasses everyone interested in early music, including scholars, amateur and professional performers, instrument builders and collectors, and concert goers. As a result, the topics covered in each issue are varied: instruments of the Middle Ages, Renaissance, and Baroque; repertory; performance practice; and problems of notation and interpretation. Some issues are devoted to a single instrument or family of instruments and contain articles on history, construction, problems of reconstruction, and repertory. Other special issues have been dedicated to individual composers, for example, Guillaume de Machaut (5.4, 1977), Jean Phillippe Rameau (11.4,

1983), and Johann Sebastian Bach (13.2, 1985). A common thread that runs through all the volumes, however, is that the information presented be of immediate use to the greatest number of people. Consequently, while articles on the Medieval, Classical, and Romantic periods sometimes appear, the focus of attention is on the music of the period 1400–1750, since this is what most of the readership performs. Critics, performers, and scholars (often nearly one and the same here) all contribute their thoughts.

The format has changed little since publication began. Each issue includes at least five articles. These are of a scholarly but not academic nature, meant to provide help and practical suggestions to all performers. Second, each issue contains review sections for books, records, and music, each with its own separate editor. Finally, correspondence describing early music activities internationally, communications from readers, and list of events is a standard feature. Early issues also contained a regular column by Christopher Monk, "Where the Wind Blows," which provided information of interest to wind players.

In addition to these standard sections, *Early Music* also includes three innovative features. The "Register of Early Music," begun earlier by Eric Hedger and Christopher Monk, was incorporated into the first issue of *Early Music* and continued until 1978. This was an international directory of performers and ensembles that provided names and addresses, phone numbers, instruments played, and self-evaluations of level of ability. The "Register of Early Instruments," discontinued after 1976, was a buyers' guide for those interested in the purchase of early instruments. Finally, Graham Wells's column "Salerooms" lists prices paid at auction for manuscripts and authentic instruments, thus constituting a guide to their value.

Like many English periodicals, *Early Music* comes equipped with a supplement. Early on this supplement was a musical one, the "Early Music Series," under the editorship of Howard Mayer Brown. It provided new editions of individual pieces drawn primarily from the Renaissance. In 1978 the "Early Music Series" was discontinued and replaced by the "Early Music Gazette," edited by Nicholas Kenyon. This was an international guide to news, groups, and events in the world of early music, and thus was, in part, a continuation of the "Register of Early Music." It was published for two years only, 1978–79. In 1980 the supplement became an index to the volume for the preceding year, edited by Peter Phillips.

Every review of *Early Music* comments on its striking visual beauty. This is the contribution of three designers at Oxford University, Roger Davies for the first volumes, then jointly Peter Campbell and Paul McAlinden. Each issue is profusely illustrated with engravings, woodcuts, manuscript facsimiles, and photographs, often covering an entire page and sometimes in color. The covers themselves were the topic of a special article by Madeau Stewart (11:22–30). Even the advertisements, usually ignored in any evaluation, come in for their share of praise. *Early Music* is a very costly journal to produce, and much of the expense is borne by the large number of advertisers. Both they and the readers are richly rewarded. Advertisements are numerous, informative, beautifully illustrated, and, taken as a body, form for the reader a compendium of information about important instrument builders and music publishers. The index to advertisers at the back of each issue suggests the importance the editors attach to this aspect of the journal.

Informtion Sources

BIBLIOGRAPHY
Baines, Anthony. "Reviews." *The Galpin Society Journal* 27 (April 1974): 156–57.
Heaton, Charles Huddleston. "Books." *Music: The AGO-RCCO Magazine* 8 (November 1974): 34.
Higbee, Dale. "Book Reviews." *American Recorder* 15 (February 1974): 28.
———. "Book Reviews." *American Recorder* 16 (August/September 1975): 101.
Lindahl, Charles E. "Book Reviews." *Notes* 32 (1975): 49–52.
Stewart, Madeau. "A Celebration of Covers." *Early Music* 11 (1983): 22–30.
Thomson, John M. "Editorial." *Early Music* 1 (1983): 1.
———. "The Spirit of Early Music." *Early Music* 11 (1983): 1–5.
INDEXES
    Internal: Each volume indexed, 1960– .
    External: Music Index, 1973– . RILM, 1973–   . Arts and Humanities Citation
    Index, 1973– . Bibliographie des Musikschrifttums, 1973– .
REPRINT EDITIONS
    Microform: UMI.
LOCATION SOURCES
    Widely available.

Publication History

TITLE AND TITLE CHANGES
    Early Music.
VOLUME AND ISSUE DATA
    Volume 1– , 1973– .
FREQUENCY OF PUBLICATION
    Quarterly.
PUBLISHERS
    Oxford University Press, 1973–89. Headley Brothers, 1989– .
PLACE OF PUBLICATION
    London, England.
EDITORS
    John Mansfield Thomson, January 1973– January 1983. Nicholas Kenyon, April
    1983– .

Vincent J. Corrigan

ETHNOMUSICOLOGY

Ethnomusicology is a relatively new discipline that studies music in its cultural context. It is also "a field [that] has never been defined to everyone's satisfaction" (7.3:iv). Since its beginning, in 1953, as the official organ of the

Society for Ethnomusicology, the journal *Ethnomusicology* has been "a testimony to the existence of variety" (7.3:iv). A quick perusal of the tables of contents from 1958 to the present reveals such topics as methodology, technology, comparison of data, dance, bibliography, instruments, language and music, musical transcriptions, and graphs. In addition to this variety of topics, the journal provides a platform for discussion and definitions: "a vehicle for exchange of ideas, news, and information among members" (7.3:iv). A consistent policy of many editors characterizes the journal's scope as "the field of ethnomusicology, broadly defined" (7.3:iv). Indeed, it is this broadness of definition that has kept the journal up-to-date with a dynamically changing, growing discipline.

In spring 1953 a group of scholars interested in maintaining closer contact with each other sent out a newsletter called *Ethno-Musicology*, inviting all concerned to use it for communication concerning their interests and research. They stressed that the effort represented a group and not one individual. The newsletter also requested opinions concerning the organization of a new society or of a new section in an existing society. The possibility of establishing a permanent organ was also recommended. The first eleven newsletters, later to be designated as v. 1 of the journal, were mailed to approximately seventy persons from an international list; within a year, the mailing list had grown to 437, with approximately one-third outside the United States.

The Society for Ethnomusicology was founded in September 1955 at the Fifty-fourth Annual Meeting of the American Anthropological Association. The first meeting took place at the University of Pennsylvania in September 1956. Willard Rhodes was elected president of the society and Alan P. Merriam editor of the journal. Both the society and its journal subsequently set the pace for unity in diversity in the newly consolidated field of "Ethnomusicology."

Although the journal appears to have changed in content and scope over the years, the changes reflect a young discipline exploring its own boundaries. The editors of the journal have endeavored to meet the needs of scholars with varying specialities. Membership input has been encouraged and acted upon. In 1967, a German reader pleaded the necessity of coming in closer contact with American scholars to strengthen lines of communication between America and Europe (11.3:iv). The editor added that collaboration with Africa, Asia, and other parts of the world also needed reinforcing. On the other hand, the society (and journal) were criticized in 1969 for not recognizing and dealing with music of the United States, particularly jazz, folksong, and popular music (13.1:iv). Responding to this criticism, the editor announced intentions to fill the "obvious gaps" with studies of urban pop music, "our own music," black music, and dance in America (15.2:iv). Concern for broadening the journal's scope was underlined again in a 1976 editorial lamenting the "silence" of Latin American, African, Asian, and European colleagues (20.1:iv).

A further source of uneasiness among ethnomusicologists were sensitive terms of possibly pejorative connotation, such as "primitive," "folk," "indigenous," and "tribal." In 1968 the journal attempted to provide guidelines for the use of these terms and their less objectionable alternatives (12.3:iv).

Responding to calls for developing ethnomusicology as a medium of education as well as research, the editor announced in 1963 that the journal would present material from time to time under the heading "The Teaching of Ethnomusicology" (7.1:iv). V. 7.3 stated that the journal "publishes many kinds of things, ranging from detailed monographs to brief notes on education, field work, and publications." A survey of the most recent issues reveals a substantial range of topics: dance, ceremonies, tempos, modes, forms, hemiola, field methods, universalism, methodology, language, ethnic groups, definitions, transcriptions, and equipment. Presently, issues range in length from forty-four to sixty-six pages and contain three to five contributors. A rubric called "Colloquy" was established in 1979 for refereed "essays and dialogues on substantive issues." Other departments range from current bibliography, discography, and filmography to record, book, and film reviews. Special issues have been devoted to the Pacific (25.3), U.S. Black Music (19.3), and the Far East (18.1); the journal's tenth and twenty-fifth anniversaries (7.3 and 26.1, respectively); and one dedicated to Willard Rhodes (13.2) and another to the memory of Charles Seeger (23.3).

The eleven newsletters consisted of "Notes & News" (mainly centered on individuals), current bibliography (divided into general theory and specific areas), recordings, exchange (to assist individuals in locating materials), needs, and problems. In 1954 (and several issues following), course surveys of various institutions were published.

V. 1 (#1–11, 1953–57), the *Newsletter*, was mimeographed on 8½" by 11" sheets and stapled. With 2.1, January 1958, the journal was initiated with a format of 6" by 9½", bearing the title "Ethno-musicology." With the exception of the short-lived hyphen, this description remains valid. The journal, appearing three times a year, is published in English; articles are amply illustrated with musical transcriptions, graphs, maps, and additional visual aids.

Advertisements for publications, discs, and scholarly information started in 1961 (v. 5). In 1977 the board of directors established a policy of accepting advertisements only for the second and third issue of each volume. Annual indexes appeared in issue n.3 of vs. 3, 6, 7, 8, 9, 10, 13, 14, 23, 26, 27, and 29. A "Decennial Index," covering 1953–66, was published separately.

Information Sources

INDEXES
>   Internal: vs. 3, 6, 7, 8, 9, 10, 13, 14, 23, 26, 27, 29. Decennial Index (1953–66) published separately.
>
>   External: Music Index, 1956– . RILM, 1967– . Bibliographie des Musikschrifttums, 1954– . Music Article Guide, 1965– . Humanities Index, 1974– . Arts and Humanities Citation Index, 1976– . Popular Music Periodicals Index, 1973–76.

REPRINT EDITION
>   Microform: UMI.

LOCATION SOURCES
Widely available.

Publication History

TITLE AND TITLE CHANGES
Ethno-Musicology Newsletter, 1953–56. *Ethnomusicology*, 1957– .
VOLUME AND ISSUE DATA
Volumes 1– , 1953– .
FREQUENCY OF PUBLICATION
3/year.
PUBLISHER
Society of Ethnomusicology.
PLACES OF PUBLICATION
Middletown, Connecticut, 1957–72. Ann Arbor, Michigan, 1972– .
EDITORS
Alan P. Merriam, 1954–58 (1.3–2.1). David P. McAllester, 1958–62 (3.1–6.1).
Bruno Nettl, 1962–66 (6.2–10.1). Frank J. Gilles, 1966–70 (10.2–14.1). Israel
J. Katz, 1970–71 (14.2–15.1). Norma McLeod, 1971–74 (15.2–22.1). Fredric
Lieberman, 1978–81 (22.2–24.3). Timothy Rice, 1981–85 (25.1–28.3). Peter
Etzkorn, 1985–88 (29.1–31.3). Charles Capwell, 1988– (32.1–).
GUEST EDITORS
Gilbert Chase, 1966 (10.1). Israel J. Katz, 1972 (16.3). Portia K. Maultsby, 1975
(19.3). Adrienne Kaeppler, 1981 (25.3).

L. JaFran Jones

ETHNO-MUSICOLOGY. See ETHNOMUSICOLOGY

ETHNO-MUSICOLOGY NEWSLETTER. See ETHNOMUSICOLOGY

ETUDE

Etude was begun in 1883, the brainchild of Theodore Presser. It was originally
conceived of as a monthly journal for private music teachers—"devoted to the
interests of the technical study of the piano." It consisted of articles giving
advice about such things as fingering technique, proper repertoire, policies on
payments for missed lessons, and the virtues of hard work and moral rectitude.
It was intended to act as an instructor or textbook for repeated use, not one-time
perusal. Presser had also been instrumental in the founding of the National Music
Teacher's Association (NMTA) and used *Etude* to further its causes. A major
feature of the magazine was the center section, which contained complete pieces
of music (*Brainard's Musical World* [q.v.] had begun this tradition in 1864).
For Presser, this center section was the start of a further venture. From the first,
many requests for additional copies of the music poured into the office. In October

1884 the following notice appeared in the journal: "Theo. Presser, Music Publisher and Dealer. We are now ready to fill all mail orders for music." The Presser Company was to become one of the major publishing houses in the world.

For the first several years Presser struggled almost single-handedly to keep his monthly journal alive. He was assisted by a young man named William E. Hetzel, who soon became the general manager, remaining with the institution for more than twenty-five years. In June 1884, a personal financial windfall allowed Presser to move the company to larger quarters in Philadelphia. By 1885 the journal began to include articles that were not purely pedagogical. A column on current events in the music world became a regular feature. In September 1886 an editorial board appeared on the masthead. The magazine began to incorporate articles pertaining to the organ, choir, and violin as well as the pianoforte. The subtitle was changed to include "all music lovers." In December 1895 *Etude* absorbed *Brainard's Musical World* and several of its prominent writers.

Etude set out to raise the general taste of the American public and to bring music into every American home. The singleness of purpose had an almost religious zeal to it. Presser's taste tended toward the practical and the conservative, and his journal did not favor modern or progressive trends in music.

In 1907 James Francis Cooke was appointed editor-in-chief, a position he held until 1949. Presser remained president of and inspiration to the company until his death in 1925. During the first half of the twentieth century, *Etude* continued to expand its coverage to various additional aspects of the musical world. It discussed the merits of music on radio, the proper diet for a burgeoning opera singer, and the proper music camp. A large number of well-known music personalities were engaged to write articles for the journal: Leopold Godowsky, Maurice Ravel, Harold Schonberg, Gerald Moore, Pablo Casals, and Enzo Pinza, to name but a few. For years, Nicholas Slonimsky wrote a regular column entitled "Music Miscellany" and later "Musical Oddities." There were book and record reviews, and regular question-and-answer columns for organists, singers, violinists, and others. A "Children's Page" was established in 1900, later evolving into several pages for young readers called "Junior Etude." Edited by Elizabeth A. Gest, it featured articles, quizzes, and a letter and pen pal column. Special issues were devoted to the music of Johann Sebastian Bach or George Frederic Handel or Franz Liszt (the latter was an especially favored figure with the journal). Occasionally a large folded poster featuring a famous composer was included with an issue. Musical epithets such as HOME MUSIC HOME HAPPINESS and MUSIC STUDY EXALTS LIFE were printed across the bottom of each page.

By 1917 *Etude* had more than doubled in size to around seventy pages with a proportionate increase in the number of its one-half to two-column articles and features. In that year, the dimensions were also altered, from the original 10″ by 14″ to 10″ by 13″. It would be further reduced to 10″ by 12″ in 1940.

The magazine was filled with photographs, drawings, and occasional cartoons. The covers often pictured portraits of famous musicians or cherubic children at the piano or in church choir and other scenes of blissful family life. There were many advertisements for music both from the Presser Company and other presses, music schools, instruments and musical accessories, as well as a classified ad section.

The music section quickly expanded to contain much more than the original piano exercises. While most of the pieces were still for the pianoforte, there were vocal works, works for piano and clarinet or violin and even, very occasionally, a set of band or orchestra parts. Most issues contained music that covered the gamut of the musical proficiency that might be found in the home. The number of pieces also increased, from three to five in early numbers, to between ten and twenty throughout much of the twentieth century.

In September 1955 the magazine boldly announced a new format; the editor reduced size (now 8½″ by 11″) and added color as well as articles on a still broader range of subjects. It seems, however, that more than format was changing. James Francis Cooke was no longer editor-in-chief, and Guy Maier, for twenty years a regular featured writer on pianoforte matters, died on 24 September 1956. The mood of the nation was changing. The circulation dropped from a peak of 250,000 to 50,000. *Etude* itself claimed that the loss of circulation was due to reduced interest in piano study, which they attributed to the growing vogue of radio and television (*Diapason* 48.6:20). The last issue appeared in May 1957.

Etude was begun as a personal labor of love, and this flavor permeated the journal throughout its history. Its popular tone was aimed at the amateur, "the music lover." Critics sometimes complain about *Etude*'s refusal to acknowledge major modern trends in music, although a September 1950 article explaining twelve-tone music to the layman (68.9:12–14), and another in March 1950 by William Grant Still discussing form in modern music (68.3:17, 61) belie that image. But *Etude* was not written for scholars. The *Musical Courier* (q.v.) stated that *Etude* was "of particular value to those who were not near large cities and had little if any other access to the information necessary to their work and development" (*Musical Courier* 155.7:6). As the musical public grew more sophisticated and urban culture became more accessible via various media, there was no longer a strong interest in or need for general musical journals such as *Etude*.

Information Sources

BIBLIOGRAPHY
"The House that Theo. Presser built." *Music Trade News*, May 1930.
"*Etude* magazine ends long service to music world." *Musical Courier*, 1957, p. 6.
"*Etude* magazine to cease publication." *Musical America* 48 (1 May 1957): 36.
"Passing of the *Etude*." *The Diapason*, May 1, 1957, p. 20.
REPRINT EDITIONS
      Microform: UMI. AMS Film Service. Opus Publications.

LOCATION SOURCES
Widely available.

Publication History

TITLE AND TITLE CHANGES
Etude, 1883–96. *Etude and Musical World*, 1897. *Etude*, 1898–1957.
VOLUME AND ISSUE DATA
Volumes 1–75, 1883–1957.
FREQUENCY OF PUBLICATION
Monthly.
PUBLISHER
Theodore Presser.
PLACE OF PUBLICATION
Lynchburg, Virginia, 1883–May 1884. Philadelphia, June 1884–1957.
EDITORS
Early editors irregularly indexed. Frequently listed names include: W. S. B. Mathews, John S. VanCleve, John C. Fillmore, and Helen D. Tretbar. James Francis Cooke, 1907–49. John Briggs, 1950–51. Guy McCoy, 1951–57.

Marilyn Dekker

ETUDE AND MUSICAL WORLD. See ETUDE

EUTERPEIAD, THE

Published in Boston from 1820 to 1823 and named for Euterpe, the flute-playing Greek muse, *The Euterpeiad, or Musical Intelligencer*, was the first American periodical to be devoted primarily to writings about music. Its editor, John Rowe Parker, was a self-confessed musical amateur, formerly a music dealer and an occasional contributor of articles on music to a local newspaper. His vision for the journal, as stated in its first issue, was to "embrace every article any ways interesting to, or connected with, the science [of music]." His audience was clearly the music lover and amateur. But the difficulties of producing a successful music periodical proved formidable, and Parker relinquished editorship after three years. Two issues later, under its new editor Charles Dingley, the journal ceased publication. Apparently unable to satisfy a sufficient readership to sustain it then, *The Euterpeiad* now provides us a valuable glimpse of New England musical life in the early nineteenth century. The breadth of its circulation and the rapid appearance of numerous American music periodicals in its wake, offers further evidence of its impact.

Content included "A Brief History of Music from the Earliest Ages," serialized throughout the first sixty issues. This and the regularly featured biographical portraits and essays on topics in European music were largely borrowed from the writings of the eighteenth-century English music historians Charles

Burney and Sir John Hawkins, and from English periodicals such as the *Musical Review*. Occupying a substantial portion of the total space in the journal, these recycled, learned, if not scholarly, music history lessons made information accessible that would have otherwise been expensive and difficult to find in print in the United States.

Writing on American music and musicians made up a relatively small but unique and important segment of the journal's content. Beginning in late 1822, a column first entitled "Musical Gossip" and soon changed to "Musical Reminiscences," provided profiles of retired or deceased American musicians, and of European musicians who had made an impact in this country and recently returned to Europe. Attributed to the editor or to an "unnamed correspondent," these essays offer biographical information and telling assessments of musicians of varied historical stature, ranging from Raynor Taylor to "Miss Hewitt." The latter, daughter of James Hewitt, is an example of a locally important teacher and performer about whom we would otherwise know very little.

Also featured in *The Euterpeiad* were reviews of local concerts and of newly published music. The writing is oratorical and peremptory; a famous review of Anthony Philip Heinrich's *The Dawning of Music in Kentucky* refers to the composer as "the Beethoven of America" (3.2:16). Editorials on topics ranging from music education to concert behavior and the social status of musicians present similarly biased but alert observations. Less subjective reflections of American musical life and taste take the form of concert programs and advertisements for music, instruments, and the services of music teachers. A song or simple piano piece was often inserted on a supplemental sheet, typically heralded as "A Favorite Song," and credited to "an amateur" or to known British and American composers like Thomas Moore, Henry Bishop, and Oliver Shaw.

Despite its avowed focus on music, *The Euterpeiad* also printed a column of poetry and a "Ladies Department." The latter, a mixture of light literary commentary and domestic advice, grew to significant enough proportions to merit the addition of *Ladies Gazette* to the title of the journal in its second year. During its last year the journal split, issuing *The Euterpeiad* alternately with *The Minerviad*, devoted to musical and "ladies" matters respectively.

The journal was issued weekly in four *quarto* pages for the first year, eight *quarto* pages biweekly for the second, and eight *octavo* pages biweekly for the first part of the third. It appeared monthly with sixteen to twenty-four *octavo* pages in its last few issues.

Information Sources

BIBLIOGRAPHY
Haskins, John C. "John Rowe Parker and *The Euterpeiad*." *Notes* 8 (June 1951): 447–56.
Johnson, H. Earle. "Early New England Periodicals Devoted to Music." *The Musical Quarterly* 26 (April 1940): 153–61.

————. *Musical Interludes in Boston, 1795–1830*. New York: Columbia University Press, 1943.

REPRINT EDITIONS

Microform: UMI.

LOCATION SOURCES

No complete set of the original exists in one place: Library of Congress and Carnegie Library of Pittsburgh, vs. 1–3; Rutgers, ns. n. 1. Reprint edition widely available.

Publication History

TITLE AND TITLE CHANGES

The Euterpeiad, or Musical Intelligencer, 1 April 1820–24 March 1821. *The Euterpeiad, or Musical Intelligencer, and Ladies Gazette*, 31 March 1821–16 March 1822). *The Euterpeiad, or Musical Intelligencer*, 30 March 1822–June 1823.

VOLUME AND ISSUE DATA

Volumes 1–3.19, 1820–March 1823. New series, volumes 1–2, May 1823–June 1823.

FREQUENCY OF PUBLICATION

Weekly, 1820–21. Biweekly, 1821–23. Monthly, 1823.

PUBLISHERS

Thomas Badger, Jr., 1820–22. True and Greene, 1822–23. Publisher of the New Series unknown.

PLACE OF PUBLICATION

Boston.

EDITORS

John Rowe Parker, March 1820–March 1823. Charles Dingley, May–June 1823.

Kathryn Reed-Maxfield

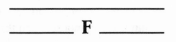

F

FEATURE. See CRAWDADDY

FILM AND TV MUSIC. See FILM MUSIC NOTES

FILM MUSIC. See FILM MUSIC NOTES

FILM MUSIC NOTES

Few journals include articles about film music. This genre, which grew to prominence as an art form in the 1930s, received its first major periodic attention with the journal *Film Music Notes*. Under the leadership of founder and editor Grace Widney Mabee and associate editor Constance Purdy, *Film Music Notes* began publication in October 1941. The principal purposes of the journal were "to provide news of the best in film music to its readers, to encourage film music, and to build an appreciation among audiences for the role of music in film" (2.1:1). Initially sponsored by the National Federation of Music Clubs Motion Picture Music Committee which Mabee chaired, *Film Music Notes* became the official organ of the newly formed National Film Music Council in 1943. The aims of this organization, founded by the editors of *Film Music Notes* themselves, included: "to foster public interest in the music of the films; to encourage film musicians to create a new art-form; and to awaken students to the artistic and worthwhile possibilities of this new medium of expression" (4.1:1).

Diverse topics ranging from analyses of single film scores and industry news to the role of film music in public school education formed the basis of the articles found in the journal. Especially noteworthy and useful were the one-page biographical articles found in the earliest volumes, which discussed film music composers who today are no longer included in biographical reference sources. Later issues devoted space to those composers whose principal area of composition was music for the many programs appearing in the newer medium of music for television.

The early volumes of this journal were published in a newsletter format, with short articles, usually less than one page in length, which discussed current events in the film industry. In successive volumes, articles which focused on various aspects of the film music industry appeared with greater regularity, although industry news still predominated. By 1948 (v. 7) a regular format had been established that included not only regular news from the membership but articles that ranged from two to four pages, complete with extensive musical examples, which discussed film score composers and their music. Title changes in 1951 from *Film Music Notes* to *Film Music* and in 1956 from *Film Music* to *Film and TV Music* reflect both the changing emphasis and attitude of the journal and its contents. Frequent contributors to this journal included noted writer on American music Siegmund Spaeth, composer Gail Kubik, and musicologist Frederick W. Sternfeld.

In addition to the articles each issue contained several regular features. These included "News and Comments" (later "Film Music Notes"), a column of short, newsy items on the industry; "Current Films," reviews of the music of recently released films; and "16mm Films," short articles which discussed films issued in that format. Beginning in v. 3, the "Portfolio series" introduced readers to actual examples of film scores from major film composers of the time. Themes from the film scores of Erich Korngold's "Constant Nymph," Miklos Rozsa's "Sahara," Aaron Copland's "North Star," Roy Webb's "The Seventh Cross" and "I Walked with a Zombie," and Max Steiner's "The Corn is Green" are only a few of the many film scores whose principal thematic materials were excerpted in the journal. From 1941 to 1948, Spaeth, in addition to serving on the advisory editorial board and contributing articles, wrote the column "After-thoughts," which contained short items on various films and their composers.

Special issues devoted to single films appeared on an irregular basis, and were usually six to eight pages in length with illustrations and musical examples. These special issues, which appeared in addition to the regular journals, included: *Carnegie Hall* (1944); *The Red Pony: A Review of Aaron Copland's Score* by Lawrence Morton (February 1949); and *Cyrano de Bergerac: A Review of Dimitri Tiomkin's Score* by Irwin A. Bazelon (January 1951).

The physical format of the journal consistently remained the standard 8½" by 11" size. Pagination of the issues varied in the early issues, with the first volume fascicles having only seven pages per issue. The subsequent five volumes increased in size from eight pages to over forty pages per issue before establishing a more or less standard twenty-two to twenty-four pages per issue. Vs. 1–5 (1941–46) were mimeographed, without photographs or musical examples interpolated within the text. Examples of film scores, varying between one and three pages were usually appended to each issue. Beginning with v. 6 (1947), issues of the journal included both black and white photographs and musical examples interpolated within the text, as well as page-long excerpts taken from film scores. Although numerous references to a change in the format of the journal were made throughout the life of the journal, the change from mimeograph to typeset pages did not occur until v. 14. Frequency of issuance varied from nine issues per year (vs. 1–6) to five issues per year (vs. 7–17). Later volumes contain indexes for the preceding year; no internal indexing is available for the early issues.

Information Sources

BIBLIOGRAPHY

Morrison, Margery. "Getting Acquainted with Some Film Music Scores." *Music Publishers Journal* 3 (September–October 1945): 38, 49.

Mabee, Grace Widney. "Work and Purpose of the National Film Music Council." *Music Publishers Journal* 3 (September–October 1945): 31, 67.

INDEXES

Internal: Later volumes individually indexed in succeeding volume.

External: Music Index, 1949–58.

LOCATION SOURCES

Library of Congress, New York Public Library, Detroit Public Library, University of California at Los Angeles (complete or lacking v. 1). Later volumes widely available.

Publication History

TITLE AND TITLE CHANGES

Film Music Notes, 1941–51. *Film Music*, 1951–56. *Film and TV Music*, 1956–58.

VOLUME AND ISSUE DATA

Volumes 1–17, 1941–58.

FREQUENCY OF PUBLICATION

9/year, 1941–47. 5/year, 1948–58.

PUBLISHER

National Film Music Council, 1943–57.

PLACES OF PUBLICATION

Hollywood, California, October 1941–May 1946. Old Greenwich, Connecticut, September 1946–March 1947. New York, April 1947–58.

EDITORS

Grace Widney Mabee, 1941–44. Constance Purdy, 1941–46. Frederick W. Sternfeld, 1946–47. Marie L. Harrison, 1947–58.

Linda M. Fidler

FONTES ARTIS MUSICAE

Fontes artis musicae (literally, "fountain-head of the art of music") is the organ of the International Association of Music Libraries, Archives, and Documentation Centres (hereafter, IAML). Founded in 1954, it remains the only journal of international music librarianship as well as an important vehicle for studies in music bibliography. It is partially sponsored by the International Music Council of UNESCO and uses three official languages: English, French, and German. More than *Notes* (q.v.) (journal of the Music Library Association) or *Brio* (q.v.) (journal of the United Kingdom branch of IAML), *Fontes* combines reports of its organization's activities with scholarly articles.

IAML's first official meeting was held in Paris in 1951, twenty years after the Music Library Association was founded in America. At first its internal communication needs were served by a *Bulletin d'information*, which appeared in two volumes (1952/3–1953). Then, in spring 1954, the Executive Council announced that the casually reproduced *Bulletin* would be replaced by a journal printed by the respected music publisher Bärenreiter. The first issue of *Fontes artis musicae* appeared in early summer 1954. Its purposes were both to facilitate the work of the organization by communicating with its scattered members between meetings and to reach a wider audience than just the members with information on music source materials (1:1). It has maintained this duality of purpose to the present day, intermixing reports of its own meetings, members, and projects with both articles on music libraries and librarianship and reports of serious musicological research (generally with a bibliographical emphasis). Contributors have likewise included both music librarians and music scholars.

For the first twenty-two volumes of its existence (1954–75), *Fontes* was edited by the remarkable Vladimir Fédorov (1901–79), a founder of IAML who served as its president (1962–65, later honorary president), the International Music Council of UNESCO (1962–66), and the International Musicological Society (1961–67). Under his editorship *Fontes* generally appeared twice a year. In 1964 *Fontes* officially moved to a publishing schedule of three issues per year, but with the exception of 1964, only two issues actually appeared, numbered either 1–2 and 3 or 1 and 2–3.

One important feature of the years under Fédorov was the regular appearance of the "Liste internationale sélective," which comprised national lists of new musical publications (both books and scores). Fédorov called them practical lists "whose sole purpose is to inform our colleagues as quickly as possible concerning the international field of musical and musicological production" (2:176). A remarkable array of twenty-eight countries participated in the *Fontes* lists in vs. 1 and 2, including all of the Western and several Eastern European countries, all of North America, and Argentina, Australia, Brazil, Egypt, India, Israel, Turkey, and Uruguay. Even though it was a perpetual problem to get the lists from each country's editor in a timely manner, at least one list appeared in every volume from 1954 to 1974 (thirty-five in all).

In 1975 Fédorov shared the editorship of *Fontes* with the American musicologist and librarian Rita Benton, who served as sole editor from 1976 until her sudden death in 1980. Under her leadership the journal was published four times a year and dropped the "Liste sélective" in favor of regular book reviews (roughly five to seven per issue, edited by François Lesure from 1976), supplemented by lists of recently published music books of a bibliographic nature. She also actively solicited newsworthy items from members for a "News" column, and added brief summaries for each major article in the two official languages not used in the body of the article.

Benton was succeeded by her associate editor, the Dutch writer André Jurres. He added several co-editors with some responsibility for overseeing the interests of specific groups within IAML (such as public libraries). The publication schedule was reduced to three times a year (without changing the numbering system) until 1984, when it again began appearing quarterly. Great Britain's Brian Redfern became editor in 1987 and announced an intention to concentrate on articles more closely related to the work of music librarians (34:79).

IAML's meetings are usually held in conjunction with those of the International Association of Sound Archives (IASA), since the interests and membership of the two organizations overlap. Reports from these meetings usually take up one full issue of *Fontes* each year and spill over into other issues as necessary. They include formal research papers that have been presented, more casual synopses of each group's actions, and reports on meetings of the executive council and general assemblies.

IAML's professional branches consist of groups affiliated with Music Information Centers as well as public, broadcasting, academic, and research libraries. It has subject commissions on bibliography, cataloguing, and service and training, and each commission has project groups working on specific topics, such as archives, classification systems, and the publishing of contemporary music. IAML's joint commissions with the International Musicological Society work on the important bibliographic tools *RISM (Répertoire international des sources musicales)* and *RILM (Répertoire international de littérature musicale)* as well as newer projects on musical iconography (*RIdIM*) and periodicals (*RIPM*). There is also a joint commission with IASA on music and sound archives. These various components of IAML are reflected in both the reports and other articles found in *Fontes*.

Besides the reports on IAML activities, *Fontes* includes several features that help to keep librarians (and interested scholars) aware of current publications, namely the "Liste internationale sélective" (appeared regularly in vs. 1–21, then occasionally), book reviews (occasionally in vs. 7–17, regularly from v. 22), lists of books received (occasionally, vs. 17–20), and the present lists of "Publications à caractére bibliographique" (regularly from v. 23). Many articles throughout the history of *Fontes* have described specific music libraries and their collections. Questions of music cataloguing have received attention, too, with a growing emphasis on cataloguing and indexing via computer in later issues. Other articles of particular interest to music librarians have addressed the training and qualifications needed for this profession, cooperation among institutions, preparing musical exhibits, and surveys of music librarianship in various countries. Both obituaries and birthday greetings for well-known members are printed occasionally.

Not only music librarians find *Fontes* useful. Many articles in its pages deal with bibliographical research, including lists of music periodicals, studies on the history of music printing and publishing, philosophies of music bibliography, and reports on data bases set up by scholars. The emphasis is consistently on the bibliographical, however, even in articles whose topics appear unrelated at first glance.

Several special issues of *Fontes* have appeared. The most important have been a series on music libraries and librarianship in certain countries. The series began in 1969 (16.3) with a number of papers on American music libraries prepared for the Eighth IAML Congress, held in New York and Washington in 1968. It has been followed by issues devoted to Italian (18.3), Dutch (21.3), Belgian (23.3), British (25.3), and Swedish (33.2) music libraries. Other special issues have included a *Festschrift* of some thirty articles to honor Vladimir Fédorov (13.1) and a survey of libraries in music teaching institutions (22.3).

Fontes has maintained a consistent size (ca. 7″ by 10″) and format throughout its history. Each issue ends with several pages (generally four to eight) of advertisements from publishers and antiquarian dealers. Illustrations are rare. Annual indexes are issued consisting of a table of contents and a name index for the volume. The length of individual volumes of *Fontes* has varied with the growth and economic status of the organization itself, but has generally been longer in years in which the triennial congress reports were published. During its first decade (1954–63) each volume averaged about 130 pages, while the average rose to over 180 pages in the second decade of publication and to over 250 pages in the third decade. Every volume since quarterly publication began in 1976 has had over 200 pages.

Information Sources

INDEXES
> Internal: each volume indexed.
> External: Music Index, 1955– . RILM, 1967– .Bibliographie des Musiksch-
> rifttums, 1954– . Arts and Humanities Citation Index, 1976– .

LOCATION SOURCES
> Widely available.

Publication History

TITLE AND TITLE CHANGES
> *Fontes artis musicae.*

VOLUME AND ISSUE DATA
> Volumes 1– , 1954– .

FREQUENCY OF PUBLICATION
> Semiannual, 1954–75. Quarterly, 1976–80. 3/year, 1981–83.
> Quarterly, 1984– .

PUBLISHER
> Bärenreiter.

PLACE OF PUBLICATION
     Kassel, West Germany
EDITORS
     Vladimir Fédorov, 1954–75. Rita Benton, Co-editor, 1975, Editor, 1976–80.
     André Jurres, Associate Editor, 1976–80, Acting Editor, 1980–81, Editor, 1981–
     86. Brian Redfern, 1987–   .

Peggy E. Daub

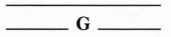

G

GALPIN SOCIETY JOURNAL, THE

Begun in 1948 as "an occasional publication" that promised to appear "not less often than once a year" (1:1), the *Journal* of the Galpin Society (an organization founded two years earlier) was devoted to the stated aims of the society: to bring together those interested in the history of European musical instruments so that they might continue to build upon the contributions of Canon Galpin (1858–1945) to organology and its place in musical scholarship. They sought to investigate the history, construction, and function of early instruments and illuminate questions of early techniques and performance styles.

A foreward by President Jack A. Westrup stated:

> It is the object of this *Journal* to pool the results of research into the history of old instruments and to provide a platform for anyone who has anything of interest to say on the subject. . . . Articles on musical instruments appear sporadically in other publications, but they are scattered over a wide field, and there is always a danger that research may lack co-ordination. . . . We need more and more to realize that the study of old instruments is no mere antiquarianism but a severely practical subject. It can cast light on many things in old music which are still imperfectly understood, and by the service it renders to interpretation can remind us that truth and beauty are one. (1:2)

This idealistic statement was followed by seventy pages of proof: a tribute to Francis W. Galpin by F. Geoffrey Rendall, Anthony Baines on James Talbot, A. R. McClure on keyboard temperaments, the genealogy of the double bass by Eric Halfpenny, and Thurston Dart on the cittern's English repertoire, as well as book reviews, illustrations, a section of "notes and queries," and relevant advertising—the latter collected in one section at the back of the issue.

This auspicious beginning was typical of following issues; contributors have included Adam Carse, Philip Bate, Martha Maas, Frank Hubbard, and Robert Donnington. Throughout its history, the *Journal* has continued to draw articles by the most highly respected scholars, many of whom also comprise the committee that directs the Galpin Society. Roughly two-thirds of these are organological in nature with much of the remainder given over to performance practice issues. The range of topics is suggested in the following list of representative major titles: Eric Halfpenny's "A Note on the Genealogy of the Double Bass" (1:41–45), Thurston Dart's "The Earliest Collections of Clarinet Music" (4:39–41), "Continuo Instruments in Italian Monodies" by Nigel Fortune (6:10–13), "A Nepalese Double Horn" by Jeremy Montagu (17:50–53), and Ian Firth's "Acoustical Experiments on the Lute Belly" (30:56–63).

By 1950 the *Journal* had begun to include reviews of music and other periodicals of interest to readers, in addition to booklists. From time to time, other lists were included—for example, the "Provisional Index of Present-Day Makers of Historical Musical Instruments (Non-keyboard)," which appeared in 1960. Pages devoted to correspondence, obituaries, or special announcements have also been added as needed. From about 1960, due to the proliferation of useful lists submitted for inclusion, the society determined a policy of publishing these separately as "occasional publications" to be announced in the *Bulletin*, which served as the organization's newsletter. In addition, the *Bulletin* contains meeting notices, sale information, queries, and other information.

The majority of articles have dealt with European musical instruments, as indicated in the original statement of purpose, though there have been notable exceptions. The 1960 issue offered Charles McNett's study of "The Chirimia: A Latin American Shawm," (13:44–51) and in 1974 we find "The New Zealand Nose Flute: Fact or Fantasy?" by Mervyn McLean (27:79–94). An occasional editorial has appeared, usually for the purpose of justifying a delay in publication of the issue at hand or calling attention to a special article or separate publication.

Principal editors since its inception have been Thurston Dart, Anthony Baines, and Maurice Byrne—all major figures in the field. Under their leadership, *The Galpin Society Journal* has had an inestimable influence on scholarship and has maintained a standard of detailed and highly respected research. The success it has had in bringing about a greater understanding of early performance practices is widely recognized. The *GSJ* has, in fact, become a model for subsequent publications of the same nature—for example, the *Journal of the American Musical Instrument Society* (q.v.) (occasionally the same article will appear in both journals).

Currently, issues have grown to an average of 130 pages in 4⅜″ by 8⅝″ format and are obtained by membership in the Galpin Society. Each includes eight to twelve articles, anywhere from five to twenty-five pages in length. An average eight pages are devoted to advertisements placed by instrument makers, publishers, and others.

Information Sources

INDEXES

    External: Music Index, 1949– . RILM, 1967– . Bibliographie des Musiksch-
rifttums, 1950, 1956– . British Humanities Index, 1968– . Arts and Humanities
Citation Index, 1976– .

REPRINT EDITIONS

    Microform: UMI.

LOCATION SOURCES

    Widely available.

Publication History

TITLE AND TITLE CHANGES

    The Galpin Society Journal.

VOLUME AND ISSUE DATA

    Volume 1– , 1948– .

FREQUENCY OF PUBLICATION

    Annual.

PUBLISHER

    The Galpin Society.

PLACE OF PUBLICATION

    Oxford, England.

EDITORS

    Anthony Baines, 1956–62, 1971–83. Eric Halfpenny, 1963–70. Jack Westrup,
1948–71. Thurston Dart, 1948–55. Maurice Byrne, 1984–88. David Rycroft,
1989– .

Ruth K. Inglefield

GRAMOPHONE, THE

The Gramophone, which first appeared at the bookstands on 23 April 1923,
was the inspiration of Sir Compton Mackenzie, who sought to launch the world's
first monthly journal solely devoted to reviewing phonograph recordings and the
equipment used in playing them. In his first editorial Sir Compton defined the
policy of the new journal as being "to encourage the recordings companies to
build up for generations to come a great library of good music"—a policy
evidently still followed with vigor by its present editor.

    The first issue contained twenty-one pages of reading matter, eleven of which
were written by Sir Compton under various signatures, one page by his wife,
Faith Stone, and a page and a half of reviews by his old friend John Hope-
Johnstone under the pseudonym James Caskett. Prominently placed was a half-
page essay concerning the royal record that King George V and Queen Mary
had made of their Empire Day messages to the children of the British Empire.

    By the autumn of 1926 the auditors presented a rather disturbing picture of
the financial side of the young journal, but a young and able accountant named

Cecil Pollard, sent to advise the magazine's editorial board, agreed to leave his job and become the business manager for *The Gramophone*. Pollard set the magazine on a solid financial base that has survived every Western European financial crisis since. With his son Anthony, Cecil Pollard even succeeded Mackenzie as editor in 1961.

Even though the publication was originally devoted to answering the needs of audiophiles throughout the United Kingdom, it has ultimately developed into an international forum for the recording industry and its related fields throughout the English-speaking world. Most of the recordings reviewed are European in origin; however, this vast array of recorded material is sought out by collectors and connoisseurs throughout the world.

The number of reviews per issue has grown from the initial 12 of the first issue to 115 in a recent counterpart. Current review sections are divided into five major musical forms: orchestral, chamber, instrumental, choral and song, and opera, with summary account of additional titles in the "Brief Reviews" section. Another regular recordings review section, "Nights of the Roundtable," treats in essay format a nonclassical genre currently popular, for example, spoken word recordings, dance band, personality, nostalgia, and brass and military. Reviews of recordings, tapes, and compact discs are all signed with the reviewer's initials.

Feature articles on all aspects of classical music and musicians and their relationship to the recording industry have been regularly offered since *The Gramophone*'s inception. These articles are based on both diligent scholarship and insightful interview techniques. Photographic illustrations generally accompany each article.

As one of the first, and certainly the earliest, major and surviving magazine to discuss sound-reproducing instruments in depth, *The Gramophone* stands alone as a source of historical and technological information on the subject. From the last waning years of the acoustic era (1923–25) and the new electronic era after 1925 to stereo, digital recording, and compact disc players, *The Gramophone* has reported on, reviewed, discussed, and advertised all major innovations in recordings playback technology. The magazine has made specific recommendations on record players and actually invited phonograph manufacturers to send them their products for testing. An excellent survey of all significant technological advances in record playback equipment to date was featured in a four-installment series written by John Gilbert, the magazine's audio consultant (May, October, and December 1983, and January 1984). This aspect of the journal, always a strong suit, has also enjoyed the greatest growth during the run, increasing several-fold.

During its more than sixty years of publication *The Gramophone* has expanded its coverage by incorporating three other related British publications: *Vox*, *Radio Guide*, and *Broadcast Review*. The monthly issues, originally less than fifty pages in length, now generally run to around a hundred 8½″ by 11″ pages. Each contains two to four articles, several pages in length, and over a hundred brief reviews and reviewer essays. There are copious advertisements for recordings and audio equipment.

Information Sources

BIBLIOGRAPHY
Mackenzie, Compton. "Editorial." *The Gramophone* 30 (December 1952): 1.
————. "How it All Began." *The Gramophone* 50 (April 1973): 1821–22.
Stone, Christopher. "Gathering Moss." *The Gramophone* 28 (January 1951): 165–66.
Pollard, Anthony. "The Gramophone: Past, Present, and Future." *The Gramophone* 50 (April 1973): 1823–24.
Wimbush, Roger, comp. *"The Gramophone" Jubilee Book.* London: General Gramophone Publications Ltd., 1973
INDEXES
    External: Music Index, 1949– .
REPRINT EDITIONS
    Microform: UMI.
LOCATION SOURCES
    Library of Congress, Boston Public Library, New York Public Library (complete run). Later volumes widely available.

Publication History

TITLE AND TITLE CHANGES
    The Gramophone.
VOLUME AND ISSUE DATA
    Volumes 1– , April 1923– .
FREQUENCY OF PUBLICATION
    Monthly.
PUBLISHER
    General Gramophone Publications Ltd.
PLACE OF PUBLICATION
    London.
EDITORS
    Compton Mackenzie, 1923–61. Cecil Pollard and Anthony Pollard, 1961–65. Anthony Pollard, 1965–72. Malcolm Walker, 1972–79. Christopher Pollard, 1980– .

William L. Schurk

GRAVESANER BLÄTTER

In the summer of 1954, the first International Conference on Music Electronics and Acoustics took place in Gravesano, Switzerland, under the auspices of the International Music Council of UNESCO. As a result of the conference, the Gravesano Experimental Studio, which was founded in 1954 with UNESCO help as well, began the first periodical devoted to "Musical, Electroacoustical, and Acoustical Issues" in July of the following year. Edited and published by conductor and champion of contemporary music Hermann Scherchen, who had helped found *Melos* (q.v.) in 1919, the *Gravesaner Blätter* ceased publication only with Scherchen's death on 12 June 1966.

Though its purpose was to report on advances in electronics and acoustics, the journal secondarily functioned as a forum for contemporary music, which is not surprising given Scherchen's interests. The first five numbers contained essays by Iannis Xenakis (1:2–4), Pierre Boulez (2/3:5), Luigi Nono (4:14–18), Hans Werner Henze (4:18–19), and Darius Milhaud (5:9–13) on various issues of contemporary music, as well as articles on technical aspects of acoustics. Composers with whom Scherchen worked continued to contribute material on their music and research, and Xenakis, in particular, became a frequent contributor. Noteworthy among the latter's submissions are "Toward a Philosophy of Music" (29:23–38), "Free Stochastic Music for the Computer" (26:54–78) and "In Search of a Stochastic Music" (11/12:112–22). Typical lead articles averaged thirty-six pages in length, including sound wave charts and other illustrative material. The contributorship is predominantly European and most articles appeared with an English translation or synopsis. The journal also published a schedule of the Gravesano studio's events as well as carrying equipment and publisher advertisements.

In 1962, in a double issue numbered 23/24, Xenakis published an article on "Musical Sounds from Digital Computers" (23/24:109–18), and from then on, the implications of the computer for music and composition became a frequent topic. Similarly, after a special television issue in 1964 (n. 25) this medium received regular coverage as well. The considerable interest generated by stereophonic sound reproduction is reflected in Robert Kolben's "Stereophony Today" (19/20: front cover).

An innovative feature of the *Gravesaner Blätter* was its accompanying 45 r.p.m. "scientific records." These recordings demonstrated the various techniques or problems discussed in the articles such as "sound transformation through frequency transposition" (*Klangumwandlungen durch Frequenzumsetzung*) (n. 4), or displayed the power of stereophonic sound with examples of music by Xenakis and others. With the interest in computers in the 1960s, the recordings contained examples of digital computer-generated music.

Planned as a quarterly publication, the journal issued twenty-nine numbers in seven volumes, with an average of 150 pages per issue in a 5¼" by 8" format. Numbering of issues is sequenced throughout the run instead of being recycled with each volume. Numbers appeared regularly for the first five volumes, but the four numbers of v. 6 were published over two years (1961–62). No issues appeared in 1963, v. 7 contained only two numbers, and the last three issues, published in 1966, appeared without a volume designation. The double issue number 23/24 (1962) contained an index for the first six volumes. No subsequent index was published.

Information Sources

INDEXES
    Internal: ns. 1–23 in n. 23/24.
    External: Bibliographie des Musikschrifttums, 1956–64, 1970.
LOCATION SOURCES
    New York Public Library, Newberry Library, University of Pennsylvania (complete runs). Later numbers widely available.

Publication History

TITLE AND TITLE CHANGES
    Gravesaner Blätter.
VOLUME AND ISSUE DATA
    Numbers 1–29, 1955–66.
FREQUENCY OF PUBLICATION
    Quarterly, 1955–60. Irregular, 1961–66.
PUBLISHER
    Ars Viva Press.
PLACE OF PUBLICATION
    Mainz, Germany.
EDITOR
    Hermann Scherchen.

Susan C. Cook

GUIDE MUSICAL, LE

On 1 March 1855, the first issue of the Belgian/French weekly *Le Guide musical* was released. Its stated intention was to chronicle Belgian musicians and composers at home and abroad, to bring news of important international events to Belgians, to provide information on upcoming events, to present the issues facing the world of music, and to enhance the quality of Belgian musical life in general. For a small additional subscription fee, magazine patrons also received, each week, a short vocal or piano work from the catalog of Schott of Brussels, the magazine's publisher and, for over three decades, sole advertiser. For the next sixty years, a succession of editors produced a remarkably consistent product that today provides a marvelously detailed view of musical life and interests in Europe from the Belgian and, later, French perspective. They also maintained a regular publication schedule without evident delays until World War I brought the entire enterprise to a halt. An effort at revival in 1917/18 failed within the year.

While the length, labeling, and subdivision of the different sections varied somewhat, the content of the magazine can be characterized as follows: (1) one to several articles, (2) news, generally subdivided by country and sometimes by city and even by major and minor stories, (3) reviews of books and music, (4) necrology, and (5) advertisements. The proportions of these sections varied widely, and all but the news section are occasionally omitted. Other more specialized departments come and go. By the end of the nineteenth century, authorship is indicated not just for some articles but for many of the major news columns as well. A table of contents was placed below the masthead from 30.34–35 through v. 50 and a yearly index first appears with v. 31.

Articles, one to two in early issues and two to three later, run from less than one page in length to more than two, with frequent longer pieces that are serialized through anywhere from two to eight issues. Topics include composers, historical issues, important musicians, festivals, new productions, genres, locales, letters by a composer, theory and acoustics, instruments, pedagogy, obituary and anniversary tributes, and commentaries on the current musical scene. They are frequently excerpted from books or other periodicals. The writings of Hector Berlioz, Richard Wagner, and even Robert Schumann, and Charles Burney appear, virtually always in reprint. Belgian composers and Richard Wagner are afforded considerable coverage. Special, multipage supplements appear up to several times a year. They may be promotional in nature or a special feature, such as the lavish, forty-four-page 11 November 1903 special supplement commemorating the one hundredth anniversary of Berlioz. Authors and music journalists are the major contributors, among them Maurice Kufferath, Hugues Imberts, Julien Tiersot, André Gédalge, Henri de Curzon, Jacques-François Fromental Halévy, Marie Escudier, Adolphe Jullien, Eugène Gigout, Edmond Vander Straeten, and Michel Brenet.

At least half of each issue is devoted to news. The most common of the several similar rubrics adopted for this section subdivides the news by country and then, usually only for Belgium and France, by city. Major concert series and theatres also receive separate headings from time to time. The majority of the space is devoted to the French-speaking nations of Europe, with Germany, England, Russia, and Italy receiving frequent, but much more concise coverage. Sporadic attention is paid to a wide variety of additional locales. Most of the reports are from a few sentences to one or two paragraphs in length, and the Brussels section can include more than a dozen such reports. The shorter are factual to mildly promotional in nature, while longer pieces may be much more opinionated. Reviews, announcements, dedications, honors, concerts, and tours all find a place here.

The "Bibliographie musicale" is usually about a half page in length and contains reviews of from one to five items. Among the music reviews, those of piano and vocal music predominate. Schott publications are clearly favored in the earlier issues as are French-language items. Likewise, Schott's domination of advertising gives way by the early 1890s to notices from other publishers, as well as performers, entrepreneurs, instrument makers and vendors, and even nonmusical enterprises.

For its first three decades, *Le Guide musicale* was produced and disseminated by Schott. It listed no specific editor, and the format was virtually unchanged.

With v. 29.36, the layout was made more pleasing to the eye and generally classier. A year later, the first volume index is included and, with v. 32, a stylish new masthead appears. V. 33, however, incorporates more substantive changes: the volume is given an ornate cover that lists major contributors and, for the first time, the editor(s); a decided reorientation toward France is seen in the placement of French news sections ahead of Belgian, the removal of any reference to Belgium in the subtitle, and the equalizing of the Belgian and French subscription prices (though the magazine is still printed in Belgium). The dimensions of the pages are increased from 8¼″ by 11¾″ to 9¾″ by 14″.

The second and last major format change occurred less than a decade later. Schott seems to have relinquished *Le Guide musicale* to its editors after v. 38, and with v. 40 the size changes once again, to 6¾″ by 10″. This is accompanied by a new subtitle, many more musical examples, and a clearer table of contents layout. The number of pages, which had doubled from four to eight in v. 9 and crept upwards toward twelve since the v. 33 format change, was now increased to between eighteen and twenty-four.

Le Guide musicale appeared every Thursday (after v. 35, every Sunday) throughout its run, with the exception of the fortnightly summer schedule traditional with such magazines. With v. 9 Schott put the journal on a 1 January to 1 January publishing schedule (previously 1 March to 1 March) by publishing double issues for two months. Starting with v. 30, issues are numbered consecutively throughout the volume. Previous issues lacked pagination entirely. Musical examples are rare at first, but common by the 1890s; illustrations (etchings and photographs) are all but nonexistent before the 1880s but also common if not plentiful by the 1890s.

Information Sources

INDEXES
     Internal: each volume indexed (vs. 31–   ).
REPRINT EDITIONS
     Microform: Library of Congress. Datamics Inc.
LOCATION SOURCES
     Partial runs available: Library of Congress, 1869–1917. New York Public Library, 1855–66, 1883–1917/18. University of Michigan, 1855–1916.

Publication History

TITLE AND TITLE CHANGE
     Le Guide musical, revue hebdomadaire des nouvelles musicales de la Belgique et de l'étranger, 1855–86. *Le Guide musical, revue hebdomadaire de la musique et des théatres*, 1887–93. *Le Guide musical, revue internationale hebdomadaire*, 1894–96. *Le Guide musical*, 1897–1904. *Le Guide musical, revue internationale de la musique et des théatres*, 1905–13. *Le Guide musical, revue internationale de la musique et des théatres lyriques*, 1914–17/18.
VOLUME AND ISSUE DATA
     Volumes 1–61, 1855–1917/18.

FREQUENCY OF PUBLICATION
   Weekly.
PUBLISHERS
   B. Schott's Sohne, 1855–89. Peter Schott, 1889–1918.
PLACE OF PUBLICATION
   Brussels.
EDITORS
   Maurice Kufferath, 1887–88, 1891–1900, 1909–14. Gaston Paulin, 1889–90.
   Hugues Imbert (Paris Editor), 1894–1904. Nelson Le Kime (Director), 1901–05.
   Robert Sand (Brussels Editor), 1904. Henri de Curzon, 1905–14.

Richard S. James

GUITAR PLAYER

Guitar Player was founded in 1967 by L. V. Eastman as a publication aimed
at guitar players young and old, amateur and professional. While much of the
magazine is made up of advertisements, the content ranges from feature articles
to newsy one-page "how to" regular columns. Information about all types of
guitars and guitar-playing styles are presented by acknowledged artists and teachers.

The feature articles include biographies of notable performers, past and present, who have made a mark in the commercial music world; pictorial essays of
guitarists, which are artistic in quality; in-depth reports on instruments and
accessories; and analyses of the music performed by leading artists. A notable
feature of the musical analyses is the inclusion of soundsheets to complement
the musical notation in the articles. Occasional special issues are devoted to such
topics as guitar synthesizers, new equipment, strat mania, and other topics.

The mainstay of *Guitar Player*, however, is its steadily evolving roster of
regular columns and workshops or "how to" columns. A list of the more
significant of these might include "Fretboard Basics" by Arnie Berle, "Studio
Log" by Tommy Tedesco, Jeff Berlin's "Bass & Beyond," "Jazz Improvisa-
tion" by Howard Roberts, Larry Coryell's "Contemporary Guitar," "Guitar
Workshop" by John Carruthers, Warren Sirota's "Electronic Guitar," Arlen
Roth's "Hot Guitar," and "Spotlight: Showcase for New Talent" by Mike
Varney. Other columns are "Back to Basics" by Rik Emmett, Keith Reinegger's
"Product Profile," Herb Mickman's "Bass Guitar Forum," and "Off the Wall"
by Teisco Del Ray.

The regularly featured departments of the magazine include "Books," "Sheet
Music," "Questions," "Guitaring," "Albums," "Action" (industry news),
"It's New," "Crosscheck" (editorial index), "Notational Symbols," and "Advertiser Index." A classified ad section assists musicians seeking instruments,
parts and accessories, instruction, and various other services.

The magazine is distributed throughout the United States and in more than
seventy other countries, both by subscription and by distribution through record

shops, instrumental music dealers, book stores, and newsstands. The circulation exceeds 170,000 and readership, according to biannual subscriber surveys, is predominantly male with an average age of twenty-six. The magazine reaches the professional and amateur reader equally well.

Perhaps the most impressive feature of *Guitar Player* is a Board of Advisors that reads like a veritable who's who of guitar artists: Will Ackerman, Laurindo Almeida, Chet Atkins, Jeff Baxter, Liona Boyd, Charlie Byrd, Stanley Clarke, Larry Coryell, Herb Ellis, Buddy Emmons, John Fahey, Tal Farlow, Jose Feliciano, Jerry Garcia, Billy Gibbons, Henry Kaiser, Carol Kaye, Barney Kessel, B. B. King, Paco de Lucia, John McLaughlin, Joe Pass, Les Paul, Howard Roberts, Juan Serrano, Johnny Smith, George Van Eps, Doc Watson, Johnny Winter, and Rusty Young. The board is active in furnishing articles, playing tips, and suggestions for stories.

The quality of writing is excellent, and the magazine is well edited. Furthermore, the *Guitar Player's* standards have steadily risen as have the quantity of music, color photographs, and pages. The editors have succeeded in bringing a great deal of information to a wide variety of readers.

The physical format of the magazine is a standard 8½" by 11" size with issues containing approximately 150 pages. It includes black and white as well as color photographs on glossy paper. Musical examples are included.

Information Sources

INDEXES
> External: Music Index, 1973–   . Magazine Index, 1977–   . Music Article Guide, 1979–   . Popular Music Periodicals Index, 1973–76.

REPRINT EDITIONS
> Microform: UMI.

LOCATION SOURCES
> Widely available.

Publication History

TITLE AND TITLE CHANGES
> *Guitar Player*.

VOLUME AND ISSUE DATA
> Volumes 1–   , 1967–   .

FREQUENCY
> Approximately 6/year though irregular, 1967–72. 8/year, 1973. Monthly, 1974–   .

PUBLISHER
> GPI Publications.

PLACE OF PUBLICATION
> Cupertino, California.

EDITORS
> L. V. Eastman, 1967–71. Jim Crockett, 1971–77. Don Menn, 1977–80. Tom Wheeler, 1980–   .

Victor Ellsworth

H

HARMONICON, THE

The Harmonicon was one of several journals devoted to the science of music that began publication during the first quarter of the nineteenth century. A monthly, it ran through eleven volumes and was edited by William Ayrton (1777–1858). The first five volumes (1823–27) bore the subtitle *A Journal of Music*. When publication ceased in 1833, the editor continued the aims of the journal in two related publications, *The Musical Library* and *The Monthly Supplement to the Musical Library*. *The Musical Library*, a compendium of music, was issued from April 1834 to March 1837, and contained eight volumes. Four of them featured vocal music, and the remainder instrumental music. The *Supplement* formed a companion to the *Library* and contained articles, reviews, biographical notices, and criticisms of performances, similar to the text portions of *The Harmonicon*. It was issued in three volumes (twenty-eight issues in all) spanning April 1834 to July 1836. Both the *Library* and the *Supplement* often reprinted material from *The Harmonicon*.

The intended audience for *The Harmonicon* was the middle-class and upper-middle-class British public, people who could afford pianos and who were eager to participate in the fashionable musical life of London. The editor's goal was to provide for this public an inexpensive periodical that would combine writings of all sorts about music with a variety of compositions to entertain and educate. The literary portion of each issue contained essays, reviews of new music, biographical memoirs of eminent musicians, criticisms of performances (including private concerts), miscellaneous correspondence, and foreign reports. Coverage of foreign news was superior to that found in contemporary journals. The topics of the essays were strikingly varied: ancient, oriental, and folk music; historical studies extending from Gregorian chant through the eighteenth century; articles on the characteristics of particular instruments; manuscript studies; music theory and acoustics; and aesthetics. These are generally of high quality, are well written, and give a clear picture of the knowledge available to a well-educated amateur. The contributors were primarily critics, music professionals, entrepreneurs, and learned amateurs.

The amount of music published in *The Harmonicon* is enormous. Each issue included between six and eight compositions; one of them was commissioned by the editor, while the rest "were selected from the best productions of the great masters" (1:1). The 829 compositions were arranged for voice and piano to permit home performance. All periods from the Renaissance to the early nineteenth century are represented.

The entire set has recently been reissued by Gregg International Publishers Limited. Each of the eleven volumes measures 7½" by 11", contains approximately 200 pages of text and lengthy musical supplements, and includes illustrations and portraits.

Information Sources

BIBLIOGRAPHY
Banfield, Stephen. "Aesthetics and Criticism." In *The Athlone History of Music in Britain: The Romantic Age 1800–1914,* edited by Nicholas Temperley, pp. 455–73. London: The Athlone Press, 1981.
Duckles, Vincent. "Musicology." In *The Athlone History of Music in Britain: The Romantic Age 1800–1914,* edited by Nicholas Temperley, pp. 483–502. London: The Athlone Press, 1981.
Temperley, Nicholas. [Letters to the Editor.] *Musical Times* 106 (April 1965): 277.
———. "MT and Musical Journalism." *Musical Times* 110 (June 1969): 583–86.
REPRINT EDITIONS
   Paper: Gregg International Publishers.
   Microform: Oxford Micro Publishing.
LOCATION SOURCES
   Library of Congress. Newberry Library (Chicago). Boston Public Library. New York Public Library. University of North Carolina. Widely available in reprint form.

Publication History

TITLE AND TITLE CHANGES
   The Harmonicon, A Journal of Music, 1823–1827. *The Harmonicon,* 1828–33. Succeeded by *The Musical Library,* 1834–37, and *The Monthly Supplement to the Musical Library,* 1834–36.
VOLUME AND ISSUE DATA
   The Harmonicon: vs. 1–11, 1823–33. *The Monthly Library:* vs. 1–8, 1834–37. *The Monthly Supplement to the Musical Library:* vs. 1–3, 1834–36.
FREQUENCY OF PUBLICATION
   Monthly.
PUBLISHER
   W. Pinnock.

PLACE OF PUBLICATION
    Westmead, Farnborough, Hants., England.
EDITOR
    William Ayrton, 1823–33.

Vincent J. Corrigan

HARP NEWS (HARP JOURNAL OF THE WEST COAST). See AMERI-CAN HARP JOURNAL

HIFI & MUSIC REVIEW. See STEREO REVIEW

HIFI REVIEW. See STEREO REVIEW

HIFI/STEREO REVIEW. See STEREO REVIEW

HIGH FIDELITY

Interest in do-it-yourself electronics increased considerably following the end of World War II when a host of U.S. servicemen trained in basic electronics joined the ranks of civilian hobbyists. Among this group were Milton B. Sleeper, a longtime publisher, and his Oxford- and Harvard-educated business manager, Charles Fowler. Determined to produce the first magazine for this growing number of what Fowler called "audio-philes" (1.1:8), Sleeper published the first issue of *High-Fidelity: The Magazine for Audio-philes* in 1951, with Fowler as editor.

The targeted "music listener" had an interest both in music, per se, and its accurate electronic reproduction. The dual nature of this listener was reflected in the magazine's content, which was divided into articles on new audio technologies with evaluations of the latest sound equipment and reviews of outstanding recordings with critiques of the performances and the recording techniques employed. The balance between the technical and the musical has varied considerably over the years.

High-Fidelity appeared quarterly during its first two years. When it went into bimonthly publication (v. 3), its format for years to come was already well established. The glossy pages (7½" by 10¾") were set in varying two- and three-column layout illustrated liberally with photographs and art work. The cover featured glossy photos of equipment, home installations, or an artist's design. The contents were divided into major sections on equipment and reviews of classical recordings; reviews of folk music, children's records, and spoken re cordings appeared occasionally. Jazz, Broadway, and other popular recordings were reviewed in a separate column. Commercial tape recordings were also reviewed. The remainder of each issue contained equipment tests, reviews of technically oriented books, letters, editorials, personal advertisements to buy or sell audio equipment, an audio company directory, and numerous record and audio company advertisements.

The earliest issues of *High-Fidelity* show a preference for the technical with articles by executives and chief engineers of major audio companies. Nonetheless, the content began to tilt in favor of music beginning with C. G. Burke's Beethoven discography ("Beethoven on Records," 1.4:33–56). It was so popular that composer discographies became a regular feature. Seeking lively musical commentary, Fowler brought in John Conly, formerly with *Atlantic Monthly* and *Pathfinder*, and several editors of *Musical America*, including James Hinton who began providing an opera review column (2.3). Book reviews started featuring biographies of musicians and music appreciation texts.

In 1954 Sleeper sold his interest in the magazine and set up Wyeth Press to publish several *High-Fidelity* spinoffs including the annual volume of *Records in Review* and the complementary *Tapes in Review* (1963). Disenchanted with the direction the magazine had taken (away from the interests of the home hi-fi tinkerer), Fowler left to direct a new Audiocom monthly, *Audiocraft*. John Conly became *High-Fidelity*'s new editor as it went into monthly publication (March 1954; 4.1). *High-Fidelity* began providing a general index to volumes in the final issue of each year.

Conly brought in Roland Gelatt of *Saturday Review* to be New York editor. Thus, he began the popular column, "Music Makers," that discussed artists' personalities as well as their recorded repertory (4.8). As special projects editor, Gelatt produced the Mozart Anniversary Issue (6.1); this issue marked both a switch to a January–December publishing year and Charles Fowler's return to *High-Fidelity* as publisher. When Gelatt became musical editor (7.5), he solicited articles from world-renowned music scholars and performers. Among such contributors were Robert Craft, Dimitri Mitropoulos, Milton Babbitt, Joseph Kerman, Andrew Porter, and Igor Stravinsky (10.6; June 1960).

In December 1958, *Audiocraft* joined *High Fidelity* to become *High Fidelity and Audiocraft*. The new magazine was approximately the same length (about 125 pages) as the old *High Fidelity* despite the inclusion of several of *Audiocraft*'s feature columns: "Audionews," "Hi-fi Shopper," and "Tape News and Views" (all eventually absorbed into the "Equipment" portion of the magazine). *Audiocraft*'s emphasis on technology gave *High Fidelity* an added dimension in the face of competition from the upstart look-alike *Stereo Review* (q.v.). Hoping to consolidate its readership, Audiocom merged with another Sleeper magazine, *Hi-Fi Music at Home*, creating *High Fidelity Including Audiocraft and Hi-Fi Music at Home* (9.6; June 1959). The new magazine's expanded equipment coverage resulted in the discontinuation of regular features such as composer discographies.

When Gelatt assumed editorship (1959), John Conly became chairman of a board of contributing editors that would include eminent musicologists H. C. Robbins Landon and Paul Henry Lang. Billboard Publishing Company obtained the magazine when it purchased Audiocom in February 1960. From the Tenth Anniversary Issue (11.4), it would simply be called *High Fidelity*. In 1962 Warren Syer, a moonlighting operatic tenor, replaced Charles Fowler as publisher, and again musical commentary began to crowd out technical discussions. During the early 1960s, reviews were expanded to cover imports and reissues, and articles on historical performance practice were written by authorities such as Denis Stevens and Noah Greenberg. Several issues focused on special themes such as FM (12.5), Claude Debussy (12.9), William Shakespeare (13.1), Richard Strauss (14.6), Wolfgang Amadeus Mozart (15.3 and 11), Richard Wagner (16.11), and rock music (17.11).

In 1963 *High Fidelity* started publishing Carnegie Hall programs, edited by Leonard Marcus, and interest in live music coverage was stirred. This inspired Billboard to acquire *Musical America* (q.v.) and incorporate it into *High Fidelity* beginning in 1965. *High Fidelity*, however, maintained two editions, one with and one without *Musical America* bound in. The integrity of equipment reports was greatly enhanced when testing was placed in the hands of CBS Laboratories in 1966. With the July 1968 issue, Leonard Marcus, then editor of the *Special Directory Issue* of *Musical America*, became editor of *High Fidelity*. Marcus promised expanded coverage of nonclassical music, and in 1977, the world of rock and pop music began receiving special attention in a section called "Backbeat." Classical music coverage included issues devoted to "New Music" (18.9), Hector Berlioz (19.3), the Beethoven Year (20.1), and Aaron Copland (20.11). Attention to jazz reached a high point with the Duke Ellington Issue (24.11).

In 1974 ABC Leisure Magazines acquired *High Fidelity* at a time when audio equipment reports were gaining prominence. Special equipment issues include the Twenty-fifth Anniversary Issue, in two parts (26.4–5), recounting audio developments since the 1950s and the centenary of the phonograph (27.1). A trend toward fewer music articles and fewer of the longer "Essay" reviews shrank the magazine to its ultimate length of approximately eighty pages per issue. In 1980 when Warren Syer and Leonard Marcus left, special projects editor, William Tynan, took over the editorship (31.1). He maintained the emphasis on equipment and furthered the trend toward more coverage of contemporary pop music. His Special Thirtieth Anniversary Issue explored the next thirty years of possible audio developments (31.4). With the July 1989 issue (39.7) *High Fidelity* ceased publication, citing changes in the consumer electronics market, and transferred subscribers to *Stereo Review* (q.v.).

Information Sources

BIBLIOGRAPHY
Keller, Michael, and Carol Lawrence, "Music Literature Indexes in Review." *Notes* 36 (1980): 598–99.

Mikkawi, Carol Lawrence. "Music Periodicals: Popular and Classical Record Reviews
and Indexes." *Notes* 34 (1977): 93, 100.
INDEXES
Internal: each volume indexed (vs. 4–).
External: Music Index, 1951– . Music Article Guide, 1965– . Readers' Guide
to Periodical Literature, 1961– . RILM Abstracts, 1969– . Popular Music
Periodicals Index, 1973–76. Classical reviews in *High Fidelity* 's annual "Records
in Review."
REPRINT EDITION
Microform: UMI.
LOCATION SOURCES
Widely available with the exception of v. 1

Publication History

TITLE AND TITLE CHANGES
High-Fidelity: The Magazine for Audio-Philes, 1951–52. *High-Fidelity: The Mag-
azine for Music Listeners*, Summer 1952–November 1958. *High Fidelity and
Audiocraft*, December 1958–May 1959. *High Fidelity Including Audiocraft and
Hi-Fi Music at Home*, June 1959–March 1961. *High Fidelity*, April 1961–January
1965. *High Fidelity Incorporating Musical America*, February 1965–89.
VOLUME AND ISSUE DATA
Volumes 1–39.7, 1951–89.
FREQUENCY OF PUBLICATION
Quarterly, 1951–52. Bimonthly, 1953. Monthly, 1954–July 89.
PUBLISHERS
Radiocom, Inc., Summer 1951. Audiocom, Inc., Fall 1951–January 1960. Bill-
board Publishing Company, February 1960–August 1974. ABC Leisure Maga-
zines, September 1974–89.
PLACES OF PUBLICATION
Great Barrington, Massachusetts, 1951–June 1981. New York, July 1981–89.
EDITORS
Charles Fowler, Summer 1951–November 1953. John Conly, March 1954–
June 1959. Roland Gelatt, July 1959–May 1968. Leonard Marcus, June 1968–
December 1980. William Tynan, 1981–1985. Michael Riggs, 1986–89.

Matthew Steel

HIGH FIDELITY AND AUDIOCRAFT. See HIGH FIDELITY

**HIGH FIDELITY INCLUDING AUDIOCRAFT AND HI-FI MUSIC AT
HOME.** See HIGH FIDELITY

HIGH FIDELITY INCORPORATING MUSICAL AMERICA. See HIGH
FIDELITY and MUSICAL AMERICA

I

IN THEORY ONLY

In Theory Only, widely known as *ITO,* is a publication of the Michigan Music Theory Society, produced by graduate students of the University of Michigan School of Music. The announced purpose of the journal is "to provide an alternative to the established theoretical organs, the *Journal of Music Theory* and *Perspectives of New Music*" (*ITO* 1.1:1). Like *Theory and Practice* (q.v.) and its sister journal *Indiana Theory Review* (q.v.) from Indiana University, its intent has been to publish shorter articles, serving as a forum even for work in progress, and to do so speedily with a minimum of editing, policies that continue to provide a welcome proliferation of outlets and opportunities for members of the profession. The range of music acceptable for discussion is wide, covering not only the classical and contemporary Western repertoire, but also jazz, popular music, and the music of other cultures. One of the most notable and refreshing features of the journal is its inclusion of humor, satire, games, crossword puzzles, and other items, all related to music theory, of course, but providing an enjoyable leavening that is conducive to a spirit of learning. Among those most involved with the founding of the journal were Professor Richmond Browne and two graduate students at that time: Henry J. Martin and Edwin Hantz. Emerging from very modest beginnings, the journal has become recognized in the discipline, with a national readership.

The journal averages about forty pages per single issue and typically contains about four feature items—articles, reviews of major music theory books, and other features—averaging eleven pages in length. The articles are wide-ranging in nature: analysis, analysis as related to performance, theoretical and philosophical speculation, pedagogy, and reviews have been the main types. Analysis symposia have appeared in six issues devoted to works by Frédéric Chopin, Wolfgang Amadeus Mozart, Johannes Brahms, Johann Sebastian Bach, Franz

Schubert, and Franz Liszt. A recently added feature (beginning with 7.3) is a series of articles under the general heading "Pedagogically Speaking." Other features that have appeared with some regularity include letters to the editor(s), announcements of journals and conferences, reports on conferences, "Comment," "Quaestionis Gratia," and "Exempli Gratia." Listings of theses and dissertations have been included, but not as often as (apparently) originally intended. In addition, special issues have included 5.1, devoted entirely to *An Annotated Bibliography of Articles on Serialism, 1955–80* by John D. Vander Weg. V. 5.6–7 is entitled *Studies in Musical Perception and Cognition.* Perhaps the most ambitious special issue was one entitled the *Index of Music Theory in the United States, 1955–70,* with subsections for "Authors," "Subjects," "Pieces," and "Theorists," edited by Richmond Browne.

By far the most prolific contributor to *ITO* has been Charles J. Smith, formerly a graduate student at Michigan and one of the early editors of the journal. The earlier issues featured primarily the writing of graduate students. Some of the other multiple contributors were Henry J. Martin, Edwin Hantz, and Marion Guck. By v. 2 some quite prominent names of professionals in the discipline began to appear, such as Richmond Browne, Roy Travis, Robert Morris, Robert Gauldin, David Lewin, Joel Lester, and Milton Babbitt, among others. More recently, prominent theorists contribute at least half of the material. Many of the younger scholars who have contributed either as graduate students or in the early stages of their teaching careers have assumed important faculty positions in more recent years.

The first volume of the journal is dated April 1975. Twelve issues appeared for each of the first three volumes, dated on a monthly basis. From v. 4 (April 1976) onward there have been eight issues per volume. The appearance of the issues under both plans lagged further and further behind the official date, and there have been several double issues (and even one designated as covering five months). This is a typical and understandable situation for a student-produced publication, dependent upon voluntary labor. It was eliminated very neatly, however, with the appearance of 5.4 (May 1981): the previous issue had been dated July 1979, and a new policy was announced whereby each issue would simply be given the actual date of its appearance. Thus there are no issues of *ITO* for 1980, and the exact calendar run of a volume is somewhat variable.

In Theory Only is published in a stapled format on standard $8\frac{1}{2}''$ by $11''$ paper, typewritten. At first the reproduction was by the ditto process; greater clarity was gradually attained by changing to mimeograph, photo offset, and other methods. Musical examples and charts are generally in the form of handwritten, camera-ready copy as provided by their authors. Internal indexing has been provided consistently in the last issue of each volume. There is no advertising, aside from announcements of conferences, calls for papers, and similar announcements.

Information Sources

BIBLIOGRAPHY
Rahn, John. "I. *In Theory Only*; II. Rhythm and Talk About It." *Perspectives of New Music* 15 (1977): 234–38.
INDEXES
Internal: each volume indexed.
External: RILM, 1976– . Music Index, 1975– . Bibliographie des Musikschrifttums, 1977–78. Music Article Guide, 1984– .
REPRINT EDITIONS
Microform: UMI.
LOCATION SOURCES
Widely available.

Publication History

TITLE AND TITLE CHANGES
In Theory Only.
VOLUME AND ISSUE DATA
Volumes 1– , 1975– .
FREQUENCY OF PUBLICATION
Irregular.
PUBLISHER
University of Michigan School of Music Graduate Theory Association
PLACE OF PUBLICATION
Ann Arbor, Michigan.
EDITORS
Henry J. Martin, April–May 1975. Edwin Hantz, 1975–76. Marion A. Guck and Charles J. Smith, 1976–78. Charles T. Horton, 1978–79. David C. Carlson and John D. Vander Weg, 1979–81. Marion A. Guck and John D. Vander Weg, 1981. John D. Vander Weg, 1981–82. David C. Carlson, 1982–83. Dave Headlam, 1984–85. William Lake, December 1985–January 1987. Robert Snarrenberg, March 1987– . Mauro Botelho, 1989– . Richmond Browne served as Supervising Editor for 3.7–11, the *Index of Music Theory in the United States, 1955–70*.

Paul B. Mast

INDIANA THEORY REVIEW

Indiana Theory Review is a publication of the Graduate Theory Association of the Indiana University School of Music. The announced purpose of the journal was to provide a means of communication among graduate theory students at Indiana University, who felt that their academic situation was overly, and detrimentally, diffuse. The president of the Graduate Association, James Skoog, was one of the principals in the founding of the journal; Vernon L. Kliewer has served as faculty adviser from v. 1 to the present.

The *Review* averages about sixty-seven pages in length and, from the first issue, has maintained the following basic format: "Open Forum," consisting variously of letters, editorial comment, reports, and similar pieces; articles; and "Potpourri," featuring, in most issues, an "Annotated Bibliography of Theses and Dissertations at Indiana University" as well as interviews, reviews, other bibliographies, and the like. One or another of these features has occasionally been omitted, and a few others inserted from time to time. V. 6:1–2 is a double issue dated Fall 1982–Winter 1983 and dedicated to Richard P. Delone (1928–84). A unique (for this journal) inclusion in this issue is the composition published in the Open Forum, "*In Memoriam*: Peter Delone" by Micah Rubenstein.

An issue typically contains three or four articles averaging fifteen pages each, but varying from seven to thirty-eight pages. The majority of articles are analytical in nature, and a large proportion of these are devoted to the twentieth century: music of Darius Milhaud, Igor Stravinsky, Carl Ruggles, Charles Ives, Arnold Schönberg, Alban Berg, Anton von Webern, Béla Bartók, Roger Sessions, Olivier Messiaen, George Crumb, John Cage, Elliott Carter, György Ligeti, and others. At the other end of the spectrum, all the articles in 2.1 (Fall 1978) are devoted to Guillaume de Machaut and the fourteenth century, and other issues have included work on the music of Gilles Binchois and Guillaumel Dufay, Don Carlo Gesualdo, J. S. Bach, J. C. Bach, Johann Kuhnau, Franz Josef Haydn, Wolfgang Amadeus Mozart, and Ludwig van Beethoven. The sixteenth and nineteenth centuries are much less represented, although both, especially the former, receive attention in the area of the history of theory, and there are some articles on Frédéric Chopin, Franz Liszt, Modest Mussorgsky Richard Wagner, Johann Strauss, and Amy Beach. All in all, the *Review*'s contents mark a welcome change in emphasis from that often encountered in the discipline.

In addition to the analytical articles and those on the history of theory, there have been others dealing with pedagogy, perception/cognition, computer research, the linguistic approach to music theory, phenomenology, aesthetic-philosophical speculation, analytical methods, and the analytically oriented subjects of "textural vocabulary" and "musical density." Some particularly useful lists or surveys include "Theory Texts 1978–1979: A Survey" by Mary Wennerstrom (2.3:39–48), "On the Teaching of Theory Teaching: A Selective Bibliography of Music Theory Pedagogy" by Michael R. Rogers (5.1:61–82), and "An Index to Schenkerian Analyses of Beethoven Piano Sonatas and Symphonies" by David Neumeyer and Rudy T. Marcozzi (6.1/2:101–17).

There have been many other contributors, far too many to name, and not all graduate students; some prominent ones are Gary Wittlich, the late Richard P. Delone, Allen Winold, Robert Gauldin, Robert S. Hatten, Laura Mattern Snyder, John L. Snyder, Sharon Boylan, Judy Lochhead, Susan Tepping, R. A. Campbelle, V. Kofi Agawu, Michael Burdick, Gary Danchenka, Richard Devore, and Reed Hoyt. As one might expect even among mature students, the quality of the articles varies, but in general it is quite high, and of course many of the others are the thoroughly professional products of faculty members at Indiana University and elsewhere. The *Review* has become a recognized journal in the discipline, with a regional-national scope.

The first volume is dated Fall 1977, and the journal has appeared three times yearly since that date with relative regularity and remarkable consistency in format, in spite of an apparent policy of the Graduate Association that has brought a change in editor approximately once per year. One significant change in editorial policy was announced in 2.2 (Winter 1979): while previous to that date the articles and reviews accepted for publication were restricted to those by graduate theory students of Indiana University, the new policy sought submissions from anyone. In the same issue, a three-year grant to the journal from the Office of Research and Development of Indiana University was announced.

Indiana Theory Review is published in a stapled paperbound format, about 6" by 9¾", typewritten (computer-formatted type, beginning with 3.1), and reduced by the photocopying process. Musical examples and charts include photocopies from printed sources as well as very legible handwritten ones. So far there has been no internal indexing in the *Indiana Theory Review*. There is also no advertising, aside from announcements of conferences, calls for papers, and the like.

Information Sources

BIBLIOGRAPHY
Notes 34 (June 1978): 888.
INDEXES
External: RILM, 1978– . Music Index, 1978– .
LOCATION SOURCES
Widely available.

Publication History

TITLE AND TITLE CHANGES
Indiana Theory Review.
VOLUME AND ISSUE DATA
Volumes 1– , 1977– .
FREQUENCY OF PUBLICATION
3/year.
PUBLISHER
Indiana University School of Music Graduate Theory Association.
PLACE OF PUBLICATION
Bloomington, Indiana.
EDITORS
Ann K. Gebuhr, 1977–78. Kate Covington, 1978–79. Robert A. Campbelle, 1979–80. Sharon H. Boylan, 1980–81. Susan Tepping, 1981–82. John Wm. Schaffer, 1982–83. Rudy Marcozzi, 1983–86. Eric J. Issacson, 1987. Raymond Foster, 1988– .

Paul B. Mast

INSTRUMENTALIST

Instrumentalist first appeared in 1946, a postwar era when many band and orchestra directors were reactivating school music programs left dormant during the war. Its purpose was clearly stated in the very first issue: "The *Instrumentalist* under the sponsorship of the Association for the Advancement of Instrumental Music—Devoted to the interests of school and college band and orchestra directors, instrumental teachers, and teacher-training specialists in music education" (1.1:3).

The first issue, which was forty-four pages long, contained articles on instrument classes, popular marches, care and repair of instruments, and other topics including one essay each (called a "clinic") for brass, woodwinds, strings, and percussion. By the tenth anniversary issue (10.1, September 1955) there were also departmental articles entitled "New Music," "Flute Facts," and "Marching Band," but none on the care and repair of instruments. There were contributing editors in the thirtieth anniversary issue (30.1, August 1975) for "Jazz," "Electronic Music," the "National Band Association," and the "National School Orchestra Association" in addition to "Flute Facts," "Woodwind," "Brass," "String," "Marching Bands," "New Music," and "Percussion." In a more recent issue (40.3) contributing editors included those found in the thirtieth anniversary issue plus one each for clarinet, saxophone, oboe, bassoon, trombone, tuba, and computers.

The above sampling of contributing editors and departments suggests a consistency in retaining areas of continuing interest as well as an adaptation to newer musical styles and technologies. *Instrumentalist* kept pace, for example, with the rise of the jazz band movement in the early 1970s, the addition of computer-assisted instruction to instrumental programs in the mid–1970s, and more recently to the continued interest in both electronic music and drum corps. *Instrumentalist* also published issues throughout the bicentennial year (beginning with 30.1; a special tribute to the armed forces) that focused on the American musical heritage and included articles on bicentennial programming, concerts, and festivals.

Feature articles in *Instrumentalist* often include interviews with noted music personalities or groups. Recent examples range from Shinicki Suzuki (June 1985) and Joseph Silverstein (February 1985), to Peter Schickele (September 1985) and the Canadian Brass (April 1985). Other articles focus on a variety of practical and pedagogical issues such as competition, fund-raising techniques, arranging, and corps style marching. A report on drum corps and color guard activities has appeared annually in *Instrumentalist* since 1975. Articles, usually ten to fifteen per issue, are between five and ten pages in length. They are most frequently contributed by public school and college band and orchestra directors, or performer/teachers on a specific instrument.

An important service is provided monthly for instrumental ensemble directors by the magazine's "New Music Reviews." New titles are catalogued according to performance group (concert band, ensemble, jazz band, marching band, orchestra, and string orchestra) and assigned grade level descriptions from 1 (for beginners in their first year) through 6 (very difficult music for advanced college players and professionals). Reviewers also single out the better pieces within performance media as being (1) of exceptional quality, or (2) highly recommended. Musical selections of lesser quality are either described in a single paragraph or appear only in a listing of the title and basic publication information.

Beginning in February 1985 (39.7) *Instrumentalist* has periodically included a "Job Guide" that ranges from various teaching positions to openings in symphony orchestras. Applicant qualifications and means for interested persons to obtain additional information are included.

A number of other regular entries in *Instrumentalist* either provide information or offer opportunities for readers to express or develop ideas. Examples of the former are: "What's the Score," which functions as a bulletin board for readers by announcing recent competition winners, personnel changes in leading symphony orchestras, and so on; a "Calendar" of upcoming symposia, festivals, and the like; "News to Us," which describes innovative products from the music industry; "Software Review," which rates the content, ease of use, sound quality, and other aspects of computer software appropriate for various student levels; and the "Music Store," which consists of brief advertisements for a variety of music materials. Columns that offer opportunities for readers to express ideas or opinions include "From Our Readers" (letters to the editor), "Idea Exchange," and "Challenge" (a forum for opinions and ideas).

An annual directory of summer camps, clinics, and workshops is presented each spring in *Instrumentalist*. The list is arranged by state and then by camp name and city with information regarding the type of camp, student age level, length and dates, cost, and best source of additional information. The 1985 directory (39.8, March 1985) contained 152 entries from forty-two states and four foreign countries.

Advertisements in *Instrumentalist* are indicative of the close association between the music industry and the music education profession. They are typically for instruments, music festivals and schools, band uniforms and accessories, instrument method books, sheet music publishers, and other music products and services.

The number of issues published per year has increased gradually. Five issues per year were published from 1946 through 1949, that is, bimonthly in September, November, January, March, and May. Between 1950 and 1957 that number increased to eleven per year. Since 1978, *Instrumentalist* has been published monthly, with individual issues ranging from 80 to 120 pages.

The page size (approximately 8¼" by 11¼") of *Instrumentalist* has remained essentially the same over its forty-year history. However, cover designs have changed markedly, becoming more and more sophisticated as evidenced by the seventeen awards that the covers have earned from the Educational Press Association of America. In the fortieth anniversary issue of *Instrumentalist* (40.1) twenty-four representative covers were reproduced as a brief visual history of the journal's style. No photographs were used on covers until September 1954 when the first black and white cover photo appeared. The first full-color covers were presented in 1959.

Information Sources

BIBLIOGRAPHY
"Tenth Anniversary Issue." *Instrumentalist* 10 (September 1955).
"Twenty-Fifth Anniversary Issue." *Instrumentalist* 25 (August 1970).
"Fortieth Anniversary Issue." *Instrumentalist* 40 (August 1985).
INDEXES
External: Music Article Guide, 1965– . Music Index, 1949– . RILM, 1976–
. Education Index, 1983– . Music Psychology Index, v. 2 (1978), and v. 3 (1984). Music Therapy Index, v. 1, 1976. Bibliographie des Musikschrifttums, 1950, 1960–61.
LOCATION SOURCES
Widely available.

Publication History

TITLE AND TITLE CHANGES
Instrumentalist.
VOLUME AND ISSUE DATA
Volumes 1– , 1946– .
FREQUENCY OF PUBLICATION
5/year, 1946–49. Increasing frequency, 1950–56. 11/year, 1957–77. Monthly, 1978– .
PUBLISHERS
The Association for the Advancement of Instrumental Music, 1946–48. The Instrumentalist Company, 1949– .
PLACES OF PUBLICATION
Glen Ellyn, Illinois, 1946–53. Evanston, Illinois, 1954–84. Northfield, Illinois, 1984– .
EDITORS
Traugett Rohner, September 1946–August 1966. James A. Mason, May 1965–August 1966. John M. Christie, September 1966–June 1970. Kenneth L. Neidig, August 1970–July 1984. John Kuzmich, Jr., August 1984–November 1984. John M. Christie, December 1984–April 1985. Jean Oelrich, May 1985–November 1985. Anne Driscoll, February 1986–October 1986. Elaine Guregian, November 1986– .

Vincent J. Kantorski

INTER-AMERICAN MUSIC REVIEW

Inter-American Music Review is quite unusual in the annals of scholarly periodical literature insofar as it is edited, published, and mostly written by one person, Robert Murrel Stevenson, long renowned as a champion of the music and musicians of the Iberian peninsula and the Americas. Stevenson, as chief contributor of articles as well as reviews, herein augments a personal bibliography of already formidable proportions.

Issued semiannually, beginning in the fall of 1978, the *Inter-American Music Review* specializes, by design, in the music of the Western Hemisphere before 1900, although material of European provenance is occasionally treated. Those familiar with Stevenson's style of writing will immediately recognize his heavily footnoted and wonderfully detailed work. Cathedral music in Latin America is one of the denser threads in the journal's tapestry, as can be noted from articles on the cathedrals at Caracas and San Juan (Puerto Rico) in the inaugural issue through the biographical essays on Puebla chapelmasters in vs. 5.2 and 6.1. Researchers in need of primary source material in this area of sacred music will find the excerpts from capitular archives of singular importance. And alongside the bibliographical treasures, complete musical addenda appear frequently. For example, five sacred choral works by Pedro Bermudez, chapelmaster at Puebla in the very early 1600s, can be found in 5:28–62.

One special issue has been published: "Caribbean Music History: A Selective Annotated Bibliography with Musical Supplement" (4.1; Fall 1981). The bibliography itself runs to eighty-four pages, and the ten-item supplement adds another twenty-eight pages. Vs. 6.2 and 7.1 contain scores only, by Latin American composers of the colonial era. A sampling of Latin liturgical works, Spanish secular part songs, and other secular pieces in native dialect by such prominent figures as Juan Gutiérrez de Padilla, Tomás de Torrejón y Velasco, Manuel de Zumaya, and Juan de Araujo can be found here.

Most of the scholarly articles, averaging ten to twenty pages, are on Latin American topics, although some have centered on the music of the United States. In this regard, v. 2.1, which contains the following—all, of course, by Stevenson—is notable: "The Eighteenth-Century Hymn Tune" (2:1–33), "Jeremiah Clarke Hymn Tunes in Colonial America" (2:35–39), "William Batchelder Bradbury in Europe 1847–1849" (2:41–44), and "Roy Harris at UCLA: Neglected Documentation" (2:59–73). V. 5.1 contains a fifty-eight-page article on "The Music that George Washington Knew: Neglected Phases."

Congratulatory essays, usually on the occasion of significant birthday anniversaries, appear prominently. Subjects of these essays include Francisco Curt Lange, Domingo Santa Cruz, Nicolas Slonimsky, Carleton Sprague Smith, Gilbert Chase, Guillermo Espinosa, John Cage, Macario Santiago Kastner, and Isabel Aretz. Necrological tributes are also provided.

Most issues contain ten or more extended book reviews, some of them running to several pages. A considerable number of the items covered are foreign language materials (usually Spanish or Portuguese) unlikely to be reviewed in other predominantly English journals. Doctoral dissertations are brought into the review column occasionally. The first issue, in fact, features reviews of five dissertations on Spanish subjects and three on Mexican subjects.

Inter-American Music Review has been thus far entirely devoid of advertisements. Its issues, 6¾" by 10" (1–6.1) and 8¼" by 10¾"(since 6.2), usually contain about 110 pages. The only illustrative material to appear has been in the form of musical excerpts or complete works. As indicated earlier, most of the articles and other contributions are in English; Spanish appears infrequently.

Information Sources

BIBLIOGRAPHY
> Thompson, Donald. "Review of 'Caribbean Music History' by Robert M. Stevenson." *Latin American Music Review* 4 (Fall/Winter, 1983): 282–86.

INDEXES
> External: Music Index, 1978– . RILM, 1969–1977. Arts and Humanities Citation Index, 1980– .

LOCATION SOURCES
> Widely available.

Publication History

TITLE AND TITLE CHANGES
> *Inter-American Music Review.*

VOLUME AND ISSUE DATA
> Volumes 1– , 1978– .

FREQUENCY OF PUBLICATION
> Semiannual.

PUBLISHER
> Robert Stevenson.

PLACE OF PUBLICATION
> Los Angeles, California.

EDITOR
> Robert Stevenson.

John E. Druesedow

INTERFACE—JOURNAL OF NEW MUSIC RESEARCH

Interface—Journal of New Music Research is "devoted to discussion of all questions which fall into the borderline areas between music on the one hand, and physical and human sciences or related technologies on the other. New fields of research, as well as new methods of investigation in known fields, receive special emphasis" (14.1–2: inside cover). The first issue appeared in April 1972 as a result of the "continuation and merger" of *Jaarboek* (Seminar for Musicology in Ghent) and *Electronic Music Reports* (Institute of Sonology in Utrecht).[1] Editors included ten prominent composers, musicologists, and theorists based in Ghent and Utrecht; with v. 6 the number was reduced to four and an international advisory board of fifteen was added.

The high scholarly intent of the journal is obvious on many levels. Technical topics range from "Micro-Frequency Modulation in Sound Synthesis" by Rafael

Bedaux (3.2:89–108) to "Design Considerations for a Multiprocessor Digital Sound System" by Stanley Haynes (10.3/4:221–44). Aside from electronic/computer music technology, a considerable number of articles address issues of music theory, for example, "Toward a Theory of Musical Cognition" by Otto E. Laske (4.2:147–208). Several articles also deal with the analysis of a specific composition—Maurice Kagel's "Anagrama," Iannis Xenakis's "Nomos Alpha," and the sketches and worksheets of electronic compositions by Stockhausen from 1952–67. Lengthy interviews with composers such as György Ligeti, Alvin Lucier, and Karlheinz Stockhausen are also included. Other articles have addressed new instrumental techniques, music education, and pedagogy. Descriptive articles have periodically appeared on important Electronic Music Studios, and for several years an attempt was made to list new compositions realized at the Institute of Sonology. Contributors are largely music professionals from Western Europe, the United States, and Canada.

To date three landmark articles or issues have been seen. In 4.1 (1975) the proceedings of the historically significant "International Conference on New Musical Notation Report" were published. Vs. 9.3/4 (1980) and 12.1/2 (1983) celebrated *Interface*'s tenth anniversary, in conjunction with a symposium that was held on 29 September 1981 at the Seminar of Musicology at Ghent as part of the ISCM World Music Days. V. 9 primed participants for the symposium and addressed the topic, "The Composer Between Man and Music." In v. 12 the proceedings of the Ghent conference, "Composer, Society," were included in a special three-language issue.

Interface contains no regular departments, although book reviews and editorials are found with some frequency. Until 1976, *Interface* was published twice yearly (approximately 70–120 pages per issue). With v. 5 the journal began quarterly publication, although issues have usually appeared in a combined format, which still averages around 120 pages in length. The size, 6¼" by 9½", has remained the same since its inception. The small amount of advertising that is included is generally placed by scholarly journals, international conferences and educational programs, and music publishing and record companies. Most articles are in English (the editors' stated preference), but entries have also been published in French and German. More recent issues have provided English abstracts, as well as a photo and biography of each article's author. Other photos appear as necessitated by content; musical examples abound. A cumulative index to vs. 1–10 (1972–81) is found in 10.3/4:251–60.

Note

1. As of 1 March 1986, the Institute of Sonology, previously part of the University of Utrecht, is now located at the Royal Conservatory, The Hague.

Information Sources

BIBLIOGRAPHY

Basart, Ann P. "Editorial Practice and Publishing Opportunities in Serious English-Language Music Journals: A Survey." *Cum Notis Variorum* 79 (Jaunary–February 1984): 39.

INDEXES
Internal: vs. 1–10 in v. 10.
External: Music Index, 1974– . RILM, 1976– . Bibliographie des Musiksch-
rifttums, 1972– . Arts and Humanities Citation Index, 1976– . INSPEC (online
file from *Interface* 1.1).
REPRINT EDITIONS
Microform: Swets & Zeitlinger Bv. (1972–85).
LOCATION SOURCES
Widely available.

Publication History

TITLE AND TITLE CHANGES
Interface—Journal of New Music Research.
VOLUME AND ISSUE DATA
Volumes 1– , 1972– .
FREQUENCY OF PUBLICATION
Semiannual, 1972–75. Quarterly, 1976– .
PUBLISHER
Swets Publishing Service.
PLACE OF PUBLICATION
Printed in the Netherlands by Offsetdrukkerij Kanters B. V., Alblasserdam.
EDITORS
Jan L. Broeckx, Lucien Goethals, K. Goeyvaerts, Walter Landrieu, Herman
Sabbe, G. M. Koenig, Otto E. Laske, Stan Tempelaars, G. Vermeulen, Frits C.
Weiland, 1972–76. Broeckx, Sabbe, Koenig, Weiland, 1977–80. Broeckx, Sabbe,
Jos Kunst, Weiland, 1981–86. Marc Leman, Sabbe, Kunst, Weiland, 1987. Le-
man, Sabbe, Weiland, 1988– .

Marilyn Shrude

INTERNATIONAL REVIEW OF MUSIC AESTHETICS AND SOCIOL-
OGY. See INTERNATIONAL REVIEW OF THE AESTHETICS AND SO-
CIOLOGY OF MUSIC

INTERNATIONAL REVIEW OF THE AESTHETICS AND
SOCIOLOGY OF MUSIC

With the support of the International Committee for Aesthetic Studies, the
Zagreb Music Academy began in June 1970 to publish a semiannual *International
Review of Music Aesthetics and Sociology* under the editorship of Ivo Supičić.
The editorial board, drawn from many countries, included Carl Dahlhaus and
Christoph-Hellmut Mahling from Germany, James Haar and Edward A. Lippman
from the United States, François Lesure and Olivier Revault D'Allones from
France, Frederick W. Sternfeld from England, and Zofia Lissa from Warsaw.
The advisory board was equally impressive, a worldwide roster of directors of

such organizations as conservatories, national and international music and philosophy associations, libraries, RILM, and UNESCO. Contributorship is likewise broadly international.

The opening article by Supičić, entitled "Instead of an Introductory Word," stated the need

> to get directly to the work and to try at least to formulate some elementary problems which inevitably arise even at the simple mention of the terms *music aesthetics* and *sociology of music*—scholarly fields to which for the first time in the world a review is especially devoted. (1.1:3)

In a highly literate exposition of the history of distinctions between "scientific" and "philosophical" knowledge as they have come to bear in the fields of musicology, sociology, and aesthetics, Supičić found that

> the more deeply the musicologist is concerned about all the problems raised by music, the more complex and deep aesthetic and philosophical problems he will be obliged to face. . . . Ultimately, the musicologist's mastery of a multiplicity of approaches and a variety of standpoints promotes musicological work towards a better scholarly knowledge and understanding of music. Music aesthetics and the sociology of music, and indirectly this review which is devoted to them, should contribute towards this direction. (1.1:14)

The periodical first appeared in much its final format: 5⅞" by 8¾", with a glossy cover on which the contents of the issue were listed. These were presented in several clearly defined sections: "Articles," "Discussions," "Reports and News," and "Reviews." Articles appeared in English, German, and French; short Slavic summaries were included, and reviewed material contained other languages as well. Perhaps the most significant change after the first issue was in the title, which became *International Review of the Aesthetics and Sociology of Music* with 2.1 (1971). Content remained the same, though the labels changed: major articles were now listed as "Original Scientific Papers," to be distinguished from "Review Papers."

The journal has maintained a standard consistent with the highest scholarly requirements and the original editorial philosophy. There is no advertising, although announcements of professional activities directly related to the field are occasionally found. Articles, six to eight per issue, range from ten to forty-five pages and include musical examples and illustrations as appropriate. Topics are fairly evenly divided between sociological and aesthetics perspectives, as suggested in the following list of representative major articles: C. Dahlhaus' "Soziologische Dechiffrierung von Musik—zu Th. W. Adorno's Wagnerkritik" (1.2:137–147), I. Supičić's "Expression and Meaning in Music" (2.2:193–212), "Linguistics: A New Approach for Musical Analysis?" by J.-J. Nattiez (4.1:51–68), Shuhei Hosokawa's "Considérations sur la musique mass-médiatisée" (12.1:21–50); and "Music in the Life of Man: Theoretical and Practical Foun dations for a World History'' by Barry S. Brook and David Bain (16.1:103–121). Occasionally there is a special focus—the first 1975 issue was devoted to the International Musicological Society Symposium held in Zagreb in the previous year.

Recent issues are still semiannual, run from 90 to 150 pages (as did previous issues) and treat such subjects as mass media and musical culture, the need for a sociology of Irish folk music, or the signifier and the signified in operas of Wolfgang Amadeus Mozart and Giuseppe Verdi (all in 15.1). The *Journal* has been well received, maintains excellent relations with the disciplines that it wishes to unite, and should continue to provide a forceful voice for broadened perspectives in musicology.

Information Sources

INDEXES
External: RILM, 1970– . Bibliographie des Musikschrifttums, 1970– . Arts and Humanities Citation Index, 1981– .
REPRINT EDITIONS
Microform: Swets and Zeitlinger Bv (1970–84).
LOCATION SOURCES
Widely available.

Publication History

TITLE AND TITLE CHANGES
International Review of Music Aesthetics and Sociology, 1970. *International Review of the Aesthetics and Sociology of Music*, 1971– .
VOLUME AND ISSUE DATA
Volumes 1– , 1970– .
FREQUENCY OF PUBLICATION
Semiannual.
PUBLISHER
Institute of Musicology, Zagreb Academy of Music.
PLACE OF PUBLICATION
Zagreb, Yugoslavia.
EDITOR
Ivo Supičić.

Ruth K. Inglefield

INTERNATIONAL SOCIETY OF BASSISTS JOURNAL

This truly international periodical is perhaps one of the most fascinating of the "specialized" journals published. It has a distinguished parentage, combines the best attributes of *Strad* (q.v.) and *American String Teacher* (q.v.), and exudes a dedication to the promotion of all aspects of the double bass that borders on fanaticism. The *International Society of Bassists Journal* is the result of a 1982 merger of *International Society of Bassists, Newsletter and Journal* (1974–82), edited by Lucas Drew, and *Bass World* edited by Barry Green and formerly titled *Probas*. Both parent periodicals were themselves the descendants of *Bass Sound Post* (1967–72), conceived by Gary Karr, double bass virtuoso and champion of the instrument as a legitimate solo vehicle. Karr inspired and encouraged double bassists to join together in a mutual undertaking to promote knowledge of and share information about the music and performers of the instrument.

The resultant periodical, now called *International Society of Bassists Journal*, is the literary arm of the International Society of Bassists (ISB). As Jeff Bradetich, current editor and executive director of the society, stated, "the *ISB* strives to communicate news, ideas, philosophies and opinions on all facets of musical life to students and professionals alike" (10.1:3).

The feature articles, four to seven per quarterly issue, encompass a variety of types: analyses of compositions, educational and philosophical essays, pedagogical articles, and profiles of artists, past and present. Contributors range from double bass performers and pedagogues to luthiers. A special pre–international convention issue promotes participation in said event. The departments section includes a "Members' Forum," "Symphony Profile" (double bass sections of orchestras), "Bass Events Around the World," "Jazz Scene," "Raising the Standards" (profiles of double bassists who have been leading contributors in performance and education), "Research Forum," "Recital Page," "New Releases," "Reviews," "Recommended Reading," "Awards," "Classified Ads," and an "Advertisers Index." Also included is a center-page foldout of a double bass of artistic or historical importance.

The current journal is highly professional in appearance and is a standard 8½" by 11" size. The covers, in color, feature unique photographs or illustrations of artistic interest. Issues, averaging forty pages, include numerous photographs, illustrations and musical examples. The journal relies heavily on advertisements and subscriptions for income.

Information Sources

INDEXES
> External: Music Index, 1974– .

LOCATION SOURCES
> Widely available.

Publication History

TITLE AND TITLE CHANGES
> *International Society of Bassists*, 1974–77. *Newsletter of the International Society of Bassists jornal*, 1977–81. *International Society of Bassists Journal*, 1982– *Bass World: Annual Journal* (1.4, 2.4, 3.4, 4.2, 5.2, 6.4, 7.3, 8.1, 8.2) *International Society of Bassists Magazine*, Fall 1983.   .

VOLUME AND ISSUE DATA
> Volumes 1– , 1974– .

FREQUENCY OF PUBLICATION
    Quarterly, 1974–79. 3/year, 1981–   .
PUBLISHER
    Northwestern University.
PLACE OF PUBLICATION
    Northwestern University, School of Music, Evanston, Illinois.
EDITOR
    Lucas Drew, 1974–81. Jack Steward, 1981–82. Jeff Bradetich, 1983–88. Paul
    Zibits, 1989–   .

Victor Ellsworth

INTERNATIONAL SOCIETY OF BASSISTS MAGAZINE. See INTER-
NATIONAL SOCIETY OF BASSISTS JOURNAL

───── J ─────

JAZZ EDUCATORS JOURNAL

In 1968, a newly formed organization of teachers and jazz artists calling itself the National Association of Jazz Educators began publishing the *NAJE Newsletter*. The base of operations for both organization and publication was Manhattan, Kansas. The editor for the first thirteen volumes, Matt Betton, Sr., proclaimed on the first pages of the *Newsletter* that theirs was "the only magazine dedicated to the development of jazz, America's only art form, in the schools."

Numerous articles on jazz pedagogy, improvisation, theory, history, and heritage have appeared, including those by such authors as Leonard Feather and Richard Rodney Bennett. Most of the information disseminated in the pages of this periodical, however, is written by college and public school teachers and deals with who played where (college and high school groups), sample programs, and "this is how I teach this aspect of jazz." Some specific article topics have included saxophone mouthpieces, vocal jazz vibrato, the use of computers and synthesizers in today's music, a brief biography of Louis Armstrong, and so on. Many of the current articles, five to ten per issue, are two pages or less, and nearly all are virtually buried among the pages and pages of advertisements, which now account for fully half of the *Educators'* length. A few of the issues have published full jazz arrangements and solo transcriptions. V. 15:3 proclaimed that each issue would thereafter be "devoted to a specific topic." Hence, all articles within an entire issue have focused on issues such as vocal jazz, improvisation, the rhythm section, and so on.

Additional features in past volumes have included "Readers Forum," the "NAJE Bulletin Board," "Jazz Festivals," "Something Worth Listening To," and "From the Editor." A standard formula of "Articles," "News," "Clinics," and "Departments" appeared when the editorship changed in 1981 from Betton to John Kuzmich, Jr. (13:3). All of v. 17 listed Roslyn Kuzmich as "interim editor,'' although no format changes were evident. John Kuzmich reappeared as editor with v. 18.

While no dates are given for v. 1.1–3, 1.4 contained twelve pages, and offered a publication date of March 1969. V. 2.3 (February/March 1970) saw a title change from *NAJE Newsletter* to *NAJE Educator*. A second title change, to the *Jazz Educators Journal*, occurred in 1981 with 13.2. The first issues were strictly in a newsletter format: announcements of the formation of NAJE, a call for members, a description of the new association's intent, and membership information. The first genuine article appeared with 2.2. The length of *Educators* began with two pages for 1.1; by 1971 (4.1), it ran forty pages and had begun to display advertising. Its standard frequency of issuance began at four per year, numbered to coincide with the academic calendar. The average issue now sports eighty to a hundred 8" by 11" pages; the pagination has been consistently separate from one number to the next. The magazine has gained an increasingly slick, professional format since its earliest days but has not altered its rather informal use of jazz vernacular in much of the prose. *Jazz Educators Journal* has always maintained its newsletter plus brief article format and remains an open forum for jazz educators to share their problems, successes, and enthusiasm with other interested musicians.

Information Sources

INDEXES
    External: Music Index, 1971– .
REPRINT EDITION
    Microform: Greenwood Press (1968–77).
LOCATION SOURCES
    Widely available.

Publication History

TITLE AND TITLE CHANGES
    NAJE Newsletter, 1968–69. *NAJE Educator*, 1970–81. *Jazz Educators Journal*, 1981– .
VOLUME AND ISSUE DATA
    Volumes 1– , 1968– .
FREQUENCY OF PUBLICATION
    Quarterly, with irregularities.
PUBLISHER
    National Association of Jazz Educators.
PLACE OF PUBLICATION
    St. Louis, Missouri.
EDITORS
    Matt Betton, Sr., 1969–81. John Kuzmich, Jr., 1981–85. Roslyn Kuzmich, interim editor, 1985. John Kuzmich, Jr., 1986– .

Paul B. Hunt

JAZZ-HOT

Jazz-Hot is a French periodical which deals exclusively with jazz. Begun in Paris in March 1935, it was among the first popular music journals, along with *down beat* (July 1934) (q.v.). Other popular music magazines have come and gone, but *Jazz-Hot* continues to be published today, fifty-one years after its founding, and the original editor, Charles Delaunay, still directs publication.

The roots of jazz can be traced to New Orleans, but the jazz appreciation movement was initially a European phenomenon. The first serious studies of jazz, as well as the early recordings collections, books, and periodicals on the subject all originated overseas. Jazz musicians of the 1920s and 1930s found a warmer reception in Europe than in America. The fascination with jazz in musical circles paralleled the effect of African sculpture and other "primitive" arts on artists in the first quarter of this century. Europeans, relatively unfamiliar with the widespread racial discrimination against blacks and not blinded by the social milieu from which jazz emerged, welcomed the new music and the black Americans who made it into their own countries.

Jazz-Hot began in 1935 as the official organ of the Fédération Internationale des Hot Clubs. By this time jazz had evolved into the swing and dance band styles of its "classical period" (1935–45). Public interest in jazz was strong, and *Jazz-Hot* made a successful debut. The first editors were Charles Delaunay and Hugues Panassié, two leading names in the world of jazz criticism. Under Delaunay and Panassié *Jazz-Hot* was a serious magazine whose mission was to present and promote an accurate account of jazz. An international troupe of writers and musicians was organized to report on the latest events. Contributors included John Hammond, Wilder Hobson, Boris Vian, Claude Luter, Claude Bolling, and Louis Armstrong.

For the first ten years of publication the magazine was printed in French and English. Great importance was attached to news from America, so that much of the reporting was simply accounts of who played what where. Correspondents tracked changes and stylistic evolution from "New Orleans" to "swing," "bop," "cool," and so on.

The magazine's contributors were rarely scholars, since jazz musicology was nonexistent, and very few classically trained musicologists were curious enough to investigate jazz. One noteworthy American contributor was John Hammond, a talent scout, recording producer, and critic who helped launch Benny Goodman, Count Basie, Teddy Wilson, Charlie Christian, and Billy Holiday. As a recording producer for Columbia and Vanguard, Hammond was a most effective catalyst in the development of jazz. Another important contributor in the early years was Boris Vian, famous French novelist and jazz trumpeter.

Jazz-Hot typically carried about six articles, two to three pages in length and mostly biographical in nature. Legendary talents like Louis Armstrong, Bessie Smith, and Coleman Hawkins were highlighted. Frequent discussions of what constituted "real" jazz as opposed to commercial imitations appeared early in the magazine. Each issue had a list of new recordings and recording reviews, concert announcements, and other news releases.

Publication ceased during the war years, 1939–45. When it resumed, *Jazz-Hot* was no longer bilingual, publishing now only in French. The editors placed a stronger emphasis on French jazz musicians while still reporting on American music. This change was warranted by the fact that after 1945 French jazz came of age. The 1920s and 1930s had been spent imitating and assimilating styles from America. Now France had its own musicians to nurture like Claude Bolling, Claude Luter, Django Reinhardt, Stéphane Grappelly, and Boris Vian.

In 1946 Panassié left *Jazz-Hot* in a dispute over the assessment of modern jazz. Composer and critic André Hodeir replaced Panassié the following year and from 1947–51 kept the journal at a formidably high musicological level. Hodeir, author of the influential book, *Hommes et Problèmes du Jazz* (1954), lent much-needed objectivity and, according to *down beat*'s Nat Hentoff, the highest standard to jazz criticism (*down beat*, 23:32). He emphasized the evolution of jazz styles and believed that the much-lauded New Orleans style was but the immature roots of real jazz. Hodeir also tried to reconcile the many warring factions of jazz fans during his years as editor.

Since 1950 *Jazz-Hot* has had numerous editors, but always under Charles Delaunay's directorship. The fundamental layout and goals of the journal have not changed. In recent years, *Jazz-Hot* has become less dogmatic in its opinions on the definition of "real" jazz. Today the magazine is more moderate and eclectic, with columns reserved for latest developments in "traditional music": blues, reggae, Brazilian music, and black sacred music.

The present format of the journal closely resembles its original one. After "Letters to the Editor" there are roughly six articles (usually biographical) about a musician or a group of musicians. These articles frequently take the form of interviews. A subsequent section, entitled "Hot Notes," reports on new recordings, concerts, and books. Top selections of the month are singled out. Following this current information are articles on traditional music, improvisation, and the history of jazz.

Jazz-Hot has played a significant role in making jazz known around the world. Their judgment has been excellent in identifying important talents. The style of writing is familiar, good-natured, and at times humorous. The quality of writing is high, especially when dealing with analyses and discussion of rhythm or the music itself. Written-out musical examples accompany many articles. *Jazz-Hot* is not, however, a musicological journal à la *Jazzforschung*. It remains an eclectic popular music magazine complete with hundreds of glossy photos and advertisements for stereo equipment and the like.

The cover is in color as are many of the advertisements. The rest of the photos are black and white. *Jazz-Hot* is 8″ by 11¾″, with issues, published on an occasionally irregular monthly basis, averaging sixty-eight to seventy pages.

Information Sources

BIBLIOGRAPHY

Carrière, Claude, Jean Delmas, and Daniel Nevers. "Infi(r)*me contribution à l'histoire de la modeste idéologie jazzoteuse des origines la guerre." *Jazz-Hot* 314 (1975): 21.

Constantin, Philippe. *Jazz-Hot* 252 (July–August 1969): 7ff.

Hess, Jacques B. *Jazz Magazine* 167 (June 1969): 5

J. D. "Jazz Hot a fêté ses 40 ans." *Jazz-Hot* 318 (July–August 1975): 23.

Jazz Journal 8 (March 1955): 12.

Jazz Magazine 206 (December 1972): 5–6.

Point du Jazz 7 (October 1972): 135–36.

REPRINT EDITIONS

Microform: Greenwood Press.

LOCATIONS

New York Public Library, v. 11– . Detroit Public Library, v. 14– .

Publication History

TITLE AND TITLE CHANGES

Jazz-Hot: Revue internationale de la musique de jazz, 1935–1939. *Le Bulletin du Hot Club de France*, 1945. *Revue de jazz hot*, 1946-1951. *Jazz-Hot*, 1951- .

VOLUME AND ISSUE DATA

Numbers 1–32, March 1935–July 1939. New series, numbers 1– , March 1945– .

FREQUENCY OF PUBLICATION

Monthly, with irregularities.

PUBLISHER

Hot Club de France.

PLACE OF PUBLICATION

Paris.

EDITORS

Charles Delaunay, 1935– . Hugues Panassié, 1935–46. André Hodeir, 1947–51. Robert Baudelet, 1951– . André Clergeat, 1951– . Phillipe Koechlin, 1951– . Laurent Goddet, 1951– .

Lyn Hubler

JAZZ JOURNAL. See JAZZ JOURNAL INTERNATIONAL

JAZZ JOURNAL INTERNATIONAL

For three decades, *Jazz Journal (International* was added to the title in 1977) reflected the passion for jazz and scholarship of its founder, Sinclair Traill, who began the magazine in May 1948. The legacy now is perpetuated by its editor and publisher, Eddie Cook, longtime jazz enthusiast and publishing executive who has directed publishing of the magazine since early 1979 and purchased it in late 1982.

A difficulty confronting any jazz magazine is defining its territory, and debates on the topic have dotted the decades of the magazine's existence. Its focus is regarded as "mainstream," a term created in its pages in the mid–1950s by Stanley Dance. However, in a 1981 article entitled "Keepers of the Flame," Bob Wilber stressed the importance of "keeping the traditionalism of jazz alive" while also developing "the idea of jazz being an individual expression" (34.11:7). Editor Eddie Cook specified, in late 1985 correspondence with the author, that the coverage includes "true" jazz from New Orleans through big band, bebop, mainstream, modern, and contemporary—but eschewing pseudic [sic] imitations and so-called avant-garde and freeform music. Diverse subcultures among jazz fans are hard to please, and an editorial in the thirty-eighth anniversary issue noted that "music must change as times and opinions change" and that *Jazz Journal* would try to "cater for the progression" but also try to retain loyal readers by continuing support of "all forms of jazz and the people who promote and create it" (38.5:2).

Features, generally one to two pages in length, are often expertly transcribed from thoughtful, in-depth interviews with leading jazz players. A notable early series profiled British jazz bands and performers, beginning with Freddy Randall in November 1948. Musicians of many nationalities have since been featured. A British emphasis is evident only in the "Jazz Diary," which lists jazz societies and live events, and in the predominence of British advertisers.

A regular early feature was "The Other Side of the Picture," explaining how various instruments work and the intricacies of playing them. A recent series, "The Forgotten Ones," reviews the careers of such stars of yesteryear as trumpeters Henry Levine and Hot Lips Page. Other special issues included surveys by the magazine of jazz in Scandinavia, Japan, and Germany.

Notable contributors over the years have included Stanley Dance, who wrote features on jazz styles and personalities and even a fiction piece; Steve Voce, whose "It Don't Mean a Thing" commentaries sometimes draw vociferous responses; former editor Mike Hennessey; and well-known jazz writers Barry McRae, Chris Sheridan, Floyd Levin, and Derrick Stewart-Baxter.

Record reviews have provided a major component of *Jazz Journal* content. Reviews were often detailed and lengthy in earlier years, but now are shorter and more numerous. In 1984, the magazine reviewed 622 albums, an average of more than fifty per issue. Selections span reissues of performances by traditionalists such as Fats Waller or the Dutch Swing College to new issues by modernists such as Stan Getz or Gerry Mulligan.

Content has been further enriched by a lively letters section, which drew international contributors from the outset. Entitled "One Sweet Letter from You"—after a popular jazz tune—it offers readers an opportunity to exchange information, ideas, and some verbal lances.

Jazz Journal was originally 8¼" by 10½" in size, then changed to a taller 8¼" by 11½" in February 1979, using larger text type. Cover photos were used from the beginning. Early issues averaged sixteen pages and gradually expanded to the usual forty- to forty-eight-page issue of today. Advertisements are mostly for records and festivals. Its monthly circulation has fluctuated from about 11,000 to over 12,000 in the late 1980s, with about 85 percent of its subscribers and newsstand buyers being Europeans. Though published only in English, its international coverage is indicated by a list of agents from thirty countries.

Traill began a smaller-scale publication entitled *Pick Up* in 1946. It was short-lived but important as the progenitor of *Jazz Journal* in that it helped develop a circle of contributors and supporters. Early issues reported on concerts, musicians, records, and the widespread English rhythm clubs, which predated the many present-day jazz societies in the United States and elsewhere. In 1974, Traill sold the magazine to its printer, Novello & Company, which combined it with another acquisition, *Jazz & Blues* magazine, then leased it in early 1977 to the United Kingdom subsidiary of *Billboard* magazine. For the next two years it included coverage of the more popular and fusion music embraced by *Billboard* (q.v.). Pitman Periodicals Ltd., of which Cook was then managing director, leased rights to *Jazz Journal* in early 1979, and Cook purchased it outright at the end of 1982.

Information Sources

INDEXES
>External: Music Index, 1950– . Popular Music Periodicals Index, 1973–76.

REPRINT EDITION
>Microform: UMI (1948–77).

LOCATION SOURCES
>Widely available.

Publication History

TITLE AND TITLE CHANGES
>*Jazz Journal*, 1948–April 1977. (Various short-lived subtitles during the early years.) *Jazz Journal International*, 1977– .

VOLUME AND ISSUE DATA
>Volumes 1– , 1948– .

FREQUENCY OF PUBLICATION
>Monthly.

PUBLISHERS
>Sinclair Traill, May 1948–December 1973. Novello & Company, January 1974–April 1977. Billboard Ltd. (United Kingdom), under lease, May 1977–December 1978. Pitman Periodicals Ltd., January 1979–December 1982. Eddie Cook, 1983– .

PLACE OF PUBLICATION
>London, England.

EDITORS
>   Sinclair Traill, 1948–78. Mike Hennessey, 1979–80. Nevil Skrimshire, 1981–82.
>   Eddie Cook, 1983–   .

Robert Byler

JEMF NEWSLETTER. See JEMF QUARTERLY

JEMF QUARTERLY

The purpose of the John Edwards Memorial Foundation (or since 1983, Forum) (JEMF) is:

> to further the serious study and public recognition of those forms of American folk music disseminated by commercial media such as print, sound recordings, films, radio and television. These forms include music referred to as "country," "western," "country & western," "old time," "hillbilly," "bluegrass," "mountain," "cowboy," "cajun," " sacred," "gospel," "race," "blues," "rhythm and blues," "soul," "rock & roll," "folk rock," and "rock."

The foundation works toward this goal by:

> gathering and cataloguing phonograph records, sheet music, song books, photographs, biographical and discographical information, and scholarly works, as well as related artifacts;

> compiling, publishing, and distributing bibliographical, biographical, discographical, and historical data;

> reprinting, with permission, pertinent articles originally appearing in books and journals;

> sponsoring and encouraging field work related to commercially recorded and published American folk music. (5: ii)

Norman Cohen, the first editor of the quarterly and later the executive secretary of the foundation, explained its genesis and growth in a 1982 editorial:

> When John Edwards, a young but knowledgeable Australian country music record collector and historian, was killed in 1960 at the age of 28, he had left a will directing that his record collection and related materials be shipped to the United States to be used to further the academic study of the music he had loved and collected. . . . Edwards had named his correspondent and fellow collector, Eugene Earle, as executor of his will, and Gene, together with four other scholars and collectors all devoted to the

study of hillbilly music . . . formed the John Edwards Memorial Foundation. (18:106)

Begun in October 1965 as the *JEMF Newsletter,* the journal has gradually
expanded from a mimeographed letter format to a fifty- to sixty-page offset
booklet. Cohen initially intended the publication merely to keep friends and
officers abreast of foundation activities; the bulk of the early *Newsletters,* contained notices of meetings, media citations, and only incidentally articles and
research data. With the inauguration of the quarterly in 1969, however, "original
articles and research" related to hillbilly music and "parallel areas of commercially recorded folk music: blues, cajun, folk-rock, etc." were sought (9:34).
The *JEMF Quarterly*'s strong interest in hillbilly music, especially "pre-hillbilly
banjo and fiddle music," as well as ethnic and humorous recorded material was
reiterated by the editor in 1973 (9:34).

Regular features of the quarterly have included "bibliographic notes," book
and record reviews (brief descriptions normally running to no more than three
paragraphs), and record lists, letters, reprinted articles from other publications,
and short articles (usually five pages or less) intended "to straddle the gap
between the scholarly and the popular orientations" (18:106). The audience and
main contributors seem to be folklorists and collectors, although some articles
by anthropologists, ethnomusicologists, and historians appear. The inclusion of
biographical capsules about academically credentialled writers in the most recent
issues suggests an attempt to demonstrate scholarly credibility and perhaps appeal
to a wider audience. The quarterly's principal contents consist of detailed discographies (often including release numbers, master numbers, titles, and individual artist names for obscure series), bibliographies, and a long-running
"graphics" department, which was started by Archie Green in 1967. This enlivening section of the journal "undertakes to explore the visual depiction of
hillbilly musicians as well as themes within their songs and instrumentals."
Specifically, these pages are devoted to articles describing and "analyzing the
origin, pattern, use and meaning for the drawings, lithographs, paintings and
other art selected to sell music" (19:174). Reprint examples of the art are always
included. One of the consistent strengths of this journal has been its generous
inclusion of pictures with most articles.

By 1982 the foundation was offering, through the journal, thirty-four items
in a "reprint series" of articles (at $1.00 apiece) as well as a "special series"
of reports of meetings, discographies, and autobiographies of country musicians
(priced from $2.50 to $6.25 each).

In 1982 the financially precarious existence of the JEMF forced its directors
to seek more solid help than could be provided by UCLA, JEMF's host institution
to that point. Accordingly, the collection was sold and by April 1983 moved to

the University of North Carolina, Chapel Hill. UCLA remains the site at which the journal is prepared. Linda Painter, who began as an editorial assistant and archivist with the journal in 1979, succeeded Cohen as chief editor in 1981 (some intermediate issues were co-edited by Painter, Cohen, and Patricia Atkinson Wells). Painter remained as editor after the transfer of the collection, but the governing body of the foundation (now forum) was streamlined; a list of some two dozen "advisors" on the masthead has been replaced by a smaller "board of directors" (including many former "advisors" and "directors").

Except for the varying size of the typeface used in the most recent volumes (to accommodate double columns on each page) and increasing the number of illustrations, the journal has seen no major changes in format since 1969, retaining its 8½" by 11" size and fifty- to sixty-page length. It contains no advertising and is indexed internally by subject at the end of each volume.

Information Sources

BIBLIOGRAPHY

Cohen, N. "JEMF." *Old Time Music* (Summer 1971): 31.

Cohen, A. and N. "The JEMF—John Edwards Memorial Foundation." *Sing Out* 19 (1969): 12–14.

Earle, Eugene. "The John Edwards Memorial Foundation, Inc." *Western Folklore* 23 (1964): 111–13.

"The John Edwards Memorial Foundation, Inc." *Western Folklore* 30 (1971): 177–81.

INDEXES

Internal: each volume indexed.

External: Music Index, 1969– . RILM, 1971– . Arts and Humanities Citation Index, 1976– . Popular Music Periodicals Index, 1973–76.

REPRINT EDITION

Microform: UMI.

LOCATION SOURCES

Widely available.

Publication History

TITLE AND TITLE CHANGES

JEMF Newsletter, 1965–68. *JEMF Quarterly,* 1969– .

VOLUME AND ISSUE DATA

Volumes 1– , 1965– .

FREQUENCY OF PUBLICATION

Quarterly.

PUBLISHER

John Edwards Memorial Foundation, 1965–1982. John Edwards Memorial Forum, 1983– .

PLACE OF PUBLICATION

Los Angeles, California.

EDITORS

Ed Kahn, 1965–68. Norman Cohen, 1965–81. Linda Painter, 1981– .

Thomas L. Riis

JOURNAL OF AESTHETICS AND ART CRITICISM

The *Journal of Aesthetics and Art Criticism,* "A Quarterly Devoted to the Advancement of Aesthetics and the Arts," was first published in the spring of 1941 under the editorship of Dagobert D. Runes of the Philosophical Library, New York. Its stated purpose has not changed during the intervening years:

> The *Journal of Aesthetics and Art Criticism* deals with the fundamental principles and problems of aesthetics and art criticism. It will concern itself also with developments in the arts, in art history, and with the relations of the artist and the arts to society. It affords a common ground for interchange of views between aestheticians, art critics, art historians, art educators, museum workers, and all who are by profession or avocation interested in the progressive development of aesthetics and the arts. It aims at constructive and critical thinking and appeals to all, professionals and laymen, who desire to keep abreast of the significant movements in aesthetics and the arts. (2.8:3)

From the first issue, book reviews and pertinent advertising were included, while in the third year of publication an editorial commentary was incorporated. Subsequent additions include an "Afterwards" (one- to two-page communications) and regular news and announcements for the American Society for Aesthetics. In the fourth year the *Journal* was turned over to the American Society for Aesthetics, which declared its wish to continue Rune's policies, and stated further that "It is hoped that a balanced diet can be provided in each issue . . . articles dealing with several different arts from different philosophic, scientific, historical and critical standpoints" (4.1:2).

While the "balanced diet" has not included a musical course in every issue, there have been many articles of direct interest to musicians: Ernst Krenek on "Music and Social Crisis" (3.1:53–58), Hugo Leichtentritt on "Aesthetic Ideas as the Basis of Musical Styles" (4.2:65–73), "Criteria of Criticism in Music" by Joyce Michell (21.1:27–30), Alfred Pike on "Perception and Meaning in Serial Music" (22.1:55–61), and "Pythagorean Mathematics and Music" by Richard L. Crocker (22.2:189–98) are typical earlier examples. More recent issues have included Herbert M. Schueller's "The Aesthetic Implications of Avant-Garde Music" (35.4:397–410); Philip Alperson's "On Musical Improvisation" (43.1:17–29); "Time in the Visual Arts: Lessing and Modern Criticism" by Jeoraldean McClain (44.1:41–58); Daniel A. Putnam on "Music and the Metaphor of Touch" (44.1:59–66); "Why Restore Works of Art?" by Yuriko Saito (44.2:141–51); "Aesthetic Experience and Psychological Definitions of Art" by Douglas J. Dempster (44.2:153–65); and Arthur C. Danto's "Art, Evolution, and the Consciousness of History" (44.3:223–44). Occasional special issues can also be useful to scholars of music; for example, v. 24.1 was devoted to "Oriental Aesthetics." The lists of books received also deserve notice. Contributors range from aestheticians to art historians and critics.

The editorship of the *Journal of Aesthetics and Art Criticism* has changed on relatively few occasions. Thomas Munro assumed this position shortly after the American Society for Aesthetics acquired the magazine; on his retirement in 1963, Herbert Schueller began a ten-year term as editor. In 1973 John Fisher became the fourth editor, pledging continuation of highest standards of scholarship and encouraging greater exchange of ideas through institution of a section for "short and pointed responses" (31.4:432).

The *Journal* has an impressive board of contributing and associate editors, a separate editor for the extensive signed book reviews and one for bibliography, and an international Editorial Council. Its influence is considerable and its reputation distinguished.

Measuring 7¹⁄₁₆″ by 10¼″ with a cover which has for most of its existence served to list the major contents, the *Journal* provides frequent charts and illustrations. It is indexed by the American Society for Aesthetics and contains internal cumulative indexes for vs. 1–20 and vs.1–40.

Information Sources

INDEXES
> Internal: vs. 1–20; vs.1–40.
> External: Music Index, 1950– . RILM, 1967– . Arts and Humanities Citation Index, 1976– . Bibliographie des Musikschrifttums, 1950–62, 1970. Humanities Index, 1982– . Arts Index, 1941– . Philosopher's Index, 1968– . RILA, 1974– . MLA International Bibliography, 1951– .

REPRINT EDITIONS
> Paper: AMS Reprints, vs. 1–9.
> Microform: UMI.

LOCATION SOURCES
> Widely available.

Publication History

TITLE AND TITLE CHANGES
> *Journal of Aesthetics and Art Criticism.*

VOLUME AND ISSUE DATA
> Volumes 1– , 1941– .

FREQUENCY OF PUBLICATION
> Quarterly.

PUBLISHER
> Philosophical Library, 1941–43. The American Society for Aesthetics, 1944– .

PLACE OF PUBLICATION
> New York.

EDITORS
> Dagobert D. Runes, 1941–45. Thomas Munro, 1945–62. Herbert Schueller, 1963–72. John Fisher, 1973– .

Ruth K. Inglefield

JOURNAL OF BAND RESEARCH

Continued interest in music education research over the past several decades has resulted in a number of research journals that focus on specific areas of music performance, teaching, and learning. An example of this trend is the *Journal of Band Research*, a periodical that serves as an outlet for scholarly efforts pertaining primarily to the wind band medium and that has become a valuable resource for band directors in this country and abroad.

The *Journal*, founded as an official publication of the American Bandmasters Association (ABA), first appeared in 1964 with a policy of publishing articles within four broad categories related to the wind band: (1) analytical discussion of band music, (2) scholarly biographical studies of composers of band music, (3) considerations of aesthetic matters related to band performance, and (4) firsthand, documented accounts of outstanding personalities or events associated with bands. In addition, the *Journal* was intended to provide for the reporting of results of studies based on materials held at the ABA Research Center at the University of Maryland in College Park. Over the years, however, the *Journal* has broadened its scope to encompass many areas of band/wind ensemble research, including historical, analytical, descriptive, and experimental studies with important implications for band and instrumental pedagogy. Most articles average eight to ten pages and are contributed by college and university band directors and music education researchers.

Several articles that have appeared in the *Journal of Band Research* are especially noteworthy because of the comprehensive information they have provided for band researchers and practitioners. These include a series of four articles (1.1:1–9, 1.2:1–5, 2.1:4–8, 3.1:39–45), on the early history of the ABA, an innovative article for its time on computer-illustrated displays for marching bands (8.2:44–47), a history of bands in the United States (13.1:47–49), an extensive bibliography of dissertations relative to the study of bands and band music (15.1:1–31 and 16.1:29–36), and a lengthy bibliography of the histories of college and university bands that includes books, dissertations, master's theses, and a variety of other sources (19.2:31–38). A special issue, appearing as 2.2, reproduced the then-current catalog of band music and recordings at the ABA Research Center.

In addition, two important research sources were also included in v. 20: (1) a comprehensive index of the *Journal's* first nineteen volumes that supersedes the three previous internal indexes and contains an Author Index, a new Title and Key-Word Subject Index, and a more traditional Subject Index with eleven major classifications (20.1:41–78); and (2) an updated overview of the ABA Research Center in College Park, Maryland, along with the announcement of future articles to appear in the *Journal* on the Goldman Band Library and other band research collections (20.1:37–40).

Three noteworthy editorial policy changes were initiated in the Spring 1984 issue (19.2): a book review section would appear regularly, an analysis of a major contemporary work for band or wind ensemble would be included in each issue, and articles that highlight major library reference sources for wind ensemble/band research would appear regularly.

The *Journal of Band Research* was published once per year for v. 1 (1964) and v. 2 (1965). It subsequently became a semiannual publication (Fall and Spring) beginning with v. 3 in 1966. Typically, there are three to six major articles per issue that report important research findings. Issue length varies from fifty to eighty-two pages, and short biographies of contributors are provided in each issue. The *Journal* is 6" by 8½".

Information Sources

BIBLIOGRAPHY
Harris, Ernest E. *Music Education: A Guide to Information Sources*. Detroit: Gale Research Company, 1978.
INDEXES
    Internal: vs. 1–19 in v. 20.
    External: Music Index, 1964–   . Music Article Guide, 1965–   . Arts and Humanities Citation Index, 1978–   . RILM, 1969–   .
REPRINT EDITIONS
    Microform: UMI.
LOCATION SOURCES
    Widely available.

Publication History

TITLE AND TITLE CHANGES
    Journal of Band Research.
VOLUME AND ISSUE DATA
    Volumes 1– , 1964–   .
FREQUENCY OF PUBLICATION
    Annual, 1964–65. Semiannual, 1966–   .
PUBLISHERS
    American Bandmasters Association, Fall 1964–Spring 1969. Iowa State University Press, Fall 1969–Spring 1977. Troy State University Press, Fall 1977–   .
PLACES OF PUBLICATION
    College Park, Maryland, Fall 1964–Spring 1969. Ames, Iowa, Fall 1969–Spring 1977. Troy, Alabama, Fall 1977–   .
EDITORS
    Hubert H. Henderson, Fall 1964–Spring 1966. Gale Sperry, Fall 1966–Fall 1973. Acton Ostling, acting editor, Spring 1974. Warren E. George, Fall 1974–Spring 1982. Jon R. Piersol, Fall 1982–   .

Vincent J. Kantorski

JOURNAL OF COUNTRY MUSIC

From Nashville, Tennessee, the home of modern-day commercial country music, comes a journal devoted to the history, study, and interpretation of this musical form—the *Journal of Country Music (JCM)*. For many years prior to the *Journal's* establishment in 1971, popular and fan-oriented publications had treated the country music scene: *Country Song Roundup* (1949–   ), *Music City News* (1963–   ), and many others. But for serious scholarly study of country music as an important musical form, the *Journal* really had only one important predecessor, the *JEMF Quarterly* (q.v.), begun in 1967 at UCLA and drawn from the resources of the late John Edward's private collection of hillbilly discs and publications. Also in 1967, the Country Music Hall of Fame and Museum opened in Nashville under the auspices of the Country Music Foundation, a nonprofit organization chartered three years earlier to preserve and interpret the history of country music. In 1970, an in-house organ of foundation news, the *Country Music Foundation Newsletter* was begun, and late the following year (Winter 1971) this became the first issue (2.4) of a more scholarly quarterly: the *Journal of Country Music*. The *Newsletter* was discontinued at that time but was reborn in 1981.

The transition of the *Newsletter* to the *JCM* was accompanied by a radical change in format, appearance, and content. Modeled on *Folklore and Folk Music Archivist*, the old 11″ by 8½″ size was reduced to 5½″ by 8½″, while photo offset from typescript was adopted. Issues came to average one hundred pages in length, featuring roughly six articles of some twelve pages each. Interpretive articles dealing with the performers, styles, and personalities of country music became the mainstay, almost to the exclusion of foundation news. The *Journal* was largely academic in tone, as professional folklorists and foundation staffers became the major contributors. The publication of primary source material, especially discographies and radio song logs, was critically lauded as the *Journal's* main contribution to country music as a field of study. Several of the interpretive articles were also hailed in academic circles, as for example Saundra Keyes's "Little Mary Phagan: A Native American Ballad In Context" 3.1:1–16).

With v. 7.1, in January 1978, several important changes took place. A square format, 8½″ by 8½″, was designed by Gary Gore. Covers became glossy, all copy was typeset, and individual issues were lengthened, while the *Journal* shifted to a thrice-yearly publication schedule. Systematic illustration of articles began (though occasional photos had been used as far back as the first issue), and a special graphic arts section, the "JCM Gallery," was inaugurated. Also, a comprehensive book review section was instituted. The latter is now one of the *Journal's* most important services, featuring reviews by major writers such as Greil Marcus, Douglas B. Green, and Bill C. Malone.

A few issues past these major changes, a further change in article content became apparent. Articles took on more of a popular tone. Journalists such as Bob Allen, Nick Tosches, Chet Flippo, Roy Blount, and Rich Kienzle contributed a succession of popular articles on major country music figures such as Waylon Jennings, Hank Williams, Jerry Lee Lewis, and Hank Penny. "Mr. Victor and Mr. Peer," an article by Nolan Porterfield which appeared in December 1978 (7.3:3–21), initiated the now-common practice of printing prepublication chapters from forthcoming books on country music. This move toward material on more popular subject matter and personalities, while not sacrificing the earlier scholarly feel and orientation, was dictated by the desire for a larger audience and a perceived decline in academic interest in the subject.

JCM editors only print ads in trade for permission to excerpt from forthcoming books; the publication's sole support besides subscription money has been Country Music Foundation funds. In spite of the critical acclaim of Gore's layout, a return to the larger 8½″ by 11″ format (of *CMF Newsletter* days), with v. 9.3 (1983), was necessitated by cost concerns. To be sure, the layout is merely an adaption of the earlier Gore design, and all other 1978 changes have remained intact.

Information Sources

BIBLIOGRAPHY
Interviews with William J. Ivey, former editor, and Kyle D. Young, current executive
    editor of the *Journal of Country Music,* January 13, 1986.
INDEXES
    Internal: Title index to vs. 1–9 in 10.1 (1985).
    External: RILM, 1977– . Arts and Humanities Citation Index, 1977– . Popular
    Music Periodicals Index, 1973–76.
LOCATION SOURCES
    Widely available.

Publication History

TITLE AND TITLE CHANGES
    Country Music Foundation Newsletter, 1970–71. *Journal of Country Music,*
    1971– .
VOLUME AND ISSUE DATA
    Volumes 1– , 1970– .
FREQUENCY OF PUBLICATION
    Quarterly.
PUBLISHER
    Country Music Foundation.
PLACE OF PUBLICATION
    Nashville, Tennessee.
EDITORS
    William J. Ivey, 1971–73. Douglas B. Green, 1974–75. Kyle D. Young, 1978–
    84. Paul Kingsbury, 1985– .

Ronnie Pugh

JOURNAL OF INTERNATIONAL FOLK MUSIC COUNCIL. See YEAR-BOOK FOR TRADITIONAL MUSIC

JOURNAL OF JAZZ STUDIES

Published by the prestigious Institute of Jazz Studies at Rutgers University, the *Journal of Jazz Studies* has added considerably, since its inception in 1973, to the scholarly literature devoted to jazz. Eleven semiannual issues of the journal were produced before a two-year hiatus after the Fall/Winter 1979 issue (6:1). It resumed as the *Annual Review of Jazz Studies* in 1982, and additional single issues were published in 1983 and 1985. A predecessor publication was *Studies in Jazz Discography*, the only issue of which was published in November 1971 with Walter Allen as editor. Its content included three papers from conferences on discographical research and jazz heritage.

Co-editors of the *Journal* and the *Annual Review* since its founding have been Charles Nanry and David Cayer. Dan Morgenstern, institute director, has been co-editor of the three annual editions and was review editor of the two issues in 1979. Of various editorial assistants, Edward Berger, institute curator, has served in that capacity since late 1976.

Though some of its articles might be equally suited for more popular jazz periodicals, the *Journal/Review*'s primary readership (currently 1,200 subscriptions) is in academia; it is not well known in general circles of jazz fans and musicians. Nor is that contrary to editorial intention. In the inaugural issue, the editors specified that the publication was designed to meet a need "for a multi-disciplinary and interdisciplinary publication for scholarly articles about jazz and related musics" (1.1:2). The editors saw no need to compete with existing periodicals, but rather to augment jazz literature with critical essays on major figures, genres or series of recordings and books, and oral history excerpts. Disciplines from which studies were intended to emerge included sociology, musicology, social history, criticism, discography, library science, and biography.

The *Journal's* subject range has spanned famous performers and their styles and social milieus, trends involving racial imagery and riverboat jazz, characteristics of the music and its environment in cities from New Orleans to Chicago, transcribed scores and improvisations for analysis by musicologists, and extensive discographies. A particularly valuable contribution, by Thomas Everett, has been an annotated bibliography of English language jazz periodicals, first published in 1976 and updated five times since. Everett's listing of some seventy-one items illustrates the expanding interest in jazz and writings about it in recent years. Book reviews have been expanded in the annual editions, flavored by Dan Morgenstern's rich background as a jazz scholar and former editor of *down beat* magazine (q.v.).

Reflecting back on how their objectives have been met, the editors, in the 1985 *Annual Review* preface, noted an "ever-widening range of scholarly approaches to this unique art form" (vii). That issue included three bio-discographical studies, an oral history, five musical analyses spanning the decades from the 1920s to 1980s, studies of early recording technology, the use of computers to analyze jazz melody, and essays examining historical, cultural, and social aspects of music. The editor's added that: "Not only has the range of disciplines and methodologies expanded, but the gradual acceptance of jazz as a field acceptable in traditional academic environments has augmented the ranks of jazz scholars seeking avenues of publication." Such scholarly efforts, they added, supplement the often-avocational efforts of nonacademic scholars and critics—mainstays of the field for many years.

The editorial board of the *Journal/Review* reads like a who's who in jazz scholarship and publishing, but is somewhat weak in performers. It includes Richard Allen of Tulane, David Baker of Indiana University's noted jazz program, archivist Frank Gillis of Indiana, Martin Williams of the Smithsonian Institution, and Gunther Schuller, composer, conductor, educator, and musicologist. Rudi Blesh, who died in 1985, was another well-known member of the twenty-nine-person board.

The format of the *Journal* has been stable, except for a change from 6″ by 9″ to 7″ by 10″ pages in v. 6.1 (1979), and a fractionally larger size for the *Annual Review* editions. At that time, the editors predicted that the text could be published more economically in the new format and that issues would be reduced from the previous range of 112 to 128 pages to only 96 pages. But the editions of the *Annual Review* have been larger rather than smaller, with prefatory material plus 170 pages in 1982, 218 pages in 1983, and 209 pages in 1985. The typical issue contains five to seven articles, ten to fifteen pages each, and about four reviews, generally one to two pages in length. A useful index to the previous ten issues was provided in late 1979, with separate sections listing contents of each issue, authors and titles, and major subjects (6.1:105–10).

Information Sources

BIBLIOGRAPHY
Letters from Marie Griffin, Librarian, Institute of Jazz Studies, December 5, 1985, and
     July 24, 1986.
INDEXES
     Internal: vs. 1–6 in v. 6.
     External: Music Index, 1974–   . RILM, 1978–   . Arts and Humanities Citation
     Index, 1976–79. Popular Music Periodicals Index, 1973–76. Music Article Guide,
     1984–   .
REPRINT EDITION
     Microform: UMI, 1973–1979.
LOCATION SOURCES
     Widely available.

Publication History

TITLE AND TITLE CHANGES
     Journal of Jazz Studies, 1973–79. *Annual Review of Jazz Studies*, 1983–   .
VOLUME AND ISSUE DATA
     Volumes 1–6.1, 1973–79. New series (*Annual Review,*) volumes 1–   , 1982–   .

FREQUENCY OF PUBLICATION
    Semiannual, 1973–79. Annual, with irregularities, 1982–   .
PUBLISHER
    Institute of Jazz Studies, Rutgers University.
PLACES OF PUBLICATION
    New Brunswick, New Jersey, and Newark, New Jersey.
EDITORS
    Charles Nanry and David Cayer, 1973–   . Dan Morgenstern added as a co-editor
    in 1983.

Robert Byler

JOURNAL OF MUSIC THEORY

The *Journal of Music Theory,* a publication of Yale University, first appeared
in 1957, at that time under the auspices of the Yale School of Music. It has
continued semiannually since that date, except for the special double issues
constituting vs. 15 and 16, without major changes in format. The only periodical
then completely devoted to the field of music theory, it has few peers, even
today, within the discipline—the most notable and similar being the annual *Music
Theory Spectrum* (q.v.). Its goal has been to restore music theory from no more
than a "didactic convenience, . . . a necessary discipline" to "a mode of creative
thought" and to serve as a forum for the exchange of ideas within the field (1:1).
All the articles are in English, but the intended readership is international in
scope.

The range of interests and musical periods addressed in the journal is very
wide. Topics are not confined to the Western tradition, and span ancient times
to the present. Included are analyses of specific works, as well as articles on
analytical methods; the history of music theory, including translations of treatises
or of portions of them, and bibliographies; speculative theory; and pedagogy.
The balance in numbers of articles on analysis, history of theory, and speculative
theory has been almost exactly even; pedagogy has been slighted by comparison.

Schenkerian theory in the United States has received considerable support in
the pages of the *Journal of Music Theory*. Landmark articles in this area include
"Schenker's Conception of Musical Structure" by Allen Forte (3:1–30), "Register and the Large-Scale Connection" by Ernst Oster (5:54–71), Schenker's
own "Organic Structure in Sonata Form," translated by Orin Grossman (12:164–
83), "Strict Counterpoint and Tonal Theory" by John Rothgeb (19:260–84),
"Schenker's 'Motivic Parallelisms' " by Charles Burkhart (22:145–75), the
"Review Symposium" (Carl Schachter, David Epstein, and William Benjamin)
on Heinrich Schenker's *Free Composition* (25:113–73), and David Beach's bibliography on Schenker (13:2–37, updated 23:275–86).

Another very useful bibliography, and an important contribution to the history
of theory, is "Music Theory in Translation: A Bibliography" by James B. Coover

(3:70–96, updated 13:230–48). Other special themes that have been pursued include the series of articles on electronic music, with Milton Babbitt serving as co-editor, which began in 7.1 (1963) and continued in vs. 8, 10.2, and 11.2.

Several of the early landmark articles dealing with set theory also appeared in the *Journal of Music Theory*, particularly Milton Babbitt's "Set Structure as a Compositional Determinant" (5:72–94), Donald Martino's "The Source Set and its Aggregate Formations" (5:224–73), and Allen Forte's "A Theory of Set-Complexes for Music" (8:136–83) and "The Domain and Relations of Set-Complex Theory" (9:173–80). Others who have contributed greatly to the journal in this area include John Rothgeb and David Lewin. Beginning in the mid–1960s there were also a number of contributions concerned with the new endeavors in computer-assisted analysis and information-theory analysis, authored by Allen Forte, Raymond Erickson, Lejaren Hiller, David Lewin, and others. A seminal article for the recent trend of linguistically oriented theory was "Toward a Formal Theory of Tonal Music" by Fred Lerdahl and Ray Jackendoff (21:111–71). Recent issues have also seen sketch studies by Carl Schachter (on Ludwig van Beethoven) and by Martha MacLean Hyde and Bryan Simms (on Arnold Schönberg).

The importance and influence of the *Journal of Music Theory* for musical scholarship in the United States can hardly be overstated. Its writing has been serious in intent and at times ground-breaking in results. Although some may object to the recondite style and nature of certain types of articles, the complexity of these is a natural consequence of the type of investigation being undertaken and demonstrates the great strides made within the field of music theory during the twenty-eight years since the journal first appeared. The very fact that so many individuals have joined in the fray, even in the most abstruse realms of *Ursatz*, set theory, and computer-assisted analysis, is evidence of the success of the journal as a forum for the exchange of ideas. Those who saw the distinctions among the endeavors of contemporary composers, music historians, and music theorists, and therefore a need for an independent outlet for the latter, were among the leaders in creating both the *Journal of Music Theory* and the later Society for Music Theory. The influence of the journal may also be said to have extended on the one hand to the creation of the music theory societies of the states of New York, Michigan, and Indiana and their journals, and on the other across the Atlantic to Great Britain and the journal *Music Analysis* (q.v.).

The average issue is about 160 pages in length and typically contains three to five substantial articles—thirty pages or more each is common—in addition to other regular features. The first several volumes include a feature called "Theory Forum," which presents very short articles (one to ten pages) on diverse topics. To this is added another, more in the nature of a true forum or roundtable discussion, in vs. 3 and 4, with several contributors writing on the topics "On the Nature and Value of Theoretical Training" and "The Professional Music Theorist," respectively. After v. 6, the original "Theory Forum" is not to be found again until very recently, but beginning with 10.1, there appears from time to time an "Analysis Symposium," in which two or more theorists present independent analyses of a chosen work: for example, the first of these featured Howard Boatwright and Ernst Oster writing on Mozart's *Menuetto in D Major*, *K. 355*. These have continued intermittently, and other special symposia of the "roundtable" type have also been featured from time to time: "National Predilections in Seventeenth-Century Music Theory" (v. 16), "Pedagogy in Perspective: Music Theory in Higher Education" (18.1), "Interval Recognition" (19.212–34), and the Schenker "Review Symposium" cited above.

Book reviews are an important aspect of the *Journal of Music Theory*; in addition, each issue contains a list of new books *not* reviewed and a bibliography of current periodical literature—articles on music in both music periodicals and nonmusic periodicals in English, and in music periodicals in other languages. In recent years the plethora of new publications has made it necessary for this bibliography to become more selective. Other, smaller features include correspondence, information regarding contributors, and an announcement of the contents of each upcoming issue. A listing of doctoral dissertations on theoretical subjects, promised in v. 1, was left to other standard sources. News items, obituaries, and similar items have been kept to a minimum. One prominent exception was "Ernst Oster (1908–1977): In Memoriam" (21:340–54).

The journal is in paper-bound format; it has varied only slightly from its basic size of 6″ by 9″ over the years. The text is typeset; musical examples in the early issues are reproduced from hand-drawn originals, but they are exceptionally clear. Later issues include both these and more formally typeset musical examples. A nice touch in the early issues was the reproduction of illustrations from various early treatises adorning the title page. With the striking change in cover design of v. 5 these disappear, but full-page illustrations from treatises are still found reproduced within the journal.

The early issues contain no advertisements, but from v. 15 onward there are several grouped together at the end of each issue, all for scholarly societies, journals, books, and so on. There is an index listing all articles, large and small (alphabetically by author), and books reviewed (by their author) for each of the following: vs. 1–2, 3–4, 5–6, 7–14, 15–17, 18–19, and individually for v. 20 and following.

Information Sources

BIBLIOGRAPHY
Mitchell, William J. "*Journal of Music Theory.*" *Musical Quarterly* 44 (1958): 540–42.
INDEXES
Internal: vs.1–2, 3–4, 5–6, 7–14, 15–17, 18–19. Each volume indexed (vs. 20–).
External: RILM, 1967– . Music Index, 1957– . Arts and Humanities Citation Index, 1976– . Music Article Guide, 1965– . Bibliographie des Musikschrifttums, 1958– .
REPRINT EDITION
Microform: UMI.

LOCATION SOURCES
     Widely available.

Publication History

TITLE AND TITLE CHANGES
     Journal of Music Theory.
VOLUME AND ISSUE DATA
     Volumes 1– , 1957– .
FREQUENCY OF PUBLICATION
     Semiannual.
PUBLISHER
     Yale University.
PLACE OF PUBLICATION
     New Haven, Connecticut.
EDITORS
     David Kraehenbuehl, 1957–59. Allen Forte, 1960–67. David Beach, 1967–70.
     Bryan Simms, 1970–74. James M. Baker, 1974–75. Bryan R. Simms, 1975–
     1976. Jane R. Stevens, 1976–79. Anthony Walts, 1980. Martha MacLean Hyde,
     1981–87. Christopher Hasty, 1988– .

Paul B. Mast

JOURNAL OF MUSIC THERAPY

The *Journal of Music Therapy* (*JMT*) is the official publication of the National
Association of Music Therapy, Inc. (NAMT). It was preceded by the *Music
Therapy Annual Books of Proceedings*, published from 1952 through 1963, which
included collections of papers presented at national conferences. *JMT* has been
published quarterly, one volume per year, since its inception in the spring of
1964.

The primary purposes of this journal are to "encourage and promote scholarly
inquiry in music therapy, to disseminate results of music therapy research and
innovations in clinical practice, and thus to advance knowledge of music therapy
theory and practice" (17.46). Diverse topics ranging from theoretical and/or
philosophical issues to case studies formed the bases of the articles found in the
early volumes of the journal. Special features in these early volumes included
"Abstracts of Research in Music Therapy" by M. L. Sears and W. W. Sears
(1.2:33–60) and "Music Therapy Bibliography" complied by E. H. Schneider
(1.3:83–111), which included references to selected articles and research studies
relating to music therapy since the 1920s.

Volumes published in the 1970s showed a rise in the emphasis on empirical
studies and the increasing use of sophisticated research techniques. Additionally,
there was a growing diversity in the research settings, from clinical laboratories
to schools and universities. Research topics expanded from a primary focus in
the 1960s on the emotionally disturbed and mentally retarded to more diverse

topics including speech and language disorders, the disadvantaged, death and dying, and applications of the concepts of people such a Jean Piaget, Carl Orff, Zoltán Kodály, and others. Throughout, the *Journal of Music Therapy* has remained at the forefront of research relating to the effects of music on various types of disabled as well as nondisabled populations. Articles appearing in the *JMT* have been contributed primarily by American music therapists, educators, and related health care professionals. Most of the discipline's major figures have appeared within its covers, with perhaps the best known being pioneer music therapist E. Thayer Gaston.

Early issues of the *Journal of Music Therapy* averaged 145 pages a volume and included articles as well as notes and comments, announcements and letters, listings of professional opportunities, association activities, conference reports, a membership directory, and a year-end index of articles. Beginning with v. 7 (1970) there was an established format including articles, a "Materials Section" (reviewing new materials for use in the field), "Book Reviews" (reviews of current books relating to music therapy and related fields), "Job Opportunities" (listing of current jobs available), "Professional News" (news related to the National Association of Music Therapy), "You Don't Say" (a place for readers to comment), and "Guest Editorials" (invited editorials by professionals in the field). V. 9 was the last time that job opportunities were published in the journal. Beginning with v. 11, all departments were dropped, and the journal included only articles and book reviews, with the last issue of each volume including an index for the complete volume. Issue 1 of vs. 18, 19, and 20 include indices of theses in music therapy completed during the respective past years. As the journal matured, the number of articles in each issue decreased, but the length of the articles and the number of pages per volume increased. As of 1986, there were approximately four to five articles per issue, and the number of pages per volume usually exceeded 200. Tables, figures, and graphs are used throughout as supporting data. A few photographs are presented in early volumes. The journal was initially 7½" by 10", but, beginning with v. 7, the size was pared down to 6" by 8¾" where it has remained to the present time.

Information Sources

BIBLIOGRAPHY

Eagle, Charles T., and Gary D. Dubler. "Recent Findings in Psychology of Music Research." *Journal of Music Therapy* 8 (1971): 152–67.

Gilbert, Janet P. "Editorial." *Journal of Music Therapy* 17 (1980): 46–49.

————. "Published Research in Music Therapy, 1973–1978: Content, Focus, and Implications for Future Research." *Journal of Music Therapy* 16 (1979): 102–10.

Jellison, Judith A. "The Frequency and General Mode of Inquiry of Research in Music Therapy, 1952–1972." *Council for Research in Music Education* 35 (1973): 1–8.

INDEXES

Internal: each volume indexed, v. 11–   .

External: Exceptional Children Education Abstracts. Psychological Abstracts. The Hospital Literature Index. Music Article Guide, 1970–   . The Selected List of

Tables of Contents of Psychiatric Periodicals. dsh Abstracts. Music Therapy Index. Music Index, 1965– . RILM, 1976– . Arts and Humanities Citation Index, 1976– . Bibliographie des Musikschrifttums, 1971– . Education Index, 1977– .

REPRINT EDITIONS
    Microform: UMI.
LOCATION SOURCES
    Widely available.

Publication History

TITLE AND TITLE CHANGE
    Journal of Music Therapy.
VOLUME AND ISSUE DATA
    Volumes 1– , 1964– .
FREQUENCY OF PUBLICATION
    Quarterly.
PUBLISHER
    National Association of Music Therapy, Inc.
PLACE OF PUBLICATION
    Lawrence, Kansas.
EDITORS
    William W. Sears, 1964–67. Ruth Boxberger, 1968–69. E. Thayer Gaston, 1970. Jo Ann Euper, 1970–74. David E. Wolfe, 1974–75. Mary J. Nicholas, 1976–79. Janet Gilbert Galloway, 1980–83. Richard Graham, 1984– .

Patricia J. Buckwell

JOURNAL OF MUSICOLOGICAL RESEARCH, THE

The *Journal of Musicological Research (JMR)* came into being in 1973 as *Music and Man,* subtitled, "An Interdisciplinary Journal of Studies on Music." The intent of this journal was to consider all facets of musical experience— music history, aesthetics, composition, and performance—in an attempt to "reach a valid philosophy of music and the arts and to promote the realization in the musician of the importance of the world that exists off-stage" (1: inside cover). The initial editors, F. J. Smith (musicology and philosophy), A. Motycka (music and aesthetic education), E. Laszlo (music and philosophy), and J. D. White (composition and performance) intended that the journal be a humanistic venture directed toward all musicians, whatever their field or type of music.

The two volumes of eight issues published under the title *Music and Man* between 1973 and 1978 were well received. The articles, by which over forty writers, did indeed address a variety of subjects, from traditional musical ap-proaches, to sociology, psychology, and philosophy. Another important facet of the journal was the book reviews, which appeared in the first four issues. These, too, considered a variety of interdisciplinary subjects.

Especially notable was the special issue of 2.1/2 (1976). It addressed a central theme of "In Search of Musical Method" and presented articles by Alfred Schutz (ed. F. Kersten), "Fragments on the Phenomenology of Music" (2.1/2:5–72); Thomas Clifton, "Music as a Constituted Object" (2.1/2:73–98); Jose Arcaya, "A Phenomenological Inquiry into the Musical Imagination: The Experience of Orchestral Conducting" (2.1/2:99–116); and, F. J. Smith, "Music Theory and the History of Ideas" (2.1/2:125–50).

Although the journal was a critical success, F. J. Smith, in his editorial of v. 2, bade farewell to *Music and Man* and introduced the *Journal of Musicological Research* as a more focused attempt "to come closer to the science as well as the wisdom of the musical experience and to the realization that science, too, is a form of humanism" (2.3/4:153). With the new title, the journal was meant to appeal more to musicologists, but also to performers and interdisciplinary friends of music. The journal also intended to deal with contemporary music. Practical matters such as a unified editorial control, improved production and editorial standards, a policy of quick response to correspondents and the publication of articles within a year of their acceptance were also cited as reasons for the transition.

V. 3.1 (1979) carried the new title, *The Journal of Musicological Research*, and a largely new, international advisory board. Smith assumed editorship, with Laszlo, Motycka, and White now appearing as advisors. More recently there has been a progressive redefining of the scope of the journal along with the addition of a distinguished new board of editors and an upgrading of both the advisory board and the quality of the contributions. This new format was fully evident with the first issue of v. 7 (1986), though the new cover and mention of the new editorial board began with 6.1 (1986). The journal now features special issues on specific topics. In accord with the modern flow system, it occasionally runs over into more than four issues yearly, though remaining with the standard four per volume.

The intention, within this redefined scope, is the publication of original articles (averaging thirty pages) in both traditional and contemporary approaches to musicological research. It also includes a broader social and cultural framework, and thus features not only historical studies but also performance analysis, criticism, sociology, and the phenomenon of sound as such. In the old format a good deal of space was given to a phenomenology of musical sound, a preoccupation, along with Medieval studies, of the editor. The new format, while not excluding a philosophy of music, will lay less formal emphasis on it. The journal will thus be closer to musicological goals as currently understood, even while musicologists are invited to take a broader view of music as such, hopefully wedding formidable historical knowledge with a critique of historicism itself.

The goal of presenting essays on contemporary music was partially met through a number of excellent articles on Béla Bartók, Charles Ives, Igor Stravinsky, and George Crumb. But the new journal *Contemporary Music Review*, also published by Gordon and Breach, has taken over this task.

In addition to articles, the journal has included as many as half a dozen regular book reviews since v. 4 (1982). Starting with 6.4 (1986), a section of shorter essays and contributions has been added as well. There have been editorials, but only to introduce the changes made either in title or purpose. *JMR* has established itself as an indispensable vehicle of the latest good thought and writing on music and a most useful tool for the working musicologist and musician.

The physical format of the journal is a consistent 6″ by 9″. Musical examples, illustrations, and photographs were interpolated with the text. Issues average eighty pages in length and include a modest quantity of professional and publisher advertising.

Publication Sources

INDEXES

> External: British Humanities Index, 1967– . Arts and Humanities Citation Index, 1976– . Bibliographie des Musikschrifttums, 1974– .

REPRINT EDITION

> Microform: Gordon and Breach Science Publishers.

LOCATION SOURCES

> Widely available.

Publication History

TITLE AND TITLE CHANGES

> *Music and Man*, 1973–78. *Journal of Musicological Research*, 1979– .

VOLUME AND ISSUE DATA

> *Music and Man:* Volumes 1–2.3/4, 1973–78. *Journal of Musicological Research*: Volumes 3– , 1979– .

FREQUENCY OF PUBLICATION

> *Music and Man:* 16/6 years. *Journal of Musicological Research*: Quarterly, with irregularities.

PUBLISHER

> Gordon and Breach Science Publishers, Ltd.

PLACE OF PUBLICATION

> London, England.

EDITORS

> Arthur Motycka, 1973–78. Ervin Laszlo, 1973–78. J. D. White, 1973–78. F. Joseph Smith, 1973– .

F. Joseph Smith and Victor Ellsworth

JOURNAL OF RENAISSANCE AND BAROQUE MUSIC. See MUSICA DISCIPLINA

JOURNAL OF RESEARCH IN MUSIC EDUCATION

Prior to 1953, reports of research findings by music educators were made in several music and nonmusic periodicals such as the *Music Educators Journal* (q.v.), *Journal of Educational Research, School and Society*, and *Musical Quarterly* (q.v.). There was no single, national outlet in which to publish the results of such studies on a regular basis. This situation was addressed at an open meeting of the Music Educators National Conference (MENC) in the spring of 1952. Among those present were members of the editorial board of the *Music Educators Journal*, members of the Music Education Research Council, and the newly elected officers of MENC. After considerable discussion, the group strongly endorsed the initiation of a research journal under the auspices of MENC: the *Journal of Research in Music Education* (*JRME*).

It was agreed that among the general purposes of the new publication would be providing a means of communication among music researchers, aiding in refining and developing research techniques, disseminating the growing amount of research information to MENC's total membership and raising the standards of music education research. The types of materials deemed appropriate for the journal included reports of experimental, historical, and survey studies; discussions of trends, practices, and philosophies of music education; bibliographic studies; digests and abstracts of theses and dissertations; reviews of important books; and reviews of major musical compositions, song series, and other materials suitable for school use. It was further agreed that initial issues would be published only as sufficient suitable materials were obtained rather than at regular intervals. However, the Executive Committee of MENC indicated that it expected to publish the journal on a quarterly basis as soon as possible.

In the years since, *JRME* has become established as the oldest national music education research journal in the country and has maintained a high level of scholarly excellence. The typical format of *JRME* over the years has included research articles (usually five to seven per issue, each averaging ten to fifteen pages), and book reviews, though the latter have not recently appeared on a regular basis. Results of a recent content analysis of *JRME* indicated that 40 percent of the articles published in the *Journal* between 1953 and 1983 were based on dissertations, 2 percent on theses, and 58 percent were not based on either. The same study revealed the following percentages of specific research types for the same period: descriptive (40 percent), experimental (32 percent), historical (17 percent), philosophical (4 percent), behavioral (1 percent), and other (6 percent). It was also indicated that a progression from experimental/control group designs to more sophisticated research designs was observed over the years under the review (32:213–22). Most contributors are college and university music education researchers.

In addition to articles and reviews, several other types of entries have been added from time to time. "News of Research," a feature that was initiated in v. 13 but no longer appears, informed readers of current research activities in various parts of the country. Letters to the editor have appeared periodically with the first one being published in v. 14. In an effort to inform the readership of additional research resources, a listing of the tables of contents of the *Bulletin of the Council for Research in Music Education* (q.v.) and *Psychology of Music* (q.v.) was included for the first time in v. 27 and continues to the present. *Psychomusicology* (q.v.) has since been added to this list.

A major new feature called Forum was added in the summer 1984 issue (32.2). The Forum consists of editorials, guest editorials, and articles that summarize previous research, speculate about future projects, explain research methodologies for readers unfamiliar with such techniques, and examines alternate or little-known research methodologies for possible use by music education researchers. The Winter 1984 Forum (32.213–42) presented a trio of articles focusing on the history and content of *JRME*.

The *Journal* has periodically published lists of completed doctoral dissertations in music and music education, either as special issues or as major portions of regular issues. These lists and the years encompassed by each are found in the following issues: 12:3–112 for dissertations completed between 1957 and 1963; 16:83–216 for 1963–67; 20:7–185 for 1968–71; and 26:131–415 for 1972–77. These bibliographies typically provide an alphabetical listing of authors and a topical index of subjects. An earlier bibliography of research studies in music education for the years 1949–56, printed as a special issue 5:69–225, contained mostly master's theses, since the terminal degree in music education at that time was normally the master's degree.

Several other special issues or major-emphasis regular issues have also been published. These include an Americana index to the *Musical Quarterly*, 1915–57 (6.2:3–144), a selected bibliography of music education materials (7.1:3–146), and a regular issue that contains a bibliography of materials on programmed instruction in music with entries from 1957–67 (18.2: 178–83).

Each article in *JRME* is prefaced with an abstract of less than 150 words. This practice was initiated in the Spring 1974 issue (22.1) as was a key word listing system to facilitate researchers' use of computer referencing. All key words were taken from a music education thesaurus and the *Thesaurus of ERIC Descriptors*. Key words were discontinued in v. 28 (Spring 1980), but abstracts are still provided with each article.

Internal indexing for *JRME* began with a cumulative index in the Fall 1962 issue (10.2:151–57) that carried materials published in vs. 1–10 (1953–62). A second index was included as part of the Winter 1964 issue (12.4:304–6) for vs. 11 and 12. Since then, yearly indexes have appeared in winter issues. In recent years, the annual indexes have listed articles both by author and by title.

V. 1.1 of *JRME* was eighty pages long and printed with two columns per page, a practice that continued until v. 14 (1966) when a change in format was made to one wide column per page for articles. Pagination from the first issue to the present one is cumulative within each volume. The physical size of the journal has remained the same (6″ by 9″) since v. 1. It was published twice yearly (Spring and Fall) for vs. 1–11 (1953–63), and changed to a quarterly schedule with v. 12 (1964).

Information Sources

BIBLIOGRAPHY

Britton, Allen P. "Founding JRME: A Personal View." *Journal of Research in Music Education* 32 (1984): 233–42.

Warren, Fred Anthony. "A History of the Music Education Research Council and the Journal of Research in Music Education of the Music Educators National Conference." Ed.D. diss., University of Michigan, 1966.

——. "A History of the Journal of Research in Music Education, 1953–1965." *Journal of Research in Music Education* 32 (1984): 223–32.

INDEXES

Internal: vs. 1–10 in v.10; vs. 11–12 in v. 12; each volume indexed (vs. 13–   ). External: Music Index, 1953–   . Music Article Guide, 1967–   . Music Psychology Index, 1983–   . RILM, 1967–   . Bibliographie des Musikschrifttums, 1961–   . Vs. 1–31 in Mark, Michael L. *Contemporary Music Education*. 2d ed. New York: G. Schirmer, 1986, pp. 309–32.

REPRINT EDITIONS

Microform: UMI.

LOCATION SOURCES

Widely available.

Publication History

TITLE AND TITLE CHANGES

Journal of Research in Music Education.

VOLUME AND ISSUE DATA

Volumes 1–   , 1953–   .

FREQUENCY OF PUBLICATION

Semiannual, 1953–63. Quarterly, 1964–   .

PUBLISHER

Music Educators National Conference.

PLACES OF PUBLICATION

Chicago, Spring 1953–56. Washington, D.C., Fall 1956–64. Baltimore, 1965–Fall 1972. Washington, D.C., Winter 1972–1973. Vienna, Virginia, 1974–Summer 1975. Reston, Virginia, Fall 1975–   .

EDITORS

Allen P. Britton, 1953–72. Robert Petzold, 1972–78. James C. Carlsen, 1978–81. George L. Duerksen, interim editorial committee chairman, 1981–82. Jack A. Taylor, 1982–88. Rudolf E. Radocy, 1988–   .

Vincent J. Kantorski

JOURNAL OF THE AMERICAN MUSICAL INSTRUMENT SOCIETY

Subscription to the American Musical Instrument Society's annual *Journal* is obtained by membership in the society, an international organization founded in 1971 "to promote study of the history, design, and use of musical instruments in all cultures and from all periods" (1: closing advertisement). One of its major projects since 1974 has been publication of the scholarly *Journal*, one each year, and three annual newsletters, "providing the membership with information on worldwide activities, book lists and comments, and general short articles of interest to museum curators, collectors, performers, and others interested in musical instruments" (1: closing advertisement).

This global approach differentiated the publication at once from its major predecessor, the *Galpin Society Journal* (q.v.), whose focus has always been on European musical instruments. The latter were not, however, excluded by the American Musical Instrument Society. The increasing interest in early performance practices and authenticity has spawned sufficient research to fill more than one publication.

Indicative of the intended breadth of content, the board of editors—headed by Thomas Forrest Kelly and including Howard Mayer Brown, Friedrich von Huene, representatives of the Smithsonian, the Henry Ford Museum, and the Museum of Fine Arts in Boston, among others—chose for its first issue an article on "Han Dynasty Musicians and Instruments" by Fong Chow (1:113–25) and one on the "North American Indian Musical Instruments: Some Organological Distribution Problems" by J. Richard Haefer (1: 56–85), but also Laurence C. Witten II's study of bowed strings in North Italy 1480—1580, "Apollo, Orpheus and David" (1:5–55), and an article by Shelley Davis on "The Orchestra under Clemens Wenzeslaus: Music at the Late Eighteenth-Century Court" (1:86–112). Book reviews, a list of recent publications, plates, and trade advertising (with instrument makers comprising the majority of ads) were included as well for a total of nearly 140 pages.

In 1979 William E. Hettrick assumed editorship of the *Journal*, now larger by some thirty pages. The newsletter, an important forum for all types of communication other than scholarly material, received its own editor, André P. Larson. A special editor was also named for the extensive section of book reviews.

The most recent issues of the *Journal* follow the format established at that time; they contain 230 or more 6″ by 9¼″ pages, including fifteen to twenty extensive, signed book reviews and a very complete list of recent books relevant to society interests. The average length of an article varies widely; a single issue may offer a five-page discussion of a historical document and a comprehensive investigation of construction and performance techniques comprising seventy pages, along with several other articles.

Although instruments of all cultures have continued to be of interest to the society, the space devoted to non-Western instruments seems proportionately less in the last ten years, perhaps due to the growth of ethnomusicology as a separate discipline. On the other hand, the number of foreign-language books reviewed has grown significantly during the life of the *Journal* and compensates in some measure for the lack of a truly international list of contributors.

Many official publications of professional societies suffer from the confusion that is engendered when scholarship is interspersed with general news and organizational business. The clear division of these functions by the American Musical Instrument Society results in a journal that is clearly devoted to sophisticated studies and a newsletter that can provide more timely dissemination of other communications. It seems an emminently logical solution and has surely contributed both to the respect for American research in the area and to the influence which the American Musical Instrument Society has had in the increasing importance of the "early instrument specialist" in the United States.

Information Sources

INDEXES
       External: RILM, 1978–   . Bibliographie des Musikschrifttums, 1978–   .
LOCATION SOURCES
       Widely Available.

Publication History

TITLE AND TITLE CHANGES
       Journal of the American Musical Instrument Society.
VOLUME AND ISSUE DATA
       Volumes 1–   , 1974–   .
FREQUENCY OF PUBLICATION
       Annual.
PUBLISHER
       The American Musical Instrument Society.
PLACE OF PUBLICATION
       Shreveport, Louisiana.
EDITORS
       Thomas F. Kelly, 1974–79. William E. Hettrick, 1979–85. Martha Maas, 1986–   .

Ruth K. Inglefield

JOURNAL OF THE INDIAN MUSICOLOGICAL SOCIETY

On Indian independence day, 26 January 1970, Amit R. and R. C. Mehta of Baroda began publishing a quarterly "English Supplement" to *Sangit Kala Vihar (SKV),* a bilingual (Hindi and Marathi) music magazine (apparently a monthly), then in its twenty-third volume. The "new feature" was offered gratis to *SKV* readers as an "experiment" and "forum." The Indian Musicological Society (IMS) entered the world in November 1970, with B. R. Deadar as founding president. V. 1.3 of *SKV* "English Supplement" announced the birth of the new society and the latter's decision to adopt the English Supplement as its official organ. The *Journal of the Indian Musicological Society* appeared for the first time in 1971 (2.1), bearing an "English Supplement . . . " reminder in its subtitle through 1972. R. C. Mehta, sole editor of the journal to date, expressed relief that the publication was no longer the "effort of an individual," but under the aegis of a bona fide institution.

The society and its founders appeared to view themselves as defenders of a somewhat embattled art, an art in need of asserting its dignity, both at home and abroad. In this context they may have been responding to a regional situation in the "syncretic" northwest, but the scope of their efforts clearly extended to the broadest reaches of Indian culture, whose curious spiritual extensions into the Western Hemisphere are sometimes reflected in the pages of the journal.

Beyond the declaration of the society, printed inside the front cover of each issue, the editor offers few direct clues to his policies. Most "editorials" are simply succinct summaries of major articles. Beyond this, they typically assume a plaintive tone: "why is nothing being done about. . . . " Such editorials champion most frequently the domestic teaching and promotion of traditional—specifically Hindustani—music (although Karnatic is not neglected elsewhere in the journal).

Other causes are the danger of using harmonium on All India Radio (AIR) (2.3:1), the "orchestra" as Indian pickings of Western refuse (3.1:3), the importance of the Raga tradition (3.2:viii; 3.3:x), praise of U.S. universitites for teaching "world music" and of Indian music/dance troupes performing abroad (1.3:vi), and an appeal to AIR to offset cheap local pop by providing "canned concerts" of India's best music (5.1:3; 5.2:3). In addition there are frequent tributes to past "pioneers" of Indian music/pedagogy and contemporary virtuosos. National music seminars/congresses also receive ample attention.

The articles themselves provide a better profile of the journal's inclination, but here the careful, "initiated" reader is called for. A superficial survey of titles suggests that interest is divided between: (1) the best of synchronic traditional and folk music throughout India, (2) musical philology of the venerable ancients, and (3) an eclectic assortment of topics from psychology, sociology, biology, aesthetics, and theosophy, as they loosely relate to music. One notes also a penchant for European electronic music and the poetry/music of Tagore. Representative special issues include: Antsher Lobo's "Indian Musical 'Ma-Grama' of Bharata: The World's Only Perfect Scale" (2.3, 3.1, 3.4, 4.1); Pandet Vishnu Narayan Bhatkhanda's "A Comparative Study of Some of the Leading Music Systems of the 15th, 16th, 17th, & 18th Centuries" (3.2, 3.3); Madhubhai Patel's "Folksongs of South Gujarat" (5.3, 5.4); and Tarkelar's monograph on "Samavedic Chants: A Review of Research" (14.2, 15.1, 15.2).

Most contributors are Indian, with a range of credentials that transcends the specifically musical. Although an occasional prominent name appears among those from Europe and America, very few are music specialists. The sympathetic lay/freelance writer from the West appears to be welcome in these pages. In salutary contrast to some European counterparts, the *Journal* presents a healthy proportion of female contributors.

Virtually every issue contains: (1) one or more articles, usually four to six, ranging from five to twelve pages in length, (2) a brief summary of each article, presented as a one to two page editorial, and (3) biographical notes on each contributor. Regular "features" begin with "News & Notes" in 4.2. "Monographs on Music" was initiated early (1.3) and realized in the special issues devoted to out-of-print books by Bhatkhanda, but the rubric was not evoked later. From v. 4.4 to 5.2 and 5.4, a "Music and Dance Chronicle" is included, listing all "significant" concerts in the country during the preceding three-month period. Rare book reviews appear in the first eleven years of publication. With v. 12 they begin in earnest with most by R. C. Mehta.

The regularity of indexing is difficult to assess at this distance. In the collection consulted there were indexes, obviously published on separate sheets, for vs. 1–3, 4–5: author/title in one sort with no subject keys.

Quantity of advertising varies sufficiently from issue to issue to suggest the local (Baroda) commercial interests may have influenced content, although this could not be affirmed without careful study. Ads were usually by local firms with no apparent connection to music, often seeming to reflect a sociopolitical orientation of the journal. Commercial advertising tapers off markedly following v. 8.2.

A format of 7¼″ by 9⅝″ has remained constant since the beginning, as well as the use of low-quality paper and the occurrence of typographical and paging errors to the threshold of distraction. Photos and other graphics not immediately realizable with typesetting techniques have been rare. Except for two to three issues, there are no transcriptions in Western music notation. On the other hand, textual citations in Devanagari are frequent.

With the exception of the Devanagari citations, the only language used is English. The journal was officially a quarterly until 1982, although apologies for "delays" were frequent and "combined issues" regular from 1978. In 1982 (v. 13) the *Journal* became a declared semiannual publication.

Information Sources

INDEXES
> External: Music Index, 1972– . RILM, 1969– .

REPRINT EDITIONS
> Microform: UMI.

LOCATION SOURCES
> Widely available, except for v. 1.

Publication History

TITLE AND TITLE CHANGES
> *Sangeet Kala Vihar,* "English Supplement," 1970, issue #1. *Sangeet Kala Vihar,* "English Supplement," "Indian Music Quarterly," 1970, issues #2–4. *Journal of the Indian Musicological Society, Incorporating Sangeet Kala Vihar English Supplement,* 1971–72. *Journal of the Indian Musicological Society,* 1973– .

VOLUME AND ISSUE DATA
> Volumes 1– , 1971– .

FREQUENCY OF PUBLICATION
  Quarterly and irregular, 1971–81. Semiannual, 1982.
PUBLISHER
  Indian Musicological Society.
PLACE OF PUBLICATION
  Jambu Bet, Dandia Bazar, Baroda, India.
EDITOR
  R. C. Mehta, 1970– .
GUEST EDITOR
  T. S. Parthasarthy, 6:3 (1975).

L. JaFran Jones

JOURNAL OF THE ROYAL MUSICAL ASSOCIATION. See ROYAL MU-SICAL ASSOCIATION, PROCEEDINGS OF

K

KEY NOTES

The Foundation for Documentation of Netherlands Music (the Donemus Foundation) was established in 1947. Its object was and still is to make known, both at home and abroad, the works of Dutch composers, especially those active during the last century. One of its early activities was the publication of a bulletin, *Muzikaal Perspectief (Musical Perspective)*. Published in Dutch, it was essentially a chronicle of new Dutch compositions, combined with lists of recordings and performances of Dutch compositions in the Netherlands and abroad. After a preliminary issue, entitled *Mededelingen van de Stichting Donemus* (December 1947), thirty-five issues of *Muzikaal Perspectief* were published (through November 1957). In most years four issues appeared, each from eight to sixteen pages in length until n. 20, thereafter from sixteen to twenty-four pages. At its tenth anniversary Donemus published a booklet, *Tien Jaar Donemus, 1947–1957*, containing a survey of its activities by André Jurres, director of Donemus.

The same year, *Muzikaal Perspectief* was superseded by *Sonorum Speculum*. After a slow start of five issues between 1958 and 1960, together about 200 pages in length, four issues a year appeared until 1971, each year containing about 200 pages. In 1972 a special double issue (n. 50/51) was published, after six more issues (1973–74), *Sonorum Speculum* was superseded by the still active *Key Notes*.

Because it was intended for an international audience, *Sonorum Speculum* was a bilingual publication, in English and German. The contents were broadened, over those of *Muzikaal Perspectief*, to contain not only documentation but also articles concerning musical life in the Netherlands. Jos Wouters, active with the journal from its inception and appointed editor with n. 6 (March 1961), moved the journal to a more active publication schedule and inaugurated two important series of articles. The first, entitled "Composer's Gallery," characterized the life and works of twentieth-century Dutch composers. The second featured detailed analyses of Dutch compositions, most of which were also released on recordings in the *Donemus Audio-Visual Series*. Musical examples are abundant.

The fifteenth anniversary of Donemus was celebrated by *Fifteen Year Donemus, 1947–1962: Conversations with Dutch Composers = Gespräche mit Niederländischen Komponisten*. In this bilingual booklet (English and German) Jos Wouters and André Jurres, president and director of Donemus respectively, published five conversations apiece with two composers. In 1971, for the twenty-fifth anniversary, the portraits of nine other composers by Jos Wouters, all of which had appeared before as articles in *Sonorum Speculum*, were reprinted in a separate bilingual publication, in Dutch and English this time: *Nederlandse Componisten Galerij, Deel 1 = Dutch Composers' Gallery, Part 1*. An intended second part never appeared.

The twenty-fifth anniversary also was celebrated by the publishing of a small but remarkable book as a double issue of *Sonorum Speculum* (n. 50/51): *Music in Paintings of the Low Countries in the 16th and 17th Centuries = Musik auf Niederländischen Gemälden im 16. und 17. Jahrhundert* by Pieter Fischer.

Until the end of 1974, the physical format of *Sonorum Speculum* had been 6″ by 9½″ and averaged from forty to fifty-six pages. At that point, however, the editors decided to change their format and their editorial policy, in conjunction with a reorientation within the Donemus Foundation itself toward the younger generation and its preoccupations. The new aim was "to form ever increasing connections with the most aware movements in musical life" (*Key Notes*, 1.2). Under the new title, *Key Notes*, they left behind "the nostalgia for the good old days" of the former journal, and sought to "follow musical life with a critical ear, indicating changes and stimulating new thought" (10.2). The scholars, critics and composers who contribute to its pages have, however, maintained the journal's traditional high standards and sophistication. The physical format was enlarged to 8¼″ by 11½″, and *Key Notes* became a semiannual magazine, published in English only, of forty-eight to sixty-four pages.

At the same time an irregular series of newsletters was started. Of these *Donemus Muzieknotities* only seven issues appeared, each eight, sixteen, or twenty-four pages in length. Published exclusively in Dutch, they contained only the chronicle, similar to the earlier *Muzikaal Perspectief*.

Through 1985, twenty-two issues of *Key Notes* have been published, and the ambitious aims of *Key Notes* are still intact. On the one hand, the traditional series of articles has been continued: the profiles of new composers and analyses of new compositions, as well as a series of articles, "Composer's Voice," in which new recordings of compositions by Dutch composers are reviewed in detail. These recordings, four issues each year, bear the same serial title, *Composer's Voice*, superseding the former *Donemus Audio-Visual Series*. Perhaps the most remarkable feature of *Key Notes* is the critical approach and tone, which provokes reactions from irritation to enthusiasm, as shown by the "Letters to the Editor," to be found in nearly every issue.

With 1986, changes in frequency of publication and in the format are foreseen, the result of economic considerations. Though there are plans to change the editorial team from year to year, the contents of *Key Notes* will remain an indispensable and unique compendium of contemporary Dutch music and composers.

Information Sources

BIBLIOGRAPHY

Finlay, I. F. "Some Reflections as a Translator for Sonorum Speculum for Nearly Ten Years." *Sonorum Speculum* 37 (Winter 1968/69): 23–26.

Moldenhauer, Hans. "Music in Europe." *Music of the West Magazine* 14 (September 1958): 3.

Wouters, Jos. "A New Phase." *Sonorum Speculum* 6 (1 March 1961): 1.

Zazlaw, Neal. "Three Music Periodicals." *Current Musicology* 10 (1970): 142–43.

INDEXES

External: Music Index, 1958– . RILM, 1967– .

LOCATION SOURCES

Widely available.

Publication History

TITLE AND TITLE CHANGES

Mededelingen van de Stichting Donemus, December 1947. *Muzikaal Perspectief: Mededelingen van Donemus,* February 1948–November 1957. *Sonorum Speculum: Mirror of Musical Life in Holland,* Summer 1958. *Sonorum Speculum: Mirror of Dutch Musical Life* (or *Mirror of Musical Life in the Netherlands*), Winter 1958/59–1974. *Key Notes: Musical Life in The Netherlands,* 1975– .

VOLUME AND ISSUE DATA

Sonorum Speculum: vs. 1–57, 1958–74. *Key Notes:* vs. 1– , 1975– .

FREQUENCY OF PUBLICATION

Sonorum Speculum: quarterly, with some irregularities. *Key Notes:* semiannual.

PUBLISHER

Stichting Donemus (all titles).

PLACE OF PUBLICATION

Amsterdam (all titles).

EDITORS

Editors of *Mededelingen, Muzikaal Perspectief,* and *Donemus Muzieknotities* are not mentioned, nor are the editors of *Sonorum Speculum* until #5 (1960). *Sonorum Speculum:* Jos Wouters, 1961–74. *Key Notes* has had an editorial board of six to nine persons.

Alfons Annegarn

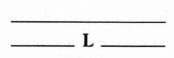

L

LEAGUE OF COMPOSERS REVIEW. See MODERN MUSIC

LISTENER'S RECORD GUIDE. See AMERICAN RECORD GUIDE

LIVING BLUES

An introduction in the forty-page first issue of *Living Blues* in 1970 stated: "We do not intend to explain, define, or confine the blues. We believe that the blues is a living tradition." Thus, while their masthead, since early 1974, has proclaimed "A journal of the black American blues tradition," the editors have noted the "changing definitions and disparate visions of blues" and cover white as well as black artists. They have also expressed faith that "the blues will continue," despite the deaths of leading performers, (n. 45/46:3). It is this faith in and devotion to the "living" quality of the music coupled with fifteen years of entrepreneurial perseverance that have made *Living Blues* the leading publication in its field.

Living Blues's coverage has encompassed traditional and contemporary blues, features on and biographies of performers, concerts and festivals, blues clubs, record companies, book and record reviews, radio station listings, and obituaries. Feature articles have averaged one to three pages, though a longer (six- to fifteen-page) special feature is included in some more recent issues. Picture coverage has been consistently strong. The first issue used a cover photo and the second issue a six-page photo feature on the Wisconsin Delta Blues Festival. Noteworthy examples of its extensive question-and-answer features on performers are a seventeen-page article in 1974 on Houston Stackhouse (17:20–36) and a twenty-six-page article with sidebars in 1975 on Jimmy Reed (21:16–40). The contributors are primarily observer/critics; readership spans both fans and performers.

On the journal's tenth anniversary, the editors noted that they tried to avoid duplication of coverage available in other magazines, on LP liner notes, or of previously published photographs. They stated: "Thus we haven't gotten around to doing features on some of the blues artists whose stories are well known already, and we won't until we feel that such features offer sufficient depth, with new and different details, insights, or perspectives" (45/46:3).

Among seven founders of the journal in the spring of 1970, Jim and Amy O'Neal gradually assumed primary responsibility for editorial duties and were its publishers until Spring 1983 (n. 56), when the publisher became the Center for the Study of Southern Culture at the University of Mississippi.

Chicago activity dominated earlier issues, because the O'Neals had the best access to touring artists there. San Francisco activity was also well covered. Since 1980, the editors have specifically sought a larger purview.

Living Blues was issued quarterly at the outset, became a bimonthly at the start of 1975 (n. 19), and then reverted to quarterly in the summer of 1979 (n. 43). It was 8¼″ by 10½″ in size and varied from forty to fifty-two pages in the early years. Since 1983 it has ranged from fifty-six to seventy-eight pages, with dimensions of 8½″ by 11″. The quality of articles and photographs has historically been respectable and improving, while production standards have soared from the journal's rather modest beginnings. Advertising includes classifieds and display ads for records, agents, clubs, artists, and instrument makers. The O'Neals' Rooster Blues Record Sales operation is a prominent advertiser.

Living Bluesletter was published monthly in conjunction with the magazine during 1983 and 1984. It contained news briefs, club listings, artists' itineraries, record releases, and radio chart ratings. Since 1985 (n. 65) this coverage has been provided as a section of the magazine itself, including a thirty-page radio program guide (n. 65).

Information Sources

INDEXES
> Internal: ns. 1–24 in n. 40.
> External: Music Index, 1971– . Abstracts of Folk Studies. RILM 1978– .
> Popular Music Periodical Index, 1973–76. MLA International Bibliography, 1976.

REPRINT EDITIONS
> Microform: UMI.

LOCATION SOURCES
> Widely available.

Publication History

TITLE AND TITLE CHANGES
> *Living Blues,* 1970– . Subtitled *Incorporating Living Bluesletter,* 1983–84.

VOLUME AND ISSUE DATA
>Volumes 1– , 1970– .

FREQUENCY OF PUBLICATION
>Quarterly, 1970–74. Bimonthly, 1975–78. Quarterly, 1979– .

PUBLISHERS
>Jim and Amy O'Neal, 1970–Spring 1983. Center for the Study of Southern Culture, University of Mississippi, Autumn 1983– .

PLACES OF PUBLICATION
>Chicago, 1970–Spring 1983. University of Mississippi, Autumn 1983– .

EDITORS
>Various co-editors listed through early 1974. Jim and Amy O'Neal, 1970–86. Jim O'Neal, 1987. Peter Lee, 1988– .

Robert Byler

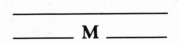

M

MAANDBLAD VOOR MUZIEK. See CAECILIA (1844–1944)

MAANDBLAD VOOR MUZIEK, EN HET MUSIEKCOLLEGE. See CAE-CILIA (1844–1944)

MEDELELINGEN VON DE STICHTING DONEMUS. See KEY NOTES

MEDELELINGENBLAD VOOR LEDEN EN DONATEURS VAN DE VERENIGING VOOR NEDERLANDSE MUZIEKGESCHIEDENIS. See TIJDSCHRIFT VAN DE VERENIGING VOOR NEDERLANDSE MUZIEK-GESCHIEDENIS

MEISTER WERK IN DER MUSIK, DAS. See TONWILLE, DER

MELODY MAKER

Melody Maker represents a uniquely British blend of the music trade weekly (exemplified in America by *Billboard* [q.v.] and *Cash Box* [q.v.]) and analytical journalism as typified by *Rolling Stone* (q.v.) and *Stereo Review* (q.v.). While this broad-based approach is largely responsible for the magazine's staying power, it has led to the rise of several more editorially focused titles most of which currently outsell *Melody Maker*.

Melody Maker was established in 1926 primarily to print song lyrics of the hits of the day. Odhams Press, Ltd., its owner and a music publisher, saw the magazine as a device for stimulating the sale of sheet music. Its pages reflected an increasingly greater coverage of the popular music of that era such as jazz, big bands, Tin Pan Alley, and the musical theatre. The appearance of its first notable competitor, *New Musical Express* (*NME*), in 1952, necessitated a gradual shift in editorial perspective; lyrics disappeared by the late 1950s and emphasis on rock music increased. *NME's* fanzine style of presentation combined with a wholehearted commitment to the lighter forms of pop music—first the crooning tradition and later rock and roll—catapulted the magazine far ahead of *Melody Maker* in the circulation sweepstakes. However, *Melody Maker's* somewhat more high brow approach began to reap dividends in the early 1960s with the rise in England of a new school of musical archaeologists dedicated to resuscitating older indigenous American forms such as the blues, rhythm and blues, and rockabilly. Many of the best rock journalists/historians of the present day started out contributing to the pages of *Melody Maker* in the 1960s and early 1970s. *Melody Maker's* informative, instructive approach earned it a reputation as the "musician's magazine." Its back pages now carried extensive information about new instruments and related products. In addition, many important bands, from Led Zeppelin to the Jam, are said to have been formed through *Melody Maker's* "Musician's Wanted" and "Musician's Available" classified ads. The magazine's preeminence was further assured by the chart success of art rock groups such as the Moody Blues, King Crimson, and Yes.

This orientation did, however, serve to hasten the gradual loss of *Melody Maker's* leadership position among British pop music periodicals. The editors appeared disinclined to cover new musical trends to any great extent throughout the seventies; the resulting vacuum came to be filled by a rash of new publications, most notably *Sounds, Smash Hits, The Face,* and *No. 1.* These titles emphasize striking visuals, terse writing aimed at the youthful reader, a monthly publication schedule, and a recognition that the all-music format is a thing of the past. In the face of this intense competition, *Melody Maker's* circulation has fallen, yet it remains secure in the fact that its importance to the more sophisticated strata of the industry enables it to turn a respectable profit.

Despite the volatile nature of the British music scene, *Melody Maker's* editorial policy has changed very little since its watershed days some fifteen years ago. A typical issue offers a highly diversified treatment of the popular music scene. The front pages of the magazine are devoted to general news briefs (emphasizing leading musicians, studio producers, and various regional markets), feature stories, and columns (for example, "U.S. News," "Mailbag") liberally interspersed with black and white photos and artwork. The middle part includes record reviews (subdivided by singles and albums, including breakdowns by specific genres such as the blues, folk, and jazz), concert reviews, concert itineraries, best-selling charts (subdivided by software format, country, and genre; for example, "U.K. Reggae Singles"), and special series reports, which typically focus on either important artists or musical trends in foreign cities or countries. The final portion includes a potpourri of columns covering British provincial centers, genre news, club calendars, equipment discussions, festival roundups, and classifieds—all with a decidedly British emphasis. No identifiable table of contents is employed, thereby limiting the reference utility of the magazine.

Melody Maker has employed numerous well-known reviewers, writers, and editors, including Ray Coleman, Chris Welch, Richard Williams, Ian Birch, Chris Brazier, Michael Oldfield, John Orme, and Harry Doherty. Many of these and other contributors have published notable books on rock music. In addition, most important British musicians have submitted articles, letters, and commentaries at one time or another to the magazine.

Melody Maker employs a tabloid newsprint format. While size has varied slightly over the past two decades, it has generally measured 13″ by 17½″. Numbering of issues begins with the establishment of a new volume series for the first weekly installment of a given year. Issues generally range from fifty to eighty pages in length.

Information Sources

BIBLIOGRAPHY
Henke, James. "British Press Shocker!" *Rolling Stone* (November 10, 1983): 53, 55–56, 88.
INDEXES
External: Music Index, 1949– . Popular Music Periodicals Index, 1973–76.
REPRINT EDITIONS
Microform: Library of Congress (1926–76); Datamics Inc. (1948–76, incomplete); UMI, 1926– (incomplete).
LOCATION SOURCES
Widely available.

Publication History

TITLE AND TITLE CHANGES
Melody Maker.
VOLUME AND ISSUE DATA
Volumes 1– , 1926– .
FREQUENCY OF PUBLICATION
Weekly.
PUBLISHERS
Odhams Press Ltd., 1926–64. 60 Magazine Ltd., 1965–66. Longacre Press Ltd., 1967–74. IPC Specialist and Professional Press Ltd., 1975– .
PLACE OF PUBLICATION
London.

EDITORS
Pat Brand, 194?–64. Jack Hutton, 1954–70. Ray Coleman, 1971–78. Richard
Williams, 1978–80. Michael Oldfield, 1981–84. Allan Jones, 1984–   .

Frank W. Hoffman

MELOS

Begun in February 1920 by Hermann Scherchen, who later founded the *Gravesaner Blätter* (q.v.), *Melos* was second only to *Anbruch* (q.v.) for its coverage of Austro-Germanic modern musical life in the 1920s. Unlike *Anbruch*, however, *Melos* was able to survive a takeover by the National Socialists and resume publication in 1947 with its dedication to contemporary music intact. *Melos* then continued to provide one of the few forums devoted solely to covering modern concert music and musical life until its merger with the *Neue Zeitschrift für Musik* (q.v.) in 1975 and its eventual absorption into the same in 1979.

Scherchen asserted, in the inaugural issue, that *Melos* intended to speak to four concerns of contemporary music: the breakdown of tonality, the relationship of music and words, music's relationship with the other arts, and the sociological foundation of music. Early issues of *Melos* contained five to six articles of three to eight pages in length on a variety of topics related to these concerns: analyses of a single composition, studies of a genre, and discussions of such ideas as the influence of folk music on modern music, musical exoticism, and the new classicism. Issues also contained several short reviews of performances as well as a list of all new scores and books pertinent to modern music, released by the major German publishers. Of special interest in the early volumes was the frequent inclusion of musical appendices consisting of a complete movement of a newly published solo or chamber work. Issues were frequently devoted to one particular topic. The very first was dedicated to Busoni and his music, and subsequent special issues were devoted to opera (4.3), music in Russia (4.9), the 1928 Baden-Baden Festival (7.7), and musical criticism (8.3). Early contributors to the journal included critics H. H. Stuckenschmidt and Paul Bekker, as well as composers Arnold Schönberg and Béla Bartók, all of whom were also part of the seventeen-member editorial board.

The Schott company of Mainz took over the publishing duties in 1927, and the journal expanded both in size and scope. Though *Melos* championed the works of Schott composer Paul Hindemith, it never became the in-house organ that *Anbruch* (q.v.) was for Universal Edition. Hans Mersmann, who continued as editor through the change to Schott, stressed the need to broaden the journal's coverage to any and all concerns pertinent to contemporary musical life. By 1928, issues contained a number of new and expanded features including "Meloskritik," written jointly by Hans Mersmann, Hans Schultze-Ritter, and Heinrich Strobel, which provided extensive reviews of most German and Austrian premieres, especially operas, as well as other performances of new music in a number of cities. Later a separate section for reviews of radio performances and recordings was added as well as coverage of film music. Other important features were the "Musical Life" and "Umschau" sections which contained short editorials, excerpts from newspaper articles, shorter concert and book reviews, reports on musical activities, and announcements.

Scherchen remained as editor until 1933, when he left Germany for political reasons and settled in Switzerland. Heinrich Strobel, who had already been a regular contributor, succeeded him. By this time *Melos* clearly mirrored the changing German political climate. Articles on topics other than modern music began to appear. In November 1934, after the virtual takeover of the German press by the National Socialist government, *Melos* became a very different publication entitled *Neues Musikblatt*. This music newspaper, with a ten-page 10¼" by 14¾" physical format, was intended for a less specialized audience. In 1943 the *Neues Musikblatt* was combined with three other music journals—*Die Musik* (q.v.), *Allgemeine Musik-Zeitung* (q.v.), and *Zeitschrift für Musik* (q.v.)— to become *Musik im Kriege*, an official National Socialist publication "united for the duration of the war" (*Musik im Kriege*: cover).

In November 1946 *Melos* returned to print and reaffirmed its prewar dedication to the cause of new music with its new subtitle "Zeitschrift für neue Musik." Heinrich Strobel returned as the editor, and a number of writers, such as H. H. Stuckenschmidt, returned as leading contributors. In order to disavow itself from the twelve years of Nazi domination, *Melos* resumed its postwar numbering with v. 14, viewing v. 13—the year before *Melos* became *Neues Musikblatt*—as representing the last true volume of *Melos*. Many of the prewar features returned in the new *Melos*, in particular its review sections, both extensive and brief, of premieres, special performances, books, radio programs, and records. Issues now contained six to seven articles of two to five pages in length on composers, specific works, and general topics. New to the postwar *Melos* was its effort to cover contemporary concert life internationally, not just those events, persons, and trends within Germany and Austria.

In 1975, Schott merged *Melos* with the historically important *Neue Zeitschrift für Musik* to form *Melos/NZ*. Both publications retained their individual numbering systems. In this new version, *Melos's* contemporary coverage was combined with the broader, more general, and historically oriented coverage of *Neue Zeitschrift für Musik*. In 1979, *Melos*, as a separate entity, disappeared, along with a good portion of its contemporary music coverage.

The physical format, size, and frequency of issuance varied over the fifty-nine year history of the journal. First advertised as a semimonthly publication, *Melos* dropped to twelve issues per year in v. 2. The first three volumes appeared in an 8⅞" by 11" physical format and grew from twenty-three to fifty-five pages per issue. In v. 4, the format was reduced to 7⁵⁄₁₆" by 9¹¹⁄₁₆" and an average issue thereafter was forty-eight to fifty-two pages long. In v. 5 the journal adopted a regular January to December monthly issuance. In the early 1930s the size dropped to below forty pages per issue and to less than thirty pages in 1934 before its reorganization as *Neues Musikblatt*. After the war the reorganized *Melos* appeared in an 8³⁄₁₆″ by 11¼″ format, and after issuing thirteen numbers in v. 14, it returned to a regular January to December monthly issuance with individual issues varying between thirty and fifty pages. In v. 34 the physical format changed again to 7⅞″ by 11½″. *Melos/NZ* was issued six times a year in an 8″ by 10³⁄₁₆″ format. *Melos* always included extensive musical examples, advertisements, appendices, and illustrations. Issues prior to World War II had unusual and often specially designed cover illustrations in keeping with the journal's modernist aesthetic. Indices were published for each volume, except for the *Neues Musikblatt* and *Musik im Kriege*.

Information Sources

BIBLIOGRAPHY

Mersmann, Hans. "Zehn Jahre 'Melos.' " *Melos* 9 (1930): 58–63.

Oesch, Hans. "Das *Melos* und die Neue Musik." In *Festschrift für einer Verleger: Ludwig Strecker zum 90. Geburtstag*, edited by Carl Dahlhaus, pp. 287–94. Mainz: Schott, 1973.

Reich, Willi. "Hermann Scherchen und 'Melos'; zum 60. Geburtstag des Dirigenten an 21 Juni." *Melos* 18 (1951): 286–88.

Strobel, Heinrich. "50 Jahre 'Melos.'" *Melos* 37 (1970): 221–23.

INDEXES

Internal: each volume indexed (except 1934–44).

External: Music Index, 1951–78. RILM, 1967–78. Bibliographie des Musikschrifttums, 1950– . Arts and Humanities Citation Index, 1976–78.

REPRINT EDITIONS

Microform: Schnase, 1920–34. Datamics, 1920–55.

LOCATION SOURCES

New York Public Library. Newberry Library (Chicago). Philadelphia Free Library. University of Houston. University of Illinois. Library of Congress (partial). Postwar volumes widely available.

Publication History

TITLE AND TITLE CHANGES

Melos, 1920–34. *Neues Musikblatt*, 1934–42. *Musik im Kriege* (joint publication with *Die Musik, Allgemeine Musik-Zeitung*, and *Zeitschrift für Musik*), 1943–44); *Melos Zeitschrift für neue Musik*, 1947–74. *Melos/NZ*, 1975–78. Ceased publication, 1979.

VOLUME AND ISSUE DATA

Vs. 1–13, 1920–34; vs. 14–45, 1947–78.

FREQUENCY OF PUBLICATION

Monthly, 1920–74. Bimonthly, 1974–78.

PUBLISHERS

Neuendorff und Moll, 1920. Melos Verlag, 1920–26. B. Schott, 1927–34. Neuen Musikblattes, 1947–73. Schott, 1974–78.

PLACES OF PUBLICATION

Berlin, February 1920–26. Mainz, 1927–78.

EDITORS

Hermann Scherchen, 1920–21. Fritz Windisch, 1921–24. Hans Mersmann, 1924–33. Heinrich Strobel, 1933–39. Fritz Bouquet, 1939–42. Herbert Gerigk, 1943–44. Heinrich Strobel, 1947–58. Heinrich Strobel and Gerth-Wolfgang Baruch, 1959–70. Gerth-Wolfgang Baruch, 1970–71. Gerth-Wolfgang Baruch and Hans Oesch, 1972–74. Carl Dahlhaus, Hans Oesch, Ernst Thomas, Otto Tomek, 1975–78.

Susan C. Cook

MELOS/NZ. See MELOS

MELOS/NZ NEUE ZEITSCHRIFT FÜR MUSIK. See NEUE ZEITSCHRIFT FÜR MUSIK

MELOS ZEITSCHIFT FÜR NEUE MUSIK. See MELOS

MÉNESTREL, LE

Le Ménestrel offers the modern reader a detailed view of French musical history and taste spanning more than a century. Founded in 1833 by journalist and amateur musician Jules Lovy, it appeared weekly until 1940 with only two wartime interruptions, 1870–71 and 1914–19. Standards of style and content evolved early in the journal's development and remained remarkably consistent throughout its life span. A typical issue contained: one or two short articles on biographical, historical, or pedagogical topics, often serialized over several issues; reviews of current performances in the major theatres and concert halls of Paris; reports from provincial and foreign music centers; and miscellaneous news items, announcements, and obituaries.

Early numbers of *Le Ménestrel* consisted of two pages of text and a popular chanson with piano or guitar accompaniment, the precursor of the musical supplements which would accompany each issue. Taking its name from the wandering performers of the Middle Ages, *Le Ménestrel's* stated intent was to provide popular music for performance and to "attend all concerts . . . and distribute praise or blame impartially" (1.6:4). Reviews of current musical events thus played a major role from the outset.

On 1 March 1840, music publisher Jacques-Léopold Heugel (1815–83) and his partner Jean-Antoine Meissonier (1783–1857) acquired the journal, expanding it to four and subsequently eight pages of double-columned text by 1858. Staples from Heugel's growing catalog comprised the musical supplements, usually in the form of excerpts from opera or operetta and salon pieces of medium difficulty.

Leo Délibes, Jules Massenet, Ambroise Thomas, and other Heugel "house composers" were frequently represented. In the twentieth century there was a shift to short original works by composers such as Gabriel Fauré, Reynaldo Hahn, Charles Widor, Jacques Ibert, Darius Milhaud, and Francis Poulenc. Taken together the supplements form an important chronicle of the musical taste of their time. Unfortunately they were easily dispersed and are only partially preserved in library collections today.

Editorially, *Le Ménestrel* espoused the views of the conservative musical establishment. Its pages document the rise of Wagnerism in France, and the critical reception accorded important works at their premieres. Arthur Pougin's ambivalent review of Claude Debussy's *Pelléas et Mélisande* (68:138–40) reflects the fundamentally cautious stance of the journal throughout much of its existence. While dramatic works (plays as well as opera) dominate the reviews, important orchestral series such as the Colonne, Lamoureux, and Pasdeloup concerts were covered, as were salons of painting and sculpture from time to time. Dance received sparse attention: the unleashing of Igor Stravinsky's *Sacre du Printemps* on Paris in May 1913 passed virtually unnoticed.

Le Ménestrel enjoyed the collaboration of numerous contributors. One of the most prolific and influential was Arthur Pougin (1834–1921) whose biographical studies (including a thirty-seven-part series on the life of Luigi Cherubini appearing between 1881 and 1882) are important landmarks in the beginnings of French musicology. Other regular contributors included François Castil-Blaze (1784–1857), Joseph d'Ortigue (1802–66; editor, 1863–66), Julien Tiersot (1857–1936), Maurice Cauchie (1882–1963), and Lionel de La Laurencie (1861–1933).

Miscellaneous events reported in *Le Ménestrel* are a frequent source of interest to the researcher. Announcements of competitions and prizes, details of private collections of manuscripts, and accounts of payments and receipts in the state-supported theatres were regularly noted. Transcribed correspondence of celebrated composers has proved invaluable in cases where original documents can no longer be traced. Letters of Hector Berlioz, Wolfgang Amadeus Mozart, and Johann Sebastian Bach appeared in vs. 45, 59, and 68, respectively.

In 1933, on the occasion of the journal's centennial, an author/title index was compiled of all general articles, reviews, and obituaries published between 1 December 1833 and 31 December 1932. Maintained on cards at the publishing offices, it is now reported lost. A new, comprehensive index is in progress at the University of Paris—Sorbonne under the direction of Daniéle Pistone.

Le Ménestrel retained an eight-page, 10¾″ by 14⅝″ format until its reappearance following World War I, when it underwent slight redesign to a smaller (9″ by 12¼″) format averaging twelve to sixteen pages in length. All but the earliest volumes are continuously paginated and include a yearly table of contents. Advertisements were infrequent and served mainly to publicize recent Heugel publications. In 1972, a reprint was issued by Minkoff Reprints, Geneva.

Information Sources

BIBLIOGRAPHY
"Cent ans d'histoire de la musique et du théâtre." *Le Ménestrel* 95 (1933): 52.
Heugel et ses musiciens: lettres à un éditeur parisien. Paris: Presses Universitaires de France, 1984.
Pistone, Daniele. "Dossier Wagner à Paris." *Revue Internationale de Musique Française* 1 (February 1980): 84.
INDEXES
External: Bibliographie des Musikschrifttums, 1937, 1939.
REPRINT EDITIONS
Paper: Minkoff Reprints.
Microform: Library of Congress, 1833–1940. Datamics, 1833–1940. Association pour la Conservation et la Reproduction Photographique de la Presse, 1833–1914.
LOCATION SOURCES
Widely available.

Publication History

TITLE AND TITLE CHANGES
Le Ménestrel.
VOLUME AND ISSUE DATA
Volumes 1–102, 1 December 1833–28 August 1870, 3 September 1871–5 September 1914, 17 October 1919–24 May 1940.
FREQUENCY OF PUBLICATION
Weekly.
PUBLISHER
Heugel & Cie.
PLACE OF PUBLICATION
Paris, France.
EDITORS
The names of the following directors of the Heugel firm appeared on the masthead: Jacques Léopold Heugel, December 1840–November 1883. Henri Georges Heugel, November 1883–September 1914. Jacques Paul Heugel, October 1919–May 1940. Editors were not consistently named, but the following are known to have served: Jules Lovy, December 1833–June 1863. Joseph d'Ortigue, June 1863–December 1866. Arthur Pougin, 1885–1914.

Ross Wood

MENS EN MELODIE

After World War II and liberation from the German occupation, musical life in the Netherlands was rekindled. In January 1946, Wouter Paap responded to this revival by starting a general monthly music journal, *Mensch en Melodie* (*Man and Melody*). The title was borrowed from a little book of the same name by Paap (Utrecht: Het Spectrum, 1940). In 1948 the title of the journal was modified to *Mens en Melodie* in accordance with the simplified spelling of the Dutch lan guage that had been introduced in 1934. As the primary, and from 1960 to 1975 only, editor, Paap labored to disseminate information on all aspects of musical life. In so doing, he made a significant contribution, during those thirty years, to the cultural development and particularly the musical education of music amateurs and music lovers as well as of professional musicians in the Netherlands.

Every issue contains short, modestly illustrated articles and essays, reports of important music events, and reviews of newly published books, music, recordings, and concerts, exclusively in Dutch. The last feature is always a compendium, two to three pages long, of short communications about musicians, orchestras, music institutions, music prizes, and so on. The subjects are not limited to Dutch music, but include, to some extent the musical life abroad. Also included are contributions on music in the schools, folk music, sociology, psychology, politics, and any other music-related subject that can be treated in a worthwhile and easily readable article. Special issues are rare. Critics, teachers, and scholarly musicians are the primary contributors.

Until 1975 Wouter Paap himself contributed many articles, as many as fifty a year, frequently writing under various pen names, usually Gerard Werker. In a retrospective, twenty-fifth anniversary piece, he suggested that *Mens en Melodie* was still necessary to provide information and publicity on "serious" music, especially since the daily papers were giving ever less attention to it.

As a rule Paap shunned interviews, which he considered a cheap way of writing an article, preferring to study a musician's work and personality by himself, as a "music spectator." For the last volume under his editorship (v. 30), however, Paap deviated slightly from this antipathy and concocted an interview between himself and his alter ego, Gerard Werker. In it he bade his readers farewell, wished his successor well, and lifted the veil on a few of his pen names.

Starting with v. 31 (1976) *Mens & Melodie* was led by a varying editorial board of three to four persons, which intended to pay more attention to avant-garde music, jazz, and music in radio and television, as well as to expand the book review section. The length of the yearly volumes, which up to 1977 had been about 350 to 400 pages, was gradually increased to about 550 to 600 pages. The physical format remained about 5½″ by 8½″.

Interest in the journal faded slightly by the late 1970s, and the number of subscribers decreased. To deal with this state of affairs, the publication of the journal was taken over by Frits Knuf of Buren early in 1982. Half a year later the editorial board was dissolved and replaced by a single editor, John Kasander. By doing so the publisher hopes to ensure the continuance of this worthwhile journal, the only one in the Netherlands devoted to the broad spectrum of music and addressed to the general public.

Information Sources

BIBLIOGRAPHY
Paap, Wouter. "Zeven jaar Mens en Melodie." *Mens en Melodie* 7 (October 1952): 317.
van der Pot, C. W. "Mens, melodie en bibliotheek: Hommage un desideratum." *Mens en Melodie* 26 (February 1971): 48–50.

"Vijb jaar Mens en Melodie." *Mens en Melodie* 5 (December 1950): 369–70.
"Tien jaar Mens en Melodie." *Mens en Melodie* 10 (November 1955): 337.
"Twentig jaar Mens en Melodie." *Mens en Melodie* 20 (November 1965): 325.
"25 jaar Mens en Melodie." *Mens en Melodie* 25 (November 1970): 321–22.
INDEXES
 External: Music Index, 1950- . RILM, 1967- . Bibliographie des Musiksch-
 rifttmus, 1950- .
LOCATION SOURCES
 Widely available.

Publication History

TITLE AND TITLE CHANGES
 Mensch en Melodie: Algemeen Maandblad voor Muziek, 1946–47. *Mens en Mel-
 odie,* 1948–73. *Mens & Melodie,* 1974- .
VOLUME AND ISSUE DATA
 Volumes 1- , 1946- .
FREQUENCY OF PUBLICATION
 Monthly.
PUBLISHERS
 Het Spectrum, 1946–February 1982. Frits Knuf, March 1982- .
PLACES OF PUBLICATION
 Utrecht and Brussels, 1946–50. Utrecht and Antwerp, 1951–February 1982.
 Buren, March 1982- .
EDITORS
 Jaap Kunst, Wouter Paap, and Hans Triebels, 1946. Jaap Kunst, Wouter Paap,
 and J. L. Broeckx, 1947–52. Wouter Paap and Jaap Kunst, 1953–60. Wouter
 Paap, 1961–75. Luc van Hasselt, Ernst Vermeulen and Bastiaan Willink, 1976–
 79. Luc van Hasselt, Ernst Vermeulen, Sabine Lichtenstein, and Job ter Steege,
 1980–October 1982. John Kasander, November 1982– .

Alfons Annegarn

MENSCH EN MELODIE. See MENS EN MELODIE

METRONOME

During its seventy-five years of publication, *Metronome* addressed the needs
and interests of the amateur and professional instrumental musician. Issues regularly featured news of happenings in the musical world, activities of performing
musicians and ensembles; reports on new developments in music and musical
instruments; notices and reviews of performances, publications, and recordings;
expert advice for performers; and news on publishing and the music trade. As
popular tastes in music changed, *Metronome* shifted its focus as well, from
classical and orchestral music, brass bands and marches, to dance music, and
ultimately, to jazz. The technological innovations of radio, film, and recorded

sound were also reflected in the pages of the magazine. With the rise of rock and roll music and the demise of the big bands at the dawn of the 1960s, however, the magazine faced overwhelming financial difficulties and ceased publication. The last issue was dated December 1961.

Metronome was founded by Carl Fischer, Sr., the head of Carl Fischer, in 1885 to serve the interests of music and musicians. Initially, the primary focus also reflected the interests of those likely to purchase Fischer's wares. Regular features in the first decades included an editorial column, letters to the editor, obituaries, news of bands and orchestras across the nation and in London, and a musical supplement including performing parts to marches, waltzes, and other popular pieces for band or orchestra. A large portion of the publication was taken up by advertisements for sheet music, instruments, uniforms, and other equipment, as well as a want ad section of professional advertisements. Feature articles ranged from profiles of bands and orchestras and biographies of or interviews with composers, instrumentalists, and conductors, to analyses of orchestral masterworks and pieces offering practical musical information on such topics as arranging, conducting, transposing, and performing. Many articles were translations and reprints from books and other musical publications (for example, *Modern Music* [q.v.]). Musical examples and portraits of musicians, bands, and orchestras were also included. Between 1897 and 1900, monthly issues averaged around twenty-four pages, plus an eight-page musical supplement, and about eight unnumbered pages of advertisements.

Regular departments on instrumental instruction began to appear in 1900 with a violin column, followed by a woodwind department in 1906 and an orchestra section in 1908. Reviews of music, methods, and books first appeared in 1901. Between 1900 and 1910, issues averaged forty pages plus an eight- to twelve-page musical supplement. The Metronome Corporation assumed publication in 1907.

Beginning in 1911, *Metronome* printed programs of band and orchestra performances from all over the country considered to be of special merit. From October 1914 to December 1924, two editions with identical numbering were issued as *The Metronome Band Monthly* and *The Metronome Orchestra Monthly*. The two editions were the same except for the musical supplement: one included arrangements for band, the other contained arrangements for orchestra. By 1919, the regular instrumental departments included ones for string instruments, brass instruments, saxophone, and drums. A regular index to advertisers debuted in 1922. Issues grew to an average of eighty pages with five to nine regular columns, five to twenty brief articles, and two to eight longer articles of 500 to 1,500 words.

In 1925, *Metronome* absorbed *The Dominant* and commenced semimonthly publication with issues, dated the first and fifteenth of each month, being called either "orchestra edition" or "band edition," through December 1931. Coverage of popular dance tunes and orchestras, Tin Pan Alley, and jazz increased, as that of classical music, brass, and military bands decreased. A banjo column was added in 1925 and a table of contents first appeared in 1926. Radio and dance music departments were introduced in 1927. The "Handy Reference Guide," an alphabetical list of popular song titles and publishers began in 1928 and continued to appear through June 1936. Regular reviews of records began in 1931. Issues averaged sixty pages with ten to fourteen regular columns, six to twelve brief articles, and five to seven longer articles.

In May 1932, the last musical supplement was included. It reappeared in a truncated, two-page form from 1936 to 1944. By 1939, *Metronome* was under the new dual editorship of George T. Simon and Richard B. Gilbert. It predominantly featured news, columns, reviews, articles, and interviews on jazz music and jazz musicians. The results of the first annual All-Star poll, a readers' poll evaluating big band instrumentalists and singers, appeared in that same year. Only one column of classical record reviews continued. The string instrument department was discontinued, and the want ad section had shrunken considerably. The remaining instrumental columns did not appear between 1944 and 1953. In 1947, the periodical *Modern Music* was absorbed. Record reviews became an increasingly large part of the magazine, and a column on high-fidelity sound started in 1954. The instrumental columns reappeared that year as well. A separate *Metronome Yearbook* was issued annually starting in 1956. The title changed to *Metronome—Music U.S.A.* in 1959, but changed back to simply *Metronome* in 1960. Issues from the 1940s on averaged fifty pages with five to ten regular columns, two to four brief articles, and two to six longer feature articles. Many photographs of jazz personalities, some half a page or larger, were included.

For most of its run, *Metronome* was issued monthly. The November and December 1906 issues were combined into one, a separate twenty-fifth anniversary supplement was issued in 1910, and the October and November 1919 issues were combined. It appeared semimonthly from January 1, 1925, until September 1927, when the frequency became monthly again. The typeface of early issues was small and rather difficult to read; the typeface improved in 1902. A new logo, improved layout, and another change of typeface appeared in 1915. In 1923 issues measured 10½" by 13½". The layout changed and the size was reduced to 8½" by 11" in 1936. A further reduction in size to 7⅞" by 10¾" occurred in 1944.

Information Sources

INDEXES
    External: Music Index, 1949–61.
REPRINT EDITIONS
    Paper: AMS Press.
LOCATION SOURCES
    Library of Congress (full run). Widely available (partial run).

Publication History

TITLE AND TITLE CHANGES

Metronome, 1885–1961, with the following exceptions: *Metronome Band Monthly, Metronome Orchestra Monthly*, 1914–24, and *Metronome—Music U.S.A.*, 1959.

VOLUME AND ISSUE DATA

Volumes 1–78, 1885–1961.

FREQUENCY OF PUBLICATION

Monthly, 1885–1924. Semimonthly, 1925–September 1927. Monthly, October 1927–1961.

PUBLISHERS

Carl Fischer, 1885–1905. Metronome Corporation, 1907–61.

EDITORS

Arthur A. Clappe, 1885–90. L. O'Reilly and other, 1891–92. Walter H. Anstead, 1893–99. Gustav Saenger, 1900–27. Dorin K. Antrim, 1928–38. George T. Simon, Richard B. Gilbert, 1939–42. Barry Ulanov, 1943–45. George T. Simon, Barry Ulanov, 1946–54. Bill Coss, 1955–60. Dave Solomon, Dan Morgenstern, 1961.

Michael Colby

METRONOME—MUSIC U.S.A. See METRONOME

METRONOME BAND MONTHLY. See METRONOME

METRONOME ORCHESTRA MONTHLY. See METRONOME

MISCELLANEA MUSICOLOGICA: ADELAIDE STUDIES IN MUSICOLOGY

Although music has been part of the curriculum in some Australian universities since their inception, the practice of "musicology" as a formal and separately named academic discipline in this country began with the creation of a senior research fellowship in musicology at the University of Adelaide in 1964. Publication of the inaugural issue (1966) of *Miscellanea Musicologica: Adelaide Studies in Musicology* coincided with the end of the first year in which musicological studies were included as part of the much older degree of Bachelor of Music at that university. When it began, *Miscellanea* provided the only forum in Australia for the reporting of scholarly work in musicology. Although it was followed quickly by the foundation of *Studies in Music* (University of Western Australia, 1967– [q.v.]), and later by *Musicology* (now *Musicology Australia*,

Musicological Society of Australia, 1976–   [q.v.]), *Miscellanea Musicologica* is unique in several respects.

It owed its genesis to the vision of Professor Andrew McCredie who was the first holder of the Adelaide Fellowship in Musicology, and who was later to become a Dent medalist, member of the executive board of the International Musicological Society, and the holder of a Personal Chair of Musicology at the University of Adelaide. McCredie saw the future of the discipline in Australia as being to some extent dependent on raising academic awareness of what musicologists do. If musicology were to take root and flourish in Australia, the results of its inquiry must be available and accessible to the scholarly community, and ideally to a wider public as well. While it had modest beginnings in a typewritten, inexpensively produced format, *Miscellanea* succeeded in increasing the scholarly community's awareness of musicology by reporting the results of research; this awareness led to greater support for the discipline, which in turn helped to provoke further research.

In its contents *Miscellanea Musicologica* reflects Australia's unique geographical position and diversified approach to musicology. Australian musicologists have consistently resisted the separation of the discipline into "Western historical musicology" and "ethnomusicology," and several of the editorial statements in *Miscellanea* address themselves to this concern (vs. 2, 4). From v. 3 (1968) on, the journal carried regular review articles, each surveying the current state of research in a particular area, for example, "Some Aspects of Current Research into Russian Liturgical Chant" (6:55–154). For the most part the contributors of these and the several standard refereed articles in each issue have been Australian scholars. Australian aboriginal music and music in colonial Australia are frequently topics for articles, most of which contain material that has not been reported elsewhere. And some of Gordon Athol Anderson's important work on thirteenth-century repertories appeared in vs. 3, 6, 7, and 8 ("Notre Dame Bilingual Motets: A Study in the History of Music," 3:50–144; "Notre Dame and Related Conductus: A Catalogue Raisonne," 6:153–229 and 7:1–81; and "Johannes de Garlandia and the Simultaneous Use of Mixed Rhythmic Modes," 8:11–31). In addition to research articles, there have been contributions that identify research materials in Australian collections (David Tunley, "The Eighteenth Century French Cantata on Microfilm—A Descriptive Bibliography of Sources held by the Reid Library, University of Western Australia," 7: 82–104). Awareness of the presence of such collections can be extremely valuable in a situation where access to European primary sources is difficult. Later issues of *Miscellanea* (vs. 13 and 14) have been devoted to the printing of summaries and selected full papers from major conferences that have been held in Australia (*Art Nouveau and Jugendstil; The Richard Wagner Centenary in Australia*, 1984).

McCredie was the founder and sole editor of *Miscellanea Musicologica* for its first eleven volumes. From v. 13 (1984) he was joined by two assistant editors, and from v. 14 (1985) he became general editor, supported by an Editorial Advisory Board, with a different editor for each volume. The physical format of the journal has remained a consistent 5¾″ by 8¼″. The early volumes were type-written, but later ones are typeset and have a pleasing appearance. The journal is nominally an annual, although its appearance has been somewhat irregular. Each issue is approximately 250 pages in length, and there is no internal indexing.

Information Sources

BIBLIOGRAPHY
"Miscellanea Musicologica." *Music Teacher* 107 (November 1966): 966.
"Miscellanea Musicologica." *Notes* 25 (1968): 38–39.
INDEXES
External: Music Index, 1967– . RILM, 1967– . Australian Public Affairs In-formation Service (APAIS): A Subject Index to Current Literature (National Li-brary of Australia). Bibliographie des Musikschrifttums, 1967– .
LOCATION SOURCES
Widely available.

Publication History

TITLE AND TITLE CHANGES
Miscellanea Musicologica: Adelaide Studies in Musicology, 1966– .
VOLUME AND ISSUE DATA
Volumes 1– , 1966– .
FREQUENCY OF PUBLICATION
Yearly with irregularities.
PUBLISHER
University of Adelaide, South Australia.
PLACE OF PUBLICATION
Adelaide, Australia.
EDITORS
Andrew D. McCredie, 1966–82. Geoffrey Moon, 1983. Andrew D. McCredie 1984– . Peter Dennison (guest editor) 1985.

Jane Morlet Hardie

MITTEILUNGEN DER INTERNATIONALEN GESELLSCHAFT FÜR MUSIKWISSENSCHAFT. See ACTA MUSICOLOGICA

MLA NOTES. See NOTES

MODERN MUSIC

In the aftermath of World War I, a young, energetic, and restless generation of American composers was eager to assert themselves but frustrated by for-midable barriers of public apathy and the neglect, even hostility of the media. Characteristic of their era, these composers reacted by forming societies, most importantly the League of Composers, and organizing aggressive concert and promotional efforts. It was also an era of "little magazines," like H. L. Mencken's *American Mercury* and Margaret Anderson's *Little Review*, so that it is only natural that the league hit upon a journalistic venture as a means of augmenting the public outreach of their concert offerings, enhancing their respectability, and balancing the poor mainstream press coverage generally accorded modern music. Initially known simply as *The League of Composers Review*, it was renamed *Modern Music: A Quarterly Review* with v. 3, evidently in an effort to clarify both its purpose and its independence from the parent organization.

Minna Lederman, the new journal's editor, took several of the established European music periodicals as models, particularly the young *La Revue musicale* (q.v.). The first few issues, in fact, look to be cast in that mold, both in format and in authorship, the latter a cross section of distinguished European critics: Emil Vuillermoz, Guido Gatti, Adoph Weissman, and Edwin Evans. There were, however, to be three crucial differences between *Modern Music* and its forebears. Within the first year of the journal's existence, league luminary Aaron Copland, freshly imbued with Nadia Boulanger's challenge to foster an American musical identity, succeeded in redirecting the journal toward the presentation of an American perspective on modern music. Emphasis was placed on American modern music and its composers, American performances of European works, and American reports on European activities and works. Second, unlike most music periodicals with a lay readership and current musical activity focus, *Modern Music* was devoted to the music and its composers, not performers and performances. The third characteristic arose, in part, from the second and partly from an editorial intent that the subject matter be "distilled by the critical rather than the reportorial mind" (1.2:1). While the contributorship includes a few critics (Pitts Sanborn, Paul Rosenfeld, Lawrence Gilman) and a number of scholars (Alfred Einstein, P. H. Lang, Charles Seeger, and Willi Reich), Lederman drew heavily on the league composers themselves for copy. Among these, Copland, Roger Sessions, Virgil Thomson, and Elliott Carter are perhaps the most significant and certainly the most frequently represented of the budding composer-critics. They were joined by a distinguished and growing pool of writers including John Cage, Henry Cowell, Lou Harrison, Leonard Bernstein, Milton Babbitt, Conlon Nancarrow, Colin McPhee, Marc Blitzstein, Arthur Berger, Frederick Jacobi, Charles Ives, and even a number of European composers: Béla Bartók, Alban Berg, Benjamin Britten, Darius Milhaud, and Arnold Schönberg.

The content of *Modern Music* was consistent: four to six articles (three to eight pages in length) and a like number of one- to two-page reports under a "Forecast and Review" heading. Articles rarely include footnotes but are well endowed with musical examples of all kinds. Additionally, the pages are graced by numerous composer caricatures and reproductions of stage and costume designs. With v. 14, five more specialized departments, one to two pages each, appeared: "Scores and Recordings," "In the Theater," "On the Hollywood Front" (later "On the Film Front"), "With the Dancers," and "Over the Air."

V. 15 saw the addition of "Recent Books" and a jazz column entitled "The Torrid Zone" begins in 20.4. The league's major committees and concert offerings were listed inside the front and back covers, respectively, and the last few pages introduced the contributors and listed tables of contents for the previous issues. The later, by v. 14, become somewhat less regular, and include only more recent issues once a cumulative index to vs. 1–12 appeared.

Both articles and the more superficial reports focused upon specific compositions, composers, composers statements and self-analyses, historical pieces (mostly devoted to ethnic and earlier American musics), and the press. Illustrative and noteworthy are the following: a series of twenty-six articles on American composers, Dmitri Shostakovich's "My Opera, Lady MacBeth of Mtzensk" (12.1:26–27), Carter's piece on Henry F. Gilbert entitled "American Figure with Landscape," a special supplement on "The Future on Tonality" by Joseph Yasser, a special symposium "On Artists and Collaboration" (with the enemy, that is) (22.1:3–11), and an entire issue on "Music and the Machine" (8.3). Igor Stravinsky and his music are the most frequent specific topics: forty-three articles comprising a remarkable and valuable collage of the widely varying reactions to and analyses of his diverse legacy. The pages of *Modern Music* also chronicle the American composer's dalliance with jazz, his/her attraction to various popular and non-Western musics, the dilemma of finding a distinctive American style, the rise and fall of classical music populism in the 1930s, and the devastating impact of Fascism and war.

Modern Music remained, throughout its twenty-three years, virtually a volunteer operation. Lederman—the editorial and diplomatic genius behind the journal—and her contributors rarely received compensation, the journal was produced out of a small room in her parents' home, and the league was forced to make up a persistent yearly operating deficit of $1,500. In an effort to remain aloof from all potentially compromising external forces, the staff refused all advertising and rigorously kept even the league at a distance. The journal's somewhat rustic appearance and occasional lapses in attention to detail as well as its final demise must be laid at the feet of the resulting economic instability.

Modern Music assumes a reader at least conversant with the contemporary music scene, though it is neither particularly scholarly nor exhaustively analytical. The composer-critics who dominate its pages occasionally digress to reportorial description, biased judgment, and matters of personality; their commentaries sometimes say almost as much about the author as the subject. In actuality, however, the degree of objectivity and paucity of bias are quite extraordinary, especially considering the emphasis on composers assessing composers and the largely New York City base of operations. One must look very hard and largely in vain for any clear, overall editorial preconception or bias. The journal provides its readers, both contemporary and future, with a marvelous window on the preoccupations and preconceptions of a very exciting musical time and place, as seen from extremely varied and largely objective perspectives. The journal also had considerable impact on its own contributorship. It acted as a mirror as much as it did a forum, and was a major force in awakening and sharpening the sensibilities of a seminal generation of American composers.

Few journals have attracted such serious attention from the American scholarly community. *Modern Music* has been extensively excerpted in books by Lederman and Carol Oja and an article by Eric Salzman, analytically indexed by Wayne Shirley, and thoughtfully explored by Michael Meckna. Lederman's book, in addition, offers a marvelous glimpse into the inner workings and personalities of the journal. A considerable *Modern Music* archive exists at the Library of Congress.

Modern Music was published on 6½″ by 9¾″ pages between bright yellow covers. The distinctive adaptations of Peruvian and Guatemalan prints that adorn the early covers and pages disappear with v. 6. The journal becomes a quarterly with v. 3, after three issues in v. 1 and two in v. 2. Pagination is continuous within each volume after v. 8, with the exception of v. 13. Issues steadily increase in size, from twenty to thirty-five pages in early issues, to around seventy by the 1940s. Readers were provided a thorough index of vs. 1–12 in 1936, an effort superseded and completed by Wayne Shirley's monumental 1976 effort.

Information Sources

BIBLIOGRAPHY

"From Modern Music: Some Representative Passages." *Perspectives of New Music* 2 (Spring 1964): 21–34.

Lederman, Minna. *The Life and Death of a Small Magazine ("Modern Music," 1924–1946).* ISAM Monographs, 18. New York: Institute for Studies in American Music, 1983.

MacDonald, Calum. "Review: *The Life and Death of a Small Magazine ("Modern Music," 1924–1946)* by Minna Lederman." *Tempo* 149 (1984): 31–33.

Meckna, Michael. Review of "The Life and Death of a Small Magazine ("Modern Music," 1924–1946)/Stravinsky in "Modern Music" (1924–1946)." *Notes* 41 (1984): 56–58.

———. "The Rise of the American Composer-Critic: Aaron Copland, Roger Sessions, Virgil Thomson and Elliott Carter in the Periodical *Modern Music*, 1924–1946." Ph.D. diss., University of California at Santa Barbara, 1984.

———. "Copland, Sessions and *Modern Music*: The Rise of the Composer-Critic in America." *American Music* 3 (1985): 198–204.

Mellers, Wilfrid. "Modern Music—Seen from America." *Musical Times* 125 (1984): 206–7.

Oja, Carol J., ed. *Stravinsky in "Modern Music" (1924–1946)."* Foreword by Aaron Copland. New York: Da Capo Press, 1982.

Salzman, Eric. "*Modern Music* in Retrospect (for the fortieth anniversary of its founding)." *Perspectives of New Music* 2 (Spring 1964): 14–20.

Shirley, Wayne D. *Modern Music: An Analytic Index.* Edited by William and Carolyn Lichtenwanger. New York: AMS Press, 1976.

INDEXES

    Internal: v. 1–12; frequent listing of past tables of contents in v. 4–23.

    External: Readers' Guide, 1945–46. Wayne Shirley (see Bibliography)

REPRINT EDITIONS
     Paper: AMS Press.
LOCATION SOURCES
     Widely available.

Publication History

TITLE AND TITLE CHANGES
     League of Composers Review, 1924–25. *Modern Music, A Quarterly Review*,
     1925–46.
VOLUME AND ISSUE DATA
     Volumes 1–23.4, 1924–46.
FREQUENCY OF PUBLICATION
     Quarterly.
PUBLISHER
     League of Composers, Inc.
PLACE OF PUBLICATION
     New York City.
EDITOR
     Minna Lederman.

Richard S. James

MONATSHEFTE FÜR MUSIKGESCHICHTE

The *Monatshefte für Musikgeschichte* was one of the earliest German music
journals dedicated to musicological rather than general reading. Founded in 1869
by Robert Eitner, the *Monatshefte* appeared monthly until shortly after Eitner's
death in 1905. The journal was sponsored by the Gesellschaft für Musikforschung
and was that society's official organ. Eitner was a founding member of the
Gesellschaft, the president and secretary of the society from 1869, and editor
of all but the final four issues of *Monatshefte für Musikgeschichte*, which appeared
after his death.

The goals of the journal were set forth in an unsigned essay by Eitner in which
he proposed to arouse public interest in music history and further efforts in its
study. Eitner called for four types of musicological work: (1) biographies of
composers of antiquity, with special emphasis on the neglected German composers; (2) general musical-historical and scientific essays and excerpts from
manuscripts; (3) description of rare published works; and (4) bibliographic works,
including critiques of music literature (1:1).

This combination of historical and bibliographic work represents the interest
of the founding members of the *Gesellschaft*. The original board was comprised
of fifty mostly German members, including representatives from important music
publishers, several well-known scholars (for example, Friedrich Chrysander,
Franz Commer, Otto Kade, A. G. Ritter), and the directors of various German
music libraries.

The types of articles found in the *Monatshefte für Musikgeschichte* inform the mainstream of twentieth-century musicology: standard life and works biographies, the history of music at a city or court, the history of a genre, manuscript studies, and translations of early theoretical works. The first two types of articles (biographies and local histories) were represented in the journal mostly by German topics with infrequent non-German contributors. Perhaps the best examples of genre and manuscript studies were Eitner's work on German song, including *Das deutsche Lied des 15. und 16. Jahrhunderts in Wort, Melodie und mehrstimmige Tonsatz*, which appeared as a supplemental to the series, and his various articles on German song manuscripts. Several translations of treatises appeared in the journal, including *Musica enchiriadis*, Sebastian Virdung's *Musica getutscht*, and Prosdocimus de Baldemandis's *Tractate*.

Some Renaissance composers, such as Heinrich Isaac, Ludwig Senfl, and Josquin des Pres, were treated often in the pages of *Monatshefte für Musikgeschichte*, as were the more famous German classical and Romantic composers. But even though one of the goals of the journal was to present material on neglected composers, some composers remained neglected in the pages of the *Monatshefte für Musikgeschichte*, for example, the important and prolific Philippe de Monte, chapel master to Emperor Rudolf II.

The outstanding quality of the *Monatshefte für Musikgeschichte* is the attention to detail with which the library catalogs, indices, and biographical materials were prepared. Corrections and addenda were regularly included. The holdings of several pre–World War I libraries are most conveniently found in the regular issues and many supplements to the series. Over fifty libraries and special collections were catalogued or indexed. While the majority of these were German collections, the Sistine Chapel, the Paris Conservatory and Opera, the Brussels Conservatory, and the Library of Congress were also catalogued. Editorial concern extended to careful indexing. Eitner included an annual subject and name index, and combined indices appeared for every ten volumes.

The *Monatshefte für Musikgeschichte* complemented Eitner's voluminous other publications, and the journal published corrections and addenda to both his *Bibliographie der Musik-Sammelwerke des XVI. und XVII. Jahrhunderts* and his monumental *Quellen-Lexicon*.[1] Although Eitner contributed more to the *Monatshefte für Musikgeschichte* than any other writer, many other scholars are also represented; the journal presented some of the finest music scholarship of its time.

Many lacunae of German musical history were addressed in the *Monatshefte für Musikgeschichte*. Much of the biographical and bibliographical information concerning German musicians from the fifteenth to the seventeenth centuries appeared in the journal for the first time. Eitner's approach to music history and bibliography was a model for developing German musicological endeavor and modern musicology as a whole. The research presented in the *Monatshefte* has frequently served as an influential basis for considerable modern scholarship.

Eitner's successor as editor was Albert Göhler, who finished the 1905 volume of the *Monatshefte für Musikgeschichte* with a shortened issue, combining ns. 7–12. In a summation essay (37:61–63), Göhler quoted Hermann Kretzschmer's inaugural address to the International Music Society extensively and suggested that the work of the new society was a direct continuation of Eitner's life work. After the abbreviated final volume of the *Monatshefte für Musikgeschichte* in 1905, all subscriptions were transferred to the International Music Society for the remainder of that year at no charge.

The physical format of the *Monatshefte für Musikgeschichte* was consistent throughout its run: 7″ by 9½″. The pagination was continuous through the twelve monthly issues of each volume, varying from 140 to 300 pages annually, with articles ranging from ten to fifty pages, sometimes divided between issues. The supplements were paginated separately. The journal and its supplements were typeset, with musical examples and occasional complete short works. Advertisements appeared only as filler on the last page of the monthly issue, and were usually devoted to works either by Robert Eitner or published by the Gesellschaft für Musikgeschichte.

Note

1. A chronological listing of Eitner's published works appeared in the final issue of the *Monatshefte für Musikgeschichte*: [Albert Göhler?] "Chronologisches Verzeichnis der im Druck erschienenen musikhistorischen Arbeiten von Robert Eitner" (vol. 37:135–38). Alec Hyatt King cites an earlier incomplete compilation in his article on Eitner in *The New Grove Dictionary of Music and Musicians,* 6th ed., s.v. "Eitner, Robert." King also provides an incorrect death date for Eitner; it should read January 22, 1905.

Information Sources

BIBLIOGRAPHY
Fellinger, Imogen. *Verzeichnis der Musikzeitschriften des 19. Jahrhunderts.* Studien zur Musikgeschichte des 19. Jahrhunderts, 10. Regensburg: Gustav Bosse Verlag, 1960.
The New Grove Dictionary of Music and Musicians. S.v. "Eitner, Robert," by Alec Hyatt King.
INDEXES
Internal: each volume indexed.
External: *I. Register,* Volumes 1–10 (1869–78). Berlin: T. Trautwein, 1879. *II. Register,* Volumes 11–20 (1879–88); *III. Register,* Volumes 21–30 (1889–98). *IV. Register,* Volumes 31–37 (1899–1905). Berlin and Leipzig: Breitkopf und Härtel, 1889, 1899, 1906.
REPRINT EDITIONS
Paper: Schnase. Dakota Graphics.
Microfilm: Research Microfilm Publishers Periodicals in Musicology.
LOCATION SOURCES
Widely available.

Publication History

TITLE AND TITLE CHANGES
Monatschefte für Musikgeschichte.
VOLUME AND ISSUE DATA
Volumes 1–37, 1869–1905.
FREQUENCY OF PUBLICATION
Monthly.
PUBLISHERS
T. Trautwein, 1869–71. Bahn, 1872–75. Leipmannssohn, 1876–77. Trautwein, 1878. Breitkopf und Härtel, 1879–1905.
PLACES OF PUBLICATION
Berlin, 1869–83. Berlin and Leipzig, 1884–1905.
EDITORS
Robert Eitner, 1869–March 1905. Albert Göhler, April 1905–December 1905.
SUPPLEMENTS
Four indices listed above, and thirty-two supplementary volumes, 1871–1905.

Carmelo P. Comberiati

MONTHLY MUSICAL RECORD

Monthly Musical Record was one of the earliest British music journals dedicated to contemporary musical criticism. Although some articles of scholarly, historical nature appear in the later volumes, the main body of work in *Monthly Musical Record* refers to the current musical scene.

Founded in 1871, the initial focus of the journal was national; however, European items appear from the first issue and a series of foreign correspondents wrote for *Monthly Musical Record.* The Journal grew steadily in its first decade, adding correspondents from Cambridge, Glasgow, North Germany, Norway, Paris, Florence, and Vienna. A listing of university music degree requirements for Dublin, London, and Oxford began to appear in v. 6, and with v. 9 the journal was registered for transmission abroad. The corresponding music agents included K. F. Koehler in Leipzig and G. Schirmer in New York.

Ebenezer Prout was the founding editor and set forth a "Raison d'être," in the opening issue calling for three types of musical contributions: (1) ample intelligence on musical matters both British and foreign, including notes on concerts, events bearing on music, and letters for correspondents, (2) review of new publications, and (3) articles of general music history and criticism (1.1:1).

The regular sections included in the early volumes were a series of three or four short articles, British commentary and concert information, foreign correspondents, and reviews. V. 5 included a section entitled "Summary of Country News" which added information on various areas not covered by the foreign correspondents, but this was discontinued and later subsumed in a section called

"Musical Notes." V. 9 added "New Music Published Last Month," which provides much useful dating information. However, some of this section duplicates the advertisements for the publisher, Augener and Company, which added as many as eight separately numbered pages to each issue. With v. 10, short musical supplements were included with the journal. Again, these were often drawn from the Augener catalog.

Occasionally, other regular sections were announced and appeared for a few issues. Beginning in v. 20, biographical "Portrait Sketches" appeared for three volumes. These articles were signed by Biographicus Minor, but were probably written by the editor, John South Shedlock. The musicians covered in the eight sketches ranged from C. P. E. Bach to Vincenzo Bellini, and the series included short articles on F. J. Fétis, C. Tausig, and A. Boucher. Beginning with v. 55, facsimile reproductions of composer's portraits appeared more or less regularly for four years.

Prout began a series of seven articles on "Franz Schubert's Masses" with the first volume, followed by a series on Schubert symphonies. Most of the early historical submissions followed Prout's model of writing, including information more useful as program notes than as analysis, and usually without bibliographical citation. The later volumes included some historical articles of note, though, for example, Gilbert Reaney's "The Musician in Medieval England" (89:3–8) and Jan La Rue's "English Paper in the British Museum: 1770–1820" (87:177–80).

The primary value of *Monthly Musical Record* is in its contemporary commentary. In the final issue, Gerald Abraham notes the solid body of criticism in the journal, including contributions by almost every important English authority, and many foreign ones (90:201–3). Notable composers contributed commentary to the journal, including Hector Berlioz on Beethoven Symphonies (1:97–100, 126–28, 141–43; 11:2–5, 15–18), Wagner on opera (5:65–67; 6:81–84; 7:97–99), and an extract from Peter Illich Tchaikovsky's diary (26:3–4). Foreign correspondents included Alfred Einstein, who wrote on Egon Wellesz, and Carl Ferdinand Pohl, who commented on Viennese musical life. Ernest Newman wrote regularly for the journal from 1898–1904, and most important musical events are covered in the journal's commentary. For example, Pope Pius X's music regulations were covered in two issues (34:25–27, 45–46).

The physical format of *Monthly Musical Record* varied from 7½" by 10" for vs. 1–54, with slight variations from 7½" by 9½" to 7½" by 11¼" for vs. 55–67, to 4¾" by 8" for vs. 68–90. The pagination was continuous for each volume. Twelve issues per year appeared from 1871 to 1955, except for a few volumes in the 1930s with only ten issues because of the shortened concert season. The early issues ranged from twelve to sixteen pages; from 1938 to 1955 this increased to thirty-two pages.

From 1956 to 1960 *Monthly Musical Record* appeared in bimonthly issues of approximately forty pages. The articles rarely were longer than four to five pages in each issue, although some were continued over consecutive issues. Advertisements were included from the earliest volumes, although mostly for materials by the publisher, Augener and Company.

Information Sources

BIBLIOGRAPHY
Fellinger, Imogen. *Verzeichnis der Musikzeitschriften des 19. Jahrhunderts.* Studien zur Musikgeschichte des 19. Jahrhunderts, 10. Regensburg: Gustav Bosse Verlag, 1960.
[Hull, A. Eaglefield?]. "The Early Years of the *Monthly Musical Record.*" *Monthly Musical Record* 50 (1920): 3–6.
Westrup, J. A. "Ebenezer Prout 1835–1909." *Monthly Musical Record* 65 (1935): 53–57.
INDEXES
Internal: each volume indexed (vs. 1–64).
External: Bibliographie des Musikschrifttums, 1937, 1939, 1950–60. Music Index, 1949–60.
REPRINT EDITION
Microform: Library of Congress (1871–1958); Datamics Inc. (1871–1958, incomplete).
LOCATION SOURCES
Widely available.

Publication History

TITLE AND TITLE CHANGES
Monthly Musical Record.
VOLUME AND ISSUE DATA
Volumes 1–90, 1871–1960.
FREQUENCY OF PUBLICATION
Monthly, 1871–1955. Bimonthly, 1956–60.
PUBLISHER
Augener and Company.
PLACE OF PUBLICATION
London.
EDITORS
Ebenezer Prout, 1871–75. Charles Ainslie Barry, 1875–79. John South Shedlock, 1879–1912. A. Eaglefield Hull, 1913–28. Richard Capell, 1929–33. J. A. Westrup, 1933–45. Gerald Abraham, 1945–60.

Carmelo P. Comberiati

MONTHLY SUPPLEMENT TO THE MUSICAL LIBRARY, THE. See HARMONICON, THE

MUSIC AND LETTERS

"Every journal that is born into the world aspires to be a journal-in-chief." So wrote A. H. Fox Strangways in the Editorial to the first issue of *Music and Letters,* January 1920 (1:3–5). He gave three interpretations to the title of the publication. Music and letters, together with gymnastics, formed the basis of Classical education. Music expresses emotion, while letters express logic. Thus the knowledge of music and letters was the hallmark of the educated, sensitive human being. Second, the coupling of the two words suggests the close association of music with literature, shown most clearly in opera, oratorio, and song. To discuss one of the arts was, at the same time, to illuminate aspects of the other. In the new journal, music would be discussed as one of a number of interrelated artistic gestures. Finally, the term "letters" implies prose; the title indicates that music could be the subject of well-expressed rational inquiry. Thus, Fox Strangways hoped that his new periodical would become an important forum for intelligent discourse on music by specialists of every kind. (More information on the founding of *Music and Letters* is given in 50:2–5, 11–14.)

Music and Letters has never attempted to be a research journal in the strict sense. Fox Strangways sought articles from, and hoped to attract an audience of, "thinkers," people who could appreciate intelligent writing about music. This audience was larger, he realized, than the body of professional musicians, and more heterogeneous. As a consequence, the first issue contained articles of little use to practicing musicians and little that would be described today as "musicological" in focus. Articles ranged from Lawrence Binyon's " 'The Shyness of Beauty': A Poem" (1:6) and "On Listening to Music" by Clutton Brock (1:12–18), to "Sailor Shanties" by R.R. Terry (1:35–44), Violet Gordon Woodhouse's, "Old Keyed Instruments and their Music" (1:45–51), and Harold Monro, "Words to Music" (1:52–59).

In his opening editorial (October 1959), Jack A. Westrup described the purpose of the journal, its readership, and its contributors in stronger terms. The journal would not publish analyses; Westrup assumed that the readership could generate them on its own. Neither would it be "a medium for those who want to record in print their enthusiasm for the great masterpieces." Westrup held in contempt those who published opinions on music uninformed by adequate musical training. The emphasis on *Music and Letters* as a literary publication was reaffirmed: "We want contributors who can write, who have a respect for the English language and are willing to take the trouble to use it effectively" (40:307).

The subject matter is eclectic. Within the limitations described above, the journal accepts articles on topics ranging from ancient to contemporary music, including those concerned with ethnomusicological topics. A survey of the articles published, however, indicates an emphasis on Western art music from 1500 to 1950. While no stated policy specifically prohibits them, articles on the newest music are rare, as are those on ancient, medieval, and non-Western topics. This situation is probably due to the nature of the articles submitted.

The style of coverage is also quite varied. All articles are scholarly and well written, but are not of the research type. Articles on general topics alternate with detailed discussions of individual composers and their works. The publication is akin in many ways to *The Musical Quarterly* (q.v.).

Music and Letters is published quarterly, in January, April, July, and October, but in some cases two numbers have been issued together. The size, 6¾" by 9⅞", has remained constant since publication began, but the number of pages in each issue has fluctuated enormously. Some are quite large (for example 50.1:218 pp.); others, especially during and shortly after World War II, are much smaller. Currently each issue averages a hundred pages and contains between three and six articles. This, too, has varied with time; earlier issues contained many more items. Editorials were a regular feature under Westrup, but appear rarely before 1959 and after 1975. In addition, each issue contains reviews of books and of music, correspondence, and a list of books received. An unusual feature of early numbers, a "Review of [articles in] Periodicals" was discontinued in July 1950. It was taken up again as "Review of Reviews" in April 1951 but disappeared by October of that year.

Throughout its first thirty-four years, *Music and Letters* was privately owned and printed. The advantage perceived in this arrangement was that the journal was independent of any publishing firm or business establishment and thus free from any biases that such associations might foster. Fox Strangways was both owner and editor from January 1920 until October 1936. When he gave up these responsibilities, Richard Capell became proprietor, and Eric Blom became editor. That arrangement lasted through January 1950. In that year Blom assumed editorship of the fifth edition of *Grove's* and resigned his post with *Music and Letters*. Capell took over editorial responsibilities in April 1950 and held them until his death in 1954.

The disadvantages of private ownership appeared clearly with Capell's passing. Apparently no one could be found to assume financial responsibility, and the future of *Music and Letters* was in grave doubt. Eric Blom returned as temporary editor and described the situation in two editorials, the first pessimistic (35:207; 1954), the second guarded (36:1; 1955). By April the problems had been solved, and Blom explained the new arrangement in a jubilant editorial (36:109; 1955). Ownership and control were in the hands of a board composed of representatives of the Royal Musical Association, Oxford University Press, and the editor of *Music and Letters*. This arrangement, with various editors, continues to the present and is described on the first page of every issue.

An index to vs. 1–40 (1920–59) was published by Oxford University Press in 1962. The index contains two sections: an index of articles, listed by author and subject in one alphabetical sequence, and an index of book reviews using the same format. No cumulative index exists for later volumes; rather, each volume contains its own index.

Information Sources

BIBLIOGRAPHY

Blom, Eric. "Editorial." *Music and Letters* 36 (January 1955): 1.

———. "Editorial." *Music and Letters* 36 (April 1955): 109.

———. "Richard Capell: March 23rd 1885–June 21st 1954." *Music and Letters* 35 (October 1954): 277.

Campbell, Frank, Gladys Eppink, and Jessica Fredricks. "Music Magazines in Britain and the United States." *Notes* 6 (March 1949): 239–62.

Fox Strangways, A. H. "Editorial." *Music and Letters* 1 (January 1920): 3–5. Reprinted: *Music and Letters* 50 (January 1969): 6–8.

Hortschansky, Klaus. "Besprechungen." *Die Musikforschung* 23 (1970): 38–60.

Howes, Frank. "A. H. Fox Strangways." *Music and Letters* 50 (January 1969): 11–14.

Keller, Hans. "The Contemporary Problem." *Tempo* 88 (Spring 1969): 56–57.

Westrup, Jack A. "Editorial." *Music and Letters* 40 (October 1959): 307–10.

———. "Editorial." *Music and Letters* 50 (January 1969): 2–5.

INDEXES

Internal: vs. 1–40 in 1962; each volume indexed (vs. 41–   ).

External: Music Index, 1949–   . RILM, 1967–   . Arts and Humanities Citation Index, 1977–   . International Index to Periodicals, 1949–73. Humanities Index, 1974–   . British Humanities Index, 1962–   . Bibliographie des Musikschrifttums, 1937, 1939, 1950–   .

REPRINT EDITION

Microform: UMI.

LOCATION SOURCES

Widely available.

Publication History

TITLE AND TITLE CHANGES

Music and Letters.

VOLUME AND ISSUE DATA

Volumes 1–   , 1920–   .

FREQUENCY OF PUBLICATION

Quarterly.

PUBLISHER

A. H. Fox Strangways, 1920–36. Richard Capell, 1936–54. Oxford University Press, 1955–   .

PLACE OF PUBLICATION

London.

EDITORS

A. H. Fox Strangways, 1920–36. Eric Blom, 1937–50. Richard Capell, 1950–54. Eric Blom, 1954–59. Jack A. Westrup, 1959–75. Denis Arnold, 1976–80. Edward Olleson, 1976–86. Nigel Fortune, 1981–   . John Whenham, 1987–   .

Vincent J. Corrigan

MUSIC AND MAN. See JOURNAL OF MUSICOLOGICAL RESEARCH

MUSIC AND MUSICIANS

Founded in 1952, *Music and Musicians* has provided its readers a steady diet of brief, generally topical articles, newsy reviews, and previews, all dealing primarily with the classical music scene in and around the London/central England region. Its contents and editorials evince stalwart belief in the importance of enlightening the music-loving public and in the enhancement of moral fiber through acquaintance with "serious music." It is well written in an educated though not scholarly tone. While not especially innovative, it has responded to the changing cultural climate with articles and programming information about radio and television. It is a most useful classical music guide for those living in and around London, and provides outsiders and historians with an invaluable catalog of the musical events, personalities, and attitudes of one of Europe's richest music capitals.

Issues appear monthly and are numbered to coincide with the concert season (No. 1 appears in September). Initially, the contents of each fifty- to sixty-page issue ranged from articles (one to three pages in length) and smaller special focus pieces on people and events, to a monthly concert guide and reviews of records, books, and music. The articles, signed and clearly intended to inform the music-loving public, most frequently deal with the lives, careers, and views of important people on the classical music scene. Other favorite topics are various musical institutions and organizations; major musical events, especially opera productions; and specific repertoires, for example, the symphonies of Vaughan Williams or contemporary piano music. There are five to eight such articles in each issue and up to a dozen in later issues. Landmark events, such as Rafael Kubelik's appointment to Covent Garden (1955), Wolfgang Amadeus Mozart's 200th anniversary, and the journal's own twentieth year, are commemorated by special issues. Most of the contributors appear to be critics and musicians, though the names of a few major scholars such as Stanley Sadie and Edward Lockspieser can be found.

A regular column entitled "Music Man's Diary" features short pieces on people and events in a chatty, even gossipy style. Initially comprised of a page of brief items averaging 200 words, this section gradually expands during the 1950s, both in length of individual entries and total length. "Music at Home and Abroad" was similar in nature and format, highlighting major events in the various music capitals of Western nations. Book, record, and music reviews are contributed by regular columnists, with record reviews heavily favored. The monthly London concert schedule is a major feature. Gradually, one finds more notices of concerts outside London.

The journal also includes a variety of smaller regular features. A monthly editorial was usually unsigned and somewhat platitudinous. Several letters to the editor were printed in each issue, while "It happened this month" listed various musical anniversaries. The reader was also acquainted with "This Month's Personality" (a noted performer, entrepreneur, composer, or teacher) and an "Up-and-coming artist" of the month. *Music and Musicians* is enhanced by numerous photographs. The equally copious advertisements promote sound equipment, publishers, instrument makers, festivals, record stores, and individual artists. A classified ad section ranges from musicians wanted and lessons offered to personals.

Well established during the journal's first decade, this format was altered several times, each time corresponding to a change of editor. In 1962, the journal's founding editor, Evan Senior, left the journal to found *Music Magazine*, a similar publication which merged with *Music and Musicians* in 1969 without having appreciable impact on the latter title. Frank Granville Barber succeeded Senior. Several news columns were revised, renamed, or eliminated, and two completely new columns were added: "Counterpoint" and "Commentary." Both offer a regular columnist(s), usually someone on the editorial staff, the opportunity to comment on current musical events and personalities. Initially a page each in length, these two columns grew steadily during the 1960s. A bias toward opera, evident throughout the 1950s, continues during the beginning of Barber's editorship but decreases substantially by the late 1960s. On the other hand, there is increased interest in composers, especially living ones, and many of the articles reveal a general tendency toward a more scholarly tone. Michael Reynolds was made editor in 1973 and, during the remainder of the 1970s, *Music and Musicians* becomes gradually shorter, ultimately about seventy pages, and slightly more scholarly, with occasional stories of primarily historical as opposed to topical significance.

Music and Musicians was briefly dormant from late 1980 to September 1981 when it reappeared with a new publisher (Brevet Publishers Ltd.), a new editor (Denby Richards), a much glossier and more striking layout (including enlargement from 8¼" by 10½" to 8¼" by 11½"), and a subtitle: "Incorporating *Records and Recording*." The latter title, another of Hanson's stable, had also been acquired by Brevet. The contents varied dramatically for a period of a year or so. Substantive articles all but disappear by late 1983 while record reviews abound earlier that year and dwindle considerably by June when the subtitle is removed. In May 1984, Robert Matthew-Walker was appointed editor and by fall, there was an obvious return to the original *Music and Musicians* concept, albeit in the new glossier production style. There are about eight articles per issue while the news items are redistributed under both new and old headings.

Information Sources

BIBLIOGRAPHY
Senior, Evan. "In the beginning." *Music and Musicians* 21 (September 1972): 18.
INDEXES
    Internal Index: 19.5 indexes 1962–1970.

LOCATION SOURCES
> Library of Congress and New York Public Library, full run. Later volumes widely available.

Publication History

TITLE AND TITLE CHANGES
> *Music and Musicians*, 1952–80. *Music and Musicians Incorporating Records and Recording*, 1981–83. *Music and Musicians*, 1983–87. *Music and Musicians International*, 1987– .

VOLUME AND ISSUE DATA
> Volumes 1– , 1952– .

FREQUENCY OF PUBLICATION
> Monthly.

PUBLISHERS
> Hanson Books Ltd., 1952–80. Brevet Publishers Ltd., 1981–88. Orpheus Publications, 1988– .

PLACE OF PUBLICATION
> London, 1952–80. Croydon, 1981–88. London, 1988– .

EDITORS
> Evan Senior, 1952–62. Frank Granville Barber, 1962–71. Tom Sutcliffe, 1971–72. Michael Reynolds, 1972–79. Keith Clarke, 1979–80. Denby Richards, 1981–84. Robert Matthew-Walker, 1984–88. Christopher James, 1989– .

Richard S. James

MUSIC AND MUSICIANS INCORPORATING RECORDS AND RE-CORDING. See MUSIC AND MUSICIANS

MUSIC AND SEWING MACHINE GAZETTE. See MUSICAL COURIER

MUSIC AND SEWING MACHINE COURIER. See MUSICIAL COURIER

MUSIC EDUCATORS JOURNAL

Music Educators Journal (*MEJ*) is the official magazine of the Music Educators National Conference (MENC), which is a nonprofit organization representing all phases of music education in schools, colleges, universities, and teacher-education institutions. All members of MENC (nearly 55,000 in 1985) receive *MEJ*.

The Music Supervisors National Conference (MENC's predecessor), founded in Keokuk, Iowa, in 1907, originally reported its activities in a privately owned journal titled *School Music Magazine*. The idea for an official magazine for the conference originated at the annual meeting in 1914. The first issue was distributed in September of that year as the *Music Supervisors' Bulletin*. This title was changed with v. 2 (1915) to the *Music Supervisors' Journal*. When the magazine's parent organization changed its name to the Music Educators National Conference in 1934, the official magazine of the organization also changed names, this time to the *Music Educators Journal*, its current title.

In general, the first two decades of the magazine contained quite a bit of conference news on the national and regional levels. The number of regional conferences grew from four in the early years to seven by 1931. Other topics of interest that appeared quite regularly concerned musical testing, measurement, and research with attention also being directed toward various problems experienced by school music directors. The quality of articles had improved noticeably by the 1920s over the almost folksy and relatively unsophisticated materials found in the earliest volumes (61.1:45–52).

Issues in the early 1920s were between forty-eight and sixty-four pages long and typically contained conference reports, book and music reviews, an editorial, the conference president's comments, and two departments—instrumental music and tests/measurements. Articles were usually three to seven pages in length. By 1928 each of the five conference reports was five to eight pages long, and a vocal music department had been added. It was also common, in issues from the late 1920s, to see one or two articles from National Conference Proceedings reprinted in the *Music Supervisors Journal*, for example, 14.5:17–28 and 14.5:29–35.

Issues by 1931 were usually about eighty-eight pages long and included seven regional conference reports (three to five pages each) and six to ten additional articles (also usually three to five pages long). The quality of writing by this time was generally impressive with articles that were relatively brief and clearly written. A large part of the credit for these improvements goes to the *MEJ's* three early editors: Peter W. Dykema, 1914–21; George Oscar Bowen, 1921–26; and Paul J. Weaver, 1926–30.

At present, *MEJ* issues are seventy-four to one hundred pages long, though some special issues have been close to 200 pages. Regular issues contain two main sections: Features and Departments. Feature articles typically comprise about 40 percent of the magazine and include a variety of topics such as philosophical inquiries, historical summaries, therapeutic uses of music instruction, composer and performer concerns, methodology presentations, and classroom management techniques. A relatively recent addition to the Features section is the "Idea Bank" in which opinions and suggestions about a single topic are presented. Another new feature called "Counterpoint" (added in February 1985) provides space for rebuttals to *MEJ* articles, particularly those considered to be controversial. Contributors are primarily music teachers, researchers, and performers at the public and postsecondary levels.

The Departments section of each issue includes an editorial page (called "Overtones"); letters to the editor ("Readers' Comments"); "News Brief" in which current information about political and conference happenings are presented; a "Bulletin Board" to announce meetings, symposia, competitions, and the like; "Market Space" in which new products are announced; "Floppy Discography" that reviews new computer software suitable for music education; "Book Reviews"; the "Ad Place" in which readers advertise goods and services; and the "Last Word" written by the president of MENC. Several issues per year include the "Changing Scene" in which announcements of newly filled teaching positions are made.

Some features found in the present journals had predecessors in much earlier volumes. For example, an early version of the "Summer Study" listing first appeared in March 1915, and both "Changing Scene" and "Book Reviews" originated in the September 1920 issue. Precursors of the current Student MENC Chapters began to appear at colleges and universities in late 1939 as "*MEJ* Clubs."

MEJ has published a variety of special issues including the following: "Electronic Music" (November 1967), "Facing the Music in Urban Education" (January 1970), "Technology in Music Teaching" (January 1971), "Music in Special Education" (April 1972), "Music in World Cultures" (October 1972), "Music in Open Education" (April 1974), "Charles Ives' Centennial" (October 1974), "Careers and Music" (March 1977 and October 1982), "The Arts in General Education" (January 1978), "Improvisation" (January 1980), "The Crisis in Music Education" (November 1981), "Teaching Special Students" (April 1982), "Technology" (January 1983), and "Multicultural Education" (May 1983). Other relatively recent issues of *MEJ* have focused on "Women in Music" (January 1979), "Opera in Education" (October 1979), "Pop Music in School" (December 1979), and "Steps Toward the Future" (May 1982).

The results of two dissertations that focused on *MEJ* contents are evidence of the magazine's impact on music education. The first of these dissertations examined the major concerns of music education between 1957 and 1967 as represented by a content analysis of *MEJ* for those years. Among the conclusions reached were the following: (1) that *MEJ* is considered an important vehicle for the expression of theoretical considerations of the music education profession, and (2) that officials of MENC carry the major responsibility for formulating and communicating music education's theoretical foundation in the United States.[1] A second dissertation was a study of values in music education from 1950 to 1970 as presented in value statements in *MEJ*. Results indicated an increase in *MEJ* value statements concerning aesthetic experience and creativity over the twenty-year time span. Values that decreased in emphasis in the *Journal* included democratic ideals, enjoyment, and socializing force.[2]

Additional information on *MEJ* contents is available in annual internal indexes found in the June/July issue for vs. 46 (1959) through 52 (1966), and in the May issue starting with v. 53 (1967). Two cumulative indexes that cover September 1959 to July 1965 (vs. 46–51) and September 1966 to May 1970 (vs. 52–56) are available for purchase from MENC.

The Editorial Board (later, Editorial Committee) of *MEJ* was first set up by the MENC Board of Directors in 1931 and currently consists of eleven members plus the chairman. All Editorial Committee members and chairmen are nominated by the MENC president and appointed by the MENC National Executive Board. Unsolicited manuscripts sent to *MEJ* are screened initially by the editor and then go to three Editorial Committee members for blind review.

Throughout the history of *MEJ* and its predecessors, the music education profession and the music industry have maintained a close relationship. For example, from 1914 to 1930 the magazine was distributed without fee to readers, with music industry advertisers providing production and circulation costs. Advertising remained an integral part of the *Journal* after the fee policy was changed with the September/October issue of 1930 and $1.00 of each $3.00 annual membership fee to MENC was designated for *MEJ*. Many music industry firms have advertised continuously in *MEJ* for more than sixty years.

The first issue of *Music Supervisors' Bulletin* was thirty-two pages long, 7" by 10" in size, and was distributed free to about 5,800 persons involved with music education. Issues were published four times a year until 1919 when a fifth issue per year was added. When the *Journal's* name was changed to its current title in 1934, the number of issues published yearly increased to six. In 1966 the number was expanded to nine issues a year, the schedule that remains to the present. The magazine's page size increased to 8½" by 11½" in 1930 and has remained essentially unchanged since. A wide variety of advertisements for music, educational aids, and so on is supplemented by a classified section called "The Ad Place."

Notes

1. Maureen D. Hooper, "Major Concerns of Music Education: Content Analysis of the *Music Educators Journal, 1957–1967*" (Ed.D. diss., University of Southern California, 1969), in *Dissertation Abstracts International* 30 (1970): 4479–80A.

2. William M. Jones, "A Study of Values in Music Education, 1950–1970, to Identify Changes and Directions of Change" (Ed.D. diss., University of the Pacific, 1973), in *Dissertation Abstracts International* 34 (1974): 1313A.

Information Sources

BIBLIOGRAPHY

Buttelman, Clifford V. "The Official Magazine of the Music Educators National Conference." *Music Educators Journal* 50 (January 1964): 34–38, 77–79.

Hooper, Maureen D. "Major Concerns of Music Education: Contents Analysis of the Music Educators Journal, 1957–1967." Ed.D. diss., University of Southern California, 1956.

Jones, William M. "A Study of Values in Music Education, 1950–1970, to Identify Changes and Directions of Change." Ed.D. diss., University of the Pacific, 1974.

"MEJ at 60." *Music Educators Journal* 61 (September 1974): 45–52.

INDEXES
> Internal: vs. 46–51; vs. 52–56; each volume indexed (vs. 46–).
> External: Music Index, 1949– . Music Article Guide, 1965– . ERIC, 1969– .
> Education Index, 1929– . RILM, 1968– .

REPRINT EDITIONS
> Microform: UMI.

LOCATIONS SOURCES
> Widely available.

Publication History

TITLE AND TITLE CHANGES
> *Music Supervisors' Bulletin,* 1914. *Music Supervisors' Journal*, 1915–33. *Music Educators Journal*, 1934– .

VOLUME AND ISSUE DATA
> Volumes 1– , 1914– .

FREQUENCY OF PUBLICATION
> Quarterly, 1914–18. 5/year, 1919–33. Bimonthly, 1934–65. 9/year, 1966– .

PUBLISHERS
> Music Supervisors National Conference, 1914–33. Music Educators National Conference, 1934– .

PLACES OF PUBLICATION
> Madison, Wisconsin, 1914–21. Ann Arbor, Michigan, 1921–24. Tulsa, Oklahoma, 1924–26. Chapel Hill, North Carolina, 1926–29. Ithaca, New York, 1929. Chicago, 1930–56. Washington, D.C., 1956–74. Vienna, Virginia, 1974–75. Reston, Virginia, 1975– .

EDITORS
> Peter W. Dykema, 1914–21. George Oscar Bowen, 1921–26. Paul J. Weaver, 1926–30. Edward Bailey Birge, Chairman of the Editorial Board, 1930–44. Clifford V. Buttleman, Managing Editor, 1930–55. Karl D. Ernst, Chairman of the Editorial Board, 1954–58. Clifford V. Buttleman, Director of Publications, 1956–65. Bonnie C. Kowall, 1960–65. Charles B. Fowler, 1965–71. Malcolm E. Bessom, 1971–77. John Aquino, 1977–September 1979. Malcolm E. Bessom, October 1979–May 1981. Arthur J. Michaels, Managing Editor, September 1981. Rebecca Grier Taylor, October 1981–May 1986. Karen Deans, September 1986–87. Maribeth Rose, January 1988– .

Vincent J. Kantorski

MUSIC MAGAZINE AND MUSICAL COURIER. See MUSICAL COURIER

MUSIC REVIEW, THE

"War babies are sometimes difficult to handle; but the life of this one, however short, will be as full as we can make it" (1:1). With these words, Geoffrey Sharp introduced the first number of the *The Music Review* in February 1940.

Sharp, studying at the Royal College of Music at the time, collaborated to found the journal with the firm of Heffer and Sons, which has published it since. During his army service from 1942 to 1944, Sharp's wife served as editor. Sharp held the position, publishing many articles in the magazine, until his death in March 1974.

The journal, based in Cambridge, was well received; in 1948 *Notes* (q.v.) hailed it as "undoubtedly the outstanding new publication to come from England in recent years."[1] Despite its financial struggles and dependence on subscriber donations during the first three years, it appeared regularly.

Even during the war years, *The Review* was scrupulously nonnationalistic, a position that Sharp cited as "a cornerstone of editorial policy" (1:1). The journal attracted writings by continental scholars early on, especially those who had fled Nazism. The early issues contained articles, many seminal, by Otto Erich Deutsch, Alfred Einstein, and Egon Wellesz as well as Donald Tovey, J. A. Westrup, and A. Hyatt King. The current editorship continues Sharp's policy.

From its inception, *The MR* aimed at balanced music journalism; according to Sharp's obituary in *The London Times*, he "hoped to provide a medium for in-depth musicological studies and critical essays."[2] Among style periods, *The MR* has consistently favored twentieth-century music, then classic and romantic, in that order; articles on pre-Baroque music are more sparse. American music, largely ignored prior to the mid–1960s, has since received increasing attention, with contributions on Charles Ives, Elliott Carter, and others. Besides new music, its main focus has been opera, with orchestral and keyboard music as important secondary interests.[3]

In its preoccupation with the current musical landscape, *The MR* has welcomed strongly articulated views and, often, controversy. Through the mid–1960s, a decided editorial slant prevailed against much new, especially twelve-tone music. In a memorable 1965 editorial, Sharp asked, "Is it . . . possible to deny that Western music is in a decline in 1965?" and decried mediocrity and a "monumental dullness" in the performance world (26:1). Nevertheless, Sharp and his successors have continued their commitment to survey contemporary music and to promote, in articles such as that on Deodat de Severac, lesser-known composers.

The articles are mainly of three types. General program notes comprise the largest category. These surveys of a composer's music with brief descriptions of some works include ones on Giacomo Meyerbeer (25:142–48) and Carl Loewe (24:134–48). Analyses are the second most frequent, followed by biographic, historical, and bibliographic studies.

According to Guy Marco, *The Review*'s greatest strength has consistently been its analyses, which include milestones in music scholarship, and in which almost every new analytical approach has been represented. Noteworthy are Hans Keller's article on functional analysis, Allen Forte's "The Structural Origin of Exact Tempo in the Brahms-Haydn Variations" (18:138–49), and Jan LaRue's "Harmonic Rhythm in the Beethoven Symphonies" (18:8–20). Especially valuable analyses of operas include Wellesz's on *Don Giovanni* (4:121–27) and Philip Friedheim's "Radical Harmonic Procedures in Berlioz" (21:282–96).

Famous bibliographic writings in *The MR* include Deutsch's "The First Edition of Brahms" (1:123–43, 255–78), Einstein's Mozart catalog revisions in seven issues, and H. C. Robbins Landon's "The Original Versions of Haydn's 'Salomon' Symphonies" and "The Symphonies of Joseph Haydn: Addenda" (15:1–32; 19:311–18). Franz Schubert's *Unfinished Symphony* has stimulated an ongoing controversy since 1941.

While historical research is not the journal's central thrust, noteworthy entries include Philip T. Barford's on eighteenth-century sonata principle (13:255–63) and D. P. Walker's five-article series on Renaissance musical humanism. Ancient classical music and acoustics were of interest in the first decade but have received less attention since (26:242–3). While *The MR*'s journalism on aesthetics has become more sophisticated since 1940, Marco maintains, it has generally not shown a broad enough grasp of recent major ideas and writings (26:241).

Special issues usually celebrate anniversaries of major composers, for example, the Mozart issue in v. 17 (eleven articles) and the several articles in vs. 18 and 21 devoted to Sir Edward Elgar and Johann Sebastian Bach, respectively. *The Review's* twenty-fifth birthday issue, v. 26, is subtitled *A Comprehensive Survey of Contemporary Music in Europe*; it also contains Guy Marco's history of *MR*.

The Review's major component, besides articles, is criticism. Reviews of concerts and festivals (live and broadcast), music, books, and recordings appeared from the earliest volume, although not in every issue. Book reviews are by far the most regular and extensive; ranging from several paragraphs to two pages, occasionally with musical examples, they vary in number from one to approximately eight per issue. Performances reviewed most often are operas and opera festivals. Since May 1977, reviews of new periodicals and articles in other journals have appeared semi-regularly. The recording and broadcast reviews have enthusiastically followed new technology in those fields since 1940.

A mainstay of modern British music journalism, *The Music Review* is directed toward the musically literate with a side interest in research as well as to students of music theory and musicology. It provides its international readership with a serious, scholarly but engaging view of music and music performance, and a sampling of leading current analysis and research relative to the contemporary and common practice repertoire.

The journal has maintained the same format since its beginning. It measures 7½″ by 10¾″, with issues averaging eighty to a hundred pages; articles usually range from fifteen to thirty pages in length. The only foreign-language entries were Einstein's on Mozart. Articles are well documented; they often have bibliographies and a few give discographies. Musical examples vary with the nature of the article, but are plentiful in the analyses. Black and white plates, portraits, and facsimiles sometimes accompany historical articles. The discreet advertising in the early issues has now nearly disappeared.

Notes

1. Frank C. Campbell, "Some Current Foreign Periodicals," *Notes* 5 (March 1948): 197.

2. *The London Times*, 10 April 1974 (no pagination). Quoted in John Boulton, "Geoffrey Sharp," *Music Review* 35 (February–May 1974):1.

3. These and all other tabulations are from Guy A. Marco. " 'And Radiate its Own Vitality': 'The Music Review' over Twenty-five Years," *Music Review* 26 (1965): 236–46.

Information Sources

BIBLIOGRAPHY

Boulton, John. "Geoffrey Sharp." *Music Review* 35 (February-May 1974): 1–3.

Campbell, Frank C. "Some Current Foreign Periodicals." *Notes* 5 (1948): 189–98.

Marco, Guy A. " 'And Radiate its Own Vitality': 'The Music Review' over Twenty-five Years." *Music Review* 26 (1965): 236–46.

The New Grove Dictionary of Music and Musicians. S.v. "Sharp, Geoffrey (Newton)," by William Y. Elias.

INDEXES

External: Music Index, 1949– . RILM, 1967– . International Index to Periodicals, 1949–74. Humanities Index, 1974– . Arts and Humanities Citation Index, 1976– . British Humanities Index, 1963– .

REPRINT EDITIONS

Microform: UMI.

LOCATION SOURCES

Widely available.

Publication History

TITLE AND TITLE CHANGES

The Music Review.

VOLUME AND ISSUE DATA

Volumes 1– , 1940– .

FREQUENCY OF PUBLICATION

Quarterly.

PUBLISHER

W. Heffer & Sons, Ltd.

PLACE OF PUBLICATION

Cambridge, England.

EDITORS

Geoffrey N. Sharp, 1940–March 1974. A. F. Leighton Thomas with John Boulton, Editorial Consultant, 1974– .

Esther Rothenbusch

MUSIC STUDENT. See MUSIC TEACHER

MUSIC SUPERVISORS' BULLETIN. See MUSIC EDUCATORS JOURNAL

MUSIC SUPERVISORS'JOURNAL. See MUSIC EDUCATORS JOURNAL

MUSIC TEACHER

The origin of the *Music Teacher* can be traced to a small group of North Country musicians headed by Dr. Percy A. Scholes who formed a network of music study circles centered upon Leeds, England, around 1907–08. These circles, which adopted Perry's *Great Composers* for study, contributed to the music appreciation movement in England. In a society that did not know the radio or the gramophone, these music study circles served a great need for music appreciation among the masses. Dr. Scholes initiated a typewritten circular in 1908, intended to advance the cause of the music circles. Within only a few months, the circular was expanded and printed as a monthly periodical with the title *The Music Student*. Two years later, this publication became the official journal of the newly organized Music Teacher's Association.

The Music Student continued to advance music education in England. It sponsored the first Vacation Conference on Music Education and the first Musician's Holiday Course, fought for higher standards in music teaching, fostered the development of ear-training and sight-singing study, and attacked the creation of unscrupulous music colleges. Alternate issues of *The Music Student* contained a chamber music supplement underwritten by W. W. Cobbett.

After World War I, the journal absorbed another popular periodical, *The Musician*, and the title was changed to *The Music Teacher*. At the same time a new numbering system was initiated: the January 1922 issue became 1.1 of the "new series." For several years following, *The Music Teacher* carried a double numbering system. In December 1937, *The Music Teacher* absorbed *The Piano Student* and again changed its title, this time to *The Music Teacher and Piano Student*. This consolidation allowed the journal to expand its service to a wider readership. In January 1968 (47.1) the journal adopted its current title: *Music Teacher*.

The focus of *Music Teacher* has been remarkably consistent throughout its publishing history: "We exist to serve music teachers of all kinds" (63.3:18). In fact, it serves two broad groups almost equally: music teachers in schools and independent music teachers, both dealing with students of all ages. Each issue contains brief articles on "popular" topics of interest to its broad readership: adjudication, piano teaching, English folk arts, music festivals, music education, master classes, music theory and history, profiles of composers, musical instruments (especially piano and organ), and music in higher education. Additionally, regular features include "Music Scene" (people and events), "Set Works for O Level" (analyses of required piano works for the General Certificate of Education, or G.C.E., examinations), "Associated Board Piano Examinations" (analyses of selected works for the Associated Board exams), " Book Reviews,"

"Music Reviews" (art music recordings), "New Music Reviews" (including solo orchestral instruments, chamber music, and school band, orchestra, and choral works), and "New Piano Music." "The Question Box" (originally "Teacher's Questions Answered by Experts") is a popular monthly feature where music teachers from remote corners of the commonwealth can receive expert advice concerning their specific teaching problems. After World War I, monthly articles on British composers contributed to a renewed interest in music of native composers. A new series of articles on contemporary composers began in May 1986 with a goal of five to six major pieces each year. *Music Teacher* has also included reviews of computer software and teaching aids of interest to music teachers.

The journal's heritage in music appreciation continues with its annual "Music Teacher Guide to Leisure Courses" and a listing of music study holidays for musicians of all ages and abilities. These courses include chamber music, music theory, recorder playing, guitar, and keyboard. Issues in the 1930s contained a new piano solo, one page in length, with a descriptive analysis as an aid to the teacher. This format was particularly useful for the adult piano student as well.

The journal plays an important role in the external examination system in Great Britain. To gain admission to a national music college, students must pass the General Certificate of Education and Associated Board examinations. The syllabi for both are discussed and required works are analyzed as monthly features of the *Music Teacher*.

Music Teacher has consistently presented musical information and opinion to a broad audience throughout the English-speaking world. It resembles a combination of three American journals, *School Musician* (q.v.), *Clavier* (q.v.), and *Music Educators Journal* (q.v.), with added emphasis on adult teaching and music appreciation. The journal's contents reflect the important trends and ideas in twentieth-century music education and chronicle the major technological advances in music and music teaching.

The physical format of *Music Teacher* is 8" by 11" with each issue averaging thirty to forty pages. It is typeset with photographs and often includes reproductions of short musical works for study purposes. Recent volumes contain a yearly index in the January issue, with listings arranged alphabetically by name and subject. *Music Teacher* presents a wide variety of advertisements relating to music publishing, music events and festivals, music schools and musical instruments.

Information Sources

BIBLIOGRAPHY

Anderson, W. R. "Our 'Music Teacher' Jubilee." *Music Teacher* (1958): 18–19.

Cady, Henry L. "Music in English Education." *Contributions to Music Education* 3 (Autumn, 1974): 43–71.

Gibbin, L. D. "Forty Years On." *Music Teacher* (1948): 11.

Scholes, Percy A. "The Story of 'Music Teacher.' " *Music Teacher* (1958): 20.

INDEXES
External: Music Index, 1950– . Bibliographie des Musikschrifttums, 1937.
REPRINT EDITIONS
Microform: UMI, 1919–71 (incomplete), 1972– .
LOCATION SOURCES
Widely available.

Publication History

TITLE AND TITLE CHANGES
Music Student, 1908–21. *Music Teacher*, 1922–37. *Music Teacher and Piano Student*, 1937–67. *Music Teacher*, 1968– .
VOLUME AND ISSUE DATA
Volumes 1–14.3, 1908–21. New series, volumes 1– , 1922– .
FREQUENCY OF PUBLICATION
Monthly.
PUBLISHERS
Evans Brothers, Ltd., 1916–81. Scholastic Publishing, Ltd., 1981–86. Rhinegold Publishing, Ltd., 1986– .
PLACE OF PUBLICATION
London.
EDITORS
Percy Scholes, 1908–21. W. R. Anderson, 1921-ca. 1926. H. S. Gordon, 1927-ca. 1933. J. Raymond Tobin, 1934-?. Barbara Fisher, 1967–73. David Renouf, 1975–79. Leonard Pearcy, 1980–85. Mariann Barton, 1986– .

Richard P. Kennell

MUSIC TEACHER AND PIANO STUDENT. See MUSIC TEACHER

MUSIC TEACHERS NATIONAL ASSOCIATION BULLETIN. See AMERICAN MUSIC TEACHER

MUSIC THEORY SPECTRUM

Music Theory Spectrum is the official journal of the Society for Music Theory. The society was founded in 1977 as a forum for scholarly work in music theory, as distinguished from the more historically oriented papers and articles emanating from the American Musicological Society (AMS) and its *Journal* (q.v.). Leading figures in this amicable separation from the AMS included Allen Forte, Wallace Berry, Richmond Browne, and Mary Wennerstrom. Relations with kindred societies are excellent; national meetings are often held jointly, and the program committees (from whose selections some, though not all, of the articles appearing in the societies' journals are chosen) consult one another during the preparatory stages for these meetings. Beyond this, however, *Music Theory Spectrum* is independent of any other journal. It operates under the dual guidance of an editor and the society's Publications Committee, chaired by David Beach until William Caplin assumed that position beginning with v. 7.

The first volume of the new society's journal appeared in 1979, and it has appeared annually since that date without changes in title or format. From its inception, *Music Theory Spectrum* has been recognized as a serious journal devoted to high-level, professional studies in music theory. Although the attention given within the discipline to Schenkerian studies and to set theory are naturally reflected in its contents, there is also sufficient breadth to avoid what might be termed an ideological position. The word "Spectrum" appearing in its title is intended to convey the breadth of interests, within the field of music theory, addressed by the journal. The editors have adhered very successfully to this goal. Articles deal with the history of music theory, analyses of music, analytical methods, and speculative theory, ranging from the Middle Ages to the present. Over sixty men and women in the field have contributed articles and reviews, with no individual appearing more than twice up to the present time. In addition to such well-known figues as David Beach, Wallace Berry, Edward T. Cone, Allen Forte, Robert Gauldin, Benito Rivera, John Rothgeb, and Lewis Rowell, younger scholars in the field are amply represented. A feature called "Teaching Music Theory," and described as "an ongoing series," appeared in vs. 2 and 3. V. 7 is a landmark issue in that it is devoted primarily to a single theme, "Time and Rhythm in Music"; it includes a bibliography by Jonathan Kramer, consulting editor for this volume, of some 850 items on these subjects, as well as eight other articles dealing specifically with time and rhythm.

"Reviews and Commentaries" is a particularly strong feature, in part because sufficient scope is allowed for the reviewer to go into meaningful detail, and in part because these features have dealt with several significant books that have appeared in recent years. Among them are the following important English translations: *Free Composition* by Heinrich Schenker, reviewed by Edward Laufer (3:158–84); *Theory of Harmony* by Arnold Schönberg, commentary by Bryan Simms (4:155–62); *Introduction to the Theory of Heinrich Schenker* by Oswald Jonas, reviewed by Bruce Campbell (5:127–31); and *The Art of Strict Musical Composition* by Johann Philipp Kirnberger, reviewed by Raymond Haggh (6:100–103).

Other features that have appeared (although not with perfect regularity) in the journal include correspondence, announcements, and editorials dealing with the founding and history of the society and its journal, the special nature of a given volume, and so on. There is no internal indexing in *Music Theory Spectrum*.

Music Theory Spectrum appears in an oblong paperbound format, 7½" by 8¾",which allows for the inclusion of Schenkerian analytical graphs and other types of charts and illustrations. The ten issues that have appeared thus far average about 160 pages in length; a volume typically contains about eight articles averaging some sixteen pages each and, beginning with v. 3, two to four substantial reviews (primarily of books; the first three issues of the new British journal *Music Analysis* are also reviewed, 6:90–100). The written text is typeset; musical examples and charts include photocopies in the various styles of the originals, and there are also a few small facsimile examples reproduced by this method. No advertisements appeared in the first five issues; in each of vs. 6 and 7 there are three—all for like-spirited journals and societies: *Music Analysis*, the *Journal of Aesthetics and Art Criticism* (q.v.), and the College Music Society and its publications. All articles are in English, but the intended readership is international in scope.

Information Sources

INDEXES
> External: RILM, 1979– . Music Index, 1979– . Music Article Guide, 1985– . Arts and Humanities Citation Index, 1984– .

LOCATION SOURCES
> Widely available.

Publication History

TITLE AND TITLE CHANGES
> *Music Theory Spectrum.*

VOLUME AND ISSUE DATA
> Volumes 1– , 1979– .

FREQUENCY OF PUBLICATION
> Annual.

PUBLISHER
> The Society for Music Theory, Inc.

PLACE OF PUBLICATION
> Bloomington, Indiana.

EDITORS
> Bryan R. Simms, 1979–82. Lewis Rowell, 1983–85. John Clough, 1986–88. Jonathan Bernard, 1989– .

Paul B. Mast

MUSICA

Musica, a German periodical first published in 1947, was the inspiration of Karl Vötterle, founder and owner of Bärenreiter-Verlag, and Fred Hamel, a musicologist who served as the journal's first editor. Their intentions for the journal were clear from the beginning. As a publication attached to no particular party or trend, *Musica* has an open editorial policy and program. Any article or piece of information concerning music might appear in the journal's pages, as the generic name, *Musica*, suggests. The journal also aims at a wide audience: anyone interested in music, both professionals and amateurs (1:1). This open-ended and open-minded approach accounts in part for the fact that *Musica* continues to thrive after nearly forty years.

Roughly one-half of each issue is devoted to musical scholarship. Articles, usually no longer than ten pages, touch on a wide variety of topics from German folk music (29:20–23) to American jazz (3:443–45) and from rhetorical devices in Johann Sebastian Bach's music (6:191–94) to the most modern compositional styles (39:151–55). There appears, despite the diversity, to be an emphasis on music from the nineteenth and twentieth centuries. Contributors include some of the leading musical figures in West Germany, among them Carl Dahlhaus, Diether de la Motte, and Peter Benary. Dahlhaus and de la Motte also serve on the editorial board.

Until 1978 most issues contained articles on a wide variety of topics. In that year the editors announced their decision that each issue would focus on one particular theme, an approach they had used occasionally in earlier issues. In 1983 they decided to alternate between the two formats, a policy that has not been strictly followed.

Among those issues that do focus on a particular theme, some feature one composer (usually German), others the music of one country, and still others address topics pertinent to contemporary musical life. Composers to whom an entire issue has been devoted include Johann Sebastian Bach (4.7/8), Dietrich Buxtehude (11.5), Franz Joseph Haydn (13.5, 36.2, and 36.5), Ernst Krenek (34.2), and Franz Schubert (32.2). One issue is devoted to Robert Schumann's *Kinderszenen* (35.5), and Richard Wagner and Johannes Brahms share the spotlight in another (37.1). The birth anniversaries of three prominent composers are recognized in an issue entitled "Bach, Händel, Schütz—Birthday in the Museum?" (38.6). Countries which have been the focus of separate issues range from Czechoslovakia (11.9/10) and France (19.3), to Great Britain (12.7/8). Finally, the titles of those issues that deal with some aspect of contemporary musical life include: "Music of the 70's" (32.1), "Music and the Media" (32.3), "Music Education outside the School" (32.4), "Guitar" (33.1), "Analysis and Interpretation" (33.2), "Television Music" (34.1), "The Politics of Music and a Society of Leisure" (34.3), "Performance Practice" (34.2), "The *Lied*" (35.3), "Can One Teach Composition?" (35.4), "The Child and His Music" (36.4), "Questions Posed to Young Composers" (37.5), and "Improvisation" (38.1).

In addition to articles, *Musica* features a number of departments designed to keep its readers abreast of current musical events. For instance, in the section labeled "Berichte/Kommentare"[1] one finds one- and two-page reviews of the latest music festivals, celebrations, and opera performances both in Germany and in other countries. In another department, "Nachrichten," one finds shorter announcements of new appointments to important musical posts, the dates of upcoming festivals and premiere performances, and obituary notices. The older issues of *Musica* can thus be useful to musicologists and music historians who seek details of particular performances and musical events. Other departments that have appeared at various times include "Das Musiktheater" (v. 22), devoted to the people and movements in opera, and a music education column entitled

"Musikpädagogik" (since v. 26). Usually there are also sections devoted to book and record reviews.

Another source of information to the reader is the abundant advertising. In addition to the usual publishers' announcements of new books and records, there are numerous advertisements placed by the organizers of music festivals and conferences. Frequently, Bärenreiter gathers this information and publishes a one- or two-page calendar listing music festivals to take place in a given year, primarily in Germany, for example, 39:99–100.

Each issue contains numerous photographs, especially of operatic productions and of famous composers and performers of this century. The early volumes contain photographs of the damage to German cities during the war, as well as of the gradual reconstruction of important landmarks.

Musica has been augmented by several supplements throughout its history. *Musica Schallplatte*, a publication that featured articles about the latest recording techniques, as well as reviews of recently released recordings, first appeared as a supplement to *Musica* in 1958. In 1962 it was renamed *Phonoprisma*, and in 1968 it was incorporated as a regular feature within the journal. In a similar manner, *Practica*, a supplement addressing performance issues, first appeared in 1962 and was incorporated into the journal in 1968.

Musica became the haven for two journals that, for various reasons, ceased independent publication. The short-lived *Neue Musikzeitschrift*, published in Munich from 1946/7 until 1950, was incorporated into *Musica* in 1951. *Hausmusik*,[2] published under various titles since 1932, was incorporated into *Musica* in 1962.

Since 1969 *Musica* has served as the official organ for the Internationale Arbeitskreis für Musik,[3] an organization founded in the 1930s by Karl Vötterle.[4] The members of the *Arbeitskreis* have, since the merger of their journal, *Hausmusik*, with *Musica*, received a subscription to *Musica* with the payment of dues. At the end of each issue there is an "IAM-Journal" with news items and brief reports of interest to the society's members.

At first, *Musica* was published bimonthly in issues of sixty-four pages. However, from 1949 (v. 3) until 1961 (v. 15) the journal appeared monthly in issues of about forty to fifty pages. In 1962 (v. 16) the journal returned to its original bimonthly schedule with issues of varying lengths. Recent volumes average about a hundred 7″ by 9½″ pages. An index is published for each volume.

Notes

1. In early volumes this feature was divided into two sections, "Berichte" and "Umschau."

2. Known as *Collegium Musicum* in 1932, as *Zeitschrift für Hausmusik* from 1933 until 1946, and as *Mitteillungen* from 1946 until 1949.

3. From 1933 until 1951 known as the *Arbeitskreis für Hausmusic* and from 1951 until 1968, as the *Arbeitskreis für Haus- und Jugendmusik*.

4. *The New Grove Dictionary of Music and Musicians*, s.v. "Bärenreiter," by Richard Baum and Wolfgang Rehm.

Information Sources

BIBLIOGRAPHY

The New Grove Dictionary of Music and Musicians. S.v. "Bärenreiter," by Richard
    Baum and Wolfgang Rehm.
Rohlfs, Eckart. *Die deutschsprachigen Musikperiodica 1945–1957: Versuch einer struk-
    turellen Gesamtdarstellung als Beitrag zur Geschichte der musikalischen Fach-
    press.* Regensburg, 1961.
INDEXES
    Internal: each volume indexed.
    External: Music Index, 1949– . RILM, 1967– . Bibliographie des Musik-
    schrifttums, 1950– .
REPRINT EDITIONS
    Microform: UMI, 1947–74 (incomplete), 1975– .
LOCATION SOURCES
    Widely available.

Publication History

TITLE AND TITLE CHANGES
    Musica.
VOLUME AND ISSUE DATA
    Volumes 1– , 1947– .
FREQUENCY OF PUBLICATION
    Bimonthly, 1947–48. Monthly, 1949–61. Bimonthly, 1962– .
PUBLISHER
    Bärenreiter-Verlag.
PLACE OF PUBLICATION
    Kassel, West Germany.
CHIEF EDITORS
    Fred Hamel, 1947–58. Günter Hausswald, 1959–70. Wolfram Schwinger, 1971–
    76. Hanspeter Krellmann, 1976–78. Clemens Kühn, 1978– .

                                                            Diane McMullen

MUSICA DISCIPLINA

In 1944 Armen Carapetyan founded the Institute of Renaissance and Baroque
Music at Cambridge, Massachusetts. The aims of the institute were twofold:
"The advancement of musical history as an integral part of history of culture in
general, and the advancement of its place in cultivated life and in the program
of humanistic studies in our universities and colleges" (1:3). He intended to
concentrate the institute's efforts on the music of the Renaissance and Baroque
periods, then little explored, although the music of the Middle Ages, insofar as
it touched on problems of the Renaissance, was also to be included.

When the institute moved to Rome in 1946, to be closer to the sources under
investigation, the organization was renamed the American Institute of Musicology (AIM), and the areas of specialization became the Middle Ages and the

Renaissance, with sporadic attention to the Baroque (2.3). AIM engages in a large number of publication projects: *Corpus mensurabilis musicae* (*CMM*, 1947–   ), *Corpus scriptorum de musica* (*CSM*, 1951–   ), *Musicological Studies and Documents* (*MSD*, 1953–   ), *Miscellanea* (*MISC*, 1952–   ), *Corpus of Early Keyboard Music* (*CEKM*, 1963–   ) and *Renaissance Manuscript Studies* (*RMS*, 1973–   ).

Musica disciplina (*MD*) is the oldest of the institute's publications. V. 1 appeared in four fascicles between 1946 and 1947 under the title *Journal of Renaissance and Baroque Music*. When v. 2 was published in 1948, the institute had moved to Rome, and the periodical was renamed *Musica Disciplina: A Journal of the History of Music*. It still comprised four fascicles annually, but was issued in irregular sizes and at irregular intervals. The fascicle format was abandoned in 1953, and yearly publication began. In 1957 this change was reflected in a title change: since then the journal has been known as *Musica Disciplina: A Yearbook of the History of Music*.

Each volume measures 7¼″ by 10½″; the length has varied from 181 to 274 pages and is usually well over 200 pages. The bulk of this space is given over to between five and thirteen articles, most of which are in English with a very few in French, German, Spanish, or Italian. The authors represent the entire European and American musicological community, although the work of American scholars tends to predominate. The subject matter is limited exclusively to music of the Middle Ages and Renaissance. Within this circumscribed area the coverage is thorough and shows the highest order of scholarship. The intended audience is the body of serious specialists interested in the finest details of Medieval and Renaissance music. Some articles present exhaustive inventories of manuscript sources; others deal with problems of notation, publication, repertories, and so on. All research articles deal with topics of a quite specific sort; there are no general articles at all.

A second department that has appeared regularly since the journal's inception is entitled "Publications of AIM." Early on, under the title "Announcements," this section presented information on forthcoming editions, various summer sessions held by the institute, and projected series. Gradually it became a list of publications available and was given its current name in 1956. Until the recent delays in publication, this section constituted the readiest guide to the enormous amount of material generated by the institute.

Beginning with v. 2, each issue contained an international bibliography of new books, editions of music, articles exclusive of those appearing in *MD*, and dissertations related to the Middle Ages and the Renaissance. From 1948 until 1957 the bibliographies were compiled by an international group of top Medieval and Renaissance musicologists, for example, Leonard Ellinwood, Nino Pirrotta, Wolfgang Schmieder, Miguel Querol, and Keith Mixter; after that, individual scholars took charge of the project. The bibliography seems to have been a continuing source of frustration—many delays in publication were attributed to it—and it was discontinued after 1975.

Some volumes honor individual musicologists. These are not *Festschriften* in the normal sense; there is no attempt to limit the subject matter or to solicit articles from specific contributors, and there is no bibliography given of a particular scholar's output. Rather they are dedications. Scholars honored in this way are: Yvonne Rokseth *In memoriam* (2.3/4), Jacques Handschin *In memoriam* (v. 10), Willi Apel on his seventieth birthday (v. 17), Donald J. Grout on his seventieth birthday (v. 17), Albert Seay on his sixtieth birthday (v. 30), and Armen Carapetyan on his seventy-fifth birthday (v. 37).

An unusual feature of *MD* is that reviews, the staple of many periodicals, here find no place at all. Indeed, since publication began, only four reviews have appeared, and these in the first two volumes. The policy against the publication of reviews was stated in detail in the editorial to v. 6 (1952) and reaffirmed in v. 30 (1976). Also, there is no department devoted to communications from readers. This does not seem to have been Carapetyan's initial intent. In an editorial he stated: "full exchange of views between scholars . . . will be published, *if* authors will restrain [themselves] and not indulge [in] excesses or polemics for the sake of polemics" (2:4). But in fact, no such exchanges have ever been published.

Each volume normally contains extended musical examples, diagrams, and tables. Plates showing manuscript facsimiles, photographs, and so on appear infrequently. An exception to this was the publication of the complete Faenza Codex in three installments (vs. 13–15: 1959–61).[1] Vs. 2–4 contained indices for the preceding year. A general index of vs. 1–20, edited by Thomas L. Noblitt, was published separately by the institute in 1968. It contains an index of authors and a separate index of subjects.

One cautionary note is in order. Readers must beware of typographical errors in the institute's publications. Some of these are minor ("uniportant" "tremselves"). Others are of more consequence. When errors of this sort, the omission of small particles or the replacement of one symbol with another closely related to it, appear in editions of music, the problems are much more profound.[2]

Carapetyan has edited the *Journal* since its inception,[3] though he has shared these duties from time to time: with Leo Schrade (v. 1) and with Gilbert Reaney (vs. 11–29). V. 37, in honor of Carapetyan, was edited by Frank D'Accone and Gilbert Reaney. In 1976, the copyright passed from the hands of Carapetyan to the publishing firm of Hänssler-Verlag, apparently to make *MD* financially secure. However, since 1978, publication of the individual volumes has been more and more irregular. It is fervently to be hoped that these delays do not signal the demise of *MD*.

Notes

1. This was later reissued as *MSD* 10. A complete transcription with parallel vocal pieces, edited by Dragon Plamenac, appears in *CMM* 57.

2. See Edward Lowinsky, "Music Reviews," *Notes* 17 (1960): 301–3, for a list of such errors in the edition of Jacobus Clemens non Papa's music (*CMM* 4). As Lowinsky

points out, it is often impossible to distinguish between compositional idiosyncrasies and misprints.

3. The logogram in use since 1948 shows a five-line staff bearing an F clef. On the staff is placed a red binaria with propriety and with perfection whose pitches represent Carapetyan's initials.

Information Sources

BIBLIOGRAPHY

Apfel, Ernst. "Besprechungen." *Die Musikforschung* 15 (1962): 186–88.

"Book Reviews." *Music Review* 10 (1949): 56–57.

Campbell, Frank, Gladys Eppink, and Jessica Fredricks. "Music Magazines of Britain and the United States." *Notes* 6 (March 1949): 239–62.

Carapetyan, Armen. "An Editorial." *Journal of Renaissance and Baroque Music* 1 (1946): 3–4.

———. "Editorial." *Journal of Renaissance and Baroque Music* 1 (1946): 253–54.

———. "Editorial." *Musica disciplina* 2 (1948): 3–4.

———. "Editorial." *Musica disciplina* 6 (1952): 3–5.

———. "Editorial." *Musica disciplina* 14 (1960): 3–12.

———. "Editorial." *Musica disciplina* 20 (1966): 7–10.

———. "Editorial." *Musica disciplina* 30 (1976): 7–11.

Davison, Archibald T. "A New Music Periodical: Its Future Influence." *Journal of Renaissance and Baroque Music* 1 (1946): 5–9.

Lowinsky, Edward E. "Homage to Armen Carapetyan." *Musica disciplina* 37 (1983): 9–26.

"Ten Years of the American Institute of Musicology: 1945–1955." *Musica disciplina* 9 (1955): 3–10.

INDEXES

Internal: vs. 1–20 in 1968.

External: Music Index, 1949– . RILM, 1967– . Arts and Humanities Citation Index, 1976– . Music Article Guide, 1966– . Bibliographie des Musikschrifttums, 1950– . Bibliographia musicologia (selective).

LOCATION SOURCES

Widely available.

Publication History

TITLE AND TITLE CHANGES

Journal of Renaissance and Baroque Music, 1946–47. *Musica disciplina: A Journal of the History of Music,* 1948–56. *Musica disciplina: A Yearbook of the History of Music,* 1957– .

VOLUME AND ISSUE DATA

Volumes 1– , 1946– .

FREQUENCY OF PUBLICATION

Annual, 1946–77. Annual but irregular, 1978– .

PUBLISHERS

Institute of Renaissance and Baroque Music, 1946–47. American Institute of Musicology, 1948–75. Hänssler-Verlag, 1976– .

PLACES OF PUBLICATION
> New Haven, Connecticut, 1946–47. Rome, 1948–75. Neuhausen-Stuttgart, 1976– .

EDITORS
> Armen Carapetyan and Leo Schrade, 1946–47. Armen Carapetyan, 1948–56. Armen Carapetyan, Editor, and Gilbert Reaney, Assistant Editor, 1957–75. Armen Carapetyan, 1976–82; 1984– . Frank A. D'Accone and Gilbert Reaney, 1983.

Vincent J. Corrigan

MUSICAL AMERICA

The founder and first editor of *Musical America*, John C. Freund, was an Oxford-educated Englishman and publisher of trade magazines. In 1898 he founded *Musical America*, a weekly paper "Devoted to Music, Drama, and the Arts" (1.1: masthead). In keeping with his background as a playwright and a would-be actor, much of the fledgling journal was devoted to the spoken theatre and light opera. A man of principle, Freund promised that the artistic and business departments would be kept separate. After only thirty-six issues *Musical America* temporarily ceased publication in 1899, probably the victim of competition from the likes of *The Musical Courier* (q.v.) and *Etude* (q.v.).[1] It took Freund six years to produce the next issue of *Musical America* (3.1; 18 November 1905); this time it was devoted exclusively to music and dance.

Reporting in the reemergent *Musical America* took on a less personal and moralizing tone. Unsigned concert reviews often centered on the size of the audience, the gate receipts, and the artist's fee. Above all, the new journal focused on opera stars, America's new idols, with numerous photographs. A chatty interview with Enrico Caruso in 1905 initiated the practice of providing each issue with an interview of a famous artist, quite often an opera star.

In Freund's day, European artists dominated the musical world and, frequently, the columns of *Musical America*. However, Freund was a staunch supporter of American musicians and musical institutions. His journal reported events ranging from major U.S. symphony concerts to recitals of small local clubs and music in educational institutions. In the fall of 1907, Freund began publishing a modest special annual issue covering the upcoming musical seasons of numerous American cities. By 1920 the "Fall Issue" had grown to nearly 250 pages with directories of artists, managements, and forthcoming seasons of 170 cities. Freund also campaigned for government support of the arts in America, proposing the establishment of The Musical Alliance of the United States (26.26:1,4; 35.5: special insert, pp. 2a–8a).

Many of the regular features of Freund's *Musical America* catered to the unsophisticated musical tastes of the majority of its readers. However, scattered between the featured artist's interviews, the humor column, and the gossipy "Mephisto's Musing," there exists an important chronicle of twentieth-century music, for example, Alfredo Casella's article on Italian Futurist music (29.1:11) and coverage of the American premiere of Arnold Schönberg's *Pierrot Lunaire* (37.16:6). At times, the magazine seemed scholarly with articles such as Carl Engel's "The Pursuit of Musicology" (36.22:3, 22); yet, rarely is any article longer than a few columns. Indeed, much of the weekly journal's prodigious length (more than fifty pages) came from reader correspondence, various concert calendars, a musicians' directory, news from abroad, obituaries, a column of miscellaneous bits called "From Ocean to Ocean," and numerous advertisements of artists and managers.

John Freund died in 1924, and in 1927, the Musical America Company was sold to Trade Publications Corporation. The new owners modernized the appearance of *Musical America* and reduced the page size from 10½" by 15" to 10" by 12" and then in 1929, to 8½" by 11½" with a double-column format. The publication schedule was changed to twice monthly; the two-volumes-per-year schedule became one starting in January 1929. A very promising American composer-critic of the day, Deems Taylor, became the new editor. New features addressed radio broadcasts and recorded music. Coverage extended to jazz in discussion of works such as Ernst Krenek's *Jonny spielt auf* and George Gershwin's *An American in Paris*.

John F. Majeski bought *Musical America* in 1929, rededicating it to the ideals of Freund and appointing A. Walter Kramer, a composer-critic and Freund disciple, as the new editor. Majeski's *Musical America* looked like Freund's in a 10" by 12" format. Now with a heavy paper cover, it was published monthly during the "off season," June through September.

Kramer was succeeded in 1936 by Oscar Thompson, another veteran of the Freund era, who brought few changes to the journal. Seemingly more sophisticated, his *Musical America* contained articles from such musicologists as P. H. Lang and Paul Nettl. Ronald F. Eyer replaced Thompson in 1943 as *Musical America* headed into a period of decline. The situation stabilized when Chicago critic Cecil Smith took over in 1948. His staff produced the momentous Fiftieth Anniversary Issue (December 1948) containing articles on the history of the publication. Another notable Smith issue, entitled "Music around the World," included accounts of many non-Western musics (70.2: most of the issue). In 1950, *Musical America* began a monthly schedule for February through October; November through January remained bimonthly.[2]

When Smith and several other staff members left in 1952, Ronald Eyer returned as editor to a shaky situation. In 1953, *Musical America* began publishing an "Annual Survey of American Orchestral Repertoire," and in 1957, Eyer launched his "Operation Symphony-Opera U.S.A." campaign in which he encouraged symphony orchestras to produce operas to earn money. Despite Eyer's efforts, the magazine's reputation continued to decline. Finally, in 1959, John Majeski, Sr., sold it to Theodate Johnson, the magazine's advertising manager.

Johnson's magazine, under the editorship of Robert Sabin, had a new look; it was smaller, 8" by 11½", and the cover was artwork instead of a celebrity's photograph. In 1961, *Musical America* became a monthly magazine, and expanded coverage of radio, television, and recordings was placed in a special section called "Audio."

Gaining respectability but not financial success, *Musical America* was sold in 1964 to an eager buyer, Billboard Publishers. Billboard merged *Musical America* with *High Fidelity* (q.v.) in 1965, creating a marriage of electronic and live music coverage. An assistant editor of *High Fidelity*, Shirley Fleming, became editor of *Musical America*. Fleming's magazine has a three-column format with fewer photographs. Since the late 1970s, the magazine has remained remarkably consistent. Issues average around forty pages. The regular departments are: "Highlights of the Month," "Education," "Television," "New Music," "Personalities," and "Book Reviews." Each department has its own contributing editor. Features include "Debuts and Reappearances" and a column on appointments, awards, and competitions. Since April 1968, a "Musician of the Month" has been featured on the cover and in an interview. A noteworthy special eightieth anniversary issue appeared in October 1978. Material is contributed primarily by critics, music journalists, and the occasional scholar. Advertisements, much less in evidence since the merger with *High Fidelity*, are placed by record and audio equipment companies, publishers, schools of music, and others. As of 1979, *Musical America* gained the subtitle "The Journal of Classical Music," obviously in response to *High Fidelity's* increased commitment to jazz and rock music. In May 1988 *Musical America* began to appear, once again, independent of *High Fidelity*, while retaining its previous format and editor.

Notes

1. See Charles Lindahl, "Music Periodicals in U.S. Research Libraries," *Notes* 38 (December 1981): 320–26, for a comparison of these and other contemporaneous journals.

2. Carol L. Mekkawi is mistaken in claiming that no issue was published September through December 1970.

Information Sources

BIBLIOGRAPHY

Lindahl, Charles. "Music Periodicals in U.S. Research Libraries in 1931: A Retrospective Survey, Part III: United States." *Notes* 38 (1981): 320–26.

Mekkawi, Carol Laurence. "Music Periodicals: Popular and Classical Record Reviews and Indexes." *Notes* 34 (1977): 92–107.

INDEXES

External: Music Index, 1949– . Readers Guide to Periodical Literature, 1949–64. RILM, 1970– . Music Article Guide, 1965– . Bibliographie des Musikschrifttums, 1937, 1939, 1950, 1960, 1961.

REPRINT EDITIONS

Microform: UMI, 1905–64.

LOCATION SOURCES

Widely available.

Publication History

TITLE AND TITLE CHANGES

>*Musical America,* 1898–1965. *High Fidelity incorporating Musical America,* 1965–70. *High Fidelity and Musical America,* 1970–88. *Musical America,* 1988– .

VOLUME AND ISSUE DATA

>Volumes 1– , 1898– .

FREQUENCY OF PUBLICATION

>Weekly, 1898–1926. Semimonthly, 1927–60 (monthly in the off season). Monthly, 1961– .

PUBLISHERS

>Musical America Company, 1898–1927. Trade Publications Corporation, 1927–29. Musical America Corporation, 1929–59. Music Publications, Ltd., 1960–65. Billboard Publishing Company, 1965–75. ABC Leisure Magazines, 1975– .

PLACES OF PUBLICATION

>New York, 1898–1965, 1981– . Great Barrington, Massachusetts, 1965–81.

EDITORS

>John C. Freund, 1898–24. Milton Weil, 1924–27. Oscar Thompson, July and August 1927. Deems Taylor, 1927–29. A. Walter Kramer, 1929–36. Oscar Thompson, 1936–43. Ronald F. Eyer, 1943–47. John F. Majeski, Jr., 1947. Cecil Smith, 1948–52. Ronald Eyer, 1952–60. Robert Sabin, 1960–62. Everett Helm, 1962–63. Jay S. Harrison, 1963–64. Shirley Fleming, 1965– .

Matthew Steel

MUSICAL AND DRAMATIC COURIER. See MUSICAL COURIER

MUSICAL COURIER

The first issue of *Musical Courier* appeared on 7 February 1880 under the title *Musical and Sewing Machine Gazette.* Howard Lockwood was publisher and William E. Nickerson editor. Nickerson had been a staff member for the by now defunct *Musical and Dramatic Times,* edited by John C. Freund (in 1898 Freund would found *Musical America* [q.v.], the future arch-rival of the *Musical Courier*). The new weekly, in newspaper format, was "devoted to the piano, organ and sewing machine trades." This odd coupling was attributed to the relationship between the internal mechanisms of the two and the fact that they were often sold in the same store. Three issues later Lockwood discovered that the word "Gazette" was currently in use for a similar publication and replaced it with " . . . Courier." On 3 April 1880, the sewing machine and music information were separated into two independent papers. The music magazine began to include more topical news from the musical world and a few items of historical interest in addition to its standard information about the music business. From the beginning until its final issue, it employed regional correspondents in various American and European cities who regularly reported on current music events. A 12 November 1880 move to include dramatic criticism proved unprofitable and was dropped in 1883.

Nickerson, feeling that the paper was beyond his capabilities, relinquished ownership and management of the *Courier* to music critic Otto Floersheim and piano manufacturer Marc A. Blumenberg. The music news and trade departments became two separate papers; the music news was issued on Wednesdays under the title *Musical Courier* and the trade news on Saturday under the title *Musical Courier Extra*. Blumenberg's bold, aggressive style of writing and his hard-nosed business tactics would set the tone of the *Musical Courier* for the next thirty years. An early champion of Richard Wagner and Johannes Brahms, he was instrumental in promoting a number of important serious musicians, both composers and performers. Under Blumenberg's editorship, various important writers consistently appeared in the pages of the *Courier*; in the early years the most notable was James Gibbons Huneker. Blumenberg's personal style was knowledgeable, opinionated, often self-congratulatory, and, according to him, totally unbiased. Outside opinion, however, consistently accuses Blumenberg of showing favoritism to his largest advertisers and attempting to drive out of business certain unfortunate parties who refused to do his bidding. During the last ten years of his editorship he was constantly involved in libel suits involving such musical personages as Victor Herbert as well as several key members of his staff.

In 1913, Leonard Liebling, who had been associated with the paper since 1902, became editor-in-chief, a position he held until his death in 1945. His column, titled "Variations (on themes moto & perpetuum)," was a standard feature for over forty years. In September 1931 the *Courier* absorbed the *Musical Observer*, a magazine devoted to the interest of the public school educator. On 15 June 1937, the journal became a semimonthly publication. The *Courier* operated without an editor-in-chief until 1954 and was published by the Music Periodicals Corporation. Managing editor Russell Kerr was a fixture on the masthead and in various columns for many years, as were associate editors Mary Craig and Rene Devries.

During the late 1950s, the journal experienced several ownership and editorial changes. At this time it began to publish monthly during the summer months, returning to a semimonthly schedule during the "season." In January 1957 the first annual *Musical Courier Directory Issue—A Standard Guidebook of the Musical Arts and Artists* was published. Essentially a booking list, it continued to appear annually through 1961. In 1960 *Musical Courier* dropped the semi-monthly schedule, appearing twelve times a year. In February 1961 the *Courier* absorbed the *Review of Recorded Music*, but the last issue appeared in October 1962. According to David K. Sengstack, president of then-owner Summy-Birchard, the magazine no longer had sufficient following to remain profitable.

The journal's importance lies with its weekly coverage of various musical events around the world for over eighty years as well as its documentation of

American musical taste and opinion during that period. While magazines like *Etude* (q.v.) were aimed at the amateur, *Musical Courier* functioned more as a newsletter for the professional musician. Gossipy items abound beside more serious reports. The magazine was not interested in "popular" music and strove continually to elevate musical taste as it viewed it. An editorial on 1 March 1945 claimed, "our files are a complete history of the musical world since 1880." Special issues were devoted to such subjects as the upcoming opera season, summer music festivals, or the present musical scene in Latin America or Hollywood. The magazine was filled with photographs of musical events and of musical personalities enjoying their leisure time. Many advertisements appeared in the paper, and their importance as a record of the contemporary music scene at any particular time is as important as the signed articles. Business cards of teachers and performers were printed in the classified advertisement section. Early issues contained thirty to forty 11" by 15" pages, but the size was gradually reduced between 1930 and 1958 to around twenty-four 8" by 11½" pages as the style of the journal changed from newspaper to magazine format.

Information Sources

BIBLIOGRAPHY

"The Conviction of William Geppert." *Music Trades* 45/1 (1913): 3.

"Light on the Methods and Finances of the *Musical Courier*." *The Music Trade* 31/21 (1906): 5–7.

Freund, John C. "First principles." *Musical America* 1 (October 8, 1898).

"Marc A. Blumenberg Dead." *The Music Trades* 45 (April 1913): 11.

"Musical Courier Quits Publication." *Billboard Music Week* (September 29, 1962): 12.

Schwers, Paul. "*Kunst und Reklame.*" *Allgemeine Musik-Zeitung* 35 (1908): 395–400.

"A Telling Resignation." *The Presto* 20 (1903): 13–18.

Waters, Edward N. *Victor Herbert: A Life in Music.* New York: Macmillan Co., 1955.

INDEXES

External: Music Index, 1949–62. Bibliographie des Musikschrifttums, 1937, 1939, 1950.

REPRINT EDITIONS

Microform: UMI.

LOCATION SOURCES

Library of Congress and New York Public Library (full runs). Later volumes widely available.

Publication History

TITLE AND TITLE CHANGES

Musical and Sewing Machine Gazette, A Weekly Paper Devoted to Music and the Music Trades, 7 February–21 February 1880. *Musical and Sewing Machine Courier, A Weekly Paper Devoted to Music and the Music Trades,* 28 February 1880– 5 November 1880. *Musical and Dramatic Courier, A Weekly Paper Devoted to Music and the Music Trades,* 12 November 1880–1882. *Musical Courier, A Weekly Paper Devoted to Music and the Music Trades,* 1883–21 April 1909. *Musical Courier, A Weekly Journal Devoted to Music and Its Allied Arts,* 28 April

1909–7 September 1916. *Musical Courier, Weekly Review of the World's Music*, 14 September 1916–May 1937. *Musical Courier*, June 1937–September 1960. *Musical Courier, Music Around the World*, October 1960–January 1961. *Musical Courier and Review of Recorded Music, Music Around the World*, February 1961–April 1961. *Musical Courier and Review of Recorded Music*, May 1961–September 1961. *Music Magazine and Musical Courier*, October 1961–October 1962.

VOLUME AND ISSUE DATA

Volumes 1–164.9, 1880–1962.

FREQUENCY OF PUBLICATION

Weekly, 1880–1936. Semimonthly, 1937–59. Monthly, 1960–62.

PUBLISHERS

Blumenberg and Floersheim, 1880–1960. Summy-Birchard, 1961–62.

PLACES OF PUBLICATION

New York, 1880–1960. Evanston, Illinois, 1961–62.

EDITORS

William E. Nickerson, 1880–83. Marc A. Blumenberg, 1884–1913. Otto Floersheim, 1884–94. Leonard Liebling, 1913–45. (No permanent editor until 1954.) Gid W. Waldrop, 1954–58. Lisa Roma Trompeter, 1958–60. Peter Jacobi 1961–62.

Marilyn Dekker

MUSICAL COURIER AND REVIEW OF RECORDED MUSIC. See MUSICAL COURIER

MUSICAL LIBRARY, THE. See HARMONICON, THE

MUSICAL QUARTERLY, THE

In a survey of "music in America" presented to the Schola Cantorum of New York in 1913, Oscar G. Sonneck mentioned the unfortunate fact that America had failed to produce a quality music periodical even while such publications flourished in Europe. Within a year, Rudolph E. Schirmer visited Sonneck at the Library of Congress to propose just such a periodical and invited him to prepare a prospectus. This document, which appeared in October 1914 after considerable study of such foreign periodicals as *Rivista musicale italiana* (q.v.) and *Die Musik* (q.v.), stated:

The appeal of the magazine will be to cultured music lovers and musicians who take an interest in more or less scholarly discussions of problems that affect the past, present and future of the art of music. It is not to be a magazine devoted to the technical or professional interests of the music teacher, virtuoso and musical antiquarian. In this respect it will be quite distinctive and it is expected to fill an apparent gap in the present structure of musical periodical literature. (10.4:460)

Sonneck was named editor, and the first comprehensive American periodical in musicology appeared in January 1915, stating that "Publisher and Editor are agreed not to throttle *The Musical Quarterly* with a program." The major intent was simply to publish work of the best scholars regardless of nationality, an overall policy that has remained in effect throughout the journal's history even while the majority of contributors are English-speaking.

During its first year of publication, articles were contributed by Percy Grainger, Edgar Istel, Hugo Leichtentritt, J. H. Fuller-Maitland, Sir Hubert Parry, Waldo S. Pratt, Cyril Scott, Carl E. Seashore, Sigmund Spaeth, William Barclay Squire, Sir Charles Villiers Stanford, and many others whose names are well known in the field of musicology. Other early contributors included Camille Saint-Saëns, Egon Wellesz, Béla Bartók, Alexander Wheelock Thayer, and Otto Ortmann.

Trade advertising was included from the beginning. In a report to the readership entitled "After Ten Years" (10.4:459–62), Sonneck stated that

The Musical Quarterly could not have survived a world-war and other impediments without the staunch support of perennial subscribers, patient contributors and publisher-colleagues who consistently drew attention through the medium of *The Musical Quarterly* to publications of theirs in which they take special pride. (10.4:461)

On the same occasion he defended the contents of the publication during its short history and entered a plea in favor of writings of direct concern to American music:

In particular, more articles on prominent American composers have been desired. The editor heartily agrees, but unfortunately the wish is but seldom the father of an acceptable article, least of all of articles on American composers which exhibit a critical sense of values, a thorough knowledge of the composer's works, and do not read like a Phantasy on superlatives. (10.4:462)

This editorial concluded with the announcement that Schirmer would provide a complete ten-year index to all current subscribers.

Within a few years some new directions were evident. "Views and Reviews" began to appear as a regular section; and v. 14.4 (1928) was devoted entirely to Franz Schubert, with contributions from Carl Engel, Guido Adler, Richard Aldrich, Edgar Istel, Olga Samaroff, Otto Kinkeldey, Hugo Leichtentritt, and others.

With v. 15, in 1929, Carl Engel assumed the position of editor of *The Musical Quarterly*. While no change in philosophy or quality was apparent during his tenure, the general usefulness of the magazine to scholars was improved through the addition of "Quarterly Book-Lists," a "Current Chronicle," and later a "Quarterly Record-List." A list of plates and illustrations was also provided at the beginning of each issue.

In 1946, beginning with v. 32.1, Paul Henry Lang began his long service as editor (having served as associate editor since 1933). His personal influence was enormous; the magazine became the most important forum for musicological debate in the country and began to publish occasional issues that were focused on a single topic (in addition to those that commemorated an important composer's anniversary). The fiftieth anniversary issue, entitled "Contemporary Music in Europe" (51.1), was later published by Norton as a book—as were other special issues of the *Quarterly*. When Lang retired, the "Publisher's Note" stated:

> For twenty-nine years Mr. Lang guided this journal, maintaining uncompromising standards of scholarship and literacy, helping, persuading, and conciliating. . . . his personality became one with *The Musical Quarterly*. (60.1:i)

Succeeding editors were Christopher Hatch, Joan Peyser, Paul Wittke, and Eric Salzman. The latter, upon assuming this position in the seventieth year of publication (1984/85), has made the first clear statement of policy change in the *Quarterly's* history. Observing that "the conditions of musical life and the state of the culture have changed in almost three quarters of a century," Salzman suggests that

> the sum, the quantity and quality of new information and scholarship, becomes truly terrifying. . . .
>
> Once there were many general music magazines; the *Quarterly* was one of the few to publish serious, scholarly work. Today, the specialist has several places to go with his or her work while outlets for high-level generalist writing on music have almost disappeared. . . . There is a dearth of high-quality, insightful writing about music—music criticism in its best and highest sense.
>
> Here, then, is an important role for *The Musical Quarterly*—in fact, a revival of its historic role. In this rethinking of the *Quarterly's* mission there will be a greater emphasis on contemporary and American music, on non-Western music, on the vernacular everywhere, on the vast issues of music in society, on the relationships between music and language and between music and the other arts. (71.1:i–ii)

Thus the role of the *Quarterly* is being redirected to fulfill its historic mission of providing a forum for all thinking musicians. This does not mean that traditional features have disappeared—the Johann Sebastian Bach and Heinrich Schütz anniversaries received special issues in 1985—but simply that the more specific and detailed articles in musicology, theory, and so on should appear in the specialty periodicals of those fields. Given its emphasis on quality scholarship, a more generalist approach should in no way diminish the prestige of this journal; in fact, "insightful criticism in its highest sense" should increase its influence on the country's musical culture.

Issues of *The Musical Quarterly,* measuring 6½″ by 9½″, currently run to approximately 150 pages. Each contains, on average, six to eight articles, ranging anywhere from ten to thirty pages or more, and four to six reviews each of books and records, with reviews running two to six pages in length. A yearly volume index appears in the fourth issue.

Information Sources

INDEXES
>   Internal: each volume indexed.
>   External: RILM, 1967– . Music Index, 1949– . Music Article Guide, 1965– .
>   Readers' Guide to Periodical Literature, 1919–53. Arts and Humanities Citation
>   Index, 1976– . Bibliographie des Musikschrifttums, 1937, 1939, 1950– .

REPRINT EDITIONS
>   Microform: UMI. Princeton Microfilm Corporation, 1915–55. Kraus Reprint,
>   1915–82.

LOCATION SOURCES
>   Widely available.

Publication History

TITLE AND TITLE CHANGES
>   *The Musical Quarterly.*

VOLUME AND ISSUE DATA
>   Volumes 1– , 1915– .

FREQUENCY OF PUBLICATION
>   Quarterly.

PUBLISHERS
>   G. Schirmer, 1915–86. Macmillan, 1986–88. Oxford University Press, 1989– .

PLACE OF PUBLICATION
>   New York.

EDITORS
>   Oscar Sonneck, 1915–28. Carl Engel, 1929–45. Paul Henry Lang, 1946–73.
>   Christopher Hatch, 1974–April 1977. Joan Peyser, July 1977–Winter 1984. Paul
>   Wittke, 1984. Eric Salzman, Fall 1984– .

Ruth K. Inglefield

MUSICAL TIMES

The large number of periodicals that were born in Britain in the early part of the nineteenth century had as their audience a wealthy middle class eager to embrace aristocratic activities. These people owned pianos, were interested in the intellectual aspects of music and its history, could read music and play with a certain amount of facility, and delighted in attending concerts. Above all, they had the leisure time and money to make all this possible. But in the early 1840s there developed a movement to bring music to the working class, people with neither knowledge nor money, for whom active musical participation had been an impossibility. These people could not be wooed by the music of the past, nor could they understand or perform the pianistic creations of contemporaneous masters; they could only be approached through vocal music. To that end, singing classes were established, some in places of employment, others in schools and churches. The widespread interest in sight-singing was largely the result of the activities of three men: John Curwen, John Hullah, and Joseph Mainzer.

John Curwen (1816–80) was not a musician but a Congregational minister. In order to train his choir, he adopted the sight-singing system advanced by Sarah Glover (1785–1867), the Tonic Sol-Fa system. In 1851 he began to publish a periodical, *The Tonic Sol-Fa Reporter* (1851, 1853–88). Later it became *The Musical Herald and Tonic Sol-Fa Reporter* (1889–90), still later *The Musical Herald* (1891–1920).

John Hullah (1812–84) adopted and adapted the continental method of Guillaume Wilhem (1781–1842), Fixed-Do, and began offering singing classes in February 1841. These singing schools for schoolmasters and schoolmistresses became extremely influential through government support. Hullah was a staunch opponent of Curwen's system.

Like Hullah, Joseph Mainzer (1801–51) adopted a Fixed-Do system and sought to promote music for laborers in his native France. Problems with political insurrections in Trier and Paris forced his removal to London, where he began to offer singing classes in May 1841. He edited and published a periodical, *The National Singing-Class Circular* (2 vs., 1841–42), later known as *Mainzer's Musical Times and Singing-Class Circular* (3 vs., 1842–44). In 1844 control of this journal was taken over by J. A. Novello and its title changed to *The Musical Times and Singing-Class Circular*. In 1904 the title was abbreviated to *The Musical Times (MT)*.[1] Thus, *MT*, dating back to 1841, stands as the oldest of all music journals with a continuous record of publication.

MT has, since its beginning, been published monthly. Over the course of nearly 150 years, the length of each issue has changed considerably. V. 1.1 contained eight pages, four of which were devoted to the musical supplement: Henry Purcell's "In these delightful pleasant groves."[2] In February 1848 *MT* expanded to twelve, and later to sixteen, pages. From then on, there is a record of continual growth: December 1853—twenty pages; January 1868—thirty-two pages; January 1872—forty-eight pages; January 1885—sixty-four pages; January 1894—seventy-two pages. Wartime conditions have forced condensation in some issues, but *MT* has always rebounded from these circumstances. Individual issues now run between sixty and eighty pages. Size, too, has varied. The most recent change (1980) was an expansion; *MT* now measures 8¼" by 10¼".

Musical supplements have, until recently, been an important part of *MT*'s contents. Indeed, in the early volumes, supplements formed the bulk of each issue. They contained both secular and sacred choral music appropriate to singing classes. Later on, the supplements were devoted almost exclusively to music for the Church of England. This concentration was reinforced in 1920 when *MT* became associated with the Royal College of Organists. More recently, the editors changed the focus of the supplements. On the one hand they published contemporary compositions, and on the other they provided editions of earlier music. These changes were not universally admired, and the musical supplements were discontinued in 1980.

Not surprisingly, the supplements contained music available only through Novello's publishing house. In the early years, in fact, only Novello's publications were advertised in *MT*. Even after other advertisers were admitted, the journal continued to be an organ of Novello and Company. This was not necessarily bad. Novello himself campaigned hard against what he called a "tax on knowledge," taxes that made printed material prohibitively expensive for the working class, and he used the pages of *MT* to do so.

Initially, the literary portion of *MT* was an adjunct to the music. The first issue contained the following: Page 1—Conditions of publication and an article, "The Amateurs of London";[3] Page 2—Novello's announcement of "Cheap Classics"; Pages 3–6—music; Page 7—"Brief Chronicle," short paragraphs on current musical activities; Page 8—List of concerts and advertisements. This changed in 1846 when Edward Holmes (1797–1859) began to contribute articles, some of which were spread over several issues.[4] Currently *MT* is divided into the following sections: "Letters to the Editor" (begun 1847); four to six articles; "Reviews" of books, records, and music; "Music in London" (reviews of performances); "Reports" from other centers, both British and foreign; "Church and Organ Music" (discussions of instruments, composers, events); "Miscellaneous" announcements (awards, appointments, competitions, conferences, obituaries); and the "London Musical Diary" for the coming month. The articles are brief, usually three to five pages in length, and are meant to be sources of general information for the public at large. Most articles deal with British composers or composers popular with the British public and concentrate either on biography or some local aspect of the composer's work. Other articles deal with particularly important British musical institutions—Glyndebourne, Covent Garden, *MT* itself. The contributors appear quite learned; some are noted scholars (A. Hyatt King, Paul Henry Lang). Editorials are rare and concern activities affecting the musical life of London.

Only recently has the name of the general editor been put in a prominent place; editorship for earlier volumes was, for the most part, anonymous. It is not certain that Novello was editor of *MT* between 1844 and 1853, but he was certainly its guiding spirit. He was succeeded by his sister, who had married writer-lecturer Charles Cowden-Clarke. It is also unclear who the editor was from 1856 to 1863; perhaps it was Henry Littleton, who assumed control of the publishing house upon Novello's retirement. As the journal has grown in importance, editorial assistance had become necessary; Stanley Sadie, editor from 1968 to 1986, was aided by Alison Latham and Robert Anderson.

Over the years *MT* has remained remarkably true to the audience it first attracted: the nonprofessional musical public of England. It fought against taxes that kept prices high, it strove to keep its own price low, it distributed issues to various institutions free of cost, and it published music of immediate use to its readership. Later on, when the interests and abilities of its audience expanded, *MT* kept pace; opera was covered under the editorship of Lunn, and reviews became increasingly important. More recently, when public interest in the musical supplements waned, they were discontinued. On the other hand, *MT* has always felt a responsibility to expand the musical horizons of the readership. Holmes's articles on Giovanni Palestrina and Henry Purcell were published at a time when the general public could hardly have been expected to know of, or be interested in, the works of these composers. It continues to maintain a balance between providing information for, and increasing the musical awareness of, its public.

Notes

1. Or 1956? See Nicholas Temperley, "MT and Musical Journalism, 1844," *The Musical Times* 110 (1969): 584.

2. From Henry Purcell's incidental music to Act IV of *The Libertine, or the Libertine Destroyed* (1692).

3. See *The New Grove's Dictionary of Music and Musicians*, s.v. "Periodicals," by Imogen Fellinger for a facsimile of the article.

4. For a listing of some of these, see Temperley, "MT and Musical Journalism," p. 585, and *Grove's Dictionary of Music and Musicians*, 3rd ed., s.v. "Periodicals, Musical," by C. B. Oldman.

Information Sources

BIBLIOGRAPHY

Banfield, Stephen. "Aesthetics and Criticism." In *The Athlone History of Music in Britain: The Romantic Age 1800–1914*, edited by Nicholas Temperley, pp. 455–73. London: The Athlone Press, 1981.

Grove's Dictionary of Music and Musicians. 3rd ed. S.v. "Periodicals, Musical," by C. B. Oldman.

Grove's Dictionary of Music and Musicians. 5th ed. S.v. "Periodicals, Musical," by A. Hyatt King.

Rainbow, Bernarr. *The Land Without Music*. London: Novello, 1967.

Sadie, Stanley. "Editorial." *The Musical Times* 110 (June 1969): 581.

Scholes, Percy A. *The Mirror of Music, 1844–1944*. London: Novello, 1947.

Temperley, Nicholas. "MT and Musical Journalism, 1844." *The Musical Times* 110 (June 1969): 583–86.

INDEXES

External: Music Index, 1949–67. RILM, 1967– . Arts and Humanities Citation Index, 1976– . British Humanities Index, 1968– . Bibliographie des Musikschrifttums, 1937, 1939, 1950– . Bibliographia musicologia.

REPRINT EDITIONS

Microform: UMI, 1844–1930.

LOCATION SOURCES

Widely available.

Publication History

TITLE AND TITLE CHANGES
   The Musical Times and Singing-Class Circular, 1844–1904. *The Musical Times,*
   1904–   .
VOLUME AND ISSUE DATA
   Volumes 1–   , 1844–   .
FREQUENCY OF PUBLICATION
   Monthly.
PUBLISHER
   Novello and Company, 1844–1988. Orpheus Publications, 1989–   .
PLACE OF PUBLICATION
   London.
EDITORS
   Joseph Alfred Novell, 1844–53. Mary Cowden-Clark, 1853–56. Henry C. Lunn,
   1863–87. William Alexander Barrett, 1887–91. Edgar F. Jacques, 1891–97. Fred-
   erick George Edwards, 1897–1909. William Gray McNaught, 1909–18. Harvey
   Grace, 1918–44. William McNaught, 1944–53. Martin Cooper, 1953–56. Harold
   Rutland, 1956–58. Robin Hull, 1958–60. Andrew Porter, 1960–67. Stanley Sadie,
   1968–86. Andrew Clement, 1987–88. Eric Wen, 1988–   .

Vincent J. Corrigan

MUSICAL TIMES AND SINGING-CLASS CIRCULAR, THE. See MU-
SICAL TIMES, THE

MUSICIAN, THE

In its fifty-three years of publication, *The Musician* had three distinct identities.
It began in 1896 as the first major American journal devoted to the concerns of
music teachers and their students, evolved into a general interest magazine for
classical music aficionados in the 1930s, and from 1943 until it ceased publication
in 1948 served as a publicity tool for a concert promotion company.

The journal was founded by Hatch Music, a music publishing company. The
original purpose of *The Musician* was to provide information to music teachers
and their students on music and techniques for effective study. In 1904 the
purpose was amended to include improving standards of musical taste and appreciation among its readers and the public at large.

During the years it served as a journal for music teachers (1896–1935), *The
Musician*'s articles offered many practical suggestions for teaching voice and a
variety of instruments. Regular columns on teaching piano, voice, chorus, organ,
strings, and wind instruments appeared under various titles during this period.
Reviews of books and music were also published. The editorial policy strongly
supported cooperation among music teachers and improvement of teaching standards.

Many of the articles from this time present a fascinating look at the history of music education in America. For example, articles can be found on Emile Jacques-Dalcroze's eurhythmics techniques, on the early years of the Music Teachers' National Association, on the burgeoning public school music teaching profession, and on Carl Seashore's "Measures of Musical Talent." The advertisements for music books, instruments, and schools (for example, New England Conservatory, Northwestern University, and Dana's Musical Institute) are also of historical interest.

The early issues of *The Musician* (1896–1907) encouraged two-way communication between the journal's readers and its editors through a series of essay contests and correspondence clubs. Subscribers who joined the clubs could send the editors questions to be answered or compositions to be evaluated in the journal. Strangely, only the editors' responses to the questions or compositions were published, making it difficult for a reader to understand the references.

In addition to the articles and columns, the journal included eight to twenty-four pages of piano music, which could be used as teaching material. The music was usually by obscure composers and written in a conservative style. The practice of publishing piano music in every issue was continued until 1939.

During the early 1930s fewer articles on music teaching were published, and the journal's publisher attempted to reach beyond the audience of music teachers. A change in publishers and editors in 1935 resulted in the acceleration of this policy. After 1935 the only reference to music teaching was in a regular column "With the Music Schools," which described events in several major conservatories.

From 1935 to 1943 the aim of *The Musician* was to serve as an advocate for classical music and a source of information about classical musicians. Each issue featured a cover photograph of a famous performer or composer with a profile of the musician inside. Reviews of concerts, books, and recordings were regular features. While some of the articles gave information about such topics as musical styles and performance techniques, most focused on current events in music and personalities and life-styles of musicians. The music scene in New York City was especially well covered.

The purpose of the journal changed dramatically in 1943 when *The Musician* became the official organ of the American Music Foundation (AMF) and the publisher became a concert promoter. AMF encouraged subscribers to *The Musician* to form local chapters for the purpose of raising money to sponsor local classical concerts, called Fellowship Concerts. The concert artists, who were usually young and without a national reputation, were then supplied by AMF for a fee. Editorials in the journal referred to this concert promotion business as "missionary work."

As the purpose of *The Musician* changed, so did its content. Articles on AMF musicians began to dominate the journal, and the cover page "celebrity of the month" was almost always an AMF musician. Outside advertising diminished after the change in policy, leaving little more than AMF promotional advertising.

The journal's troubles began in 1945 when two editorials in *The Musician* inspired a libel suit from Columbia Concerts. Publication problems also developed, and in 1946 the journal began using cheaper paper and decreased the number of pages per issue to sixteen. After that, issue length, quality, format, and even regularity declined to a final demise after the November 1948 issue.

Despite radical changes in the editorial policy during the fifty-three years of the journal's publication, two editorial positions remained constant: (1) criticism of popular music, primarily jazz, and (2) a call for the creation of a federal, cabinet-level Department of Fine Arts. The crusade against popular music was typified by editor Nicholas de Vore, who wrote that jazz "is not an American idiom, but an American Disease."

A critical assessment of *The Musician* should consider each of the journal's three phases. In its first phase, as the only national journal then addressed to music educators, *The Musician* served important functions by showing teachers improved methods of instruction and by providing an inexpensive source of piano music suitable for lessons. The quality of the articles during this period was quite good, especially after the correspondence clubs were discontinued in 1907. *The Musician*'s second phase, as a journal for the general music-loving public, helped to popularize classical music with interesting, usually well-written articles. However, in the journal's third phase, as the organ of the American Musical Foundation, the content of the articles amounted to little more than puffery, and the success of the "missionary" work of the Fellowship Concerts is dubious.

The Musician was published monthly from January 1896 to November 1948. The physical format of the journal was 10¼″ by 13¾″ from 1896 to 1917. The size was changed to 9″ by 12″ in 1917 (v. 22) and was increased to its former size in 1922 (v. 27). The number of pages per issue ranged from a high of sixty-four in the early days of its publication to a low of twelve in 1948. The length of articles ranged from a few paragraphs to several pages. An internal index for each year's articles appeared in the December issue beginning in 1927 (v. 32).

Information Sources

INDEXES
>   Internal: each volume indexed (vs. 32–   ).
>   External: Readers' Guide to Periodical Literature, 1909–48.
LOCATION SOURCES
>   Widely available.

Publication History

TITLE AND TITLE CHANGES
>   *The Musician.*
VOLUME AND ISSUE DATA
>   Volumes 1–53.11, 1896–1948.
FREQUENCY OF PUBLICATION
>   Monthly.

PUBLISHERS

Hatch Music Co., 1896–1903. Oliver Ditson Co., 1904–18. Henderson Publi-
cations, 1919–22. Paul Kempf, 1922–35. Eugene Belier, 1935–40. Brant Music
Corp., 1940–42. Gerstner Publications, 1942. Detner Associates, 1942. American
Music Foundation, 1943. AMF Artists Service, 1943–48. Fellowship Concerts
Services, 1948.

PLACES OF PUBLICATION

Philadelphia, 1896–1903. Boston, 1904–18. New York, 1919–38. East Strouds-
burg, Pennsylvania, 1938–41. Hoboken, New Jersey, 1941–42. New York, 1942–
48.

EDITORS

Arthur L. Manchester, 1896–1093. Thomas Tapper, 1904–07. W. J. Baltzell,
1907–18. Glad. Henderson, 1919–22. Paul Kempf, 1922–35. Nicholas de Vore,
1935–47. Ned Jaakobs, 1947–48.

John K. Kratus

MUSICOLOGY. See MUSICOLOGY AUSTRALIA

MUSICOLOGY AUSTRALIA

Musicology Australia is the journal of the Musicological Society of Australia,
founded by a Sydney-based group begun in 1963 under the founding presidency
of Donald Peart of Sydney University. The society's expressed aim was:

> directly encouraging research into old music, instruments and performance;
> theory of music, acoustics, aesthetics and psychology; ethnomusicology
> and folk music—and of developing public interest in them. The Society
> hopes to sponsor, in addition to a journal, musicological studies such as
> periodic reports, learned works and musical editions, at the same time
> organizing lectures, discussion and demonstration at a local level. (1:43)

Despite such brave founding words, the society did not become a national organization with chapters in each state until 1976, and its journal, *Musicology
Australia,* did not become an annual publication until 1985.

Musicology Australia began (under the title *Musicology*) in 1964, as a special
issue of the already long-established journal *Canon.* From v. 2 *Musicology*
became an independent journal published by the Musicological Society of Australia. Vs. 1–4 were published irregularly and their contents largely featured
work from the music department at Sydney University. In 1976 the Musicological
Society of Australia became a national organization. The first national issue of
Musicology, v. 5 (1979), contained an article that documented the progress of
the society in its first three years (Michael Kassler and Graham Pont, "Progress
of the Musicological Society of Australia 1976–1979," 5:231–33), and several
shorter pieces on collections or items of special musicological interest in Aus-

tralia. These included reports from the Mitchell Library in New South Wales and the National Library of Australia; a report on the Chinnery/Viotti papers held in the Museum of Applied Arts and Sciences in Sydney; and a discussion of the then newly established Australia Music Centre in Sydney. V. 6 (1980) included a list of all papers given to the society since its inception (Gordon Anderson, "The Musicological Society of Australia: A Chronicle of Meetings 1963–1976," 6:5–11). V. 6 also inaugurated the practice of including a section entitled "Abstracts of Honours Theses Accepted by Australian Universities." This list supplemented those in *Studies in Music* (q.v.) and *Miscellanea Musicologica* (q.v.) V. 7 included a posthumous article by the first president of the national society, Gordon A. Anderson (1928–81), entitled "New Sources of Medieval Music," 7:1–26, and a complete bibliography of his published work up to the time of his death (Jane Morlet Hardie, "Gordon A. Anderson: A Bibliography," 7:140–53). Following earlier practice, the Reports Section of v. 7 included material on interesting collections or discoveries (Stephen Dowland Page, "Early Printed Monographs on Music in Australian Libraries").

With v. 8 (1985), the title of the journal changed to *Musicology Australia* and became an annual with an editorial board elected for a three-year term. The new format of the journal added "Reviews" and "Register of Members' Publications" to the traditional "Articles" and the "Register of Australian Undergraduate Theses in Music." Issues are about seventy-five pages in length (with a few much longer) and generally include from six to nine articles, ten to twelve pages long. Authorship is approximately 90 percent Australian. The dimensions of the journal appear to have been standardized at 8⅛″ by 11¼″.

Since its inception the contents of *Musicology Australia* have reflected the Musicological Society of Australia's profound commitment to maintaining a nondivisive approach to Western historical musicology, ethnomusicology and music theory. Contemporary and popular music have received attention as well, albeit less frequently. The editorial board consists of representatives of each discipline, and an attempt is made to maintain a balance between these interests, in each issue of the journal.

Information Sources

INDEXES
   External: Music Index, 1968– . RILM Abstracts, 1969– . Australia Public Affairs Information Service (APAIS): A Subject Index to Current Literature (National Library of Australia, Canberra).
LOCATION SOURCES
   Widely available.

Publication History

TITLE AND TITLE CHANGES
   V. 1 of the journal, titled *Musicology 1*, was in fact *Canon* 17.3 (1964). *Musicology*, 1967–82. *Musicology Australia*, 1985– .

VOLUME AND ISSUE DATA
Volumes 1– , 1964– .
FREQUENCY OF PUBLICATION
Irregular, 1964–84. Annual, 1985– .
PUBLISHER
Musicological Society of Australia.
PLACE OF PUBLICATION
Varies. Copies obtainable through The Musicological Society of Australia, Union Box 67, University of New South Wales, P.O. Box 1, Kensington, NSW 2033, Australia.
EDITORS
Donald Peart, 1964 (v. 1). Dene Barnett, Doreen Bridges, Martin Long, 1965–67 (v. 2). Martin Long, 1968–69 (v. 3). Francis Cameron, 1974 (v. 4). Jamie C. Kassler, Graham Hardie, Michael Kassler, Graham Pont, 1979 (v. 5). Gordon A. Anderson, Margaret Kartomi, Gordon Spearitt, 1980 (v. 6). Margaret Kartomi, Jamie C. Kassler, Gordon Spearitt, 1982 (v. 7). Stephen Wild, Warren Bebbington, Graham Hardie, Gordon Spearitt 1985 (v. 8). Stephen Wild, 1986 (v. 9).

Jane Morlet Hardie

MUSIEKCOLLEGE, HET. See CAECILIA (1844–1944)

MUSIEKCOLLEGE CAECILIA, HET. See CAECILIA (1844–1944)

MUSIK, DIE

Die Musik was begun in 1901 as an illustrated bimonthly music journal and revue. The founding editor, Bernhard Schuster, envisioned a revue similar to those of the literary and other fine and performing arts. He also wished to support an exploration of all forms of expression and all stages of musical development. Most importantly, Schuster called for impartial criticism of the musical scene.

The early volumes of *Die Musik* were illustrated with pen and ink drawings, and the issue covers were adorned with either musical quotations or poetry. The journal began to appear in a less ornamented format in 1911 (v. 11) when the review sections began to appear in double-column or newspaper style.

These early volumes reflected the editor's musical activities. Schuster was moderately active as a composer in the late Romantic style. He wrote lieder, a few chamber works, two large choral works, and two operas. Not surprisingly, the early volumes of *Die Musik* contained considerable information about the contemporary opera scene.

The journal was predominantly concerned with German musical life. A particularly valuable feature was the detailed chronicle of stage and concert music in Germany, and selected other European centers. The first issue contained thirty-seven pages of review and criticism of German musical life, including "A Look at the Musical Life of the Past Summer," seventeen book and music reviews, a review of important articles in contemporary journals, a listing of the lecture classes given at German-speaking universities, a listing of newly released books and music, and the programs of the major European opera and concert halls, with a listing of new operas in their repertory.

Die Musik also noted the invention of new musical instruments, the sale of important manuscripts and autographs, and various items of historical interest. For example, Schuster quoted an 1813 advertisement by Carl Maria von Weber in which the composer was seeking a suitable opera text (1:99–100). In the same issue, Schuster mentioned the erection of a new marble monument for the grave of Heinrich Vogl and that Lilli Lehmann donated 1,000 kronen to the Salzburg music festival. The extent of like contemporary commentary makes *Die Musik* an extremely valuable resource for the reconstruction of the early twentieth-century musical scene.

Because of World War I, *Die Musik* indefinitely suspended publication with v. 14 in 1915. It reappeared on a monthly schedule in 1922. New to the format was the inclusion of photographs, portraits, facsimiles of letters and manuscripts, and musical inserts. The European musical scene still received ample coverage in a reorganized section of criticism. "Echo der Zeitschriften" reviewed articles in foreign, as well as German, periodicals; book and music reviews were included in "Kritik"; and the opera and concert halls were covered in "Das Musikleben der Gegenwart." A new section, entitled "Zeitgeschichte," covered the remaining news, gossip, and other contemporary events.

The lead essay in the revived journal was an editorial by Paul Bekker on the state of German music since 1915. Bekker details the chaos of the postwar years, mentions the growing political influence on the arts, and strongly condemns the mixture of music and politics. He also scorns the anti-Semitic interference with Fritz Reiner in Dresden and Bruno Walter in Munich (15:3).

Bekker's appraisal of German music in 1922 is instructive; he evaluated the major prewar musicians and suggested that the future musical leadership would be inherited by Arnold Schönberg (15:7). However, the same issue demonstrated a darker side of the political *Zeitgeist*. In "Spieltalent und Rasse," Rudolf Maria Breithaupt described the various playing abilities of the races. Breithaupt attributed the piano and violin talent of the Slavs and Semites to their similar abilities in juggling and acrobatics, and contended that true creative ability was beyond either race (15:37). The history of German periodicals from 1920 to 1940 is full of similar examples. As the Third Reich prospered, the journals became attached to various state offices, losing their independent voice to state propaganda.

Die Musik began to include many advertisements for various music stores, publishers and music-related items in the late 1920s to offset inflation. Schuster remained editor until his death in 1934. The journal, under his editorship, continued to produce musical articles of quality. Of particular interest were the contemporary reports of the new media of film music and recordings, and the growing interest in folk music. Each issue usually contained four or five essays of approximately five to seven pages.

After Schuster's death, *Die Musik* became the official newsletter of the Reich's youth leadership, with Johann Gunther as editor. In 1937, the journal also became the official "Organ der hauptstelle Musik beim Beauftragten des Fuhres für die Überwachung der gesamten Geistigen und weltanschaulichen Schulung und Erziehung der NSDAP."

Herbert Gerigk assumed editorial duties in 1935 and set a new tone for the journal. Gerigk is probably best known as co-editor of the infamous *Lexikon der Juden in der Musik*. An example of the new editorial philosophy is an article by Willi Kalil, "Mendelssohn und Hiller im Rheinland: Zur Geschichte der Judenemanzipation im deutschen Musikleben des 19. Jahrhunderts" (31:166–77), which traces the nineteenth-century Jewish infiltration of German music.

Under Gerigk, *Die Musik* began to be typeset in *Fraktur*, and the corners of some pages were given over NSDAF slogans. Gerigk remained editor as *Die Musik* combined with *Neues Zeitschrift für Musik* (q.v.) *Allgemeine Musik-zeitung* (q.v.), and *Neues Musikblatt* to form the Gemeinschaftzeitschrif (community magazine), *Musik im Kreige*. The combined journal was a necessary response to the wartime economic hardships. The format of the new journal further reflected these conditions. A cheaper paper was used, the typesetting returned to Roman type, and all text was double column, newspaper style. The final issue of *Musik im Kriege* "for the duration of the war" appeared in 1944 (2:7/8). Gerigk addressed the readers with the need for the entire population to concentrate on the war effort.

Some significant musicological work continued to appear in the journal until the final issue. For example, articles by Wolfgang Boetticher on Lassus, by Karl Gustav Fellerer on sixteenth-century musical style, and by Max Unger on the Beethoven conversation books appeared in the final volume. Although this material was valuable in its time, it has mostly been superseded by modern scholarship. The value of this journal lies in the amount of contemporary social reference found in its pages. German musical life is presented in great detail. In its listing of all new productions, concert reviews, and the fascinating "Zeitgeschichte," *Die Musik—Musik im Kriege* vividly reproduces the official NSDAP position on music.

The physical format of the journal was consistent throughout its run: 7½" by 10". The pagination was continuous through the twenty-four issues of each vs. 1–14 (1901–15) with approximately 300 to 350 pages per volume, and through the twelve issues of each vs. 15–37 (1922–43) with 250 to 300 pages per volume. The supplements to the journal appeared in the early years: a centennial celebration of music history in 1901, and three calendars devoted to German masters: Ludwig van Beethoven in 1907, Richard Wagner in 1908, and Johannes Brahms in 1909. A quarterly index appeared in vs. 2–14 (1902–15), a biannual table of contents in v. 26 through v. 2 of *Musik im Kriege* (1934–44).

Information Sources

BIBLIOGRAPHY

Fellinger, Imogen. *Verzeichnis der Musikzeitschriften des 19. Jahrhunderts.* Studien zur Musikgeschichte des 19. Jahrhunderts, 10. Regensburg: Gustav Bosse Verlag, 1960.

Moser, H. J. *Musik Lexikon.* 2nd ed. Berlin: Max Hesses Verlag, 1943.

Die Musik in Geschichte und Gegenwart. S.v. "Schuster, Bernhard," by Bernhard Stockmann.

New Grove Dictionary of Music and Musicians. S.v. "Periodicals," by Imogen Fellinger.

INDEXES

Internal: Quarterly, vs. 2–14. Biannually, v. 15—*Musik im Kriege*, v. 2.

External: Bibliographie des Musikschrifttums, 1937, 1939.

REPRINT EDITIONS

Paper: Kraus. Brookhaven Press.

Microform: Datamics. Schnase.

LOCATION SOURCES

Boston Public Library, Newberry Library (Chicago), Harvard University Library, New York Public Library, Sibley Music Library of Eastman School of Music, University of Illinois Music Library, University of Michigan Music Library (full run).

Publication History

TITLE AND TITLE CHANGES

Die Musik, Illustrierte Halbmonatschrift, 1901–15. *Die Musik, Monatschrift*, 1922–43. Joined with *Allgemeine Musikzeitung, Zeitschrift für Musik*, and *Neues Musikblatt* to become *Musik im Kriege, Organ des amtes Musik beim Beauftragten des Führers für die Überwachung der gesamten Geistigen und weltanschaulichen Schulung und Erziehung der NSDAP*, 1943–44.

VOLUME AND ISSUE DATA

Volumes 1–35.6, 1901–43.

FREQUENCY OF PUBLICATION

Bimonthly, 1901–15. (Ceased publication, 1916–21.) Monthly, 1922–43.

PUBLISHERS

Schuster & Löffler, 1901–15. Deutsche Verlags-Anstalt, 1922–27. Max Hesses Verlag, 1928–43. Geschäftsstelle *(Musik im Kriege)*, 1943–44.

PLACES OF PUBLICATION

Berlin and Leipzig, 1901–15. Stuttgart, Berlin, and Leipzig, 1922–27. Berlin, 1928–43. Berlin-Hellensee, 1943–44.

EDITORS

Bernhard Schuster, 1901–33. Johannes Günther, 1933–37. Herbert Gerigk, 1937–44.

SUPPLEMENTAL VOLUMES

Einhundert Jahre Musikgeschichte, 1902. *Beethoven-Kalendar, Herausgegeben von den "Musik,"* 1907. *Wagner-Kalendar, Herausgegeben von den "Musik,"* 1908. *Brahms-Kalendar, Herausgegeben von den "Musik,"* 1909.

Carmelo P. Comberiati

MUSIK IM KRIEGE. See MUSIK, DIE; see also ALLGEMEINE MUSIK-ZEITUNG; MELOS; NEUE ZEITSCHRIFT FÜR MUSIK

MUSIK UND GESELLSCHAFT

Musik und Gesellschaft, published by the Henschel-Verlag in East Berlin, provides the most comprehensive account of musical life in the German Democratic Republic (DDR; East Germany). Founded by Ernst Hermann Meyer in March 1951, it has served as the official publication of the Verband der Komponisten und Musikwissenschaftler der DDR[1] since April of the same year. As a journal founded soon after the establishment of the German Democratic Republic, *Musik und Gesellschaft* offers a unique view into the evolution of a socialist music culture in a new country. The quality of submissions is relatively high; practical, analytical, and philosophical issues are often addressed with the professional in mind.

One of the journal's main goals is to serve as a forum in which the "most urgent problems of contemporary music composition and performance can be aired and resolved" (21:145). The most common problem addressed in various articles and editorials is summarized by Walter Siegmund-Schultze in the following words: "We cannot deny the fact that present-day socialist music in its more developed forms has not yet reached the majority of listeners in our Republic. . . . The question that follows is how we write better, more popular music and how we spread it among the working classes" (18:652).[2] The pages of *Musik und Gesellschaft* contain both stories of success and stories of frustration as composers try to realize the goal of writing art music that appeals to the masses.

The editors of *Musik und Gesellschaft* have taken it upon themselves to try to overcome any rifts that might arise between modern art music and the people. For instance, they encourage composers to enter into dialogue with the working classes and to try to express these people's feelings, wishes, and emotions in their music (25:390). In this way they hope for the public to become a partner in the creative process (21:241). They also strive to educate the people about art music. Throughout the journal, for instance, there are biographical portraits of East German composers and performers. New compositions are introduced occasionally in a feature labeled "Neue Werke unserer Komponisten," and for music connoisseurs and composers there are detailed analyses of compositions.

A certain nationalistic pride runs through the journal. In 1979, for instance, *Musik und Gesellschaft* commemorated the thirtieth anniversary of the DDR with a chronological calendar tracing the development of East German music culture since 1951 and a series of observations on the progress of the nation's musical culture. In honor of the thirtieth anniversary of the Verband der Komponisten und Musikwissenschaftler der DDR every issue published in 1981 features a portrait of musical life in a different part of the country. Political rhetoric can be found in some editorials and even in some articles. However, given that the journal aims to improve music culture in a socialist country, praise of socialist values is to be expected.

Great Germanic composers of the seventeenth, eighteenth, and nineteenth centuries are sometimes the topic of an article, especially on the anniversaries of their births or deaths. However, emphasis is placed on modern composers, usually from socialist countries. Two of the most popular East German composers of the twentieth century, Hanns Eisler and Paul Dessau, have received considerable attention in the journal.

Occasionally, individual issues have focused on one theme. Since 1983 it seems that the editors have made this format a policy. Some of the titles of these issues are "Music in Nazi Germany" (33.1), "Brahms" (33.5), "Music and the Mass Media" (34.5), and "Paul Dessau" (34.12).

Among the regular features are book and record reviews. Two features, "Kurz berichtet" and "Wir informieren," keep readers abreast of important musical events and conferences. There are also regular summaries of music programs broadcast over the radio and television. Advertising, usually of music editions and scholarly books from East German publishers, is limited to the back cover.

The journal has appeared in monthly issues since its founding, and each issue is seventy to eighty pages long in a 6½" by 9⅜" format. The later volumes contain a volume index, but there is no cumulative index.

Notes

1. Until 1972 known as the Verband Deutscher Komponisten und Musikwissenschaftler.

2. "Jedenfalls kommen wir nicht über die Tatsache hinweg, dass die sozialistische Gegenswarts-musik in ihren entwickelteren Formen die Hörermassen unserer Republik noch nicht erreicht hat. . . . Da steht zunächst die Frage, wie wir bessere, volkstümlichere Musik schreiben und sie unter den Werktätigen verbreiten."

Information Sources

BIBLIOGRAPHY

Blum, Fred. "East German Music Journals." *Notes* 19 (1961–62): 401.

Brockhaus, Heinz Alfred, and Konrad Niemann. *Musikgeschichte der Deutschen Demokratischen Republik 1945–1976.* Berlin: Verlag Neue Musik, 1979.

Prieberg, Fred K. *Musik im anderen Deutschland.* Cologne: Verlag Wissenschaft und Politik, 1968.

INDEXES

External: Music Index, 1959– . RILM, 1967– . Bibliographie des Musikschrifttums, 1950– .

LOCATION SOURCES

Cornell University, University of Chicago, New York Public Library, University of Illinois, University of California (complete). Library of Congress (all but v. 1).

Publication History

TITLE AND TITLE CHANGES
  Musik und Gesellschaft.
VOLUME AND ISSUE DATA
  Volumes 1– , 1951– .
FREQUENCY OF PUBLICATION
  Monthly.
PUBLISHER
  Henschel-Verlag.
PLACE OF PUBLICATION
  East Berlin.
EDITORS
  Ernst Hermann Meyer, 1951. Karl Laux, 1951. Eberhard Rebling, 1952–59. Horst
  Seeger, 1959–60. Hansjürgen Schaefer, 1960–72. Liesel Markowski, 1973–83.
  Michael Dasche, 1983– .

Diane McMullen

MUSIK UND KIRCHE

Founded by Christhard Mahrenholz (1900–80), Wolfgang Reimann (1887–
1971), and Karl Vötterle (1903–75), *Musik und Kirche* traces its history back
to the title *Siona,* which began publication in 1876 and was succeeded by the
Zeitschrift für evangelische Kirchenmusik (1923–32); the latter merged with
Musik und Kirche in 1932. (A substantial article on the history of *Siona* and the
Zeitschrift für evangelische Kirchenmusik by Oskar Stollberg is listed in the
bibliography.) In the inaugural issue (January/February 1929), Dr. Mahrenholz
set forth the aims of the journal in a short essay, "Die Aufgabe der Zeitschrift
'Musik und Kirche' " (1:1–4), making the point that "music" and "church"
are to be considered co-equal in importance and coverage. The "church" in this
case is understood to be centered in the Protestant (*evangelische*) movement of
Western Europe, with special emphasis on German Lutheranism. From 1933 to
1938 (vs. 2–6), the journal was also listed as the organ of the Neue Schütz-
Gesellschaft.

During the pre–World War II years, *Musik und Kirche* assumed a progressive
stance, becoming a voice for some of the leaders in the organ reform movement
(see, for example, Hans Klotz, "Imperativ der Orgelbewegung," 5:166–74; also
the same author's "Zur Orgelreform von den klassischen Principalchören,"
7:250–60) and those espousing authentic performance practice (for example,
Willy Maxton, "Zur Aufführungspraxis Dietrich Buxtehudes," 4:268–77). Articles on German baroque composers (especially J. S. Bach, Heinrich Schütz,
and Dietrich Buxtehude) were numerous, but some contemporary figures (Hugo
Distler and Ernst Pepping in particular) were not neglected. Distinguished writers
such as H. J. Moser, Friedrich Blume, and Wilhelm Ehmann were frequent
contributors. In the liturgical area, articles of a general nature frequently men-

tioned renewal and reform (for example, Friedrich Gebhardt, "Was erwarten wir Jungen von der liturgischen Bewegung?" 4:25–29). A very few articles explicitly mentioned music under National Socialism (for example, Bernhard von Plinen, "Kirchenmusik im dritten Reich," 5:174–89; Ernst Schieber, "Die Singwoche im neuen Reich," 6:103–4). As World War II approached and became a reality, the individual issues became slimmer and fewer in number; publication was then suspended for two years (1945–46).

The first of the postwar volumes gave evidence of stocktaking (as in Walter Blankenburg, "Die Gegenwartslage der evangelischen Kirchenmusik," 17:33–39) and a certain ecumenism (Walter Lipphardt, "Zur Lage der katholischen Kirchenmusik in der Gegenwart," 17:13–17). Eminent theologians were occasionally called upon for contributions (Karl Barth, "Der Mensch im 18. Jahrhundert," 18:130–34), and the concern for *Aufführungspraxis* continued, even intensified. In the first of two "Bach-year" volumes (v. 20, 1950, and v. 55, 1985), Alfred Dürr contributed "Zur Aufführungspraxis der vor-Leipziger Kirchenkantaten J. S. Bachs" (pp. 54–64). Articles on the organ, its history, construction, and literature continued in abundance. Photographs of organs of all sizes—from the humblest home instrument to the most resplendent cathedral organ—continued to grace the pages of this journal. Articles on organs and organ technology outside Germany began to appear somewhat more frequently. In general, a greater number of scholarly articles per issue could be found. Investigation into such subjects as twelve-tone music, Romantic music, and jazz emerged. Alongside J. S. Bach, Heinrich Schütz, and Dietrich Buxtehude, new names as subjects—most notably, Max Reger and Olivier Messiaen—proliferated. Dialogues, for example, between Alfred Dürr and Wilhem Ehmann in vs. 30 and 31 (on the matter of the *concertino* and *ripieno* in J. S. Bach's B-minor Mass) added zest to scholarly inquiry. Numerology in the works of J. S. Bach was the subject of several articles (for example, Wolfgang Hösch, "Motivische Integration, Proportion, and Zahlsymbolik in Johann Sebastian Bachs Magnificat," 46:265–69). And general articles on church music by noted authorities (such as Hans Heinrich Eggebrecht, "Kirchenmusik in Krise?" 46:214–22) continued but were less frequent than during the prewar years.

As a physical object, *Musik und Kirche* originally appeared in a 6⅛" by 9" format, later decreased to 5¾" by 8½". Six issues per year, with continuous pagination, has been the consistent standard, except for the years 1943 and 1944 (vs. 15 and 16), during which only two issues per year were published. The typical volume now contains about 325 pages plus advertisements. About half of each issue in the recent past has consisted of scholarly articles and congratulatory or memorial notices; the articles range, on the average, between three and ten pages in length. The remainder has been devoted to reviews, listings of festivals and congresses, notices of premiere performances of new church music, obituaries and birthday anniversary notices, and descriptions (with stop lists) of new organs. An annual index is provided.

Four ancillary publications have come and gone: (1) *Des musikalische Schrifttum: Ein Führer durch werfolle Noten und Musikbücher*, a review pamphlet issued only twice (Winter 1929–30, Spring 1930); (2) *Der Kirchenchor*, issued from 1959 to 1970; (3) *Acta Sagittariana*, the bulletin of Internationalen Heinrich Schütz-Gesellschaft, from 1963 to 1966; and (4) *Schallplatte und Kirche: Beihefte zu Musik und Kirche*, from 1966 to 1973. In connection with the last title, it should be noted that *Musik und Kirche* has carried reviews and listings of recordings from its earliest years; the second issue of *Das musikalische Schrifttum* includes an index of the early historical series, "2000 Jahre Musik auf der Schallplatte" (pp. 45–46).

Information Sources

BIBLIOGRAPHY

Blankenburg, Walter. "50 Jahre 'Musik und Kirche'—Rückschau und Ausblick." *Musik und Kirche* 50 (1980): 285–95.

————, and Christhard Mahrenholz. "Zum Anschluss des 40, Jahrgangsvon 'Musik und Kirche.' " *Musik und Kirche* 40 (1970): 397.

"Grussworte zum Beginn des 25, Jahrgangavon 'Musik und Kirche.' " *Musik und Kirche* 25 (1955): 1–13.

Mahrenholz, Christhard. "Die Aufgabe der Zeitschrift 'Musik und Kirche.' " *Musik und Kirche* 1 (1929): 1–4.

————. "Dem 30, Jahrgang zum Geleit." *Musik und Kirche* 30 (1960): 1–7.

Stollberg, Oskar. "Siona." *Musik und Kirche* 46 (1976): 115–25.

"Ein Vierteljahrhundert Musik und Kirche: Chronik der Ereignisse." *Musik und Kirche* 25 (1955): 14–25.

INDEXES

Internal: each volume indexed.

External: Musik Index, 1949– . RILM, 1967– . Bibliographie des Musikschrifttums, 1937, 1939, 1950– .

REPRINT SOURCES

Microform: Schnase, 1929–44.

LOCATION SOURCES

Widely available.

Publication History

TITLE AND TITLE CHANGES

Musik und Kirche.

VOLUME AND ISSUE DATA

Volumes 1– , 1929– .

FREQUENCY OF PUBLICATION

Bimonthly.

PUBLISHER

Bärenreiter-Verlag.

PLACE OF PUBLICATION

Kassel, West Germany.

EDITORS
Christhard Mahrenholz, 1929–80. Wolfgang Reimann, 1929–71. Johannes Wolgast, 1929–32. Günter Ramin, 1947–56. Walter Blankenburg, 1952–86. Kurt Thomas, 1957–59. Eberhard Wenzel, 1960–65. Hans Pflugbeil, 1966–70. Renate Steiger, 1981– .

John E. Druesedow

MUSIKAAL PERSPECTIEF. See KEY NOTES

MUSIKALISCHES WOCHENBLATT. See NEUE ZEITSCHRIFT FÜR MUSIK

MUSIKBLÄTTER DES ANBRUCH. See ANBRUCH

MUSIKFORSCHUNG, DIE

Die Musikforschung first appeared in 1948 under the aegis of the Gesellschaft für Musikforschung, which had begun in November 1946. Frederick Blume, founding president of the *Gesellschaft*, explained, in the first issue of the journal, that the organization was intended to create a postwar system of support for all friends of musicology. The *Gesellschaft's* journal would thus both supplant earlier internal membership publications and act as a "scientific specialty organ" (*Fachorgan*) to encourage more work in the discipline and to provide another postwar forum for German scholarship. Blume further stated that *Die Musikforschung* was intended to follow in the tradition of such scholarly German-language journals as the *Zeitschrift für Musikwissenschaft* (q.v.), which ceased publication in 1935 and had been superseded by the *Archiv für Musikforschung* (q.v.).

The scholarly bent of *Die Musikforschung* is apparent from the outset, with issues containing three to four major articles, several shorter reports, and a number of short book reviews. Articles aptly reflect the continuing state of German-speaking musicology with coverage initially stressing topics in the Medieval, Renaissance, and Baroque eras, with occasional articles on eighteenth-century and nineteenth-century issues and comparative musicology. In the 1960s, articles on twentieth-century music became more common, and today, the coverage is wide-ranging in keeping with contemporary scholarly concerns. Early contributions included such well-known scholars as Heinrich Bessler, Helmuth Osthoff, Curt Sachs, and Erich M. von Hornbostel. With only a few notable exceptions, contributors were and continue to be German-speaking scholars; East German participation is, however, minimal.

Die Musikforschung began in its first volumes and continues today a number of special features in keeping with its goal to increase scholarly activity and support. Starting with v. 1, it provided a semiannual list of all music courses given in German-speaking universities. Of even greater interest is the journal's yearly compilation of all German-language dissertations completed during the previous year. This feature first appeared in v. 3. Both features were present in the editor's prewar model, *Zeitschrift für Musikwissenschaft*. Also appearing in the first volume was a necrology honoring important scholars, especially those who had died unnoticed during the war years. Although this necrology department no longer appears, the journal continues to recognize with cover articles the deaths of major German-speaking scholars. Added later were other sections sharing information on the *Gesellschaft*'s membership—names, addresses, and other information.

By v. 5 (1952), the journal was well established and acknowledged on its masthead the support and cooperation of the institutes for musicological research at Kiel and Regensburg. In the first number of that year, Frederich Blume, then president of the *Gesellschaft*, noted the journal's growth and restated the need for German musicologists to continue to work to regain their preeminence in the discipline, which had been lost during World War II.

No editor is given for the first two volumes. With v. 3, editorship was assumed by Hans Albrecht, who remained the editor until his death in 1960. He was succeeded, with v. 14, by Ludwig Finscher. The following year, 1962, saw the creation of an advisory board composed of Georg von Dadelsen, Hans Engel, Thrasybulos Georgrades, and Georg Reichert, with Finscher retaining primary editorial control. The announcement of this new board further stated that an effort had been made to include two representatives from East Germany, but that such had not proved possible. In v. 21 Christoph-Hellmut Mahling joined Finscher, and with v. 24 the advisory committee was dropped. Editorial duties have since been shared by two scholars, who change with some frequency.

From the start, each quarterly issue of *Die Musikforschung* was approximately eighty pages in length in an 5½″ by 8⅞″ format. A new title page format appeared in v. 3 and again in v. 27. The journal increased in length somewhat over the years, gradually expanding to as much as 560 pages per volume, with three to four major articles of ten to fifteen pages in length, nine to ten shorter reports and contributions of one to five pages, twenty to thirty, two- to three-page book reviews, plus the other regular features. In 1982 the format changed to 7″ by 9⅞″, and the number of pages per volume has since fluctuated between 230 and 330 pages. The actual content of each issue has remained much the same as before, although an occasional issue contains only a single major article plus the shorter reports and departments. Musical examples are common and sometimes even extensive; black and white photographs are printed infrequently. Books, music, and other periodicals are advertised. An internal index appears for each volume.

Information Sources

INDEXES
>   Internal: each volume indexed.
>   External: Music Index, 1949– . RILM, 1967– . Arts and Humanities Citation
>   Index, 1976– . Bibliographie des Musikschrifttums, 1952– .

LOCATION SOURCES
>   Widely available.

Publication History

TITLE AND TITLE CHANGES
>   *Die Musikforschung.*

VOLUME AND ISSUE DATA
>   Volumes 1– , 1948– .

FREQUENCY OF PUBLICATION
>   Quarterly.

PUBLISHER
>   Bärenreiter.

PLACE OF PUBLICATION
>   Kassel, West Germany.

EDITORS
>   Hans Albrecht, 1950–60. Ludwig Finscher, 1961–67. Ludwig Finscher and Chris-
>   toph-Hellmut Mahling, 1968–75. Christoph-Hellmut Mahling and Wolfgang
>   Doewling, 1976–80. Martin Just and Wilhelm Seidel, 1981–86. Detlef Altenburg
>   and Ulrich Tank, 1987– .

Susan C. Cook

MUSIQUE ET INSTRUMENTS

Musique et instruments began publication in January 1911 under the leadership
of Auguste Bosc, a successful businessman and a director of the Costallat music
publishing firm. In a sample "avant premier numero," dated 30 December 1910,
Bosc set forth the purpose of the weekly journal as providing information and
documentation through articles and advertisements that would be helpful to all
industrial and commercial interests involved with music, be they in the manu-
facturing of instruments, the publication of scores, or the various retail channels.
This innovative periodical was to provide a forum whereby the growing music
industry worldwide would be apprised of the latest products, inventions, and
publications, primarily—but not exclusively—of French origin. Bosc intended
this journal to be totally independent and impartial, devoted exclusively to the
business end of music, eschewing polemics and political affiliation, and disre-
garding scholarly articles common to other music periodicals.

By 1912 *Musique et instruments* (now issued twice a month) had established
the pattern of regular features and columns that were to remain standard for most
of its publication history. These included: (1) information relative to all com

mercial activity in music; (2) official lists of new French patents and registered trademarks, governmental regulations, and legal matters; (3) descriptions and diagrams of recent inventions; (4) extensive lists of the latest—primarily French—publications of musical scores; (5) membership rosters of various professional societies, lectures delivered at and minutes of their meetings, schedules of forthcoming music contests, and citations of winners; (6) information covering the world of music performance including premiers at concerts, opera, and ballet (in Paris, the provinces, and some foreign countries), schedules of upcoming seasons, obituaries, news, and gossip; (7) want ads for jobs and for the sale or purchase of businesses, instruments, books, and so on.

Under Bosc's guidance *Musique et instruments* witnessed a steady growth in size during the years preceding World War I. New rubrics kept being added, and the number of advertisements rose significantly. The diversity and content of the advertisements provide a unique insight into the world of music just prior to the war. A special issue featuring extensive listings of French music publications came out in May 1914 in connection with the exhibition of the Book Industry and the Graphic Arts at the Leipzig fair. The outbreak of the war a few weeks later forced the magazine to suspend publication from 25 July 1914 to 10 March 1919.

The resurgence of the economy after the war had a wide impact on the music business, and this is reflected in the giant strides made by *Musique et instruments* into the late 1920s. Bosc now envisioned his magazine as playing a leadership role in all commercial aspects of music. To this end he succeeded in having the various professional organizations (instrument builders, publishers, engravers, retail associations, and so on) accept *Musique et instruments* as the official organ reporting on their activities. Moreover, he founded the Office Général de la Musique, a centralized clearinghouse for the dissemination of information and publicity for all commercial interest in music. The journal was to serve as its major publication. To further help the industry Bosc was instrumental in organizing (starting in 1923) the Salons de Musique at the annual industrial fairs in Paris. Expanded issues of the magazine promoted these events.

During the 1930s the periodical expanded its coverage further by providing lengthier articles and offering reviews of concerts, books, and scores. Gradually, however, one notes a steady decline in advertisements, and by 1937 the number of pages is drastically curtailed, all reflecting the deteriorating financial situation of the Depression. By summer 1939 Bosc, reacting to the growing paralysis of industrial production and fears of an imminent war in Europe, decided to consolidate *Musique et instruments* with another of his journalistic endeavors, *Machines parlantes et radio*. Now called *Musique et radio* the new periodical came out as a bimonthly beginning with the September/October issue. Upon Germany's occupation of France, Bosc, whose wife was Jewish, fled Paris, selling the magazine to Horizons de France, a publishing firm. On Bosc's recommendation Eric Sarnette, who had been writing articles for *Musique et instruments* for several years, took over as editor. Sarnette managed to keep the magazine afloat during the war years, but it was a pale reflection of its former self.

With war's end, *Musique et radio* was gradually accorded a more international flavor, with many of its articles summarized in foreign languages (including English and German). Bosc returned to the journal, though Sarnette remained as "directeur musical." Throughout the 1950s the magazine broadened its outlook in order to reach a wider music-loving public. Though adhering to the informative rubrics and advertising policies of its earlier years, it had veered noticeably from its original intent of addressing itself exclusively to the professional musical trade.

In a major attempt to reverse this post–World War II orientation, the editors decided in 1964 to start afresh with a new physical, editorial, and bimonthly format. The first issue, now reverting to its original title *Musique et instruments*, emerged that September. The effort was marginally successful: though seeking again to speak to and further the French commercial musical enterprises at home and abroad, it continued to include the types of articles of the years immediately preceding, dropping only the critical reviews of concerts and recordings. But with the accession of Jean Deit as publisher in 1981, and Sarnette's departure as editor, the magazine saw a definite shift in focus. Again a monthly and now emphasizing almost exclusively articles dealing with aspects of music education, it changed its name to *Enseignement musical*, in effect establishing a new periodical bearing no resemblance to the publication envisaged by either Bosc or Sarnette.

Throughout its history *Musique et instruments* published numerous special issues. The previously mentioned, expanded issues in May and June of the 1920s and 1930s printed in conjunction with the annual Salons de Musique in Paris were revived after the war. Starting with the periodical's new format in 1964 there appeared special supplements in the July/August issues providing up-to-date listings of interest to the music world, for examples, 1965, orchestras in France; 1968, French conservatories of music, enumerating faculties; 1976, concert societies and series in the United States. Also during the 1970s come special issues discussing problems and reforms in music education. A high point is the 1976 issue detailing the twelfth conference of the International Society for Music Education in Montreux. Perhaps the most ambitious special issue is the 1960 celebration of the fiftieth anniversary of the founding of *Musique et instruments*. It features highly informative articles by Bosc, Sarnette, and others describing the history of the magazine and the significant trends in French music since 1911.

The volume of information contained in the pages of *Musique et instruments* should prove of inestimable value to scholars dealing with musical life during the years the magazine flourished. It can shed light on evolving musical tastes and French society's acceptance of what the music industry was marketing during much of the twentieth century. It provides historical data on the fluctuating financial health and distinctive developments within the instrument building and publishing trades, it demonstrates the steady advances in the technology of radio, high-fidelity equipment, phonograph recordings, and serves as a barometer of what the publishing firms considered significant and saleable. The magazine is a gold mine for ascertaining dates and locales of first performances and publications of old and new music, for identifying and discussing compositions or personalities in the music world, for gauging the myriad foreign influences on the French musical scene, for defining the role and changing nature of popular music, and for establishing a host of other informative facts and figures.

Musique et instruments's physical format, overall size, and printing style varied widely over its publishing history. The dimensions of the pages remained a constant 9½″ by 12¼″ from 1911 to 1964; thereafter it was modified to 8″ by 10½″. Originally only twelve pages in length the journal grew to thirty-two pages by the time of World War II. The 1920s and early 1930s saw dramatic increases, and the special May and June issues coinciding with the Salons de Paris could well contain over 120 pages. By the late 1930s, however, the number dwindled to twenty-four pages, not to increase again until the 1950s when the average was around forty pages. With the new format in 1964 the average number was sixty pages, but this too was pared down by the late 1970s. Paralleling the vicissitudes of the size of the magazine was the quality of paper, typography, binding, and thickness of covers, with the fat years of the 1920s and 1930s revealing a thoroughly modern, slick style. Photographs were rather sparse at first, but again by the 1920s many were included, particularly within advertisements for instruments. The issues of the magazine were numbered consecutively until n. 640 in June 1964. With the ensuing new format, the numbering began anew and lasted till n. 29 (January/February 1969), thereafter listing only the year of the magazine's publication, for example, "59ᵉ année."

Information Sources

INDEXES
    External: Bibliographie des Musikschrifttums, 1937, 1939.
LOCATION SOURCES
    Library of Congress, v. 30– .

Publication History

TITLE AND TITLE CHANGES
    Musique et instruments, 30 December 1910–July/August 1939. *Musique et radio*, September 1939–June 1964. *Musique et instruments*, September/October 1964–June/July 1981. For one year starting October 1981 the periodical was published in two identical versions, one entitled *Musique et instruments*, the other *Enseignement musical*; starting in September 1982 both titles are combined as *Musique et instruments—Enseignement musical*.
VOLUME AND ISSUE DATA
    Numbers 1–640, 1910–June 1964. New series, numbers 1– , August 1964– .
FREQUENCY OF PUBLICATION
    Semimonthly, 1910–18. Monthly, 1919–38. Bimonthly, 1939– .

PUBLISHERS
    Auguste Bosc, 1911–19. Office général de la musique, still under A. Bosc, 1919–
    30. Fédération nationale du commerce et de l'industrie de la musique, still under
    A. Bosc, 1931–39. Horizons de France, 1939–76—starting with the March 1943
    issue Jacques Lagrange is listed as *Directeur général*. E.G.P., 1976–   . Jean Deit
    listed as *Directeur* starting October 1981.
PLACE OF PUBLICATION
    Paris.
EDITORS
    Auguste Bosc and V. Counille, 1911–39. Eric Sarnette, 1939–81.

Sylvan Suskin

MUSIQUE ET INSTRUMENTS—ENSEIGNEMENT MUSICAL. See MU-
SIQUE ET INSTRUMENTS

MUSIQUE ET RADIO. See MUSIQUE ET INSTRUMENTS

MUZIEK, DE. See CAECILIA (1844–1944)

MUZIEK WERELD, DE. See CAECILIA (1844–1944)

MUZYKA

The record of outstanding Polish musicological accomplishment since World
War II is most clearly embodied in the pages of the foremost contemporary
Polish musicological journal *Muzyka,* which began appearing in 1956 under
Józef M. Chominski's editorship. The full title *Muzyka: Kwartalnik poswiecony
historii i teorii muzyki oraz krytyce naukowej i artystycznej* (*Music: Quarterly
Devoted to the History and Theory of Music as well as its Scholarly and Artistic
Criticism*) conveys both an accurate and a somewhat deceptive impression of
this quarterly's topic coverage. On the one hand, *Muzyka* editors have assembled
research on all periods of European music history (especially on source materials)
and included ethnomusicological, music-analytical, and less readily categorized
studies as well, for example, the discussion of cybernetics and music in v. 11.
It also offers frequent discussion of contemporary music, for example, the first
issue includes a presentation by Chominski on twelve-tone composition, still a
politically risky subject in Communist Poland at the time the issue was published.
On the other hand, although many *Muzyka* articles deal with non-Polish matters,
by far the largest percentage address issues connected in some fashion with
Polish music and its history, even the relatively rare piece by a non-Polish author.

As might be anticipated, considerations of Frédéric Chopin and Karol Szymanowski occur with some frequency, but many authors offer what is usually thorough and sound research into the history of lesser-known and earlier Polish music. The reader of this periodical quickly learns a great deal about the at first Latin, then mainly Italianate Western European musical culture that flourished in Poland between 1200 and 1700. The sustained investigation of Polish source material seems to be motivated by Polish musicologists' awareness of the musical manuscripts and data lost during World War II before scholars had time to document them. Many later studies in *Muzyka* consider the work of Witold Lutoslawski, Krysztof Penderecki, and other composers active in Poland during the last few decades.

Muzyka deserves a special measure of attention because of the significant opportunity it affords for studying a special kind of musical explanation that has become dominant in Poland. The early volumes of *Muzyka* contain a number of articles by Chominski and others that cogently present and develop his "sonoristic" theory, the outstanding formulation of the Polish mode of music-analytical thought. These contributions permit the reader to achieve a solid grasp of the intellectual framework underlying recent Polish musical scholarship. They are also invaluable in comprehending many more recent *Muzyka* articles, since Polish writers on music have come to take this indigenous approach for granted to such an extent (it now forms the backbone of Polish musicological and compositional training) that they tend to employ it as if it were self-evident and did not require any explanation or justification. As a result, the actual implications of current Polish musicological literature often elude the reader from abroad who has otherwise managed to overcome the language barrier. Sonoristic theory accords very well in many respects with characteristics of Polish music composed in the 1960s and 1970s. Inasmuch as the *Muzyka* articles appeared at about the same time or even prior to the emergence of the Polish "new music," it seems possible to suggest a certain indebtedness of Polish composition to Polish musicology.

Muzyka regularly reviews Polish publications and often offers valuable bibliographical data. Illustrations of scholarly interest also appear. Issues frequently conclude with a chronicle that reports on scholarly conferences, awards, and other kinds of news of interest to readers of *Muzyka*. Later volumes contain English summaries. Issues can run over a hundred pages while double issues are frequent. The physical format is 6¾" by 9½". It is to be hoped that future issues of *Polish Musicological Studies*, the Polish English-language musicological periodical which first appeared in 1977, will include further translations from *Muzyka*.

Two earlier Polish journals bore the title *Muzyka*. These should not be confused with the post–1956 *Muzyka*. The first of these, a monthly which appeared from 1924 to 1938, was edited by Mateusz Glinski who was later to champion the authenticity of the Delphine Potocka–Chopin letters. Apparently modeled on the French *La Revue musicale* and the German *Die Musik*, it reputedly familiarized the Polish musical scene with many new trends of that time, for example, neo-Classicism, and, in a special 1927 issue, jazz. Another *Muzyka*, published from 1950 to 1956 by Polskie Wydawnictwo Muzyczne (PWM) in Kraków and edited by the composer Witold Rudzinski, superseded the *Ruch Muzyczny* that had been published in Kraków between 1945 and 1949. It offered monthly issues at first, but then began to appear bimonthly. It ceased publication in early 1956, shortly before the first issue of the post–1956 *Muzyka* became available. Footnotes in Polish scholarly studies referring to the 1950–56 *Muzyka* suggest that it combined some scholarly work with more popular material of a kind similar to that associated with the current *Ruch Muzyczny* (q.v.), rather than the current *Muzyka*. One suspects that a good deal of 1950–56 *Muzyka* bore the stamp of a required Stalinist orientation. The post–1956 *Muzyka* is probably more correctly seen as heir to *Studia Muzykologiczne (Musicological Studies)*, which was published in Kraków by the Panstwowy Instytut Sztuki (State Institute of Art) under Chominski's editorship between 1953 and 1956, as well as to *Kwartalnik Muzyczny (Musical Quarterly)*, the chief prewar Polish journal for musicological scholarship.

Information Sources

BIBLIOGRAPHY
Michalowski, Kornel. "Bibliographical Resources for Music Periodicals in Poland." *Periodica Musica* 1 (1983): 14–15.
INDEXES
    External: Music Index, 1961– . RILM, 1967– . Bibliographie des Musikschrifttums, 1950– .
REPRINT EDITIONS
    Microform: UMI, 1956–73 (incomplete), 1974– .
LOCATION SOURCES
    University of California, Berkeley; University of Illinois, Urbana; New York Public Library; Harvard (full runs). Later volumes widely available.

Publication History

TITLE AND TITLE CHANGES
    Muzyka: Kwartalnik poswiecony historii i teorii muzyki oraz krytyce naukowej i artystycznej.
VOLUME AND ISSUE DATA
    Volumes 1– , 1956– .
FREQUENCY OF PUBLICATION
    Quarterly.
PUBLISHERS
    Panstwowy Instytut Sztuki, 1956–60. Instytut Sztuki Polskiej Akademii Nauk, 1961– .
PLACES OF PUBLICATION
    Kraków, 1956–60. Warsaw, 1961– .
EDITORS
    Józef M. Chominski, 1956–71. Elzbieta Dziebowski, 1971– .

                                                                    Stefan M. Ehrenkreutz

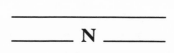

N

NACWPI BULLETIN. See NACWPI JOURNAL

NACWPI JOURNAL

The National Association of College Wind and Percussion Instrument Instructors was founded on the University of Michigan campus in 1951. The organization was affiliated with the Music Educators National Conference (MENC) and set as its primary goal "the advancement of wind and percussion instrument music" (1.1:4). The organization has always been interested in commissioning new works, sponsoring composition contests, and providing a forum, primarily though its publication, for the sharing of ideas germane to the college wind and percussion teacher.

The *Nat'l Assn. of College Wind and Percussion Inst. Instructors Bulletin* was first published in Ann Arbor in October 1952. V. 3 (October 1954) saw an alteration of the publication's name to the *Nat'l Assn. of College Wind and Percussion Instructors "Nack-Wappy" Bulletin*. The organization dropped the word "instrument" from its name in 1953 and the *Bulletin* accordingly reflected the change. The name was shortened to the *NACWPI Bulletin* with 7.1 (Fall 1958). The *Bulletin* became the *NACWPI Journal* in 1970 with 19.1.

First edited by Sanford M. Helm, the early *Bulletin* consisted of six to twelve loose pages of 8½″ by 11″ paper, typeset in three columns and printed on both sides. Earl Boyd succeeded Helm as editor (4.1), and the publication location moved to Charleston, Illinois, although the format and length did not change appreciably. The early publication schedule was posted as "several times a year," an irregular pattern that amounted to two releases of the *Bulletin* during the academic year (NACWPI also allowed its members to purchase its other publications, the commissioned works, and composition contest winners, at a reduced price).

Roger Phelps of Hattiesberg, Mississippi, took over the editorship with v. 7, and the publication changed not only location, but name, format, and appearance as well. It was now printed in booklet style (sheets folded and center-stapled with no additional binding), 6″ by 9″ pages, and in two columns of print rather than three. The publishing schedule was expanded to quarterly, a rate that still stands although the exact release times of September, December, March, and June were changed to Fall, Winter, Spring, and Summer with 13.1. Phelps added many regular features to the content of the *Bulletin* and increased issue length to between twenty-four and thirty-six pages. The inclusion of advertisements (with 7.2) helped finance the expansion of length and frequency.

The next two editors, Paul Wallace and Thomas A. Ayres, maintained the appearance, format and size of the *Bulletin* set by Phelps. The current editor, Richard K. Weerts, began his duties with v. 17. Weerts initiated a change in printers to Simpson Publishing Company of Kirksville, Missouri, with 17.3. The size of the publication changed slightly in 1981 (35.1) to page dimensions of 5½″ by 8½″, and the two-column layout was gradually abandoned in favor of no columns at all. The length of the publication expanded with Weerts's editorship to a current average of fifty-four pages.

The first seven volumes were mostly concerned with announcements of the organization and its governing documents, information on the composition projects, and a few news items related to the activities, especially the recital programs of its members. The programs began to appear in 4.1, were removed with 5.1 due to space considerations, then reappeared with 7.2 as a regular feature under the heading "A Little Night Music." They were last published in 29.4 (1981), although for three years after that a separately published program booklet "A Little Night Music" was offered to the members. Photographs of officers and performing ensembles abounded in the publication through the editorship of Wallace. Very few photographs now appear in the publication, although musical examples and illustrations are still prevalent. Pedagogical features of one to two pages, titled "Reed & Ligature," "Slide and Valve," "Membranophones & Idiophones," appeared regularly beginning with v. 7.2. These features changed with v. 23.4 to "Woodwind Forum," "Brass Forum," and "Percussion Forum," then disappeared altogether with 27.1. Reviews of music, records, and books varying in length from a few sentences to involved articles have been a mainstay of the publication since v. 3.1.

The expansion begun by Phelps was consummated under the editorial leadership of Weerts. The general trend since the 1960s toward more learned music scholarship in academia has been reflected in the contents of the *NACWPI Bulletin*. Even its change in title to *Journal* demonstrated the interest in providing a scholarly publication for its readers. The articles became longer (four to eight pages) and the topics more substantial as evidenced in the seven-part article by William C. Willett entitled "An Investigation of Clarinet Reed Contour and Its

Relation to Tone Quality'' (9.3–11.2), the two-part article by Betty Bang entitled
"Quantz and Tromlitz on Where to Breathe" (18.3:22, 27–28; 18.4:45–48),
"The Wind Music of Alvin Etler" by William Nichols (26.3:3–9; 26.4:7–16),
and "The Shakuhachi: Make It and Play It" by Donald P. Berger (35.1:8–21).
V. 28.2 inaugurated a new recurring column called "Recent Research in Instrumental Music," and v. 35.1 saw the development of "Composer Profile,"
a short biographical sketch and a selected list of compositions of a featured
composer.

While the NACWPI publications have never been as lofty in content as comparable periodicals in the fields of musicology or theory, it is refreshing to see
a publication maintain an ever-evolving stance for the academic interests of its
members.

Information Sources

INDEXES
    External: Music Index, 1975– . RILM, 1976– . Music Article Guide,
    1967– .
LOCATION SOURCES
    Widely available.

Publication History

TITLE AND TITLE CHANGES
    Nat'l Assn. of College Wind and Percussion Inst. Instructors Bulletin, 1952–54.
    Nat'l Assn. of College Wind and Percussion Instructors "Nack-Wappy" Bulletin,
    1954–58. *NACWPI Bulletin,* 1958–70. *NACWPI Journal,* 1970– .
VOLUME AND ISSUE DATA
    Volumes 1– , 1952– .
FREQUENCY OF PUBLICATION
    Semiannual with irregularities, 1952–57. Quarterly, 1958– .
PUBLISHER
    National Association of College Wind and Percussion Instructors.
PLACES OF PUBLICATION
    Ann Arbor, Michigan, 1952–55. Charleston, Illinois, 1955–58. Hattiesberg, Mis-
    sissippi, 1958–68. Kirksville, Missouri, 1969– .
EDITORS
    Sanford M. Helm, 1952–55. Earl Boyd, 1955–58. Roger Phelps, 1958–62. Paul
    Wallace, 1962–67. Thomas A. Ayres, 1967–68. Richard K. Weerts, 1968– .
                                                                Paul B. Hunt

NAJE EDUCATOR. See JAZZ EDUCATORS JOURNAL

NAJE NEWSLETTER. See JAZZ EDUCATORS JOURNAL

NATIONAL ASSOCIATION OF COLLEGE WIND AND PERCUSSION INSTRUMENT INSTRUCTORS BULLETIN. See NACWPI JOURNAL

NATIONAL ASSOCIATION OF COLLEGE WIND AND PERCUSSION INSTRUMENT INSTRUCTORS "NACK-WAPPY" BULLETIN. See NACWPI JOURNAL

NATS BULLETIN. See NATS JOURNAL, THE

NATS JOURNAL, THE

The National Association of Teachers of Singing (NATS) was founded in 1944. The first issue of *The NATS Bulletin* followed six months later as the official organ of the association. *The NATS Journal,* as it became known with v. 42 (September/October 1985), represents the organization's objectives as stated in the revised bylaws (28.4:1): "to encourage the highest standards of the vocal art and of ethical principles in the teaching of singing; and to promote vocal education and research at all levels, both for the enrichment of the general public and for the professional advancement of the talented." *The NATS Journal* has for many years served as the record of all official NATS activities (although most official business is now transmitted through an additional NATS organ, *Inter Nos.*). At the same time, it represents the state of the art of singing, in reporting current scholarship in voice research, announcing new and significant publications in relevant areas, and addressing pertinent topics in the teaching of voice and vocal performance.

The earlier issues, in newsletter format and comparatively brief (initially four pages), chronicled the activities of the fledgling national organization and its regional chapters, even to the regular inclusion of names and addresses of the membership and subsequent changes in membership status. Short articles, usually not more than one page in length, on singing technique and pedagogy, performance practice and interpretation, and announcements and follow-up reports of national and regional NATS meetings, were the substance of the first years' efforts. During the second decade, a traditional journal format was adopted, with the physical characteristics (8½" by 11") remaining generally unchanged today. The bimonthly (except in summer) issuance continued and somewhat lengthier issues were the norm, averaging thirty-six pages during the 1960s, and reflecting the varying needs and interests of a broadly based readership. Short articles on research in singing, choral performance, church music, or secondary school vocal music were to be seen alongside, for example, essays on the songs of a particular genre or perhaps a short study of operas by American composers. Special attention continued to be given to the organizational activities of NATS. Of particular historical interest, in addition, were the listings of the recital programs of important guest artists at the conventions, as well as those of the recipients of the NATS Singer of the Year awards.

With a larger readership and an expanded stable of advertisers (primarily publishers and educational institutions), the issues of the third decade and beyond increased in size to forty-five pages or more per issue. In 1975 Bernard Underhill Taylor had occasion to note that *The NATS Journal* "has moved away from the house organ status and is known as a learned journal of national and international importance to teachers of singing" (31.1). Indeed, the late 1970s and early 1980s ushered in an era of regular attention to current scientific investigation on singing and voice production, including papers by leading scholars whose fields were not necessarily music—medical specialists, speech pathologists, and audiologists, for example—in addition to important writers and representatives of the field of voice teaching. In the earlier years of the *Journal*, writings by Raoul Husson and especially, William Vennard, were prominent. Later, articles or even regular columns by Berton Coffin, Van Lawrence, Richard Miller, Ingo Titze, and others were featured.

Issues generally include three to four articles, four to fourteen pages in length. Reviews of selected books, music (art song, opera, and choral literature), and recordings became a regular feature. The question-and-answer column, by which a wide range of vocal performance and teaching problems were posed by the readership and addressed by experts, later gave way to another approach ("Point-Counterpoint") in which selected NATS members were given the opportunity to respond to a particular pedagogical topic posed by the editorship, with the resulting opinions published in a forthcoming issue.

Currently, significant areas of coverage include brief but informative analyses of selected contemporary vocal music ("New Directions") and Baroque performance practice in vocal music ("Baroque Corner"), a column on the singing of popular music styles, and a continuing series on famous singers from the past, in addition to matters of current voice research. Essays on the oeuvre of particular song composers, or unusual recital literature, often with musical illustrations, continue to be an important feature.

Information Sources

INDEXES
> External: Music Index, 1955– . Music Article Guide, 1965– . RILM, 1967– .
>
> Huizenga, Ann Huisman. "An Index of the National Association of Teachers of Singing Bulletin, 1945–1954." Ph.D. diss. Michigan State University, 1979.

REPRINT EDITIONS
> Paper: Johnson Reprint, 1944–62.
>
> Microform: UMI, 1944–68, incomplete. 1969– .

LOCATION SOURCES
> Widely available.

Publication History

TITLE AND TITLE CHANGES
    The NATS Bulletin, 1944– . *The NATS Journal,* 1985– .
VOLUME AND ISSUE DATA
    Volumes 1– , 1944– .
FREQUENCY OF PUBLICATION
    Five times per year, bimonthly except July–August.
PUBLISHERS
    National Association of Teachers of Singing, Inc.
PLACE OF PUBLICATION
    2800 University Boulevard North, JU Station, Jacksonville, Florida 32211.
EDITORS
    Howard G. Mowe, 1944–48. Leon Carson, 1944–55. Harvey Ringel 1955–80.
    Richard Miller, 1980–87. James McKinney, 1987– .

David Knapp

NEDERLANDSCH MUZIKAAL TIJDSCHRIFT. See CAECILIA (1844–1944)

NEUE LEIPZIGER ZEITSCHRIFT FÜR MUSIK. See NEUE ZEIT-SCHRIFT FÜR MUSIK

NEUE MUSIK-ZEITUNG

The *Neue Musik-Zeitung* was founded at the beginning of 1880 as a publication devoted to providing interesting musical information to that large body of German-speaking musicians whose participation in the art was primarily recreational, not professional. The subtitle "Illustriertes Familienblatt" attests this purpose. Each newspaper-format issue contains several articles, mostly five to ten columns in length, about musical compositions, performance issues, or composers. Important figures in European art music dominate the biographical sketches. Authors like Marie Lipsius (La Mara) write about famous and popular classical composers and their repertory. Lighter topics receive attention in the briefer *Feuilltons* and humorous inserts. Also included are musical examples, concert reviews, letters written to the paper, and complete pieces of music. The many advertisements appeal to those wanting music, instruments, musical instruction, and the like.

The publication history parallels the fortunes of Germany over the fifty-year history of the magazine. Born in 1880, during the political and social heyday of the new German nation, the *Neue Musik-Zeitung* dissolved during the difficult years after World War I. Yearly volumes contained twenty-four numbers, each consisting of twelve to sixteen pages and measuring 10½" by 13".

Supplements include the *Conversations-Lexicon der Tonkunst* (1881–87), a *Musikalischer Anzeiger* (1882), as well as a partial index, the *Verzeichnis einer Auswahl bemerkenswerter Aufsätze aus den Jahrgängen 1880–1908 der Neuen Musik-Zeitung* (1908). A parallel Austro-Hungarian edition appeared until 1923, issued by Moritz Perles.

Information Sources

BIBLIOGRAPHY
Fellinger, Imogen. *Verzeichnis der Musikzeitschriften des 19. Jahrhunderts*. Studien zur musikgeschichte des 19. Jahrhunderts, 10. Regensburg: Gustav Bosse, 1968.
REPRINT EDITIONS
    Paper: Kraus, Brookhaven Press.
    Microform: Library of Congress. Schnase. Datamics, Inc.
LOCATION SOURCES
    Library of Congress, New York Public Library, Rutgers University (complete). University of Minnesota, Detroit Public Library (partial holdings).

Publication History

TITLE AND TITLE CHANGES
    Neue Musik-Zeitung.
VOLUME AND ISSUE DATA
    Volumes 1–49.24, 1880–1928.
FREQUENCY OF PUBLICATION
    Semimonthly.
PUBLISHERS
    H. Alexander, 1880 (ns. 1–14). P. J. Tonger, 1880 (n. 15)–87. C. Grüninger, 1888–1918. Grüninger nach folger Klett, 1918–28.
PLACES OF PUBLICATION
    Leipzig, 1880 (ns. 1–14). Cologne and Leipzig, 1880 (n. 15)–87. Stuttgart and Leipzig, 1888–1918. Stuttgart, 1918–28.
EDITORS
    H. Alexander, 1880. August Reiser, 1880–90. August Svoboda, 1890–1901. Ernot Ege, 1901–3. Oswald Kühn, 1903–16. Willibald Nagel, 1916–22. Hugo Holle, 1922–26. Hermann Ensslin, 1926–28. Algred Burgetz, 1928.

Paul W. Borg

NEUE ZEITSCHRIFT FÜR MUSIK

Neue Zeitschrift für Musik (*New Journal for Music*) is actually a misnomer for this venerable publication, which has had one of the longest continuous (or nearly continuous) runs of any music periodical being issued today. Founded in

1834, *NZM* has been published every year since then with the exception of the seven-year period during and immediately following World War II. Over the years there have been many changes of publisher, a number of mergers with other journals, and a few temporary alterations of the title, but the present editors can justly claim that the *Zeitschrift* still preserves its original character. It is and always has been a journal of international scope (though published in German only), addressed primarily to professional musicians but also to persons interested in the arts generally, featuring informational reporting on all manner of current events in the world of music, along with sophisticated criticism of compositions, performances and books about music, and articles on specialized topics concerning music of the past as well as of the present.

The journal was originally the brainchild of Robert Schumann, who served as editor from 1835 through 1844. Schumann's name is not mentioned in the journal during its first year (1834)—the title page describes the editorship cryptically as "a society of artists and friends of art," and research reveals that the official editor was Julius Knorr, but Schumann was the real driving force behind the enterprise from its inception. Nor could this have been a secret to anyone acquainted with Schumann either personally or through his previous work, for numerous articles in the first year bear the signatures of Schumann's favorite fictional personae—Florestan, Eusebius, and Raro.

For Schumann's purposes the word *neue* in the journal's title was indeed appropriate, since his venture was very much a reaction against the established musical periodicals. Ironically, the new journal was founded in the same city— Leipzig—that was already home to one of the most important musical periodicals in the world at that time, the *Allgemeine musikalische Zeitung* (q.v.) (Schumann's journal was titled *Neue Leipziger Zeitschrift für Musik* during its first year). But there was never any question of a duplication of efforts. The *Allgemeine*, in fact, was of all the established journals the one that Schumann most loathed, and the one whose influence he sought most strenuously to combat.

Schumann perceived the early 1830s as a period of low ebb in music history, particularly as regards the tastes of the musical audience (and from a modern vantage point his perception seems correct). Ludwig van Beethoven, Franz Schubert, and Carl Maria von Weber had recently died and seemed already to be fading from memory, while the new talents of Felix Mendelssohn, Frédéric Chopin, Hector Berlioz (and Schumann!) had not yet gained wide recognition. Concert stages and amateur music making alike were dominated by a taste for the bombast of Giacomo Meyerbeer's opera and the empty virtuosity of a host of pianistic showmen. The musical journals of the time only served to perpetuate this state of affairs, in part because most of them were controlled by music publishers whose aim was to enhance their sales, and not necessarily the appreciation of great music (The *Allgemeine* ... , for instance, was the organ of Breitkopf und Härtel). It was not by chance that the *Neue Zeitschrift* had no association with a music publisher.

In format the new journal was remarkably similar to the *Allgemeine*. . . . Issued weekly, it consisted as a rule of four pages containing short articles on various topics, reviews of new books and music, and reports on performances both in Germany and abroad. A few advertisements of various sorts were typically interspersed, while occasional issues featured a supplementary "Intelligenzblatt" devoted to advertising exclusively. The difference from the older journal was not outward appearance, but rather content. In the reviews of new music especially, the new journal's dedication to high artistic standards was always evident—composers of genius were praised unreservedly, but on the other hand no holds were barred in criticizing the inferior.

Schumann's crusade for good music turned out to be a great success. The music that he and his contributors championed gained rapidly in popularity, and the new journal flourished. By the time Schumann retired from the editorship in 1844, the rival *Allgemeine* . . . had disbanded (though it was later revived).

In succeeding decades the *Neue Zeitschrift* continued to be an important forum for the ideas of prominent musicians, and its pages contain many valuable historical documents. In 1853, for instance, Schumann made a final contribution entitled "Neue Bahnen" ("New Paths"), which introduced the young Johannes Brahms as the potential leader of the next musical generation. However, the journal's new editor, Franz Brendel, did not become an advocate for Brahms, but rather inclined toward the "New-German" school of Franz Liszt and Richard Wagner. In 1860 Brahms and several others declared in a famous manifesto their contempt for what they saw as the journal's lack of dedication to traditional values. It should be pointed out that this criticism, whether justified or not, is applicable only to a relatively brief period in the long history of the journal.

In the twentieth century the *Neue Zeitschrift* continued to be one of the most influential journals in the world of music. The passing decades saw several mergers with other journals and some temporary changes of title, though the overall character remained substantially the same. Thus, starting in 1906, we encounter the *Musikalisches Wochenblatt/Neue Zeitschrift für Musik: Vereinigte musikalischen Wochenschriften*. In 1911 the title reverted simply to *Neue Zeitschrift für Musik*. The word *"neue"* was dropped from the title in 1920, but it was restored in 1955. From 1943 to 1945 the journal was combined with several others to form an instrument of Nazi propaganda, *Musik im Kriege* (q.v.), published in Berlin. Thereafter publication was suspended altogether until the original journal was resuscitated at Regensburg (West Germany) in 1950. The 1950s saw the absorption of two lesser journals—*Der Musikstudent* (1953) and *Das Musikleben* (1955) and another relocation, also in 1955, to Mainz, where the journal was taken over by B. Schotts Söhne. The size of the periodical has also varied considerably. Volumes slightly in excess of 200 pages were standard in the nineteenth century, but the journal blossomed to over 1,000 pages by 1905 and over 1,500 by 1936, with sharp declines to 336 in 1918 and 568 in 1942 (the depths of war), and a post–1950 average of approximately 700. Page dimensions also varied, through less dramatically.

An important milestone was reached in 1975 when the journal merged with another Schott publication, *Melos* (q.v.), to form *Melos/NZ Neue Zeitschrift für Musik*. *Melos* was dropped from the title in 1979, but the effects of the merger were lasting. *Melos* had been devoted exclusively to contemporary music, and from 1975 on the *Neue Zeitschrift* . . . has been outstanding among general musical periodicals in the amount of attention given to new works in the realm of "serious" music—about as much attention, proportionately, as was given by Schumann to music of his contemporaries.

Part of the reason for this latest merger was, the editors admitted, to overcome financial difficulties, and indeed the issues from 1975 through 1981 do seem to show the signs of an austerity program. The journal was reduced from Schumann's weekly publication schedule to a bimonthly plan, and though it still offered far more than Schumann's four pages per issue, the total number of pages per year still seemed relatively meager. In 1982, however, the journal began publishing once a month, without significantly cutting back on the number of pages per issue. That number has recently been averaging about seventy, with the pages measuring 8¼″ by 10¼″.

The format of each issue has varied considerably during the journal's long history, but is currently as follows: "Editorial," "Letters from Readers" (recently including, for example, a tirade from Karlheinz Stockhausen regarding an unfavorable review of one of his works); "Themen des Heftes" (two or three articles on varying topics, for example a research article on music of Alkan, or one by Pierre Boulez on problems of composing in our time); a column entitled "Komponieren Heute," a "Glosse" (short commentary of less than one page); "Das actuelle Porträt" (an interview, usually with a performer or conductor); "Im Konzertsaal gehört"; "Informationen aus dem Musikleben" (about six to eight short reports); numerous record and book reviews (the latter mostly of books in German, but occasionally including French or English items); and finally a series of brief "Notizen" of important performances in Germany and elsewhere. Musical examples are adequate and illustrations, especially photographs, have become common since the late nineteenth century.

In its overall stance, *Neue Zeitschrift* . . . lies somewhere between a scholarly journal and a more amateur-oriented publication like, for instance, *Stereo Review* (q.v). While on the one hand it avoids the lengthy articles on esoteric topics that characterize musicological publications (especially in America), on the other hand, it maintains the high critical standards and concern for serious music that Schumann had already established in 1834. The background and training of recent editors-in-chief—Carl Dahlhaus, Wolfgang Burde, Harold Bedweg, and since January 1985, Sigfried Schible—are symptomatic of the broad coverage and serious intent of the journal. Most are trained in musicology, but are also active as composers and/or performers, and while deeply involved in the study of music history, they also have a special interest in music of our own time.

Information Sources

BIBLIOGRAPHY

Heuss, A. "Augenblicksaufnahmen der *Zeitschrift für Musik* aus ihren drei letzten Jahr-zehnten." *Zeitschrift für Musik* 100 (1933): 30–33.

Kinsky, George. "Zur Geschichte der Grundung der *Neuen Zeitschrift für Musik.*" *Zeitschrift für Musik* 87 (1920): 1–5.

Plantinga, Leon. "The Musical Criticism of Robert Schumann in *Neue Zeitschrift für Musik*, 1834–1844." Ph.D. diss., Yale University 1964.

Plantinga, Leon. *Schumann as Critic.* New Haven: Yale University Press, 1967.

Schering, Arnold, W. Niemann, and Max Unger. "Ein Wort zum Jubilumsjahrgang der *Zeitschrift für Musik* aus den Reihen ihrer früheren Schriftleiter." *Zeitschrift für Musik* 100 (1933): 27–30.

Wustmann, G. "Zur Entstehungsgeschichte der Schumannischen *Zeitschrift für Musik.*" *Zeitschrift der Internationalen Musik-Gesellschaft* 8 (1906–07): 396–403.

INDEXES

External: Music Index, 1949– . Bibliographie des Musikschrifttums, 1955– . RILM, 1967– .

REPRINT EDITION

Microform: Krauss Reprints, 1864–1924. Mikrofilmarchiv der deutschsprachen-igen Press, 1864–1912. Mikropress Gmbh, 1864–1912.

LOCATION SOURCES

Widely held.

Publication Sources

TITLE AND TITLE CHANGES

Neue Leipziger Zeitschrift für Musik, 1834. *Neue Leipziger für Musik*, 1835–1905. *Musikalisches Wochenblatt/Neue Zeitschrift für Musik: Vereinigte Musikalische Wochenschriften*, 1906–10. *Neue Zeitschrift für Musik*, 1911–19. *Zeitschrift für Musik*, 1920–43. *Musik im Kriege*, 1943–45. *Zeitschrift für Musik*, 1950–55. *Neue Zeitschrift für Musik*, 1956–74. *Melos/NZ Neue Zeitschrift für Musik*, 1975–78. *NZ Neue Zeitschrift für Musik*, 1979– .

VOLUME AND ISSUE DATA

Volumes 1– , 1834– .

FREQUENCY OF PUBLICATION

Weekly, 1834–74. Bimonthly, 1975–81. Monthly, 1982– .

PUBLISHERS

Numerous.

PLACES OF PUBLICATION

Leipzig, 1834–1928. Regensburg, 1929–43. Berlin, 1943–45. Regensburg, 1950–55. Mainz, 1955– .

EDITORS

Robert Schumann, 1834–44. Franz Brendel, 1845–68. C. F. Kahnt, 1869–86. Oskar Schwalm, 1887–89. Paul Simon, 1890–99. Edmund Rochlich, 1900–03. Carl Kipke, 1904–7. Ludwig Frankenstein, 1908–11. Friedrich Brandes, 1912–19. Max Unger, then Wolfgang Lenk, 1920. Steingräber-Verlag, 1921. Alfred Heuss, 1922–30. Gustav Bosse, 1931–43. Erich Valentin, 1950–55. Karl H.

Wörmer, 1956. Heinz Joachim et al., 1957. Erich Valentin et al., 1958–59. Karl Hartmann et al., 1960–63. Ernst Thomas, 1964–66. Ernst Thomas et al., 1967–74. Carl Dahlhaus et al., 1975–78. Wolfgang Burde, 1979–81. Harald Budweg, 1982–84. Sigfried Schiblie, 1985–   .

David R. Beveridge

NEUES MUSIKBLATT. See MELOS

NEWSLETTER: AMERICAN SYMPHONY ORCHESTRA LEAGUE, INC. See SYMPHONY NEWS

NEWSLETTER OF THE AMERICAN SYMPHONY ORCHESTRA LEAGUE, INC. See SYMPHONY NEWS

NZ NEUE ZEITSCHRIFT FÜR MUSIK. See NEUE ZEITSCHRIFT FÜR MUSIK

19th CENTURY MUSIC

19th Century Music is a journal of serious, scholarly intent, directed primarily toward the musically educated reader. It can claim the distinction of being the only major periodical (scholarly or otherwise) devoted particularly to music of the Romantic era. The journal was founded in 1977 by a group of musicologists from various branches of the University of California (most notably Joseph Kerman from Berkeley) who felt that the traditional musicological publications of the United States tended to overlook the growing tide of research and analysis being conducted in the field of nineteenth-century music in favor of music of earlier periods (1:90–91). A secondary factor in the new journal's desiderata appears to have been an effort to broaden the traditional scope of musical scholarship in the United States to include not just historical research but also analysis and, especially, criticism. The defense of criticism as an important endeavor within the broader study of music has always been one of Kerman's foremost concerns.

To date, *19th Century Music* has published a wide variety of essays: sketch studies (for example, D. Kern Holoman, "The Berlioz Sketchbook Recovered," 7:282–317), harmonic and linear analysis (Nicholas Temperley, "Schubert and Beethoven's Eight-Six Chord," 5:142–54), archival source materials, performance practice (Will Crutchfield, "Vocal Ornamentation in Verdi: The Phonographic Evidence," 7:3–54), stylistic evolution, and critical appraisals of particular works have all been represented and copiously illustrated. The music covered has been for the most part that prescribed by the journal's title, although the boundaries of the century have occasionally been extended at the latter end to include articles on late Gustav Mahler, Claude Debussy, Aleksander Scriabin, and even one piece on Igor Stravinsky. Inevitably, the journal reflects the biases of American musicology (biases that do not always coincide with the interests of the concert-going public). For example, while Richard Wagner, Giuseppe Verdi, and Franz Schubert have each been the focus of at least ten articles, no article on Peter Tchaikovsky has yet appeared.

Contributors to *19th Century Music* have included many of the most respected musicological figures active today, not just in the area of nineteenth-century studies, but in musical scholarship in general. A high representation of faculty, graduate students, and former students of the University of California is noticeable, but the Californians' articles are liberally interspersed with essays from around the country, especially from the Ivy League schools, as well as from Great Britain and Germany (the latter in English translation). The journal can truly claim to be a compendium of the most sophisticated current thought in Western culture on music of the nineteenth century.

The format of the journal has remained remarkably consistent, with each of the three yearly issues comprising approximately ninety pages. Issues begin with four or five major articles, sometimes devoted to a unified theme (for example, Verdi, 2.2; Debussy, 5.2; and French Archives, 7.2), but usually not. A column on "Performers and Instruments" usually follows, commenting on particular performances or groups of performances (live or recorded) or broader issues in the area of performance theory. Next comes a series of extended reviews of books (often up to five pages in length) on pertinent topics, then, occasionally, a column entitled "Viewpoint" which presents a position, often controversial, regarding some important aspect of the study of nineteenth-century music. "Viewpoint" frequently is the highlight of the issue, at least as a source of food for thought, for example, when Kerman, in the November 1978 issue, delivered a stinging attack on the obsession many analysts have with discovering dramatic symbolism in a composer's use of keys (2:186–91). (Kerman's immediate target for demolition was an article on Verdi: Siegmund Levarie, "Tonal Relations in Verdi's *Un Ballo in maschera*" in 2:143–47).

Near the end of each issue appears an unsigned "Comment and Chronicle" section, always informative and frequently amusing. For the lay reader "Comment and Chronicle" may well be the most valuable part of the journal, since it often provides information on music festivals, new editions of music, and other matters of interest to more than just a narrow circle of musicologists.

The last two or three pages of each issue are generally occupied by advertisements from publishers, listing performing and scholarly editions of music as well as journals and books about music. An index follows at the end of the third and last issue (the Spring issue) for each volume, listing the journal's contents for the year just being completed. A ten-year index, compiled by Michael Rogan, appeared in 10.3:297–307.

The editorship of *19th Century Music* has generally been a triumvirate, listed alphabetically. Always present among the three have been D. Kern Holoman and Joseph Kerman; holders of the (unofficially) rotating third position have been, in chronological order, Robert Winter, Richard Swift, and Walter Frisch. From the Fall 1981 issue through Spring 1983, Kerman was listed first as the chief editor. The editorial board for the journal has comprised from twelve to sixteen persons. Membership has included all of the above names in addition to several others from the University of California, along with nine others including such luminaries as Gerald Abraham, Jacques Barzun, and Andrew Porter.

The physical design of the journal, by Edwin Pinson, is exceptionally handsome, and received an award from the American Association of University Presses in 1979. Each volume features a different cover pattern, always taken from a series of nineteenth-century floral chintzes by William Morris. The dimensions are 8½" by 9⅞".

Information Sources

INDEXES
    Internal: each volume indexed; vs. 1–10 in v. 10.
    External: Music Index, 1977– . RILM, 1977– . Music Article Guide, 1984– . Arts and Humanities Citation Index, 1977– . Humanities Index, 1983– . Bibliographie des Musikschrifttums, 1978– .
REPRINT EDITIONS
    Microform: UMI.
LOCATION SOURCES
    Widely available.

Publication History

TITLE AND TITLE CHANGES
    19th Century Music.
VOLUME AND ISSUE DATA
    Volumes 1– , 1977– .
FREQUENCY OF PUBLICATION
    3/year.
PUBLISHER
    University of California Press.
PLACE OF PUBLICATION
    Berkeley, California.
EDITORS
    Joseph Kerman and D. Kern Holoman, 1977– . Robert Winter, 1977–79. Richard Swift, 1983–84. Walter Frisch 1984– .

David R. Beveridge

NORDISK MUSIKKULTUR. See DANSK MUSIKTIDSSKRIFT

NOTES, THE QUARTERLY JOURNAL OF THE MUSIC LIBRARY ASSOCIATION

Notes, the oldest continuous periodical of music librarianship, is the principal publication of the Music Library Association (MLA), an organization founded at Yale University in June 1931 by librarians attending an American Library Association conference. The number of music librarians was small and music librarianship was in its infancy, occupied with collection development, standard procedures, cataloguing/classification of *musicalia*, development of bibliographic aids, and interlibrary communication. To address such concerns *Notes for the Members of the MLA* was begun in July 1934 by Eva J. O'Meara, editor, and, for its earliest issues, its sole contributor.

Between 1934 and 1942 the fifteen numbers of the First Series were issued occasionally in mimeographed form on 8½" by 11" paper, ranging from seventeen to sixty-two pages in length. The sometimes informal tone of *Notes* belies the merit of its contents: plate numbers for cataloguing and identification; calls for cataloguing codes and music subject headings; checklists of music and publications; compilation of bibliographic tools; proposals for periodical indexing, current, and retrospective; and descriptions of music libraries in the United States. Proceedings, minutes, reports, and membership lists were eventually included, and with n. 7 (1940) the title became *Notes for the MLA*.

O'Meara was succeeded as editor by Charles Warren Fox in 1941. By the following year, with membership growing dramatically and concerns of librarians being enunciated with increasing urgency, the time had come for *Notes* to become a bona fide scholarly journal, and with n. 15 the First Series ended.

The Second Series began in 1943 with *The MLA Notes* 1 appearing as a printed journal in octavo format. The new editor was Richard S. Hill, eventually known as the "Father of *Notes.*" In spite of its new appearance, clearly defined sections, and quarterly publication schedule, *Notes* remained true to its original aims. No break occurred in the continuity of its contents. Once established, the Series II departments and layout have remained constant, although they have kept abreast of the times.

Individual feature articles, three to ten pages in length, run a wide gamut of subjects but tend to fall into broad categories: bibliographic accounts—checklists, indexes; historical and biographical essays; current technology; items of current interest; and "state of the art" in research and librarianship. Their authors include not only librarians but also composers, publishers, musicologists, and critics.

Notes has abounded in articles about periodicals and their literature. Moreover, many lists of magazines have appeared in Series II, for example, Latin American titles (2:120–23); German wartime journals (5:199–206); foreign periodicals (5:189–98); and East German issues (19:399–410). More recently, Charles Lindahl has treated a variety of periodicals, current and retrospective, in a "Periodical Review" column (32.1–39.1), for which Linda I. Solow compiled her "Index to Music Periodicals Reviewed in *Notes* (1976–1982)" (39:585–90).

Since 1983 Stephen M. Frey has prepared annotated lists of "New Music Periodicals."

Book reviews first appeared in Series I, n. 15, with short essays about seven books. They became a regular feature with Series II, 1.4, and at present an average of sixteen to twenty books about music, in the major languages, are reviewed. Music reviews began in 1945 (2.3). In recent issues, works by some fifty composers, from any historical period and for all media, as well as from scholarly editions to books for children, are reviewed.

The book and music lists appearing in each issue were both begun in 1946 (4.1) and contain names of authors/composers, titles, publication data, and prices. "Books Recently Published," currently compiled by William C. Parsons, is a list of some 300–400 titles, arranged alphabetically by language. "Music Received," since 1967 compiled by Ruth Watanabe, with "Pops" lists by Norma Jean Lamb, includes 300–350 collections and individual compositions, arranged by type of edition and by performance medium.

In George R. Hill's annual "Music Publishers' Catalogs," about a hundred firms are represented. Together with Joseph Boonin, Hill also prepares an annual analysis of prices of *musicalia*. Because of the scope of Kurtz Myers's "Index to Record Reviews," started in 1947 (5.2), no record reviews as such appear in *Notes*. A unique reference tool, the Myers index summarizes reviews from many critical sources, its aim being to present a poll of different opinions.

Appearing first in 1966, the "Index to Musical Necrology," now compiled by Kären Nagy, is an annual feature in the June issue. It gives information on recently deceased musicians, the source(s) of the obituary, and reference works in which biographical data can be located.

Notes abounds in bibliographic studies, usually complete within a single issue. But among compilations in multiple installments included in Series II are the "Bibliography of Asiatic Musics" by Richard A. Waterman and associates, a significant contribution to ethnomusicological research (fifteen installments, vs. 5–8); Alfred Einstein's revision of Vogel's *Bibliography of Italian Secular Vocal Music* (thirteen installments, vs. 2–5); Margaret M. Mott's "Bibliography of Song Sheets" (three installments, vs. 6, 7, 9); and Gerald D. McDonald's "Songs of the Silent Films" (two installments, v. 14).

Many fine studies of Americana have appeared. Special attention is called to Dena J. Epstein's "Music Publishing in Chicago Before 1871" (nine installments, vs. 1–3) and her "Slave Music in the U.S. Before 1860" (two installments, v. 20).

Series I, n. 4, was a special issue of forty pages completely devoted to Robert Bruce's "Partial Index to the *Encyclopédie de la musique et dictionnaire du conservatoire* of Lavignac," providing access to a multivolume reference work published without a working index. While several issues have contained tributes to deceased dignitaries, the *Festschrift* in celebration of Otto Kinkeldey's seventieth birthday (6.1) was a special issue of a more joyous nature.

Advertisements did not appear in Series I, although a few short announcements of duplicates for sale by member libraries were sometimes found. In Series II, however, they are a regular and valuable part of each issue. Forty-one firms, most of them publishers and dealers, were represented in a recent issue (42.3). Advertisements are printed on both inside covers, the outside back cover, and a section of up to forty numbered pages preceded by an "Index to Advertisers" at the end of the issue.

Although no cumulative index exists for the complete run of *Notes*, an index to Series I, compiled by Frank C. Campbell, appears in Series II, 1:2. Indexes to earlier volumes of Series II, also compiled by Campbell, were for a two-year cumulation, and since 1966–67 there have been annual indexes for all volumes.

To attend to the internal affairs of the association a *Supplement for Members* was issued between 1947 and 1964 as a house organ. Matters of technical and bibliographical import are dealt with in MLA's *Technical Reports, Music Cataloging Bulletin*, and *Bibliographic Series*. News of chapter and association activity is now found in the quarterly *MLA Bulletin*. These are separate publications.

Notes itself, originally intended for MLA members, has not been merely a library journal. Indeed, it defies classification. It is true that its many lists, reviews, and advertisements are purchasing guides for music librarians, and its bibliographies and indexes are an aid to reference services, but *Notes* serves a much larger public than librarians. Articles that are at once enlightening and often amusing, with some interesting illustrations and plates, cannot help attracting all persons interested in music, to say nothing of students, teachers, and researchers.

Information Sources

BIBLIOGRAPHY

Bradley, Carol June. "History of the MLA." *Notes* 37 (1980/81): 763–822.
Lichtenwanger, William. "When *Notes* Was Young: 1945–1960." *Notes* 39 (1982/83): 7–30.
Krummel, Donald W. "Twenty Years of *Notes*: A Retrospect." *Notes* 21 (1963/64): 56–82.
———. "The Second Twenty Volumes of *Notes*: A Retrospective Re-Cast." *Notes* 41 (1984/85): 7–25.

INDEXES

Internal: ns. 1–15 in n.s. v.2; n.s. vs. 1–23 indexed biennially; each volume indexed (vs. 24–   ).
External: Music Index, 1949–   . Bibliographie des Musikschrifttums, 1950–   . Music Article Guide, 1965–   . Der Zeitschriftendienst Musik, 1965–   . RILM, 1967–   . Arts and Humanities Citation Index, 1977–   .

REPRINT EDITION

Paper: AMS Press, ns. 1–15.

LOCATION SOURCES

Widely available.

Publication History

TITLE AND TITLE CHANGES

> *Notes for the Members of the MLA*, 1934–37. *Notes for the MLA*, 1940–42. *MLA Notes*, 1943–47. *Notes, Quarterly Publication by the MLA*, 1947–66. Also described on the cover as *Notes, A Magazine Devoted to Music and Its Literature, with Bibliographies and Reviews of Books, Records, Music*, 1947–66. *Notes, The Quarterly Journal of the MLA*, 1966–   .

VOLUME AND ISSUE DATA

> Ns. 1–15, 1934–42. N.s., vs. 1–   , 1943–   .

FREQUENCY OF PUBLICATION

> Irregular, 1934–42. N.s.: quarterly, 1943–   .

PUBLISHER

> The Music Library Association, Inc.

PLACE OF PUBLICATION

> Ann Arbor, Michigan.

EDITORS

> Eva J. O'Meara, 1934–41. Charles Warren Fox, 1941–42. Richard S. Hill, 1943–60. William Lichtenwanger, 1961–63. Edward N. Waters, 1963–65. Harold Samuel, 1966–70. Frank C. Campbell, 1971–74. James Pruett and Frank C. Campbell, co-editors, 1974. James Pruett, 1975–77. William McClellan, 1977–82. Susan T. Sommer, 1982–86. Michael Ochs, 1987–   .

Ruth Watanabe

NUOVA RIVISTA MUSICALE ITALIANA

In its wide scope and its format, *Nuova rivista musicale italiana* is a true heir to *Rivista musicale italiana*, published from 1894–1932, 1936–43, and 1946–55. The latter journal, in 1894, introduced a format that embraced two categories of articles: "Memorie" (studies of aesthetics, historical investigations, biographical research, and so on as it pertains to a broad range of music) and "Arte contemporanea" (studies relating to "present-day" musical life). (The categories were not mutually exclusive; Richard Wagner, for instance, figures in both.) Extended reviews of books and music were accompanied by shorter "bibliographical notes." News of the musical year (concert life), publications, forthcoming works, and so on appeared, as did a summary review of current periodicals. Cumulative indices for vs. 1–20 were prepared by Luigi Parigi (1917); for vs. 21–35 by A. Salvatori and G. Concina (1931). An independent index to the remaining volumes was prepared by Francesco Degrada in 1966.

Nuova rivista musicale italiana (*NRMI*) published continuously from 1967, perpetuates the broad scope and important contributions of its fifty-seven-volume predecessor. The journal's wide range of items—critical essays, archival studies and chronicles of the contemporary musical life (concert reports, news of musical institutions, and so on) are all regularly included—make it a useful tool for scholars, performers, composers, and concert enthusiasts alike.

NRMI has appeared quarterly since 1972; the previous schedule brought forth an issue every two months. Its typical format includes the following items, always in Italian: essays and articles, documentary presentations, correspondence from Italy, correspondence from foreign countries, radio music, content summaries of current musical journals, news column, reviews (books, music, and recordings), and a cumulative index for the volume.

Expectedly, the essays and articles are prominent features of each issue. Twentieth-century topics are the most plentiful, embracing the European "mainstream" (Béla Bartók, Igor Stravinsky, Luigi Dallapiccola, Pierre Boulez, *inter alia*), as well as investigations of jazz and rock. The nineteenth century is also well represented with both Italian and non-Italian subjects. However, an Italian focus sometimes emerges even in coverage of non-Italian topics. Vs. 4–8, for example, present an extended ten-article series entitled "La Fortuna di Beethoven nella vita musicale italiana di ieri." Here Beethoven's part in the nineteenth-century musical life of Turin, the Piedmont, Naples, Rome, Florence, Lombardy, Sardegna, Genoa, Veneto, Bologna, and Messina is assessed by various authors. An Italian bias is more evident in coverage of earlier periods. Topics pertaining to the seventeenth and eighteenth centuries are often published; the seventeenth-century coverage is almost entirely Italianate. Renaissance subjects are only occasionally offered; Medieval ones even less often. The contributorship is predominantly Italian.

Thematic organization of articles occurs within some volumes. In commemoration of the tercentenary of Antonio Vivaldi's birth, for example, v. 13 is devoted entirely to studies of his work and milieu, including a catalogue of his many works and a discography.

Some essays and articles of course resist "period" classifications. The editors of *NRMI* have included organological investigations (for example, Leonardo Pinzauti's "Conservazione e restauro degli antichi strumenti" (10:617–22) or Pietro Righini's "Dalle trombe egizie per l'"Aida" alle trombe di Tut-Ankhamon" (11:591–605)), the occasional study pertaining to "musics of the world" ("La notazione musicale strumentale del Buddismo Tibetano" by Ivan Vandor (7:335–51) or Paolo Santarcangeli's "Cenni sulla storia della musica ungherese" (11:26–43) are two examples), and "conceptual" studies (for instance, the famous French structuralist Roland Barthe's "La musica, la voce, il linguaggio" (12:362–66), or Steven Scher's "Il concetto di realismo nella musica" (11:167–84)).

Also found among the essays are profiles (*ricordi*) of prominent composers and scholars, mostly Italian. And in the earlier volumes of *NRMI*, colloquia with major European composers (for example, Hans Werner Henze, Krzysztof Penderecki, Karlheinz Stockhausen, Luciano Berio, and Gian Carlo Menotti) are frequently featured.

The documentary presentations found in most volumes of *NRMI* present the fruits of archival research, generally in the form of commentary on and transcription of a document(s). Not surprisingly, the scope of these documents is broad, consistent with the aims of the journal as a whole. Letters are a mainstay of this category, and the correspondence investigated covers a range of several centuries. Letters studied include those by well-known Baroque composers—Claudio Monteverdi and Antonio Vivaldi, for example—and those by more obscure figures like Gian Andrea Fioroni (a late eighteenth-century Milanese composer). Other correspondence is more modern. Scholars have presented, for instance, the letters of Alfredo Casella and Goffredo Petrassi, Wagner and Giovanni Lucca, and Giacomo Puccini and Giulio Ricordi, to name but a few. Institutional records, musical transcriptions, and manuscript catalogues also make up an important part of this aspect of the journal.

The essays, articles, and documentary presentations show *NRMI* fulfilling its scholarly goals. As the periodical addresses a wide audience, however, other aspects are more journalistic. "Correspondence from Italy" and "Correspondence from foreign countries" give reports of concert life, festivals, and so on in the musical centers of the world. "Radio music," often divided into a "listening chronicle" and reports of the "public seasons" ("Le staggioni pubbliche"), also addresses the more general reader. The impact of *NRMI*'s publisher, Edizione RAI Radiotelevisione Italiana, is seen not just in the appearance of "Radio Music," but in the fact that the reports of the "public seasons" come from Rome, Milan, Naples, and Turin, the homes of the four RAI orchestras.

Among the most useful and unusual sections of *NRMI* is the brief content summaries of current periodicals: an annotated table of contents for an international range of music journals that include *Melos* (q.v.), *Musica disciplina* (q.v.), *Musical Quarterly* (q.v.), *Chigiana* (q.v.), and *Musik und Kirche* (q.v.). The utility of this feature is clear, but should be underscored: one may quickly gain an overview of the contents of many music periodicals—an invaluable aid to those with limited access to extensive library holdings.

The "news column," advertising, and moderate-length book, music, and record reviews are standard features that require little comment. More unusual among music periodicals, though extremely helpful, are the multifaceted indices—typical features of *NRMI*—that detail the contents of a single volume. Characteristically the index includes a cumulative table of contents, an index of subjects, of names and works, and of illustrations. Annual volumes run 700–900 pages in length in a 6″ by 9″ format.

Information Sources

INDEXES

Internal: *Rivista musicale italiana*, vs. 1–20; vs. 21–35. *Nuova rivista musicale italiana*, each volume indexed.

External: *Rivista musicale italiana*. Bibliographie des Musikschrifttums, 1937, 1939, 1950–55.

Nuova rivista musicale italiana., Music Index, 1969–   . RILM, 1967–   . Bibliographie des Musikschrifttums, 1970–   . Arts and Humanities Citation Index, 1976, 1984–   .

Degrada, Francesco. ''Indice della rivista musicale italiana annate XXXVI–LVII.'' In *Quaderni della rivista italiana di musicologia a cura della Societa' Italiana di Musicologi*. Florence, 1966.

REPRINT EDITION

Microform: *Rivista musicale italiana:* Library of Congress. Schnase. Kraus International. Scholars' Facsimiles and Reprints, 1894–1920.

LOCATION SOURCES

Widely available.

Publication History

TITLE AND TITLE CHANGES

Rivista musicale italiana, 1894–1932, 1936–43, 1946–55. *Nuova rivista musicale italiana*, 1967–   .

VOLUME AND ISSUE DATA

Volumes 1–   , 1967–   .

FREQUENCY OF PUBLICATION

Bimonthly, 1967–71. Quarterly, 1972–   .

PUBLISHERS

(*RMI*) Fratelli Bocca Editori; (*NRMI*) Edizioni RAI Radiotelevisione Italiana.

PLACES OF PUBLICATION

(*RMI*) Turin, later Milan, and other places (*NRMI*) Rome.

EDITORS

(*NRMI*) A board of directors oversees the publication of each volume. Remo Giazotto, Segretario di direzione, 1967–76. Giancarlo Rostirolla, Segretario di redazione, 1973–76. Giancarlo Rostirolla, Redazione, 1977–   . Leonardo Pinzauti, Responsabile, 1967–   .

Steven Plank

O

OPERA

Beginning in 1948, the monthly magazine *Ballet* began to include articles and current information about opera (1.1). Such was the response from operaphiles who became acquainted with the expanded *Ballet and Opera* and such were the demands to increase further the opera-related topics and news that the potential for a successful separate venture, at least bimonthly, seemed assured. And so began *Opera*, which, after a few bimonthly issues in early 1950, instituted a monthly and firmly regularized schedule of publication which continues to this day. The Earl of Harewood, founder and editor for its first three years, wrote in the premier issue: "We mean to cover in prospect and retrospect any form of serious operatic activities, amateur or professional, that is in our opinion of interest to the intelligent opera-goer. The views of those who practice opera and of those who only criticise it will appear side by side, and detailed articles on individual operas and composers will supplement news of British and foreign productions of operas ancient and modern. Letters or articles from readers will be welcome, and we shall try in every number to describe one or another of the great operatic figures of the day, be it singer, conductor, or producer" (1.1). That there were even more ambitious hopes for *Opera* became clear when upon Harold Rosenthal's succession to the editorship in 1953 Lord Harewood stated: "*Opera* came into being because we felt there was a need for a magazine in which we could set forward certain principles. . . . We believed that opera should be sung in English (with certain exceptions, festival performances and the like), and that an English school of opera should be developed by encouraging native composers, librettists and singers to devote their time and efforts to opera" (3.7).

Opera has made its mark as an important and distinguished publication in the field of opera. It has amply proven its devotion to the coverage of current activities of the international scene as well as Great Britain, sometimes covering world premieres of major operas with separate articles by two or even three writers. It has included, in addition, reviews and essays on specific operas, matters of general operatic interest, plus studies of singers past and present, and well-written reviews of books on opera and recordings. Reviews range from 500 to 1,500 words while feature articles, usually one or two per issue, are at least twice that size. Reviewer Patrick J. Smith has remarked:

> the level of writing, both in the articles and in the reviews, is amazingly high. In the early years, Lord Harewood provided a number of reviews, and his stable of writers included Harold Rosenthal, Andrew Porter, Desmond Shaw-Taylor, William Mann, Donald Mitchell, Eric Walter White, Martin Cooper, Winton Dean, Hans Keller, Erwin Stein, Lincoln Kirstein, and, in one review of *Marriage of Figaro,* Benjamin Britten . . . and many of the reviews were in the very capable hands of Cecil Smith and James Hinton.[1]

In the determination to incorporate the perspective of the contemporary British composer, *Opera* included, in an entire issue devoted to Giuseppe Verdi (v. 2), a symposium consisting of Ralph Vaughan Williams, Arthur Bliss, Benjamin Britten, and Lennox Berkeley, opera composers all. It goes practically without saying that major attention was lavished on new works by British composers in particular, practically an entire issue (4.8) was given over to Britten's coronation opera, *Gloriana*.

Over the years, *Opera* has explored topics which lend themselves well to the symposium format. The general topic of v. 3.3 was music criticism in Great Britain and included contributions from Britten, Kenneth Clark, Winton Dean, Erwin Stein, and the French critic and musicologist Fred Goldbeck. Years later, *Opera* would explore in depth the subject of opera libretti in translation with articles by leading translators, which would cover the course of several consecutive issues.

A typical issue of the 1950s covered, in addition to the in-depth topics described earlier, news about current or former opera stars, a feature entitled "Opera Diary," which contained reviews of the major British houses' recent efforts, and "News," which contained reviews of the activities of the major foreign houses, including the United States. Beginning in the 1960s, matters of scheduling and forthcoming events in both Great Britain and throughout the operatic world were afforded greater prominence in a "Coming Events" section, distinctive by its printing on tinted paper and insertion into the center of the issue. Most of the advertising supplements this function by promoting upcoming opera performances. Contributors continued to be chosen with an eye to quality, with such names as E. M. Forster, Arnold Haskell, Brigid Brophy, Victor Gollancz, Neville Cardus, Pierre Boulez, and Rolf Liebermann as examples. Contributions from areas of the operatic art other than singing specifically would also include the names of Franco Zeffirelli, Peter Hall, and Dennis Arundell (producers),

John Pritchard and Charles Mackerras (conductors), or Hans Werner Henze (composer). These have provided a welcome and substantive addition.

The physical format of *Opera* has varied little since the first issues, except to increase in numbers of pages. Published twelve times per year, its relatively small size (5½" by 8½") and small but attractive type face serve to announce its serious, scholarly, and self-effacing manner with no particular emphasis on the glamorous element of opera. Within this framework *Opera* traditionally devoted part of its coverage to the events of major operatic summer festivals of the world. To relieve the strain of this burgeoning enterprise, a separate "Festival Issue" began in 1960, at first containing eighty pages instead of the sixty-five to seventy-five of standard issues, and covering seventeen different operatic festivals, with a special emphasis on Glyndebourne. Today the festival issue has grown proportionately, with recent issues at well over one hundred pages. *Opera* has also seen fit to include a thorough index to the contents of each volume, from the very first. Thus one may access its contents via the principal "General Index" or the three component indices (for contributors, operas, or artists), which also include indication of any photographs printed.

Notes

1. Patrick J. Smith, "Opera: Reprint of the First Six Years of Opera Magazine (1950–1955) in Five Volumes." *High Fidelity/Musical America* 30 (September 1980): 16–17.

Information Sources

BIBLIOGRAPHY

Katz, Bill, and Linda Sternberg Katz. *Magazines for Libraries,* 5th ed. New York: R. R. Bowker, 1986.

Marconi, Joseph V. *Indexed Periodicals.* Ann Arbor, Mich.: Pierian Press, 1976.

Rosenthal, Harold. *My Mad World of Opera.* New York: Holmes & Meier, 1982.

Sjoerdsma, Richard Dale. "Opera."[Review of the DaCapo Press reprint of the first six volumes]. *National Association of Teachers of Singing* 37 (May 1981): 41–42.

Smith, Patrick J. "Opera: Reprint of the First Six Years of Opera Magazine (1950–1955) in Five Volumes." *High Fidelity/Musical America* 30 (September 1980): 16–17.

INDEXES

Internal: each volume indexed.

External: Music Index, 1950– . British Humanities Index, 1962– . RILM, 1967– . Humanities Index, 1974– . Arts and Humanities Citation Index, 1979– . *Opera* ("Index" vol. 1–).

REPRINT EDITIONS

Paper: DaCapo, vs. 1–6.

Microform: UMI.

LOCATION SOURCES

Widely available.

Publication History

TITLE AND TITLE CHANGES

Opera.

VOLUME AND ISSUE DATA
 Volumes 1–   , 1950–   .
FREQUENCY OF PUBLICATION
 Monthly, plus festival issue and index.
PUBLISHER
 Opera, DSB.
PLACE OF PUBLICATION
 Wickford, Essex, England.
EDITORS
 The Earl of Harewood, 1950–53. Harold Rosenthal, OBE, 1953–85. Rodney
 Milnes, 1986–   .

David Knapp

OPERA NEWS

In 1935 the redoubtable Eleanor Robson Belmont founded the Metropolitan
Opera Guild. Eager to publicize the guild's work, officials launched its *Bulletin*
in May 1936. A one-page affair, it was almost immediately renamed *Opera
News*, and by this title the magazine remains known today. Its coverage was
divided between news of the Met and news of the guild. Belmont soon appointed
Mary Ellis Peltz as editor, a position she would retain with great success for the
next twenty years, and *Opera News* was firmly established. Upon the occasion
of the tenth anniversary of *Opera News*, Peltz described the genesis of the
magazine and made what was in fact the first public record of the magazine's
goals and objectives:

> What is *Opera News?* . . . Is it a bulletin of Metropolitan Opera Guild
> activities? Is it a house organ of the Metropolitan Opera Association? Is
> it an opera magazine? Is it a listeners' guide for the radio audience which
> listens to the Saturday afternoon broadcasts? Frankly speaking, *Opera News*
> attempts to be all of these things. . . . As the Opera Guild expanded to
> include groups in Philadelphia and San Francisco, it became advisable to
> give space to the operatic affairs in the country at large. . . . Meanwhile,
> *Opera News* was expanding to meet new needs. In its second season,
> 1937–38, it was increased to sixteen pages, in a bright blue cover. Volume
> 3 . . . offered a total of twenty pages with a new feature, "The Opera
> Shelf," a series on opera scores and manuscripts. Volume 4 included
> several new departments: "This Week in Operatic History," "Arias on
> the Air," and an operatic quiz, entitled "Answer me That" with increased
> space devoted to the broadcasts. Volume 5 was professionally designed,
> increasing the contents to thirty-two pages, initiating "This Week and
> Next," "Names, Dates, and Places," and the "Opera of the Week,"
> section, and increasing the size and number of pictures. In 1941–42 we
> started the "Personality of the Week" feature, which ran for two years

and was eventually published in book form. Herbert F. Peyser started his popular series, "For Deeper Enjoyment" of the broadcast in volume 7, while the following year we introduced the broadcast program as a center spread, surrounded by pictures of the artists in costume. Meanwhile, the Metropolitan's sixtieth season (1943–44) was celebrated by a series of six articles on "Jubilee Memories" by outstanding personalities. (8.1:4–8.9:5)

Under Peltz's editorship, *Opera News* was published weekly during the so-called opera season and biweekly during October, November, and April. Issues contained, in addition to the aforementioned topics, occasional essays ("Past Glories of Opera in New Orleans" in several installments—10.3:10–10.4:10), special attention to new Met productions or the very occasional new opera ("Backstage with 'Peter Grimes'"—12.21:18) and news about opera performances elsewhere in the country or abroad. In addition, special attention was paid to the activities of the Guild Chapters throughout the United States. Reviews are generally under 500 words in length though major new productions can merit 1,000 or more and feature articles, four to six per issue, exceed 3,000 words.

In 1947 (v. 11) began an "Annual Survey of Opera Performances" which summarized the wide range of professional, semiprofessional, and amateur opera activities in this country, a forerunner of the extensive work undertaken later by the Central Opera Service. Opera in college and university opera departments was also occasionally described, with an eye to world premieres and productions of unusual repertory such as would not likely be undertaken by the Met. Some book and recording reviews appeared, too. Discography for the Saturday broadcast opera, including reviews of complete operas on record as well as individual arias, was a constant feature of these early years of *Opera News*. Among the notable contributors during Peltz's editorship were John Erskine, Olga Samaroff Stokowski, Walter Damrosch, William Lyon Phelps, Samuel Chotzinoff, Sir Thomas Beecham, Bruno Walter, and others.

Frank Merkling, assistant editor for two years, assumed the editorship in 1957. Three years later (v. 24), he increased the size from 6¾" by 9¾" to 8½" by 11", and *Opera News* became a monthly. Increased advertising revenues (from a variety of musical and nonmusical enterprises) and the advent of new printing methods allowed the introduction of color photos within the magazine as well as the cover. Writers and musicians of a high caliber such as Virgil Thomson, Paul Henry Lang, Georg Solti, Sacheverell Sitwell, André Maurois, Jacques Barzun, Vincent Sheehan, John Culshaw, and Martin Mayer were featured.

With v. 39 (1974–75) Robert Jacobson became editor. In response to a 1973 survey of readers that revealed that the mean age of the *Opera News* subscribership was fifty-two, Jacobson sought to perk up what was considered a very conservative publication and to give the magazine a youthful accent. Another nagging problem was the relationship between *Opera News* and the Met. While not truly a house organ, the periodical was, in fact, controlled and even censored by the Met, particularly when the material dealt with Met stars and productions.

Jacobson eventually found a middle ground with much more distant yet intact ties to the Met, a middle ground retained by Jacobson's successors, Patrick O'Connor and Patrick J. Smith.

Today's *Opera News* surely fulfills the same goals envisioned by Eleanor Belmont and developed so well by editors Peltz and Merkling. Published monthly May through November and biweekly December through April (seventeen issues per year), the contents reflect appropriately both the international opera scene and the activities and performance schedules of the Met. Reviews of opera performances from around the world continue to be featured while Met performances are reviewed without any hint of overt censorship. Issues run from fifty-five to sixty-five pages and include short essays or longer articles on a variety of topics by such writers as Gary Schmidgall, William Ashbrook, George Marek, Irving Kolodin, and of course Robert Jacobson. News about the guild is still appropriately included, and the Met is still well represented in interviews with star singers, conductors, artistic advisors, and the entire gamut of production personnel. The annual "U.S. Opera Survey" by Maria F. Rich continues to supply important survey statistics.

Information Sources

BIBLIOGRAPHY

Eaton, Quaintance. *The Miracle of the Met: An Informal History of the Metropolitan Opera, 1883–1967*. New York: Meredith Press, 1968.

Farber, Evan Ira. *Classified List of Periodicals for the College Library*. 5th ed. Westwood, Mass.: F. W. Faxon, 1972.

Katz, Bill, and Linda Sternberg Katz. *Magazines for Libraries*. 5th ed. New York: R. R. Bowker, 1986.

Rubin, Stephen E. *The New Met in Profile*. New York: Macmillan, 1974.

Schonberg, Harold C. *Facing the Music*. New York: Summit Books, 1981.

INDEXES

External: Music Index, 1949– . Readers' Guide to Periodical Literature, 1961– . Music Article Guide, 1965– . RILM, 1967– . Arts and Humanities Citation Index, 1976– . Humanities Index, 1982– .

Opera News ("General Index," Vol. 25–37); *All-time Index to Opera News* (1936–1981); New York, Wayner Publications, n.d.

REPRINT EDITION

Microform: UMI. Bell and Howell.

LOCATION SOURCES

Widely available.

Publication History

TITLE AND TITLE CHANGES

Bulletin of the Metropolitan Opera Guild, 1936 (1.1). *Opera News*, 1936 (1.2)– .

VOLUME AND ISSUE DATA

Volumes 1– , 1936– .

FREQUENCY OF PUBLICATION

Weekly during the season, then biweekly, 1936–1959. Biweekly during the season, then monthly (17/year), 1960–   .

PUBLISHER

Metropolitan Opera Guild.

PLACE OF PUBLICATION

1865 Broadway, New York, NY 10023.

EDITORS

Mrs. John Dewitt (Mary Ellis) Peltz, 1936–56. Frank Merkling, 1957–73. Robert Jacobson, Editor-in-Chief, 1974–87. Patrick O'Connor, 1988–89. Patrick J. Smith, 1989–   . Jane Poole, managing editor, October, 1983–   .

David Knapp

OPERNWELT

The pervasive allure of opera—its aura of glamour, tradition of spectacle, and emphasis on performer-as-personality—are inevitably reflected in the medium of the specialized opera magazine. Unlike many learned journals, the opera magazine must not only support the needs of the opera professional, but also consider the interests of die-hard opera aficionados. If occasional attention can also be given to the concerns of opera historians and musicologists, then an additional service has been rendered. For the German-speaking countries of the world the chief source of opera-as-current-event is *Opernwelt,* with its international scope and special focus on the activities of West Germany, Austria, and Switzerland. Published originally in thirteen issues per year, it switched to twelve per year in 1980, with a combined August/September issue and yearbook. Relying on a basic format which has varied but little since the first issue in October 1960, *Opernwelt* has maintained a successful and admirable consistency of presentation within a carefully prescribed scope—an initial, additional attention to dance was short-lived. With unflagging attention to high quality photography, the highly attractive, well-organized, and dependably informative *Opernwelt* has commanded a devoted following throughout its years of publication.

Each issue is from sixty to seventy-five pages in length—earlier issues were less ambitious—and features current events coverage, biographical and related essays, criticism, and reviews. Current events coverage chronicles the activities of selected leading singers and conductors, including dates and locations of forthcoming performances—a representative issue touched upon fourteen singers of world-class importance. Upcoming festivals, premieres of new operas, and new productions are announced. Other timely information includes schedules of performances at the leading opera theatres in West Germany and abroad (cast lists are supplied for the larger houses), notices of forthcoming competitions, major personnel appointments, or brief newsworthy feature stories.

Biographical essays, with a strong emphasis on person-as-personality, focus on current opera singers, conductors, directors, scenic designers, and other personnel, in short articles or interviews. A typical issue may contain a one-page feature about a leading stage director, biographical sketches of three or four selected leading opera singers, and an interview with a leading opera figure, or perhaps a small piece composed of several brief interviews with singers. Copious studio portraits or informal poses are included. In addition, an extended biographical essay on an historically important singer from the past is sometimes included. Related essays are occasionally to be seen, such as a series on prominent opera houses of the world, with a different theatre featured in each issue. Most of these articles are two to three pages long and rarely over five, though lengthier pieces are sometimes serialized over several installments. Most are by staff reporters and editorial assistants.

Informative reviews of current operatic performances, primarily but by no means exclusively in Europe, are standard fare. Great attention is paid to the activities of the large number of opera theatres great and small in West Germany. Lengthier articles are frequently afforded new productions in the major houses as well as new operas by leading composers. Important revivals are likewise not neglected.

Two or three book reviews appear per issue on aspects of the operatic art or singing in general. Surprisingly, recordings reviews often include the performances of leading instrumental soloists, sometimes over and above the usual vocal and operatic performances one would rather expect. Recordings, however, are usually limited to only a half-dozen or so titles in any event.

The yearbook (twelfth issue) is entitled simply *Oper* and is included in the price of the annual subscription. Originally oblong in format, and then increased to 8½″ by 9½″, it was further enlarged in 1979 to the identical size (9½″ by 12″) of *Opernwelt*. The modest quantity of advertising is largely given over to the promotion of various luxury items, particularly food and beauty aids. Frequently running to well over 100 pages, *Oper* evinces the same general goals as *Opernwelt* only in an expanded format, without the need for schedules of current performances and the like. Of chief importance are analyses of the events of the year in opera including coverage of the major opera festivals and additional reviews of new books and recordings. Of considerable historical interest is the documentation of the past season, theatre by theatre, for all the houses of West Germany, Austria, and Switzerland, including lists of all works performed (separate lists for premieres) and the major artists and guest personnel employed at each theatre. The final portion of the yearbook consists of a listing of the full official title and address of each opera house for the above-mentioned countries.

Information Sources

INDEXES

External: Bibliographie des Musikschrifttums, 1960–64, 1970. Der Zeitschriftendienst Musik, 1965– . Music Article Guide, 1965– . Music Index, 1967– .

LOCATION SOURCES
    Widely available.

Publication History

TITLE AND TITLE CHANGES
    Opernwelt.
VOLUME AND ISSUE DATA
    Volumes 1– , 1960– .
FREQUENCY OF PUBLICATION
    Monthly; August and September issues are combined. Price of annual subscription
    includes the yearbook *Oper: Jahrbuch der Zeitschrift "Opernwelt."*
PUBLISHER
    Orell Fuessli & Friedrich Verlag.
PLACE OF PUBLICATION
    Dietzingerstrasse 3, CH–8036 Zurich, Switzerland.
EDITORS
    Hans Otto Spingel, 1960–68. Imre Fabian, 1972– .

David Knapp

**ORGAAN DER FEDERATIE VAN NEDERLANDSCHE TOONKUNSTE-
NAARS-VEREENIGINGEN.** See CAECILIA (1844–1944)

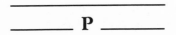

P

PERCUSSIVE NOTES/THE PERCUSSIONIST

Percussive Notes is a periodical primarily devoted to information of interest to percussionists. It began in 1962 as the private project of the first editor, James L. Moore of Columbus, Ohio, and was at first written and published solely by him. *Percussive Notes* started as an unaffiliated publication which appeared four times "during the school year." The first seven volumes were printed in a simple 8½" by 11" mimeograph style; the print was crude and the illustrations were hand-drawn stick figures and line drawings. It became an "official publication of the Percussive Arts Society" (P.A.S.) in 1967 (v. 6) and was simultaneously reduced to three issues per year. The periodical took on a more professional, printed format with v. 8 and has since then grown in terms of the number of pages, the use of color ads, and the frequency of publication—six issues per year since 1980, v. 18.

The development of *Percussive Notes* was paralleled, more or less, by a second quarterly publication: *The Percussionist*. First appearing in 1963 as the "Official publication of P.A.S.," *The Percussionist* featured, then as now, a 5½" by 8½" format. P.A.S. underwrote both journals separately from 1967 through 1980. A change in the editorship of *Percussive Notes*, from Moore to Michael Combs, occurred with 18.3 (1980), and *The Percussionist* was retitled *Percussive Notes: Research Edition, The Percussionist*. This was a merging of sorts of the two magazines, but *Percussive Notes* retained separate volume numbers until 1983 (21.4), when Robert Schietroma succeeded Combs as editor of *Percussive Notes* and Stuart Smith became editor of *The Percussionist*. Both publications began to appear under the same volume number with v. 22 (Fall 1983). The *Percussive Notes* issues of that volume consist of ns. 1, 2, 4, and 5 and *Research Edition, The Percussionist* issues appear as ns. 3 and 6. In v. 24, for instance, ns. 3 and 6 were combined for a special edition of 184 pages devoted solely to an historic reprint of a collection of catalogues for the J. C. Deagun company, dating from the turn of the century. In 1985 the *Research Edition* again changed editors, this time to Jean Charles François. Charles Lambert became executive editor of *Percussive Notes* in 1986 (25.1), except for v. 25.6, the PASIC '87 preview issue edited by Thomas Siwe and David Via (both designated executive editors). A new format for *Percussive Notes* was announced with 25.6 (9 September 1987) (retrospectively, since it describes the published format of v. 25). With this new format, ns. 1, 2, 4, and 5 are designated *Percussive Notes*; n. 3 is *Percussive Notes Research Edition*, and n. 6 is now titled *Percussive Notes PASIC Preview*. The pagination is not continuous and only the *Research Edition* is printed on 5½" by 8½" paper.

The Percussionist always maintained the more scholarly approach of the two publications. Its articles are primarily concerned with items of pedagogical and technical interest, for example, acoustics, notation, the historical use of percussion, analysis, and performance guides to specific samples of the percussion repertoire. V. 17.2, for example, offered articles solely on timpani: performance techniques in Baroque music, a treatise on a method dated 1845, contemporary techniques, the Viennese Timpani and Percussion School, and so on. The authors of both articles and reviews are predominantly educators and performers in the United States. The average issue of *The Percussionist* runs fifty to a hundred pages, and the pagination has varied erratically between separate numbering for each issue and continuous pagination within a volume. No advertising appears on its pages.

Percussive Notes, on the other hand, is a magazine with an informal, newsy format and a single editor. It features personal interviews, new events, reviews, coverage of the yearly P.A.S. convention, programs, and many articles of a "how-to-build-equipment" or "this-is-how-I-approach-this-problem" nature. The latter issues especially are filled with advertisements of percussion equipment firms and endorsements from popular artists. *Percussive Notes* currently retains twenty or more people assigned to edit the various aspects of each issue, for example, "Chapter News," "Industry News," "Programs," "Reviews," "Drum Set Forum," and "Percussion on the March." The reviews in more recent issues are brief (150–300 words) and cover published music, records, tapes, and texts. Authors, like those in *The Percussionist*, are primarily American teachers and performers. *Notes* has consistently held to a practice of separate pagination for each issue. The earliest issues were only two or three pages in length; the current issues run consistently to ninety pages or more.

Information Sources

BIBLIOGRAPHY
Sewrey, J. "The Percussive Arts Society." *School Musician* 35 (1963): 30.
INDEXES
          External: Music Index, 1963– . Music Article Guide, 1966– . RILM, 1967– .

REPRINT EDITIONS
Microform: *Percussionist*. UMI.
LOCATION SOURCES
Widely available.

Publication History

TITLE AND TITLE CHANGES
The Percussionist, 1963–80. *Percussive Notes: Research Edition, The Percussionist*, 1980–82. *Percussive Notes, Research Edition*, 1983–   . *Percussive Notes*, 1962–   .
VOLUME AND ISSUE DATA
The Percussionist: Volumes 1–(24), 1963–(85). From 1980, published as ns. 3 and 6 of *Percussive Notes*. *Percussive Notes*: Volumes 1–   , 1962–   .
FREQUENCY OF PUBLICATION
The Percussionist, Quarterly, 1963–1977. 3/year, 1977–81. Semiannual 1982–85. Annual, 1986–   . *Percussive Notes*, Quarterly, 1962–66. 3/year, 1967–1979. Bimonthly (with three issues/year constituting the legacy of *The Percussionist*), 1980–   .
PUBLISHERS
The Percussionist: Percussive Arts Society. *Percussive Notes*: James L. Moore, 1962–66. Percussive Arts Society, 1967–   .
PLACES OF PUBLICATION
The Percussionist: Terre Haute, Indiana, 1963–80. Knoxville, Tennessee, 1980–83 (18.3–21.3). Traverse City, Michigan, 1983–   (21.4–   ). *Percussive Notes*: Columbus, Ohio, 1963–80 (vs. 1–18.2); Knoxville, Tennessee, 1980–83 (18.3–21.3). Traverse City, Michigan, 1983–   (21.4–   ).
EDITORS
The Percussionist: Neal Fluegel, 1963–80. Michael F. Combs, 1980–83. Stuart Smith, 1983–84. Jean Charles François, 1985. *Percussive Notes*: James L. Moore, 1962–80. Michael F. Combs, 1980–83. Robert Shietroma, 1983–87. Charles Lambert, 1987–   .

Paul B. Hunt

PERSPECTIVES OF NEW MUSIC

Perspectives of New Music was founded with sponsorship from the Fromm Music Foundation in 1962. Among the individuals most active in the founding were Paul Fromm, Arthur Berger, and Benjamin Boretz. Milton Babbitt, Aaron Copland, and Erich Leinsdorf (then director of the Berkshire Music Center) were also involved in two projects that helped spawn the new journal: the Princeton Seminars in Advanced Musical Studies and the Fromm Fellowship Players at Tanglewood. In recent years financial support has been provided by Princeton University and the University of Washington.

The stated purposes of the new journal were ''to meet the widely recognized need for an American journal devoted to the serious consideration of contem porary music," to open "avenues of communication between composers and interested performers and listeners" (1.1:1), and "to probe as deeply as possible into fundamental issues that by their nature must be treated concretely and analytically with sophisticated methods, and that require investigation from many different sides" (1.1:4).

The articles are not devoted exclusively to contemporary music or even contemporary music theory, although that is of course the dominating theme. In some articles the attempt to explore the relations between contemporary music and tradition has resulted in a focus largely on the tradition itself. Books reviewed have also represented such traditional disciplines of music theory as harmony, form, and modal and tonal counterpoint.

Because of the technical nature of many articles, *Perspectives of New Music* has long had a reputation for being particularly difficult reading, or of having a particularly Princetonian manner of verbal expression. The trend of *Perspectives* away from the hard-core analytical, set-theory articles of the 1960s and 1970s to the art, graphics, and poetry of recent years is one of the most striking phenomena in American scholarly journalism. If there was a period during which this journal ran relatively parallel to certain aspects, at least, of the *Journal of Music Theory* (q.v.), there is little resemblance between the two at the present time. For many years it was one of the two serious journals in the field of music theory; now that field is more crowded, although not overly so, and while *Perspectives* has from its inception held a distinguished and unique position, it has now struck out on a path that is even more singular. The future direction of the journal in this respect is difficult to predict, but one trusts that it will continue to enlighten, inform, and challenge its readers in the years to come.

Many prominent individuals have contributed to *Perspectives of New Music*. Some of the most recurrent names are: Milton Babbitt, Elaine Barkin, Arthur Berger, Benjamin Boretz, Edward T. Cone, David Lewin, John Rahn, J. K. Randall, Claudio Spies, Peter Westergaard, and Charles Wuorinen. Among others who have contributed less frequently one encounters many of the best-known contemporary composers: Pierre Boulez, Elliott Carter, Luigi Dallapiccola, Ross Lee Finney, Lukas Foss, Ernst Krenek, Donald Martino, George Perle, Henri Pousseur, George Rochberg, Gunther Schuller, and Roger Sessions, among others. Many younger scholars and composers have also been represented, this being a goal of editorial policy from the beginning.

The format of early issues typically included about six articles averaging around fifteen pages in length, in addition to other features. The most regular of the latter was called "Colloquy and Review," and it comprised several items in each issue, including such fairly regular subcategories as "Communications," "Books and Articles," and "Reports" (for example, from music festivals). In v. 2 another feature appeared between the articles and the "Colloquy and Review," called "Some Younger American Composers." This was continued in several subsequent volumes (3.2, 6.1, 7.1, 7.2, 8.1, and 10.1) and then disappeared. This is typical of the way in which the journal's format has varied over the years; with v. 12 the "Colloquy and Review" disappeared, only to reappear in v. 22 (as just "Colloquy"), along with sections headed "Events" and "Books"; at the end there are "Editorial Notes," "Correspondence," "Personae," "Errata," "Acknowledgements," and, in recent volumes, a cassette. V. 23.1 maintains the same format for the end materials, but the "Events," "Books," and "Colloquy" sections are not to be found; there are, however, eighteen articles, compositions, sections of poetry or other texts, and so on, including a Varése Forum (three articles), and numerous graphics.

One of the most interesting features of *Perspectives of New Music*, and part of the reason that it is so hard to generalize about its format, is that many issues (including some of the double issues) have been devoted to a special topic, generally a major composer, and the format has been adjusted, appropriately, so as to serve this purpose best. The first of these special themes was the Igor Stravinsky memorial double issue, 9.2 and 10.1 (1971). Six portions of vs. 11 through 14 were designated "Toward the Schoenberg Centenary." Issues 14.2 and 15.1 (1976) constitute another special double issue, a "Critical Celebration of Milton Babbitt at 60." Vs. 18 (1979–80) and 19 (1980–81) were also double issues, in honor of Kenneth Gaburo and Aaron Copland at eighty, respectively. Shorter dedications have also appeared, for example, "In Memoriam: Paul Hindemith" (2.2) and "In Memoriam: Stefan Wolpe" (11.1).

Another notable feature that has created irregularities in the format of *Perspectives of New Music* is the "Forum." In vs. 3 through 9 a series of these appeared with irregularly recurring subtitles: "Talking About Music," "Notation," and "Computer Research," later "Electronic Music and Computer Research." This type of feature has not been continued consistently, however.

The first volume of the journal is designated Fall 1962, and it has generally appeared twice yearly—a Fall-Winter issue and a Spring-Summer issue—with frequent double issues, including several recent volumes. Beginning with v. 22 (1983–84) a cassette tape was included as part of the publication.

Perspectives of New Music is a paperbound serial, about 6″ by 9″ in size. The written text is typeset; musical examples and charts include those especially set for the journal, photocopies in the various styles of printed sources, and photocopies of manuscript. All the articles are in English, but the intended readership is international in scope. The trend in the past decade has been toward greater and greater size, with an average length of some 260 pages, whereas the earlier issues ran closer to 175 pages. Double issues are literally that: v. 22 (1983–84) weighs in at 659 pages, plus cassette.

An index first appeared in v. 2, for vs. 1–2, organized in two sections: an alphabetical listing by contributors, and one by names and works mentioned. This practice was continued with every even-numbered volume through v. 12, and thereafter with individual volumes through v. 15. A cumulative, detailed author and subject index to the first twenty volumes was prepared by Ann P. Basart. Numerous advertisements are to be found at the end of later issues of *Perspectives of New Music*. These are mainly for publishers of music, the pub

lished works of individual composers, recordings, and other journals and musical
or scholarly societies.

Information Sources

BIBLIOGRAPHY
Kerman, Joseph. *Contemplating Music: Challenges to Musicology.* Cambridge, Mass.:
     Harvard University Press, 1985.
INDEXES
     Internal: volumes indexed biennially, vs. 1–12; each volume indexed, vs. 13–   .
     External: Music Index, 1962–   . Music Article Guide, 1965–   . RILM, 1967–   .
     Bibliographie des Musikschrifttums, 1969–   . Arts and Humanities Citation In-
     dex, 1976–   .
     Basart, Ann P. *Perspectives of New Music: An Index, 1962–1982.* Berkeley,
     Calif.: Fallen Leaf Press, 1984.
REPRINT EDITIONS
     Microfilm: UMI, 1972–   .
LOCATION SOURCES
     Widely available.

Publication History

TITLE AND TITLE CHANGES
     Perspectives of New Music.
VOLUME AND ISSUE DATA
     Volumes 1–   , 1962–   .
FREQUENCY OF PUBLICATION
     Semiannual.
PUBLISHERS
     Princeton University Press, 1962–72. Perspectives of New Music, Inc., 1972–
     81. University of Washington Press, 1982–   .
PLACE OF PUBLICATION
     Princeton, New Jersey, 1962–81. Seattle, Washington, 1982–   .
EDITORS
     Arthur Berger, 1962–63. Arthur Berger and Benjamin Boretz, 1963. Benjamin
     Boretz, 1964–65. Benjamin Boretz and Edward T. Cone, 1965–69. Benjamin
     Boretz, 1969–82. Elaine Barkin as Co-Editor, 1972–82. Elaine Barkin and John
     Rahn, 1982–84. John Rahn, 1984–   .

Paul B. Mast

PIANO QUARTERLY, THE

For the legions of private piano teachers in this country, frequently self-
employed and occasionally working in conditions of greater or lesser isolation
from one another and lacking essential professional support, the specialized
journal is a valuable means of resource sharing and continuing education. For
many years such teachers had to rely on a few very general magazines, for

example, the venerable *Etude* (q.v.). In 1952 the Piano Teachers Information Service proposed to address the specific needs of private piano teachers with a new publication: *Piano Quarterly Newsletter*. Founded by Mary Vivian Lee, who served for a number of years as managing editor, the issues, thirty pages on the average by the fifth year of publication, had as a central focus a list of "Recommended Music" for piano solo. Selected by an "expert panel of judges" (who were never identified), the music was presented in graded categories ("Easy," "Intermediate," "Early Advanced," and "Advanced"). The foreword stated: "Our Board of six musicians have tried to include among the accepted works all those that demonstrated creative ability regardless of how small, or in what idiom: conservative, mildly venturesome, or fiercely so." The works chosen for review were generally shorter pieces of the "miniature" category. Some were by major or at least well-known composers such as Robert Starer, Federico Mompou, Francis Poulenc, or Herbert Elwell, for example, whose works generally represented the more advanced levels of difficulty; others were contributed by lesser-known figures whose offerings would be more appropriately described as "teaching pieces." An accompanying column, "Music Reviews," provided commentary on the music selected for presentation, publication information and an incipit. Written for many years by Hubert Doris, this column provided a brief analysis of each piece and an evaluation of its suitability for pedagogical needs. In the final issue of each year, a "Best of the Year" feature was included. A brief but thoughtful biographical sketch and studio portrait were provided for each of the ten or so composers who had contributed pieces of superior merit.

With n. 25 (Fall 1958) the *Newsletter* adopted the new title of *The Piano Quarterly* but otherwise retained the goals and standards previously articulated. The American musicologists William J. Mitchell and William S. Newman served jointly for a number of years as contributing editors, and they were eventually assisted by Irwin Freundlich, Luise Eitel, and Hubert Doris. Mitchell and Newman both contributed occasional articles on matters of history and interpretation. Newman also wrote, for a time, full-length book review articles that gave an unmistakable scholarly tone to the *Quarterly* in its early years. Other important features were compilations of new publications: "New Editions" of piano music, "Pedagogy Albums" and new music for piano ensemble; lists of new books on music plus publication information and occasionally a brief abstract; and lists of new piano recordings for the quarter.

By 1960, "Letters" to the editor began to be incorporated and a "Topics" section provided readers a forum for the sharing of concepts and problems. The "Music Reviews" columns of this period decried the lack of an abundance of excellent teaching material. Doris's description and criticism of even those pieces selected for inclusion frequently tended toward the acidulous. Nevertheless, n. 44 (1963) consisted entirely of the "best of the best" pieces from the past ten years.

With the sixteenth year (Fall 1967), the four-year editorship of Harold Schramm began. His input can be seen in the improved physical appearance of the *Quarterly* (the 8″ by 11″ size was slightly reduced) with its attractive paper stock and typeface. The format otherwise remained largely unchanged except that the authors' contributions were somewhat more ambitious than formerly. N. 68 (Summer 1969) includes two serial articles: "Some Nineteenth-Century Consequences of Beethoven's 'Hammerklavier' Sonata" (68:24) by Newman and a compendium of piano technical exercises with commentary entitled "A Rational Approach to Piano Technic," a regular feature by Martin Canin, based on his private study with Rosina Lhevinne, which later became "The Open Forum." The list of contributing editors was expanded to include Stanley Babin, Saul Dorfman, F. E. Kirby, and Peter Yates.

With n. 78 (Winter 1971–72) Hubert Doris concluded twenty years' service, and the selection and presentation of new teaching pieces, for so long a major thrust of the *Quarterly*, was temporarily suspended. The column was permanently reestablished by Margaret Tolson with the assistance of a number of others with n. 87. The music reviewed began to cover a broader range of difficulty than previously, and newly discovered works by older composers and new editions of standard pieces were also presented.

Martin Winkler became publisher—publication was now handled by Belwin-Mills—with n. 79 and at the same time the American pianist Robert Silverman became editor, replacing Schramm. Canin inaugurated a short-lived "Open Forum" for pianists' questions, which was later replaced by a regular essay feature entitled "Pianists' Problems" in which Canin would address a particular area of piano playing technique. By this time issues began to reach forty-eight pages and were published in a new, consistently attractive format. The *Quarterly* sought and accepted articles from a wider circle of authors than previously. Special topics were explored, taking up the entire issue—for example, the piano music of Schubert (n. 104), Mozart (n. 95), Busoni (n. 108), or group teaching (n. 62)—with articles by master pianists or noted musicologists. A regular feature, "Pianists' World," sought to put readers in greater touch with current events (appointments, and so on) of leading pianists, listings of forthcoming piano competitions and the like. Issues began to include occasionally a short piano composition in its entirety. The newly discovered, so-called "Images oubliées" by Claude Debussy, "Nightmusic II" by Donald Erb, and a recently unearthed piano sonata by Felix Mendelssohn were all given their first publications in the pages of the *Quarterly*.

With the 1980s the list of contributing editors continued to expand and now included Paul Badura-Skoda, Joseph Banowetz, Joseph Block, Dika Newlin, and Konrad Wolff, in addition to Lawrence Chaikin, Dorfman, Hinson, and Newman, in all an impressive array of esteemed pianists and music historians. Alfred R. Weil was appointed associate editor. Now some fifty-six pages in length, issues included interviews with master pianists and research essays, the latter frequently important and of serial length (for example, "The American

Beginning Piano Method'' which spanned nine consecutive issues), added additional depth to the *Quarterly*. Later issues were expanded, sometimes to sixty-four pages, undoubtedly supported by the subsidy of increased advertising revenues from publishers, instrument manufacturers, and educational institutions.

Currently, the six to eight feature articles in each issue continue to cover the areas of pedagogy (at all levels), scholarly analysis of piano literature and current biography, as well as book and recording reviews, current events, and the long-established reviews of new music. The growth of the journal in size and scope indicates an intention to appeal to a multitude of piano teachers of all levels, the advanced piano student, and the master pianist alike. The publication of correspondence to the editor likewise reveals an enthusiastic, loyal and international readership, now more than 13,000. *The Piano Quarterly* has made impressive strides from humble but vital beginnings. It stands in the forefront of current thought on the art of piano performance and teaching.

Information Sources

BIBLIOGRAPHY

Katz, Bill, and Linda Sternberg Katz. *Magazines for Libraries*. 5th ed. New York: R. R. Bowker, 1986.

Skaggs, Hazel Ghazarian. "Teachers' Organizations." In *Teaching Piano: A Reference Book for the Instructor,* edited by Denes Agay, p. 665. New York: Yorktown Music Press, 1983.

Zaimont, Judith Lang. "Twentieth-Century Music for the Developing Pianist: A Graded Annotated List." In *Teaching Piano: A Reference Book for the Instructor,* edited by Denes Agay, pp. 389–90. New York: Yorktown Music Press, 1983.

INDEXES

External: Music Index, 1961– . Music Article Guide, 1965– . RILM, 1973– . Arts and Humanities Citation Index, 1976– . *The Piano Quarterly* ("A Complete Listing of all Articles Published in the 32 Years of PQ's History; Indexes by Author, Title, and Category") available for $5.00 from the publisher.

REPRINT EDITIONS

Microform: UMI.

LOCATION SOURCES

Widely available.

Publication History

TITLE AND TITLE CHANGES

Piano Quarterly Newsletter, 1952–58. *The Piano Quarterly,* 1958– .

VOLUME AND ISSUE DATA

Volumes 1– , 1952– .

FREQUENCY OF PUBLICATION

Quarterly.

PUBLISHER

The Piano Quarterly, Inc.

PLACE OF PUBLICATION

Wilmington, Vermont.

EDITORS

Mary Vivian Lee, 1952–67. Harold Schramm, 1967–71. Robert Joseph Silverman, 1971–   .

David Knapp

PIANOFORTE, IL. See QUADERNI DELLA RASSEGNA MUSICALE

POPULAR MUSIC AND SOCIETY

While there have always been countless publications devoted to popular music and the rock phenomenon in particular, there have been few academic outlets for scholarship in this area; pop music was not considered worthy of serious academic attention.[1] When the *Journal of Popular Culture* (*JPC*) first appeared in 1967, it was alone in providing a forum for scholarly studies of popular culture. Soon, however, the *JPC* found itself unable to publish the increasing number of manuscripts on pop music that it was receiving. It was this situation that motivated the *JPC's* publisher, the Center for the Study of Popular Culture at Bowling Green State University, Ohio, to found a second journal in 1971: *Popular Music and Society* (*PMS*).

Edited since its inception by sociologist R. Serge Denisoff, *PMS* was conceived as an interdisciplinary journal covering all genres of popular music. Papers were sought from record company executives, musicians, and journalists, as well as academics. While *PMS* has become the premier journal for sociological studies of pop music, it has not been as successful in attracting papers from outside the social sciences. Only 8 percent of the authors published in the first eight years of *PMS* were from the industry, while 78 percent were from the scholarly community. Half of the latter were sociologists, and most of the remainder were from other social science disciplines (7.1:2).

Popular Music and Society has been more successful in meeting its goal of including a breadth of subject matter. While rock has been the most extensively explored, articles have also appeared on jazz, country, punk, semiclassical, rhythm and blues, and in fact, practically all but the more esoteric styles of pop music. Treatments have included audience studies, sociological themes (for example, music and feminism), and single artist studies.

Most authors have preferred a qualitative approach: literary criticism and historical analysis being the most popular methods, while others used content analysis, journalistic approaches, or submitted an interview or article on a single act. Only 15 percent of the authors have used a quantitative methodology.

A number of scholars have appeared repeatedly in the pages of *Popular Music and Society*. Most notable are Peter Hesbacher, who has researched the music industry, and sociologist George Lewis—both represented by over ten papers. Others who have appeared with some regularity include H. F. Mooney, who has extensively investigated trends in popular music, sociologist Richard Dixon, and, of course, editor R. Serge Denisoff himself.

Two special issues appeared in 1978–79. Country music was featured in v. 6.4 while reprints of articles from past issues on radio were collected in v. 6.2. The sociological orientation of *Popular Music and Society* is emphasized by two notable literature surveys: "The Sociology of Popular Music: A Selected and Annotated Bibliography" by George H. Lewis (7.1:57–68), and "The Sociology of Popular Music: A Review" by R. Serge Denisoff and John Bridges (9.1:51–62).

Book and record reviews appear in each issue. Both the number and length of the record reviews have been rather inconsistent over the years. Recently, music video reviews have been added. The few advertisements are primarily for other Bowling Green State University Popular Press publications.

Early in its existence, Denisoff stated that

> The journal has not established a clear identity, at times containing short *Crawdaddy* [q.v.]-type record reviews more suited for a *L. A. Free Press* audience along with highly technical and esoteric papers such as "Responding to Popular Music: Criteria of Classification and Choice Among English Teenagers" or . . . "Popular Music and Research Design: Methodological Alternatives." *Popular Music and Society* certainly is not a challenge to any of the trades, prozines or even many of the privately published fanzines.[2]

However, it is undeniable that *PMS* is a valuable forum for scholarly studies of pop music and that it has played a significant role in legitimizing such work in the academic world.

Published on a quarterly basis for its first four years, subsequent publication had been irregular. V. 5 (1977) consisted of only one issue, and its current frequency is closer to biannual, although the four numbers per volume is still maintained, along with an average length of seventy to eighty pages and a 6″ by 9″ format. The decreased and uneven publication frequency is attributable to a lack of submissions; unlike the situation attendant to the birth of *PMS*, many scholarly papers on pop music are now being published in the more traditional journals.

NOTES

1. A summary of early academic studies is provided in: R. Serge Denisoff, *Solid Gold: The Popular Record Industry* (New Brunswick, N.J.: Transaction Books, 1975), pp. 450–61.

2. Ibid., p. 460.

Information Sources

INDEXES

External: Music Index, 1971– . Popular Music Periodicals Index, 1973–76. Annual Index to Popular Music Record Reviews, 1972–77. RILM, 1978– . Arts

and Humanities Citation Index, 1977– . Book Review Index, 1980– . Index
to Book Reviews in the Humanities, 1983– .
REPRINT EDITIONS
Microform: UMI.
LOCATION SOURCES
Widely available.

Publication History

TITLE AND TITLE CHANGES
Popular Music and Society.
VOLUME AND ISSUE DATA
Volumes 1– , 1971– .
FREQUENCY OF PUBLICATION
Quarterly, 1971–74. Irregular, close to semiannual, 1975– .
PUBLISHERS
Department of Sociology, Bowling Green State University, 1971–82. Bowling
Green State University Popular Press, 1982– .
PLACE OF PUBLICATION
Bowling Green, Ohio.
EDITOR
R. Serge Denisoff, 1971– .

David D. Ginsburg

PROCEEDINGS OF THE ROYAL MUSICAL ASSOCIATION. See
ROYAL MUSICAL ASSOCIATION PROCEEDINGS

PSYCHOLOGY OF MUSIC

Music education and the psychology of music are two fields that share common
borders. Researchers in the psychology of music examine musical processes that
often bear on musical development and instruction. Music education researchers
examine musical processes that often relate to musical perception and cognition.
One journal that publishes empirical and philosophical research in both fields is
the British journal *Psychology of Music*. The journal's articles are "directed at
increasing scientific understanding of any psychological aspect of music, including listening, performing, creating, memorizing, analyzing, describing,
learning, teaching, applying, and social, developmental, and attitudinal factors"
(15.1: inside cover).

The journal's origins are found in the University of Reading Conferences on
Research in Music Education, which began in 1966 with the purpose of bringing
together British music education researchers semiannually to share research ideas
and results. At the October 1971 meeting, Desmond Sergeant proposed that a
new research journal be developed to encourage further research in the United

Kingdom in music education and the psychology of music, and he offered to be the journal's first editor. Those attending the Reading Conference agreed and formed the Society for Research in Psychology of Music and Music Education as an umbrella organization to publish the new journal and to plan future research meetings. The first issue of *Psychology of Music* was published fifteen months later in January 1973.

For the most part, the editorial staff of the journal is comprised of faculty from the music education and psychology departments of British universities. Contributors to the journal typically are college faculty from European and North American departments of music education and psychology. The articles in earlier issues are almost exclusively by British authors, but later issues attracted articles from an international group of contributors.

Each issue contains five or six articles of approximately 3,500 words. Other regular features include "Proceedings of the Society for Research in Psychology of Music and Music Education" (abstracts of papers presented), brief book reviews (usually on music education books published in Great Britain), and tables of contents for the *Journal of Research in Music Education* (q.v.) and the *Council for Research in Music Education* (q.v.).

Articles are written in a scholarly style, and each begins with an abstract. The topics of articles published in *Psychology of Music* can be grouped into four broad categories: (1) psychomusicology (for example, melodic perception, musical cognition), (2) aesthetics (musical preferences, attitudes toward music), (3) music education (instructional methods, curriculum development), and (4) musical abilities (musical development, musical aptitude). This fourth category is especially well represented, perhaps because of the influence of editor Rosemund Shuter-Dyson, a prominent scholar in this area. In keeping with the focus of the journal, many articles offer educational implications.

Special series of articles appearing in *Psychology of Music* include a four-part series by Anthony Kemp in 1981 and 1982, "The Personality Structure of the Musician" (9.1:3–14, 9.2:69–75, 10.1:48–58, 10.2:3–6), which examined personality traits of performers and composers, compared personalities of male and female musicians, and developed a comprehensive model of musicians' personality. A three-part series in 1983 and 1984 (11.2:86–96, 12.1:25–33, 12.2:75–82) on "Innovation in the Music Curriculum" by Robert Walker discussed new curriculum ideas from Canada and Great Britain, the Manhattanville Music Curriculum Project, and the use of experimental music in schools. Authors who have contributed notable articles on a single topic include Rudolf E. Radocy (studies on pitch judgment) and John Sloboda (the process of music reading).

In 1982 *Psychology of Music* published an extra issue devoted to the Proceedings of the Ninth International Seminar on Research in Music Education, which was held in London on 13–20 July 1982. The issue features brief articles by each of the seminar's speakers.

Two cumulative internal indexes of *Psychology of Music* have been published and were distributed to subscribers as separate publications. The index for vs.

1 through 5 (1973–77) is organized alphabetically by author, title, and subject. The index for vs. 1 through 10 (1973–82) follows the same format. Another useful index, "A Bibliography of Dissertations Relevant to Psychology of Music and Music Education Presented for Higher Degrees in the Universities of the United Kingdom up to the Year 1970," appeared in 1975 (3.1:41–46). An update of this bibliography was published in 1982 (10.2:32–38).

To some extent, *Psychology of Music* serves as a British counterpart to the older American journals *Council for Research in Music Education* and *Journal of Research in Music Education*. All three journals publish empirical philosophical articles on psychological processes in music with a special emphasis on music learning. Some articles in *Psychology of Music* focus on dimensions of psychomusicology outside the realm of music education, and in this respect *Psychology of Music* is similar to another American journal, *Music Perception* (q.v.), which began publication eleven years after *Psychology of Music* first appeared.

Psychology of Music has played a significant role in encouraging British research in music education and the psychology of music. Recent books on the psychology of music from Britain's John Sloboda, John Booth Davies, and Peter Howell, Ian Cross, and Robert West attest to this trend. The journal's articles are well written and usually interesting; knowledge of statistical techniques is necessary to understand some of them. Also of special interest are the numerous philosophical and theoretical articles, which are typically found less frequently in American music education research journals. The combination of music education, psychology of music, and aesthetics has been a successful mix for *Psychology of Music* and has earned the journal an international reputation.

Psychology of Music is published twice yearly, approximately in the spring and fall. Each issue contains about sixty pages. Consecutive page numbering within volumes did not begin until 1983 (v. 11). Prior to that, each issue began with page 1. From its inception in 1973 until 1984 (v. 12) the size of the journal was 5½″ by 8½″. The type size was very small and somewhat difficult to read. Beginning in 1985 (v. 13) the journal's size increased to 6″ by 9¼″, and a larger, more legible type size was adopted.

Information Sources

INDEXES
    Internal: vs.1–5; vs. 1–10.
    External: British Education Index, 1973– . Psychological Abstracts, 1976– .
    RILM, 1976– . Bibliographie des Musikschrifttums, 1976– .
LOCATION SOURCES
    Widely available.

Publication History

TITLE AND TITLE CHANGES
    Psychology of Music.
VOLUME AND ISSUE DATA
    Volumes 1– , 1973– .

FREQUENCY OF PUBLICATION
   Semiannual.
PUBLISHER
   Society for Research in Psychology of Music and Music Education.
PLACE OF PUBLICATION
   Eastbourne, Sussex, England.
EDITORS
   Desmond Sergeant, 1973–78. Rosamund Shuter-Dyson, 1979–85. John Sloboda,
   1986–   .

John K. Kratus

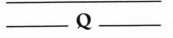

QUADERNI DELLA RASSEGNA MUSICALE (Formerly: LA RASSEGNA MUSICALE; IL PIANOFORTE: RIVISTA DI CULTURA MUSICALE)

These three journals comprise one of the most significant historical documents of Italian music in the twentieth century. Each journal represents a somewhat different initial motivation and direction; yet, their overall contribution to contemporary Italian thought on performance, scholarship, and aesthetics is truly without peer for much of the pre–World War II period. A major unifying feature of these journals is that they share the same principal editor and mentor, Guido Maggiorino Gatti.

The first of these, *Il pianoforte*, was begun in 1920 and ran for eight years on a monthly schedule. This periodical, in Gatti's words, had been "born essentially as a propaganda periodical for a piano factory, but little by little [it was] transformed to a high level of general discourse. It attracted well-known and respected scholars and critics, in addition to younger writers who subsequently pursued musicological studies." In fact, the journal became a significant voice in the 1920s for music criticism and research.

Il pianoforte was superseded in 1928 by *La rassegna musicale* (the most important of these three journals), which embodied a transformation of the goals of its predecessor. Gatti, who served as general editor for this as well, later wrote:

> With *La rassegna musicale* I did not intend to change direction, but to present with greater depth and efficiency the problems already posed but not addressed in *Il pianoforte* ... *La rassegna musicale* would not be a musicological journal in the technical sense the word implies (this task has been admirably served by the authoritative *Rivista musicale italiana* ...),

but rather it would be a music journal in the full and living sense, dedicating abundant space to contemporary music and to its problems, announcing and illustrating for the first time both works and composers. . . . In the revival of music of the past it would study the purely technical-philological aspects, putting into relief the true and accurate spirit and form of these works on an aesthetic level. And above all, it would initiate a discussion of ideas of criticism both of letters and of the figurative arts, which today arouses such particular interest within music. (*Quaderni* 1:5–6)

Probably one of the most significant aspects surrounding *La rassegna musicale* are the many commentaries on the interaction of music and politics. Political sensitivity had early been a point of argument in the journal (see for example Adriano Lualdi's "Concerning Musical Crisis" in 1.4:247–49), and increased with the events of World War II. Most of these discussions appeared in the "Notes and Commentary" section of each issue. Also of particular strength are the many discussions of music criticism. Full-length essays on this topic, for example, appeared by Alfredo Parente (6.3:197–218, 1933), Guido Pannain (6.1:1–15, 1933), Hans Mersmann (12.9/10:369–79, 1939), and Alfredo Casella (13.1:7–11, 1940), as well as by many others. Articles related to contemporary music—its composers, style, and aesthetics—flourished in nearly every issue. Other historical studies appear as well, although the major emphasis dwells on composers and music of Italian heritage. Despite Gatti's assertion, *La rassegna musicale* did become a rather musicological endeavor.

Each issue of *La rassegna musicale* consists of several regular sections, as well as articles on broad topics. Articles usually open each volume, and are frequently serialized, appearing over several issues within a single volume. These are followed by the regular departments of "Musical Life," "Reviews" (of both books and records), and "In Other Journals." This last is a report of articles that have appeared elsewhere, both foreign publications and domestic, and which have particular interest for the Italian reader. Finally, editorials and bulletins of various kinds are found under the heading "Notes and Information"—later "Notes and Commentary."

An excellent and extensive discussion of the history of *La rassegna musicale* can be found in the lengthy "Introduction" to an anthology of articles drawn from the journal and published in 1966 by Feltrinelli of Milan as *La rassegna musicale: antologia*. Luigi Pestalozza, who collected this material and edited the volume offered a massive (169-page) discourse on the history of the journal, with emphasis on its relationship to the sociological and political climate of Italian music in the twentieth century. Reprints of articles and editorials are gathered in the remaining 700 pages of this volume, which is conveniently indexed by composers and authors, and which contains a lengthy bibliography as well.

La rassegna musicale was published in thirty-two volumes from 1928–43 and 1947–62. During the last years of World War II and for a short time thereafter the journal ceased publication (1944–46). It appeared monthly for vs. 1–2 (1928–29), bimonthly in vs. 3–8 (1930–35), reverted again to a monthly format in vs. 9–16 (1936–43), and after v. 17 appeared on a quarterly basis. It ceased publication in 1962, to be superseded by the *Quaderni della rassegna musicale*. A separate cumulative index appeared in 1952: *Indice generale della annate 1928–1952*, edited by Riccardo Allorto. It includes alphabetical indexes by author, as well as indexes of reviews and general subjects.

The *Quaderni della rassegna musicale*, which appeared in five volumes from 1964–72 and was likewise under the direction of Gatti, was not a periodical in the strict sense at all. It appeared without a regular publishing schedule or price (which varied according to the length of the volume). In his introductory essay, Gatti expounded on the difficulties that had been imposed on music journals since World War II, and which included not only the initial financial, physical restraints, but also the subsequent proliferation of musicological journals. Of the nature of the *Quaderni*, he noted that it would:

> be published without any fixed date, but would appear three or four times each year. . . . Each *Quaderno* . . . would contain essays and notes, preferably on a unified theme (composers, movements and trends, time periods, etc.), in addition to reviews of books and music.

All volumes were published by Einaudi, and the articles are both longer and more scholarly. V. 1 appeared in 1964, dedicated to the works of Goffredo Petrassi. It included six essays, plus a bibliography and discography, as well as reviews of various kinds and a list of works received. V. 2 was delayed until 1965 and contained essays on the works of Luigi Dallapiccola, in a format similar to that of the first volume. Appearing in the same year, v. 3 addressed the state of Italian musicology in twelve essays devoted to various historical topics. Included was Guglielmo Barblan's notice of "The first Year of the Italian Musicological Society" (3:7–12). V. 4 appeared three years later, in 1968, under the general title of "Music and the Figurative Arts," while v. 5 (published with the editorial assistance of Giorgio Pestelli) appeared in 1972 with the title "Aspects of music of our day." Upon the death of Gatti in 1973, the *Quaderni* ceased publication.

All three journals share the same physical format: 7¾″ by 9¼″. The number of pages varies, although the later volumes generally fluctuate from 500–800 pages. Content varies widely over time though as a broad average, the journal contains fifteen to twenty-five articles, averaging fifteen pages in length. The scholarly level steadily improved, becoming nearly equal to major American and German musicology publications. Illustrations (occasionally lavish), such as line drawing, music examples, and black and white photograph plates are included. All text is in Italian, and the vast majority of authors are therefore Italian as well. Each volume is indexed at the end of the year.

Information Sources

INDEXES

External: *La rassegna musicale*: Music Index, 1950–63. Bibliographie des Musikschrifttums, 1954–62. *Quaderni della rassegna musicale*: Music Index, 1968–72. RILM, 1967–72. Bibliographie des Musikschrifttums, 1937, 1939, 1950–62, 1970–72.

REPRINT EDITION

Microform: *Il Pianoforte*. Schnase, 1921–27. *Rassegna Musicale*. Schnase, 1928–43.

LOCATION SOURCES

Widely available (with the exception of *Il pianoforte*).

Publication History

TITLE AND TITLE CHANGES

Il pianoforte: Rivista di cultura musicale, 1920–27. *La rassegna musicale*, 1928–62. *Quaderni della rassegna musicale*, 1964–72.

VOLUME AND ISSUE DATA

Il pianoforte: Rivista di cultura musicale: v. 1–8, 1920–27. *La rassegna musicale*: v. 1–32, 1928–1962. *Quaderni della rassegna musicale*: v. 1–5, 1964–72.

FREQUENCY OF PUBLICATION

Il pianoforte: Rivista di cultura musicale: Monthly. *La rassegna musicale*: Monthly, 1928–29; Bimonthly, 1930–35; Monthly, 1936–43; none issued, 1943–47; Quarterly, 1947–62. *Quaderni della rassegna musicale*: Irregular—5/9 years.

PUBLISHERS

Il Pianoforte: Rivista de cultura musicale. *La rassegna musicale*: Fratelli Buratti Editore, 1928–33. Guido Einaude Editore, 1934–35. Felice Le Monnier Editore, 1936–43. None published, 1943–47. Edizione della Bussola, 1947–48. Casa Editrice Valentino Bonpiani, 1949. Rassegna musicale, 1950–55. Guido Einaudi Editore, 1956–62. *Quaderni della rassegna musicale*: Einaude Editore, 1964–72.

PLACES OF PUBLICATION

Il Pianoforte: Rivista de cultura musicale. *La rassegna musicale*: Torino, 1928–36, 1956–62. Firenze, 1936–43. Rome, 1947–48, 1950–55. Milan, 1949. *Quaderni della rassegna musicale*: Torino, 1964–72.

EDITOR

Guido Maggiorino Gatti, 1920–73.

Dale E. Monson

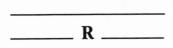

R

RASSEGNA MUSICALE, LA. See QUADERNI DELLA RASSEGNA MU-
SICALE

RECHERCHES SUR LA MUSIQUE FRANÇAISE CLASSIQUE

Recherches sur la musique française classique is a French periodical confined
to the study of French music during the reign of the Bourbon kings, 1589–1830.
But it would be fair to say that the majority of the articles are concerned with
music during the reign of Louis XIV, the so-called Golden Age of French history
(1661–c. 1715).

The goal of the journal is to render account of all historical, technical, and
aesthetic discoveries surrounding French classical music (1:5). Consequently,
Recherches includes a very wide range of articles, from the organ works of Jean
Titelouze to the music attending Charles X's coronation. In effect, *Recherches*
presents a stained-glass-window image of early French music, each article contributing a tiny amount of detail to the overall picture. The analogy holds especially true for this journal, as the articles tend to be quite arcane. Often an
obscure composer or unknown work is the topic of lengthy discussion. But for
the connoisseur of French seventeenth- and eighteenth-century music, *Recherches* is an invaluable resource.

The editors today, Marcelle Benoit and Norbert Dufourcq, founded the journal
in 1960. Dufourcq (b. 1904) has been the organist at the church of St. Merry
in Paris for over sixty years and, until 1975, taught music history and musicology
at the Paris Conservatory. He has also been editor of *L'Orgue, Orgue et liturgie,
Les grandes heures de l'orgue* as well as *Recherches*. A complete list of Dufourcq's voluminous writings on music appears in the fifteenth issue of *Re-

cherches (1975), dedicated to the editor on the occasion of his retirement from the conservatory. Marcelle Benoit (b. 1921) was a student under Dufourcq. She was editorial assistant to Dufourcq for the *Larousse de la musique* (1957) and has been a regular contributor to *Recherches*.

Recherches has been published annually since 1960 except for 1982. Each volume is approximately 240 pages long and contains from eight to ten modestly illustrated articles, some in English. The length of articles is by no means predictable; some are just a few pages long while others are extended over two or three volumes and total perhaps a hundred pages.

Much of the material in *Recherches* is documentary in nature. Benoit and Dufourcq as a team have unearthed a tremendous amount of information by foraging in old church, municipal, and other institutional records. As one example, they have been going through the Minutier Central for musical references. Such discoveries supply facts about a musician's life, what kind of instruments he or she owned and how many, or announce new musical events. The documentary and archival bias of the editors is clearly felt in many of the articles published. Roberte Machand's "Les Musiciens en France au temps de Jean Philippe Rameau d'après les acts du Secretariat de la maison du Roi" (11:7) devotes over a hundred pages to records taken from the royal household and concludes with a long list of all the musicians employed at the court. In another article, Ariane Ducrot provides a lengthy account of the productions staged by the royal music academy during the time of Louis XIV with information drawn chiefly from contemporary gazettes and correspondence (10:19).

Not all of the material is strictly documentary, and issues are frequently divided into two parts: articles, and reprints from archives. Biographies of musicians, analyses of their works, histories of instruments (especially organs) and cities, such as musical life outside Paris, can all be found. *Recherches* sometimes publishes parts of theses or doctoral dissertations. The names of Dufourcq's many students at the Paris Conservatory turn up frequently as contributors. The journal is as eclectic as it is detailed, with scholarly works for every taste; violinists, stage directors, balletomanes, church musicians, singers, aficionados of the opera, and more.

A regular feature of *Recherches* is the reviews at the end of each issue, written predominantly by Dufourcq. Dufourcq remarks on anything concerning seventeenth- and eighteenth-century French music: new books, music editions, records and performances, and so on. Musicologist James Anthony has on occasion supplemented this section with a checklist of research in progress on early French music (20:261).

For the most part the articles are well researched and written. Criticism of the journal has centered on the sparse attention generally paid to analysis and in-depth studies of the music itself. Analyses published are sometimes superficial and descriptive without providing insight into the style or historical placement of the work. Little effort is made to relate the articles to more general topics of music history. Facts are presented in an isolated fashion without attempting to define their significance. Some reviewers protest that articles deal with unknown composers and works too frequently.

For twenty years *Recherches sur la musique française classique* was supported by the Centre National de la Recherche Scientifique (CNRS), France's most prestigious source of grant funds. That funding was discontinued in 1980, a move protested in an open letter to the CNRS that was written and signed by numerous important American and British musicologists, including Albert Cohen, James Anthony, H. Wiley Hitchcock, and David Fuller. They asserted that *Recherches* is an important research and reference source for the study of French music and strongly defended the quality of its endeavors. The CNRS did not resume funding, but two years later the Centre National des Lettres (CNL) picked up the journal and ensured its continuation.

Recherches sur la musique française classique is a hardbound periodical 6⅜″ by 10″. For the last few years the cover has been peach color with red and black lettering. The central figure on the cover is an engraving of Apollo with his lyre seated on a pedestal and surrounded by musical instruments.

Information Sources

BIBLIOGRAPHY
Giazotto, Remo. "Recherches sur la musique française classique, volumes 8 and 9." *Nuova rivista musicale italiana* 3 (1969): 1195–99.
Käser, Theodor. "Recherches . . . vol. 11." *Musikforschung* 28 (1975): 221–22.
Kneif, Tibor. "L'historie de l'orgue français." *Neue Zeitschrift für Musik* 134 (1973): 752.
Morche, Gunther. "Recherches . . . vol. 10." *Musikforschung* 27 (1974): 114–15.
Thomson, J. T. "Recherches . . . vol. 18." *Early Music* 8 (1980): 237.
Tunley, David. "Recherches . . . 15." *Music and Letters* 58 (1977): 90–91.
Viret, Jacques. "Recherches . . . vol. 13." *Revue de musicologie* 61 (1975): 136–37.
INDEXES
    External: Bibliographie des Musikschrifttums, 1960– . RILM, 1967– .
LOCATION SOURCES
    Widely available.

Publication History

TITLE AND TITLE CHANGES
    Recherches sur la musique française classique.
VOLUME AND ISSUE DATA
    Volumes 1– , 1960– .
FREQUENCY OF PUBLICATION
    Annual.
PUBLISHER
    A. et J. Picard.
PLACE OF PUBLICATION
    Paris.

EDITORS
   Norbert Dufourcq and Marcelle Benoit, 1960–   .

                                                                     Lyn Hubler

RECORDED SOUND

One cannot properly summarize *Recorded Sound,* as published by the British Institute of Sound (London), without making reference to its predecessor, the *Bulletin of the British Institute of Recorded Sound*, published from the summer of 1956 to 1961. Throughout its short history the *Bulletin* was always printed somewhat informally on up to twenty, 8½" by 11" offset pages and circulated to Friends of the Institute "from time to time" (1:1). Most of the content was comprised of two to four page articles on classical music, musical instruments, discography, and recording instruments for language teaching. One entire issue was devoted to the British Archives of Folk and Primitive Music. The *Bulletin* also included information about acquisitions of special interest and the activities of the institute. In addition to its articles and news, plus discographies, bibliographies, and book reviews (the latter perhaps 20 percent of each issue), the *Bulletin* published periodic pleas to its friends with automobiles to drive to outlying areas around London that had phonograph recordings to donate to the Institute. In 1956, the institute had amassed a modest 25,000 recordings; by January 1965, it could boast a collection of 100,000 discs and 1,000 hours of taped materials; and by the early 1980s, the count exceeded a half million discs.

Recorded Sound was a natural outgrowth of the less sophisticated *Bulletin*, not to mention the strength of the institute's collection. Its contents clearly embody the principal objective of the institute: "to preserve for posterity sound recordings of all kinds and to serve as a center for their study." The first issue of *Recorded Sound* included the statement that the journal "would contain the texts of some of the lectures given on behalf of the institute, articles on recorded sound in all its aspects, discographies, and other matters relating to the institute's objects." *Recorded Sound* quickly established itself as an excellent discographic research tool for classical and nature recordings.

Articles appearing in *Recorded Sound* focus on all forms of classical music, folk music, the history of sound recording and libraries, some spoken word and wildlife sound, and to a much lesser extent, jazz. Two major series have appeared in the journal: "History of Sound Recording" by Peter Ford, which was based on his lectures given at the institute during the autumn and winter of 1961, and "Discographies of British Composers," which ran from 1977 to 1982. There have been articles on such personalities as Sarah Bernhardt, Jane Bathori, and Percy Grainger, and an entire issue devoted to Sir Edward Elgar (January 1963). *Recorded Sound* has featured articles on the care of LP and stereo recordings by Cecil Watts, problems of record cataloguing, acquisition of recordings, copyright and performing rights, and a milestone statement on "Censorship and Spoken Literature" by Aldous Huxley.

A unique facet of *Recorded Sound* lies in the fact that it has endeavored to publish discographies on the obscure and unusual, for example, insect sounds on records, Paleoarctic mammal sound recordings (whales, and so on), and bird songs. Not as unusual but most timely have been occasional articles on film music, electronic music and *musique concrète*, and dance orchestras. The scattered dance-orchestra listings that did appear were compiled by the legendary Brian Rust and featured such personages as Bert Ambrose and Paul Whiteman. This work in turn laid the groundwork for Rust's later two-volume set of discographical data for all artists in this genre.

In addition to the articles and discographies in every issue, *Recorded Sound* also included abstracts of recent articles about recordings libraries, book reviews, and announcements of programs, especially those sponsored by the institute. It was a slick academic journal, published on glossy paper or on high quality rag stock. Illustrations, though sparse, were well chosen and beautifully reproduced. Contributors range from archivists and discographers to musicians, musicologists, and naturalists.

Recorded Sound was published quarterly, starting with the May 1961 issue, until cessation in July 1984 (Number 86) due to time pressures at the institute. The archive had hoped that by early 1986 it would once again begin publishing, this time in the form of a series of journals, each dealing with a single subject area, such as Western art music, spoken literature, oral history, and wildlife sounds. To date, however, nothing has been forthcoming.

The institute has published various reference books, which since have proven to be valuable research aids to discographers. Titles include Elgar and Monteverdi discographies, *Vertical-Cut Cylinders and Discs, a Catalogue of all Hill and Dale Recordings of Serious Worth Made Between 1897–1932 circa*, and *The Music of Some Indian Tribes of Colombia*. All have been promoted in the pages of *Recorded Sound*. It also arranges lectures and recitals and acts as a center for information and documentation. The institute library contains books and periodicals relating to all aspects of recorded sound and catalogs of record companies.

Information Sources

BIBLIOGRAPHY
"Two Very Promising New Periodicals." *Notes* 19 (1961): 56.
INDEXES
      External: Music Index, 1961–84. Library & Information Service Abstracts, 1961–84. RILM, 1968–84.
LOCATION SOURCES
      Widely available.

Publication History

TITLE AND TITLE CHANGES
      Recorded Sound.

VOLUME AND ISSUE DATA
    Numbers 1–86, 1961–84.
FREQUENCY OF PUBLICATION
    Quarterly.
PUBLISHER
    British Institute of Recorded Sound.
PLACE OF PUBLICATION
    London.
EDITORS
    Editorial Board.

William L. Schurk

REIHE, DIE

For the brief period of its publication, 1955–62, *Die Reihe* was the all but official organ of the group of German avant-garde composers centered around Karlheinz Stockhausen and Herbert Eimert, the journal's editors. As such, it provides an invaluable window on this highly influential group for whom electronic music and indeterminacy were exciting new frontiers, post-Webern serialism was the *raison d'être*, and Anton Webern the idol. Their doctrinaire reasoning, insightful yet frequently distorted views of history and aesthetics, and highly (often excessively) cerebral and analytical approach to music—in short, the spectrum of their brilliance and their myopia—are fully revealed in the pages of *Die Reihe*. As a result, the journal enjoys both contemporaneous and future significance all out of proportion to its eight slender volumes.

Averaging just over a hundred pages, each volume of *Die Reihe* contains from five to eighteen articles, rarely footnoted but frequently provided with abundant musical and graphic illustrations of all kinds. There are no departments, reviews, or advertisements. The contributors are mostly German, mostly composers, and all male, though one finds articles by Frenchmen Pierre Boulez and Henri Pousseur, Americans John Cage, Christian Wolff, and John Whitney, Italian György Ligeti, author H. H. Stuckenschmidt, and physicist Werner Meyer-Eppler. Frequent contributors include Stockhausen (six articles), Eimert (five), Ligeti (two), Cage (two), Wolff (two), Meyer-Eppler (two), Pousseur (three), Boulez (two), Ernst Krenek (two), and one each by Stuckenschmidt, Stravinsky, Schönberg, Webern, and Mauricio Kagel. The complex, intellectual prose of most of these authors deliberately limits *Die Reihe* to a readership of composers and serious students of contemporary music, preferably those with a thorough grounding in the German musical heritage and in the fundamentals of serial technique.

Each volume of *Die Reihe* has a topical focus that the editors indicate with a volume title on the cover. V. 1 is devoted to electronic music, and opens with editor Eimert's "What Is Electronic Music?" (1:1–10). This is followed by provocative and widely varied commentaries on the subject by Stuckenschmidt, Boulez, Krenek, Pousseur, Stockhausen, and others. The final article, "Statistic and Psychologic Problems of Sound'' (1:22–28), is the particularly erudite work of Werner Meyer-Eppler, the phonetician, acoustician, and information science specialist who provided much of the theoretical foundation for the German electronic music school.

V. 2 is dedicated to Anton Webern on the tenth anniversary of his death. This is a first-rate piece of work, with a foreword by Igor Stravinsky, a biographical sketch, several reprints of Webern's own writings, Schönberg's foreword to Webern's *Six Bagatelles*, excerpts of Webern's correspondence, and analytical tributes by Eimert, Stockhausen, Boulez, Pousseur, Wolff, and others.

A projected third volume, parallel to the second but given over to Claude Debussy, reached fruition only in scattered articles in later issues. Instead, v. 3 addressed the topic of musical craftsmanship. It is dominated by Pousseur's complex explication of his applications of post-Webern serialism and Gestalt theory, and leavened by Cage's description of I-Ching-based indeterminacy. Most controversial, however, was Stockhausen's hefty discourse on temporal aspects of music: ''how time passes . . . '' (3:10–40). In v. 8, Adriaan D. Fokker examined this article in his ''Wherefore, and Why?'' (8:68–79) and both Stockhausen and Fokker were revisited by Gottfried Michael Koenig (8:80–98). See also Perle and Karkoschka (on Stockhausen) in the bibliography below.

V. 4 features ten thoughtful, largely sympathetic, and highly analytical sketches of young composers, including Stockhausen, Pousseur, Luciano Berio, and Bo Nilsson. These are balanced by Heinz-Klaus Metzger's fascinating look at twentieth-century German music, its trends and its critics all seen against the backdrop of philosophers Theodor Adorno and Hellmut Kotschenreuther. The next volume is a less unified one with analytical essays on Boulez's Third Piano Sonata and Debussy's *Jeux*, a Cage lecture on indeterminacy, and two lectures by Stockhausen. Under the wide-open volume title ''Speech and Music,'' the editors of v. 6 have assembled an intriguing assortment of articles including Hans Rudolf Zeller's ''Mallarmé and Serialist Thought'' (6:5–32) and Nicolas Ruwet's ''Contradictions within the Serial Language'' (6:65–76).

The last two volumes of *Die Reihe* continue this trend toward more diverse contents. V. 7, entitled ''Music—Form'' contains appropriate articles by Ligeti, Wolff, and Kagel, but also the unusual ''Project for 200,000 Inhabitants'' (7:72–75) by Rainer Fleischhauer and Jorn Janssen. The final volume, in addition to the two articles already mentioned, includes Eimert's memorial tribute to Meyer-Eppler (8:5–6), an address by the latter entitled ''Musical Communication as a Problem of Information Theory'' (8:7–10), Walter O'Connell's highly mathematical ''Tone Spaces'' (8:34–67), and the visually striking work of Walter Schulze-Andresen's ''The Three-dimensional Music Stave'' (8:25–33).

An unusual feature of this journal is the parallel English translation, also titled *Die Reihe*. The individual volumes of this series appeared at first three but then anywhere from two to six years after their German counterparts. Major translators included Leo Black (parts of vs. 2, 3, 4, 5), Cornelius Cardew (parts of vs. 3, 7, 8), and Ruth Koenig (parts of vs. 5, 6, 8). The English series was published by Theodore Presser in the same 5⅞″ by 8¼″ format, but the subtitle of the original was replaced, on the inside title page, by the descriptor "a periodical devoted to developments in contemporary music." At least one article, Eimert's "What is Electronic Music?" was substantially rewritten for the translation, and the one-page introduction to v. 1 was, unfortunately, cut.

Information Sources

BIBLIOGRAPHY
Drew, David. "Spinner, Die Reihe, and Thematicism: Notes Towards a 13th Question." *Tempo* 146 (1983): 9–12.
Karkoschka, Erhard. "Stockhausen wird attackiert und verteidigt." *Melos* 30 (1963): 121–3.
———. "Junge Komponisten unter der Lupe." *Melos* 27 (1960): 268–69.
Perle, George. "Die Reihe. Vol. III: Musical Craftsmanship." *Journal of Music Theory* 4 (1960): 102–4.
RLH. "Die Reihe." *Music and Letters* 41 (1960): 184–85.
INDEXES
      External: Music Index, 1958–68. RILM, 1967.
LOCATION SOURCES
      Widely available.

Publication History

TITLE AND TITLE CHANGES
      Die Reihe.
VOLUME AND ISSUE DATA
      Volumes 1–8, 1958–68.
FREQUENCY OF PUBLICATION
      Annual.
PUBLISHER
      Universal Editions AG. English edition: Theodore Presser.
PLACE OF PUBLICATION
      Vienna. English edition: Bryn Mawr, Pennsylvania.
EDITORS
      Herbert Eimert and Karlheinz Stockhausen.

Richard S. James

REVISTA DE MUSICOLOGÍA

Revista de musicología (1978–   ) is the scholarly journal of the Sociedad Española de Musicología (Spanish Society of Musicology) and is devoted primarily to Spanish music history, with emphasis on sacred music of the Medieval, Renaissance, and Baroque periods. A semiannual publication, *Revista de musicología* typically contains about 150–200 pages per 6″ by 9½″ issue. Double issues appeared in 1978 (v. 1), 1980 (v. 3), and 1983 (v. 6). All articles are in Spanish, and most are by Spanish musicologists, including such figures as Macario Santiago Kastner, Daniel Vega, Samuel Rubio, Dionisio Preciado, Lothar Siemens Hernández, and Francisco José León Tello. The typical issue has contained a number of longer articles ("Estudios"), followed by several shorter essays ("Miscelanea"), somewhat comparable to the "Studies and Reports" section of the *Journal of the American Musicological Society* (q.v.) and reissues, with commentary, of brief documents of historical importance ("Textos"). Medium-length reviews and annotated lists of books and articles ("Información Bibliográfica," which should prove of considerable importance to the bibliographer of Spanish music) began to appear in v. 2. Musical examples (including some complete compositions), facsimiles, photographs, and line drawings are all part of the illustrative support for the scholarly material presented. No advertisements appear. Beginning with v. 3, indexes for proper names and for place-names are appended to the complete volume.

Liturgical music—including its composers, practitioners, sources, and instruments—has been the subject of perhaps half of the articles and essays in this periodical thus far. The archives of cathedrals, parishes, and monastic orders (for example, Benedictine, Hieronymite), have received much attention, and various extant organs (such as those at Santa Cruz de Zaragoza, San Martín de Tours in Ataun, Bornos in Cádiz, and La Seo de Zaragoza) are described in detail. Some of the articles on instruments are accompanied by illustrations showing various perspectives and measurements. Lists of names (including chapelmasters, organists, and other instrumentalists) accompanying some articles provide a convenient point of departure for further research.

A very few articles have concentrated on ethnomusicological matters. Occasionally, an article dealing with aesthetic analysis appears. Secular music (with an emphasis on the Baroque period) is treated with increasing frequency. Only rarely are contemporary music and composers considered.

One of the founders of the society, its first president, and the founding editor of this periodical as well, is Samuel Rubio (b. 1912), O.S.A., whose work on Cristobal de Morales, Tomás Luis de Victoria, and Antonio Soler has been widely recognized; his monograph *La Polífonia Clásica*[1] shed light on Spanish applications of the techniques of Roman-school polyphony. V. 6 (1983), a substantial double issue of 630 pages, is devoted in its entirety to Father Rubio as a *Festschrift* on the seventieth anniversary of his birth. Among the twenty-eight articles appearing here are an eighty-six-page bio-bibliographical study by Luis Hernández, "Samuel Rubio: Una Vida para la Música" (6.1/2:21–106), which cites 133 publications by the subject, and an appreciation of Father Rubio's place in Spanish musicology by Ismael Fernández de la Cuesta.

Although a relatively young journal, *Revista de musicología* has published an impressive number of extended articles by respected musicologists. It should be considered an essential tool for research on the early history of Spanish music.

Note

1. El Escorial: Biblioteca "La Ciudad de Dios," 1956; English trans., *Classical Polyphony*, Toronto: University of Toronto Press, 1972.

Information Sources

BIBLIOGRAPHY

"Revista de musicología." *Die Musikforschung* 35 (April–June 1982): 181.

INDEXES

Internal: each volume indexed beginning with v. 3.

External: RILM, 1978– .

LOCATION SOURCES

Widely available.

Publication History

TITLE AND TITLE CHANGES

Revista de musicología.

VOLUME AND ISSUE DATA

Volumes 1– , 1978– .

FREQUENCY OF PUBLICATION

Semiannual, with some irregularities.

PUBLISHER

Sociedad Española de Musicología.

PLACE OF PUBLICATION

Madrid.

EDITORS

Samuel Rubio, 1978–79. Antonio Gallego, 1979–80. Dionisio Preciado, 1980–84. Lothar Siemens Hernandez, 1985– .

John E. Druesedow

REVISTA MUSICAL CHILENA

Revista musical chilena, which began publication in May 1945, is one of the most respected musical journals emanating from Latin America. Its first editor was Vicente Sales Viu (1911–67), a musicologist whose survey of Chilean music and musicians during the first half of the twentieth century (*La creación musical en Chile, 1900–1951,* Santiago, 1952) has become a standard source. Salas Viu, historian Eugenio Pereira Salas (1904–79; author of *Historia de la música en Chile, 1850–1900,* Santiago, 1957), and composers Alfonso Letelier (b. 1912) and Juan A. Orrego-Salas (b. 1919) were among the most frequent contributors to the journal during its first two decades; in later years, the musicologist Samuel Claro (b. 1934), among others, contributed significantly. To the present time, it has been published under the auspices of the Universidad de Chile (at first within the Instituto de Extension Musical, later within the Facultad de Ciencias y Artes Musicales y de la Representación, and most recently the Facultad de Artes division).

Revista musical chilena has always provided significant coverage of contemporary musical life in general and of current musical events in particular, mostly within the Americas and with an emphasis on Chile (notices of recitals, festivals, meetings of musical societies, and reviews of various musical programs, somewhat after the fashion of the U.S. periodical *Musical America* [q.v.]. The overall high quality of both production and subject matter has been consistent and the latter gradually more scholarly. Many articles are by prominent Latin American composers who write on other composers or address the aesthetics or philosophy of contemporary (including avant-garde) music (for example, Aurelio de la Vega, "Problemática de la música latinoamericana" in n. 61; an article with the same title by Marlos Nobre appeared in ns. 142–44 about twenty years later). Indeed, biographical articles on composers (mostly native Chileans), with appended lists of works, comprise a particular strength of the journal. Such composers as Pedro Humberto Allende (1885–1959), Alfonso Leng (1884–1974), Carlos Isamitt (1887–1974), Domingo Santa Cruz (b. 1899), Jorge Urrutia Blondel (1905–81), and Juan A. Orrego-Salas (b. 1919), among others, have been honored with dedicatory issues and catalogs of their compositions.

A second strain of emphasis has been on traditional or ethnic music. Outstanding ethnomusicologists—for example, Carlos Vega, George List, and Erich M. von Hornbostel—have contributed articles, and a special monograph of ethnic interest, *El Romancero chilena*, by Raquel Barro and Manuel Dannemann, appeared as n. 111. There have also been a significant number of articles on music education: n. 11 included the first appearance of a new (and subsequently somewhat regular) column, "Educación Musical," and one entire double issue (n. 87–88), including fifteen articles, was devoted to the subject.

Historical articles have added subsequently to the scholarly fund of musical knowledge concerning Central and South America. Lauro Ayesterán, Eugenio Pereira Salas, Dom León Toloza, Pablo Hernández Balaguer, and Robert Stevenson's articles on aspects of colonial music in Latin America, beginning with 81–82:153–71 ("La música colonial en Colombia" and "Música en Quito"), provide seminal information on cathedral archives and early composers. Stevenson's article, "Francisco Correa de Arauxo, New Light on His Career" (103:7–42), is the only non-Spanish article published so far.

Reviews of monographs and other printed publications appear regularly; reviews of recordings are somewhat more sporadic. Necrological notices (with emphasis on Latin American composers) are frequently included. Illustrative material (for example, musical examples and photographs) can be found throughout.

Issues have been numbered consecutively (that is, they are not linked to the volume number) from the beginning. For the first several years of its existence, the journal was published monthly, with some irregularities. It then became a quarterly (with n. 37, Fall 1950), was subsequently transformed into a bimonthly (n. 52–74, April–May 1957 through 1960), and finally reverted to, and remains, a quarterly (beginning with n. 75, January–March 1961). Double issues are frequent; page dimensions are 6″ by 9½″. With few exceptions, each volume is indexed in either the last issue of the volume or the first of the subsequent volume. A comprehensive index for the first two decades (from May 1945 to December 1966) is contained in n. 98 (October–December 1966); a supplement to this index appears in the thirtieth anniversary issue (129/130:17–103, January–June 1975).

Information Sources

INDEXES
    External: Music Index, 1950–   . RILM, 1967–   . Bibliographie des Musik-schrifttums, 1950, 1960–   .
LOCATION SOURCES
    Widely available.

Publication History

TITLE AND TITLE CHANGES
    Revista Musical Chilena.
VOLUME AND ISSUE DATA
    Volumes 1–   , 1945–   .
FREQUENCY OF PUBLICATION
    Monthly, with irregularities, 1945–Summer 1950. Quarterly, Fall 1950–March 1957. Bimonthly, April/May 1957–60. Quarterly, 1960–   .
PUBLISHER
    Universidad de Chile, Facultad de Artes.
PLACE OF PUBLICATION
    Santiago, Chile.
EDITORS
    Vicente Salas Viu, 1945–49. Juan A. Orrego-Salas, 1949–53. Leopoldo Castedo, 1954. Pedro Mortheiru, 1954–56. Alfonso Letelier, 1957–60. Magdalena Vicuña, 1960–71. Cirilo Vila, 1971–72. Luis Merino, 1973. Magdalena Vicuña, 1974–75. María Ester Grebe, 1975–78. Magdalena Vicuña, 1979–   .

John E. Druesedow

REVUE BELGE DE MUSICOLOGIE

The idea for the Société Belge de Musicologie arose on 3 November 1945 at a meeting in honor of Charles van den Borren, dean of Belgian musicology, on the occasion of his admission to emeritus status at the University of Liège. On 2 March 1946, the society was formally constituted. With van den Borren its president, it consisted of his students and former students from the Universities of Liège and Brussels; professors of musicology from Universities of Gand, Louvain, and Liège; and personalities from the musical world of Belgium.

The society began publication of the *Revue belge de musicologie,* subtitled *Belgisch tijdschrift voor muziek-wetenschap,* in 1949. Its goals were

to promote musicological studies in Belgium on a vast scale, placing principal emphasis upon the study of music in our country. Far from considering musicology uniquely as a science of the past, these studies will engage resolutely in studies of music of today, organizing concerts of contemporary music as well as performances of early music, and encouraging those who wish to apply themselves to problems of comparative musicology, of acoustics, and of speculations of a philosophical order. They propose, moreover, to undertake studies such as determining the terminology of their discipline, publishing archival sources relative to music, making known the contents of churches where entire collections of old music have gathered dust, those of library sources still not catalogued, centralizing a vast bibliographic documentation on everything concerned with our musical past (fiches and photographic documentation), etc. (1:1)

The *Revue* has steadfastly fulfilled these goals and changed little since its inception. Van den Borren's expertise in the music of the Renaissance provided the model for the emphasis of early issues. Articles by Suzanne Clercx, "Introduction à l'histoire de la musique en Belgique" (5.9:114) and "Contribution à l'histoire de la musique belge de la Renaissance" (9:103) by René Lenaerts (the journal's first editor) are significant. The *Revue* rapidly expanded its scope to cover all historical periods: articles often appear in the language of the contributor (French, Flemish, English, German, and Italian). Noteworthy are C.P.E. Bach's complete *Versuch* translated into French by Jean-Pierre Muller (23:8–121 and 26–27:159–236) and some dozen essays on Franz Schubert by Reinhard Van Hoorickx.

The format of the *Revue* has remained much the same from its first issue. Contents consist of reports of the society (moved from the front to the back of issues in 1953), several essays running between ten and twenty-five pages, several modest articles of two to four pages ("Miscellanea") that cover individual letters, documents, chronologies, inventories, and reports of festivals and conferences, and some dozen one-page reviews of books. Early issues sometimes included a review of periodicals, a necrology, and correspondence. The *Revue* measures 6⅞" by 10¼", contains black-and-white illustrations, and is indexed by volume. The journal contains no advertisements and is printed by Nederlandsche Boekhandel (Antwerp).

Information Sources

INDEXES
    External: Music Index, 1951– . Bibliographie des Musikschrifttums, 1950– .
    RILM, 1967– .
LOCATION SOURCES
    Widely available.

Publication History

TITLE AND TITLE CHANGES
    Revue belge de musicologie. Belgisch tijdschrift voor muziek-wetenschap.

VOLUME AND ISSUE DATA
Volumes 1– , 1949– .
FREQUENCY OF PUBLICATION
Quarterly.
PUBLISHER
Société Belge de Musicologie (Belgische vereniging voor muziekwetenschap).
PLACE OF PUBLICATION
Antwerp.
EDITORS
Suzanne Clercx and René Lenaerts, 1945–57. Floris Vander Mueren, 1958–66.
Albert Vander Linden, 1958–77. Robert Wangermée, 1958– . Henri Vanhulst,
1971– .

J. Scott Messing

REVUE DE JAZZ HOT. See JAZZ-HOT

REVUE DE MUSICOLOGIE

During the two decades that preceded World War I, all parts of the French
musical community participated in the evocation of their national heritage. Composers made self-conscious references to pre-Romantic traditions, "early music"
performances burgeoned, and the first generation of professional French musicologists produced historical editions of a hitherto moribund repertoire as well
as a wealth of commentary and criticism. This environment provided a rich
background to the inauguration of the Société Française de Musicologie.

The idea for the society originated with Lionel Dauriac in 1904, the year in
which the Paris section of the International Music Society was founded, but it
was only on 17 March 1917 that it was formally constituted. The first volume
of the *Bulletin de la Société Française de Musicologie* reported the goals of the
organization: "the study of the history of music and musicians, of aesthetics,
and of the theory of music. Its means of activity consists of the publication of
a periodic bulletin and, eventually, of documents, texts, and all types of works
of a thorough nature concerning musicology" (1:vi). The first issue of the *Bulletin*
also recorded the elections of the governing body of the society (Lionel de La
Laurencie, president; Elie Poirée, vice-president; Jacques-Gabriel Prod'homme,
secretary; Henri Quittard, recording secretary; and Charles Mutin, treasurer), its
statutes and rules, and the minutes of its early meetings (1:1–12).

In March 1922 a "nouvelle série" was begun, and *Bulletin* was superseded
by *Revue* in the journal's title. The war had clearly hampered regular operation
of the original *Bulletin*; the first issue of the new *Revue* stated that "Our Society
wishes to try to give a new impulse to a movement so unfortunately arrested or
more or less slowed down. It will continue to apply itself as best it can, and it
is to emphasize this goal that it has proposed to substitute the old title of its

'Bulletin' with that of *Revue de musicologie*" (6:1–2). Julien Tiersot was elected the society's new president, and he shared editorial responsibilities with La Laurencie and Marie-Louise Pereyra.

Due to the vigilance of the society, both the *Bulletin* and the *Revue* offered essays that maintained high standards of scholarly inquiry. Like the *Bulletin*, the *Revue* emphasized documentary and archival studies especially of French music before 1800. Path-breaking research on manuscripts, composers, instruments, and performance practice of the Renaissance, Baroque, and Classical periods by the first generation of professional French musicologists (Lionel de La Laurencie, Paul Marie Masson, André Pirro, Yvonne Rokseth, Geneviève Thibault, and others) was characteristic of the journal between the two world wars. After World War II, the scope of the *Revue* broadened; unpublished correspondence of many nineteenth- and twentieth-century composers was reproduced and noteworthy special issues were devoted to Claude Debussy (1962) and Hector Berlioz (1977). André Schaeffner's presence among the society's officers (vice-president, 1948–58; president, 1958–61) encouraged an increase in the number of essays with ethnomusicological subjects. (A special issue honoring him appeared in 1982.) The list of authors is now international, although all contributions remain in French.

Publication of the original *Bulletin* was irregular: ten issues in two volumes, each of the two numbered consecutively, appeared between 1917 and 1921 with indexes after numbers 5 and 10. The format consisted of the society's minutes followed by several articles (rarely longer than ten pages each), necrology, and a bibliography consisting of one-page reviews of some dozen books. A more extensive bibliography entitled "Essai de bibliographie des périodiques musicaux de langue française" appeared in v. 2:76–90.

Between 1922 and 1939 the *Revue* appeared four times per year: the first issue in 1922 was considered to be the "sixième année," but also ns. 1–4. Thus 1939 saw the twenty-third "année" of the journal's publication (dating from the original *Bulletin* in 1917) as ns. 69–72. As war intervened again, publication was suspended during 1940 and 1941. A "série spéciale," constituting the society's "rapports et communications," appeared between 1942 and 1944 without volume numbers (*sans périodicité*). The "nouvelle série" continued in 1945, ns. 73–76 (the twenty-seventh "année," counting 1942–44 as the twenty-fourth through twenty-sixth "années"; whole numbering was dropped in 1954 with the thirty-sixth "année" now listed as v. 36), when the journal began to appear twice yearly.

The number and length of the articles in the *Revue*, supplemented with photographic reproductions, remained similar to that of the *Bulletin*. In addition to the bibliography and the society's minutes (placed at the end of issues in the *Revue*), there appeared brief notices of events of musical interest and modest articles of several pages concerning individual documents, letters, inventories, and so on ("Nouvelles musicologiques-documents" and later "Notes et documents") and listings of musical articles in French newspapers and foreign journals ("Périodiques"). A separate bibliography of editions of music began in 1927. Consecutive pagination appeared on a yearly basis. Between the wars the average length of an issue of the *Revue* ran to about seventy-five pages. After 1950, the length doubled, due mostly to greater detail and depth of the main essays. Neither the *Bulletin* nor the *Revue* has included advertisements.

Fischbacher, the original printer of the *Revue*, was superseded by Heugel in 1951, and by Durand in 1979. The latter change introduced the current cover and type, although the 6¼" by 9" size remained relatively constant since the journal's inception. Kraus (Nendeln/Liechtenstein) has issued a reprint of the early issues. There is a separate index for the years 1917–66.

Information Sources

BIBLIOGRAPHY
Schaeffner, André. "Cinquantenaire de la Société Française de Musicologie." *Revue de musicologie* 53 (1967): 103–9.
INDEXES
Internal: 1917–66.
External: Bibliographie des Musikschrifttums, 1937, 1939, 1952– . Music Index, 1959– . RILM, 1967– . Arts and Humanities Citation Index, 1977– .
REPRINT EDITIONS
Paper: Kraus Reprint Limited.
Microfilm: UMI, 1942– .
LOCATION SOURCES
Widely available.

Publication History

TITLE AND TITLE CHANGES
Bulletin de la Société Française de Musicologie, 1917–22 (vs. 1–2, ns. 1–10).
Revue de musicologie, 1922– (v. 3– , new series n. 1–).
VOLUME AND ISSUE DATA
Volumes 1–2 (ns. 1–10), 1917–22. New series, volumes 1– , 1922– .
FREQUENCY OF PUBLICATION
Irregular, 1917–22. Quarterly, 1922 (new series) –53. Semiannual, 1954– .
PUBLISHER
Société Française de Musicologie.
PLACE OF PUBLICATION
Paris.
EDITORS
(N.B.: Editors were not always listed in the journal. Where not indicated, the president of the society is given.) Lionel de La Laurencie (president), 1917–21. La Laurencie, Julien Tiersot, Marie-Louise Pereyra, 1922–25. La Laurencie, Tiersot, Pereyra, Maurice Cauchie, André Tessier, 1925–26. Tiersot (president), 1927. Théodore Reinach (president), 1928. Georges Saint-Foix (president), 1929–31. La Laurencie (president), 1932–33. Amédée Gastoué (president), 1934–37. Léon Vallas (president), 1938–43. J.-G. Prod'homme (president), 1944. Paul-Marie Masson (president), 1945–47. Marc Pincherle (president), 1948–55. Com-

tesse de Chambure, 1955. Elizabeth Lebeau, 1955. André Schaeffner, 1955–58. François Lesure, 1955–73. André Verchaly, 1956–73. Mme. H. de Chambure, 1968–73. Jean Gribenski, 1974–84. Christian Meyer, 1985–   .

J. Scott Messing

REVUE MUSICALE, LA

The name *La Revue musicale* has been carried by four French periodicals.[1] The present discussion will concern itself solely with the most recent of these journals, which continues to be published today. It was founded in 1920 by Henry Prunières as a general music periodical for amateurs wishing to increase their knowledge of music history as well as specialists, professionals, and artists. There have only been three editors in the sixty-six years of the *Revue*'s history. The design and execution of the magazine have, however, gone through considerable revision. In 1952 the *Revue* changed under the influence of both a new editor and a new publisher. For the sake of clarity, therefore, the journal will be discussed as it existed from 1920 to 1952 and then from 1952 to the present.

In the 1920s and 1930s the *Revue* enjoyed the largest circulation of any magazine of its kind.[2] The editorial staff included Henry Prunières, André Coeuroy, and Fred Goldbeck. With the assistance of the best musicians and musicologists the *Revue* covered a wide range of topics as well as devoting special issues to specific composers (Johann Sebastian Bach, Ludwig van Beethoven, Franz Liszt, Jean Lully, Claude Debussy, Maurice Ravel, Paul Dukas, and others).

Two clear predilections of the journal manifest themselves in the earlier years. The first is to serve as a forum for contemporary music with articles by and about people like Eric Satie, Ravel, Arthur Honegger, Wallingford Riegger, Béla Bartók, Igor Stravinsky, and Ernst Krenek. Reviews of new music and concert performances around the world made up a sizable portion of every issue. André Coeuroy (b. 1891), the co-founder of *Revue* and a distinguished music critic and writer on contemporary music (*Panorama de la musique contemporaine*, 1928), was clearly instrumental in guiding the direction of the magazine toward contemporary music.

The other major emphasis of the *Revue* reflects Prunières's own area of expertise as a musicologist: seventeenth-century music, especially French and Italian opera. Noteworthy examples include André Tessier's "Messes d'orgue de Couperin" (6.1:26–48), Lionel de La Laurencie's "L'opera francais au XVIIe siècle" (6.3:26–43), and many articles by Prunières himself.

The *Revue* of the 1920s and 1930s typically had about ninety pages and six articles. The topics ranged from the life and works of living composers and jazz and its influence, to seventeenth-century correspondence on music, and opera and ballet. Major musicologists like André Tessier, Marc Pincherle, Egon Wel lesz, Charles Van den Borren, and Paul Brunold contributed articles. Composers and performers offered their own perspective in articles by Ernest Ansermet, Alfred Cortot, Robert Casadeseus, Alfredo Casella, Zoltán Kodály, Francis Poulenc, and Virgil Thomson.

A regular feature of each issue was the section entitled "Chroniques et Notes," one of the most enlivening and enlightening features of the prewar *Revue*. With the aid of correspondents in Europe and North and South America, *La Revue* reported on musical activities in twenty countries: concerts, theatre productions, operas, and recitals. New music editions, books, courses and conferences, recordings, and even new films also received comment. "Chroniques et Notes" captured first impressions of new music by Stravinsky and concert performances by people like Wanda Landowska or Gustav Furtwängler. Prunières and Coeuroy wrote many of the reviews themselves.

Each issue of *La Revue musicale*—there was an average of ten a year—was meticulously indexed, on a yearly basis, from 1920 to 1939. Not only were authors and titles cross-indexed but every piece of music and every reviewer's name will be found. There is some advertising throughout the journal.

In 1939 Prunières resigned as editor-in-chief of the *Revue* and was succeeded by Robert Bernard. Bernard continued Prunières's editorial policies where possible, but publication ceased during the war years and suffered several interruptions after 1946 until a new publisher, Richard Masse, bought the magazine. Masse gathered together the staffs of three newly acquired journals, *Polyphonie*, *Contrepoint*, and *La Revue musicale* into one office. By the mid–1950s he had merged them into one journal, the "new" *Revue musicale*. Editor under the new management was Albert Richard, who continues to serve as director of the magazine today.[3]

"Chroniques et Notes" was dropped, and the average length of the articles increased. In-depth studies and special issues became the rule rather than the exception. In the new journal, many issues are devoted to conference proceedings. One such instance was a conference on Franz Schubert organized by the Institut Autricien. Four of the papers presented at the meeting were compiled for *La Revue musicale* and entitled "Carnets Critiques." In fact, proceedings issues as well as some shorter issues of a more documentary nature are regularly entitled "Carnet Critiques," though officially brought out by *La Revue musicale*.

Under Albert Richard the *Revue* has continued to support contemporary music, especially in France. In fact, the majority of the issues today are devoted to modern music. Special issues combining two or three *numerós* have been written on Edgard Varèse, Iannis Xenakis, Luciano Berio, and Pierre Henry (ns. 265–66), Henri Sauguet (ns. 361–363), Lili and Nadia Boulanger (ns. 353–354), and Claude Ballif (ns. 370, 371), to name just a few. Questions facing modern composers, aesthetics, or compositional systems are the subject of other issues.

Aside from modern music there are some studies on Romantic composers. One such work on the songs of Franz Liszt by Suzanne Montu-Berthon (1981) occupied five issues (ns. 342–46). Three volumes contained the text and two the musical examples. These issues were very positively reviewed.[4] Camille Saint-Saëns, Frédéric Chopin, Franz Schubert, and other nineteenth-century composers are featured in other issues.

Articles on early French music are almost nonexistent. With the arrival on the scene in recent years of specialist journals restricted to early music, the disappearance of this area of study is perhaps understandable: 1953 saw the founding of *Annales musicologiques* (q.v.) and 1960 the *Recherches sur la musique française classique* (q.v.).

The format of the *Revue Musicale* since 1952 has vacillated along with the quality of the content. There are supposedly ten *numéros* per year, and the number of pages for a single issue is around ninety. Many of the issues appear as double or triple numbers, though, and have 200–300 pages. Issues may be authored by a single person or by many contributors. Reviews of the journal have frequently been enthusiastic, and articles on the whole tend to be very well documented. Tables, indices, and bibliographies can be found at the end of most studies.

The physical layout of the *Revue* was altered after the 1952 transition. The new version is taller (7⅛″ by 10⅛″ than the original (7″ by 9½″), and printed on much better quality paper. The cover changed, so that instead of having the table of contents on the front, the cover is now cleaner with only a drawing or photo. Currently, the overall presentation is very handsome. Articles are profusely illustrated with photos, drawings, and even fold-out musical examples. There are no advertisements.

Notes

1. *Larousse de la musique*, 1957, s.v. "Revue musicale."
2. Ibid.
3. *Contrepoints* was edited by Fred Goldbeck, former secretary of *La Revue musicale* under Prunières. It was hailed, in the 1954 edition of *Groves*, as one of the best new periodicals to come out of France. *Polyphonie* had Albert Richard as its editor.
4. Donald Windham, "Suzanne Montu-Berthon: Un Liszt meconnu," *Journal of the American Liszt Society* 11 (1982): 83–84.

Information Sources

BIBLIOGRAPHY:

"Claude Ballif: Essais, Etudes, Documents." *Music and Letters* 50 (1969): 408–9.

Lyon, Raymond. "Musiciens de France." *Le Courrier musicale de france* 70 (1980): 70–71.

Onnen, Frank. "Activiteit in de Franse muzikale pers." *Mens en Melodie* 5 (February 1950): 60–62.

Petersen, Peter. "Jean Gergely: Béla Bartók: Compositeur hongrois." *Musikforschung* 36 (1983): 165–67.

Reed, John. "Franz Schubert et la symphonie. Numéro special 258: Claude Debussy." *Musikforschung* 23 (1970): 90–91.

Reich, Willi. "La Revue musicale." *Melos* 19 (October 1952): 285.

"La Revue musicale." *Notes* 9 (1951): 67–68.

Rogge, Wolfgang. "La Revue musicale. Numéro special 258: Claude Debussy." *musikforschung* 23 (1970): 90–91.

tonietti, Tito. "Musique et Technologie." *Nuova rivista musicale italiana* 9 (1975): 479–81.

Windham, Donald. "Suzanne Montu-Berthon: Un Liszt meconnu." *Journal of the American Liszt Society* 11 (1982): 83–84.

INDEXES
>   Internal: each volume indexed (1920–39).
>
>   External: Bibliography des Musikschrifttums, 1937, 1939, 1952–65. Music Index, 1952. RILM, 1967–   . Arts and Humanities Citation Index, 1977–   .

REPRINT EDITIONS
>   Paper: Brookhaven Press.
>   Microform: Kraus.

LOCATION SOURCES
>   Widely available.

Publication History

TITLE AND TITLE CHANGES
>   *La Revue musicale,* 1920–   . Some volumes also known as "Carnets critiques" since 1952.

VOLUME AND ISSUE DATA
>   Volumes 1–   , 1920–   .

FREQUENCY OF PUBLICATION
>   Monthly, November 1920–March 1921. 11/year, April 1921–May 1932. 10/year, June 1932–December 1936. Suspended, 1940–46. Irregular/occasional, 1946–49. 9/year, 1949–52. 10/year, 1952–   .

PUBLISHERS
>   Editions de la Nouvelle revue française, 1920–51. Editions Richard-Masse, 1952–   .

PLACE OF PUBLICATION
>   Paris.

EDITORS
>   Henry Prunières, 1920–39. Robert Bernard, 1939–52. Albert Richard, 1952–   . Richard and Jean Jacques DuParcq appear alone and together as editors of numerous issues since 1952. Editors are also frequently not indicated.

Lyn Hubler

RIVISTA ITALIANA DI MUSICOLOGIA

One of the most significant developments for the international musicological community since World War II has been the emergence of a strong and influential organization of Italian scholars. From the early years of the twentieth century, only a relatively small number of outstanding Italian scholars were active in musicological research. In the 1950s and 1960s, however, attitudes and procedures began to change. Symptomatic of the rising prevalence and sophistication of Italian scholarship was the establishment, in February of 1964, of the Società Italiana di Musicologia, or SIDM (Italian Musicological Society). Two years later the society began publication of a journal as its official voice, patterned in format and content after the *Journal of the American Musicological Society* (q.v.) and entitled *Rivista italiana di musicologia* (*Italian Journal of Musicology*).

The opening editorial of the first volume recognized the importance of the establishment of the SIDM, as well as the journal itself:

In the last two years, that is since the birth of the Società Italiana di Musicologia on 29 February 1964 a new direction has been noticed among the activities of our scholars in musicology: that of coordinating common interests, to be more individually efficient in research projects and other purposes. Such a desire [for cooperation] . . . seems to us to be the long awaited sign of a conscious, widespread maturity.

The Journal is issued as the official organ of the SIDM and reflects, and will always continue to reflect, the efficacy of Italian musicology. While it is not an old tradition, . . . it has successfully adopted the ideals of musicology in other nations.

Rivista moved with assurance to the forefront of Italian musicological publications. The appearance, high standard, and stated goals of the SIDM and its journal were immediately and widely applauded. Jan LaRue, then president of the American Musicological Society, called the journal "a splendid new periodical," and continued: "The distinction of the first issue of the new *Rivista* augurs a brilliant future for the new society."

The format of the journal follows that of other major musicology journals, wherein the principal emphasis usually lies with major, extended articles treating a wide spectrum of musicological topics. These are frequently followed by smaller reports, bibliographies, reviews of recent publications, and announcements or other communications from the sponsoring society.

The first and largest section (whether entitled "Saggi" ["essays"] as in vs. 1–8 or "Articoli" ["articles"] from v. 9 onward) is devoted to articles of twenty to thirty-five pages in length that develop some musicological topic in depth. These primarily address issues of Western art music scholarship, whether discussions of musical style, history, bibliography, theory, biography, aesthetics, analysis, or other such issues. There is no apparent attempt to limit the articles by chronology; they extend from topics of the Middle Ages to the present. Unlike many musicological journals, articles discussing aesthetic issues are frequently found, for example, G. Stefani's "Analisi, semiosi, semiotica" (11:106–25) or M. Baroni's "Sulla nozione di grammatica musicale" (16:240–79).

Many articles of particular note could be mentioned. The tone for high scholarship was set from its first issue, which opened with the eminent Italian musicologist Nino Pirotta's appraisal of "Ars nova e stil novo," a discussion of music and Dante. The second volume, which included the proceedings of the Monteverdi Convention held in Sienna in April 1967, contains numerous im portant contributions to Monteverdi scholarship. The Italian authors found in the journal range from such established figures as Pier Luigi Petrobelli, Francesco Degrada, and Ulisse Prota-Giurleo, to the important contributions of a new, rising generation of Italian scholars, such as Franco Piperno's "Buffa e buffi (considerazioni sulla professionalità degli interpreti di scene buffi ed intermezzi" [18:240–84]). Contributions come from the world over.

Bibliographic studies are occasionally found, and beginning with v. 9 (1974) these receive their own subject heading, "Rassegna bibliografiche." The single, largest bibliographic study appears in v. 6 (1971): an index to the various monuments of music by Alberto Basso.

For most of the journal's history it has been particularly strong in reviews of contemporary musicological literature, although in recent years these have been less numerous. Ranging from one to six pages, these reviews are usually rather comprehensive. They are augmented (also since v. 9) with a list of publications received ("Libri ricevuti").

Since the journal is the official organ of the SIDM, periodic reports and announcements by the society are found. These inventory the activities and publications of various conferences or professional societies, announce new scholarly ventures and offers or calls for cooperation, and report on activities or affairs of the SIDM itself. Periodic lists of the members of SIDM are found (12:350–59 and 15:298–308). Editorials are rare, although in the early history of the journal, lengthy obituaries were common. In recent years, letters to the editor have been added. A few advertisements are found, as in American musicological journals, grouped at the end and are intended primarily to draw attention to the publisher's own book list.

The *Rivista*, from its inception, has been published by Olschki of Florence, under the general direction and editing of a SIDM committee, the membership of which, in recent times, has rotated about every three years. It is numbered yearly by volume, with each volume containing either one or two issues. At times a single-issue volume is motivated by a special purpose, as with the issue in honor of Nino Pirotta, but at other times no explanation is offered (as with v. 5, 1970). Volumes vary widely from around 250 pages to over twice that number, with individual issues from 120 pages in length. The journal is softbound in a standard 6" by 9" format. It is typeset in a large clear font, with liberal provision for musical illustrations and examples. Occasional black and white glossy photographs are also found.

For the most part, the journal publishes all its contributions in Italian, with foreign language articles translated into Italian before publication. Approximately 75 percent of submissions are the work of native Italians. In the early years of the journal, however, an occasional article did appear in English, such as James Haar's "A Gift of Madrigals to Cosimo I . . . " (1:167–89), and a few of the contributions to the special Pirotta issue.

Information Sources

INDEXES
   External: Bibliographie des Musikschrifttums, 1966– . Music Index, 1967– .
   RILM, 1967– .
LOCATION SOURCES
   Widely available.

Publication History

TITLE AND TITLE CHANGES
   Rivista italiana di musicologia, 1966– .
VOLUME AND ISSUE DATA
   Volumes 1– , 1966– .
FREQUENCY OF PUBLICATION
   Varies between annual and semiannual.
PUBLISHER
   Olschki.
PLACE OF PUBLICATION
   Florence.
EDITORS
   Guglielmo Barblan, 1966. Guglielmo Barblan, Francesco Degrada, Mario Fabbri,
   Claudio Gallico, Federico Ghisti, Mario Medici, Federico Mompellio, 1967. Al-
   berto Basso, Gianluigi Dardo, Alberto Gallo, Pierluigi Petrobelli, 1968. Nino
   Albarosa, Alberto Basso, Gianluigi Dardo, Pierluigi Petrobelli, 1969. Nino Al-
   barosa, Alberto Basso, Pierluigi Petrobelli, 1970–73. F. Alberto Gallo, Lorenzo
   Bianconi, Andrea Lanza, Pierluigi Petrobelli, 1974–76. F. Alberto Gallo, Lorenzo
   Bianconi, Paolo Fabbri, Andrea Lanza, Giorgio Pestelli, 1977–79. Giulio Cattin,
   Marcello Conati, Renato Di Benedetto, Paolo Fabbri, Giulia Giachin, Giorgio
   Pestelli, 1980–82. Marcello Conati, Renato Di Benedetto, Paolo Fabbri, F. Alberto
   Gallo, Giorgio Pestelli, Angelo Pompilio, 1983–85. Anna Laura Bellina, Amalia
   Collisani, Fabrizio Della Seta, Renato Di Benedetto, Giovanni Morelli, Angelo
   Pompilio, Thomas Walker, 1986.

                                                                    Dale E. Monson

RIVISTA MUSICALE ITALIANA. See NUOVA RIVISTA MUSICALE IT-
ALIANA

ROLLING STONE

Rolling Stone is generally credited with creating a viable alternative to trade
magazines and fanzines with respect to contemporary popular music coverage—
that is, a professionally produced publication adapting the trappings of the ''counterculture'' ethic for a mainstream audience. The first issue was published on 9
November 1967 by owner and editor Jann Wenner. The magazine prospered

almost immediately, largely because Wenner's journalistic instincts struck a responsive chord with the 1960s youth generation. Success was solidified by obtaining widespread newsstand distribution (as opposed to the initial strategy of using street vendors and head shops) and securing large-scale record company advertising.

Over the years, *Rolling Stone* has employed many of the finest rock journalists in the business, including Ralph Gleason, Jon Landau, Dave Marsh, Greil Marcus, Lester Bangs, Ben Fong-Torres, Jonathon Cott, David Fricks, Kurt Loder, Nick Tosches, Jan Pareles, and Christopher Connelly. While offering insightful analysis unsurpassed in the rock literature, the magazine's writers and reviewers have continued to reflect a distinct bias in favor of progressive rock artists going back to the counterculture leanings of the 1960s. Musicians embodying a profound social commitment, but possessed of limited musical expertise, are generally given far greater positive coverage—indeed, more attention is general—than are highly accomplished stylists such as Barbra Streisand, George Benson, Al Jarreau, and Aretha Franklin. In fact, analysis of the youth subculture and the political significance of rock music received major coverage right beside the more radical rock scenes like San Francisco.

Appearing fortnightly, the magazine currently includes two to three pages of news briefs ("Random Notes"), short features (combined under the heading, "Music News"), exhaustive articles (including "The Rolling Stone Interview"), approximately six pages of record reviews, reports of related multimedia and equipment developments (the "Sight and Sound Special," which focuses on home video, compact discs, car stereo, and so on), music charts (subdivided by "U.S. Singles," "Dance Tracks," "Videos," "Top Fifty Albums," based on a continuous nationwide telephone survey of sales in rock-oriented record stores; "College Albums," "British LPs," and "British Singles"), concert itineraries as well as a listing of "Top Ten Concert Grosses," and an extensive classifieds section—all aimed at the discerning music enthusiast.

During the past decade, *Rolling Stone* has had to contend with the problem of retaining its core audience while attracting a new generation of readers. The 1960s youth have gradually settled into a yuppie life-style in which music is no longer such a driving force. *Rolling Stone* has responded with expanded coverage of a variety of nonmusical subjects, such as articles devoted to the rest of the entertainment industry (the cinema, television, theatre, and so on), current events, and life-style concerns as well as fiction and poetry, now staples of the magazine.

This shift actually had its beginnings a full decade earlier with the appearance of award-winning articles on the Altamont disaster and the Charles Manson family. Throughout the 1970s *Rolling Stone* continued to garner respect for its investigative reporting—typified by features on Patty Hearst's SLA activities and the Karen Silkwood coverup—as well as for its analysis of political affairs. A key move with respect to this expanded political coverage was the hiring, in the early 1980s, of William Greider, former assistant national news editor of the *Washington Post*. Greider has been a prime exponent of the "advocacy journalism" concept as typified by his second column for *Rolling Stone* dealing with the nuclear freeze movement. The magazine has also invited back three of its big names from the 1960s—Hunter Thompson, Tom Wolfe, and Timothy Crouse—to cover sociopolitical issues in the 1980s.

Another source of evidence of *Rolling Stone's* maturation has been the active solicitation of advertisers of mainstream products such as autos, cameras, sportswear, liquors, and cigarettes. The appeal of these ads has been enhanced by the use of an increasingly more attractive physical format. The magazine shifted from cheap newsprint to a higher quality paper stock in 1981. In January 1984 an even heavier, glossy stock was employed. In addition, *Rolling Stone* has downsized its dimensions slightly to the current 10" by 12" format while gradually employing more colorful, eye-catching graphics.

The prognosis appears good for *Rolling Stone's* continued growth and success. Significant inroads have been made into the adult magazine market. A media marketing sheet compiled by Simmons reveals that the magazine compares favorably with *Esquire* and *GQ* in attracting the twenty-five- to thirty-nine-year-old market, many of whom have household incomes in excess of $30,000 and have attended or graduated from college. This demographic cross section of American consumers is highly prized by advertisers. *Rolling Stone's* shift into nonmusic areas in the 1980s has led to the healthiest years in its history. Consumer research conducted by the magazine during the mid–1980s has revealed a demand for renewed emphasis on music coverage on the part of readers. While *Rolling Stone* has made minor adjustments in that direction, it continues to maintain a precarious balance between music and nonmusic subjects. The result: although lacking the bite, conviction, and sense of community characterizing its early years, *Rolling Stone* now clears a profit of approximately $3 million a year, and as of 20 September 1985, total paid circulation surpassing Wenner's long-stated goal of 1 million copies.

Information Sources

BIBLIOGRAPHY
Blum, David. "Wenner in Wonderland." *New York* 18 (February 25, 1985): 28–37.
Canape, Charlene. "Playing Politics in a Big Way: National, World Affairs Are Ever More Vital for These Magazines." *Advertising Age* 53 (July 26, 1982): M2–3, 6.
Cooper, Ann. "Jann Wenner Grows from Gonzo to Gotham." *Advertising Age* 56 (January 28, 1985): 3ff.
Dougherty, Philip H. "Advertising: Rolling Stone Goes Platinum." *New York Times*, May 28, 1985, sec. 4, p. 14, col. 3.
Edelstein, Andrew J. "Underground Newspapers," in *The Pop Sixties*. New York: World Almanac, 1985, pp. 211–13.
Emmrich, Stuart. "Bonanni Guides 'Rolling Stone' to Center." *Advertising Age* 53 (March 29, 1982): 4ff.

Hafferkamp, Jack. "Rolling Moves into Mainstream." *Advertising Age* 55 (October 18, 1984): 13–14.
Helander, Brock. "Jann Wenner/Rolling Stone Magazine." In *Rock Who's Who*, pp. 620–22. New York: Schirmer, 1982.
Love, Barbara. "Henry W. Marks: 'We Have No Competitor But Ignorance,' Contends Persuasive Sales Exec." *Folio* 3 (February 1984): 48ff.
INDEXES
> External: RILM, 1967– . Music Index, 1968– . Popular Music Periodical Index, 1973–76. Popular Periodical Index, 1974– . Magazine Index, 1977– . Readers' Guide, 1978– .

REPRINT EDITION
> Microform: UMI. AMS Film Service, 1967–79.

LOCATION SOURCES
> Widely available.

Publication History

TITLE AND TITLE CHANGES
> *Rolling Stone.*

VOLUME AND ISSUE DATA
> Volumes 1– , 1967– .

FREQUENCY OF PUBLICATION
> Semimonthly.

PUBLISHER
> Straight Arrow Publishers, Inc.

PLACES OF PUBLICATION
> San Francisco, 1967–76. New York, 1976– .

EDITOR
> Jann Wenner, 1967–

Frank W. Hoffman

ROYAL MUSICAL ASSOCIATION, PROCEEDINGS OF THE

The Musical Association was founded by John Stainer in 1874. The early history of the society and its annual publication, *Proceedings of the Musical Association,* was compiled by J. Percy Baker in the fiftieth volume of the journal (50:129–38). The society originated as a learned society "for the investigation and discussion of subjects connected with the art and science of music" (100:x). The purpose of the journal was to reproduce the spoken proceedings of the society. Thus, it appealed to the informed musician as entertaining discourse and was not meant to be scholarly.

Associated with the International Music Society as its London chapter from 1899–1914, the Musical Association fostered a broadened range of interests. The *Proceedings* began to include historical essays, even welcoming some non-English topics. By the 1930s the journal began to adopt a tighter focus; articles of scholarly interest began to appear along with those intended for the informed amateur. However, compared to German musicology, the topics remained general.[1]

The journal changed its name to *Proceedings of the Royal Musical Association* in 1944 (v. 71), and from that time the society experienced an increase in membership and the number of chapters. No longer could all the papers read at the association meetings be printed. The activities of the association also broadened. In 1951, the Royal Musical Association initiated the publication of *Musica Britannica*; in 1961 the *Royal Musical Association Research Chronicle* was inaugurated.

Since the 1960s the materials in the *Proceedings of the RMA* have more closely approximated international musicological scholarship. The details of the association meetings have been omitted and the written essays have appeared in a format intended for written scholarly discourse, with ample documentation and supporting material. The landmark *Centenary Essays* (v. 100; 1974) was received as a notable contribution to international musicology, with essays by Austrian, German, Hungarian, and American, as well as British scholars.

The format of the journal has varied slightly since 1874. It has appeared annually with occasional internal and external indexes. The page size has varied from 5" by 8" to 5½" by 8½"; the volumes have ranged from 60 to 225 pages. Pagination is renewed for each volume. The journal has included advertisements only for other publications of the Royal Musical Association, including the *Royal Music Association Research Chronicle* (q.v.) and *Musica Britannica*.

As of February 1986, the *Proceedings of the Royal Musical Association* was superseded by the semiannual publication of the *Journal of the Royal Musical Association*. Continuing as editor, David Greer announced an editorial board consisting of eight prominent British scholars.[2] The new *Journal* presents[3] new research in "all branches of musical scholarship," and has continued the *Proceedings*'s recent trend toward a more international scholarship. Issues average close to 200 pages in length and contain 5 to 10 articles, 20 to 30 pages each in length. Abstracts of conference papers presented in Great Britain along with a handful of reviews and advertisements round out each issue. The spring 1989 issue included selected papers read at the association's 23rd annual conference.

Notes

1. For examples, see Donald J. Grout, "Review of *Royal Musical Association Centenary Essays,*" *Music and Letters* 59 (1978): 55.

2. Kristine K. Forney, "Editor's Column," *AMS Newsletter* 16 (1986): 8.

3. Originally the editing of the *Proceedings of the Musical Association* was the responsibility of the honorable secretary of the association. This title changed to secretary in 1892. From 1945 an honorary editor was included on the roster of the association (except for 1951/2). From 1969 the phrase "Edited by_____" has appeared on the title page of the journal. Therefore all these titles are included under the category of editor.

Information Sources

BIBLIOGRAPHY

Abraham, Gerald. "Our First Hundred Years." *Proceedings of the Royal Musical Association* 100 (1973–1974): 7–13.

Baker, J. Percy. "The Musical Association: A Fifty Years Retrospective Compiled with the Authority of the Council by the Secretary." *Proceedings of the Musical Association* 50 (1923–24): 129–38.

Grout, Donald J. "Review of *Royal Musical Association Centenary Essay.*" *Music and Letters* 59 (1978): 52–55.

Lunn, Henry C. "The London Musical Season." *The Musical Times* 17 (1976): 551–52.

REPRINT EDITION

Microform: Brookhaven Press, 1874–1962.

INDEXES

Internal: v. 25 (1899), v. 30 (1904), v. 33 (1909), v. 40 (1914), and v. 50 (1924). External: Bibliographie des Musikschrifttums, 1936, 1950– . Music Index, 1952– . British Humanities Index, 1965– . RILM, 1967– .

Loewenberg, Alfred, and Rupert Erlebach. *Index to Papers Read Before the Members of the Royal Musical Association, 1874–1944*. London: Whitehead and Miller, 1948.

The Royal Musical Association: Proceedings Vols. 1–90 (1874–1964). Classified List of Contents. Compiled by Alan Smith. London: The Royal Musical Association, 1966.

LOCATION SOURCES

Widely available.

Publication History

TITLE AND TITLE CHANGES

Proceedings of the Musical Association: For the Investigation and Discussion of Subjects Connected with the Arts and Sciences of Music, founded May 29, 1874, 1874–1943/4. *Proceedings of the Royal Musical Association*, 1944/5–February 1986. *Journal of the Royal Music Association*, 1987– .

VOLUME AND ISSUE DATA

Volumes 1– , 1874/5– .

FREQUENCY OF PUBLICATION

Annual, 1874/5–1981. Semiannual, 1982–86, 1987– .

PUBLISHERS

Spottiswoode & Co., 1874–78. Novello & Co., 1878–18.

Whitehead and Miller, 1918–48. The Royal Musical Association, 1948–86. Oxford University Press, 1987– .

PLACE OF PUBLICATION

London.

EDITORS

Honorable Secretary: Charles K. Salaman, 1874/5–76/7. James Higgs, 1877/8–82/3. F. W. Davenport, 1883/4–90/1. J. Percy Baker, 1891/2. Secretary: J. Percy Baker, 1892/3–1935/6. Rupert Erlebach, 1936/7–55/6. Nigel Fortune, 1956/7–75/6. Hugh Cobbe, 1976/7– . Honorary Editor: Marion M. Scott, 1945/6–50/1.

A. Hyatt King, 1952/3–56/7. Frederick Sternfeld, 1957/8–62/2. Peter Le Hurray, 1962/3–66/7. Edward Olleson, 1967/8–68/9. Editor: Edward Olleson, 1969/70–74/5. Geoffrey Chew, 1975/6. David Greer, 1976– .

Carmelo P. Comberiati

ROYAL MUSICAL ASSOCIATION RESEARCH CHRONICLE

The *Royal Musical Association Research Chronicle* has undergone various changes of purpose and format in its somewhat irregular publication history since 1961. The original editor, Thurston Dart, intended the *Research Chronicle* as a clearing house for the "large quantities of musicological raw material—lists, indexes, catalogues, calendars, extracts from newspapers, new fragments of biographical information, and so on" (1:i). An inexpensive format allowed for the convenient circulation of valuable research material.

V. 3, with Jeremy Noble as editor, introduced a "Register of Theses on Music Presented in British Universities." Updates on theses continue to appear in the later volumes and represent a valuable service. Thanks to the financial support of the British Academy, the *Chronicle* began to appear regularly with v. 7. Michael Tilmouth became editor in 1969 and started to encourage narrative articles, rather than the original documentary materials, a trend continued by Geoffrey Chew, editor since 1978. In a lengthy editorial (16:2), Chew proposed that "the primary commitment and loyalty of the *Chronicle* must be to nitty-gritty historical musicology." Included in v. 16 for the first time were a "Book Review" section and the announcement of a reader's "Forum."

With the new editorial policy, recent issues of the *Research Chronicle* have been less parochial. V. 17 included articles about the music of Dufay, thirteenth-century Paris, Alfonso Ferrabosco, and singers at San Marco in Venice. The commitment to "nitty-gritty" musicology still seems to be somewhat narrowly defined as articles concerning European art music; however, it is clear that the *Research Chronicle* will have to be consulted as an important source of musicological commentary, with emphasis on musical "raw material."

The *Research Chronicle* has remained approximately the same size, 8″ by 10½″, throughout its changes in format. Although the quality of paper and the clarity of typesetting has improved with later issues, the early mimeographed issues can be easily read. The articles range from short two-page notices to lengthy compilations over consecutive issues, usually with four to six articles in each thirty- to fifty-page issue.

Information Sources

BIBLIOGRAPHY

Fallows, David, Arnold Whittall, and John Blacking, edited by Nigel Fortune. "Musicology in Great Britain since 1945." *Acta musicologica* 52 (1980): 38–68.

INDEXES
    Internal: annual cumulative tables of contents in Vols. 4–13 (1964–76); with an
    inlaid sheet in Vol. 14 (1978).
    External: Music index, 1968–   (retrospective from 1961). RILM, 1967–   .
LOCATION SOURCES
    Widely available.

Publication History

TITLE AND TITLE CHANGES
    Royal Musical Association Research Chronicle.
VOLUME AND ISSUE DATA
    Volumes 1– , 1961– .
FREQUENCY OF PUBLICATION
    Annual.
PUBLISHER
    Royal Musical Association.
PLACES OF PUBLICATION
    Cambridge, England, 1961–62. Taunton, Somerset, England, 1963–76. London,
    1975– .
EDITORS
    Thurston Dart, 1961–62. Jeremy Noble, 1963 and 1966. Nigel Fortune, Acting
    Editor, 1964–65. Michael Tilmouth, 1969–77. Geoffrey Chew, 1978–   .

Carmelo P. Comberiati

RUCH MUZYCZNY

Since 1957, the eminently readable, highly stimulating Polish biweekly musical newsmagazine *Ruch Muzyczny* (in German: *Musikalische Bewegung*—the
title cannot be adequately rendered into English) had kept track of current musical
events in Poland and abroad. Its pages contain reports and reviews of concert
and opera life as well as of Polish festivals (such as the Warsaw Autumn and
the *Vratislavia Cantans)* and competitions (including the Chopin and Wieniawski). It also endeavors to bring Polish music lovers information about the
present musical scene abroad. It is, however, a good deal more than a newsmagazine; in many respects, it is the musical equivalent of the central European
literary journal where the major intellectual issues of the day are the subject of
often heated debate.

Much of this publication's success seems to stem from the excellence of its
staff of musical "scholar-essayists" (such as Bohdan Pociej), who manage to
engage the interest of the nonspecialist reader without trivializing the content.
Established Polish musicologists often give their newest ideas a first public trial
here, while younger musicologists may obtain their initial public exposure by
writing for it. Discussions of Polish new music figure prominently and Polish
composers frequently explain their music and ideas. When Polish musicians seek

to question some aspect of Polish musical life, they often submit a polemic to this serial. Discussion of concert policy is also frequent. *Ruch Muzyczny* contains numerous interviews. Important statements by foreign musical personalities are regularly translated. Mycielski's courageous 1960 reply to Shostakovich's mean-spirited published denunciation of the Warsaw Autumn festival deserves notice. The journal also offers numerous special issues. After Nadia Boulanger's death, it published remembrances by her Polish students (24.1–2, 1980). It contains copious photographs and other illustrations, as well as announcements of publications, concerts, and festivals.

In short, *Ruch Muzyczny* has been established as a significant aspect of contemporary Polish musical culture. Future music historians will no doubt value its vivid portrayal of contemporary musical life. Issues run to about twenty 8″ by 13″ pages, usually of three to four long narrow columns. During the summer, *Ruch Muzyczny* appears less frequently than twice a month.

Two earlier and quite distinct Polish musical newsmagazines bore the same title. The first was published between 1857 and 1862 and provides an important record of Polish musical life before the January Insurrection. The second was begun by Stefan Kisielewski (also the first editor of *Ruch Muzyczny*) in 1945 in Kraków even before the war was over, and ceased publication in 1949.

Information Sources

BIBLIOGRAPHY
Michalowski, Kornel. "Bibliographical Resources for Music Periodicals in Poland."
    Periodica Musica 1 (1983): 14–15.
INDEXES
    External: Bibliographie des Musikschrifttums, 1958– . Music Index, 1960– .
    RILM, 1967– .
LOCATION SOURCES
    Widely available.

Publication History

TITLE AND TITLE CHANGES
    Ruch Muzyczny.
VOLUME AND ISSUE DATA
    Volumes 1– , 1957– .
FREQUENCY OF PUBLICATION
    Semimonthly.
PUBLISHERS
    PWM (Polish Musical Editions), 1957–59. "Prasa—Ksiazka—Ruch," 1960– .
PLACES OF PUBLICATION
    Kraków, 1957–59. Warsaw, 1960– .
EDITORS
    Stefan Kisielowski, 1957–59. Zygmunt Mycielski, 1960–68. Ludwik Erhardt,
    1968– .

Stefan M. Ehrenkreutz

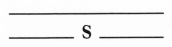

S

SANGEET KALA VIHAR. See JOURNAL OF THE INDIAN MUSICO-
LOGICAL SOCIETY

SCHOOL MUSICIAN, THE

During his tenure as an advertising editor with Buescher Instrument Company,
Robert L. Shepherd was impressed with the growth of instrumental ensembles
in the American Midwestern states. After leaving Buescher in 1928, he founded
a new magazine, *The School Musician* (SM), "exclusively for school band and
orchestra musicians and their directors" (25.2:17). The magazine parallels and
chronicles the development of public school music in America, and its contributors include major figures in instrumental music from 1929 to the present day.

The School Musician was founded as a popular magazine with a simple message: See how others have achieved success in music? You can do it too! The
feature articles and regular departments have been reinforced by glossy advertising to get this message to music students and teachers. The journal has presented practical articles by major figures and aspiring major figures in
instrumental music over the years. The nature and quality of these articles has
reflected the popular origins of the journal. As its readers became more sophisticated and professional through the 1960s and 1970s, the journal has responded
with a more focused coverage of instrumental music and a corresponding attempt
to improve the content of its feature articles while preserving its upbeat style
and popular approach.

Early issues of the magazine feature roughly ten articles, usually between one
and two pages long, contributed by a noted group of authors, as well as columns
of coming events, humor, and musical achievements. Articles were often continued from month to month, and advertising was prominent. The periodical

presented a positive if not enthusiastic view of instrumental school music and, in particular, championed the popular national music competition movement. A monthly column highlighting a successful national figure in instrumental music, "We Are Making America Musical," was prominent in the magazine's founding issue and continues today. The editors take pride in tracing many prominent contemporary music leaders to early issues: Frederick Fennell, singer/composer Mel Torme, violinist Yehudi Menuhin, and Chicago Symphony Orchestra hornist Frank Brouk, to name but a few.

Since the journal addressed the interests of both students and teachers, its articles cover a broad range of topics: music contests, summer camps (especially Interlochen), master classes, self-development and continuing education, musical acoustics, twirling techniques, repertoire lists, new technologies, uniforms, fund-raising programs, musical interpretation and pedagogy, music fundamentals, biographies of prominent band directors, festival and convention news, marching and show bands, and student motivation. New columnists and feature topics supplemented established coverage as the music profession evolved.

The School Musician began publishing a monthly series of specific tips on playing techniques in 1937 with columns on playing the clarinet, trombone, and saxophone. These monthly columns have remained a prominent feature of the journal to the present day although undergoing many changes in authorship, as well as additions and deletions of topics. Current issues, for example, include the following regular columns: "Band Music Reviews" by Richard Strange, "Jazz Ensembles" by Don Verne Joseph, "Computers" by Gary Wittlich, "Clarinet and Saxophone Topics" by Harry R. Gee, "Show Choirs" by Paul E. Thoms, and "Brass Workshop" by Gloria J. Flor. Over the years, columns on percussion, flute, strings, accordion, twirling, composition and arranging, audiovisual aids, piano, organ, parent booster clubs, and choral music were introduced and withdrawn at various irregular intervals.

"The School Music News" was introduced in 1938 as a compilation of coming events and other announcements of interest to directors and students. It featured a "newspaper" format within the magazine and ran until 1957. A similar layout dedicated to teenagers, "The Teenager Section," was introduced in 1952. Other "newspaper" sections included "Baton Twirling" and "Choral Section."

A number of issues are of interest to the researcher. The January 1937 issue (8.5) included a reprint of A. R. McAllister's address at the National School Band Association's December convention. This speech addresses the need for ethical behavior by music teachers in their dealings with music and instrument companies and students. The address is doubly significant because it precipitated the decline of the N.S.B.A. (National School Band Association) as a viable professional association. The twenty-fifth anniversary issue included "The Passing Parade" (25.2:17–18, 48–49, 52–55) and a special article by Robert L. Shepherd, which provides a valuable history of the early band movement in the United States. The fiftieth anniversary volume included an eight-part series,

"The School Musician Time Capsule" which chronicles the years 1929 to 1968, and the history of *The School Musician* and instrumental music in America.

The relationship between *The School Musician* and professional music organizations is also significant. From the start, Shepherd provided space in *The School Musician* to the officers of the new National School Band and Orchestra Association (N.S.B.O.A.) as as device to promote instrumental music in the schools and to increase circulation of the magazine. The journal has since catalogued the organization and reorganization of such groups. "The Band Stand" was created as a regular column in 1951 as a bulletin board for the College Band Directors National Association. In 1952, *The School Musician* adopted the Modern Music Masters (Tri-M), a high school music honorary society. The American School Band Directors Association replaced the N.S.B.O.A. in 1954 with *The School Musician* playing an important promotional role for the organization. Phi Beta Mu, the national band honorary fraternity, joined *The School Musician* in 1954, and the National Catholic Bandmaster's Association first appeared in the magazine in 1955. In 1970, the Women's Band Directors National Association became the most recent addition to the journal's correspondents.

In February 1951, Robert L. Shepherd was replaced by Forrest McAllister (son of A. R. McAllister) under whose leadership *The School Musician* continued to expand. In the January 1965 (36.5) issue, the name of the journal became *The School Musician/Director & Teacher*, signaling an important shift in emphasis toward increased service to music professionals. An advisory board is listed for the first time in the September 1972 (44.1) issue. Forrest McAllister became consulting editor in 1976 when George Littlefield was named editor. The final editor, Dr. Edgar B. Gangware, Jr., took over with the September 1979 (51.1) issue. Issues in the 1980s reveal a reduced number of pages, apparently a part of the editors' effort to reduce *SM*'s overlap with other journals—for example, coverage of choral and piano music—in favor of a tighter focus on school band issues. In March 1987 (53.7) the journal ceased publication.

Advertising and news of the music industry were prominent throughout the history of the journal. Advertisers ranged from instrument manufacturers and music publishers to uniform and accessory companies. An editorial by Forrest McAllister encouraged subscribers to patronize the journal's advertisers. "It is through the cooperation of these advertisers that this magazine will continue to expand into new and greater phases of Music Education" (23.1:9). The introduction of new technologies in music was an important contribution of the journal.

The School Musician/Director & Teacher appeared in a 8¼″ by 11¼″ format that changed little in the journal's history. It expanded from twenty pages in early issues to over sixty pages in the early 1970s. Subsequent issues decreased to approximately forty pages, reflecting the more limited scope. Photographs were a prominent part of v. 1 and continued to be of high quality. *The School*

Musician/Director & Teacher was published in English and appeared monthly except for July and August. A yearly index was included for vs. 37–50.

Information Sources

INDEXES
>External: Music Index, 1949–   . Education Index, 1949–   . Music Article Guide, 1965–   .

REPRINT EDITIONS
>Microform: UMI.

LOCATION SOURCES
>Widely available.

Publication History

TITLE AND TITLE CHANGES
>*The School Musician*, 1929–65. *The School Musician/Director & Teacher*, 1966–87.

VOLUME AND ISSUE DATA
>Volumes 1–53.7, 1929–87.

FREQUENCY OF PUBLICATION
>10/year.

PUBLISHER
>School Musician, Inc., 1929–87.

PLACES OF PUBLICATION
>Chicago, Illinois, October 1929–June 1954. Joliet, Illinois, September 1954–June/July 1978. Chicago, Illinois, September 1978–87.

EDITORS
>Robert L. Shepherd, 1929–51. Forrest McAllister, 1951–76. George Littlefield, 1976–79. Edgar B. Gangware, Jr., 1979–87.

Richard P. Kennell

SCHOOL MUSICIAN/DIRECTOR/TEACHER, THE. See THE SCHOOL MUSICIAN

SCHWEIZERISCHE MUSIKZEITUNG

The *Schweizerische Musikzeitung* is the oldest and most distinguished music journal still being published in Switzerland. In 1861 the Bern Kantionalgesangverein initiated a *Sängerblatt* containing articles and information of interest to the choral societies that made up the association. Very quickly the journal broadened its scope both with respect to its audience and to the materials included in it. By 1866, as the *Schweizerisches Sängerblatt*, it served the Eidgenössischen Sängerverein, and in 1900 it was named the official organ of the Schweizerisches Tonkünstlerverein. Since 1906 it has also been associated with the Schweizerischen Gesang- und Musiklehrerverein (later called the Schweizerisches Musik-pädagogischen Verband).

The materials included in the journal reflect the ever-increasing scope of the readership. Originally concentrating on singing and choral topics as well as notices about the member groups in the association, the subject matter expanded gradually during the first twenty-five years of publication. By the turn of the century major essays, several per issue, on historical topics, genres, new compositions, and composers formed the central emphasis of each issue. Swiss, German, and Austrian topics are clearly favored. Along with the continued notices about local and foreign choral societies, increased space was devoted to reviews of performances and new compositions. From about 1876 the final two pages or so were given to advertisements. This section has expanded to eight to ten pages of notices devoted to music, books, recordings, instruction, and competitions.

After surviving World War I without too many difficulties, the *Schweizerische Musikzeitung* became more explicitly international in scope under the editorship of Karl Heinrich David. Material devoted to singing and singers came to be centralized under the heading "Sängerblatt/Chronique des chanteurs." The "Sängerblatt" portion established itself as a separate periodical by 1937. The journal has maintained its present format since that time and has enjoyed the editorial guidance of a succession of noted scholars. Early articles tended to be short, but they occasionally were continued in later issues. Contributions such as G. Güldenstein's "Phenomenologie der Musik" (71:100–103) suggest the more scholarly level occasionally attained at this time. Special issue topics include Othmar Schoeck (71.2) and the 1932 Tagung des Schweizerische Tonkünstlervereins (71.8). The latter, yearly event was traditionally well covered in the journal. Articles after World War II range from five to ten pages and reveal a slightly greater scholarliness and emphasis on modern music as suggested in such titles as Romain Rolland's "Romain Rolland über die Zukunftsausgaben der Musikwissenschaft" (85:50–51), "Universität und Musik in der USA" by Bruno Nettl (95:7–9), "Alban Berg als Apologet Arnold Schoenberg" by Willi Reich (95:475–77), János Liebner's "Une oeuvre oubliées de Bartók" (100:357–59), and Ivo Supičić's "La pédagogie musicale et l'historicisme interpretatif" (100:351–57). Half of the journal is still devoted to local, regional, national, and international reports, as well as reviews of concerts, books, and other musical publications. Musical examples regularly accompany the articles and since 1974 occasional photographs appear. A trend toward more topical articles and a reduction in news and advertisements in the 1960s has since been reversed.

The *Sängerblatt* began as a bimonthly paper of from four to six pages. In 1876 the typeface changed from Fraktur to Roman type, and each issue was expanded to eight to ten pages. Continuing pagination throughout a year started in 1878, and the total length of a yearly volume grew from around 200 pages in 1878 to some 350 by the outbreak of World War I. Following 1898, thirty-six issues appeared each year; after the war began, the frequency returned to bimonthly. After 1887 each yearly accumulation included an index. In 1929 the format changed. The newspaper-sized 10" by 13" was replaced by a smaller 7" by 10", a title page was added, and a new typeface was used. In 1940 the journal became a monthly, and since 1960 it has been issued every other month.

Since the change in format and editorial policy in 1929, the *Schweizerische Musikzeitung* has maintained a reputation as a major journal for music professionals. Articles appear in German and French and are contributed by an international body of scholars.

Information Sources

BIBLIOGRAPHY
Becker, Hugo. "Die Geschichte der Schweizerische Musikzeitung." *Schweizerische Musikzeitung* 101 (1961): 2–15.
Fellinger, Imogen. *Verzeichnis der Musikzeitschriften des 19. Jahrhunderts*. Studien zur Musikgeschichte des 19. Jahrhunderts, 10. Regensburg: Gustav Bosse, 1968.
INDEXES
    Internal: each volume indexed, vs. 26– .
    External: Bibliographie des Musikschrifttums, 1939, 1950– . Music Index, 1957– . RILM, 1969– .
REPRINT EDITION
    Microform: Schnase, 1861–1928.
LOCATION SOURCES
    Library of Congress, vs. 1–74. New York Public Library, vs. 72– . Detroit Public Library, vs. 79– .

Publication History

TITLE AND TITLE CHANGES
    Schweizerische Musikzeitung.
VOLUME AND ISSUE DATA
    Volumes 1– , 1861– .
FREQUENCY OF PUBLICATION
    Semimonthly, 1861–97. 36/year, 1898–1917. Semimonthly, 1918–39. Monthly, 1940–59. Bimonthly, 1960– .
PUBLISHERS
    Johann R. Weber, 1861–79. Gebrüder Hug, 1879– .
PLACES OF PUBLICATION
    Bern, 1861–79. Zürich, 1879– .
EDITORS
    R. Weber, 1861–75. Karl G. Weber, 1875–84. August Glück, 1884–90. Arnold Niggli, 1891–98. Karl Nef, 1898–1909. Ernst Isler, 1910–27. Karl Heinrich David, 1928–41. Willi Schuh, 1941–68. Rudolf Kelterborn, 1969–74. Jürg Stunzl, 1975– .

Paul W. Borg

SCHWEIZERISCHES JAHRBUCH FÜR MUSIKWISSENSCHAFT

In 1924 the Neue schweizerische Musikgesellschaft published a *Festschrift* containing papers presented that year at its twenty-fifth anniversary congress in Basel. Thus began what the organization envisioned as an annual journal for Swiss musicological research, the *Schweizerisches Jahrbuch für Musikwissenschaft*. Although announced for the following year, the second volume appeared only in 1927, and the entire project ended within fifteen years after only seven numbers. The plan to issue different volumes under the sponsorship of the various local chapters, though perhaps admirable and democratic, ultimately proved too unreliable to sustain the journal after only a single issue per chapter.

The contents of the *Schweizerisches Jahrbuch* represent the best in Swiss musical scholarship between the two world wars. Jacques Handschin contributed articles throughout the journal's run, including "Eine wenig beachtete Stilrichtung innerhalb der mittelalterlichen Mehrstimmigkeit" (1:56–75), "Über reine Harmonie und temporierte Tonleitern" (2:145–66), and "De différentes conceptions de Bach" (4:7–35). Other scholars of the stature of Willy Hess dealt with a broad range of topics that include Othmar Schoeck and Ludwig van Beethoven ("Beethovens Werke und ihre Gesamtausgabe" [5:163–88]). Previously unpublished letters by Richard Wagner, Hector Berlioz, and Franz Liszt appear in the first few issues. Musical examples accompany several of the articles. Although the subject matter is international in character, there is a certain reliance on Swiss source materials. Topics range from composer studies, poets and poetry, and folk music, to organs, religious music, choral music, and aesthetics. Reports on the activities of the Neue schweizerische Musikgesellschaft and obituaries for important Swiss scholars, which appear in vs. 2–5, form a relatively insignificant portion of the journal's information.

The first five issues of the journal contain between five and ten signed articles, ranging from five to forty-five pages in length and averaging twenty. Most are in German, although the volume issued from Geneva contains articles in French. Vs. 6 and 7 are devoted, respectively, to the dissertations of two young Swiss scholars of the time, Arnold Geering (*Die Vokalmusik in der Schweiz zur Zeit der Reformation. Leben und Werke von Bartholomäus Frank, Johannes Wannenmacker, Cosmas Alder*) and Walter Robert Nef (*Der St. Galler Organist Fridolin Sicher und seine Orgeltabulatur*).

Each volume runs to approximately 130 to 150 pages and measures 5½" by 8½". There are no advertisements and very few illustrations. Although vs. 1–5 each contain a table of contents, no general index exists for the *Schweizerisches Jahrbuch*.

Information Sources

LOCATION SOURCES

    Library of Congress, Rutgers University, University of Pennsylvania, Indiana University, University of North Carolina (complete). University of Chicago, New

York Public Library, Columbia University, Harvard University, University of Minnesota (partial run).
REPRINT EDITION
Microform: Swets and Zeitlinger Bv.

Publication History

TITLE AND TITLE CHANGES
Schweizerisches Jahrbuch für Musikwissenschaft.
VOLUME AND ISSUE DATA
Volumes 1–7, 1924–38.
FREQUENCY OF PUBLICATION
Annual, with irregularities.
PUBLISHER
Neue schweizerische Musikgesellschaft.
PLACES OF PUBLICATION
Basil, 1924, 1933, 1938. Winterthur, 1927.
Bern-Freiburg-Solvthurn, 1928. Geneva, 1929. Zürich, 1931.
EDITORS
Each volume edited by the officers of a different regional chapter of the Neue schweizerische Musikgesellschaft.

Paul W. Borg

SIGNALE FÜR DIE MUSIKALISCHE WELT

Signale für die musikalische Welt[1] was founded in 1843 by Bartholf W. Senff. An enterprising young publisher, Senff sensed that the townspeople's curiosity about the music world was not entirely satisfied by the two prominent journals published in Leipzig at the time, the *Allgemeine musikalische Zeitung* (q.v.) and the *Neue Zeitschrift für Musik* (q.v.). These two journals were intended primarily for the connoisseur and the professional musician. Senff, on the other hand, wanted to reach "not just the musically-educated, but the entire world of the educated."[2]

Senff's intuition appears to have been correct, for *Signale* not only became popular, but it survived for almost a century and succumbed only to the chaos of World War II. While *Allgemeine musikalische Zeitung* and *Neue Zeitschrift* contained primarily scholarly, reflective articles, *Signale* offered its readers the very latest news in the music world. The reports are usually only a paragraph long, but they contain the essential information. The tone of the journal is generally objective and uncommonly free of polemics. The unpresuming contents and writing style are only two factors that made *Signale* accessible to and popular with the average Leipzig resident. It also cost less than the other two Leipzig music journals.

Issues usually open with one or two short articles, of one to four pages. Some address practical issues, such as voice training (30:529–31, 593–97, 609–12,

673–77, and 689–92) and teaching children to play the piano (30:721). Others focus on the lives and works of contemporary composers and on music festivals or concert series. A regular feature is "Dur und Moll" (later "Kleinere Mitteilungen von hier und dort"), where diverse news items from around the world are assembled in an abbreviated form. One issue, for instance, reports that Clara Schumann performed with great success in London and that a new music journal had been founded in Madrid (30:155). Entire paragraphs are devoted to reviews of important concerts. These reports focus primarily on solo voice, violin, and piano recitals, a journalistic prejudice of the times. Occasionally, there are short novels of interest to music lovers, as well as excerpts from travelogues kept by the editors and other correspondents.

Of use to music historians are the "address books" that appear occasionally. Here one finds the names of prominent people in the music world, along with their positions and the cities in which they lived. The final pages are always reserved for advertisements by music publishers (including Senff's own press), music stores, music organizations, and conservatories.

While many issues are filled primarily with articles by Senff himself (or after Senff's death, with articles by later editors), the editor did rely on material from co-workers, especially for reports on concert life in other cities. Some of these contributors included Moritz Hauptmann, Leipzig composer and theorist; Christian Louis Heinrich Köhler, Königsberg music critic and journalist; Dr. Ernst Kossak, music critic in Berlin; and Richard Pohl, journalist and composer in Munich.

After publishing a trial issue in November 1842, Senff officially inaugurated *Signale* on 2 January 1843. Appearing on a weekly basis, the journal, printed in *Frakturschrift*, was published at first in issues of eight pages. From 1849 on the issues were of different sizes, from sixteen to thirty-two pages. In 1869 the journal began to appear more frequently, allowing Senff to fulfill one of his main goals: to offer the most up-to-date news. The journal did not vary from large octavo format (5½″ by 8½″), in spite of the fact that it was printed over the years by four different printers. Each volume contains a directory of contents.

Notes

1. Only nineteen of the journal's ninety-nine volumes were available to the author of this review. Many of the general statements are borrowed from Rudolf Vogler's *Die Musikzeitschrift "Signale für die musikalische Welt" 1843–1900*, published as v. 81 in the series *Kölner Beitäge zur Musikforschung* (Regensburg: Gustav Bosse Verlag, 1975).

2. "Die *Signale* gehören nicht nur der musikalischen, sondern der ganzen gebildeten Welt." Quoted in Vogler, *Die Musikzeitschrift*, p. 154.

Information Sources

BIBLIOGRAPHY
Fellinger, Imogen. *Verzeichnis der Musikzeitschriften des 19. Jahrhunderts*. Studien zur Musikgeschichte des 19. Jahrhundert, 10. Regensburg: Gustav Bosse Verlag, 1968.

Vogler, Rudolf. *Die Musikzeitschrift "Signale für die musikalische Welt" 1843–1900.*
    Kölner Beitäge zur Musikforschung, 81. Regensburg: Gustav Bosse Verlag, 1975.
INDEXES
    External: Bibliographie des Musikschrifttums, 1937.
REPRINT EDITION
    Microform: Schnase (incomplete).
LOCATION SOURCES
    Library of Congress, University of Michigan, University of California—Berkeley,
    University of Pennsylvania, Stanford University, Boston Public Library, Harvard
    University, Yale University (all partial runs).

Publication History

TITLE AND TITLE CHANGES
    Signale für die musikalische Welt.
VOLUME AND ISSUE DATA
    Volumes 1–99, 1843–1941.
FREQUENCY OF PUBLICATION
    Weekly, and occasionally more frequently.
PUBLISHERS
    Expedition, 1843–47. Verlag von Bartholf Senff, 1847–1907. Publisher unknown,
    1907–20. Redepennig, 1920–27. Signale für die musikalische Welt, 1927–41.
PLACES OF PUBLICATION
    Leipzig, 1843–1907. Berlin-Leipzig, 1907–20. Berlin, 1920–41.
EDITORS
    Bartholf Senff, 1843–1900. Detlef Schultz, 1902–07. August Spanuth, 1907–28.
    Max Chop, 1928–30. Walther Hirschberg, 1930–33. Walter Petzet, 1933–37.
    Richard Ohlekopf, 1937–41.

Diane McMullen

SING OUT

Sing Out was founded by People's Artists, Inc., in May 1950 to fill the void
left in the American left-wing folk music movement by the demise of *People's
Songs Bulletin* (1946–49). Its title was taken from a phrase in "The Hammer
Song" by Lee Hays and Pete Seeger featured in its debut issue. The journal's
stated purpose was to promote "people's music," which was defined in the first
issue as a music in which folk and concert traditions "shall now join in common
service to the common people . . . by one thing above all else we will judge it:
How well does it serve the common cause of Humanity?"

The heart of *Sing Out* has always been the songs. Each issue contains lyrics
and music to about a dozen "homemade" songs. Many important folksongs saw
their first publication in the pages of *Sing Out*. Accordingly, a flexi-disc providing
first verse and chorus to songs in the magazine has accompanied every other
issue beginning in July/August 1971 until 1977. *Sing Out* has also produced a
respected series of songbooks.

Pete Seeger has been associated with the magazine since its inception; his "Johnny Appleseed, Jr." column made its debut in the Fall 1954 issue. Each issue also includes book and record reviews, feature articles up to six pages in length, and interviews with folk musicians, a folk festival calendar, instructional columns, the "Songfinder" (a column where publications and recordings of songs desired by readers are identified), news notes, and letters. Advertising has always been music-related, including a large number from small folk labels and specialty shops. Several special issues devoted to themes in American music appeared in 1976–77, for example, "Native American Music" (24.5) and "Songs of Labor Struggle" (25.1). The January/February 1981 (29.1) issue was devoted to "Folk Music and Disabled People."

Support for the magazine initially was limited to the New York City leftwing, but in the mid–1950s the sectarianism and polemics were somewhat curtailed and folk music became more prominently featured. With the decline of the Old Left, People's Artists was dissolved in 1957. In 1959, near financial collapse, the magazine was bailed out by Moses Asch of Folkways Records, just in time to ride the burgeoning tide of the folk music revival. By the mid–1960s *Sing Out* had achieved its editorial and commercial peak. However, an attempt at expanding newsstand distribution at the time the folk music revival was winding down proved disastrous.

The editor of *Sing Out* during its most influential years was co-founder Irwin Silber, who assumed this role in 1951 and retained it for seventeen years. During the early years of his tenure, the pages of *Sing Out* featured such notables as Paul Robeson, Walter Lowenfels, Waldemar Hille, and Alan Lomax. Contributors during the 1960s included Julius Lester, Israel Young, John Cohen, Josh Dunson, Pete Welding, A. L. Lloyd, Frederic Ramsey, Jon Pankake, and photographer Dave Gahr. Coverage included American and international folk music, traditional to contemporary styles, and relevant political commentary.

By the late 1960s, however, Silber found himself at political and musical odds with many of the staff and readers. One area of dissention was the emerging genre of folk rock, which to Silber was not appropriately political. Paul Nelson, on the other hand, articulately championed folk rock in important early examples of rock criticism, circa 1966–68. *Sing Out*, however, soon dropped the rock coverage. Another, and perhaps more significant, issue was Silber's increasing desire to emphasize again partisan politics in the publication. In 1971 he left the magazine.

The magazine was again in a precarious financial situation in the early 1980s; only one issue dated 1981 (29:1) appeared, and none were published in 1982. Regular publication of *Sing Out* resumed in April 1983 at a more realistic quarterly frequency, in a reduced 5¼" by 8½" format of about a hundred pages.

The physical appearance and frequency of *Sing Out* have varied over the years. For its first four years it was published monthly in a sixteen-page, 5" by 8" format. Frequency was reduced to quarterly and the size increased to thirty-two pages with 4.7 (Fall 1954). The size increased to fifty-two pages and continued to increase through the 1960s, occasionally to over a hundred pages. Frequency varied from four to six issues a year. The format was enlarged to 8½" by 11" in 1966 (16.1), and then was reduced to 7" by 10" (18.2).

Information Sources

BIBLIOGRAPHY
Denisoff, R. Serge. *Great Day Coming: Folk Music and the American Left*. Urbana: University of Illinois Press, 1971.
Dunson, Josh. *Freedom in the Air: Song Movements of the Sixties*. New York: International Publishers, 1965.
Reuss, Richard A. "American Folklore and Left-Wing Politics: 1927–1957." Ph.D. diss., Indiana University, 1971.
Senauke, Alan. "You've Got to Reap Just What You Sow: Roots of Sing Out Magazine." *Sing Out* 25 (May/June 1976): 3–7.
Silber, Irwin. "15 Years of Sing Out!" *Sing Out* 16 (February/March 1966): 43–49, 53.
Traum, Happy. "Sing Out! 25 Years Old This Month." *Guitar Player* 9 (May 1975): 16, 29.
INDEXES
External: Music Index, 1959– . Music Article Guide, 1965– . MLA International Bibliography, 1971– . Annual Index to Popular Music Record Reviews, 1972–77. Popular Music Periodicals Index, 1973–76. Access, 1976– . Magazine Index, 1977– . Arts and Humanities Citation Index, 1977–82. Alternative Press Index, 1980– .
REPRINT EDITIONS
Microform: UMI.
LOCATION SOURCES
Widely available.

Publication History

TITLE AND TITLE CHANGES
Sing Out! A People's Artists Publication, May 1950–Summer 1956 (1.1–6.3). *Sing Out!,* Winter 1956/57–Spring 1959 (6.4–8). *Sing Out! The Folk Song Magazine,* Summer 1959– (9–).
VOLUME AND ISSUE DATA
Volumes 1– , 1950– .
FREQUENCY OF PUBLICATION
Monthly, 1950–Summer 1954. 4–6/year, Fall 1954–82. Quarterly, 1983– .
PUBLISHERS
People's Artists, Inc., 1950–56. Sing Out, Inc., 1957–81. Sing Out Corporation, 1983– .
PLACES OF PUBLICATION
New York, 1950–81. Easton, Pennyslvania, 1983– .
EDITORS
Robert Wolfe, 1950. Waldemar Hille, 1950. Ernie Lieberman, 1950–51. Irwin Silber, 1951–68. Ed Badeaux, 1967–68. Julius Lester, 1967–68. Paul Nelson, 1967–68. Ethel Raim, 1967–68. Happy Traum, 1968–71. Rob Fleder, 1971. Bob Norman, 1971–77. Rhoda Mattern, 1975–79. Alan Senauke, 1975–77. Estelle

Schneider, 1976–78. Peter Wortsman, 1977–79. Nan Silver, 1978. Jennifer Block, 1978. Mimi Bluestone, 1979–80. Sarah Plant, 1979–80. Maise McAdro, 1980. Carolyn Bevis, 1980. Don Palmer, 1980. Mark D. Moss, 1983–   .

David D. Ginsburg

SONORUM SPECULUM. See KEY NOTES

SOURCE: MUSIC OF THE AVANT GARDE

"*Source,* a chronicle of the most recent and often the most controversial scores, serves as a medium of communication for the composer, the performer, and the student of the avant grade" (1:1).[1] Founded in 1967 under the leadership of Larry Austin of the University of California at Davis, it remains one of the finest documentations of the musical avant grade in the late 1960s and early 1970s. Although only eleven issues were published (1967–73), no other periodical has rivaled its unique, colorful, and timely presentation of contemporary music.

The journal's contents included compositions, articles, photo essays, and sound recordings. During the seven years of its existence, around 200 scores appeared by a variety of composers, some of the more notable being John Cage, "4'33"" (1961); Cornelius Cardew, "The Great Learnings" (1968–70); Barney Childs, "Nonet" (1967); Morton Feldman, "Between Categories" (1969); Lukas Foss, "Etudes for Organ" (1976); Ben Johnston, "Knocking Piece"; Anna Lockwood, "Piano Burning"; Alvin Lucier, "Gentle Fire" (1971); Robert Moran, "39 Minutes for 39 Autos"; Pauline Oliveros, "Sonic Meditations" (1971); Nam June Paik, "My Symphonies"; Harry Partch, "—And on the Seventh Day Petals Fell in Petaluma" (1963–64); and Steve Reich, "Four Organs" (1970). These scores, usually included in their entirety, span the stylistic gamut; several have become true classics of the era. Performance instructions for each piece were usually provided, along with a biography and photo.

Besides raising the reader's consciousness through the presentation of provocative compositions, *Source* also published articles that raised stimulating questions. Most notable were the extensive commentary, "Events/Comments: Is New Music Being Used for Political or Social Ends?" with statements by Feldman, Ashley, Cage, Tudor, Foss, Reich, and others (6:7–9, 90–91); Ben Johnston's, "How to Cook an Albatross" (7:63–65); and "Editorial: Is the Concerto Dead? Yes," "But Is It Music?" "Music is Dead—Long Live Music?" (8:55–58) by Larry Austin. Other articles take the form of interviews or conversations—John Cage and Lejaren Hiller, the ONCE Group, Karlheinz Stockhausen, Frederic Rzewski. Photo essays by David Freund are included on Harry Partch and David Tudor.

Although almost every score and article are worth special mention, several rise above the overall high level. The unique collaboration of John Cage and Calvin Sumsion, "Plexigram IV: Not Wanting to Say Anything About Marcel," is presented with special acetate reproductions of the original plastic overlays (7:1–19). The composition of Jocy de Oliveira, "Probabilistic Theatre I," comes with a slide for performance (4:34–36). The scores of Daniel Lentz's "Three Pieces" are noteworthy for their colorful and engaging design (3:43–49). The boldness of Dick Higgins' "The Thousand Symphonies: Symphony #585" is seen in an excerpt complete with bullet holes in the score (6:1–3, 35). Finally, Nelson Howe's "Fur Music" is presented with various strips of "fake fur" glued into the score (9:60–63).

As a special collaboration between *Source* and Columbia Masterworks, six records were produced, the first two appearing in n. 4 and subsequent offerings being found in ns. 6, 8, and 9/2. Largely the work of John McClure, director of Columbia Masterworks, Larry Austin, and David Behrman, some of the featured composers included Larry Austin, Robert Ashley, Alvin Lucier, Anna Lockwood, and Arthur Woodbury. Performance materials for all the works are found in the journal.

A valuable guide to the entire run of *Source* can be found in Michael D. Williams's *Source: Music of the Avant Garde, Annotated List of Contents and Cumulative Indices* (1978). Williams gives background information on the journal, as well as an annotated list of the contents and both name and title indices. In providing an analytical retrospective of *Source*, Williams points out that "there is a gradual trend from works and articles by well-known composers using relatively traditional media and notations in the early issues to multi-media events using graphic and verbal notations in the later issues" (Williams, p. 7). This obviously reflects Austin's editorial policy, for in n. 5 he says, "the time-honored concept of 'writing-and-notating-music-equals-composition' is dead" (5:77). By n. 11 (the final issue), we have then editor Stanley Lunetta writing (according to Williams) an apologia: "He did not know what he was getting into when he opened *Source* to guest editors—'music' with few notes, intermedia, and happenings. 'The definition of music which has been stretched (as seen in earlier issues of *Source*) to extreme length finally snaps" (Williams, p. 8, quoting *Source* 11:1). It is perhaps this later emphasis, as well as the lack of a strong financial base, that caused the demise of the journal. Each issue of *Source* was a masterpiece in itself. A typical volume might contain ten to twelve articles/compositions with full color illustration and varied typography on paper of several different textures and shapes. The overall size was large, 13½" by 10¾", and pages were bound together with a plastic spiral. Published semiannually, each issue averaged around one hundred pages. The journal contained no regular features, although editorials appeared with some frequency. The advertising at the end of each issue (and as a special supplement in ns. 7/8) was directed to a new music audience—such things as journals, records, and symposia.

Note

1. For purposes of this article, citations are listed by issue, rather than volume number. The more prominent and widely used reference system for the journal was its consecutive issue number, although a volume number was also provided in the publication information.

Information Sources

BIBLIOGRAPHY

Williams, Michael D. *Source: Music of the Avant Grade, Annotated List of Contents and Cumulative Indices.* MLA Index and Bibliography Series, n. 19. Ann Arbor, Mich.: MLA, 1978.

Snyder, Ellsworth. "[Review]." *Notes* 24 (1967): 348–49.

INDEXES

External: RILM, 1967–76. Music Article Guide, 1967–72. Music Index, 1968–73. See also Williams in Bibliography.

LOCATION SOURCES

Widely available.

Publication History

TITLE AND TITLE CHANGES

Source: Music of the Avant Garde.

VOLUME AND ISSUE DATA

Numbers 1–11, 1967–72.

FREQUENCY OF PUBLICATION

Semiannual.

PUBLISHER

Composer/Performer Edition.

PLACES OF PUBLICATION

Davis, California, 1967–69. Sacramento, California, 1969–72.

EDITORS

Larry Austin, 1967–70. Stanley Lunetta, 1969–72. Arthur Woodbury, 1969–71.

GUEST EDITORS

John Cage, 1970. Alvin Lucier, 1971. Stan Friedman, 1972.

Marilyn Shrude

SOVETSKAIA MUZYKA

Founded in 1933 as the official organ of the newly formed Union of Soviet Composers, *Sovetskaia muzyka* (*Soviet Music*) is the foremost music journal of the Soviet Union. It attempts to cover a broad range of material and to serve several audiences, offering reviews of concerts and theatrical events for the public, articles on pedagogy for educators, and critical articles and printed documents for historians and scholars. Contributors are almost exclusively the musicologists, critics, and composers who constitute the membership of the Union of Soviet Composers. As a source of edited texts of primary materials that would otherwise be very difficult to obtain, it is valuable. As the official journal of the

Union of Composers of the USSR and as a record of music in the Soviet Union since 1933, it is itself a unique primary source.

Various topics are taken up in the pages of *Sovetskaia muzyka*. Critical articles dealing with either Soviet or prerevoluntionary Russian music appear in every issue. Traditional subjects appearing somewhat less regularly include the native musical cultures of the various national minorities of the Soviet Union, the music of foreign composers, roundtable discussions of specific works or "problems," performance and pedagogy, reviews of concerts and theatrical premieres in Moscow and elsewhere, and reviews of books and printed music. Many issues contain a feature that amounts to a daily "chronicle of Soviet musical life." Of exceptional value, and appearing in nearly every issue, are documents from the archives of the Soviet Union pertinent to the history of Russian music, edited and published for the first time in this journal.

As one might expect, *Sovetskaia muzyka* has always been sensitive to the concerns of the Communist party, and to an extent its contents have been dictated by those concerns. The journal first appeared at a critical time in the history of Soviet music, just after the party had dissolved various modernistic and proletarian musical organizations and while composers, critics, and scholars were trying to give musical meaning to the party's new artistic doctrine, Socialist Realism. Thus, an editorial in the first issue stated that the journal's first task was to develop a Marxist-Leninist musicology and to combat the discredited ideologies of modernism and proletarianism. In addition, an article by Viktor Gorodinskii, appearing in this same issue, tried to define Socialist Realism in music. Throughout the 1930s, *Sovetskaia muzyka* led the discussion of "the fundamental questions of Soviet musical creativity." As Boris Schwarz has noted in his book *Music and Musical Life in Soviet Russia*,

> the editorial policy of *Sovetskaia muzyka* was based on the assumption that the [party's] Resolution of 1932 had eliminated all intra-musical factionalism. Discussion was permitted, but not dissent; the cultural policy dictated by the Party's Central Committee could not be questioned. Within this framework, however, there was still room for lively discussion of musical subjects in the fields of theory, history, aesthetics, and performance. There were important debates on the problems of genres—the opera, the symphony—there were analyses of new compositions, book reviews, critical columns on new operas, ballets, concerts, interviews with foreign visitors, [and] translated excerpts from foreign publication. (Schwarz, p. 113)

In 1948, at the height of the Zhdanov purge, the journal served as one platform for the denunciation of Sergey Prokofiev, Dmitri Shostakovich, and others. And, in response to the more liberal currents of the 1970s, it led the discussion of such avant-grade works as Alfred Schnittke's Symphony No. 1.

From time to time, special issues of *Sovetskaia muzyka* have been devoted to specific events or composers. For example, the double issue of September–

October 1937 (n. 10–11) commemorated the twentieth anniversary of the Great October Socialist Revolution, and the issue of June 1954 (n. 26) was devoted entirely to Mikhail Glinka, an observance of the 150th anniversary of his birth. The journal has marked other occasions with several articles within a single issue addressing a specific topic, for example, the articles collectively entitled "On the Study of Mussorgski's Heritage" that marked the one hundredth anniversary of that composer's death in 1981 (45:94–112, 1981).

Sovetskaia muzyka was published bimonthly in its first year and then monthly (with an occasional double issue) from January 1934 through May 1941, when publication was suspended. From 1943 through 1945 six essay collections appeared irregularly under the title *Sovetskaia muzyka: Sbornik statei (Soviet Music: A Collection of Articles)*. Publication resumed in 1946, and by 1949 a monthly schedule was restored and continues to the present day. Printed music appears in many issues; in n. 10–11 for 1937, for example, we find a "Song about Stalin" by Aram Khachaturian. Most issues contian from 112 to 160 pages, but a few exceed 200 pages; there are no advertisements. Later issues are uniformly of the size 7¾" by 10".

Information Sources

BIBLIOGRAPHY
Horecky, Paul, ed. *Basic Russian Publications*. Chicago: University of Chicago Press, 1962.
Keldysh, Yu. V., ed. *Muzykal'naia entsiklopediia (Musical Encyclopedia)*, 6 vols. Moscow: Sovetskii Kompozitor, 1973–82.
Schwarz, Boris. *Music and Musical Life in Soviet Russia: Enlarged Edition, 1917–1981* Bloomington: Indiana University Press, 1981.
INDEXES
 Internal: for 1933–35, in no. 8 of 1936, annual index in many years' final issues, including 1940–41, 1946– .
 External: Bibliographie des Musikschrifttums, 1950/51– . Music Index, 1959– . RILM, 1967– .
REPRINT EDITIONS
 Microform: Inter Documentation Center. UMI, 1962– .
LOCATION SOURCES
 Library of Congress and University of California at Berkeley (complete). New York Public Library (nearly complete). Widely available (partial run).

Publication History

TITLE AND TITLE CHANGES
 Sovetskaia muzyka, 1933–41, 1946– . *Sovetskaia muzyka: Sbornik statei*, 1943–45.
VOLUME AND ISSUE DATA
 Volumes 1– , 1933– .
FREQUENCY OF PUBLICATION
 Bimonthly, 1933. Monthly, 1934–41. Irregular, 1946–49. Monthly, 1949– .

PUBLISHER
Union of Composers of the USSR and the USSR Ministry of Culture.
PLACE OF PUBLICATION
Moscow.
EDITORS
N. I. Cheliapov, 1933–37. M. A. Grinberg, 1937–40. D. B. Kabalevsky, 1940–
46. A. A. Nikolaev, 1947. M. V. Koval', 1948–52. G. N. Khubov, 1952–57.
Yu. V. Keldysh, 1957–61. E. A. Grosheva, 1961–70. Yu. S. Korev, 1970–   .

Robert W. Oldani

STEREO REVIEW

In May 1958, stereophonic sound reproduction was just being introduced
commercially and a columnist for the then three-month-old *HiFi & Music Review*
remarked that manufacturers' marketing strategy would decide whether or not
stereo was to become "a magnificent new listening medium for the home or a
fiasco like color TV." Stereo became the surprise of the mid-twentieth century,
of course, establishing itself so quickly that by February 1960 the name of this
monthly magazine was changed to *HiFi/Stereo Review*, and in November of the
same year, *Stereo Review*. The word "music" had already been dropped permanently from the title, thus emphasizing the intended focus on recordings.

From its very inception *Stereo Review* has consistently addressed itself to the
home consumer market for first high fidelity and then stereophonic hardware
and recordings. Its aim has been to increase the pleasure its readers take in their
musical hobby by providing information first for the music enthusiast, second
for the listener who is interested in collateral reading relating to the music and
high fidelity industry, and third for those who seek technical and practical knowledge about listening equipment. The initial editors knew that Americans would
gradually have more leisure time and thus more inclination to spend disposable
income on their various leisure-time activities. Clearly their intuition was correct.
According to editor William Livingstone (1982–87), the magazine had a paid
circulation of 175,000 in 1965; as of 1985 it was 575,000. He also states that
the average age of their readers in 1965 was thirty-seven, and that after a drop,
in the early 1970s, to about twenty-three, that figure has matured with the
population as a whole and now stands at thirty-one. It is still written for a
predominantly male audience, mostly young, and considerably above the national
average in education and income. Although it shares the market with several
similar publications, *Stereo Review* has succeeded with an emphasis on the
consumer and offers some of the best, most knowledgeable articles about the
music itself.

Since 1958, *Stereo Review* has published hundreds of laboratory test reports
on audio equipment and thousands of new-product entries and record reviews.
Many of these articles, including ones on the audibility of distortion, piracy in

the recording industry, and the difference made by the use of heavy copper connecting cables, have had a major impact on the stereo/hi-fi trade.

Even though one would expect a considerable bias for the technically oriented article in *Stereo Review*, this is actually far from the truth. Excellent biographical studies have appeared on a regular basis, one series in particular being devoted to "Great American Composers." There are also featured essays on various musical styles and trends, the history of the recording industry, and record collecting, care, and storage. Newer popular, rock, soul, country, and reggae music are treated with the same respect as the more traditional classics, jazz, and folk music. The proportion of technical to musical coverage has varied somewhat over the years, but they receive approximately equal attention in both articles and reviews.

Stereo Review also presents a yearly record award: the Mabel Mercer Certificate of Merit for Outstanding Contributions to the Quality of American Musical Life. Recipients include Eugene Ormandy, Mable Mercer, Jascha Heifetz, Arthur Fiedler, Richard Rodgers, Beverly Sills, Earl Hines, Aaron Copland, and Benny Goodman.

During its thirty year existence the magazine has had only five editors—the late Oliver Perry Farrell, who helped to found it; Furman Hebb, who succeeded Farrell in 1960; William Anderson, who had been Hebb's managing editor and succeeded him in 1965; William Livingstone, who was on the staff throughout Anderson's tenure succeeded him in 1982; and Louise Boundas, who had served as managing editor to Livingstone prior to moving to editor-in-chief in May 1987. This relative continuity means that there has been tight editorial control and that the outlook and editorial policy have stayed fairly constant throughout the magazine's history.

A classified section in the back lists sales on and wanted advertisements for electronic gear, recordings, and related items. There is also an index each month of all advertisers. After using a slightly taller format for its initial few issues, the editors adopted an 8″ by 11″ norm that remains to the present. *Stereo Review* has continually included well-produced photographs and graphics, all printed on good high-rag stock.

Information Sources

BIBLIOGRAPHY
Anderson, William. "The Logocracy We Live In." *Stereo Review* 21 (November 1968): 4.
Foster, E. J. "High Fidelity Gurus: They Write the Reviews the Audiophiles Read."
    Village Voice 23 (October 9, 1978): 79–80.
Livingstone, William. "Speaking My Piece: Twenty-Five." *Stereo Review* 48 (February
    1985): 4.
Read, Oliver. "Why Another Magazine?" *Stereo Review* 1 (February 1958): 6.
INDEXES
    External: Music Index, 1959– . Music Article Guide, 1965– . RILM,
    1967– . Popular Music Periodical Index, 1973–76. Magazine Index, 1977– .
    Readers' Guide, 1978– . Popular Magazine Review. Consumers Index to Product
    Evaluations and Information Sources.

REPRINT EDITIONS
Microform: UMI.
LOCATION SOURCES
Widely available.

Publication History

TITLE AND TITLE CHANGES
HiFi & Music Review, February–November 1958. *HiFi Review*, December 1958–
January 1960. *HiFi/Stereo Review*, February 1960–October 1968. *Stereo Review*,
November 1968– .
VOLUME AND ISSUE DATA
Volumes 1– , 1958– .
FREQUENCY OF PUBLICATION
Monthly.
PUBLISHERS
Ziff-Davis Publishing Company, 1958–85. CBS Magazines, 1985– .
PLACE OF PUBLICATION
New York, 1958–85. Los Angeles, 1985– .
EDITORS
Oliver Perry Farrell, 1958–60. Furman Hebb, 1960–65. William Anderson, 1965–
82. William Livingston, 1982–87. Louise Boundas, 1987– .

William L. Schurk

STRAD

The *Strad,* subtitled "For all those who play stringed instruments with a bow,"
began its prestigious publication history in England in 1890. The content of the
journal is aimed at amateurs and professionals in all fields connected with the violin family: making, playing, teaching, dealing, collecting, and so on. The journal was founded by Harry Lavendar and remained in the Lavender family until
1964 when it was bought by Novello. E. W. Lavendar remained as the editor until
1982 when he became a consulting editor. The magazine was then jointly edited
by Anne Inglis and Jaak Liivoja-Lorius for three years and, after that, solely by Anne
Inglis. Eric Wen succeeded Inglis in 1986 followed by Christopher James in 1989.
Orpheus Publications acquired the *Strad* from Novello in 1988.

Throughout the last century, the *Strad* has maintained its high standard as it
has grown, become somewhat more eclectic, and changed with the times, for
example, adding record and video reviews. Its contents are distinctive, ranging
from international coverage of events in the stringed instrument world, and
profiles and interviews with famous instrument makers, to reports of instru-
ment-making and playing competitions, pedagogical essays, and articles dealing with restoration and string aesthetics. Of particular note are the articles
concerned with the analysis of fine instruments, supplementary color photographs featuring a great instrument with detailed measurements and history,

and the four-color covers featuring string instruments. Extensive use is made of commissioned photography and illustrations. Articles average 1,000 to 2,000 words and are authored by leading scholars, performers, and makers. The violin is clearly favored over other members of the string family. Regular features include book, record, and music reviews as well as correspondence from readers, and reviews of concerts in the United Kingdom and New York.

Outstanding features include a commemorative issue for David Oistrakh (October 1984), supplements, containing color instrument photographs and instrument drawings in the April 1984 and February 1985 issues, and past issues with extensive authoritative articles on instrument making by George Wulme Hudson.

Advertising, particularly by instrument makers, string publications, and the like, is integral to the magazine and occupies nearly half the available space. There is no index as of this writing. The dimensions were changed from 7" by 9½" to 8" by 11" in 1979, with issues averaging approximately eighty pages, a notable increase from its fifteen-page inaugural issue. The *Strad* has been published monthly throughout its run.

Information Sources

INDEXES
> External: Bibliographie des Musikschrifttums, 1937, 1939, 1950– . Music Index, 1949– . British Humanities Index, 1967– . Arts and Humanities Citation Index, 1976– .

REPRINT EDITION
> Microform: World Microfilms Publications, 1921–85.

LOCATION SOURCES
> Widely available.

Publication History

TITLE AND TITLE CHANGES
> *Strad*. Subtitle: *A Monthly Journal for Professionals and Amateurs of All Stringed Instruments Played with the Bow,* 1890–1979.

VOLUME AND ISSUE DATA
> Volumes 1– , 1980– .

FREQUENCY OF PUBLICATION
> Monthly.

PUBLISHER
> Novello & Co. Ltd., 1890–1988. Orpheus Publications, 1988– .

PLACE OF PUBLICATION
> London.

EDITORS
> Lavendar Family (Harry and E. W.), 1890–1982. Jaak Liivoja-Lorius, 1982–85. Anne Inglis, 1982–86. Eric Wen, 1986–89. Christopher James, 1989– .

Victor Ellsworth

STUDI MUSICALI

The inspiration to establish *Studi musicali* in 1972 came from Renzo Silvestri, the thirtieth president of the Accademia Nazionale de Santa Cecilia in Rome. It was during Silvestri's presidency that the *academia*, with assistance from two Italian governmental agencies, completed a five-year project in which its four centuries of history were collected. Silvestri suggested the establishment of a periodical, sponsored by the *accademia*, in which both its past and its present activities could be documented and issued in installments.

Guido M. Gatti assumed the task of producing the new journal, and publication was placed in the hands of Leo S. Olschki, Editore of Florence. The only editorial statement of any kind appears in the initial fascicle. Here, the journal is dedicated to the discipline of musicology, and studies from scholars throughout the world are solicited. Topics of major significance from any historical period and any civilization are welcome. Special interest is claimed for subjects that show particular sensitivity to the problems of history and criticism.

In reality, the scope of the journal has been somewhat more restricted than the initially purported interest in studies of all epochs and all civilizations from scholars throughout the world. To this date, not a single ethnomusicological article has appeared in the journal. The first issue did, in fact, contain articles on subjects from all six major Western musicological eras, and one article of a general nature. However, over the years the trend has been toward publishing more articles on Renaissance and Baroque music, a leaning that cannot be directly related to the prejudices of the editor or the director of the board. A distant third is the twentieth century, followed closely by the Medieval, Romantic, and Classic eras, respectively. Ironically, articles that treat the general nature of history and criticism are fewest in number. Footnotes are employed rather than endnotes, with the number per article varying widely. The journal permits authors to insert a generous amount of musical notation, which is professionally set. Moreover, articles are often enhanced with eight or more glossy pages of illustrations per issue.

From the very beginning, the contributors to *Studi musicali* have come from among the most highly respected musicological scholars in the Western world, for example, K. G. Fellerer, Heinrich Husmann, Ludwig Finscher, Nino Pirrotta, Oliver Strunk, Emmanuel Winternitz, Lewis Lockwood, Claude Palisca, Edward Lowinski, and Solange Corbin. Moderately interspersed among the contributors are a few lesser-known musicologists, especially local Italians. A short-lived feature of the journal (vs. 1 and 2) was the presentation of biographical sketches of contributors on its last page. Unlike most scholarly journals, it has only once (9.2) offered any departments such as reviews of books, music, or records.

Studi musicali is a multilingual journal with articles appearing in their original language. A certain degree of provincialism cannot be denied, given the preponderance of articles in Italian (roughly 50 percent). After Italian come English (33 percent), German (15 percent), and French (2 percent). In the first two volumes of the journal, an Italian synopsis of articles in other languages is provided along with an offer to translate, on request, entire German and English articles into Italian.

During the first years of publication the journal was issued semiannually. Then, in 1974 through 1979, the journal appeared in single annual issues. Thereafter, it returned to its twice-a-year schedule. The change in publication schedule may have been due to the unexpected death of Gatti in 1973 and the assumption of editorial duties by Agostino Ziino (2:2). However, v. 3 (1974) was also a landmark special issue containing fifteen articles devoted to a single subject, "Mannerism in art and music," taken from an international congress held at the *accademia* in October 1973, and was, no doubt, conceived as a single issue. Since 1977, production of the journal has been passed on to a managing board directed by Nino Pirrotta; members of the board include Giorgia Vigolo, Mario Zafred, and Ziino. Remo Giazotto joined the board in 1984. Nonetheless, since 1973 Ziino has continued to function as the *redattore responsibile*.

The physical format of the journal has remained very consistent throughout its publication history. The page size is typical, 6½" by 9", and issues are bound with a stiff, gray paper cover. Each contains six to ten articles with the length of individual articles ranging from ten to fifty pages. Semiannual issues range in length from 150 to 215 pages; annual issues are approximately twice that length. These figures do not include the eight to twenty pages of Olschki advertisements discreetly placed at the back of the journal on orange paper.

Studi musicali stands beside the journal *Acta musicologica* (q.v.) in its scholarship, care of production, subject matter, and languages. It has a worldwide circulation, but today it is found only in more astute university, college, and municipal libraries in the United States.

Information Sources

INDEXES
    External: Bibliographie des Musikschrifttums, 1972– . RILM, 1976– .
LOCATION SOURCES
    Widely available.

Publication History

TITLE AND TITLE CHANGES
    Studi musicali.
VOLUME AND ISSUE DATA
    Volumes 1– , 1972– .
FREQUENCY OF PUBLICATION
    Semiannual, 1972–73. Annual, 1974–79. Semiannual, 1980– .
PUBLISHER
    Leo S. Olschki, Editore, for the Accademia Nazionale di Santa Cecilia, Rome, Italy.
PLACE OF PUBLICATION
    Florence.

EDITORS

Guido M. Gatti, 1972. Agostino Ziino, 1973–   . Since 1977, the journal has been managed by a council consisting of Georgia Vigolo, Mario Zafred, and Ziino under the direction of Nino Pirrotta.

Matthew Steel

STUDIA MUSICOLOGICA ACADEMIA SCIENTIARUM HUNGARICAE

The establishment of the Hungarian Academy of Sciences (Magyar Tudom-ányos Akadémia) in 1833 marks the beginning of a unified effort on the part of the Hungarian intellectuals and scholars to organize a forum for the discussion and dissemination of findings in all areas of modern scientific research. Over a hundred years later, in 1961, the Committee on Musicology within the academy published a new journal: *Studia musicologica*. The journal officially claims as its honorary founder Zoltán Kodály, who was also its chief editor until his death in 1966. He was succeeded by Bence Szabolcsi (1967–73), and József Ujfalussy (1974–   ).

The committee recognized that Hungarian musicology was deeply rooted in the study of the interrelationship between folk music and art music. Thus, the journal consistently features articles, predominately by Hungarian musicologists, on Hungarian folk music or on music of a Hungarian composer, or folk and "art" music of other lands as they relate to Hungarian or Eastern European music. Topics of international interest, or articles that contribute to questions of universal music history, appear on a regular yet less frequent basis.

Each volume of the journal is organized into several topical segments, not all of which are necessarily present in each volume. The first and unnamed part contains full-length scholarly articles, annotated and illustrated with photographs and musical examples as the topic dictates. Some volumes have musical inserts that are not paginated and not indexed. Studies on or descriptions of manuscript material or manuscript collections located in Hungary appear in the "Documenta" section. These may pertain to Hungarian music or music of various Western European composers as their holographs are represented in Hungarian collections. The "Miscellanea" section is devoted largely to reports on a great variety and number of conferences, from those of the International Folk Music Council to special conferences on specific composers. The sections also may contain "in memoriam" tributes, special discographies, polemics on certain disputed topics, and short descriptive articles or notices. "Recensiones" contains reviews of books published in subject areas that are within the stated "interests" of the journal. These signed reviews are often lengthy (averaging two pages) and very thorough.

In v. 16, another more or less regular section called "Varia" appears, featuring shorter articles on a variety of topics. In vs. 4 and 6 a new section entitled "Discographia" documents record production in Hungary.

It is a fairly frequent practice of this journal to present topical "special" issues within the regular issue numbering rubric. They usually contain only articles and feature a special editor. Vs. 3 and 11 are *Festschriften* for Kodály and Szabolcsi, respectively. V. 5 is essentially a *Kongressbericht* containing studies on Franz Liszt and Béla Bartók presented at the Second International Musicological Conference held in Budapest in 1961. Similarly, v. 7 contains papers read at the International Folk Music Council Conference held in Budapest in 1967. V. 23 is another issue devoted to Bartók. V. 24 contains Bartók studies presented at the Musicological Congress of the International Music Council and papers from the International Bartók Symposium, both of which were held in Budapest in 1981.

The journal features a great many articles on subjects related to Hungarian composers, music, or folk music. Liszt, Bartók, Kodály, and Erkel receive the most attention (in decreasing order of frequency). Discussions range from their correspondence and source materials on particular works, to studies of the interrelationships between their music and either folk music or the music of other composers. Articles on folk music cover areas of analysis, classification, and comparative research. They may deal with music from Africa to Poland, with the folk music of Hungary being the central or underlying theme. In the chronology of music, topics of articles range from antiquity to the twentieth century with the Middle Ages and the nineteenth and twentieth centuries predominating. Topics of interest to both systematic and historical musicology are well represented. Discussion of manuscript and document materials (located in Hungary) range from those of Johann Georg Albrechtsberger, Bartók, Alban Berg, Joseph Haydn, Franz Liszt, Thomas Stolzer, and Franz Xaver Süssmayr to those on organ building in Hungary and Bösendorfer's activities in Hungary. Among works that are more bibliographic in nature, "The Discography of Gustav Mahler's Works" in v. 26 is the most extensive (200 pages!).

V. 21 contains an index to the first twenty volumes of the journal, including an alphabetically arranged list of studies and reviews, and another of works reviewed. A separate index of names and subjects is provided. Beginning with v. 22, the journal publishes an "Index Personarum" as an insert to each volume. Supplements are not self-indexed by the journal.

The physical format of the journal has remained the same since its founding. Each volume measures 6¾" by 9½", with continuous pagination of 250 to 450 pages. The indication of "faciculi 1–4" on the title page is, however, misleading: the journal has really been published most of the time in one annual volume, with occasional publication in two volumes (fasciculi 1–2 and 3–4, respectively), and very rarely with an additional supplement (1982). The journal is usually two to three years behind in its publication schedule. It publishes articles in

German, English, French, Italian, and Russian, all signed and footnoted. Beginning with v. 8, advertisements and other notices appear in the journal.

Information Sources

BIBLIOGRAPHY
Szepesi, Zsuzsanna, and András Wilhelm. "Studia musicologica, Index for vs. 1–19, 1961–78." *Studia musicologica academia scientiarum hungaricae* 21 (1979): 1–77.
INDEXES
Internal: vs. 1–20 in v. 21; each volume indexed, v. 22– .
External: Music Index, 1961– . Bibliographie des Musikschrifttums, 1962– . RILM, 1967– .
LOCATION SOURCES
Widely available.

Publication History

TITLE AND TITLE CHANGES
Studia musicologica academia scientiarum hungaricae.
VOLUME AND ISSUE DATA
Volumes 1– , 1961– .
FREQUENCY OF PUBLICATION
Annual, occasionally semiannual.
PUBLISHER
Akadémiai Kiadó.
PLACE OF PUBLICATION
Budapest.
EDITORS
Zoltán Kodály, 1961–66. Bence Szabolcsi, 1967–73. Jozsef Ujfalussy, 1974– .

Béla Foltin, Jr.

STUDIEN ZUR MUSIKWISSENSCHAFT

Studien zur Musikwissenschaft was founded by Guido Adler as a supplement to the *Denkmäler der Tonkunst in Oesterreich (DTOe)* in 1913. Adler had been general editor of the *DTOe* series from its inception, having originally proposed the idea of a national music monument to the Austrian government in 1888.[1] He was also editor of the *Studien* until 1934 (v. 21), supervising volumes ranging from 26 to 300 pages. The journal appeared annually throughout this time, except for 1917.

Political and economic conditions within the Third Reich affected most musicological work on the continent; *Studien zur Musikwissenschaft* suspended publication between 1934 and 1953. The *Denkmäler* had lost independent status during the German annexation of Austria but continued to appear. The appearance of the journal in the postwar years, with Erich Schenk as editor, has been somewhat less regular. After intermittent volumes until 1966, publication was again suspended until 1977 when Othmar Wessely took over as editor.

Volumes appeared annually from 1977 until 1982, when publication was again temporarily suspended due to financial problems.

As professor of musicology at the University of Vienna, Adler founded the Musikwissenschaftliches Institut and developed an active cadre of scholars that came to be known as the "Vienna School" of music history. The work of the first twenty-one volumes of *Studien zur Musikwissenschaft* is informed by the methods emphasized at the institute and bears the stamp of Adler's considerable influence.

In a short preface to the first volume, Adler outlines the purpose of the new journal (1.1:iii). The folio format of *DTOe* was not appropriate for scholarly writings concerning the music. A separate publication would allow for better reference to materials in various volumes of the series and could more conveniently present the relevant bibliographical and biographical materials. Furthermore, the separate format encouraged wider writings concerned with Austrian topics and provided a platform for the stylistic studies fostered by Adler.

Many of the early articles in *Studien* refer to materials in the accompanying volumes of the *Denkmäler*, though ample musical examples and, at times, complete pieces are included in the journal. Other articles are excerpts of doctoral dissertations at the University of Vienna, or concern bibliographical matters of Austrian musical history. The articles were all historical, rather than being concerned with contemporary musical events. Leading scholars contributed to the journal, with notable essays by Alfred Einstein on Italian music and musicians (21:3–32), by Paul Pisk on parody treatment in Masses by Jacob Gallus (5:35–48), and by Rudolf Ficker on the Trent Codices, (7:5–47 and 11:3–58).

Adler strongly encouraged archival and manuscript study. He had recommended that the Austrian government acquire the Trent Codices, and much of the archival work that he encouraged remains useful for current scholarship. Both Adolf Koczirz (1:278–303) and Albert Smijers (6:139–86, 7:102–42, 8:176–206, and 9:43–81) reproduced material on the Imperial court organizations of the Austro-Hungarian empire. Although their work was sloppy at times, their catalogs stimulated much further research by scholars in Austria.

Due to the rising cost of publication, *DTOe* appears less regularly than in its earlier years, and its continued existence may be threatened.[2] Because of this diminished activity, the recent articles in *Studien* have not always referred to volumes in the *DTOe*. An exception is Milton Steinhardt's "A Musical Offering to Emperor Maximilian II: A Political and Religious Document of the Renaissance" (28:19–27). This article is also exceptional in that it appeared in English. However, the financial strain shows in the recent volumes of *Studien*. Only one article since 1977 has had typeset musical examples; all others have been handwritten.

Most articles continue to deal with matters of Austrian musical history, especially with musical events in Vienna. For example, Wessely compiled a catalog of selected writings at the Musicology Institute at the University of Vienna. Generally, however, *Studien* has been less identified with the university in recent years than during Schenk's tenure when listings of the lectures and publications of the Musicology Institutes of Austrian universities were regularly included.

The prime usefulness of *Studien zur Musikwissenschaft* relates to matters of Austrian musical history. The content is scholarly and covers music history from the Middle Ages to the early twentieth century. Research on Austrian folk music occasionally appears, but the majority of essays are concerned with traditional musicological topics. These include bibliography, biography, musical instruments, and style studies. Although v. 34 was delayed (it should have appeared in 1983), the journal continued to accept articles and has now returned to its annual schedule.

The *Studien* appeared annually from 1913 to 1934, except for 1917. After vs. 22 and 23 (1953 and 1956) the journal appeared every other year from 1960 to 1966, and then again annually since 1977. Vs. 1–21 (1913–34) were 6½″ by 9½″; the remaining volumes have been 6″ by 9″.

Advertising for the *DTOe* appeared inside the back cover of the journal for vs. 1–23. V. 22 also included advertisements for publications of the Wiener Musikwissenschaftliches Institut and the Wiener Musikwissenschaftliche Beiträge. Occasional photographs have appeared since v. 25, and the issues since 1977 have been on a somewhat better paper stock. Although infrequent essays catalogued the articles of vs. 1–27, these are marginally useful. A thorough catalog was prepared separately by Max Shonherr for the first twenty-seven volumes.

Notes

1. *The New Grove Dictionary of Music and Musicians,* s.v. "Adler, Guido," by Mosco Carner.
2. Author's conversation with Othmar Wessely, 1981.

Information Sources

BIBLIOGRAPHY

Fellinger, Imogen. *Verzeichnis der Musikzeitschriften des 19. Jahrhunderts.* Studien zur Musikgeschichte des 19. Jahrhunderts, 10. Regensburg: Gustav Bosse Verlag, 1960.

Lindahl, Charles. "Music Periodicals in U.S. Research Libraries in 1961: A Retrospective Survey. Part II: Other European Countries." *Notes* 38 (1981): 78.

The New Grove Dictionary of Music and Musicians. S.v. "Adler, Guido," by Mosco Carner.

The New Grove Dictionary of Music and Musicians. S.v. "Periodicals," by Imogen Fellinger.

Pass, Walter. "75 Jahre Denkmäler der Tonkunst in Oesterreich." *Oesterreichische Musikzeitschrift* 23 (1968): 686–89.

INDEXES
> External: Bibliographie des Musikschrifttums, 1954–67. Music Index, 1956–58.
> Schonherr, Max. *Kompendium zur Publikationsreihe Denkmäler der Tonkunst in Oesterreich (Vol. 1–27) (1913–1966)*, pp. 273–303. Graz: Akademische Druck— und Verlagsantalt, 1974.

REPRINT EDITIONS
> Microform: Inter Documentation Co., 1913–20. Dakota Graphics (incomplete).

LOCATION SOURCES
> Widely available.

Publication History

TITLE AND TITLE CHANGES
> *Studien zur Muzikwissenschaft: Beihefte der Denkmäler der Tonkunst in Oesterreich.*

VOLUME AND ISSUE DATA
> Volumes 1– , 1913– .

FREQUENCY OF PUBLICATION
> Annual, 1913–34. Irregular, 1953–66. Annual, 1977– . Suspended, 1917, 1935–52, 1967–76.

PUBLISHERS
> Breitkopf und Härtel and Artaria & Co., 1913–34. Oesterreichischer Bundersverlag, 1953–56. Hermann Bohlaus Nachf, 1960–66. Hans Schneider, 1977– .

PLACES OF PUBLICATION
> Leipzig and Vienna, 1913–34. Vienna, 1953–56. Graz, Vienna, and Cologne, 1960–66. Tutzing, West Germany, 1977– .

EDITORS
> Guido Adler, 1913–34. Erich Schenk, 1954–66, except for v. 25, 1962. Othmar Wessely, 1962, 1977– .

Carmelo P. Comberiati

STUDIES IN MUSIC

Studies in Music has, since its inception in 1967, been a refereed journal with an editorial board of Australian scholars and an advisory panel of internationally known musicologists. Unlike its older sibling *Miscellanea musicologica* (q.v.), it did not seek to promote the cause of musicology in Australia, but rather, recognizing the "marked growth of musicological studies in Australia and New Zealand," it sought to "report the results of some of this activity, often in company with contributions from scholars of other countries, and to provide a forum for all facets of musical thought" (1:1). From the beginning, *Studies in Music* made no apology for the infant state of the discipline in Australia and New Zealand. Instead, as proper for an emerging study, it devotes space regularly to articles by Australians and internationally respected scholars that ponder the nature of musicology, its strengths and weaknesses as it is practiced elsewhere, and ways in which Australia could contribute its unique voice to international discussion.

Australia itself is comprised of an array of contradictions. Physically it is one of the oldest continents of the world, with an ancient, indigenous Aboriginal culture that is marked by a rich oral tradition in music. Geographically, it is a Southeast Asian nation, and its closest neighbors all have complex and extensive musical cultures. This makes it one of the most privileged areas in the world for the study of world musics. It also has a colonial history, which looks to the British cultural tradition and Western European intellectual heritage for validation and impetus. More recently, Australia has become a truly mutlicultural society, with a population whose roots are as dispersed and varied both geographically and culturally as Eastern Europe, South America, and the Middle East. Twentieth-century immigration and patterns of resettlement have given birth in Australia to a rich tapestry of "urban ethnic" musical expression. Out of this fascinating and often contradictory mixture, Australian musicologists struggle to extract their own "Australian voice." It may be that Australia's unique contribution to musical scholarship will lie in its study of all these varied musical traditions as equally valid and often mutually informing aspects of musicology, and its rejection of the compartmentalization of methodologies into "Western historical," "ethnomusicological," "analytical," and so on that has character- ized much scholarship elsewhere.

Historically, *Studies in Music* has been marked by a healthy tension between reporting results of individual scholarly effort, and perspective-gaining, reflec- tive, longer looks at aspects of the discipline as a whole. Research reported in this journal has maintained a balance between topics in Western historical mu- sicology, music of non-Western cultures, and Australian music (Aboriginal, colonial, and twentieth-century). Contemporary and, to a lesser extent, popular musics receive more modest but occasionally quite serious attention. Some in- ternationally known Australian musicologists have chosen to report the results of their research here rather than in international journals (Gordon Anderson, David Tunley), and nearly a quarter of the contributions come from outside Australia. In addition to the articles that one might expect to find in such a journal, *Studies in Music* contains several other interesting features. Some issues have a section following the articles that may be devoted to a forum on a special topic ("Musical Composition in Australia and New Zealand," 7:77–90); may contain short pieces of a more general, conceptual nature ("Forward to First Principles—An Article of Faith," 1:89–97); or book reviews, conference reports, and bibliographies ("Discography of Music by New Zealand Composers," 8:91– 93). This section is variously titled "Music Forum" or "Miscellany." Each issue also carries a "Register of Theses." This classified list is based on Paul Doe's register of theses on music undertaken by students of British universities (see *R.M.A. Research Chronicle* [q.v.], v. 3, 1963), and lists completed theses and research projects in progress for higher degrees at Australian and New Zealand universities.

In addition to the journal itself, *Studies in Music* has, since its inception, carried a series of Supplements. Two series of Supplements (*Music Series* and *Music Monograph*) have been issued irregularly. The *Music Series* consists of performing editions, primarily of works discussed in research articles or new music by Australian composers. The aim of this series is to "assist the study of both established and contemporary musical styles, and will frequently include works discussed in the journal *Studies in Music*." The monograph series has been devoted mostly to bibliographies of non-Australian materials in Australian collections (Patricia Brown, *Early Published Handel Scores in the Dalley-Scarlett Collection, Music Monograph 1*. Supplement to *Studies in Music*, v. 5, 1971), or material relating to Australian composers and Australian colonial musical life (Therese Radic, *G.W.L. Marshall-Hall: Portrait of a Lost Composer, Music Monograph*, n. 5). Items in both series can be purchased separately from the journal. A special volume of *Studies in Music* (v. 16, 1982) was devoted to Percy Grainger, on the occasion of his centenary.

The physical format of the journal has been a consistent 5¾" by 8¼". It is nominally an annual, although publication has not always been completely regular. Each issue is approximately 200 pages in length, later issues carry some advertising, and there is no internal indexing.

Information Sources

INDEXES
> External: Music Index, 1967– . RILM, 1967– . Bibliographie des Musikschrifttums, 1970– . Australian Public Affairs Service (APAIS): A Subject Index to Current Literature (National Library of Australia).

REPRINT EDITION
> Microform: Krauss International, 1967–70, suppl. 1–4.

LOCATION SOURCES
> Widely available.

Publication History

TITLE AND TITLE CHANGES
> *Studies in Music.*

VOLUME AND ISSUE DATA
> Volumes 1– , 1967– .

FREQUENCY OF PUBLICATION
> Annual, with irregularities.

PUBLISHER
> University of Western Australia Press.

PLACE OF PUBLICATION
> Nedlands, Western Australia, 6009.

EDITORS
    Frank Callaway, 1967–84. David Tunley, 1967– . David Symons, 1985– .
                                                              Jane Morlet Hardie

SVENSK TIDSKRIFT FÖR MUSIKFORSKNING

The *Svensk Tidskrift för Musikforskning* (*STM*) was among the magazines
devoted to specialized music interests founded during the rapid expansion of
Swedish musical life in the late nineteenth and early twentieth centuries. First
published in 1919, *STM* is the principal publication of the Swedish Musicological
Society and has played a central role in the history of musical scholarship in
Sweden. In the introduction to the inaugural issue, Tobias Norlind, editor-in-
chief, evoked the symbiotic duality of researcher/scientist and poet/philosopher
embodied in Wagner and Faust, and in Eusebius and Florestan, as the essential
ingredient in the quest for understanding greatness in art. Hence, Norlind dedicated the journal to the persistent study of traditions and thought in the legacy
of the past which he considered an inexhaustible fund of knowledge and inspiration for present-day thinking and creativity (1:1–3). This statement articulated
the journal's policy and the modest adjustments in the editorial approach over
the years have come primarily in response to change in the profession of musicology. Kurt Atterberg took the occasion of the final publication of the annual
report from the Royal Swedish Music Academy (1942) to comment on the
inability of the Swedish musical public, particularly that of the students and the
"upper classes," to withstand the infiltration of international music styles (musical variety shows and jazz, in particular) into Swedish musical life, which had
traditionally centered around concert and opera performance and conserved established Swedish musical traditions ("house music," for example) (24:153–
54). Although aware of these changes, the *STM* continued to pursue its policy,
to observe the neutral political stance of the country, and to persist in publishing
meticulously researched musical studies in fields acceptable to prevailing traditional and nationalistic standards.

One result of this policy has been the absence of "theme" issues devoted to
a particular topic of widespread interest. The rare exceptions have been one issue
devoted to studies concerning Jenny Lind on the one hundredth anniversary of
her birth (2.3); an issue containing a study of Joseph Martin Kraus (6.2); a
collection of essays dedicated to Carl-Allen Moberg (v. 43); and a single issue
in 1980 with the theme of "Swedish Music in the 50s" (62.1). The areas of the
journal that catered to changing musical interests have been the review section
and the bibliographies of music history. K. Malm's several reviews of jazz
literature in 1962 (v. 44) were some of the first indications of the present-day
all-inclusive character of these sections where references to commercial popular,
country and western, and rock and roll are regularly included.

The consistency of the editorial policy of the journal has been due, in part, to the stability in its editorial staff. The editors-in-chief have often served eight consecutive years in addition to having been assistant editors and consultants. The notable exceptions have been Carl-Allen Moberg who served as chief editor for sixteen years (1945–60), and Tobias Norland, who served the first eight years, then returned in difficult times during mid–World War II, to shepherd the journal through its twenty-fifth and twenty-sixth volumes.

Contributions fall into two main categories: scholarly articles and reviews of recordings and music literature. The majority of the articles are biographical studies or research in music history and they mostly concern Swedish musical life and Swedish musicians. Subject matter treated less frequently includes bibliographic studies, acoustics and organology, ethnology and folk music, music theory, and sociology and psychology of music. Principal contributors have been Swedish musicologists and music professionals, particularly bibliographers. The most active authors frequently have been among the members of the editorial staff and include the formidable musicologists Tobias Norlind and Daniel Fryklund (organology, Swedish music history, folk music topics), Ingmar Bengtsson (music research), Richard Engländer and Carl Fredrik Hennerberg (classical and eighteenth-century studies), Irmgard Leux-Henschen (eighteenth century, especially aesthetics), and Carl-Allen Moberg, whose numerous publications include studies of Gregorian chant and Buxtehude, and an essay on the "Function of music in modern society."

The principal language is Swedish. The occasional articles in Danish, Norwegian, and English are less numerous than those in German, since, particularly in the formative years, *STM* published the work of German scholars as well as articles in German by Swedish scholars. Since the 1960s, the growing influence of research written in English has been evident. Contributions in French are extremely rare.

V. 1 was self-contained; vs. 2–7 were quarterly, published in combined issues (1, 2, 3–4 or 1, 2–3, 4); vs. 8–21 were quarterly, published as a yearbook; vs. 22–55 were annual; and vs. 56–62 were semiannual, paginated separately. Since 1981 (v. 63), *STM* has been a yearbook. The average number of pages has grown slowly from 129 in the early years to 240. The average number of pages per article varies considerably; contributions are either somewhat short (average fifteen pages) or quite long (average twenty-eight). Presently the issues contain four articles, reviews, a list of music (prepared by the Swedish Music Information Center) that was either composed or first performed in the previous year, and a bibliography listing sources concerning Swedish music and Swedish authors, including those with value as primary sources found in the newspapers. Dissertation abstracts and reports of musicological papers are found together with lists of literature received. Illustrations are modest, but include musical examples, charts and tables, drawings and photographs, and an occasional photographic facsimile. Advertising is music-related. The size of the volumes has remained a constant 6½" by 9½".

Information Sources

INDEXES
Internal: vs. 1–15 in v. 16; vs. 16–25 in v. 25; vs. 26–41 in v. 41; vs. 1–50 (1919–68) printed separately in 1969.
External: Bibliographie des Musikschrifttums, 1939, 1950– . Music Index, 1951– . RILM, 1967– . Arts and Humanities Citation Index, 1982– .
LOCATION SOURCES
Widely available.

Publication History

TITLE AND TITLE CHANGES
Svensk Tidskrift för Musikforskning.
VOLUME AND ISSUE DATA
Volumes 1– , 1919– .
FREQUENCY OF PUBLICATION
Quarterly, with frequent combined issues, 1919–25. Quarterly, published as a yearbook, 1926–39. Annual, 1940–73. Semiannaul, 1974–80. Annual, 1981– .
PUBLISHER
Svenska Samfundet för Musikforskning (Swedish Society for Musicology).
PLACE OF PUBLICATION
Uppsala, Sweden.
CHIEF EDITORS
Tobias Norlind, 1919–26. Gunnar Jeanson, 1927–34. Einar Sundström, 1935–42. Tobias Norlind, 1943–44. Carl-Allen Moberg, 1945–60. Ingmar Bengtsson, 1961–71. Anders Lönn, 1972–80. Erik Kjellberg, 1981– . Important assistant editors: C. F. Hennenberg, 1919–35. Anna Johnson, 1972–76. Present assistant editors: Sten Dahlstedt, 1979– . Lennart Stenkvist, 1981– .

Jean Christensen

SYMPHONY MAGAZINE. See SYMPHONY NEWS

SYMPHONY NEWS/SYMPHONY MAGAZINE

The special concerns of symphony orchestras in America are ardently addressed in the pages of *Symphony Magazine,* the official publication of the American Symphony Orchestra League. The current title and format are only the latest for the league's official journal; beginning in 1948 as the *Newsletter* (actually, *News Letter* until 1952), it was renamed *Symphony News* in 1971 (v. 22), and finally received its present title in 1980. Throughout, it has remained faithful to the aims of the league: to develop and stimulate the growth of all types of orchestras in the United States, to encourage interchange of ideas, to promote American orchestral composers and conductors, and to bolster the standards of performance. Over its nearly forty-year history, the publication has evolved from an eight-page news bulletin to its present hundred-page glossy format with feature articles and regular departments.

The existence of *Symphony Magazine* is due, in no small way, to the diligence and dedication of the original editor of the *Newsletter*, Helen M. Thompson. Thompson was a violinist in the Charleston, West Virginia, Symphony and secretary-treasurer of the league when she accepted the responsibility of reviving the sporadically published league news sheet, the *Inter-Orchestra Bulletin*, in 1948 (the league, itself, was only six years old at the time). Almost single-handedly she produced the *Newsletter*. It appeared infrequently at first, but contained the kinds of information emblematic of all subsequent league publications: league news, news of various grants and awards of interest to orchestras, reports on fund-raising techniques for smaller orchestras, news of college and youth symphonies, samples of symphony programs, and lists of new league members. In 1950, the league gave Thompson the paid position of executive secretary. She left the Charleston Symphony and devoted all her energies to writing and editing the *Newsletter*. With the July 1950 issue (2.1), the *Newsletter* began a six-issues-a-year publication schedule. There soon appeared new departments such as a Concert Calendar for league member orchestras and a Talent Mart, a kind of placement service listing performing members' resumes for a small fee. The first feature article appeared in 1953.

The *Newsletter* initially faced competition from a monthly publication called *Symphony*, also inaugurated in 1948. Although the content of the two publications overlapped, the *Newsletter* devoted more space to the practical matters of managing and funding orchestras. Lacking the financial security provided the *Newsletter* by league memberships, *Symphony* was forced to cease publication in 1954.

With a spectacular increase in league memberships over the early years, the *Newsletter*'s financial base was adequate and advertising was not directly solicited. By 1960, the *Newsletter* had expanded to about thirty pages with no increase in the number of advertisements.

A history of the league appeared in a special Twentieth Anniversary Issue of the *Newsletter* (13.3–4, April–May 1962). After 1962 the *Newsletter* switched from a July to June publication schedule to the more conventional January to December schedule. Slowly, the production values improved as the number of advertisements increased. In 1969, the Helen Thompson era came to a close when she left the *Newsletter* to become manager of the New York Philharmonic.

Under new editor Barbara Mosgrove, the *Newsletter* emerged in 1970 with a newly designed logo and a new double-column format. Her tenure was brief; with a change in name to *Symphony News* in 1971 came a new editor, Benjamin S. Dunham. His seven years as editor of the *News* saw many improvements in production values. Beginning in 1973 (24.4), the *News* cover featured a photo on the front and a half page of Late News tipped in inside the cover. News coverage expanded with regular columns given to "Urban and Community Orchestras"; "Youth Orchestras"; "College, University, and Conservatory Or chestras"; "World Premieres"; "Media" (book reviews); and reader "Correspondence." In 1974, league Executive Director Ralph Black began his regular column called "Black Notes." The *News* expanded to over sixty pages by 1977 with a smaller typeface on glossy paper (page size remained 8½" by 11" throughout its history). The most notable feature article of the *News* was the seven-part, scholarly article (with numerous footnotes) entitled "A Conductor's Guide to the Community Orchestra" by James Van Horn (appearing from June 1975 to February 1977).

When Benjamin Dunham left *Symphony News* in 1978, his replacement was Robin Perry. Under Perry, the *News* has continued to grow to over a hundred pages per issue, though much of that growth has been in advertisements— primarily publishers and booking agencies. In 1980 the latest metamorphosis occurred; the *News* became *Symphony Magazine*, and a revised format was adopted. The news departments were reorganized into the following four categories: "Onstage" (various musical concerns), "Backstage" (orchestral administration), "Behind the Scenes" (volunteer work), and "Education and Outreach" (orchestras in community service).

With the exception of a few biographical and historical feature articles, *Symphony Magazine* has little to offer the average symphony enthusiast or scholar. It is a professional association journal and, consequently, often reads like a business report. It is, however, essential reading for all professional orchestra performers, conductors, managers, and volunteer organizations.

Information Sources

INDEXES
> External: Music Index, 1949– . Bibliographie des Musikschrifttums, 1950. Music Article Guide, 1971– .

REPRINT EDITIONS
> Microform: UMI.

LOCATION SOURCES
> *Symphony News* and *Symphony Magazine* are widely available. The *Newsletter* can be found in very few libraries, and complete holdings are extremely rare.

Publication History

TITLE AND TITLE CHANGES
> *News Letter of the American Symphony Orchestra League, Inc.*, October 1948– January 1952. *Newsletter: American Symphony Orchestra League, Inc.*, March 1952– September 1971. *Symphony News: The Newsletter of the American Symphony Orchestra League*, October 1971–April 1980. *Symphony Magazine*, May/ June 1980– .

VOLUME AND ISSUE DATA
> Volumes 1– , 1948– .

FREQUENCY OF PUBLICATION
> Irregular, 1948–50. 6/year, 1950– .

PUBLISHER

American Symphony Orchestra League.

PLACES OF PUBLICATION

Charleston, West Virginia, 1948–62. Vienna, Virginia, 1962–83. Washington, D.C., 1983–   .

EDITORS

Helen M. Thompson, 1948–69. Barbara Mosgrove, 1970. Benjamin S. Dunham, 1971–78. Robin L. Perry, 1978–   .

Matthew Steel

T

TEMPO

Tempo, A Quarterly Review of Modern Music, the journal of the British publishing firm Boosey and Hawkes, was first issued in 1939. The introduction to the inaugural edition states a twofold purpose: (1) to be a "source of information for those with an interest in present-day composers and musical activities," thereby establishing a closer connection between composers and the public, and (2) to list new publications of Boosey and Hawkes and the foreign firms it represented. Throughout the almost fifty years of its existence, *Tempo* has had a sophisticated and scholarly thrust, making it of interest to professional composers, performers, and musicologists, as well as astute amateurs.

In the early years the difficulty of maintaining a regular publishing schedule was compounded by the onslaught of World War II, thus the apparent confusion with the journal's numbering system.[1] Ns. 1–15, printed in London and dated January 1939–June 1946, are designated as the "First Series." Temporarily abandoned from 1941–44, it resumed quarterly publication in February 1944 (n. 6). An independent "American Series" was begun in March 1940 and ran through September 1942; however, only seven issues appeared. A "New Series" was inaugurated in September 1946 and for a short time a double numbering system was used (n. 1 in "New Series" = n. 16 in "First Series").[2] Aside from the "American Series," which was published in two volumes, the journal is numbered consecutively; since 1948, it has appeared four times a year.

During World War II, *Tempo* provided a valuable chronicle of the music publishing and performing environment in Great Britain. An editorial from August 1941, "Music and War," describes the climate: "The classics are indeed the order of the day, although we are inclined to think that this is due more to economic considerations on the part of concert promoters than to a modification of public taste. Contemporary music having but rarely 'paid' in peaceful days, its wartime prospects are naturally yet further diminished" ("First," 5:1). Despite less-than-ideal conditions and a publication suspension of nearly three years, *Tempo* promptly resumed in 1946 with its usual optimism: "With the present issue this paper acquires a new lease on life" ("First," 7:1). It is then that the following became the policy of all issues to follow: "We live in an era of social, cultural, and economic upheaval, and the world of music being no more immune from change than any other sphere of human activity, it will not be out of place to discuss such changes in these columns insofar as they affect the art of music and those for whom it is either a livelihood or recreation, or both" (Ibid.).

Presently *Tempo* maintains a consistent format with an average of four articles (eight to ten pages each) on various facets of contemporary music, followed by relatively brief reviews of records, books, festivals, and/or first performances. Editorials appear only occasionally and, at that, only for specific reasons—one hundredth anniversary issue, obituaries, commentary on the world situation. Frequent contributors, largely though not exclusively British, have included prominent musicians from every phase of the profession: Brian Dennis, Peter Evans, G. W. Hopkins, Hans Keller, Anthony Payne, Eric Roseberry, Stanley Sadie, Willi Schuh, Erwin Stein, Tim Souster, Harold Truscott, Eric Walter White, and Stephen Walsh, to name a few. Short announcements highlighting the recent accomplishments of Boosey and Hawkes composers comprise the final section of each issue, entitled "Music in the Making" (mainly in the "First Series"), later "Allotria" and "News and Notes," and currently "News Section."

Boosey and Hawkes has published the music of some of the greatest composers of the twentieth century, and it is partially through their efforts that the world has come to know the works of Béla Bartók, Benjamin Britten, Aaron Copland, and Igor Stravinsky, as well as a host of composers of less prominent stature. Through *Tempo*'s reviews of first performances and new publications, we get a candid view of these composers in their early years. Some of the typical enthusiasm can be seen in this announcement of the yet-to-be-titled "Contrasts" by Béla Bartók: "A new work by Béla Bartók for violin, clarinet, and piano has been announced. . . . The first performance will be given on January 9th by Joseph Szigeti, Benny Goodman, and Endre Petre (piano), at Carnegie Hall, New York, and the prospect of an audience consisting jointly of Szigeti admirers and Benny Goodman 'fans' fraternizing over a new Bartók work is, to say the least, a piquant one" ("First," 1:3). Furthermore, works of each of these composers are analyzed in the pages of *Tempo* by some of the most prominent theorists and musicologists of the century: Erwin Stein, Peter Evans, Hans Keller on Britten; Colin Mason, Benjamin Suchoff, and John S. Weissmann on Bartók; Peter Evans, Hugo Cole, Arthur Berger on Copland; Eric Walter White, Erwin Stein, Colin Mason, Robert Craft, and Anthony Payne on Stravinsky.

Several "landmark" issues have appeared, mainly on individual composers. Of interest are the three issues on Stravinsky—a mid-career overview (n. 8), "Stravinsky at 85" (n. 81) with color sketches from "The Rite of Spring" and

"Stravinsky Remembrance" (n. 97), commemorating the composer's death with articles and a large insert of "Canons" and "Epitaphs" by Edison Denisov, Alfred Schnittke, Michael Tippett, Maxwell Davies, Luciano Berio, and others. The next issue continued the musical tribute with pieces by Pierre Boulez, Copland, Robert Sessions, Elliott Carter, and others. Special issues on other composers have appeared as well: Copland (n. 9), Sergey Prokofiev (n. 11), Richard Strauss (n. 12), Bartók (ns. 13 and 14), Sergei Rachmaninoff (n. 22), Frederick Delius (n. 26), Zoltán Kodály (n. 63), and Benjamin Britten (ns. 66–67, 106, 120).

Several articles are worth special mention. These include the ethnomusicological writings of Béla Bartók—"The Influence of Peasant Music on Modern Music" (14:19–24) and "Some Linguistic Observations" ("First," 14:5–7)—and Copland's commentary on his own music, "The Story Behind My 'El Salon Mexico' " ("First," 4:2–4). Noteworthy for their scholarship are the theoretical writings of G.W. Hopkins—"Schoenberg and the 'Logic' of Atonality" (94:15–20) and "Stravinsky's Chords," Part I (76:6–12) and Part II (77:2–9). Also significant is the eclectic view of the twentieth century through the eyes of Hans Keller in both his regular feature, "The Contemporary Problem" (ns. 82–89), and the many articles he authored between ns. 3–98. A short, but pithy chronicle of musical life in postwar Germany is found in an article by J. Bornoff, "Music in Germany" ("First," 14:13).

Early issues in the "First" and "American" series were printed on inexpensive paper and ranged from twelve to twenty-eight pages in length. In the "New Series" we see a gradual increase in content until the present average of around fifty-six pages per issue. The size has remained 7″ by 10⅜″. Variations in the subtitle are also evident (see Publication History below). Advertisements are of a professional nature—new publications, conference announcements, and the like. Photos and musical examples appear as necessitated by an article's content.

Notes

1. For precise clarification of the early publication history, as well as an index by author and subject, see Thomas Noblitt's *Index to Tempo, January, 1939–June, 1972.*

2. For the purposes of this essay, citations for the original and American series will be distinguished by the prefixes "First" and "Am," as suggested in Noblitt.

Information Sources

BIBLIOGRAPHY
Noblitt, Thomas L. *Index to Tempo, January 1939–January 1972.* Millwood, N.Y.: KTO Press, 1977.
MacDonald, Calum. "A Short History of *Tempo* (I): 1939–1946." *Tempo* 168 (March, 1989): 2–3.
———. "A Short History of *Tempo* (II): 1946–1962." *Tempo* 169 (June 1989): 2–3.
INDEXES
External: Music Index, 1949– . Bibliographie des Musikschrifttums, 1950, 1960–66, 1974– . Music Article Guide, 1966– . British Humanities Index,

1966–   . RILM, 1967–   . Arts and Humanities Citation Index, 1976–   . See also Noblitt in Bibliography.

REPRINT EDITION

Paper: First series: Kraus Reprint.

Microform: UMI, 1946–69 (incomplete), 1970–   .

LOCATION SOURCES

Widely available.

Publication History

TITLE AND TITLE CHANGES

Tempo. The Boosey and Hawkes News-Letter, 1939–44 ("First Series" ns. 1–6 and "American Series" 1.1–2.3). *Tempo. The Boosey and Hawkes Quarterly,* 1944–46 ("First Series" ns. 7–15). *Tempo. A Quarterly Review of Modern Music,* 1946–   ("New Series").

VOLUME AND ISSUE DATA

Volumes 1–15, 1939–45. New series, volumes 1–   , 1946–   .

FREQUENCY OF PUBLICATION

Quarterly.

PUBLISHER

Boosey and Hawkes Publishers Ltd.

PLACE OF PUBLICATION

London.

EDITORS

Ernest Chapman, 1939–49. Anthony Gishford, 1950–58. Donald Mitchell, 1958–62. Colin Mason, 1962–71. David Drew, 1971–82. Calum MacDonald, 1982–   .

Marilyn Shrude

THEORY AND PRACTICE

Theory and Practice first appeared in 1975 with the subtitle "Newsletter-Journal of the Music Theory Society of New York State." Its original purpose was to provide a means of communication, of both a pragmatic and a substantial nature, among the members of that society. John R. Hanson, first president of the Music Theory Society of New York State (MTSNYS), was instrumental in all the society's early activities, including the formation of its journal. The designation "Journal" was dropped with issue 4.2 (December, 1979), and it has developed into a journal that is primarily topical in its focus and is recognized within the discipline well beyond its statewide and regional origins.

The early issues were especially heavy on such matters pertaining to MTSNYS as details of membership, announcements of meetings, and their programs, and so on, and one still finds an occasional membership list published even in the most recent issues. V. 1, only eleven pages long, contained only one three-page book review, a two-page "Letter from the Editor" (Donald Bohlen) on matters of academic philosophy, and an announcement of the appearance of the new journal *In Theory Only* (q.v.) from the University of Michigan. It also printed its own call for submissions: short articles on a variety of topics, including bibliography, pedagogy, and reviews, as well as editorials of general interest, along with a promise of prompt publication of those accepted, with a minimum of editing. The latter has been a keynote of editorial policy with this journal—an opportunity for scholars to publish without the long delays often associated with the process. V. 2.1 consists primarily of the bylaws, constitution, lists of officers, committees, and so on of the society; in addition there is one eight-page article on species counterpoint. Beginning with vs. 2.2. and 2.3 (still only seventeen and eighteen pages, respectively), the following more or less regular features are to be found: "News and Announcements" (and "Reports"), "Aural Perception" (discontinued with 3.2), "Book Reviews," "New Books and Periodicals," and "Editor's Note," in addition to articles, analyses, and, often, "Responses" to previous articles and analyses. Since taking on its present format with v. 3.1, the length of the journal has increased, ranging from thirty-six to seventy-seven pages, with an average of about fifty-five to sixty pages. Hedi Siegel was principally responsible for this change from a newsletter to a journal.

In the beginning, articles and reviews tended to be quite short—two to five pages—but again, beginning with v. 3, this has changed considerably. The average length is now nearer fifteen pages (articles ranging from five to fifty pages and reviews up to fifteen page long). The music under discussion spans sixteenth-century modal counterpoint to the most recent concepts in set theory, with little preceding that and nothing, so far, outside the realm of completely specified notes for human performance. In contrast to *In Theory Only* and *Indiana Theory Review* (q.v), the majority of contributors are not graduate students, but faculty members at institutions in New York State and elsewhere. Some who have appeared most often in the pages of *Theory and Practice* include John R. Hanson, John Rothgeb, Harold F. Lewin, and Pozzi Escot; Robert Gauldin and Larry Laskowski have engaged in an enlightening exchange of article and responses concerning Bach preludes (vs. 4 and 5), as have Philip Hough and Bruce McKinney, on Béla Bartók's "Autumn Tears" (vs. 3 and 4), and L. Poundie Burstein, Arthur Maisel, and Bruce McKinney on *Tristan* (vs. 8 and 9). Other notable contributors have been David Beach, Jonathan Bernard, Martin Brody, Roger Kamien, David Lewin, Robert Morris, William Rothstein, Hedi Siegel, David Stern, and Jurgen Thym. Richard Brooks has edited and compiled the "New Books and Periodicals" sections. Two documents have appeared in translation: Ernst Oster's "On the Meaning of the Long Appoggiatura" (Robert Kosovsky, 7.1:20–37) and Heinrich Schenker's letter on the opening of Beethoven's Sonata, Opus 111 (John Rothgeb and Hedi Siegel, 8.1:3–13). Obituaries have appeared for Ernst Oster (v. 3.1:4) and for Justine Shircliff (5.2:5–6).

V. 1 appeared in June 1975 and consisted of only one issue. V. 2 comprised three issues (May and September 1976, and February 1977). From v. 3 to the present the journal has appeared twice yearly, with slight irregularity: the first issue of each year is variously dated February, March, July, August, or September, while the second is more consistently dated December. V. 9 is a double issue dated July–December 1984. An index ("Authors," "Books Reviewed") for vs. 1–6 is found in 7.1:44–50. There are no advertisements. All articles are in English. The journal is sent to all members of MTSNYS.

Theory and Practice is published in a simple 8½" by 11" photocopy format. Only with v. 3 did it gain a cover made of heavier, colored paper. The text is typed (or word-processor-printed). Musical examples are reproduced from original sources or from clear hand-written copies (especially for analytical graphs, and the like). Vs. 1 and 2.1 do not even have a table of contents, but beginning with 2.2 the journal has had a recognizable consistency in its appearance and regular features.

Information Sources

BIBLIOGRAPHY
Lindahl, Charles. Review of "Theory and Practice." *Notes* 33 (1976): 314.
INDEXES
    External: RILM, 1979–
LOCATION SOURCES
    Widely available.

Publication History

TITLE AND TITLE CHANGES
    Theory and Practice. Newsletter-Journal of the Music Theory Society of New York State, 1975–79 (4.1). *Theory and Practice. Journal of the Music Theory Society of New York State*, December 1979–   .
VOLUME AND ISSUE DATA
    Volumes 1–   , 1975–   .
FREQUENCY OF PUBLICATION
    Seminanual, with irregularities.
PUBLISHER
    Music Theory Society of New York State.
PLACE OF PUBLICATION
    Ithaca, New York.
EDITORS
    Donald Bohlen, 1975–78. Hedi Siegel, 1979–80. Larry Laskowski and Hedi Siegel, 1981–82. Channan Willner, with Larry Laskowski and Hedi Siegel as editors-at-large, 1982–85. Frank Samarotto, 1986–   .

Paul B. Mast

TIJDSCHRIFT DER VERENIGING VOOR NOORD-NEDERLANDSCHE MUZIEKGESCHIEDENIS. See TIJDSCHRIFT VAN DE VERENIGING VOOR NEDERLANDSE MUZIEKGESCHIEDENIS

TIJDSCHRIFT VAN DE VERENIGING VOOR NEDERLANDSE MUZIEKGESCHIEDENIS

The *Tijdschrift van de Vereniging voor Nederlandse Muziekgeschiedenis* (*TVNM*) (*Journal of the Society for the History of Netherlands Music*) "forms an impressive monument of music historiography, and it occupies a unique place in the world of musicology, which is unique in the sense that no other journal has the same objective of limiting its musical historiography to The Netherlands, i.e. the entire geographical area commonly known as the Low Countries" (32:1). Founded in 1868 as a section of the Maatschappij tot Bevordering der Toonkunst (Society for the Promotion of Music) on the initiative of the latter's secretary, Jan Pieter Heije, the Vereniging voor Nederlandse Muziekgeschiedenis (VNM) is the oldest surviving musicological organization of its kind.

In 1869 the VNM published a volume entitled *Berigten* (literally "Communications"), containing a chronicle of its activities, as well as short communications from several contributors. After this single volume, sixty-four pages in length, communications were gathered over several years and published in volumes entitled *Bouwsteenen* (literally, "Building Blocks"). Three such volumes appeared, in 1872, 1874, and 1881, containing materials about composers, musicians, music, books, musical instruments, publishers, and so on. Totaling nearly 600 pages in all, the *Bouwsteenen* offered basic data as it was found in libraries and archives, not yet studied and compiled in coherent articles.

In 1882 the VNM published the first issue of its *Tijdschrift (Journal)*. With minor irregularities, one issue appeared every year until 1972 (v. 22). Four of these "yearly" issues are bound together with a special title page and an index to form one volume of 200–300 pages. Starting in 1973 one volume of 100–200 pages in two issues was published every year.

All these publications, the *Berigten, Bouwsteenen*, and *Tijdschrift*, have roughly the same physical format of 6″ by 9¼″. To v. 3 (1891) all articles were written in Dutch and contributed mostly by members of the board of the VNM. Notable are the more than twenty contributions by J.P.N. Land, at that time president of the VNM. These include his article in seven installments (v. 1.3–3.1), entitled "Het Luitboek van Thysius," a nearly 400-page study which is still the only extant guide to this manuscript lute book. With the addition of a title page, preface, and register, this work was also published as a one-volume book in 1889.

V. 4.1 (1892) opened with an article by Max Seiffert, "Über Sweelinck und seine deutschen Schüler." This first non-Dutch contribution was followed by other articles in German, French, English, and Italian, though prior to 1965 they never outnumbered those written in Dutch. The article by Seiffert was one of a long series of contributions on Jan Pieterszoon Sweelinck that were later developed into several editions of the composer's complete works. Randall H. Tollefsen summarized earlier research on Sweelinck in his article, "Jan Pietersz.

Sweelinck: a Bio-bibliography, 1604–1842'' (22:87–125). The same is true, *mutatis mutandis*, referring to two other Netherlandish composers, Jacob Obrecht and Josquin des Prez.

The *TVNM* also traditionally publishes research on the life and works of minor Netherlandish composers. In addition to polyphonic music, a number of short studies deal with monophony. The Dutch national anthem "Wilhelmus van Nassouwe" was the subject of five articles (vs. 5, 7, and 9). Of equal importance are the articles dealing with original sources. The notation problems of the songs in the Gruuthuse manuscript were the subject of a detailed study by Cornelis Lindenburg (17:44–86); a number of controversial articles on this subject appeared in the following years (vs. 21–25, 34; 1971–75 and 1984).

It is of course not possible here to make a complete survey of a journal that has been published for more than a century. It would be amiss, however, not to mention Daniel François Scheurleer, banker and maecenas, who was the VNM's president from 1896 until his death in 1927. During this period he also contributed over one hundred articles of varying length. His successor, Albert Smijers, contributed about twenty-five articles to the *TVNM*. Noteworthy is his musicological dissertation, *Karel Luython als Motetten-Komponist*, published as a double volume of the *TVNM* in 1923 (11.1/2). Of equal importance is his study of Renaissance choir books in "'s-Hertogenbosch (Bois-le-Duc)'' (16:1–30), and the edition of the records relating to the Illustre Lieve Vrouwe Broederschap (Brotherhood of Our Illustrious Lady), owner of the choirbooks (11.4–17.3; 1925–51). Smijers was the editor of the *TVNM* from 1921 to 1955, and, after 1934, president of the VNM as well.

During a short period, from 1948 to 1959, the VNM wished to expand its journal's purview to musicology in general. Under the title *Tijdschrift voor Muziekwetenschap (Journal for Musicology)* eight such issues (vs. 17–18) were published. Since only a small number of the articles in these two volumes went beyond the scope of the music of the Low Countries, it was agreed in 1960 that the journal return to its previous name and activities.

After the death of Smijers in 1957, Eduard Reeser became president of the VNM and, together with John Daniskas, the editor of the *TVNM*. About 1965 the editorial policy was changed, and beginning with v. 20 the greater number of the contributions to the *TVNM* were written in German and English and contributed by foreign scholars.

An account of the activities of the VNM has always been a regular feature of its journal. To address the more specific interest of the members of the VNM, the secretary, Rudolf Lagas, started the *Mededlingenblad (Bulletin)* in December 1961. It reached twenty-six issues in its nearly seven years' existence. All contributions were written in Dutch, and included announcements and reviews of new editions by the VNM and summaries of articles by members of the VNM published elsewhere, as well as short studies on all kinds of musical subjects. In September 1968, after the death of Lagas, his successor, Clemens von Gleich, edited the last number (n. 26), containing a register of all published issues of the *Mededelingenblad*.

In the same year, Willem Elders took over the editorship of the *TVNM*. He introduced reviews of recently published books and music concerning the Low Countries, a feature that has been continued regularly ever since.

In commemoration of the VNM's seventy-fifth anniversary (1943), Eduard Reeser edited a *Gedenkboek (Memorial Volume)*, containing a history of the VNM and a chronological list of its publications, including the tables of contents for all past volumes of *TVNM*. The chronology was twice updated by the same author, in *Addenda* (19:102–118), and in *Chronologie*, a separate publication for the one hundredth anniversary of the VNM. The first centennial of the *TVNM* was celebrated with a survey by Willem Elders, in which he showed how the *TVNM* had attained a position of importance in the international musicological world.

Information Sources

INDEXES
> External: Bibliographie des Musikschrifttums, 1937, 1939, 1950– . Music Index, 1961– . RILM, 1967– .

REPRINT EDITION
> Microform: *Bouwsteenen*. Library of Congress, 1872–81.

LOCATION SOURCES
> Widely available.

Publication History

TITLE AND TITLE CHANGES
> *Berigten / Vereeniging voor Nederlandsche Muziekgeschiedenis, 1869. Bouwsteenen: Eerste Jaarboek der Vereeniging voor Nederlandsche Muziekgeschiedenis, 1869–72. Bouwsteenen: Tweede (-Derde) Jaarboek der Vereeniging voor Noord-Nederlands Muziekgeschiedenis, 1872–1874, 1874–81. Tijdschrift der Vereeniging voor Noord-Nederlands Muziekgeschiedenis, 1886–1910. Tijdschrift der Vereeniging voor Nederlandsche Muziekgeschiedenis, 1912–46. Tijdschrift voor Muziekwetenschap, 1948–59. Tijdschrift van de Vereniging voor Nederlandse Muziekgeschiedenis, 1960/61– . Mededelingenblad voor Leden en Donateurs van de Vereniging voor Nederlandse Muziekgeschiedenis*, December 1961– September 1968.

VOLUME AND ISSUE DATA
> Volumes 1– , 1882– .

FREQUENCY OF PUBLICATION
> Annual, 1882–1972. Semiannual, 1973– .

PUBLISHERS
> *Berigten, Bouwsteenen*, and *Mededelingenblad:* VNM. *Tijdschrift:* J. C. Loman, 1882–83. Frederik Muller & Co., 1884–1904. Johannes Müller, 1905–08. G. Alsbach & Co., 1909–57. VNM, 1958– .

PLACE OF PUBLICATION (all titles)
> Amsterdam.

EDITORS

Berigten and *Bouwsteenen*: Jan Pieter Heije. *Mededelingenblad*: Rudolf Lagas. *Tijdschrift*: Editors were not mentioned until 1940, but certainly a member of the board of the VNM acted also as editor of the *TVNM*. In the early years this was most probably the secretary, H. C. Rogge. Thereafter: E. W. Moes, 1897–1911. S. Bottenheim, 1912. E. Pijzel, 1913–20. Albert Smijers, 1921–39. Editors explicitly mentioned since 1940: Albert Smijers, 1940–55. Eduard Reeser and John Daniskas, 1956–67. Willem Elders, 1968–   .

Alfons Annegarn

TIJDSCHRIFT VOOR MUZIEKWETENSCHAP. See TIJDSCHRIFT VAN DE VERENIGING VOOR NEDERLANDSE MUZIEKGESCHIEDENIS

TONWILLE, DER and DAS MEISTERWERK IN DER MUSIK

Der Tonwille is a series of pamphlets that appeared more or less periodically from 1921 to 1924. It consists entirely of articles and analyses by the renowned music theorist Heinrich Schenker (1868–1935). N. 1 was published in 1921, ns. 2 and 3 in 1922, ns. 4–6 in 1923, and ns. 7, 8/9, and n. 10 in 1924; the issues of 1924 are also known as "4. Jahrg., Hefte 1., 2./3., und 4." *Der Tonwille* was succeeded by the three "Yearbooks" of 1925, 1926, and 1930, known as *Das Meisterwerk in der Musik*, and actually referred to by Schenker as a continuation (*Fortsetzung*) of *Der Tonwille*. The title *Der Tonwille*, which might be translated as "The Will of the Tone," reflects Schenker's belief in the organic nature of the "masterworks" of tonal music and in certain immutable principles governing artistic musical composition. The articles in both publications are of two general types: essays on music and analyses of specific works. Among the former in *Der Tonwille* are such celebrated articles as "Die Urlinie" (1:22–26), "Die Kunst zu hören" (3:22–25), and "Wirkung und Effekt" (8/9:47–48). Those in *Das Meisterwerk* include "Die Kunst der Improvisation" (1:9–40) based on the work of C.P.E. Bach, "Fortsetzung der Urlinie-Betrachtungen" (continuing, that is, from *Der Tonwille*; this title appears in both 1:185–200 and 2:9–42, with the latter developing the concept still further), "Vom Organischen der Sonatenform" (2:43–54) and "Das Organische der Fuge" (2:55–95).

The analyses also include some of Schenker's most significant: in *Der Tonwille*, the three articles on Ludwig van Beethoven's Fifth Symphony (1:27–37; 5:10–40, 6:9–35), those on sonatas by Joseph Haydn, Wolfgang Amadeus Mozart, and Beethoven, on Johannes Brahms's "Handel" Variations (8/9:3–46), and on shorter works by J. S. Bach, C.P.E. Bach, Haydn, Franz Schubert, Felix Mendelssohn, and Robert Schumann; in *Das Meisterwerk*, the famous analysis of Beethoven's "Eroica" Symphony (3:25–101), of the "Representation of

Chaos'' from Haydn's *Creation* (2:159–70), of Mozart's Symphony No. 41 in G minor (2:105–56), and of shorter works by J. S. Bach, Domenico Scarlatti, and Frédéric Chopin. These lists define fairly completely the range of music addressed in both publications, to which hardly more than George Frederick Handel can be added for most of Schenker's entire output. One might note also in v. 2 the "negative example" *(Gegenbeispiel)*, an analysis of Max Reger's *Variations and Fugue on a Theme of J. S. Bach*, Op. 81 (2:171–92). Other such attacks, on Arnold Schönberg and Igor Stravinsky, may also be found within some of the articles.

Although Schenker's concepts continued to evolve, leading to his culminating work, *Der freie Satz*, the articles and analyses in *Der Tonwille* and *Das Meisterwerk in der Musik* are central to an adequate understanding of his work, which is today the most influential of any theorist in the realm of tonal music.

In addition to the articles, a feature entitled "Vermischtes" (Miscellanea) appeared in most issues of *Der Tonwille* and in *Das Meisterwerk*. It consists of short essays on various topics, poetry, and quotations of correspondence to or from such composers as Mozart, Beethoven, Schubert, and Brahms. The latter several issues of *Der Tonwille* also give a table of abbreviations, a practice continued in *Das Meisterwerk*, and each of the last two, as well as vs. 1 and 2 of *Das Meisterwerk*, contains a short essay intended as clarification (*Erläterungen*) of Schenker's basic analytical principles. There is no real indexing in either publication, although the contents of *Der Tonwille* are listed in cumulative fashion in succeeding issues and in each volume of *Das Meisterwerk*; v. 3 of the latter also contains a complete listing of contents for the two preceding volumes. There are a few advertisements at the end of each of the three bound volumes of *Der Tonwille*, primarily for Schenker's other published writings and for other musical works published by Universal-Edition; ironically, among these is a large advertisement for Arnold Schoenberg's *Harmonielehre*. There is no advertising in *Das Meisterwerk* except for the complete listing of Schenker's writings.

The issues of *Der Tonwille* average in length about forty-five pages (approximately 7″ by 9⅝″) and contain from three to nine articles each. There are of course numerous musical examples; at the end of each issue one finds longer, fold-out analytical graphs. The paper used during those years is unfortunately quite acidic and is now deteriorating rapidly.

Das Meisterwerk in der Musik is slightly smaller in format (6¾″ by 9⅜″). Each is a hardbound book—219, 216, and 121 pages, containing thirteen, seven, and two articles, respectively. In addition to the normal musical examples found imbedded in the text and a few fold-out graphs in v. 1, there are very extensive analytical graphs contained in pockets at the end of each volume.

All the articles in both publications are in German, with the text set in the older Gothic (*Fraktur*) style, although Schenker clearly intended to address readers not only in Austria and Germany but ultimately those in all nations that share in the Western cultural tradition.

Information Sources

BIBLIOGRAPHY

Kalib, Sylvan S. "Thirteen Essays from the Three Yearbooks Das Meisterwerk in der Musik by Heinrich Schenker: An Annotated Translation" (3 volumes). Ph.D. diss., Northwestern University, 1973.

INDEXES

External: Laskowski, Larry. *Heinrich Schenker: An Annotated Index to his Analyses of Musical Works*. New York: Pendragon Press, 1978.

REPRINT EDITION

Microform: *Der Tonwille*. New York Public Library.

Paper: *Dus meisterwerk in der Musik*: Georg Olms, 1974.

LOCATION SOURCES

Der Tonwille: Library of Congress, New York Public Library, Oberlin College Conservatory Library, Kansas State University (Manhattan), Swarthmore College, Duke University, Yale University Music Library, Harvard University, University of Chicago.

Das Meisterwerk in der Musik: widely held.

Publication History

TITLE AND TITLE CHANGES

Der Tonwille, 1921–24. *Das Meisterwerk in der Musik*, 1925–30.

VOLUME AND ISSUE DATA

Der Tonwille: Volumes 1–10, 1921–24. *Das Meisterwerk in der Musik*: Volumes 1–3, 1925–30.

FREQUENCY OF PUBLICATION

Der Tonwille, 10/4 years. *Das Meisterwerk in der Musik*, 3/6 years.

PUBLISHERS

A. Gutman, F. Hoffmeister, Universal-Edition; Drei Masken Verlag.

PLACES OF PUBLICATION

Vienna, Leipzig, Vienna, Munich. Reprint edition: Hildesheim.

EDITOR

Heinrich Schenker, 1921–30.

Paul B. Mast

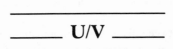

U/V

UP BEAT. See DOWN BEAT

VEREENIGDE TIJDSCHRIFTEN CAECILIA, DE. See CAECILIA (1844–1944)

VEREENIGDE TIJSCHRIFTEN CAECILIA EN HET MUZIEKCOL-LEGE, DE. See CAECILIA (1844–1944)

VIERTELJAHRSCHRIFT FÜR MUSIKWISSENSCHAFT

The *Vierteljahrschrift für Musikwissenschaft* (*VfM*), published in Leipzig from 1885–94, is recognized as a landmark publication in the field of musicology. Whereas earlier music periodicals had focused mainly on music readily heard in the concert houses, with occasional items devoted to historical studies, the *Vierteljahrschrift* "completed the separation of the general music periodical and the musicological one foreshadowed by Chrysander's *Jahrbücher* and Robert Eitner's *Monatshefte für Musikgeschichte* (q.v.)."[1] The editors of the journal acknowledged their decisive step in the preface to the first issue:

The *Vierteljahrschrift für Musikwissenschaft* wishes to take up the attempt, which was first made with the *Jahrbücher für musikalischen Wissenschaft* then set forth in the *Allgemeine musikalische Zeitung* [q.v.], as much as was possible in its weekly format. The undersigned do not deceive themselves about the difficulties of the undertaking, but hope . . . to overcome them and create a viable publication . . . whose sole purpose shall be the service of scholarship. Besides actual musical subjects, the *Vierteljahr-schrift* will also consider auxiliary areas as much as is possible and pertinent. . . .

Invited to participate are all who have the furtherance of musicology at heart.

The three scholars issuing this invitation all figured prominently in late nineteenth-century musicology: Friedrich Chrysander, Philipp Spitta, and Guido Adler. Not only did they set the standards for future musicological journals, but their own contributions to the journal helped to define the new field of scholarship itself. In particular, Guido Adler's article "Umfang, Methode und Ziel der Musikwissenschaft" (1:5–20) describes parameters and criteria for research that still have validity today.

Adler distinguishes between historic and systematic musicology, a distinction that can be seen in the variety of articles appearing in *VfM*. In the former category are studies devoted to: notational/transcription problems (Oswald Koller's "Der Liederkodex von Montpellier: Eine Kritische Studie," 4:1–82), historical forms (Rudolph Schwartz's "Die Frottole im 15. Jahrhunderts," 2: 427–66), discussion of broader style periods (Hermann Kretschmar's "Die Venetianische Oper und die Werke Cavalli's und Cesti's," 8:1–76), and musical biography (F. A. Voigt's "Reinhard Keiser," 6:151–203). Systematic musicology, according to Adler, encompasses a wide range of topics and auxiliary areas, including: speculative theory (Hugo Riemann's "Wurzelt der musikalische Rhythmus in Sprachrhythmus?" 2:488–96); aesthetics, which Adler considered to be topics relating music to nature, and so on (Paul Fischer's "Zittauer Konzertleben vor hundert Jahren," 5:582–88); ethnomusicology (Carl Stump's article "Phonographirte Indianermelodien," 8:127–44); and various auxiliary areas such as acoustics and psychology (Richard Wallaschek on "Das musikalische Gedächniss und seine leistungen bei Katalepsie, im Traume und in der Hypnose," 8:204–51). The categories and trends seen in the journal articles were continued in twentieth-century German musicology, especially the emphasis on *kleinmeister*, musical life in German cities, and manuscript studies.

As the articles began to define the field of musicology, they also began to lay the ground rules for scholarly apparatus and research techniques. Many of the studies are based on archival research and present their results by means of elaborate and extensive charts and tables, obviously reflecting the desire to begin to attempt bibliographic control of a vast amount of material. The elegantly printed musical examples, sometimes running to forty or fifty pages, seem excessive by modern standards, but served to make the material accessible to scholars in an age without extensive collected editions and monuments of music. Most of the articles have been superseded by later research, many contain outright false information, but some remain as examples of outstanding scholarship, for example, Emil Vogel's article "Claudio Monteverdi" (3:315–450) and Max Seiffert's essay "J. P. Sweelinck und seine direkten deutschen Schüler" (7:145–

260). Flawed and inaccurate though they may be, Friedrich Chrysander's critical notes on George Frederick Handel's instrumental works should be recognized as one of the first such studies. Moreover, it is exciting to read about the discoveries in this new field: Hermann Kretschmar's report on the newly found score of Monteverdi's *Poppea* (10:483–530) or Philipp Spitta's "Eine neugefundene altgriechische Melodie" (10:103–10). If nothing else, the articles are of interest to those concerned with the history of musicological method and discovery.

VfM was issued quarterly with consecutive pagination, the yearly total running between 500 and 700 pages. Articles vary in length from brief reports to extended essays of up to a hundred pages; longer articles appear in installments. In addition to two to four articles, issues include numerous reviews of books in English, French, Italian, and German. Each volume (and sometimes each individual issue) also contains a bibliography of recent musicological and related publications; some volumes expand this feature to include a listing of articles in music periodicals of various countries, a useful tool for scholars doing research in that period. The *Vierteljahrschrift* itself includes a cumulative table of contents and index for each volume, plus a cumulative index brought out in 1895.

The journal's tenth volume contains a notice of the death of Philipp Spitta, and though Chrysander assumed the editorship, the journal ceased publication at the end of the year. Despite its brief tenure, the *Vierteljahrschrift* laid a solid foundation for the scholarship yet to come.

Note

1. *The New Grove Dictionary of Music and Musicians,* s.v. " Periodicals, II, 6," by Imogen Fellinger.

Information Sources

BIBLIOGRAPHY
Fellinger, Imogen. *Verzeichnis der Musikzeitschriften des 19. Jahrhunderts*. Studien zur Musikgeschichte des 19. Jahrhunderts, 10. Regensburg: Gustav Bosse, 1968.
INDEXES
Internal: each volume indexed.
REPRINT EDITIONS
Microform: Inter Documentation Co. Dakota Graphics.
LOCATION SOURCES
Widely available.

Publication History

TITLE AND TITLE CHANGES
Vierteljahrschrift für Musikwissenschaft.
VOLUME AND ISSUE DATA
Volumes 1–10, 1885–94.
FREQUENCY OF PUBLICATION
Quarterly.

PUBLISHER
   Breitkopf und Härtel.
PLACE OF PUBLICATION
   Leipzig, Germany.
EDITORS
   Friedrich Chrysander, Philipp Spitta, and Guido Adler, 1885–94.

Mary Sue Morrow

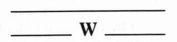

W

WEEKBLAD VOOR MUZIEK. See CAECILIA (1844–1944)

WERELD DER MUZIEK, DE. See CAECILIA (1844–1944)

WESTERN MUSICAL WORLD. See BRAINARD'S MUSICAL WORLD

WOODWIND WORLD—BRASS AND PERCUSSION

Symphony magazine offered a quarterly supplement periodical in the spring of 1950 called *The Clarinet*. Edited by James Collis, it offered twenty-four to thirty-six pages of brief articles and news items of interest to clarinetists and, later, saxophonists. All twenty-six issues of *The Clarinet*, published over seven years, were numbered within v. 1. In 1957 Collins moved *The Clarinet* from New York City to Mt. Kisco, New York, changing its format and scope as well as the title. The first three issues of the new publication, *Woodwind World* (beginning again with v. 1), appeared in a newspaper format: 12½″ by 18″ with five columns of print per page. Collis described the objectives in the new periodical: "We shall tell the news about woodwind players, publish technical articles of lasting value, bring to the performer and teacher the latest information about instruments, music, and related material, and endeavor to sharpen the interest of the student" (1.1:2).

Woodwind World changed to a magazine format, 8¼″ by 10¾″ with 2.1

(February 1958) in response to complaints from readers that the newspaper format was unsuitable for binding and preservation (2.1:3). Issues 2.1–2.8 (February 1958 to November 1958) of *Woodwind World* were published monthly except for July and August. Its layout featured a cross between newspaper format for the news items (a header with the location and printed in three columns) and magazine format (full page articles plus photographs). The twelve issues of v. 3 were published in Bedford Hills, New York, and released five times per year on the first days of January, March, May, September, and November. With v. 3.2 the release dates were changed to 1 February, 10 April, 1 June, 15 September, and 1 December. This rather unusual frequency rate was maintained, but the numbering of volumes was completely unpredictable. Vs. 4.1 through 4.11 began with 1 June 1962 and ended with 1 June 1963; v. 5 had only five numbers: 15 September 1963 through 1 June 1964; v. 6 featured eleven issues: 15 September 1964 through 14 September 1966; v. 7 had six issues: 1 December 1966 through 1 December 1967; v. 8 only released three issues: 1 February, 10 April, and 1 June 1968.

The publisher of *Woodwind World* changed to Swift-Dorr Publications of Oneonta, New York, in 1970. Harry Dorr was the printer/publisher, and Frederic Fay Swift took over the duties of managing editor. The 1970 *Woodwind World* began with v. 9, but contains three issues only: June, September, and December; the publication date became merely the name of the month in which it was released. The size of the publication remained consistent with previous issues, but the length of each issue expanded from sixteen to twenty pages to twenty-eight to forty pages each. The periodical returned to being released five times a year with v. 10 but each year now marked a new volume number. Indices were published in the last number of each volume beginning with v. 9 (1970).

Woodwind World merged in January 1975 with another Swift-Dorr Publication, *B&P: Brass and Percussion* to become *Woodwind World—Brass and Percussion*. The publication continued the *Woodwind World* volume numbering (beginning with v. 14), but the release schedule changed from the preceding pattern to Winter, Spring, Fall, and a Holiday Issue (December). V. 15 (1976) expanded to a six-issue schedule by adding a Vacation Issue (late summer). The expansion reflected in the frequency of release was also made apparent in the periodical's length; each issue of *Woodwind World—Brass and Percussion* ran fifty to sixty pages.

Woodwind World—Brass and Percussion changed owners/editors in 1980 to Sarah M. Evans of Evans Publications, Deposit, New York. In 1981 (v. 20), the journal altered its publication frequency to eight issues per year but released only seven. The title changed to *Woodwind/Brass & Percussion* with v. 20.4. Vs. 21–23 (1982–84) reflected the eight-issue schedule; v. 24 only reached number four before publication ceased.

Woodwind World was the official publication of the National Flute Association from 13.1 to 15.4. *Woodwind World—Brass and Percussion* was the official publication of the Association of Concert Bands of America from v. 16.4 to the periodical's cessation.

Throughout the run, the periodical's style remained fundamentally the same. The articles were written by performers and pedagogues, and later by students. The articles were brief (generally one page), the news items were focused on members of the woodwind (later including the brass and percussion) community. Certain recurring features came and went with the various editors, affiliations, and the ever-changing scope of the periodical. Examples include "Clarinet Music Since 1900," "It's a Fact," "Daniel Bonade's 'Reed Tontebook,' " "Clarinet Quiz," "New Records," "The Bandmaster's Corner," "Letters from Our Readers," and "Happenings in the Musical World." Advertisements and photographs are plentiful while musical examples are sometimes included in articles.

While the style of the publication was quite consistent, the content of these periodicals changed quite perceptibly during the years of publication. *The Clarinet* and *Woodwind World*, under the editorship of Collis, were aimed primarily at the professional woodwind player; the college teacher and student were of secondary focus. The pedagogical articles, the musical announcements, and even the covers drew attention to the master teachers and performers in the orchestral/professional recitalist world. Collis's successors, John Gerstner, Swift, and Evans shifted that focus to the world of the college musician. The affiliations with the National Flute Association and the Concert Bands Association as well as the addition of brass and percussion music as part of the magazine's topics were reflected in altered content. These various changes are suggested in the following list of notable feature articles: "The Plastic Reed" by Curtis Craver, Jr. (1.7:5–6), Collis's own article on Aaron Copland's Clarinet Concerto (1.3:24–25), Samuel Baron's "The Flute Music of J. S. Bach" (1.1:6–7), "The Young Professional Clarinetist" by Bernard Portnoy (3.5:9), Dr. Maurice Whitney's "Recorder: Toy or Musical Instrument?" (9.2:7), "Some Thoughts on Percussion" by Karel Husa (14.3:28–29), and Catherine P. Smith's four-part article entitled "Expressiveness in Pre-Boehm Transverse Flutes" (14.2:18–21 to 14.5:22).

The primary reason, however, for the shift in focus was probably the reader market itself. The publication that began as a supplement to Carnegie Hall's *Symphony* magazine could not maintain itself through its rather limited appeal to only the professional clarinetist or, later, woodwind players in general, and then the entire woodwind, brass, and percussion families. The 1970s and 1980s saw the organization and/or strengthening of many instrument-oriented societies, each of which publishes a journal or newsletter. While no written evidence for cessation of publication can be found in the magazine, the last publishers may have ended *Woodwind World/Brass & Percussion* because there were too many journals and magazines competing for the same readers.

Information Sources

INDEXES

    Internal: each volume indexed, v.9– .

    External: Music Index, 1950–65, 1970– . Music Article Guide, 1965– . Arts and Humanities Citation Index, 1976– .

LOCATION SOURCES
> University of Illinois, University of Michigan, University of Texas at Austin, Vancouver Public Library (partial run). Later volumes widely held.

Publication History

TITLE AND TITLE CHANGES
> *The Clarinet* (1.1–1.26; 1950–57); *Woodwind World* (1.1–13.5; 1957–74); *Woodwind World—Brass and Percussion* (14.1–20.3; 1975–81); *Woodwind/Brass & Percussion* (20.4–24.4; 1981–April 1985).

VOLUME AND ISSUE DATA
> *The Clarinet*: Volumes 1.1–1.26, 1950–57. *Woodwind World*: Volumes 1.1–24.4, 1957–85.

FREQUENCY OF PUBLICATION
> 26/7 years, 1950–57. Monthly, 1958 (2.1–2.8). 5/years, 1959–75. 6/year, 1976–80. 8/year, 1981–85.

PUBLISHERS
> *Symphony Magazine*, 1950–57. *Woodwind World*, 1957–69. Swift-Dorr Publications, 1970–79. Evans Publications, 1980–85.

PLACES OF PUBLICATION
> New York, 1950–57. Mt. Kisco, New York, November 1957–October 1958. Bedford Hills, New York, January 1959–June 1968. Oneonta, New York, June 1970–December 1979. Deposit, New York, January 1980–April 1985.

EDITORS
> James Collis, 1950–62. John Gerstner, 1962–68. Frederic Fay Swift, 1970–79. Sarah M. Evans, 1980–85.

Paul B. Hunt

WOODWIND/BRASS & PERCUSSION. See WOODWIND WORLD

WORLD OF MUSIC, THE

The World of Music emerged in 1959 as an update of the *Bulletin of the International Music Council* (IMC). Its subtitle continued to reflect this nativity for two decades. The first issue announced "published quarterly"; however, there appear to have been six issues per year until 1967.

Mario Balroca (Italy), president of the council at the onset of the journal, stated its purpose simply: to reflect the council's action. Initial volumes aimed at informing readers on different conceptions of music language, contributing to a better understanding of music values, and establishing cooperation on the cultural level between continents. These goals were pursued by publishing such materials as aesthetic debates, features on new composers, and roundtable discussions from congresses. Space was also devoted to reports on meetings, information on festivals, and events of the season. There were short articles on musicianship.

In 1967, under the leadership of council president Narayana Menon, the *Bulletin* changed to a quarterly publication. The International Institute for Comparative Music Studies and Documentation (ICMSD) joined efforts with the IMC for the newly styled publication. The journal also set a new goal: to present the readers a broader and more comprehensive spectrum of the "world of music." Further objectives were to "give music lovers and scholars around the world an informative and provocative view of international music life and of what leading experts think about it" (10.2:3). As the journal took on a more professional appearance, substantive articles became more scholarly and increased in length to an average of ten pages, while the feature "Critics Column" was added (10.2). Issue length ranges widely, from around seventy pages to more than twice that. The number of articles per issue varies accordingly, from four to nine.

Other changes came in 1978 when the editor announced that "the journal was obliged to change presentation and publishers." At this time frequency of publication decreased from quarterly to three times per year. One-third of the space was still to be devoted to the IMC and associated organizations, with two-thirds remaining for its "world music" vocation. The preference was for descriptive articles on various aspects of specific music traditions. The approach tended to be sociocultural rather than technical/analytic. Editorials, book and record reviews, press opinions, and competitions were among the features added at this time. Although not expressed by the editor, it appears that a tacit decision had been made to give each issue a central theme (see below). In 1980 the editor indicated (22.3) that a council committee was developing a "world history of music," and a preliminary study was being carried out with the collaboration of the IMC, IFMC, and IMS. This study appeared in a special issue entitled "Toward a World View of Music" (22.3). Other special issues were devoted to various countries—Germany (6.4), Japan (25.1), Korea (27.2); specific topics—Sacred Music (24.3, 26.3), Masks (22.1, 23.3); and professional issues—Methodology—Symposium '80 (23.2) and Aesthetics (25.3).

The bulletins contained many advertisements in all three languages. Use of photographs was generous, including centerfolds. Since 1978 the journal has also incorporated charts, graphs, diagrams, and musical transcriptions.

Vs. 1–8 were published as a bulletin on 8½″ by 11″ sheets with paper cover. Each bulletin had a photo of a musician, record cover, or the like, centered; the title—*The World of Music*—was (until 1961) followed by subtitle "Bulletin of International Music Council" in three languages: English, French, and German. Each article or rubric appeared in only one of the three languages; however, the president's remarks were in all three. In 1972 the entire journal was published in three languages, divided into more or less equal blocks on each page. Since 1978 all articles have appeared in English followed by substantive summaries in German and French. When the bulletin became a journal (1967), the format changed to 5⅝″ by 7¼″; the cover, now glossy, retained the photograph and gave the title in three languages: *World of Music, die Welt der Musik*, and *Le monde de la musique*.

Information Sources

INDEXES
> External: Music Index, 1958–   . Bibliographie des Musikschrifttums, 1962–   .
> RILM, 1967–   . Arts and Humanities Citation Index, 1976–   .

LOCATION SOURCES
> Widely available.

Publication History

TITLE AND TITLE CHANGES
> *The World of Music. Bulletin of International Music Council, Bulletin du conseil international de la musique, Organ des internationalen Musikrates*, 1958–67. *The World of Music. Die Welt der Musik, Le monde de la musique. Journal of . . .*, 1968–77. *The World of Music*, 1978–   .

VOLUME AND ISSUE DATA
> Volumes 1–   , 1959–   .

FREQUENCY OF PUBLICATION
> Bimonthly, 1959–66. Quarterly, 1967–77. 3/year, 1978–   .

PUBLISHERS
> International Music Council with assistance of UNESCO, 1959–76. International Music Council with assistance of UNESCO and Berlin Senate, 1976–77. IMC, UNESCO, Berlin Senate, and IICMSD, 1978–   .

PLACES OF PUBLICATION
> Paris, 1959–77. Berlin, Germany, 1978–   .

EDITORS
> John Evarts, associate executive secretary, 1959–60. Egon Kraus, Jack Bornoff, and John Evarts, 1960–66. John Evarts, Rudolf Heinemann, 1967–68. Ivan Vandor, 1969–87. Max Peter Baumann, 1988–   .

L. JaFran Jones

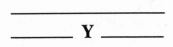

Y

YEARBOOK OF INTERNATIONAL FOLK MUSIC COUNCIL. See
YEARBOOK FOR TRADITIONAL MUSIC

YEARBOOK FOR TRADITIONAL MUSIC

The annual *International Folk Music Council Journal* served, from 1949, to
communicate the status, goals, and objectives of the International Folk Music
Council (IFMC). Vs. 1–20 (1949–68) of the journal featured conference papers
on general principles and problems of folksong studies, regional ethnic investigations, and modal analyses of folk melodies. The scope of the journal has
now expanded to include such themes as "music of a complex society," "technology in music of urban or urbanized popularization," and "the processes by
which music communicates."

In 1947 a conference was convened in London by the International (advisory)
Folk Dance Council. The council's discussion on whether to widen its scope to
include folk music resulted in the founding of the International Folk Music
Council. This new council held its first general conference in Basel, Switzerland,
in September 1948, and launched a journal the next year. Dr. Ralph Vaughan
Williams was elected honorary president and served in that capacity until his
death in 1958. Succeeding in the presidency were Dr. Jaap Kunst (until 1961)
and Zoltán Kodály (1961–67).

Maud Karpeles was instrumental in organizing the council and made a major
contribution as the first editor of the journal (1949–61, 1963–64). She styled it
as a manual for in-the-field collectors. As the official organ of the council, the
journal's chief policy was to publish major papers of the periodic council conferences. At this time they were deeply concerned with the survival and revival
of folk music throughout the world.

As the council matured, this concern persisted, alongside a growing recognition of the impact of technology on the social and artistic aspects of folk music. The council acquired a more international flavor in 1950, when the conference was held at Indiana University. In 1952 the council attempted to decentralize, so that responsibility for implementing its objectives would be more equally shared.

By 1956 the council had succeeded in enlisting the collaboration of radio stations in expeditions throughout the world for collecting priceless musical documents. The council/*Journal* also encouraged comparative study of folk music. In 1963 the IFMC objectives were updated (15:1): (1) to assist the present discussion and practice of folk music in all countries; (2) to further comparative study of folk music; and (3) to promote understanding and friendship between nations through communication and interest in folk music.

In 1969 (v. 1, new series) the council chose to replace "Journal" with "Yearbook" in the title. The change was intended to reflect more accurately the nature of this annual publication. The same issue brought other important changes: volume numbers were recycled to v. 1, each issue contained a larger variety of lengthier articles, and the quality and "depth" of articles were upgraded.

Another change came in 1981, when the current title, *Yearbook for Traditional Music*, was adopted. According to the General Assembly, the change from "folk" to "traditional" "does not signify any change in policy, in goals or in works of the Council. The IFMC (now ICTM) has been concerned, from the beginning, with all kinds of traditional music, not only with 'folk.' This has not always been understood by 'outsiders' " (15:ix). The change came about because the council saw itself "as an open-minded, non-dogmatic organ." However, it also recognized that the study of traditional (or folk) music was being introduced in many other disciplines and societies, and it found "itself in healthy competition with other international organs" (15:ix). The ITMC cited the founding of the Society for Ethnomusicology and the Hungarian Academy of Science (15:ix).

The nature of the *Yearbook* was redefined at that time "as a vehicle for extensive studies dealing in depth with aspects of the membership's original research, presenting surveys of complete or in-progress work with specific cultural entities and/or regions." In 1984 the *Yearbook* reaffirmed its policy of reflecting more closely the work of the council. The general plan was to coordinate, in principle, one or more themes of the *Yearbook* with the conference held the preceding year. Such special issues have, in fact, been common: Yugoslavfest (v. 4), Report of IFMC and East & West in Music Conference Organization (v. 16), Studia Musicologica, Academiae Scientarium Hungaricae (v. 17, part 2), a 25th Anniversary Issue (n.s., v. 4), and East Asia (n.s., v. 15).

From the outset (1949) the journal regularly featured editorial statements, festival information, dance and music at the IFMC festival, proceedings of the congress, "Notes & News," and correspondence from other organizations in addition to articles. Book, pamphlet, record, and music reviews began to appear in 1962 (v. 14). Four years later, advertisements for records, journals, and scholastic material were first included.

The *Yearbook* measures 7″ by 10″ and is published in English. Only in earlier volumes was there a rare article in French or German; many, however, are accompanied by musical transcriptions. An "official" index (by author, title, and subject) was published for vs. 1–15 (old series).

Information Sources

INDEXES

External: Music Index, 1949–. Bibliographie des Musikschrifttums, 1950–67, 1972– . RILM, 1967– . Arts and Humanities Citation Index, 1976– .

LOCATION SOURCES

Widely available.

Publication History

TITLE AND TITLE CHANGES

Journal of International Folk Music Council, 1949–68. Yearbook of International Folk Music Council, 1969–81. Yearbook for Traditional Music, 1982– .

VOLUME AND ISSUE DATA

Volumes 1–20, 1949–68. New series, volumes 1– , 1969– .

FREQUENCY OF PUBLICATION

Yearly.

PUBLISHERS

International Folk Music Council, 1949–52. International Folk Music Council with assistance of United Nations Education, Scientific, and Cultural Organization (UNESCO), 1952–82. International Folk Music Council in cooperation with "East and West in Music" Conference, 1964. International Council of Traditional Music and UNESCO, 1982– .

PLACES OF PUBLICATION

London, 1964–67. Copenhagen, 1968–69. Urbana, Illinois, 1970–71. Kingston, Ontario, 1971–80. New York, 1980– .

EDITORS

Maud Karpeles, 1949–61. Laurence E. R. Picken, 1962. Maud Karpeles, 1963–64. Peter Crossley-Holland, 1965–68. Alexander L. Ringer, 1969–70. Charles Haywood, 1971–74. Bruno Nettl, 1975–76. Israel J. Katz, 1977–79. Norma McLeod, 1980–81. Dieter Christensen, 1982– .

GUEST EDITORS

Erich Stochmann (Europe), 1981. Yoshihiko Tokumaru (Far East), 1981. Hahn Man-Young, 1983. Adelaida Reyes Schramm, 1984.

L. JaFran Jones

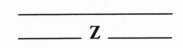

Z

ZEITSCHRIFT FÜR MUSIK. See NEUE ZEITSCHRIFT FÜR MUSIK

ZEITSCHRIFT FÜR MUSIKTHEORIE

The *Zeitschrift für Musiktheorie* (*Journal for Music Theory*) was established in 1971 as the first German periodical expressly devoted to music theory. This biannual's founding co-editors were Peter Rummenhöller and Karl Michael Komma, both then members of the music theory staff of the Stuttgart *Musikhochschule*. Rummenhöller remained as either co-editor or, after v. 4.1, sole editor until publication was suspended due to loss of publisher after completion of the 9.2 (1979). The *zfmth*, as its title is abbreviated by its editors, may shortly resume publication.

Despite a wide range of theoretical topics covered and the evident desire to draw submissions and readership from scholars, composers, teachers, performers, and listeners alike (1.1:1), the contents will mainly be of interest to readers with the following six special concerns: (1) radical twentieth-century composition; (2) harmonic function analysis in the Riemann tradition; (3) hermeneutic analysis of tonal music (at times reflecting historical consciousness); (4) psychoanalytic interpretation of music and musical questions; (5) music in relation to various forms of Marxist theory; and (6) recent and future development of music theory in Germany. Noteworthy articles include Carl Dahlhaus's consideration of sentence and period structure (9.2:16–26), Josef Rufer's examination of Arnold Schönberg's attitudes toward music theory (2.1:1–3), Helmut Lachermann's groundbreaking discussion of sound categories of new music (1.1:20–30) with its supplementary recording, Tibor Kneif's comments on Adorno and Stockhausen (4.1:34–38), Hans Oesch's exegesis of Schönberg's Op. 23/3 in terms of this composition's significance in the development of twelve-tone technique (5.1:2–10), Jens Peter Reiche's remarks on Gamelan Music and Claude Debussy (3.1:5–15), Rudolf Heinz's curious psychoanalytic interpretations (4.1:3–6, 5.1:21–28, and 7.2:6–24), William Earl Caplin's stimulating explanation of musical accent (9.1:17–28), as well as Albrecht Dümling's demonstration of a youthful leftist period in Schönberg's life and Hansjörg Pauli's speculations regarding the relationship between the avant garde and popularity (6.1:11–21 and 6.1:4–10, respectively). The early issues also contain quite revealing editorial statements on the nature of music theory and similar methodological points.

Unfortunately, two flaws (either singly or conjointly) tend to mar many *zfmth* papers. First, nearly all the contributors simply ignore relevant work from outside of Germany. As a result, there is too much reliance on ideas and approaches that are already outdated elsewhere. Second, many of the authors devote much space to largely irrelevant, often clumsy, and sometimes extremely self-righteous Marxist applications. All too often, these writers seem to believe that mere assertion is enough to make some conceivable connection between a music and social conflict true.

Each issue offers several substantial articles. There are several single topic issues: v. 4.1 focuses on Adorno (a supplement provides a facsimile score of Adorno's Op. 8 women's choruses); 4.2 is an analysis issue; 5.1 concentrates on Schönberg, and 7.2 deals with group psychoanalytic interpretation of the ''Emperor'' Concerto's second movement. Some issues, but not all, contain a few, often lengthy, book reviews. At times, these seem intended to settle scores with German theorists of a more conservative inclination than acceptable at the Stuttgart Hochschule. Advertisements (like the book reviews) often concern rather obscure German titles. As befits a theory journal, there are copious musical examples and diagrams. Early issues conclude with a bibliography of the publications on theory by teachers from a particular West German Musikhochschule (1.1:46—Stuttgart, 1.2:45—Hamburg, 2.1:46—Saarbrücken, and 3.1:45—Munich).

The two annual issues usually ran to about fifty pages apiece; numbering of pages is consecutive only in v. 6. The approximately 8″ by 10″ pages generally contained two columns of offset print. However, some parts of vs. 6 and 7 were printed with one column per page or with a wide column of German text accompanied by a minimally useful, very brief English summary in a narrow column at the side. It is regrettable that this laudable experiment was not better executed. Most of the articles require a sophisticated command of the German language.

Information Sources

INDEXES

    External: Music Index, 1971–   . RILM, 1969–   . Bibliographie des Musikschrifttums, 1970–78.

LOCATION SOURCES
   Widely available.

Publication History

TITLE AND TITLE CHANGES
   Zeitschrift für Musiktheorie.
VOLUME AND ISSUE DATA
   Volumes 1–9.2, 1970–78.
FREQUENCY OF PUBLICATION
   Biannual.
PUBLISHERS
   Icythys Verlag, 1971–75. Gustav V. Döring Verlag, 1975–79.
PLACE OF PUBLICATION
   Stuttgart.
EDITORS
   Peter Rummenhöller, 1971–79 (1–9.1). Karl Michael Komma, 1971–74 (1–4.1).
   Hermann Danuser, 1979 (9.2).

Stefan M. Ehrenkreutz

ZEITSCHRIFT FÜR MUSIKWISSENSCHAFT

In December 1917 a group of scholars met in Berlin to begin a musicological organization that professed national and international aims. Headed by Berlin professor Hermann Kretzschmar, they sought to unite those involved in German musicology, to facilitate the exchange of ideas and research, and to renew efforts to create a German-speaking arm of an international musicological organization, efforts that had been disrupted by World War I. The following January these scholars, now identified as "Die deutsche Musikgesellschaft," drew up bylaws and elected a board of directors, headed by Hermann Kretzschmar, which included Guido Adler and Johannes Wolf. The first issue of the *Zeitschrift für Musikwissenschaft*, the *Gesellschaft*'s monthly journal, appeared in October 1918, free to members. Nonmembers could purchase the journal for 2 marks an issue. The journal appeared regularly until 1935, when once again the German musicological community was disrupted by political events. After the war the journal was superseded by the *Archiv für Musikforschung* (q.v.).

Die deutsche Musikgesellschaft stressed the scholarly nature of the journal from the outset; an average issue contained five to six articles of two to five pages in length. Occasionally an article ran to ten pages. Most dealt with Medieval, Renaissance, and Baroque topics, reflecting the interests of German musicology of the time. They are more in the nature of "works in progress" reports than major musicological discourses by modern standards. In the 1920s a rare article on Arnold Schönberg, the Donaueschingen Chamber Music Festival, and other contemporary music issues appeared. Archival investigations and articles devoted to single works were also included. Ernst Krohn's "Musikwis senschaft in Amerika'' (8:297–98) illustrates the occasionally broader perspective. Contributors included the major, primarily German scholars of the day, including Egon Wellesz, Alfred Lorenz, and Paul Nettl. Alfred Einstein, well known at the time as both a scholar and as the leading musical critic for the *Berliner Tageblatt*, edited the journal from its first issue until 1933, when he was forced into exile by the National Socialist government.

Regular departments which appeared in the first issue were the ''Book Display'' section which listed, without reviews or annotations, all new book-length publications on music; a second list of all new editions of Baroque and pre-Baroque compositions; a compilation of all musical courses offered at German-speaking universities; and a section for organization business. Each year, again beginning with v. 1, the journal published a bibliography, compiled by Gustav Beckmann, of articles on musical topics that appeared in other newspapers or journals. A later feature, begun in v. 5, was an annual record of all German-language musicological dissertations completed the previous year. In v. 11, the journal began a separate miscellany section for responses from scholars and reports of works in progress.

The *Zeitschrift für Musikwissenschaft* retained its 5⅞'' by 9'' size throughout its existence. An average volume consisted of 730 pages including musical examples, although in the 1930s the size decreased considerably to an average of 430 pages. Occasional numbers were published as joint issues, and with v. 16 the journal switched to the standard January to December publishing year from its earlier October to September calendar. With v. 12 (1929–30) the journal discontinued its *Fraktur* typeface. Each volume contained a volume index compiled by Kurt Fischer. Musical examples and other illustrative materials are rare.

Information Sources

INDEXES
>   Internal: Each volume indexed.
>   External: Bibliographie des Musikschrifttums, 1936.

REPRINT EDITIONS
>   Papers: Johnson Reprint. Kraus Reprints.
>   Microform: Datamics, Inc. Dakota Graphics. Brookhaven.

LOCATION SOURCES
>   Widely available.

Publication History

TITLE AND TITLE CHANGES
>   *Zeitschrift für Musikwissenschaft.*

VOLUME AND ISSUE DATA
>   Volumes 1–17.12, 1918–35.

FREQUENCY OF PUBLICATION
>   Monthly.

PUBLISHER
    Breitkopf und Härtel.
PLACE OF PUBLICATION
    Leipzig, Germany.
EDITORS
    Alfred Einstein, 1918–33. Max Schneider, 1934–35.

Susan C. Cook

New Journals of the 1980s

During the 1980s, a number of new journals with significant subject orientation began publication. With their relatively short publication run, it is too soon to assess the significance to music research of these periodicals; however, note must be made of these titles as there is every indication that articles published in these journals are making and will continue to make a notable contribution to the literature.

AMERICAN MUSIC

Dedicated, as the subtitle emphasizes, "to all aspects of American music and music in America," *American Music* is an outgrowth of the rapidly expanding interest in and high quality exploration of American music during the past two decades. In the 1983 inaugural issue, founding editor Allen P. Britton announced that the journal would deal with:

> genres and forms; geographical and historical patterns; composers, performers, and audiences; sacred and secular traditions; cultural, social, and ethnic diversity; the impact and role of the media; the reflection of social, political, and economic issues; problems of research, analysis, and archiving; education; criticism and aesthetics; and more. We disown chauvinistic intent, wishing only to provide for the musical sector of the general field of American studies. . . . Neither are we trying to prove anything, seeking only to provide a forum for all who have studies to report, histories to tell, or arguments to develop. (1.1:prepagination)

Britton was joined in this endeavor by Irving Lowens (book review editor) and Don L. Roberts (record review editor/discographer) along with an impressive editorial board featuring the likes of John Cage, Gilbert Chase, Richard Crawford, Charles Hamm, H. Wiley Hitchcock, Cynthia Hoover, Bruno Nettl, Vivian Perlis, Nicolas Slonimsky, Eileen Southern, and Virgil Thomson. The journal is co-published by the Sonneck Society and the University of Illinois Press.

As Britton promised, virtually no stone in American music has been left unturned. The following list of a few of the many fine articles that have appeared to date is indicative: Lawrence Gushee's, "A Preliminary Chronology of the Early Career of Ferd 'Jelly Roll' Morton" (3.4:389–412); "Conlon Nancarrow: Interviews in Mexico City and San Francisco," by Roger Reynolds (2.2:1–24); Richard Crawford's, "Musical Learning in Nineteenth-Century America" (1.1:1–11); and "David Medoff: A Case Study in Interethnic Popular Culture," by Mark Slobin and Richard K. Spottswood (3.3:261–276). It would likewise be difficult to defend any accusation of chronological, geographical, ethnic, reportorial, or methodological bias. *AM* has included two fascinating special issues to date: "Music of the American Theatre" (2.4) and "British-American Musical Interactions" (4.1), the latter a product of the Third American Music Conference, University of Keele, 2–5 July 1983. Most contributors are American music scholars, both famous and emerging, with no particular scholar or school dominating. The endnoting is frequently extensive and the visual and musical examples excellent, if sparse.

Each issue includes six to eight articles, fifteen to twenty pages long, and twenty to twenty-five scholarly reviews—mostly of books, the rest of recordings—that average one to two pages. The remainder of each 120-page issue contains five to eight pages of advertisements, primarily placed by presses, journals, record labels, and both the Sonneck Society and the Institute for Studies in American Music. Each volume of *AM* is meticulously indexed in the final issue by author, title, and subject—one integrated but thoroughly differentiated listing.

Pagination became continuous within the volume in v. 3 and with v. 4 the journal's overall dimensions were reduced from 7″ by 10″ to 6″ by 9″ while the covers lost their glossy finish. Otherwise, the format of *American Music* has remained unchanged and the journal continues to appear quarterly on acid-free paper.

Information Sources

INDEXES
　　Internal: each volume
　　External: Music Index, 1983– . RILM, 1983– . Arts and Humanities Citation
　　Index, 1983– .
LOCATION SOURCES
　　Widely available.

Publication History

TITLE AND TITLE CHANGES
　　American Music.
VOLUME AND ISSUE DATA
　　Volumes 1– , 1983– .

FREQUENCY OF PUBLICATION
    Quarterly.
PUBLISHER
    The Sonneck Society and the University of Illinois Press.
PLACE OF PUBLICATION
    Champaign, Illinois.
EDITORS
    Allen P. Britton, 1983–85. John Graziano, 1986–88. Wayne Shirley, 1989–   .

Richard S. James

JOURNAL OF MUSICOLOGY

The American quarterly *The Journal of Musicology,* subtitled *A Quarterly Review of Music History, Criticism, Analysis, and Performance Practice,* aims to present a "balanced perspective of musicological activity" ("Guidelines for Authors" in each issue). It welcomes articles addressing "aspects of musical style in all periods, from the historical, analytic, or critical points of view; articles on performance practice, reports of works in progress, and of library holdings and conferences" (3.4:inside back cover).

Historical articles outweigh those on music theory and aesthetics, although the latter two are represented in most issues. The Classical era is the most discussed in *JM* with Renaissance music next. Leading scholars, as well as newer writers contribute in all areas, for example, William S. Newman's "Beethoven's Fingerings as Interpretive Clues" (1:171–91), "H. C. Koch, The Classical Concerto, and the Sonata-Form Retransition" (2:45–61) by Shelley Davis, and Allan Atlas' "Paolo Luchini's *Della Musica*: A Little-Known Source for Text Underlay from the late Sixteenth Century" (2:62–80).

The journal's one special issue to date, v. 3.3, treats ancient Greek and medieval music both historically and theoretically. Entitled *The Ancient Harmoniai, Tonoi, and Octave Species in Theory Practice,* this number contains papers and discussions from the American Musicological Society meeting in Louisville, 1983. Claude Palisca's "Introductory Notes on the Historiography of the Greek Modes" (3:221–28) and "Octave Species" (3:229–41) by André Barbera are especially noteworthy.

The journal's progressive welcoming of popular music scholarship, a distinctive feature, is evident in both articles and reviews, such as Paul Oliver's "Blues Research: Problems and Possibilities" (2:377–90), and Charles Hamm's report on the International Conference on Popular Music Research in Amsterdam in 1982 (1:466–69). Like the other items, conference reports represent the journal's broad spectrum of interest. Usually two to five pages long, they cover events ranging from major early music festivals to Debussy and Schumann conferences.

The layout, on 6″ by 8¾″ pages, usually consists of four to six articles, ranging from fifteen to twenty-five pages, one or two book reviews and, in most issues,

at least one conference report. Analyses are richly illustrated with musical examples; a few include extensive charts also. Facsimiles and engravings are
frequent in historical articles such as Dorothy S. Packer's *"Au boys de dueil*
and the Grief-Decalogue Relationship in Sixteenth-Century Chansons'' (3:19–
54). A dozen pages of publisher's advertising at the back of each issue reflect
JM's scholarly tone and audience.

Information Sources

INDEXES
> External: Music Index, 1982– . RILM, 1982– . Arts and Humanities Citation
> Index, 1982– .

LOCATION SOURCES
> Widely available.

Publication History

TITLE AND TITLE CHANGES
> *The Journal of Musicology, A Quarterly Review of Music History, Criticism,
> Analysis, and Performance Practice.*

VOLUME AND ISSUE DATA
> Volumes 1– , 1982– .

FREQUENCY OF PUBLICATION
> Quarterly.

PUBLISHER
> Imperial Printing Company.

PLACE OF PUBLICATION
> St. Joseph, Michigan.

EDITOR
> Marian Green, 1982– .

Esther Rothenbusch

LATIN AMERICAN MUSIC REVIEW/REVISTA DE MUSICA LATINO AMERICANA

The *Latin American Music Review,* even though a semiannual publication, is
in many ways the successor to the *Yearbook for Inter-American Musical Research*, a scholarly annual whose eleven issues (1965–75) were editorially over-
seen by Gilbert Chase. The associate editor of the *Yearbook* during most of its
existence was Gerard Béhague, another noted specialist in Latin American music,
who in 1980 became the founding editor of the *The Latin American Music Review.*
While the *Yearbook* covered the music of the Americas in general, the *Latin
American Music Review* is limited to the music of Mexico and Central America,
the Caribbean Islands, and South America. Ethnic music (including folklore,
dance, and instruments), art music (from post-Columbian times to the present),
and contemporary popular music form the spectrum of coverage, with most

articles falling into the ethnic segment. Articles average twenty pages in length. English is the predominant language of the contributions; Spanish appears somewhat frequently and Portuguese occasionally. Contributors are mostly well-known specialists (e.g., Luiz Heitor Corrêa de Azevedo, Juan A. Orrego-Salas, George List) or experienced doctoral candidates.

Regular features include extended reviews of books and recordings, several pages of "Communications and Announcements," and brief statements about the contributors. Extended bibliographies and discographies are not at all unusual. So far there have been few advertisements per issue. Illustrations, such as photographs, diagrams, line drawings, and musical examples appear frequently. Issues measure 5¾" by 8¾" and run, on the average, from 125 to 150 pages in length.

Since the inaugural issue (Spring/Summer 1980), the *Latin American Music Review*, has assumed a position of prominence among scholarly journals in the subject area.

Information Sources

BIBLIOGRAPHY
"Latin American Music Review/Revista de Música Latinoamericana." *Inter-American Music Review* 3 (Fall 1980): 115.
INDEXES
    Music Index, 1980– . RILM, 1980– . Arts and Humanities Citation Index, 1980– .
REPRINT EDITION
    Microfrorm: Microforms International Marketing Co. UMI.

Publication History

TITLE AND TITLE CHANGES
    Latin American Music Review/Revista de música latino americana.
VOLUME AND ISSUE DATA
    Volumes 1– , 1980– .
FREQUENCY OF PUBLICATION
    Semiannual.
PUBLISHER
    University of Texas Press.
PLACE OF PUBLICATION
    Austin, Texas.
EDITOR
    Gerard Béhague, 1980– .

John E. Druesedow

MUSIC ANALYSIS

Music Analysis is the creation of a dynamic group of the established British scholarly discipline of musical analysis who regard London as their intellectual home base. Its editors conceive of it not only as "a forum for academic exchange," but also as a means "to provide a flow of views of interest to critics, performers and all those who are concerned with what musicians think about particular musical works and how musicians go about examining musical structure and effect" (1.1:1). In its pages, the reader can encounter a very broad range of the most outstanding American (e.g., Allen Forte, George Perle, Carl Schachter), British (e.g., Ian D. Bent, Hans Keller, Arnold Whittall), continental European (e.g., Theodor Adorno, Ernö Lendvai, Erwin Ratz), as well as other (e.g., Roy Howat) work presently being done in the field known in the United States as music theory.

Due to the exceptionally wide scope of its contents, this handsomely-produced journal vividly demonstrates just how well music-theoretical questions can be approached successfully from many positions beyond those recognized by any single contemporary theoretical milieu. Reviews from outside an author's own scholarly community as well as editorials introducing an issue's content produce actual confrontation between the ideas of the diverse theoretical traditions represented. In accordance with its editor's semiotic inclinations, *Music Analysis* has finally made writings by such significant continental European music semioticians as Jean Jacques Nattiez (1:243–340) and Giorgie Baroni (2:175–208) readily available in English. Despite the recent founding date (1982), its forthright book reviews and extended review articles already constitute a thorough assessment of the music theory of the last few decades. Commencing with v. 2, an "Article Guide" is located at the end of each volume. It presents summaries of significant recent theory articles published elsewhere. Volume 1.2 includes a symposium on Giuseppe Verdi's *Trovatore*. Someone contemplating becoming a music analyst or music theorist would do well to read *Music Analysis* carefully from cover to cover.

Individual issues, three per annum, run to over one hundred pages. Articles average ten pages, though individual pieces can far exceed that. Numbering of pages, which are approximately 7″ by 10″, is consecutive within each annual volume. Musical examples, graphs and illustrations are abundant; advertising is of a predictably scholarly nature.

Information Sources

INDEXES
External: Music Index, 1984– . Arts and Humanities Citation Index, 1984– .
LOCATION SOURCES
Widely available.

Publication History

TITLE AND TITLE CHANGES
Music Analysis.
VOLUME AND ISSUE DATA
Volumes 1– , 1982– .

FREQUENCY OF PUBLICATION
    3/year.
PUBLISHER
    Basil Blackwell.
PLACE OF PUBLICATION
    Oxford, England.
EDITORS
    Jonathan Dunsby, 1982–87. Derrick Puffett, 1987–   .

Stefan M. Ehrenkreutz

MUSIC PERCEPTION

Music psychology is an interdisciplinary field encompassing theoretical and experimental approaches to studying the psychological processes involved in composing, performing, and listening to music. One journal that has been successful in bringing together authors from these diverse fields, and thereby contributing significantly to the understanding of perceptual processes in music, is *Music Perception*. The journal "publishes original theoretical and empirical papers, methodological articles and critical reviews covering the study of music." Articles are published "from a broad range of disciplines, including music theory, psychology, psychophysics, linguistics, neurology, neurophysiology, ethology, artificial intelligence, computer technology, and physical and architectural acoustics" (1.1: inside, back page). *Music Perception* was founded in the Fall of 1983 by its first editor, Diana Deutsch, a prominent researcher on melodic perception and the editor of a book on the psychology of music. The list of associate and contributing editors is truly international in scope, representing leading scholars in music, psychology, and acoustics. Contributors to the journal are primarily faculty from American and European college departments of psychology and music theory.

Each issue contains approximately five articles and one or two book reviews. Articles are written in a scholarly style, and each one begins with an abstract. Many articles offer theoretical models of music cognition, focusing on the perception of such elements as meter, phrase structure, and consonance. Other articles describe empirical studies of music perception. Several issues feature articles on a single topic, such as rhythm and meter (1.4), and pitch structures and tonality (2.1). The quality of the articles is excellent.

One problem with the journal is the assumption, made by some contributors, that music is merely an auditory stimulus and that humans approach the processing of non-musical sounds in the same way they approach listening to music. While this assumption reflects the current views of many in the field and allows for easier experimentation and model building, it does not take into account the complexity of music as an *aesthetic* stimulus, nor the complexity of human emotional responses to music.

Music Perception is 7″ by 10″ with approximately 130 pages per issue. The high quality shown in the articles extends to the physical production of the journal. The cover is glossy, and the journal is printed on good quality off-white paper. Charts, tables, and musical examples are usually very clear. Two to four pages of advertising appear in the back of each issue. Four issues per year are published (Fall, Winter, Spring, Summer). An internal index appears in the back of Summer issues (no. 4).

Information Sources

INDEXES
   Internal: each volume
   External: Music Index, 1985–   . RILM, 1983–   . Arts and Humanities Citation Index, 1984–   . Psychological Abstracts, 1983–   .
LOCATION SOURCES
   Widely available.

Publication History

TITLE AND TITLE CHANGES
   Music Perception.
VOLUME AND ISSUE DATA
   Volumes 1–   , 1983–   .
FREQUENCY OF PUBLICATION
   Quarterly.
PUBLISHER
   University of California Press.
PLACE OF PUBLICATION
   La Jolla, California.
EDITOR
   Diana Deutsch, 1983–   .

John K. Kratus

THE OPERA QUARTERLY

The Opera Quarterly, one of the youngest periodicals devoted to opera, appeared in the spring of 1983, under the general editorship of its founders, Sherwin and Irene Sloan. The Sloans are assisted by a host of contributing and consulting editors which include some of the most familiar names in opera: George Marek, Tito Capobianco, Edward Downes, Richard Woitach, James Levine, Carlisle Floyd, and Marilyn Horne.

The journal is intended to appeal to audiences of widely diverging tastes and sophistication: amateur opera lovers, professional performers, and scholars. The subject matter and style of coverge is also quite varied, though never chatty or gossipy. The focus is on opera as a humanistic, literary topic of inquiry. A single issue commonly includes articles on history, libretti, stage direction, performance, major composers, and discussions and interpretations of individual works. An unusual feature is the so-called "Quarterly Quiz" which made its first appearance in v. 1.4.

The format has not changed since publication began. Each issue is 7″ by 9⅞″ high and contains nearly 200 pages. There are between eight and eleven articles in each issue, and reviews of approximately forty books and recordings. Each issue also contains a "Reader-Author Interchange" and a list of books and scores received. Two issues to date have been dedicated to individual composers: Wagner (1.3), and Puccini (2.3). In those issues all reviews as well as the articles concern the works of those composers. Finally, each issue contains beautifully printed musical examples, figures, and photographic reproductions.

Information Sources

BIBLIOGRAPHY
Central Opera Service Bulletin 24.3 (1983): 48.
Central Opera Service Bulletin 25.1 (1983): 61.
Fry, Stephen M., "Periodicals." *Notes* 39 (1983): 835.
INDEXES
        External: Music Index, 1983– . RILM, 1983– . Music Article Guide, 1986/
        87– . Arts and Humanities Citation Index, 1983– .
LOCATION SOURCES
        Widely available.

Publication History

TITLE AND TITLE CHANGES
        The Opera Quarterly.
VOLUME AND ISSUE DATA
        Volumes 1– , 1983– .
FREQUENCY OF PUBLICATION
        Quarterly.
PUBLISHER
        University of North Carolina Press.
PLACE OF PUBLICATION
        Chapel Hill, North Carolina.
EDITORS
        Sherwin and Irene Sloan, 1983– .

Vincent J. Corrigan

PERIODICA MUSICA

In 1981, after several years of discussion and work, a proposal to establish a cooperative group to document scholarship in the nineteenth century was made at the annual meeting of the International Association of Music Libraries (IAML). In 1982 IAML formally approved the creation of the Repertoire International de la Presse Musicale de XIXe siecle (RIPM); the following year the International Musicological Society added its approval. The goals of the project are: 1) to direct attention to nineteenth-century press as a resource for music history; 2) to develop a method for cataloging and indexing writings on music and musical iconography in nineteenth-century periodical literature;[1] 3) to offer an opportunity for those interested in working in this area to do so within an internationally sanctioned structure; 4) to oversee the publication of the resulting reference volumes of the Repertory itself; 5) to make available copies of articles and iconography brought to light by the cataloging effort; 6) to develop in North America and in Europe, an extensive microfilm research archive of nineteenth-century periodical literature concerning music; and 7) to disseminate information concerning writings on music and musical iconography through the publication of a journal entitled *Periodica Musica*.[2]

Periodica Musica, the newsletter of the RIPM, provides an opportunity for the exchange of information concerning nineteenth-century music periodical literature. Published annually, the newsletters contain such diverse information as articles about journals or groups of journals and significant collections, reports of current works in progress or meetings of interest, bibliographies of relevant materials and other related research.

In the first issue articles ranged from a discussion of Hungarian periodicals from 1800–30 to a list of Polish music journals. Subsequent annual issues have surveyed nineteenth-century Russian music periodicals (v. 2), Italian journals (entire v. 3), nineteenth-century eastern European journals (v. 4). All articles are by noted scholars, archivists, and librarians, and provide needed documentation for the field.

The physical format of the newsletter is 8½" by 11", with issues ranging from twenty-four to thirty-six pages.

Notes

1. H. Robert Cohen and Marcello Conati, "Le Repertoire de la Presse Musicale." *International* Acta musicologica 59 (1987): 310.
2. Cohen and Conati, 309.

Information Sources

BIBLIOGRAPHY
Cohen, H. Robert and Marcello Conati. "Le Repertoire International de la Presse Musicale." *Acta Musicologica* 59 (1987): 309–24.
"Periodica Musica." *Notes* 40 (December 1983): 277.
LOCATION SOURCES
 Widely available.

Publication History

TITLE AND TITLE CHANGES
 Periodica Musica, 1983– .
VOLUME AND ISSUE DATA
 Volumes 1– , 1983– .

FREQUENCY OF PUBLICATION
    Annual.
PUBLISHER
    University of British Columbia for Repertoire International de la Presse Musicale
    de XIXe siecle, 1983–86. University of Maryland, College Park, 1986– .
PLACE
    Vancouver, British Columbia, Canada, 1983–86. College Park, Maryland,
    1986– .
EDITORS
    Editorial Board: H. Robert Cohen, Elvidio Surian, Marcello Conati. Editors: Joel
    H. Kaplan, Peter Loeffler, Zoltan Roman, 1983– .

Linda M. Fidler

PSYCHOMUSICOLOGY

"Psychomusicology" is a relatively new term, appropriately chosen as the
title for a recent journal founded to improve communication among those interested in "re-examination of the nature of human response to music and of the
models upon which our inquiry has been founded" (1.1:3). Thus *Psychomusicology: A Journal of Research in Music Cognition* was introduced by editor
David Brian Williams. Joined by James C. Carlsen and W. Jay Dowling in a
position statement, they suggested an initial taxonomy and emphasized the intention to disseminate experimental research reports through "a comprehensive,
rigorously refereed publication" (1.1:4). An article by Roger Brown entitled
"Do We Need a Psychomusicology?" (1.1:7–11) elaborated on the potential of
such research and the necessity of providing a forum for scholars in this area.

Successive issues—two each year, seventy to eighty pages each in 5⅞" by
8⅝" format—have been no less impressive, and have contained some valuable
added features: the "Psychomusicology Forum" (for exchange of ideas and short
communications), a section for book reviews, a listing of events, and a "Research
Notes" department devoted to a variety of short communications. The early
issues have been marked by an American focus, although the board of consulting
editors includes scholars from Canada and England. Contributors number among
leading experts in cognition. The high quality of the journal's contents suggests
that *Psychomusicology* will be a formidable companion to the British *Psychology
of Music* (q.v.).

Information Sources

INDEXES
    External: Psychological Abstracts, 1981– .
LOCATION SOURCES
    Widely available.

Publication History

TITLE AND TITLE CHANGES
> *Psychomusicology: A Journal of Music Cognition*, 1981. *Psychomusicology: A Journal of Research in Music Cognition*, 1982– .

VOLUME AND ISSUE DATA
> Volumes 1– , 1981– .

FREQUENCY OF PUBLICATION
> Semiannual.

PUBLISHER
> Stephen F. Austin State University for the Psychomusicology Society.

PLACE OF PUBLICATION
> Nacogdoches, Texas.

EDITOR
> David Brian Williams, 1981– .

Ruth K. Inglefield

UPDATE: THE APPLICATIONS OF RESEARCH IN MUSIC EDUCATION

First appearing in May 1982, *Update* is unique as a research-based journal in that it is designed for a readership of school music teachers. Contributors are asked to submit articles that can be read and understood by music teachers who may not be specially trained in research methodologies and statistics. Consequently, the writing style is, for the most part, free of most research and statistical terminology. Instead, the author offers his or her interpretation of a study and makes specific suggestions for practical applications of the findings to the classroom setting.

Each issue of *Update* is divided into two main sections: "Features" and "Articles." The "Features" section includes: "Comments from the Editor"; "Reflections," a column devoted to historical issues in music education; and "Have You Ever Wondered," a one-page entry that features topics of interest to readers. There are typically five to seven articles per issue, each of which is usually four to six pages long. Topics range from Darwinian explanations for the origins of music to early identification of the musically gifted and the effects of anxiety on musical performance. In addition, the editors occasionally include articles of a philosophical or editorial nature as well as some which may be of interest or assistance to music teachers even though not written specifically for them, such as an article reprinted from a nonmusic journal.

By only the fourth issue (Summer 1983), *Update* had attracted subscribers from all fifty states and several foreign countries, including the Soviet Union. This popularity suggests that *Update* has answered a significant need in the music education research field by effectively bridging the gap between researchers (typically but not exclusively university faculty) and K–12 music teachers.

The organizational structure of *Update* includes an editor and an advisory board comprised of about fifteen members, several of whom are public school music teachers. The majority of articles are unsolicited and are channeled through a blind review process that involves several members of the advisory board. The contributors are almost exclusively college and university music educators and researchers. *Update* is published three times a year (Spring, Summer, and Fall) and is usually twenty-four to twenty-eight pages in length. Page size is 8½″ by 10½″ and pagination is for each issue only. Advertisements and illustrative material are modest. In addition to the usual subscription structure, a group rate for eight or more subscribers was initiated in the Fall 1983 issue in response to requests by university faculty and students in music education methods classes.

Information Sources

BIBLIOGRAPHY
Fry, Stephen M. "New Music Periodicals." *Notes* 40 (1983): 278.
INDEXES
    External: Music Article Guide, 1983– .
LOCATION SOURCES
    Widely available.

Publication History

TITLE AND TITLE CHANGES
    Update: The Applications of Research in Music Education.
VOLUME AND ISSUE DATA
    Volumes 1– , 1982– .
FREQUENCY OF PUBLICATION
    3/year.
PUBLISHER
    Department of Music, University of South Carolina.
PLACE OF PUBLICATION
    Columbia, South Carolina.
EDITOR
    Charles A. Elliott, 1982– .

Vincent J. Kantorski

Music Periodical Indexes

Although the history of music periodicals can be traced to the beginning of the eighteenth century, systematic indexing of music journals is a mid-twentieth century phenomenon. Prior to *Music Index* (1949–), music periodicals were indexed in general periodical literature indexes such as *Readers' Guide to Periodical Literature* or periodical indexing that appeared in music journals such as the *Zeitschrift der Internationalen Musikgesellschaft* (1899–1914) and *Zeitschrift für Musikwissenschaft* (1918–35) (q.v.). One index devoted exclusively to music journals—*Bibliographie des Musikschrifttums*—was issued only three times (1936, 1937, 1939) prior to World War II and did not resume publication until 1950.

The general periodical indexes failed to include many music journals. For example, *Readers' Guide* (1901–) indexed only five music journals prior to 1949: *Etude* (1919–57) (q.v.), *Modern Music* (1945–47) (q.v.), *Music* (1900–04, *Musical Quarterly* (1921–53) (q.v.), and *Musician* (1910–48). *International Index to Periodicals* (1916–63) (later *Social Sciences and Humanities Index*, 1963–73; *Humanities Index*, 1974–) did not include any music periodicals until 1949 when *Music and Letters* (q.v.), *Music Review* (q.v.), *Notes* (q.v.), and in 1952 *Musical Quarterly* (q.v.) were added to the list of journals indexed.

Neither the *Zeitschrift der Internationalen Musikgesellschaft* nor *Zeitschrift für Musikwissenschaft* provided adequate indexing for the journals of the period. Frequently only authors were indexed and the indexes were not cumulative.

At the 1938 Music Library Association meeting in Kansas City, a report presented by the Committee on Periodical Indexing identified the major problems that confronted librarians who needed access to the periodical literature. The committee proposed three different plans for meeting librarians' needs. These included: 1) indexing all periodicals, past and present, by author and subject; 2) indexing important foreign titles which had ceased publication in addition to a selected list of *festschriften* and congress reports, by both author and subject; and 3) current periodicals to 1939, by author and subject. The first two proposals were to result in indexes in book form, the third would be an index in card format. Although MLA did not act on any of the three proposals, the third option was implemented with the W.P.A. Newberry Project for Indexing Music Periodicals, which began in October 1938. Unfortunately, this project remains unfinished.[1]

Throughout the war years, the need for systematic indexing of music periodicals continued to be a topic of discussion, and not only with the Music Library Association. In 1948 a group of librarians and music specialists led by Kurtz Meyer and H. Dorothy Tilly formed Information Services, Inc. in Detroit, Michigan. Their purpose was to establish an indexing service for music journals. At the December 1948 meeting of the Music Teachers National Association, a sample index was presented to conference attendees, who received the index with enthusiasm. With the January 1949 monthly issue, the first major index devoted to music journals—*Music Index*—was begun.

The next twenty-eight years (1949–77) saw the establishment of five publications devoted to the indexing of music periodicals: *Bibliographie des Musikschrifttums* (1950–   ); *Music Article Guide* (1965–   ); *RILM Abstracts of Music Literature* (1967–   ); *Popular Music Periodical Index* (1973–76); and *Jazz Index* (1977–   ).

Meanwhile, the general periodical indexes began to include more music titles. *Readers' Guide* added *Musical America* (q.v.) in the 1950s and *American Record Guide* (q.v.), *High Fidelity* (q.v.), and *Opera News* (q.v.) in the 1960s. By the late 1970s, *Readers' Guide* also indexed *Crawdaddy* (q.v.), *down beat* (q.v.), *Rolling Stone* (q.v.), and *Stereo Review* (q.v.). *Humanities Index* increased its coverage of music titles with its 1974 volume to include the *Journal of the American Musicological Society* (q.v.), *Ethnomusicology* (q.v.), *Opera* (q.v.), and later *Current Musicology* (q.v.), *19th Century Music* (q.v.), and *Opera News*. *British Humanities Index* (1962–   ) which superceded the *British Subject Index to Periodicals* (1915–61) was broad in its coverage of music periodicals, primarily from Great Britain. From five music titles in 1962, *British Humanities Index* increased its coverage of music titles to nineteen titles in 1967 and to over forty titles by 1975. In 1978, the Institute for Scientific Information, known for its *Science Citation Index* and *Social Science Citation Index*, began publication of the *Arts and Humanities Citation Index* which from the very first issue indexed over forty "scholarly" titles in music.

In 1987 University Microfilms International (UMI) announced a collaborative project with the Center for Studies in 19th Century Music. This project, an index series entitled Répertoire International de la Presse Musicale (RIPM), will include over one hundred volumes that index selected journals from the late eighteenth to the early twentieth century. Unlike the other periodical indexes which index groups of journals usually by year, RIPM will issue separate index volumes for each title (for the duration of the title's run).

NOTE

1. For a more detailed discussion of the W.P.A. periodicals indexing project, see Dena J. Epstein, "The Mysterious WPA Music Periodical Index," *Notes* 45 (1988/89): 463–82.

BIBLIOGRAPHIE DES MUSIKSCHRIFTTUMS

Several attempts at indexing music periodicals began as early as the beginning of the twentieth century. During its fifteen-year history the *Zeitschrift der International Musikgesellschaft* (1899/1900–1913/14) included indexing of some eighty-four periodicals. From 1918 until it ceased publication in 1935 the *Zeitschrift für Musikwissenschaft* (q.v.) included indexing for two hundred periodicals. The first volume retrospectively covered from 1914 through 1918, including the literature which had appeared since the *Zeitschrift (IMS)* had ceased. It remained for noted scholar and bibliographer Kurt Taut to begin a publication, *Bibliographie des Musikschrifttums*, devoted solely to the indexing of not only over two hundred periodical titles but also *festschriften*, congress reports, and other serial publications.

Bibliographie des Musikschrifttums was an outgrowth of bibliographic work which appeared in *Jahrbuch der Musikbibliothek Peters* (1895–1941). Many of the *Jahrbuch* issues contained a section entitled "Verzeichnis der in allen Kulturländern erschienenen Bücher und Schriften über Musik" which reported various literature; however, this section excluded periodical literature. Taut, who had served as one of the editors of the *Jahrbuch*, incorporated the "Verzeichnis" into periodical indexing from both musical and nonmusical journals to form the basis of *Bibliographie des Musikschrifttums*. Four volumes, also called *Jahrbuch*, appeared before the publication suspended publication, due in part to the beginning of World War II, and in part to the death of Taut before the second volume appeared. George Karstädt assumed the editorship for the remaining volumes prior to the war. *Bibliographie des Musikschrifttums* resumed publication on a biennial basis in 1950 under the leadership of Bach scholar and archivist Wolfgang Schmieder and in 1960 it began an annual publication schedule.

Although *Bibliographie des Musikschrifttums* covers the range of musical types, its primary focus is classical music. Its annual coverage includes over five thousand citations to scholarly books and articles from over two hundred serial titles including a great number of nonmusical periodicals in all major European languages. Entries are alphabetically arranged within eight broad classifications: 1) Bibliographies, dictionaries, catalogs; 2) Musicology as a discipline; 3) Comparative musicology; 4) Philosophy, psychology, and physiology; 5) History (to 1900); 6) History (1900–   ); 7) Instrumental music; and 8) Single biographical studies. The latter four classifications are further divided into subclassifications. Four indexes—authors, names as subjects, places, and general subjects—appear at the end of each volume. Each volume lists titles included at the front.

Information Sources

LOCATION SOURCES
Widely available.

Publication Information

TITLE AND TITLE CHANGES
Bibliographie des Musikschrifttums.
VOLUME AND ISSUE DATA
1936– . Publication suspended 1940–1949.
FREQUENCY OF PUBLICATION
Semiannual, 1936. Annual, 1937–38. Biennial, 1950/51–1958/59. Annual, 1960– .
PUBLISHER
F. Hofmeister, 1936–68 [1936–1960]. B. Schott's Söhne, 1969– [1961–].
PLACE OF PUBLICATION
Frankfurt am Main, West Germany, 1936–1968. Mainz, 1969– .
EDITORS
Kurt Taut, 1936–37. George Karstädt, 1938–39. Wolfgang Schmieder, 1950–59. Werner Bollett, 1960. Dieter J. Frecot, 1960–68. Bärbel Schleyer, 1960–64. Heinz-Lothar Fichter, 1965. Elizabeth Wilker, 1969–75. Claudia Wegner, 1976– . Norbert Böker-Heil, 1977– .

JAZZ INDEX

Jazz Index was established in 1973 by two West German librarians, Norbert Ruecker and Christa Reggentin-Scheidt, to bring the periodical literature of jazz under systematic bibliographic control. In the first issue, the editors stated that their aim was "to give complete coverage of relevant articles and reviews published in jazz periodicals" and to provide an "overall picture of activities on the jazz scene and in jazz research." (1:1.1) Titles for inclusion were selected on an international basis. While in the first volume blues was excluded, they stated that it was their intention to include coverage of blues in v. 2 as well as to provide a listing of unpublished materials. A "List of Unconventional Literature" (later called "Hard-to-Get Literature") was featured in each issue, and an annual authors' index was provided. However, by the fourth issue of the first volume, the editors noted that with the increase from twenty-two journal titles in issue one to forty titles in issue four, it was clear that their plans might be too ambitious. Announced in the preface to v. 2 was the decision to include only those blues articles which appeared in journals already being indexed. Also removed from the index was the selective inclusion of individual record reviews.

As the number of journals increased and the number of articles grew (from 1000 in the first volume to over 5000 in later volumes), other deletions appeared. Concert reviews, festival reviews, and news items, unless a feature article, were dropped, as was a plan to include lists of soon-to-be-published titles. However, selective indexing of collections of essays did continue. Significant articles concerning jazz or blues from journals not indexed fully also continued to be included.

Although announced as a quarterly publication with potential for a bi-monthly schedule, it became all too apparent that this project, which depended on the volunteer time of two full-time librarians, could not maintain even a quarterly publication schedule. Each of the first two volumes contained four issues; the next two volumes contained two issues each. With v. 5 (1981) publication was shifted from quarterly to semi-annually, although v. 6 contained only a single issue. With v. 7 (1983), which appeared in 1987, *Jazz Index* ceased publication. The final two volumes lacked the author index announced as an annual feature.

Each issue of *Jazz Index* contained a number of sections. Following the list of periodicals and collections indexed, the section on jazz, arranged alphabetically by subject appeared. The section covering blues, also arranged alphabetically by subject followed. The "List of Unconventional Literature" closed each issue. After the first volume, all subject headings appeared only in English; the citations, however, appear in the language of the original.

Information Sources

BIBLIOGRAPHY
Erskine, Gilbert M. "Jazz Index." *The Second Line* 29 (Fall 1977): 29–30.
Hodgson, Julian. "Jazz Index." *Brio* 14 (1977): 24–25.
LOCATION SOURCES
    Widely available.

Publication History

TITLE AND TITLE CHANGES
    Jazz Index: Bibliography of Jazz Literature in Periodicals and Collections.
VOLUME AND ISSUE DATA
    1977–83.
FREQUENCY OF PUBLICATION
    Quarterly, 1977–80. Semi-annually, 1981–82. Annual, 1983.
PUBLISHER
    Norbert Ruecker.
PLACE OF PUBLICATION
    Frankfurt, West Germany
EDITORS
    Norbert Ruecker, 1977–83. Christa Reggentin-Scheidt, 1977–82.

MUSIC ARTICLE GUIDE

Music Article Guide, which began in 1965, indexes over 150 American music periodicals from scholarly journals and journals of professional societies to house organs and periodicals of a more ephemeral or specialized nature. Although the best known American journals are found in both *Music Index* and *Music Article Guide*, the latter tends to index those journals less sophisticated or of a more practical orientation and offers unique coverage of specialty interests including regional music education journals, popular music, music industry, and individual instrument society research. Unlike *Music Index* or *RILM Abstracts*, *Music Article Guide* is directed toward the college/university user with a strong music education background.

Music Article Guide excludes from coverage all unsigned articles and most brief features and items of news. Reviews of books, recordings, and concerts are also excluded. All articles are entered by author, title, and subject although the title entry is by far the fullest and includes capsule descriptions describing the contents of the article. A "Directory of American Music Periodicals" appears in most issues.

The first volume of *Music Article Guide* appeared as a small, loose-leaf book. With v.2 (1966/67) the *Guide* adopted the 8'' x 11½'' format which it maintains today. The early volumes were typescript; in 1988, production changed from typescript to a computer-generated typeface. *Music Article Guide* has maintained an on-time quarterly publication schedule.

Information Sources

BIBLIOGRAPHY
Ludden, Bennet. "Review of *Music Article Guide*." *Notes* 24 (1967): 719–20.
REPRINT EDITION
    UMI.
LOCATION SOURCES
    Widely available.

Publication History

TITLE AND TITLE CHANGES
    Music Article Guide: A Comprehensive Quarterly Reference Guide to Significant Signed Feature Articles in American Music Periodicals, 1966–72. *Music Article Guide: An Annotated Comprehensive Quarterly Reference Guide to Significant Signed Feature Articles in American Music Periodicals*, 1973–75. *Music Article Guide: The Nation's Only Annotated Guide to Feature Articles in American Music Periodicals*, 1975– .
VOLUME AND ISSUE DATA
    V. 1– , 1966– .
FREQUENCY OF PUBLICATION
    Quarterly.

PUBLISHER
  Music Article Guide, 1966–77. Information Services, 1977– .
PLACE OF PUBLICATION
  Philadelphia.

MUSIC INDEX

Music Index made "readily available for the first time a key to current music periodical literature."[1] It first appeared in 1949 under the direction of Kurtz Meyer and Dorothy Tilly of the Detroit Public Library, and editor Florence Kretzschmar. During the first year, eleven monthly issues appeared; the twelfth was the annual accumulation. Beginning with 1950, twelve monthly issues plus the annual accumulation were scheduled for publication. In the first issue forty-one English-language periodicals were indexed; by December of that year, eighty periodicals, including ones in French, German, Italian, and Danish, as well as English were being indexed.

The basic arrangement for entries in *Music Index* has remained constant. V. 1 was organized in dictionary format with subjects and composers arranged in a single alphabetical file. Authors of individual articles did not receive entries, a practice which continued until the 1957 issue when the decision was made to include authors of articles within the listing. In 1950 Book Reviews, formerly listed only under that heading, were now also listed under the specific subject of the book. By 1952 reviews of recordings and music appear under both the composer and the medium of performance. The initial subject list, compiled from the suggestions of librarians and music teachers in the 1940s, has continued to evolve, reflecting not only the changing society but also the diversification of research and the proliferation of new journals.

Two concerns of periodical indexing—periodicals which appeared before 1949, and indexing of periodicals from 1949 which had not been originally included in the early volumes of *Music Index*—were discussed by Kretzschmar in the preface to the 1956 *Music Index*. To meet one of these concerns, she announced the beginning of retrospective indexing of titles from 1949 not originally included in the initial list of titles, a practice which continued for several years. In January 1962, under an arrangement with the New York Public Library, an additional twenty-one periodical titles as well as program notes from twenty-four American orchestras were added to the one hundred twenty-five titles indexed by the staff of *Music Index*. After a two-year hiatus, from 1965 to 1967 during which time these titles were absent from *Music Index*, contributions from the staff of the New York Public Library again appeared.

In the November 1984 monthly issue, Nadia Stratelak assumed the position of managing editor. With the retirement of Florence Kretzschmar as editor in 1985 and a subsequent change from Information Coordinators to Harmonie Press in 1987, a new editorial board adopted several changes. The most significant of these was the committment to improve the publication schedule. In the preface to the first two-year cumulation, managing editor Stratelak commented that "publication of the annual cumulation is several years behind, therefore the decision has been made to publish a two-year cumulation combined into one volume this year and each year thereafter, until printing is up-to-date. Once current an annual cumulation will then be published."[2] The first double cumulation (1979/80) appeared in 1986, with double cumulations appearing annually.

The format of *Music Index* has undergone a number of changes in the last forty years. From 1949 until 1958 the index appeared in a double column format; in 1959 the listing appeared in a single column per page. The single column format remained until the 1979/80 double cumulation (1986), when a double column format returned. From 1949 until 1965 *Music Index* was 6½" x 9½"; from 1966 to 1978 the size was reduced to 6" x 9". Monthly issues through 1986 remained 6½" x 9½". The double cumulations increased to 8½" x 11" while monthly issues are slightly smaller at 8¼" x 10½".

Notes

1. Several small indexing projects were undertaken prior to *Music Index*. These included Ernst Krohn's *The History of Music: An Index to the Literature Available in a Selected Group of Musicological Publications* (St. Louis: Washington University, 1952) and *A Bibliography of Periodical Literature in Musicology* (Washington, D.C.: American Council of Learned Societies, 1940–43).

2. "The Music Index" *The Strad* 60 (November 1949): 208.

Information Sources

BIBLIOGRAPHY
"The Music Index." *The Strad* 60 (November 1949): 208, 210.
"Music Index Enlarges." *Symphony* 4 (1950): 13.
LOCATIONS SOURCES
Widely available.

Publication History

TITLE AND TITLE CHANGES
Music Index.
VOLUME AND ISSUE DATA
1949– .
FREQUENCY OF PUBLICATION
Monthly with annual cumulations.
PUBLISHERS
Information Coordinators, 1949–87. Harmonie Press, 1988– .
PLACE OF PUBLICATION
Detroit, MI, 1949–87. Warren, MI, 1988– .
EDITORS
Florence Kretzschmar, 1949–85. Nadia Stratelak, 1984– .

POPULAR MUSIC PERIODICALS INDEX

Many periodicals which focus on popular music—rock, country, folk, jazz, blues, shows, soul—began publication in the late 1960s and early 1970s. Popular music had begun to develop as a legitimate field to study. To meet the need to access the body of literature on popular music, Dean Tudor started *Popular Music Periodicals Index*, an index which focused on English-language periodicals featuring articles on popular music. The initial volume contained forty-seven journals indexed comprehensively, with an additional seventeen which received selective coverage. By 1977 that number had risen to sixty-one titles comprehensively indexed. Many titles found in *PMPI* were not included in *Music Index*, including such specialized titles as *Jazz Hot* (q.v.). Excluded from the index were news items, obituaries with fewer than 250 words, advertisements, unsigned notes, editorials, and film reviews unless the motion picture focused on the music. Recording reviews were also excluded as they appeared in Tudor's *Annual Index to Popular Music Record Reviews*.

Each volume of the index was divided into two section: subject and author. Subjects include genres with standard subdivisions, such as artists, geographical regions, instruments, songs which appeared in magazines (lyrics and music), concerts, contests, and awards, as well as some nonmusical subjects such as payola and humor. Entries were arranged alphabetically within each of the two sections. A bibliography of recent books on popular music was also included.

Information Sources

BIBLIOGRAPHY
Seidel, Richard. "Two New Jazz-Popular Reference Books: A Review." *Journal of Jazz Studies* 3 (1976): 85–88.
LOCATION SOURCES
    Widely available.

Publication History

TITLE AND TITLE CHANGES
    Popular Music Periodicals Index.
VOLUME AND ISSUE DATA
    1973–77
FREQUENCY OF PUBLICATION
    Annual.
PUBLISHER
    Scarecrow Press.
PLACE OF PUBLICATION
    Metuchen, New Jersey.
EDITORS
    Dean Tudor, 1973–77. Nancy Tudor, 1973. Andrew D. Armitage, 1974–76. Linda Biesenthal, 1976.

RILM ABSTRACTS

RILM Abstracts (Répertoire international de la littérature musicale) is a computer-based bibliography of significant scholarly literature on music. It was established in the summer of 1966 by the International Musicological Society (IMS) and the International Association of Music Libraries (IAML) as a counterpart to RISM (Répertoire international de la sources musicale), and is governed by an international group of scholars (Commission Internationale Mixte) working in conjunction with national groups of scholars. Although international in scope and participation, it is headquartered at City University of New York. In the United States, RILM receives additional support from the Music Library Association (MLA), the American Musicological Society (AMS), and the American Council of Learned Societies (ACLS).

Editor and president of the Commission Internationale Mixte, Barry S. Brook, conceived the project in two parts: current literature and retrospective literature (prior to December 1966). The retrospective project was to be undertaken once the current indexing phase was successfully implemented. To date, this retrospective aspect of RILM has not yet begun.

The primary objective of RILM is "to attempt to deal with current literature by compiling and publishing abstracts and computer-generated indexes of all scholarly writings on music appearing after 1 January 1967."[1] Taken from over 280 journals, this literature includes articles, books, dissertations, essays, congress reports, *festschriften*, bibliographies, catalogs, reviews, and introductions to collected works. Informational notices, ephemera, concert and record reviews normally are excluded from *RILM Abstracts*. Since the information is viewed as more important than the format in which it is presented, even formats designated as excluded may be indexed.

Periodicals to be included in *RILM Abstracts* were placed into three categories: (1) Major musicological periodicals and yearbooks to be fully abstracted; (2) Music periodicals selectively abstracted; and (3) Nonmusical periodicals selectively abstracted and not listed in the list of journals in each issue. The national committees are responsible for assigning titles to a category. Over 280 titles currently receive attention, either comprehensively or selectively.

RILM Abstracts is a classified index arranged alphabetically by author within assigned classifications. All abstracts, whether written by the author or by a volunteer abstractor, appear in English. Each volume contains three quarterly issues of abstracts plus a fourth issue which is a subject/author index of the preceeding three quarterly issues. Each of the first three issues contain an author index. Two five-year cumulative indices (1967–71, 1972–76) are available. V. 10 (1976) was a lacunae issue, containing citations omitted from the first ten years of *RILM Abstracts*. RILM has also been available as an online computer file since 1971.

Note

1. Barry S. Brook, "RILM Inaugural Report: January 1967," *Notes* 23 (1967): 463.

Information Sources

BIBLIOGRAPHY

Brook, Barry. S. "RILM Inaugural Report: January 1967." *Notes* 23 (1967): 462–67.

———. "RILM Report No. 2: September 1967." *Notes* 24 (1968): 457–66.

———. "Music Literature and Modern Communication: Revolutionary Potentials of the ACLS/CUNY/RILM Project." *College Music Symposium* 9 (1969): 48–59.

Keller, Michael A., and Carol A. Lawrence. "Music Literature Indexes in Review: *RILM Abstracts* (On-Line) and the *Arts and Humanities Citation Index*, *Music Therapy*, *Music Psychology*, and *Recording Industry* Indexes." *Notes* 36 (1980): 575–600.

LOCATION SOURCES

    Widely available.

Publication History

TITLE AND TITLE CHANGES

    RILM Abstracts. Répertoire International de la Littérature Musicale. International Inventory of Musical Literature.

VOLUME AND ISSUE DATA

    V. 1– . 1967– .

FREQUENCY OF PUBLICATION

    Quarterly.

PUBLISHER

    International RILM Center.

PLACE OF PUBLICATION

    New York City.

EDITORS

    Barry S. Brook, Editor-in-Chief, 1967– . Murray Ralph, 1969–73. Howard Accurso, 1974–76. John Morris, 1975. Carl Skoggard, 1977–81. Terence Ford, 1980–81. Nicolas Schidlovsky, 1982. Robert Estrine, 1983.

Chronological Listing of Periodicals by Title

In the following listing of periodicals by the year of initial publication, the most recent or best-known title is used rather than the title under which the journal might have begun. For example, although *Key Notes* began in 1958 under the title *Sonorum Speculum*, the only title which appears in the listing is *Key Notes*. For alternate titles under which the journals might have been known, see the individual essay.

1798   *Allgemeine musikalische Zeitung*

1820   *Euterpeiad*

1823   *Harmonicon*

1824   *Caecilia* (Germany)

1833   *Le Ménestrel*

1834   *Neue Zeitschrift für Musik*

1843   *Signale für die musikalische Welt*

1844   *Caecilia* (Netherlands)
       Musical Times

1852   *Dwight's Journal of Music*

1855   *Le Guide musical*

1861   *Schweizerische Musikzeitung*

1864   *Brainard's Musical World*

1869   *Monatshefte für Musikgeschichte*

1871   *Monthly Musical Record*

1874   *Allgemeine Musik-Zeitung*
       Royal Musical Association Proceedings

1880   *Musical Courier*
       Neue Musik-Zeitung

1883   *Etude*

1885   *Metronome*

Tijdschrift van de Vereniging voor Nederlandse Muziekgeschiedenis
Vierteljahrschrift für Musikwissenschaft

1890 *Strad*

1894 *Billboard*
Nuova rivista musicale italiana

1896 *Musician*

1898 *Musical America*

1901 *Die Musik*

1908 *Music Teacher*

1910 *Musique et instrument*

1913 *Studien zur Musikwissenschaft*

1914 *Music Educators' Journal*

1915 *Musical Quarterly*

1917 *Revue de musicologie*

1918 *Archiv für Musikwissenschaft*
Zeitschrift für Musikwissenschaft

1919 *Anbruch: Monatshefte für Musikgeschichte*
Svensk Tidskrift för Musikforskning

1920 *Melos*
Music and Letters
Quaderni della rassegna musicale
Revue musicale

1921 *Der Tonwille*

1923 *Gramophone*

1924 *Modern Music*
Schweizerisches Jahrbuch für Musikwissenschaft

1926 *Dansk musik tidsskrift*
Melody Maker

1928 *Acta musicologica*

1929 *Musik und Kirche*
School Musician

1933 *Sovetskaia Muzyka*

1934 *down beat*

1935 *American Record Guide*
Jazz-Hot

1936 *Archiv für Musikforschung*
Bibliographie des Musikschrifttums
Opera News

1939 *Tempo*

1940 *Music Review*

1941   *Film Music Notes*
       Journal of Aesthetics and Art Criticism

1942   *Cash Box*

1943   *Musik im Krieg*
       Notes

1944   *NATS Bulletin*

1945   *Revista musical chilena*

1946   *Anuario musical*
       Instrumentalist
       Mens en melodie
       Musica disciplina
       Revue belge de musicologie

1947   *Musica*

1948   *Galpin Society Journal*
       Jazz Journal (International)
       Journal of the American Musicological Society
       Die Musikforschung
       Opera
       Symphony News
       Yearbook for Traditional Music (International Folk Music Council)

1949   *Music Index*

1950   *American Harp Journal*
       Sing Out!
       Woodwind World Brass and Percussion

1951   *American Music Teacher*
       American String Teacher
       High Fidelity
       Musik und Gesellschaft

1952   *Music and Musicians*
       NACWPI Journal
       Piano Quarterly

1953   *Annales musicologiques*
       Ethnomusicology
       Journal of Research in Music Education

1954   *African Music*
       Fontes artis musicae

1955   *Gravesaner Blätter*

1956   *Muzyka*

1957   *Brass Quarterly*
       Journal of Music Theory
       Ruch Muzyczny
       World of Music

1958   *American Choral Review*

Coda: Canada Jazz Magazine
Composer (London)
Die Reihe
Stereo Review
Key Notes

1959 *Beiträge zur musikwissenschaft*
Choral Journal

1960 *Opernwelt*
Recherches sur la musique française classique

1961 *College Music Symposium*
Recorded Sound
Royal Musical Association Research Chronicle
Studia musicologica

1962 *Clavier*
Percussive Notes
Perspectives of New Music

1963 *Council for Research in Music Education*
Percussionist

1964 *Brio*
Chigiana
Journal of Band Research
Journal of Music Therapy
Musicology Australia

1965 *Canadian Composer/Le Compositeur canadien*
Current Musicology
JEMF Quarterly

1966 *Crawdaddy*
Miscellanea Musicologica: Adelaide Studies in Musicology
Music Article Guide
Rivista italiana di musicologica

1967 *American Organist*
Association for Recorded Sound Collections Journal
Guitar Player
Rolling Stone
Source: Music of the Avant Garde
Studies in Music

1968 *Asian Music*
Jazz Educators Journal

1969 *Creem*

1970 *Canada Music Book/Les Cahiers canadiens de musique*
International Review of the Aesthetics and Sociology of Music
Journal of Country Music

Journal of the Indian Musicological Society
Living Blues
Zeitschrift für Musiktheorie

1971   *Brass Bulletin*
       Popular Music and Society

1972   *Contributions to Music Education*
       Interface: Journal of New Music Research
       Studi musicali

1973   *Black Perspective in Music*
       Early Music
       Journal of Jazz Studies
       Journal of Musicological Research
       Psychology of Music

1974   *International Society of Bassists Journal*
       Journal of American Musical Instrument Society

1975   *In Theory Only*
       Theory and Practice

1977   *Computer Music Journal*
       Dialogue in Instrumental Music Education
       Indiana Theory Review
       Jazz Index
       19th Century Music

1978   *Inter-American Music Review*
       Revista de musicología

1979   *Music Theory Spectrum*

1980   *Black Music Research Journal*
       Latin American Music Review

1981   *Psychomusicology*

1982   *Journal of Musicology*
       Music Analysis
       Update: Applications in Music Education

1983   *American Music*
       Music Perception
       Opera Quarterly
       Periodica Musica

Geographical Listing of Periodicals by Title

The following listing represents the countries of origin for the periodicals in this volume. For subsequent places of publication, see the individual essays.

Australia

Miscellanea Musicologica: Adelaide Studies in Musicology
Musicology Australia
Studies in Music

Austria

Der Tonwille

Belgium

Le Guide musical

Revue belge de musicologie

Canada

Canada Music Book/Les Cahiers canadiens de musique

Canadian Composer/Le Compositeur canadien

Coda

Periodica Musica

Chile

Revista musical chilena

Denmark

Dansk Musiktidsskrift

France

Annales musicologiques

Fontes artis musicae

Jazz-Hot

Le Menestrel

Musique et instrumente

Recherches sur la musique française classique

Revue de musicologie

La Revue musicale

World of Music

Germany

Acta musicologica

Allgemeine Musik-Zeitung

Allgemeine musikalische Zeitung

Anbruch

Archiv für Musikforschung

Archiv für Musikwissenschaft

Beitrage zur Musikwissenschaft

Bibliographie des Musikschrifttums

Caecilia (1824–1848)

Gravesaner Blätter

Jazz Index

Melos

Monatshefte für Musikgeschichte

Musica

Die Musik

Musik im Krieg

Musik und Gesellschaft

Musik und Kirche

Die Musikforschung

Neue Musik-Zeitung

Neue Zeitschrift für Musik

Opernwelt

Die Reihe

Signale für die musikalische Welt

Studien zur Musikwissenschaft

Vierteljahrschrift für Musikwissenschaft

Zeitschrift für Musiktheorie

Zeitschrift für Musikwissenschaft

Great Britain

Brio

Composer (London)

Early Music

Galpin Society Journal

Gramophone

Harmonicon

Jazz Journal (International)

Melody Maker

Monthly Musical Record

Music Analysis

Music and Letters

Music and Musicians

Music Review

Musical Times

Opera

Psychology of Music

Recorded Sound

Royal Musical Association Proceedings

Royal Musical Association Research Chronicle

Strad

Tempo

Yearbook for Traditional Music (International Folk Music Council)

Hungary

Studia musicologica

India

Journal of the Indian Musicological Society

Italy

Chigiana

Nuova rivista musicale italiana

Quaderni della rassegna musicale

Rivista italiana di musicologia

Studi musicali

Netherlands

Caecilia (1844–1944)

Interface: Journal of New Music Research

Key Notes

Mens en Melodie

Tijdschrift van de Vereniging voor Nederlandse Musiekgescheicdenis

Poland

Muzyka

Ruch Muzyczny

South Africa

African Music

Spain

Anuario musical

Revista de musicología

Sweden

Svensk Tidskrift för Musikforskning

Switzerland

Brass Bulletin

Schweizerisches Jahrbuch für Musikwissenschaft

Schweizerische Musikzeitung

Union of Soviet Socialist Republics

Sovetskaia Muzyka

United States

American Choral Review

American Harp Journal

American Music

American Music Teacher

American Organist

American Record Guide

American String Teacher

Asian Music

Association of Recorded Sound Collections Journal

Billboard

Black Music Research Journal

Black Perspective in Music

Brainard's Musical World

Brass Quarterly

Cashbox

Choral Journal

Clavier

College Music Symposium

Computer Music Journal

Contributions to Music Education

Council for Research in Music Edcucation

Crawdaddy

Creem

Current Musicology

Dialog in Instrumental Music Education

down beat

Dwight's Journal of Music

Ethnomusicology

Etude

Euterpeiad

Film Music Notes

Guitar Player

High Fidelity

In Theory Only

Indiana Theory Review

Instrumentalist

Inter-American Music Review

International Society of Bassists

Jazz Educators Journal

JEMF Quarterly

Journal of Aesthetics and Art Criticism

Journal of Band Research

Journal of Country Music

Journal of Jazz Studies

Journal of Music Theory

Journal of Music Therapy

Journal of Musicological Research

Journal of Musicology

Journal of Research in Music Education

Journal of the American Musical Instrument Society

Journal of the American Musicological Society

Latin American Music Review

Living Blues

Metronome

Modern Music

Music Article Guide

Music Educators Journal

Music Index

Music Perception

Music Teacher

Music Theory Spectrum

Music: The A.G.O. and R.C.C.O. Magazine

Musica Disciplina

Musical America

Musical Courier

Musical Quarterly

Musician

NACWPI Journal

NATS Bulletin

19th Century Music

Notes

Opera News

Opera Quarterly

Percussive Notes

Percussionist

Perspectives of New Music

Piano Quarterly

Popular Music and Society

Psychomusicology

Rolling Stone

School Musician

Sing Out!

Source: Music of the Avant Garde

Stereo Review

Symphony News

Theory and Practice

Update: Applications in Music Education

Woodwind World Brass and Percussion

Yugoslavia

International Review of the Aesthetics and Sociology of Music

Subject Listing of Periodicals by Title

While many of these titles are adequately described by a single catagory, others, such as the *Dansk Musiktidsskrift* and *Sovetskaia Muzyka*, deserve a listing in several categories. Still others began as one sort of journal and have evolved into different orientations. The list below assembles the journals in this volume into all pertinent categories. For clarification, see individual essays. The category "General/Appreciation" warrants explanation. It includes all those journals intended primarily to inform amateurs, music lovers, and musicians of current events and topics of general interest. While articles in these journals may carry very historical or pedagogical titles, they are only moderately scholarly and are intended for public education, not for scholarly interchange.

Composition

Anbruch

Canadian Composer/Le Compositeur canadien

Composer (London)

Computer Music Journal

Dansk Musiktidsskrift

Gravesaner Blätter

Interface: Journal of New Music Research

Key Notes

Melos

Modern Music

Musik und Gesellschaft

Perspectives of New Music

Die Reihe

Source: Music of the Avant Garde

Sovetskaia Muzyka

Tempo

Computer Music

Computer Music Journal

Ethnomusicology

African Music

Asian Music

Dansk Musiktidsskrift

Ethnomusicology

Inter-American Music Review

Journal of the Indian Musicological Society

Latin American Music Review

La Revue musicale

Studia musicologica

World of Music

Yearbook of Traditional Music

Music Periodical Indexes

Bibliographie des Musikschrifttums

Jazz Index

Music Article Guide

Music Index

RILM Abstracts

General Appreciation

Allgemeine Musik-Zeitung

Allgemeine musikalische Zeitung

American Record Guide

Brainard's Musical World

Caecilia (1824–1848)

Caecilia (1844–1944)

Canada Music Book/Les Cahiers Canadiens

Dansk Musiktidsskrift

Dwight's Journal of Music

Etude

Euterpeiad

Film Music Notes

Le Guide musical

Harmonicon

Le Ménestrel

Mens en Melodie

Metronome

Modern Music

Monthly Musical Record

Music and Musicians

Musica

Musical America

Musical Courier

Musical Times

Musician

Die Musik

Musik und Gesellschaft

Neue Musik-Zeitung

Neue Zeitschrift für Musik

Opera

Opera News

Opernwelt

Revue musical chilena

Royal Musical Association Proceedings

Ruch Muzyczny

Signale für die musikalische Welt

Sovetskaia Muzyka

Interdisciplinary

International Review of the Aesthetics and Sociology of Music

Journal of Aesthetics and Art Criticism

Popular Music and Society

Psychology of Music

Psychomusicology

Music Librarianship

Brio

Fontes artis musicae

Notes

Musicology

Acta musicologica

Allegmeine Musik-Zeitung

American Music

American Musicological Society Journal

Anbruch

Annales musicologique

Anuario musical

Archiv für Musikforschung

Archiv für Musikwissenschaft

Beitrage zur Musikwissenschaft

Black Music Research Journal

Black Perspectives in Music

Caecilia (1824–1848)

Caecilia (1844–1944)

Chigiana

College Music Symposium

Current Musicology

Dansk Musiktidsskrift

Early Music

Galphin Society Journal

Gravesaner Blätter

Inter-American Music Review

Interface: Journal of New Music Research

JEMF Quarterly

Journal of Country Music

Journal of Jazz Studies

Journal of Musicological Research

Journal of Musicology

Journal of the Indian Musicological Society

Key Notes

Latin American Music Review

Melos

Miscellanea Musicologica: Adelaide Studies in Musicology

Modern Music

Monatscheft für Musikgeschichte

Monthly Musical Record

Music and Letters

Music Perception

Music Review

Musica

Musica disciplina

Musical Quarterly

Musicology Australia

Musik im Krieg

Musik und Gesellschaft

Musik und Kirche

Die Musikforschung

Muzyka

Neue Zeitschrift für Musik

19th Century Music

Nuova rivista musicale italiana

Opera Quarterly

Periodica Musica

Quaderni della rassegna musicale

Recherches sur la musique française classique

Die Reihe

Revista de musicologia

Revue belge de musicologie

Revue de musicologie

Revue musicale chilena

Rivista italiana di musicologia

Royal Musical Association Proceedings

Royal Musical Association Research Chronicles

Schweizerische Musikzeitung

Schweizerisches Jahrbuch für Musikwissenschaft

Source: Music of the Avant Garde

Sovetskaia Muzyka

Studi musicali

Studia musicologica

Studien zur Musikwissenschaft

Studies in Music

Svensk Tidskrift för Musikforschning

Tempo

Tijdschrift van de Verenging voor Nederlandse Musiekgeschiedenis

Vierteljahrschrift für Musikwissenschaft

Zeitschrift für Musikwissenschaft

Organology

Galpin Society Journal

Journal of the American Music Instrument Society

Musik und Kirche

Strad

Pedagogy

American Choral Review

American Music Teacher

American String Teacher

Choral Journal

Clavier

College Music Symposium

Contributions to Music Education

Council for Research in Music Education

Dansk Musiktidsskrift

Dialog in Instrumental Music Education

Etude

Instrumentalist

Jazz Educators Journal

Journal of Band Research

Journal of Research in Music Education

Music Educators Journal

Music Perception

Music Teacher

Musician

NATS Bulletin

Piano Quarterly

Psychology of Music

Psychomusicology

School Musician

Sovetskaia Muzyka

Strad

Update: Applications in Music Education

Performance

American Choral Review

American Harp Journal

American Organist

Brass Bulletin

Brass Quarterly

Choral Journal

Clavier

International Society of Bassists Journal

Journal of Band Research

Musik und Kirche

NACWPI Journal

NATS Bulletin

Opera

Opera News

Opernwelt

Percussive Notes/Percussionist

Strad

Symphony News

Woodwind World Brass and Percussion

Popular Music

Billboard

Cash Box

Coda

Crawdaddy

Creem

Dansk Musiktidsskrift

down beat

Film Music Notes

Jazz Educators' Journal

Jazz Journal (International)

Jazz-Hot

JEMF Quarterly

Journal of Country Music

Journal of Jazz Studies

Living Blues

Melody Maker

Popular Music and Society

Rolling Stone

Sing Out!

Sound Recordings

American Record Guide

Association for Recorded Sound Collections Journal

Gramophone

High Fidelity

Recorded Sound

Stereo Review

Theory

College Music Symposium
In Theory Only
Indiana Theory Review
Interface: Journal of New Music Research
Journal of Music Theory
Key Notes
Melos
Music Analysis
Music Theory Spectrum
Perspectives of New Music
Die Reihe
Source: Music of the Avant Garde
Tempo
Der Tonwille
Zeitschrift für Musiktheorie

Therapy

Journal of Music Therapy

Trades

Billboard
Canadian Composer/Le Compositeur canadien
Cash Box
Melody Maker
Musician
Musique et instrument

Selected Bibliography

With the exception of writings which chronicle the publication history of various music periodical titles and a very few articles which survey the periodical output of an entire country, little research on the journals themselves appears in the literature. The history, the significance, the content of periodicals in general, and the interrelationship of titles are areas which, for the most part, remain unresearched. The following represent the most important studies that have been done. For writings which focus on specific titles, check the bibliography section of the entry for that periodical.

Blum, Fred. "East German Music Journals: A Checklist." *Notes* 19 (1961/62): 399–410.

Campbell, Frank. "Some Current Foreign Periodicals." *Notes* 5 (1947/48): 189–206.

Campbell, Frank, Gladys Eppink, and Jessica Fredricks. "Music Magazines of Britain and the United States." *Notes* 6 (1948/49): 239–62, 457–59; 7 (1949/50): 372–76.

Clough, F. F., and G. J. Cuming. "Phonographic Periodicals." *Notes* 16 (1957/58): 537–58.

Coover, James B. "A Bibliography of East European Music Periodicals." *Fontes Artis Musicae* 20 (1956): 219–25.

Fairley, Lee. "A Check-List of Recent Latin American Music Periodicals." *Notes* 2 (1944/45): 120–23.

Fellinger, Imogen. *Verzeichnis der Musikzeitschriften des 19. Jahrhunderts*. Studien zur Musikgeschichte des 19. Jahrhunderts, v. 10. Regensburg: Gustav Bosse Verlag, 1968.

Fétis, François. "Revue des journaux de musique publies dans les divers pays de l'Europe." *Revue musicale* 2 (1828): 313–20.

Freystatter, Wilhelm. *Die musikalischen Zeitschriften seit ihrer Entstehung bis zur Gegenwart*. Munich: Theodor Riedel, 1884.

Gregoir, Edouard G.- J. *Recherches historiques concernant les journaux de musique depuis les temps les plus reculés jusqu'à nos jours*. Anvers: Chez Louis Legris, 1872.

Meggett, Joan M. *Music Periodical Literature: An Annotated Bibliography of Indexes and Bibliographies*. Metuchen, N.J.: Scarecrow Press, 1978.

Prod'homme, J.- G. "Essai de bibliographie des périodiques musicaux de langue française." *Bulletin de la société française de musicologie* 2 (1918): 76–90.

Riedel, A. *Répertoire des périodiques musicaux belges*. Bibliographia belgica, v. 8. Bruxelles: Commission belge de bibliographie, 1954.

Rohlfs, Eckart. *Die deutschsprachigen Musikperiodica, 1945–1957*. Forschungsbeiträge zur Musikwissenschaft, v. 11. Regensburg: Gustav Bosse Verlag, 1961.

Straeten, Edmond vander. *Nos périodiques musicaux*. Gand: J. Vuylsteke, 1893.

Thoumin, Jean-Adrien. *Bibliographie rétrospective des périodiques française de littérature musicale, 1870–1954*. Paris: Union française des organismes de documentation, 1957.

Weichlein, William J. *A Checklist of American Music Periodicals, 1850–1900*. Detroit Studies in Music Bibliography, v. 16. Detroit: Information Coordinators, 1970.

Index

A. et J. Picard, 359
ABA Research Center, 189
Abbott, Curtis, 95–98
ABC Leisure Magazines, 159–60, 270–71
Abeles, Hal, 115
Abendroth, Walter, 12
Abraham, Gerald, 242–43, 318, 384
Academiae Scientarium Hungaricae, 450
Accademia Musicale Chigiana, 81
Accademia Nazionale de Santa Cecilia, 410
Ackerman, Will, 153
Acta musicologica, xii, 3–5, 411
Acta Sagittariana, 294
Adderley, Cannonball, 88
Adelson, David, 80
Adler, Guido, 9, 275, 414–15, 417, 440, 442, 455
Adolf of Bückeburg, 40
Adorno, Theodor, 363, 453–54, 463
African Music, 5–7
African Music Society, 5, 7
Agawu, V. Kofi, 164
Akadémia Kiadó, 412, 414
Albarosa, Nino, 379
Albert, George, 79–80
Alberti, Luciano, 82
Albrecht, Hans, 5, 35, 296–97
Albrecht, Theodore, 93
Albrechtsberger, Johann Georg, 413
Alder, Cosmas, 395
Aldrich, Richard, 275
Aletti, Vince, 103, 105
Alexander, H., 311

Alexander, J. Heywood, 61–62
Alkan, Charles-Henri, 314
All India Radio (AIR), 208
Allen, Bob, 191
Allen, Red, 88
Allen, Richard, 194
Allen, Walter, 193
Allende, Pedro Humberto, 367
Allgemeine (deutsche) Musik-Zeitung, xi
Allgemeine deutsche Musik-Zeitung, 11
Allgemeine musikalische Zeitung, xi–xii, 7–11, 312–13, 396, 439
Allgemeine Musik-Zeitung, 11–14, 223, 288
Allison, Mose, 88
Allorto, Riccardo, 355
Almeida, Laurindo, 153
Alperson, Philip, 187
Altenburg, Detlef, 297
Altmann, Wilhelm, 12
Ambrose, Bert, 361
American Anthropological Association, 126
American Bandmasters Association (ABA), 189–90
American Choral Directors Association (ACDA), 15, 83, 85
American Choral Review, 14–16
American Choral Foundation, Inc., 14–16
American Federation of Musicians, 117
American Guild of Organists (AGO), 24–27
American Guild of Organists Quarterly, 25
American Harp Journal, The, 16–17
American Harp Society, 16–17
American Institute of Musicology (AIM), 264–65, 267

American Library Association, 319
American Mercury, 235
American Music, xiv
American Music Foundation, 282–84
American Music Lover, 27, 29
American Music Teacher, 18–21
American Musical Instrument Society, 206–7
American Musicological Society, Inc., 24
American Organist, 24–27
American Record Guide, 27–29
American Society for Aesthetics, 187–88
American String Teacher, 29–31, 175
American String Teachers Association, 29–31
American Symphony Orchestra League, 422,
    424
AMF Artists Service, 284
Anbruch, 31–33, 222
Anderson, Chester, 103, 105
Anderson, Gordon Athol, 233, 285–86, 418
Anderson, Margaret, 235
Anderson, Robert, 279
Anderson, W. R., 258–59
Anderson, William, 407–8
Anderson, William M., 99
Anglés, Higinio, 36–38
Annales musicologiques, Les, xiii, 33–36, 375
Annegarn, Alfons, 75, 213, 229, 436
Annual Review of Jazz Studies, 193–94
Ansermet, Ernst, 374
Anstead, Walter H., 232
Antheil, George, 32
Anthony, James, 358–59
Antrim, Dorin K., 232
Anuario musical, 36–38
Apel, Willi, 266
Apfel, Ernst, 267
Appleton, Jon, 96
Apthorp, W. F., 120
Aquino, John, 253
Araujo, Juan de, 169
Arauxo, Francisco Correa de, 367
Arazi, Ishaq, 30
Arban, Jean Baptiste, 62
Arbeitskreis für Haus- und Jugendmusik, 263
Arbeitskreis für Hausmusik, 263
Arcaya, Jose, 201
Archiv für Musikforschung, xiii, 38–40, 41,
    295, 455
Archiv für Musikwissenschaft, xiii, 40–43
Aretz, Isabel, 169
ARG American Record Guide Publishing, 29
Armstrong, Louis, 88, 177, 179

Arnell, Richard, 93, 95
Arnheim, Rudolf, 108
Arnold, Denis, 64, 246
Arnold, Malcolm, 93
Ars Viva Press, 149
ARSC Bulletin, 45, 47
ARSC Newsletter, 45–46
Artaria & Co., 417
Artificial Intelligence, 96
Arts Council of Great Britain, 94
Arundell, Dennis, 328
Asch, Moses, 399
Ashbrook, William, 332
Ashley, Robert, 401–2
Asian Music, 43–45
Askegaard, Paul, 31
Associated Pipe Organ Builders of America,
    26
Association for Recorded Sound Collections
    (ARSC), 45, 47
Association for Recorded Sound Collections
    Journal, 45–47
Association for the Advancement of Instru-
    mental Music, 166, 168
Association of Concert Bands of America,
    444–45
Association of Professional Vocal Ensembles,
    16
Atkins, Chet, 153
Atlantic Monthly, 158
Atlas, Allan, 460
Atterberg, Kurt, 420
Atwood, Jody, 31
Audiocom, Inc., 158–60
Audiocraft, 158
Audiocraft and Hi-Fi Music at Home, 158
Auftakt, 32
Augener and Company, 243
Austin, Larry, 401–3
Ayesterán, Lauro, 367
Ayres, Thomas A., 306–7
Ayrton, William, 155, 157
Azevedo, Luiz Heitor Corrêa de, 462

B&P: Brass and Percussion, 444
B. Schott's Söhne, 151–52, 313
Baalen & Zonen, J. van, 72, 74
Babbitt, Milton, 158, 162, 196, 235, 339–41
Babin, Stanley, 344
Bach, C. P. E., 242, 436
Bach, J. C., 164
Bach, J. S., 9, 30, 61, 108, 120, 123, 129,

161, 164, 226, 255, 262, 276, 292, 369, 373, 395, 431, 436–37
Badeaux, Ed, 400
Baden-Baden Chamber Music Festivals, 12
Baden-Baden Festival, 222
Badger, Thomas, Jr., 132
Badura-Skoda, Paul, 344
Bagge, Selmar, 9–11
Baglivi, Anthony, 27
Bahn, 241
Bain, David, 174
Baines, Anthony, 125, 143–45
Baker, David, 194
Baker, David M., 67
Baker, J. Percy, 382, 384
Baker, James M., 198
Balaguer, Pablo Hernandez, 367
Balch, Edward L., 121
Baldemandis, Prosdocimus de, 239
Ballet, 327
Ballet and Opera, 327
Ballif, Claude, 374
Ballola, Giovanni Carli, 82
Balroca, Mario, 446
Baltzell, W. J., 284
Banfield, Stephen, 156, 280
Bang, Betty, 307
Bangs, Lester, 105–7, 380
Banowetz, Joseph, 344
Barber, Frank Granville, 248–49
Barber, Gail, 17
Barbera, André, 460
Barblan, Guglielmo, 355, 379
Barbour, J. Murray, 10
Bärenreiter-Verlag, 4–5, 138, 140, 261–64, 294, 297
Barford, Philip T., 255
Barker, John W., 28
Barkin, Elaine, 340, 342
Barlow, Clarence, 96
Barnett, Dene, 286
Baron, Samuel, 445
Baroni, Giorgie, 463
Baronis, M., 377
Barrett, William Alexander, 281
Barriere, Jean-Baptiste, 96
Barro, Raquel, 367
Barry, Charles Ainslie, 243
Barth, Karl, 293
Bartha, Denes, 38
Barthe, Roland, 323
Bartholf Senff, Verlag von, 398

Bartlett, Clifford, 66–67
Bartók, Béla, 32, 164, 201, 222, 235, 275, 323, 373, 413, 428–29, 431
Barton, Mariann, 259
Baruch, Gerth-Wolfgang, 225
Barzun, Jacques, 318, 331
Basart, Ann P., 171, 341
Basch, Peter J., 27
Basie, Count, 179
Bass Sound Post, 175
Bass World, 175
Basso, Alberto, 378–79
Bastianelli, Giannotto, 81
Bate, Philip, 144
Bathori, Jane, 360
Battier, M., 97
Baudelet, Robert, 181
Bauerlein, Charles Robert, 104
Baum, Richard, 263–64
Baumann, Max Peter, 448
Bax, Arnold, 109
Baxter, Jeff, 153
Bazelon, Irwin A., 136
Beach, Amy, 164
Beach, David, 195, 198, 260, 431
Beach Boys, The, 103
Beatles, The, 103
Bebbington, Warren, 286
Becker, C. F., 11
Becker, Hugo, 394
Beckmann, Gustav, 456
Bedaux, Rafael, 170
Bedweg, Harold, 314, 316
Beecham, Sir Thomas, 331
Beecroft, Norma, 77
Beethoven, Ludvig van, xi, 8–9, 22, 91, 158, 164, 196, 242, 254, 288–89, 312, 316, 323, 373, 395, 431, 436–37, 460
Béhague, Gerard, 461–62
Behrman, David, 402
Beiträge zur Musikwissenschaft, xiii, 49–51
Bekker, Paul, 12, 32, 222, 287
Belgisch Tijdschrift voor Muziek-wetenschap, 368
Belier, Eugene, 284
Bellina, Anna Laura, 379
Bellini, Vincenzo, 242
Belmont, Eleanor Robson, 330, 332
Benary, Peter, 262
Benjamin, William, 195
Bengtsson, Ingmar, 421–22
Bennett, Richard Rodney, 177–78

Benoit, Marcelle, 357–58, 360
Benson, George, 380
Bent, Ian D., 463
Benton, Rita, 138–39, 141
Berg, Alban, 164, 235, 393, 413
Berg, Sigurd, 114
Berger, Arthur, 235, 339–40, 342, 428
Berger, Donald P., 307
Berger, Edward, 193
Berigten, 433, 435–36
Berio, Luciano, 323, 363, 374, 429
Berkeley, Lennox, 328
Berle, Arnie, 152
Berlin, Jeff, 152
Berlioz, Hector, 150, 159, 226, 242, 254,
    312, 316, 371, 395
Bermudez, Pedro, 169
Bernard, Jonathan, 261, 431
Bernard, Robert, 374, 376
Bernardini, Nicola, 96
Bernhardt, Sarah, 360
Bernstein, Lawrence F., 24
Bernstein, Leonard, 46, 235
Berry, Wallace, 259–60
Besseler, Heinrich, 38, 40, 295
Bessom, Malcolm E., 253
Betton, Matt, Sr., 177–78
Beulah Publishing Co., 105
Beveridge, David R., 43, 316, 318
Bevis, Carolyn, 401
Bhatkhanda, Pandet Vishnu Narayan, 208–9
Bianconi, Lorenzo, 379
Bie, Oscar, 12, 32
Biel, Michael, 46
Biggs, E. Power, 26
Billboard, 51–55, 159, 183, 219, 270
Billboard Advertising Co., 51, 55
Billboard Ltd., 183
Billboard Publishing Co., 55, 159–60, 271
Binchois, Gilles, 164
Biographicus Minor, 242
Birch, Ian, 221
Birge, Edward Bailey, 253
Bishop, Henry, 131
Black, Leo, 363
Black, Ralph, 424
Black Music Research Bulletin, 56
Black Music Research Journal, 55–57
Black Music Research Newsletter, 56
Black Perspective in Music, xiv, 57–59
Black Sabbath, 106
Blacking, John, 385

Blackwell, Basil, 464
Blakey, Art, 88
Blankenburg, Walter, 293–95
Blesh, Rudi, 194
Bliss, Arthur, 328
Blitzstein, Marc, 235
Bloch, Ernest, 109
Block, Jennifer, 401
Block, Joseph, 344
Blois, Louis, 28
Blom, Eric, 245–46
Blondel, Jorge Urrutia, 367
Blount, Roy, 191
Bluestone, Mimi, 401
Blum, David, 381
Blum, Fred, 50, 291
Blume, Frederick, 292, 295–96
Blumenberg, Marc A., 272–74
Boatwright, Howard, 197
Bode, Wilhelm, 70
Boetticher, Wolfgang, 288
Bogart, Neil, 80
Bohlen, Donald, 430, 432
Bolling, Claude, 179–80
Bonade, Daniel, 445
Bonnen, Helge, 114
Boonin, Joseph, 320
Boosey and Hawkes, 94, 427–28, 430
Boretz, Benjamin, 339–40, 342
Borg, Paul W., 311, 394, 396
Bornoff, J., 429
Bornoff, Jack, 448
Bosc, Auguste, 297–99, 301
Bosse, Gustav, 315
Bossert, William, 27
Botelho, Mauro, 163
Bottenheim, S., 436
Boucher, A., 242
Boulanger, Lili, 374
Boulanger, Nadia, 235, 374, 387
Boulez, Pierre, 97, 109, 148, 314, 323, 328,
    340, 362, 429
Boulton, John, 256
Boundas, Louise, 408
Bouquet, Fritz, 225
Bouwsteenen, 433, 435–36
Bowen, George Oscar, 250–53
Bowling Green State University Popular Press,
    347–48
Boxberger, Ruth, 200
Boyd, Earl, 305, 307
Boyd, Liona, 153

Boylan, Sharon, 164–65
Bradbury, William Batchelder, 169
Bradetich, Jeff, 175–76
Bradley, Carol June, 321
Bradley, Jack, 88
Bradshaw, Susan, 93
Brahms, Johannes, 11, 161, 254–55, 262, 272, 289, 291, 313, 436–37
Brainard, Charles S., 62
Brainard, Nathan, 59
Brainard's Musical World, 59–62, 128–29
Brainard's Sons, 62
Brand, Pat, 222
Brandes, Friedrich, 315
Brandt, Thompson, 115
Brant Music Corp., 284
Brass Bulletin, 62–63
Brass Quarterly, 63–65
Braxton, Anthony, 88
Bray, Lesley, 93
Brazier, Chris, 221
Breithaupt, Rudolf Maria, 287
Breitkopf und Härtel, 5, 8, 11, 13, 39–40, 43, 69, 241, 312, 417, 442, 457
Brendel, Franz, 313, 315
Brenet, Michel, 150
Brevet Publishers Ltd., 248
Bridges, Doreen, 286
Bridges, John, 347
Briggs, John, 131
Brincker, Jens, 114
Brinkmann, Jesper, 114
Brio, 65–67, 138
British Archives of Folk and Primitive Music, 360
British Humanities Index, 66
British Institute of Sound, 360, 362
Britten, Benjamin, 235, 328, 428–29
Britton, Allen P., 205, 458–60
Broadcast Review, 146
Brock, Clutton, 244
Brockhaus, Alfred, 49
Brockhaus, Heinz Alfred, 291
Brody, Martin, 431
Broeckx, Jan L., 172, 229
Brook, Barry S., 174
Brooks, Richard, 431
Brooks, Tim, 46
Brophy, Brigid, 328
Brouk, Frank, 390
Brown, Howard Mayer, 124, 206
Brown, Patricia, 418

Brown, Roger, 468
Browne, Richmond, 161–63, 259
Bruce, Robert, 320
Bruckner-Bigenwald, Martha, 10
Brün, Herbert, 97
Brunold, Paul, 374
Brylawski, Sam, 47
Buck, Dudley, 60
Buckner, Milt, 88
Buckwell, Patricia J., 200
Buelow, George J., 93
Buescher Instrument Company, 389
Bukofzer, Manfred, 34
Bulletin, 93
Bulletin d'information, 138
Bulletin de la Société Française de Musicologie, 370
Bulletin of the AMS, 21
Bulletin of the British Institute of Recorded Sound, 360
Bulletin of the Council for Research in Music Education, 100–102, 204, 349–50
Bulletin of the International Music Council, 446–47
Bulow, Hans von, 12
Burchu, Guido, 83
Burde, Wolfgang, 314, 316
Burdick, Michael, 164
Burgetz, Algred, 311
Burke, C. G., 158
Burkhart, Charles, 195
Burney, Charles, 131, 150
Burrows, David, 108
Burrs, Glenn, 118–19
Burstein, L. Poundie, 431
Busoni, Ferruccio, 222, 344
Bussotti, Sylvano, 81
Buttelman, Clifford V., 252–53
Buxtehude, Dietrich, 262, 292–93
Buxton, William, 97
Byler, Robert, 90, 119, 184, 195, 217
Byrd, Charlie, 153
Byrne, Maurice, 145

Cabanilles, Juan, 37
Cabezón, Antonio de, 37
Cabinet Press, Inc., 65
Cady, Henry L., 99–100, 258
Caecilia (1824–1848), 69–71
Caecilia (1844–1944), 71–75
Caecilia en De Muziek, 72
Caecilia en Het Muziekcollege, 72

Cage, John, 43, 164, 169, 235, 362, 401–3, 458
Caine, Milton A., 29
Caldara, Antonio, 82
Caldwell, Sarah, 108
Callaway, Frank, 420
Calo, José López, 36
Cambray Publishing, 106–7
Cameron, Francis, 286
Campbell, Bruce, 260
Campbell, Frank C., 23, 246, 256, 267, 321–22
Campbell, Peter, 124
Campbelle, R. A., 164–65
Canada Council, 89
Canada Music Book, 75–77
Canadian Brass, 166
Canadian Composer, The, 77–78
Canadian League of Composers, 76
Canadian Music Council, 75–76
Canadian Music Journal, 76
Canape, Charlene, 381
Canin, Martin, 344
Cann, Richard, 96
Canon, 284
Capell, Richard, 243, 245–46
Caplin, William Earl, 260, 454
Capobianco, Tito, 465
Capwell, Charles, 128
Carapetyan, Armen, 264, 266–68
Cardew, Cornelius, 363, 401
Cardus, Neville, 328
Carl Fischer, 230, 232
Carlsen, James C., 205, 468
Carlson, David C., 163
Carner, Mosco, 416
Carpenter, Patricia, 108
Carriere, Claude, 181
Carroll, Charles M., 93
Carruthers, John, 152
Carse, Adam, 144
Carson, Leon, 27, 310
Carter, Elliott, 46, 164, 235–36, 254, 340, 429
Caruso, Enrico, 268
Casa Editrice Valentino Bonpiani, 356
Casadeseus, Robert, 374
Casals, Pablo, 129
Casella, Alfredo, 81, 269, 324, 354, 374
Cash Box, 78–80, 219
Caskett, James, 145
Castedo, Leopoldo, 368

Castil-Blaze, François, 226
Cattin, Giulio, 379
Cauchie, Maurice, 226, 372
Cavalli, Pier Francesco, 440
Cayer, David, 193, 195
CBMR Digest, 56
CBS Laboratories, 159
CBS Magazines, 408
Center for Black Music Research (Columbia College), 56
Center for Computer Research in Music and Acoustics (CCRMA), 95
Center for the Study of Popular Culture, 346
Center for the Study of Southern Culture (University of Mississippi), 216–17
Central Opera Service, 331
Centre National de la Recherche Scientifique, 35, 359
Centre National des Lettres, 359
Cesti, Marc Antonio, 440
Chadabe, Joel, 96
Chaikin, Lawrence, 344
Chalfin, Doris, 29
Chamber of Mines of South Africa, 6
Chambure, Comtesse de, 373
Chapman, Ernest, 430
Charles X, King, 357
Chase, Gilbert, 26, 128, 169, 458, 461
Chase, Sam, 55
Chazanoff, Daniel, 30
Cheliapov, N. I., 406
Cherubini, Luigi, 226
Chesterian, xiv
Chew, Geoffrey, 385–86
Chicago Symphony Orchestra, 390
Chigiana, 81–83
Chigiana: Rassegna annuale di studi musicologici, xiv, 324
Childs, Barney, 401
Chominski, Józef M., 301, 303
Chop, Max, 398
Chopin, Frédéric, 9, 61, 161, 164, 302, 312, 375, 386, 437
Choral Conductors Forum, 14
Choral Journal, The, 83–85
Chotzinoff, Samuel, 331
Chou Wen-Chung, 43
Chow, Fong. See Fong Chow
Chowning, John M., 96
Christensen, Dieter, 451
Christensen, Jean, 114, 422
Christgau, Robert, 105

Christian, Charlie, 179
Christie, John M., 168
Chrysander, Friedrich, xiii, 9, 70, 238, 439–42
Chusid, Martin, 108
Clappe, Arthur A., 232
Clarinet, 443
Clark, Dick, 80
Clark, Frances, 86
Clark, Kenneth, 328
Clarke, Jeremiah, 169
Clarke, Keith, 249
Clarke, Stanley, 153
Clarkson, Austin, 110
Claro, Samuel, 366
Clavier, 85–87, 258
Clemencic, René, 82
Clemens, Jacobus (non Papa), 266
Clement, Andrew, 281
Clercx, Suzanne, 35, 369–70
Clergeat, Andre, 181
Clifton, Thomas, 201
Clough, John, 261
Cluck, Nancy, 31
CMS Newsletter, 90
CMS Proceedings, 90–92
Cobbe, Hugh, 384
Cobbett, W. W., 257
Coda, 87–90
Coeuroy, André, 373–74
Coffin, Berton, 309
Coffman, Wesley, 85
Cohen, Albert, 359
Cohen, H. Robert, 467–68
Cohen, Harold, 96
Cohen, John, 399
Cohen, Norman, 184–86
Colby, Michael, 232
Cole, Hugo, 428
Coleman, David, 27
Coleman, Ray, 221–22
Collaer, Paul, 37
College Band Directors National Association (CBDNA), 391
College Music Association, 90
College Music Society (CMS), 90–93, 261
College Music Symposium, 90–93
Collegium Musicum, 263
Collis, James, 443–46
Collisani, Amalia, 379
Columbia, 179
Columbia College, 57

Columbia Masterworks, 402
Columbia University, 107–8, 110
Colwell, Richard J., 100, 102
Comberiati, Carmelo Peter, 241, 243, 289, 385–86, 417
Combs, Michael F., 337, 339
Commer, Franz, 238
Composer (London), 93–95
Composer/Performer Edition, 403
Composers Authors and Publishers Association of Canada (CAPAC), 77
Composers' Guild of Great Britain, 93–95
Compositeur Canadien, Le, 77
Computer Music Journal, 95–98
Conati, Marcello, 379, 467–68
Concina, G., 322
Cone, Edward T., 108, 260, 340, 342
Conly, John, 158–60
Connelly, Christopher, 380
Cons, Carl, 118–19
Consejo Superior de Investigaciones Científicas, 36–37
Constantin, Philippe, 181
Contemporary Music Review, 201
Contrepoint, 374–75
Contributions to Music Education, 98–100
Cook, Eddie, 181–84
Cook, Susan C., 5, 11, 14, 33, 149, 225, 297, 456
Cooke, George Willis, 121
Cooke, James Francis, 129–31
Cooper, Ann, 381
Cooper, Martin, 281, 328
Cooper, Matt, 29
Coover, James B., 195
Copland, Aaron, 136, 159, 235, 339–41, 407, 428–29, 445
Corbin, Solange, 410
Cornell University Music Review, 94
Corporon, Eugene, 115
Corrigan, Vincent J., 24, 125, 157, 246, 268, 281, 466
Cortot, Alfred, 374
Coryell, Larry, 152–53
Coss, Bill, 232
Costallat, 297
Costanza, A. Peter, 115
Cott, Jonathon, 380
Counille, V., 301
Country Music Foundation, 191–92
Country Music Foundation Newsletter, 191–92
Country Music Hall of Fame and Museum, 191

Country Song Roundup, 191
Couperin, François, 373
Covent Garden, 247, 279
Covington, Kate, 165
Cowden-Clarke, Charles, 279
Cowden-Clarke, Mary, 281
Cowell, Henry, 235
Craft, Robert, 158, 428
Craig, Mary, 272
Craver, Curtis, Jr., 445
Crawdaddy, 102–5, 347
Crawdaddy Enterprises, 104
Crawdaddy Publishing Company, 103, 105
Crawford, Richard, 23, 458–59
Creative Arts Company, 78
Creem, 105–7
Creem Magazine, Inc., 107
CRI, 28
Critica musica, x
Critischer Musicus, xi
Crocker, Richard L., 108, 187
Crockett, Jim, 153
Cronin, John, 29
Cross, Ian, 350
Crossley-Holland, Peter, 451
Crouse, Timothy, 381
Croy, Jamie, 110
Crumb, George, 164, 201
Crutchfield, Will, 316
Cuesta, Ismael Fernández de la, 365
Culshaw, John, 331
Current Musicology, 107–10
Curtis Circulation Company, 105
Curwen, John, 278
Curzon, Henri de, 150, 152

D'Accone, Frank, 266, 268
D'Allones, Olivier Revault, 172
Dadelsen, Georg von, 296
Dahlhaus, Carl, 23, 42, 172, 225, 262, 314,
    316, 453
Dahlstedt, Sten, 422
Dallapiccola, Luigi, 323, 340, 355
Dalton, Mark, 85
Damrosch, Leopold, 60
Damrosch, Walter, 60, 331
Dan Morgenstern Institute, 193, 195
Dance, Stanley, 182
Danchenka, Gary, 164
Daniskas, John, 434, 436
Dannemann, Manuel, 367
Dansk musiktidsskrift, 111–14
Danto, Arthur C., 187

Danuser, Hermann, 455
Dardo, Gianluigi, 379
Darling, Robert, 108
Darrell, Rob, 27
Dart, Thurston, 143–45, 385–86
Das Meisterwerk in der Musik, 436–37
Das Musikleben, 313
Dasche, Michael, 292
Daub, Peggy, 67, 141
Dauriac, Lionel, 370
Davenport, F. W., 384
David, Karl Heinrich, 393–94
Davies, John Booth, 350
Davies, Maxwell, 429
Davies, Roger, 124
Davis, Shelley, 206, 460
Davison, Archibald T., 14, 267
Davison, Mary Veronica, 61
de Lerma, Rene-Dominique, 58
De Martino, Dave, 107
Deadar, B. R., 208
Deagun, J. C., 338
Dean, Winton, 328
Deans, Karen, 253
Debussy, Claude, 16, 159, 226, 317, 344,
    363, 371, 373, 454, 460
Decker, Marilyn, 131, 274
Degrada, Francesco, 82, 322, 378
Dehn, Sigfried Wilhelm, 70–71
Deit, Jean, 299, 301
Del Ray, Teisco, 152
Delaunay, Charles, 88, 179–81
Délibes, Leó, 226
Delius, Frederic, 429
Delmas, Jean, 181
Delone, Richard P., 164
DeMicheal, Don, 119
Dempster, Douglas J., 187
Demuth, Norman, 93
Denisoff, R. Serge, 346–48, 400
Denisov, Edisson, 429
*Denkmäler der Tonkunst in Öesterreich
    (DTÖe)*, 414–15
Dennis, Brian, 428
Dennison, Peter, 234
Des Pres, Josquin, 239, 434
Dessau, Paul, 291
Det unge Tonekunstnerselskab (DUT), 111,
    114
Detner Associates, 284
Deutsch, Diana, 464–65
Deutsch, Otto Erich, 254–55

Deutsche Gesellschaft für Musikwissenschaft, 38–39
Deutsche Musikgesellschaft, Die, 455
Deutsche Verlags-Anstalt, 289
Deutsches Jahrbuch der Musikwissenschaft, xiii
Devore, Richard, 164
Devries, Rene, 272
Di Benedetto, Renato, 379
Dialogue in Instrumental Music Education, 114–16
Diapason, 24–25, 130
Dickinson, Peter, 93
Dineen, Murray, 110
Dingley, Charles, 131–32
Dircknick-Holmfeld, Gregers, 114
Distler, Hugo, 292
Ditson, Oliver, 120
Dixon, Richard, 347
Dodgson, Stephen, 95
Doewling, Wolfgang, 297
Doherty, Harry, 221
Dolejsi, Robert, 30
Dominant, 230
Dompierre, François, 77
Don Giovanni, 8
Donaldson, William H., 51–52
Donastia, José A. de, 36
Donaueschingen Chamber Music Festival, 12, 455
Donemus, Stichting, 213
Donemus Foundation, 211–12
Donemus Muzieknotities, 212–13
Donnington, Robert, 144
Dorfman, Saul, 344
Doris, Hubert, 343–44
Dorr, Harry, 444
Dougherty, Philip H., 381
Dow, Paul, 418
Dowling, W. Jay, 468
down beat, 116–19, 179
Downes, Edward, 465
Drei Masken Verlag, 438
Drew, David, 364, 430
Drew, Lucas, 175–76
Driscoll, Anne, 168
Druesedow, John E., 38, 170, 295, 366, 368, 462
Dubler, Gary D., 199
Duckles, Vincent, 156
Ducrot, Ariane, 358
Duerksen, George L., 205

Dufay, Guillaume, 164, 385
Dufourcq, Norbert, 357–58, 360
Dukas, Paul, 373
Dümling, Albrecht, 454
Dunham, Benjamin S., 423–25
Dunsby, Jonathan, 464
Dunson, Josh, 399–400
DuParcq, Jean Jacques, 376
DuParcq, Richard, 376
Durn, Sebastian, 37
Dürr, Alfred, 15, 293
Dutch Swing College, 182
Dwight, John Sullivan, 119–20
Dwight's Journal of Music, xii, 119–21
Dykema, Peter W., 250–53
Dziebowski, Elzbieta, 303

Eagle, Charles T., 199
Earle, Eugene, 185–86
Early Music, xiv, 15, 123–25
Eastman, Eddie, 77
Eastman, L. V., 152–53
Eaton, Quaintance, 332
Edelstein, Andrew J., 381
Eder, Terry, 85
Editions de la Nouvelle revue française, 376
Editions Richard-Masse, 376
Editore, Guido Einaude, 355
Edizione della Bussola, 356
Edizione RAI Radiotelevisione Italiana, 324–25
Educational Press Association of America, 167
Edwards, Frederick George, 281
Edwards, John, 184, 191
Ege, Ernot, 311
Eggebrecht, Hans Heinrich, 42–43, 293
Ehinger, Hans, 10
Ehmann, Wilhelm, 292–93
Ehrenkreutz, Stefan, 303, 387, 455, 464
Eidgenössischen Sängerverein, 392
Eimert, Herbert, 362–64
Einstein, Alfred, 235, 242, 254–55, 320, 415, 456–57
Eisler, Hanns, 291
Eitel, Luise, 3, 34
Eitner, Robert, xiii, 238–41, 439
Elders, Willem, 435–36
Electronic Music Reports, 170
Elgar, Edward, 255, 360–61
Elias, Robert, 19, 21
Elias, William Y., 256
Ellington, Duke, 159
Ellinwood, Leonard, 265

Elliott, Charles A., 470
Ellis, Herb, 153
Ellsworth, Victor, 31, 153, 176, 202, 409
Elsenaar, E., 74
Elwell, Herbert, 343
Emmett, Rik, 152
Emmons, Buddy, 153
Emmrich, Stuart, 381
Engel, Carl, 269, 275, 277
Engel, Hans, 39, 296
Engláder, Richard, 421
Enoch, Yvonne, 87
Enseignement musical, 299
Ensslin, Hermann, 311
Ephland, John, 119
Eppink, Gladys, 23, 246, 267
Epstein, David, 195
Epstein, Dena J., 320
Erb, Donald, 344
Erhardt, Ludwik, 387
Erickson, Raymond, 196
Erkel, Ferenc, 413
Erlebach, Rupert, 384
Ernst, Karl D., 253
Ernst, Roy E., 115
Erskine, John, 331
Erven H. van Munster & Zoon, de, 74
Escot, Pozzi, 431
Escudier, Marie, 150
Espinosa, Guillermo, 169
Esquire, 381
Ethno Musicology, 125–28
Etler, Alvin, 307
Etude, 60, 128–31, 268, 273, 343
Etude and Musical World, 60
Etzkorn, Peter, 128
Euper, Jo Ann, 200
Euterpe, 131
Euterpeiad, The, xii, 131–33
Evans, Edwin, 235
Evans, Peter, 428
Evans, Sarah M., 444–46
Evans Brothers, Ltd., 259
Evans Publications, 444, 446
Evarts, John, 448
Everett, Thomas, 193
Expedition, 398
Eyer, Ronald F., 269, 271

Fabbri, Mario, 82–83, 379
Fabbri, Paolo, 379
Fabian, Imre, 335
Face, 220

Fahey, John, 153
Fallows, David, 385
Farber, Evan Ira, 332
Farlow, Tal, 153
Farrell, Oliver Perry, 407–8
Faubert, Jacques, 77
Fauré, Gabriel, 226
Feather, Leonard, 177
Feature Publishing Co., 105
Federatie van Nederlandsche Toonkunstenaars-
    Vereenigingen, 72, 74
Fédération Internationale des Hot Clubs, 179
Fédération nationale du commerce et de l'in-
    dustrie de la musique, 301
Federhofer, Hellmut, 5
Fédorov, Vladimir, 138, 140, 142
Feintuch, Burt, 55
Feldman, Morton, 401
Felice Le Monnier Editore, 356
Feliciano, Jose, 153
Fellerer, Karl Gustav, 288, 410
Fellinger, Imogen, x, xv, 10, 39, 70, 240,
    243, 289, 311, 394, 397, 416, 441
Fellowship Concerts Services, 284
Feltrinelli (of Milan), 354
Fennell, Frederick, 390
Ferrabosco, Alfonso, 385
Fétis, F. J., xii, 242
Ficker, Rudolf, 415
Fidler, Linda M., 57, 137, 468
Fiedler, Arthur, 407
Figueras, José Romeu, 36
Fillmore, John C., 131
Film Music Notes, 135–37
Fink, Gottfried Wilhelm, 9, 11
Finlay, I. F., 213
Finney, Ross Lee, 340
Finney, Theodore M., 18, 20
Finscher, Ludwig, 296–97, 410
Fioroni, Gian Andrea, 324
Firth, Ian, 144
Fischer, Carl, Sr., 230, 232
Fischer, Kurt, 456
Fischer, Kurt von, 42
Fischer, Paul, 440
Fischer, Pieter, 212
Fisher, Barbara, 259
Fisher, John, 188
Fisk University, 57
Fisk University Institute for Research in Black
    American Music, 55–56
Fleder, Rob, 400

Fleischhauer, Rainer, 363
Fleming, Shirley, 270–71
Fleury, Albert, 70
Flippo, Chester W., 104, 106, 191
Floersheim, Otto, 272–74
Flohil, Richard, 77–78
Flor, Gloria J., 390
Floyd, Carlisle, 465
Floyd, Samuel A., Jr., 55–58
Fluegel, Neal, 339
FM (Special Issue), 159
Fokker, Adriaan D., 363
Folklore and Folk Music Archivist, 191
Folkways Records, 399
Follet, Grace, 16–17
Foltin, Béla, Jr., 414
Fong Chow, 206
Fong-Torres, Ben, 380
Fontes artis musicae, xii, 66, 137–41
Foote, Arthur, 60
Forbes, Elliot, 15
Forchhammer, Sverre, 114
Ford, Peter, 360
Forkel, J. N., xi
Forney, Kristine K., 383
Forster, E. M., 328
Forsythe, Jere, 102
Forte, Allen, 195–96, 198, 254, 259–60, 463
Fortune, Nigel, 144, 246, 384, 385–86
Foss, Lukas, 340, 401
Foster, E. J., 407
Foster, Raymond, 165
Foundation for Documentation of Netherlands
    Music, 211
Foundation for Research in the Afro-American
    Creative Arts, Inc., 58–59
Fowler, Charles, 157–60
Fowler, Charles B., 253
Fox, Charles Warren, 23–24, 319, 322
Fox, Gerald S., 28
Francis, John W. N., 47
François, Jean Charles, 338–39
Frankenstein, Ludwig, 315
Franklin, Aretha, 380
Fratelli Bocca Editori, 325
Fratelli Buratti Editore, 356
Frederik Muller & Co., 435
Fredricks, Jessica, 23, 246, 267
Freedman, Harry, 77
Freund, David, 401
Freund, John C., 268–69, 271, 273
Freundlich, Irwin, 343

Frey, Stephen M., 320
Fricker, Peter Racine, 93
Fricks, David, 380
Friedheim, Philip, 255
Friedman, Stan, 403
Frisch, Walter, 318
Frith, Simon, 105
Fromm, Paul, 339
Fromm Music Foundation, 339
Fry, Christopher, 96
Fry, Stephen M., 466
Fryklund, Daniel, 421
Fuller, David, 359
Fuller-Maitland, J. H., 275
Fulton, Dave, 80
Fürstliche Forschungsinstitut, 40–41
Fürtwängler, Gustav, 374

G. Alsbach & Co., 435
G. Schirmer Inc., 241, 275, 277
*G.W.L. Marshall-Hall: Portrait of a Lost
    Composer, Music Monograph*, 419
Gabrieli, Andrea, 64
Gabrieli, Giovanni, 64
Gaburo, Kenneth, 341
Gahr, Dave, 399
Galilei, Galileo, 81
Gallay, Martin, 119
Gallego, Antonio, 366
Gallico, Claudio, 379
Gallo, Alberto, 379
Galloway, Janet Gilbert, 200
Galloway, Jim, 88
Gallus, Jacob, 415
Galpin, Canon, 143
Galpin, Francis W., 143
Galpin Society, 144–45
Galpin Society Journal, 143–45
Gangware, Edgar B., Jr., 391–92
Garcia, Jerry, 153
Gaston, E. Thayer, 199–200
Gastoué, Amédée, 372
Gatti, Guido Maggiorino, 235, 353–56, 410–
    12
Gauldin, Robert, 162, 164, 260, 431
Gavaldá, Miguel Querol, 36–38
Gazette musicale de Paris, xii
Gazzetta musicale di Milano, xii
Gebhardt, Friedrich, 293
Gebuhr, Ann K., 165
Gedalge, André, 150
Gee, Harry R., 390
Geering, Arnold, 5, 395

Gefors, Hans, 114
Gelatt, Roland, 158–60
Geminiani, Francesco, 82
General Gramophone Publications Ltd., 147
Gentleman's Journal, x
George, Warren E., 190
George V, King, 145
Georgrades, Thrasybulos, 296
Gerigk, Herbert, 13–14, 225, 288–89
Gershwin, George, 269
Gerson-Kiwi, Edith, 4
Gerstner, John, 445
Gerstner Publications, 284
Geschäftsstelle, 289
Gesellschaft für Musikforschung, 238, 295–96
Gesellschaft für Musikgeschichte, 240
Gest, Elizabeth A., 129
Gesualdo, Don Carlo, 164
Getz, Stan, 182
Ghisti, Federico, 379
Giachin, Giulia, 379
Giazotto, Remo, 325, 359, 411
Gibbin, L. D., 258
Gibbons, Billy, 153
Gibson, Gerald, 46, 47
Giesy, Marya H., 30
Gigout, Eugene, 150
Gilbert, Henry F., 236
Gilbert, Janet P., 199–200
Gilbert, John, 146
Gilbert, Richard B., 231–32
Gilles, Frank J., 128
Gillette, D. C., 55
Gillis, Frank, 194
Gilman, Lawrence, 235
Gilmore, Patrick S., 60
Ginsburg, David D., 104–5, 107, 348, 401
Gishford, Anthony, 430
Gleason, Ralph, 380
Gleich, Clemens von, 10, 434
Glinka, Mikhail, 405
Glinski, Mateusz, 302
Glover, Sarah, 278
Glück, August, 394
Gluck, Christoph Willibald, 81
Glyndebourne, 279, 329
Goddet, Laurent, 181
Godowsky, Leopold, 129
Goebbels, Joseph Paul, 38
Goethals, Lucien, 172
Goethe, Johann Wolfgang von, 70

Goeyvaerts, K., 172
Göhler, Albert, 240–41
Gold, Don, 119
Goldbeck, Fred, 328, 373, 375
Goldin, Milton, 16
Goldschmidt, Harry, 50
Gollancz, Victor, 328
Goodman, Benny, 179, 407, 428
Goodrich, A. J., 62
Gordon, Dexter, 88
Gordon, H. S., 259
Gordon and Breach Science Publishers, Ltd., 201–2
Gore, Gary, 191–92
Gorodinskii, Viktor, 404
Gosset, Philip, 108
Gottschalk, Louis, 60
GPI Publications, 153
GQ, 381
Grace, Harvey, 281
Graham, Richard, 200
Grainger, Percy, 275, 360, 419
Gramaphone, The, 145–47
Grand Funk, 106
Grandjany, Marcel, 16
Grappelli, Stephane, 88, 180
Graves, Robert, 43
Gravesaner Blätter, 147–49, 222
Gravesano Experimental Studio, 147
Gray, Michael, 46, 47
Gray, Robert, 64
Graziano, John, 460
Grebe, María Ester, 368
Green, Archie, 185
Green, Barry, 175
Green, Douglas B., 191–92
Green, Marian, 461
Greenberg, Noah, 159
Greer, David, 383, 385
Gregg International Publishers Limited, 156
Greider, William, 380–81
Gribenski, Jean, 373
Griffel, Margaret Ross, 110
Griffel, Michael, 110
Griffin, Marie, 194
Grinberg, M. A., 406
Grosart, Allister, 77–78
Grosheva, E. A., 406
Grossman, Orin, 195
Grout, Donald J., 21, 23–24, 266, 383–84
Grüninger, C., 311
Gubbins, Bill, 107

Guck, Marion, 162–63
Guide musical, Le, 149–52
Guitar Player, 152–53
Güldenstein, G., 393
Gunther, Johann, 288
Günther, Johannes, 289
Gunther, Siegfried, 38, 39
Guregian, Elaine, 168
Gurlitt, Wilibald, 42–43
Gushee, Lawrence, 22, 459
Gutman, A., 438
Gutman, Hanns, 32

Haack, Paul, 115
Haar, James, 24, 172, 378
Haden, Walter Darrell, 45
Haefer, J. Richard, 206
Hafferkamp, Jack, 382
Haggh, Raymond, 260
Hahn, Renaldo, 226
Halévy, Jacques-François Fromenatal, 150
Halfpenny, Eric, 143–45
Hall, David, 47
Hall, Peter, 328
Hambleton, Ronald, 78
Hamburger, Poul, 113
Hamel, Fred, 261, 264
Hamm, Charles, 459–60
Hammond, John, 179
Handel, George Frederick, 129, 262, 419,
    437, 441
Handel Festival, 12
Handschin, Jacques, 266, 395
Hansen, Ivan, 114, 323, 448
Hanslick, Eduard, 9
Hanson, John R., 430–31
Hanson Books Ltd., 248–49
Hänssler-Verlag, 266–67
Hantz, Edwin, 161–63
Hardie, Graham, 286
Hardie, Jane Morlet, 234, 285, 286, 420
Harewood, Earl of, 327–28, 330
Harmonicon, The, xii, 155–57
Harp News, 16
Harris, Ernest E., 190
Harris, Roy, 169
Harrison, Jay S., 271
Harrison, Lou, 235
Harrison, Marie L., 137
Härtel, Gottfried Christoph, 7–9, 11
Hartmann, A. C., 55
Hartmann, Karl, 316

Harvard Musical Association, 119
Harvey, Jonathan, 94, 96
Hase, Oskar von, 10
Haskell, Arnold, 328
Haskins, John C., 131
Hasty, Christopher, 198
Hatch, Christopher, 276–77
Hatch, Martin, 45
Hatch Music, 281, 284
Hatten, Robert S., 164
Hauptfuerer, George, 90
Hauptmann, Moritz, 11, 397
Hausmusik, 263
Hausswald, Günter, 264
Hawkins, Coleman, 179
Hawkins, John, 132
Haydn, Joseph, 8–9, 164, 255, 262, 413,
    436–37
Haynes, Stanley, 171
Hays, Lee, 398
Haywood, Charles, 451
Headlam, Dave, 163
Headley Brothers, 125
Hearst, Patty, 380
Heaton, Charles Huddleston, 125
Hebb, Furman, 407–8
Hedden, Steven, 115
Hedger, Eric, 124
Heerup, Gunnar, 114
Heifetz, Jascha, 407
Heije, Jan Pieter, 433
Heinemann, Rudolf, 448
Heinrich, Anthony Philip, 131
Heinz, Rudolf, 454
Helander, Brock, 382
Helen Dwight Reed Educational Foundation,
    29
Helm, Everett, 271
Helm, Sanford M., 305, 307
Henahan, Donal, 94
Henderson, Charles N., 25, 27
Henderson, Glad, 284
Henderson, Hubert H., 190
Henderson Publications, 284
Henke, James, 221
Hennegan, James F., 51–52, 55
Hennenberg, Carl Fredrik, 421–22
Hennessey, Mike, 182, 184
Henninger, Ernst, 14
Henry, Pierre, 374
Henry Ford Museum, 45
Henschel-Verlag, 290, 292
Hentoff, Nat, 180

Henze, Hans Werner, 148, 323, 329
Herbert, Victor, 272–73
Herlinger, Jan, 93
Hernández, Lothar Siemens, 365–66
Hernández, Luis, 365
Herztka, Emil, 31
Hesbacher, Peter, 346
Hess, Jacques B., 181
Hess, Willy, 38, 395
Het Muziekcollege, 72
Het Spectrum, 229
Hettrick, William E., 206–7
Hetzel, William E., 129
Heugel, Henri Georges, 227
Heugel, Jacques-Léopold, 225–27
Heugel, Jacques Paul, 227
Heugel & Cie, 227, 372
Heuss, A., 315
Hewitt, James, 131
HiFi & Music Review, 406
Hi-Fi Music at Home, 158
HiFi/Stereo Review, 406
Higbee, Dale, 125
Higgins, Dick, 402
Higgins, Jon, 43
Higgs, James, 384
High-Fidelity, 157–60, 270
Hilbert, Lloyd, 4
Hill, George R., 320
Hill, John W., 24
Hill, Richard S., 39, 319, 322
Hille, Waldemar, 399–400
Hiller, Ferdinand, 288
Hiller, J. A., xi
Hiller, Lejaren, 96, 196, 401
Hillis, Margaret, 14
Hindemith, Paul, 112, 222
Hines, Earl, 407
Hinson, Maurice, 344
Hinton, James, 158, 328
Hirschberg, Walther, 398
*Historisch-kritische Beyträge zur Aufnahme
    der Musik*, xi
Hitchcock, H. Wiley, 359, 459
Hitler, Adolf, 32, 38
Hobson, Wilder, 179
Hodeir, André, 180–81
Hoernlé, Winifred, 5
Hoffding, Finn, 113
Hoffman, Frank W., 80, 222, 382
Hoffmann, E.T.A., 8
Hoffmann, Mark, 70

Hoffmeister, F., 438
Holdship, Bill, 107
Holdship, J. K., 107
Holdsworth, Sam, 55
Holiday, Billy, 179
Holle, Hugo, 311
Holmboe, Vagn, 113
Holmes, Edward, 279–80
Holoman, D. Kern, 23, 316, 318
Holten, Bo, 114
Honegger, Arthur, 373
Hooper, Maureen D., 252
Hoover, Cynthia, 459
Hope-Johnstone, John, 145
Hopkins, G. W., 428
Horecky, Paul, 405
Horizons de France, 298, 301
Hornbostel, Erich M. von, 296, 367
Horne, Marilyn, 465
Horowitz, Linda, 14
Horton, Charles T., 163
Hortschansky, Klaus, 246
Hösch, Wolfgang, 293
Hosokawa, Shuhei, 173
Hot Club de France, 181
Hough, Philip, 431
Houghton, Osgood, 121
Howat, Roy
Howe, Nelson, 402
Howell, Peter, 350
Howes, Frank, 246
Hoyt, Reed, 164
Hubbard, Frank, 144
Hubler, Lyn, 36, 181, 360, 376
Hudson, George Wulme, 409
Huene, Friedrich von, 206
Huetteman, Albert, 20
Hug, Gebrüder, 394
Hughes, David G., 23–24
Hugoboom, R. Wayne, 83, 85
Huizenga, Ann Huisman, 309
Hull, A. Eaglefield, 243
Hull, Robin, 281
Hullah, John, 278
Huneker, James Gibbons, 272
Hunt, Paul B., 63, 65, 178, 307, 339, 446
Husmann, Heinrich, 35, 410
Husson, Raoul, 309
Hutton, Jack, 222
Huxley, Aldous, 361
Hyde, Martha MacLean, 196, 198

Ibert, Jacques, 226
Il Pianoforte, 353, 356

Illinois Music Education Association, 100
Imberts, Hugues, 150, 152
Imperial Printing Company, 461
In Theory Only, 161–63, 431
Indian Musicological Society (IMS), 207–8, 210
Indiana Theory Review, 161, 163–65, 431
Indiana University, 163–65
Inglefield, Ruth K., 17, 145, 174, 188, 207, 277, 469
Inglis, Anne, 408–9
Ingo Titze, 309
Institut de recherche et de coordination acoustique musique (IRCAM), 95
Institute for Studies in American Music, 459
Institute of Jazz Studies, 193–95
Institute of Renaissance and Baroque Music, 264, 267
Institute of Social and Economic Research (Rhodes University), 6, 7
Institute of Sonology, 171
Institutes for the Contemporary Music Project for Creativity in Music Education (CMP), 91
Instituto Español de Musicología, 36–37
Instrumentalist, 85, 166–68
Instrumentalist Publishing Co., 85, 87, 168
Instytut Sztuki Polskiej Akademii Nauk, 303
Inter-American Music Review, 168–70
Interface: Journal of New Music Research, xiv, 170–72
International Association of Music Libraries, Archives, and Documentation Centres (IAML), 65–67, 137–39, 466
International Association of Sound Archives (IASA), 139
International Committee for Aesthetic Studies, 172
International Conference on Music Electronics and Acoustics, 147
International Folk Music Council (IFMC), 412, 449–51
International Folk Music Council Journal, 449
International Institute for Comparative Music Studies and Documentation (IICMSD), 447–48
International Library of African Music (ILAM), 5, 7
International Music Council, 448
International Music Council of UNESCO, 138, 147
International Music Society (IMS), xii, 240, 370, 382

International Musicological Society (IMS), 3–4, 138, 233, 466
International Musikgesellschaft, 3
International Review of the Aesthetics and Sociology of Music, 172–74
International Society of Bassists Journal, 174–76
Internationale Arbeitskreis für Musik, 263
Inter-Orchestra Bulletin, 423
Iowa State University Press, 190
IPC Specialist and Professional Press Ltd., 221
Isaac, Heinrich, 239
Isamitt, Carlos, 367
ISCM, 112, 171
Isler, Ernst, 394
Issacson, Eric J., 165
Istel, Edgar, 275
Ives, Charles, 164, 201, 235, 251, 254
Ivey, William J., 192

Jaakobs, Ned, 284
Jaarboek, 170
Jackendoff, Ray, 196
Jackson, Milt, 88
Jackson, Paul T., 46–47
Jacobi, Frederick, 235
Jacobi, Peter, 274
Jacobson, Robert, 331–33
Jacques, Edgar F., 281
Jacques-Dalcroze, Emile, 282
Jahn, Otto, 9
Jahrbücher für musikalische Wissenschaft, xiii, 70, 439
Jam, The, 220
James, Christopher, 249, 408–9
James, Richard S., xv, 77, 152, 238, 249, 364, 460
Jamet, Pierre, 17
Janssen, Jorn, 363
Jarreau, Al, 380
Jazz & Blues, 183
Jazz & Blues Centre, 89
Jazz Educators Journal, 177–78
Jazz-Hot, 179–81
Jazz Journal International, 181–84
Jazzforschung, 180
Jeanson, Gunnar, 422
Jellison, Judith A., 199
JEMF Newsletter, 185
JEMF Quarterly, 184–86
Jenkins, Newell, 82
Jennings, Waylon, 191
Jensen, Vagn, 114

Jeppesen, Knud, 3, 5, 113
Jeske, Lee, 80
Joachim, Heinz, 316
John Edwards Memorial Forum, 186
John Edwards Memorial Foundation, 184–86
Johnson, Anna, 422
Johnson, H. Earle, 131
Johnson, Theodate, 269
Johnston, Ben, 401
Jonas, Oswald, 260
Jones, Allan, 222
Jones, Kelsey, 77
Jones, L. JaFran, 7, 45, 128, 210, 448, 451
Jones, Malcolm, 66–67
Jones, S. Turner, 20
Jones, William M., 252
Jorgenson, Dale, 10
Joseph, Don Verne, 390
Journal of Aesthetics and Art Criticism, 187–88, 261
Journal of Band Research, 189–90
Journal of Country Music, 190–92
Journal of Educational Research, 203
Journal of Jazz Studies, 88, 193–95
Journal of Music Theory, xvi, 15, 161, 195–98, 340
Journal of Music Therapy, 198–200
Journal of Musicological Research, 200–202
Journal of Musicology, xiv
Journal of Popular Culture, 346
Journal of Renaissance and Baroque Music, 265
Journal of Research in Music Education, 100–101, 203–5, 349–50
Journal of the American Musical Instrument Society, 144, 206–7
Journal of the American Musicological Society, xiv, 21–24, 259, 365, 377
Journal of the Indian Musicological Society, 207–10
Journal of the International Folk Music Council, xii
Journal of the Royal Musical Association, 383
Journal of the Royal Society of Arts, 94
Jullien, Adolphe, 150
Jurres, André, 139, 141, 211–12
Just, Martin, 297

Kabalevsky, D. B., 406
Kade, Otto, 238
Kaeppler, Adrienne, 128
Kagel, Mauricio, 171, 362–63
Kahn, Ed, 186

Kahnt, C. F., 315
Kaiser, Henry, 153
Kalib, Sylvan S., 438
Kalil, Willi, 288
Kamien, Roger, 431
Kantionalgesangverein, Bern, 392
Kantorski, Vincent J., 102, 168, 190, 205, 253, 470
Kaplan, Joel H., 468
Karkoschka, Erhard, 363–64
Karpeles, Maud, 449, 451
Karr, Gary, 175
Kartomi, Margaret, 286
Kasander, John, 228–29
Käser, Theodor, 359
Kaske, Stephan, 96
Kassler, Jamie C., 286
Kassler, Michael, 284
Kastner, Macario Santiago, 169, 364
Kastner, Santiago, 36
Katz, Bill, 87, 329, 332, 345
Katz, Israel J., 128, 451
Katz, Linda Sternberg, 87, 329, 332, 345
Kaufmann, Henry W., 93
Kaye, Carol, 153
Keiser, Reinhard, 440
Keldysh, Yu. V., 405–6
Keller, Hans, 246, 254, 328, 428–29, 463
Keller, Michael, 159
Kelly, Thomas Forrest, 206–7
Kelterborn, Rudolf, 394
Kemink & Zoon, 71, 74
Kemp, Anthony, 349
Kempers, K. Ph. Bernet, 75
Kempf, Paul, 284
Kendall, Gary, 96
Kennell, Richard, 100, 116, 259, 392
Kenney, Sylvia W., 35
Kenton, Egon F., 64
Kenyon, Nicholas, 123–25
Kerman, Joseph, 23, 158, 316–18, 342
Kerr, Russell, 272
Kersten, F., 201
Kessel, Barney, 153
Key Notes, xiv, 211–13
Keyes, Saundra, 191
Khachaturian, Aram, 405
Khubov, G. N., 406
Kienzle, Rich, 191
Kimball, Horace E., 62
King, Alec Hyatt, 240, 254, 279–80, 385
King, B. B., 153

King Crimson, 220
Kingsbury, Paul, 192
Kinkeldey, Otto, 22–24, 275, 320
Kinsky, George, 315
Kipke, Carl, 315
Kirby, F. E., 344
Kirchenchor, Der, 294
Kirnberger, Johann Philipp, 260
Kirstein, Lincoln, 328
Kist, F. C., 71, 74
Kjellberg, Erik, 422
Kliewer, Vernon L., 163
Klotz, Hans, 292
Knapp, David, 87, 310, 330, 333, 335, 346
Kneif, Tibor, 359, 453
Knepler, George, 49–51
Knobler, Peter, 103, 105
Knorr, Julius, xi, 312
Knowles, Rosalind, 16
Knuf, Frits, 228–29
Koch, H. C., 460
Koczirz, Adolf, 415
Kodály, Zoltán, 14, 199, 374, 412–14, 429,
    449
Koechlin, Phillipe, 181
Koehler, K. F., 241
Koenig, Gottfried Michael, 96, 172, 363
Koenig, Ruth, 363
Köhler, Christian Louis Heinrich, 397
Kolben, Robert, 148
Kolinski, Mieczyslaw, 109
Koller, Oswald, 440
Kolodin, Irving, 332
Komma, Karl Michael, 453, 455
Koprowski, Richard, 110
Korea, 43
Korev, Yu. S., 406
Korngold, Erich, 136
Korolosh, John, 107
Kosovsky, Robert, 431
Kossak, Ernst, 397
Kotschenreuther, Hellmut, 363
Koval, M. V., 406
Kowall, Bonnie C., 253
Kraehenbuehl, David, 198
Kramer, A. Walter, 269, 271
Kramer, Barry, 105–6
Kramer, Connie, 106
Kramer, Jonathan, 260
Kratus, John K., 21, 93, 100, 284, 351, 465
Kraus, Egon, 372, 448
Kreader, Barbara, 87

Krellmann, Hanspeter, 264
Krenek, Ernst, 32, 187, 262, 269, 340, 362,
    373
Kretschmar, Hermann, 240, 440–41, 455
Krohn, Ernst, 455
Krummel, Donald W., 321
Krupa, Gene, 88
Kubelik, Rafael, 247
Kubik, Gail, 136
Kufferath, Maurice, 150, 152
Kühn, Clemens, 264
Kühn, Oswald, 311
Kuhn, Terry Lee, 99–100
Kuhnau, Johann, 164
Kunst, Jaap, 229, 449
Kunst, Jos, 172
Kuzmich, John, Jr., 168, 177–78
Kuzmich, Roslyn, 177–78
Kwabena Nketia, J. H., 58
Kwartalnik, Muzyczny, 303

L. A. Free Press, 347
L. E. Bosch en Zoon, 71–72
La Laurencie, Lionel de, 226, 370–73
Lachenmann, Helmut, 453
Ladies Gazette, 131
Lagas, Rudolf, 434, 436
Lagrange, Jacques, 301
Lake, William, 163
Lamb, Norma Jean, 320
Lambert, Charles, 115, 338–39
Land, J.P.N., 433
Landau, Jon, 103, 380
Landon, H. C. Robbins, 159, 255
Landowska, Wanda, 374
Landré, Willem, 72, 74
Landrieu, Walter, 172
Lang, Paul Henry, 15, 26, 159, 235, 269,
    276–77, 279, 331
Lange, Art, 119
Lange, Francisco Curt, 169
Lanza, Andrea, 379
Larsen, Jens Peter, 15, 113
Larson, André P., 206
LaRue, Jan, 65, 242, 254, 377
Laske, Otto E., 96, 171–72
Laskowski, Larry, 431–32
Lassus, Roland de, 288
Laszlo, E., 200–202
Latham, Alison, 279
Laufer, Edward, 260
Laux, Karl, 292
Lavendar, E. W., 408–9

Lavendar, Harry, 408–9
Lawrence, Arthur, 27
Lawrence, Carol, 159–60
Lawrence, Van, 309
Le Hurray, Peter, 385
Le Kime, Nelson, 152
League of Composers, Inc., 238
League of Composers Review, 235
Lebeau, Elizabeth, 373
Lebow, Marcia Wilson, 121
Led Zeppelin, 220
Lederman, Minna, 235–38
Ledsham, Ian, 66–67
Lee, David, 88
Lee, Mary Vivian, 343, 346
Lee, Peter, 217
Lees, Gene, 119
Lehman, Paul R., 115
Lehmann, Lilli, 287
Lehrsten, Paul, 13
Leichtentritt, Hugo, 12, 187, 275
Leinsdorf, Erich, 339
Leipmannssohn, 241
Leipzig Gewandhaus, 9
Leipzig Hochschule für Musik, 9
Leipziger allgemeine musikalische Zeitung, 9
Leman, Marc, 172
Lenaerts, René, 369, 70
Lendvai, Erwin, 463
Leng, Alfonso, 367
Lenk, Wolfgang, 315
Lentz, Daniel, 402
Lerdahl, Fred, 196
Les grandes heures de l'orgue, 357
Lessmann, Otto, 14
Lester, Joel, 162
Lester, Julius, 399–400
Lesure, François, 34, 36, 138, 172, 373
Letelier, Alfonso, 366, 368
Leux-Henschen, Irmgard, 421
Levende Musik, 112
Levin, Floyd, 182
Levine, Henry, 182
Levine, James, 465
Levy, Kenneth, 34
Levy, Morten, 113
Lewin, David, 162, 196, 340, 431
Lewin, Harold F., 431
Lewis, George, 88
Lewis, George H., 346–47
Lewis, Jerry Lee, 191
Lhevinne, Rosina, 344

Lichtenstein, Sabine, 229
Lichtenwanger, William, 321–22
Lichtman, Irv, 80
Lieberman, Ernie, 400
Lieberman, Fredric, 43, 128
Liebermann, Rolf, 328
Liebling, Leonard, 272, 274
Liebner, János, 393
Ligeti, György, 164, 171, 362
Liivoja-Lorius, Jaak, 408–9
Lincoln Center, 45
Lind, Jenny, 420
Lindahl, Charles E., 76, 125, 270, 319, 416, 432
Lindenburg, Cornelis, 434
Lipphardt, Walter, 293
Lippman, Edward A., 172
Lipschultz, Albert, 119
Lipsius, Marie, 310
Lispet, J. J., 74
Lissa, Zofia, 172
List, George, 367, 462
Listener's Record Guide, 27, 29
Liszt, Franz, 11, 120, 129, 162, 164, 313, 373, 374–75, 395, 413
Little Review, 235
Littlefield, George, 391–92
Littleford, Roger S., 54–55
Littleton, Henry, 279
Living Blues, 215–17
Living Bluesletter, 216
Livingstone, William, 406–8
Llorens, José M., 38
Lloyd, A. L., 399
Lobe, J. C., 9, 11
Lobo, Antsher, 208
Lochhead, Judy, 164
Lockspieser, Edward, 247
Lockwood, Anna, 401–2
Lockwood, Howard, 271
Lockwood, Lewis, 24, 410
Loder, Kurt, 380
Loeffler, Peter, 468
Loewe, Carl, 254
Lohner, Henning, 96
Loman, A. D., Jr., 74
Loman, J. C., 435
Lomax, Alan, 399
London Times, 254
Long, Martin, 286
Longacre Press Ltd., 221
Longsworth, Carol, 14

Lönn, Anders, 422
Lorenz, Alfred, 456
Louis XIV, King, 357–58
Love, Barbara, 382
Lovy, Jules, 225–27
Lowenfels, Walter, 399
Lowens, Irving, 458
Lowinski, Edward, 266–67, 410
Loy, D. Gareth, 96
Lualdi, Adriano, 354
Lucca, Giovanni, 324
Luchini, Paolo, 460
Lucia, Paco de, 153
Lucier, Alvin, 171, 401–3
Luckhardt, 13
Lully, Jean Baptiste, 373
Lunetta, Stanley, 402–3
Lunn, Henry C., 281, 384
Luter, Claude, 179–80
Lutoslawski, Witold, 302
Luython, Karel, 434
Lyke, James, 87
Lyon, Raymond, 375
Lyons, James, 28–29

Maas, Martha, 144, 207
Maatschappij tot Bevordering der Toonkunst, 433
Mabee, Grace Widney, 135, 137
McAdro, Maise, 401
McAlinden, Paul, 124
McAllester, David P., 128
McAllister, Forrest, 391–92
McAllisters, A. R., 390–91
McClain, Jeoraldean, 187
McClellan, William, 322
McClure, A. R., 143
McClure, John, 402
McCorkle, Donald M., 90, 93
McCoy, Guy, 131
McCray, James, 14, 85
McCredie, Andrew, 233–34
MacDonald, Calum, 237, 429–30
McDonald, Gerald D., 320
McGahey, Beverly, 87
McGinty, Doris, 58
Machand, Roberte, 358
Machaut, Guillaume de, 123, 164
MacKenzie, Compton, 145–47
Mackerras, Charles, 329
McKinney, Bruce, 431
McKinney, James, 310
McLaughlin, John, 153

McLean, Mervyn, 144
McLeod, Norma, 128, 451
Macmillan, 277
MacMillan, Ernest, 77
McMorrow, K., 76
McMullen, Dianne, 71, 264, 293, 398
McNabb, Michael, 96
McNaught, William, 281
McNaught, William Gray, 281
McNett, Charles, 144
McPhee, Colin, 235
McRae, Barry, 182
Madurell, José, M., 36
Maegaard, Jan, 113
Magyar, Tudományos Akadémia, 412
Maher, John, Jr., 118–19
Maher, John, Sr., 118–19
Maher Publications, 119
Mahler, Gustav, 32, 317
Mahling, Christoph-Hellmut, 172, 296–97
Mahrenholz, Christhard, 292, 294–95
Maier, Guy, 130
Mainka, Jurgen, 50
Mainzer, Joseph, 278
Mainzer's Musical Times and Singing-Class Circular, 278
Maisel, Arthur, 431
Majeski, John F., 269, 271
Malm, K., 420
Malone, Bill C., 191
Manchester, Arthur L., 284
Mann, Alfred, 15–16, 108
Mann, Edith White, 14
Mann, William, 328
Manson, Charles, 380
Man-Young, Hahn, 451
Marco, Guy, 254–55
Marconi, Joseph V., 329
Marcozzi, Rudy T., 164–65
Marcus, Greil, 105, 191, 380
Marcus, Leonard, 159–60
Marek, George, 332, 465
Mark, Michael, 115
Markowski, Liesel, 292
Marpurg, F. W., xi
Marsh, Dave, 105, 380
Marsh, Warne, 88
Martin, Henry J., 161–63
Martino, Donald, 196, 340
Martinotti, Sergio, 82
Mason, Colin, 428, 430
Mason, James A., 168

Massachusetts Institute of Technology (MIT), 95
Masse, Richard, 374
Massenet, Jules, 226
Masson, Paul-Marie, 371–72
Mast, Paul B., 163, 165, 198, 261, 342, 432, 438
Mathews, Max, 96–97
Mathews, W.S.B., 120, 131
Mathez, Jean-Pierre, 62–63
Matos, M. García, 36
Mattern, Rhoda, 400
Mattheson, Johann, x
Matthew-Walker, Robert, 248–49
Maultsby, Portia K., 128
Maurois, Andre, 331
Maximilian II, Emperor, 416
Maxton, Willy, 292
Mayer, Martin, 331
Meckna, Michael, 237
Mededelingenblad, 434–36
Medici, Mario, 379
Medoff, David, 459
Mehta, Amit R., 207
Mehta, R. C., 207–10
Meissonier, Jean-Antoine, 225
Mekkawi, Carol Laurence, 270
Mellers, Wilfrid, 237
Melody Maker, 219–22
Melos, xiv, 31, 148, 222–25, 314, 324
Melos/NZ, 223–24
Melos/NZ-Neue Zeitschrift für Musik, 314
Meltzer, Richard, 103, 105
Mencken, H. L., 235
Mendelssohn, Felix, 288, 312, 344, 436
Mendelssohn Scholarship Foundation, 94
Ménestrel, Le, xi, xii, 225–27
Menn, Don, 153
Menon, Narayana, 447
Menotti, Gian-Carlo, 323
Mens en melodie, xiv
Mensch en Melodie, 227–29
Menuhin, Yehudi, 390
Mercer, Mable, 407
Mercure galant, x
Merino, Luis, 368
Merkling, Frank, 331–33
Merriam, Alan P., 108, 126, 128
Mersmann, Hans, 222, 224–25, 354
Merz, Karl, 61–62
Meske, Eunice Boardman, 115
Messiaen, Olivier, 92, 164, 293

Messina, Anthony, 31
Messing, J. Scott, 370, 373
Metronome, 229–32
Metronome Band Monthly, 230
Metronome Corporation, 231–32
Metronome Orchestra Monthly, 230
Metronome Yearbook, 231
Metronome-Music U.S.A., 231
Metropolitan Opera Association, 330
Metropolitan Opera Guild, 330, 333
Metzger, Heinz-Klaus, 363
Meyer, Christian, 373
Meyer, Ernst Hermann, 290, 292
Meyerbeer, Giacomo, 254, 312
Meyer-Eppler, Werner, 362–63
Michaels, Arthur J., 253
Michalowski, Kornel, 303, 387
Michelangelo, 81
Michell, Joyce, 187
Michigan Music Theory Society, 161
Mickman, Herb, 152
Mikkawi, Carol Lawrence, 159
Milhaud, Darius, 148, 164, 226, 235
Miller, D. Antoinette Handy, 58
Miller, Phillip L., 29
Miller, Richard, 309–10
Milligan, Samuel, 16–17
Milligan, Stuart, 26
Milnes, Rodney, 330
Minerviad, 131
Minkoff Reprints, 226
Minsky, Marvin, 96
Miscellanea Musicologica, 232–34, 285, 417
MIT Press, 97–98
Mitchell, Donald, 328, 430
Mitchell, William, 90
Mitchell, William J., 197, 343
Mitropoulos, Dimitri, 158
Mitteilungen der Internationalen Gesellschaft für Musikwissenschaft, 3–4
Mixter, Keith, 265
Mizler, Lorenz, x
Moberg, Carl-Allen, 420–22
Modern Music Masters, 391
Modern Music, xiv, 230, 231, 234–38
Moes, E. W., 436
Moldenhauer, Hans, 213
Mompellio, Federico, 379
Mompou, Federico, 343
Monatschefte für Musikgeschichte, xiii, 238–41, 439
Monde de la musique, Le, 448
Monk, Christopher, 124

Monro, Harold, 244
Monson, Dale E., 110, 356, 379
Montagu, Jeremy, 144
Monte, Philippe de, 239
Monteverdi, Claudio, 324, 361, 440–41
Monteverdi Convention, 377–78
Monthly Musical Record, 241–43
Monthly Supplement to the Musical Library, 155
Montparker, Carol, 87
Montu-Berthon, Suzanne, 374–75
Moody Blues, 220
Moog, Robert, 96
Moon, Geoffrey, 234
Mooney, H. F., 346
Moore, F. Richard, 96
Moore, Gerald, 129
Moore, James L., 337, 339
Moore, Thomas, 131
Moorer, James A., 96–97
Morales, Cristóbal de, 36–37, 365
Moran, Robert, 162, 401, 431
Morawetz, Oskar, 77
Morche, Gunther, 359
Morelli, Giovanni, 379
Morgenstern, Dan, 119, 232
Morrill, Dexter, 96–97
Morris, William, 318
Morrison, Margery, 137
Morrow, Mary Sue, 40, 51, 442
Mortheiru, Pedro, 368
Morton, Ferd "Jelly Roll," 459
Morton, Lawrence, 136
Moser, Hans J., 289, 292
Mosgrove, Barbara, 423, 425
Moss, Mark D., 401
Mott, Margaret M., 320
Motte, Diether de la, 262
Motycka, A., 200, 202
Mowe, Howard G., 310
Mozart, Wolfgang Amadeus, 8–9, 38, 69, 158–59, 161, 164, 174, 197, 226, 247, 250, 344, 436–37
Muck, Karl, 46
Mueller, Joseph, 11
Mueller-Blattau, Joseph, 10
Mueren, Floris Vander, 370
Muller, Jean-Pierre, 369
Müller, Johannes, 435
Mulligan, Gerry, 182
Munksgaard, Ejnar, 5
Munksgaard, Levin, 5

Munro, Thomas, 188
Music Analysis, 196, 261
Music and Letters, xiii, 244–46
Music and Man, 200–201
Music and Musicians, xiv, 247–49
Music City News, 191
Music Education Research Council, 203
Music Educators Journal, 19, 203, 249–53, 258
Music Educators National Conference (MENC), 18–19, 30, 83, 99–100, 203, 205, 249–53, 305
Music Industry Council, 30
Music Information Centers, 139
Music Library Association, 138, 319, 322
Music Lover's Guide, 27
Music Magazine, 248
Music Perception, 350
Music Periodicals Corporation, 272
Music Publications, Ltd., 271
Music Review, The, xiii, 253–56
Music Student, 257
Music Supervisors' Bulletin, 250, 252
Music Supervisors' Journal, 250
Music Supervisors National Conference, 249, 253
Music Teacher, The, 257–59
Music Teacher and Piano Student, The, 257
Music Teacher's Association (MTA), 112, 257
Music Teachers National Association (MTNA), 18, 20, 30, 282
Music Teachers National Association Bulletin, 18
Music: The A.G.O. and R.C.C.O. Magazine, 25
Music Theory Society of New York State, 430, 432
Music Theory Spectrum, 195, 259–61
Music Therapy Annual Books of Proceedings, 198
Musica, 261–64
Musica disciplina, xiv, 264–68, 324
Musica Schallplatte, 263
Musical America, xii, 158–59, 268–71, 366, 368
Musical America Company, 269, 271
Musical and Dramatic Times, 271
Musical and Sewing Machine Gazette, 271
Musical Association, 382
Musical Courier, 130, 268, 271–74
Musical Courier Extra, 272
Musical Criticism, x

Musical Herald, 278
Musical Herald and Tonic Sol-Fa Reporter, 278
Musical Library, 155
Musical Observer, 272, 274
Musical Quarterly, The, xiv, 119–20, 203, 204, 245, 274–77, 324
Musical Review, 132
Musical Times, xi, xii, 94, 277–81
Musical Times and Singing Class Circular, xii
Musical World, xii, 60
Musicalische Patriot, Der, x, xi
MUSICANADA, 76
Musician, The, 281–84
Musicians Benevolent Fund, 94
Musicological Society of Australia, 284–86
Musicology, 232, 284
Musicology Australia, 232–33, 284–86
Musik, Die, xi, 13, 223, 274, 286–90, 302
Musik im Kreige, 13, 223–24, 288, 313
Musik und Gesellschaft, 290–92
Musik und Kirche, 292–95, 324
Musikalische Schrifttum, Des, 294
Musikalisches Wochenblatt, xi
Musikalisches Wochenblatt/Neue Zeitschrift für Musik: Vereinigte musikalischen Wochenschriften, 313
Musikalisch-kritische Bibliothek, xi
Musikblatter des Anbruch, xiv
Musikforschung, Die, xiii, 42, 295–97
Musik—Musik im Kreige, Die, 288–89
Musikstudent, Der, 313
Musikwissenschaftliche Literatur sozialistischer Länder, 50
Musikwissenschaftliches Institut, 415–16
Musik-Zeitung, 223
Musique en jeu, xiv
Musique et instruments, 297–301
Musique et radio, 298–99
Mussorgsky, 164
Mutin, Charles, 370
Muziek, De, 72
Muzikaal Perspectief, 211–13
Muzyka, 301–3
Muzyka (1950–1956), 303
Mycielski, Zygmunt, 387
Myers, Kurtz, 320

N. V. Seyffardt's Boek-en Muziekhandel Orgaan, 74
Nachf, Hermann Bohlaus, 417
NACWPI Bulletin, 305
NACWPI Journal, 305–7

Nagel, Willibald, 311
Nagy, Christine A., 87
Nagy, Kären, 320
NAJE Educator, 178
NAJE Newsletter, 177–78
Nan Silver, 401
Nancarrow, Conlon, 235, 459
Nanry, Charles, 193, 195
National Association of College Wind and Percussion Instructors "Nzck-Wappy" Bulletin, 308
National Association of College Wind and Percussion Instrument Instructors Bulletin, 305
National Association of Jazz Educators, 177–78
National Association of Music Therapy, Inc. 198–200
National Association of Teachers of Singing, 308, 310
National Catholic Bandmaster's Association, 391
National Federation of Music Clubs Motion Picture Music Committee, 135
National Film Music Council, 137
National Flute Association, 444–45
National Music Teacher's Association, 128
National School Band and Orchestra Association (NSBOA), 391
National School Band Association, 391
National Singing-Class Circular, 278
National Socialists, 38, 222–23
NATS Bulletin, The, 308
NATS Journal, The, 308–10
Nattiez, Jean Jacques, 173
Neal, 213
Near East-Turkestan, 43
Nederlandsch Muzikaal Tijdschrift, 71
Nef, Karl, 394
Nef, Walter Robert, 395
Neidig, Kenneth L., 168
Nelson, David, 115–16
Nelson, Paul, 399–400
Nelson, Philip F., 91, 93
Nettl, Bruno, 108, 128, 393, 451, 459
Nettl, Paul, 269, 456
Neue eröffnete musikalische Bibliothek, oder Gründlich Nachricht nebst unpartheyischem Urtheil von musikalischen Schifften und Büchern, x
Neue Leipziger Zeitschrift für Musik, 312
Neue Musik-Zeitung, xi, 310–11
Neue Musikzeitschrift, 263
Neue Schütz-Gesellschaft, 292

Neue schweizerische Musikgesellschaft, 395–96

Neue Zeitschrift für Musik, xi, xv, 8–9, 13, 222, 288, 311–16, 396

Neuendorff and Moll, 224

Neues Musikblatt, 13, 223–24, 288

Neumeyer, David, 164

Nevers, Daniel, 181

New Crawdaddy Ventures, 104

New Grove Dictionary of Music and Musicians, xv

New Musical Express, 220

New York Band Instrument Company, 27

New York Philosophical Library, 187–88

New York Times, 94

Newcomb, Anthony, 24

Newlin, Dika, 344

Newman, Ernest, 242

Newman, William S., 23–24, 109, 343–44, 460

Nicholas, Mary J., 200

Nichols, William, 307

Nickerson, William E., 271–72, 274

Nicolaï, W. F. G., 72, 74

Nielsen, Anne Kristine, 114

Nielsen, Hans Jørgen, 114

Nielsen, Poul, 114

Niemann, Konrad, 51, 291

Niemann, W., 315

Nieuwenhuysen, W. J. F., 74

Niggli, Arnold, 394

Nijhoff, Martinus, 72, 74

Nikolaev, A. A., 406

Nilsson, Bo, 363

19th Century Music, xiv, 316–18

No. 1, 220

Noack, Fritz, 26

Noble, Jeremy, 385–86

Noblitt, Thomas L., 266, 429

Nobre, Marlos, 367

Nolthenius, Hugo, 74

Nono, Luigi, 148

Nordisk Musikkultur, 112

Norgaard, Per, 113

Norlind, Tobias, 422

Norman, Bob, 400

Norris, John, 87–90

North Central Music Educators Conference, 100

Northern California Harpists Association, 16

Northwestern University, 176

Norton, 109, 276

Notes, 21, 66, 138, 254, 319–22

Novello, Joseph Alfred, xii, 279–80

Novello and Co., 94, 183, 278–79, 281, 384, 408–9

Nuova rivista musicale italiana, xii, 322–25

Nzewi, Mezi, 58

O'Connell, Walter, 363

O'Connor, Patrick, 332–33

O'Meara, Eva J., 319, 322

O'Neal, Amy, 216–17

O'Neal, Jim, 216–17

O'Reilly, L., 232

Obetz, John, 26

Obrecht, Jacob, 434

Ochs, Michael, 322

Odhams Press, Ltd., 220–21

Oelrich, Jean, 168

Oesch, Hans, 224–25, 453

Office Général de la Musique, 298, 301

Ohio Music Educators Association, 98–99

Ohlekopf, Richard, 398

Oistrakh, David, 409

Oja, Carol J., 237

Oldani, Robert W., 406

Oldfield, Michael, 221–22

Oldman, C. B., 280

Oliveira, Jocy de, 402

Oliver, Paul, 460

Oliver Ditson Co., 121, 284

Oliveros, Pauline, 401

Olleson, Edward, 246, 385

Olms, Georg, 438

Olschki, Leo S. (Editore), 82, 378–79, 410–11

Olsen, Poul Rovsing, 113

Olson, Gerald B., 114–16

ONCE Group, 401

Onnen, Frank, 375

Ontario Arts Council, 89

Oper, 334

Opera, 327–30

Opera, DSB, 330

Opera News, 330–33

Opernwelt, 333–35

Opus One, 28

Orell Fuessli & Friedrich Verlag, 335

Orff, Carl, 199

Organization of German Music Teachers, 12

Orgue, L', 357

Orgue et liturgie, 357

Ormandy, Eugene, 407

Orme, John, 221

Orpheus Publications, 249, 280, 408–9

Orr, Buxton, 93
Orrego-Salas, Juan A., 366–68, 462
Orselli, Cesare, 83
Ortigue, Joseph d', 226–27
Ortmann, Otto, 275
Orval, Francis, 62
Osburn, Mary Hubbell, 61
Oster, Ernst, 195, 197, 431
Österreichische Musikzeitung, xi
Österreichische Zeitschrift für Musik, 32
Österreichischer Bundersverlag, 417
Osthoff, Helmuth, 295
Ostling, Acton, 190
Ostrow, Marty, 80
Otto Spingel, Hans, 335
Owl, 28
Oxford University Press, 123, 125, 245–46, 384

Paap, Wouter, 227–29
Packer, Dorothy S., 86–87, 461
Padgett, Stephen, 80
Padilla, Juan Gutiérrez de, 169
Page, Hot Lips, 182
Page, Stephen Dowland, 285
Paik, Nam June, 401
Paillard, Jean-Francois, 82
Painter, Linda, 186
Palestrina, Giovanni, 9, 92, 280
Palisca, Claude, 4, 410, 460
Palmer, Don, 401
Palmer, Robert, 94
Panassié, Hughes, 179–81
Pankake, Jon, 399
Pannain, Guido, 354
Panstwowy Instytut Sztuki, 303
Paolucci, Giuseppe, 82
Papers of the AMS, 21
Pareles, Jan, 380
Parente, Alfredo, 354
Parigi, Luigi, 322
Parker, Charlie, 88
Parker, John Rowe, 131–32
Parry, Sir Hubert, 275
Parsons, William C., 320
Partch, Harry, 401
Parthasarthy, T. S., 210
Pass, Joe, 153
Patel, Madhubhai, 208
Pathfinder, 158
Patterson, Daniel W., 45
Paul, Angus, 56
Paul, Les, 153

Pauli, Hansjörg, 454
Paulin, Gaston, 152
Payne, Anthony, 428
Payzant, Geoffrey B., 76
Pearcy, Leonard, 259
Pearlman, Sandy, 103
Peart, Donald, 284, 286
Pedrell, Felipe, 37
Peltz, Mary Ellis, 330–33
Penderecki, Krysztof, 302, 323
Penny, Hank, 191
People's Artists, Inc., 398–400
People's Computer Company, 95, 98
People's Songs Bulletin, 398
Pepping, Ernst, 292
Percussive Arts Society, 337–39
Percussive Notes, 337–39
Pereyra, Marie-Louise, 370
Pergolesi, Giovanni, 81
Perle, George, 340, 363–64, 463
Perles, Moritz, 311
Perlis, Vivian, 459
Perosi, Don Lorenzo, 81
Perry, Richard, 47
Perry, Robin, 424
Perspectives of New Music, xiv, 161, 339–42
Perspectives of New Music, Inc., 342
Pestalozza, Luigi, 354
Pestelli, Giorgio, 355, 379
Peters, David, 115
Petersen, Peter, 375
Petrassi, Goffredo, 81, 324, 355
Petre, Endre, 428
Petrobelli, Pier Luigi, 378–79
Petzet, Walter, 398
Petzold, Robert, 205
Petzoldt, Richard, 14
Peyser, Herbert F., 331
Peyser, Joan, 276–77
Pflugbeil, Hans, 295
Phelps, Roger, 306–7
Phelps, William Lyon, 331
Phi Beta Mu, 391
Phillips, Peter, 124
Phonograph Monthly Review, 27
Phonoprisma, 263
Piaget, Jean, 199
Piano Quarterly, The, 85–86, 342–46
Piano Quarterly, Inc., 345
Piano Quarterly Newsletter, 343
Piano Student, 257
Piano Teacher, 85

Piano Teachers Information Service, 343
Pick Up, 183
Picken, Laurence E. R., 451
Picker, Martin, 24
Piersol, Jon V., 190
Pijper, Willem, 75
Pijzel, E., 436
Pike, Alfred, 187
Pincherle, Marc, 373
Pinnock, W., 156
Pinson, Edwin, 318
Pinza, Enzo, 129
Pinzauti, Leonardo, 325
Pipernos, Franco, 378
Pirotta, Nino, 265, 377–78, 410–12
Pirro, André, 371
Pisk, Paul, 32, 415
Pistone, Danièle, 226
Pitman Periodicals Ltd., 183
Pius X, Pope, 242
Plamenac, Dragan, 34, 266
Plank, Steven, 83, 325
Plant, Sarah, 401
Plantinga, Leon, 315
Platt, Melvin C., 100
Plinen, Bernhard von, 293
Pociej, Bohdan, 386
Pohl, Carl Ferdinand, 242
Pohl, Richard, 397
Poirée, Elie, 370
Polk, Keith, 64
Pollard, Anthony, 146–47
Pollard, Cecil, 145–47
Pollard, Christopher, 147
Polskie Wydawnictwo Muzyczne (PWM), 387
Polyphonie, 374–75
Pont, Graham, 284
Poole, Jane, 333
Popular Music and Society, 346–48
Porter, Andrew, 158, 281, 318, 328
Porter, Lewis, 58
Porterfield, Nolan, 191
Portnoy, Bernard, 445
Potvin, Gilles, 75–77
Pougin, Arthur, 226–27
Poulenc, Frances, 226, 343, 374
Pousseur, Henri, 340, 362
Practica, 263
Prasa—Ksiazka—Ruch, 387
Pratt, Waldo S., 275
Preciado, Dionisio, 365–66
Presser, Theodore, 60, 128–29, 364

Presser Co., 129–131
Prieberg, Fred K., 291
Princeton University Press, 342
Pritchard, John, 329
Probas, 175
Proceedings of the Royal Musical Association, xiii, 382–85
Proceedings of the Musical Association, 382
Proctor, David Paul, 104
Prod'homme, Jacques-Gabriel, 370, 372
Prokofiev, 404, 429
Prota-Giurleo, Ulisse, 378
Prout, Ebenezer, 241–43
Pruett, James W., 4, 322
Prunières, Henry, 373–76
Psychology of Music, 101, 204, 348–51, 468
Psychomusicology, 101, 204
Puccini, Giacomo, 324, 466
Puffett, Derrick, 464
Pugh, Ronnie, 192
Pult und Taktstock, 32
Purcell, Henry, 278, 280
Purdy, Constance, 135, 137
Putnam, Daniel A., 187

Quaderni della Rassegna musicale, xiv, 353–56
Quarterly Musical Magazine and Review, xii
Querol, Miguel, 265
Quintes, Nicolás A. Solar, 36
Quittard, Henri, 370

Rabinowitz, Peter J., 28
Rachmaninoff, Sergei, 429
Radic, Therese, 419
Radio Guide, 146
Radiocom, Inc., 160
Radocy, Rudolf E., 205, 349
Rahn, John, 163, 340, 342
Raim, Ethel, 400
Rainbow, Bernarr, 280
Rameau, Jean Phillipe, 123, 358
Ramin, Günter, 295
Ramsey, Frederic, 399
Randall, Freddy, 182
Randall, J. K., 340
Randel, Don M., 24
Randolph Publishing, Inc., 104
Raney, Carolyn, 93
Rasmussen, Mary, 64–65
Rassegna musicale, La, xii, xiv, 353–56
Rattenbury, Ken, 94
Ratz, Erwin, 463

Ravel, Maurice, 129, 373
Read, Oliver, 407
Reaney, Gilbert, 242, 266, 268
Rebling, Eberhard, 292
Recherches sur la musique française classique, 357–60, 375
Record Guide Productions, 29
Record Research, 88
Recorded Sound, 360–62
Records and Recordings, 248
Records in Review, 158
Redepennig, 398
Redfern, Brian, 139, 141
Reed, Jimmy, 216
Reed, John, 375
Reed, Peter Hugh, 27, 29
Reed-Maxfield, Kathryn, 132
Reese, Gustave, 23–24, 35
Reeser, Eduard, 74, 434–36
Reger, Max, 293, 437
Rehm, Wolfgang, 263–64
Reich, Howard, 56
Reich, Steve, 401
Reich, Willi, 224, 235, 375, 393
Reiche, Jens Peter, 454
Reichert, Georg, 296
Reihe, Die, 362–64
Reimann, Wolfgang, 292, 295
Reinach, Théodore, 372
Reinegger, Keith, 152
Reiner, Fritz, 287
Reinhardt, Django, 180
Reinsdorf, O., 11, 14
Reiser, August, 311
Reisser, Marsha J., 57
Rendall, F. Geoffrey, 143
Renouf, David, 259
Répertoire international de iconographie musicale (RIdIM), 139
Répertoire international de la presse musicale (RIPM), 139, 466
Répertoire international de littérature musicale (RILM), 66, 139, 173
Répertoire international des sources musicales (RISM), 139
Research Chronicle, 383
Reuss, Richard A., 400
Review of Recorded Music, 272
Review of the Aesthetics and Sociology of Music, xii
Revista de musicología, 364–66
Revista musical chilena, 366–68

Revue belge de musicologie, 368–70
Revue d'histoire et de critique musicales, xiii
Revue de musicologie, xiii, 370–73
Revue et gazette musicale de Paris, xii
Revue musicale, La, xii–xiv, 235, 302, 373–76
Reynolds, Michael, 248–49
Reynolds, Roger, 235, 340, 459
Rheinische-Westfälische Musikzeitung, 12
Rhinegold Publishing, Ltd., 259
Rhodes, Willard, 44, 126–27
Rice, Timothy, 128
Rich, Maria F., 332
Richard, Albert, 374–76
Richards, Denby, 248–49
Richter, Clifford G., 27
Ricordi, Giulio, 324
Riegger, Wallingford, 373
Riemann, Hugo, 12, 40, 440, 453
Riesenfeld, Paul, 12
Rieter-Biedermann, J., 11
Riggs, Michael, 160
Righini, Pietro, 323
Riis, Thomas, 59, 121, 186
Riley, John Terrence, 58
Riley, W. J., 55
Ringel, Harvey, 310
Ringer, Alexander L., 451
Risset, Jean-Claude, 96
Ritter, A. G., 238
Ritter, F. L., 120
Rivera, Benito, 260
Rivista de cultùra musicale, 356
Rivista italiana di musicologia, xiv, 376–79
Rivista musicale italiana, xii, xiv, 274
Roads, Curtis, 95–98
Roberts, Don L., 458
Roberts, Howard, 152–53
Robeson, Paul, 399
Robins, Wayne, 107
Rochberg, George, 340
Rochlich, Edmund, 315
Rochlitz, Johann Friedrich, xi, 7–9, 11
Rock music (Special Issue), 159
Rodet, Xavier, 96
Rodgers, Richard, 407
Rodgers and Hammerstein Archives of Recorded Sound, 45
Rogan, Michael, 317
Rogers, Michael R., 164
Rogge, H. C., 436
Rogge, Wolfgang, 376

Rohlfs, Eckart, 70, 264
Rohner, Traugett, 168
Rokseth, Yvonne, 266, 371
Rolland, Paul, 29
Rolland, Romain, 393
Rolling Stone, 103, 105–6, 219, 379–82
Roman, Zoltan, 468
Rooster Blues Record Sales, 216
Rosand, Ellen, 24
Rose, Maribeth, 253
Roseberry, Eric, 428
Rosenfeld, Paul, 235
Rosenthal, Harold, 327–30
Rostirolla, Giancarlo, 325
Roth, Arlen, 152
Rothenbusch, Esther, 256, 461
Rothgeb, John, 195–96, 260, 431
Rothstein, William, 431
Routh, Francis, 93–95
Rowell, Lewis, 260–61
Rowen, Ruth Halle, 108
Royal Canadian College of Organists (RCCO), 25
Royal College of Music, 254
Royal College of Organists, 279
Royal Conservatory (The Hague), 171
Royal Musical Association, 245, 384, 386
Royal Musical Association Research Chronicle, 383, 385–86, 418
Royal Swedish Music Academy, 420
Rozsa, Miklos, 136
Rubenstein, Micah, 164
Rubin, Stephen E., 332
Rubinstein, Reanne, 103, 105
Rubio, Samuel, 365–66
Ruch Muzyczny, 386–87
Rudolf II, Emperor, 239
Rudzinski, Witold, 303
Rufer, Josef, 453
Ruggles, Carl, 164
Rummenhöller, Peter, 453, 455
Runes, Dagobert D., 187–88
Russell, Bill, 88
Rust, Brian, 361
Rutgers University, 193
Rutland, Harold, 281
Rutters, Herman, 74
Ruwet, Nicolas, 363
Ryder, Jeane, 110
Rzewski, Frederic, 401

S.I.M. Revue musicale mensuelle, xiii
Sabbe, Herman, 172

Sabin, Robert, 269, 271
Sachs, Curt, 23–24, 41, 295
Sackville Records, 89
Sadie, Stanley, 247, 279–81, 428
Saenger, Gustav, 232
Saint-Foix, Georges, 372
Saint-Saëns, Camille, 275, 375
Saito, Yuriko, 187
Salaman, Charles K., 384
Salas, Eugenio Pereira, 366, 367
Salem Research (Millbrook), 29
Salvatori, A., 322
Salzedo, Carlos, 17
Salzman, Eric, 237, 276–77
Samaroff, Olga, 275
Samarotto, Frank, 432
Sammelbände der Internationalen Musik-Gesellschaft, xii, 41
Sample, Duane, 100
Samuel, Harold, 322
Sanborn, Pitts, 235
Sand, Robert, 152
Sanders, Paul F., 75
Sangit Kala Vihar (SKV), 207–8
Santa Cruz, Domingo, 169, 367
Santarcangeli, Paolo, 323
Saracini, Count Guido Chigi, 81
Sarnette, Eric, 298–99, 301
Sartori, Claudio, 34
Satie, Erik, 373
Saturday Review, 158
Sauguet, Henri, 374
Scarlatti, Domenico, 437
Schaal, Richard, 70
Schachter, Carl, 195–96, 463
Schaefer, Hansjürgen, 292
Schaeffner, André, 371–73
Schafer, R. Murray, 76
Schaffer, John Wm., 165
Schallplatte und Kirche: Beihefte zu Musik und Kirche, 294
Scheibe, J. A., xi
Schenk, Erich, 414, 416–17
Schenker, Heinrich, 195, 197, 260, 431, 436–38
Scher, Steven, 323
Scherchen, Hermann, 148–49, 222–23, 225
Schering, Arnold, 38, 41, 315
Scheurleer, Daniel François, 434
Schible, Sigfried, 314, 316
Schickele, Peter, 166
Schieber, Ernst, 293

Schiørring, Nils, 114
Schirmer, Rudolph E., 274
Schlacter, Marv, 80
Schlager, Ken, 55
Schmidgall, Gary, 332
Schmieder, Wolfgang, 265
Schmitt-Thomas, Reinhold, 10
Schneider, E. H., 198
Schneider, Estelle, 400
Schneider, Hans, 417
Schneider, Marius, 36
Schneider, Max, 40, 457
Schnittke, Alfred, 404, 429
Schoeck, Othmar, 393, 395
Schoenberg, Arnold, 32, 111–12, 164, 196,
    222, 235, 260, 269, 287, 341, 362–63, 393,
    429, 437, 453–54, 455
Schola Cantorum of New York, 274
Scholastic Publishing, Ltd., 259
Scholes, Percy A., 257–59, 280
Schonberg, Harold C., 129, 332
Schonherr, Max, 416
School and Society, 203
School Music Magazine, 249
School Musician, The, 258, 389–92
School Musician/Director & Teacher, 391
Schott (Brussels), 149, 152
Schott, 222, 224
Schott, B., 224
Schott-Verlag, 71
Schrade, Leo, 34, 38, 266, 268
Schramm, Adelaida Reyes, 451
Schramm, Harold, 43, 344, 346
Schrank, Donald, 78
Schreker, Franz, 32
Schrøder, Jens, 114
Schubert, Franz, xi, 61, 161, 242, 255, 262,
    275, 312, 316, 317, 344, 369, 374–75,
    436–37
Schueller, Herbert M., 187–88
Schuh, Willi, 394, 428
Schuller, Gunther, 194, 340
Schultz, Detlef, 398
Schultze-Ritter, Hans, 222
Schulze-Andresen, Walter, 363
Schumacher, Elly, 14
Schumann, Clara, 397
Schumann, Robert, xi, xv, 9, 120, 150, 262,
    312–15, 436, 460
Schuneman, Georg, 39, 40
Schunke, Ludwig, xi
Schurk, William L., 29, 47, 55, 147, 362,
    408

Schuster, Bernhard, 286–89
Schuster & Löffler, 289
Schutz, Alfred, 201
Schütz, Heinrich, 262, 276, 292–93
Schutz-Gesellschaft, Heinrich, 294
Schwalm, Oskar, 315
Schwartz, Rudolph, 440
Schwarz, Boris, 404–5
Schweizerische Muzikzeitung, 392–94
Schweizerischen Gesang- und Musiklehrerver-
    ein, 392
Schweizerisches Jahrbuch für Musikwissen-
    schaft, 395–96
Schweizerisches Musikpädagogischen Ver-
    band, 393
Schweizerisches Sängerblatt, 392
Schweizerisches Tonkünstlerverein, 392
Schwers, Paul, 12, 273
Schwinger, Wolfram, 264
Scoppa, Bud, 103
Scott, Cyril, 275
Scott, Marion M., 384
Scriabin, Alexander, 317
Sears, M. L., 198
Sears, William W., 198, 200
Seashore, Carl E., 275, 282
Seaton, Douglass, 110
Seay, Albert, 266
Second Viennese School, 42
Seeger, Charles, 23–24, 127, 235
Seeger, Horst, 292
Seeger, Pete, 398
Seger, Bob, 105
Seidel, Wilhelm, 297
Seiffert, Max, 40, 43, 433, 440
Seijff, A.P.F. de, 71, 74
Senauke, Alan, 400
Senff, Bartholf W., 396–98
Senfl, Ludwig, 239
Sengstack, David K., 272
Senior, Evan, 248–49
Sentiment d'un harmoniephile sur differents
    ouvrages de musique, xi
Sergeant, Desmond, 348, 350–51
Serrano, Juan, 153
Sessions, Roger, 164, 429
Seta, Fabrizio Della, 379
Settimana Musicale Senese, 81–82
Severac, Deodat de, 254
Sewrey, J., 338
Shakespeare, William, 159
Shapiro, Julian, 80

Sharp, Geoffrey, 253–54
Shaw, Arnold, 55
Shaw, Greg, 105
Shaw, Oliver, 131
Shaw, Robert, 84
Shaw, Ronnie, 85
Shaw-Taylor, Desmond, 328
Shedlock, John South, 242–43
Sheehan, Vincent, 331
Shepherd, Robert L., 389–92
Sheridan, Chris, 182
Shietroma, Robert, 337, 339
Shircliff, Justine, 431
Shirley, Wayne, 237, 460
Shostakovich, Dimitri, 236, 387, 404
Shrude, Marilyn, 78, 95, 98, 172, 403, 430
Shumann, William, 46
Shuter-Dyson, Rosamund, 349, 351
Siegel, Hedi, 431–32
Seigmund-Schultze, Walter, 290
Signale für die musikalische Welt, 396–98
Silber, Irwin, 399–400
Silkwood, Karen, 380
Sills, Beverly, 407
Silverman, Robert Joseph, 344, 346
Silverstein, Joseph, 166
Silvestri, Renzo, 410
Simms, Bryan, 196, 198, 260–61
Simon, George T., 231–32
Simon, Paul, 315
Simpson Publishing Company, 306
Sing Out, 398–401
Sing Out, Inc., 400
Sing Out Corporation, 400
Siona, 292
Sirota, Warren, 152
Sitwell Sacheverell, 331
Siwe, Thomas, 338
60 Magazine Ltd., 221
Sjoerdsma, Richard Dale, 329
Skaggs, Hazel Ghazarian, 345
Skoog, James, 163
Skrimshire, Nevil, 184
Sleeper, Milton B., 157
Sloan, Irene, 465–66
Sloan, Sherwin, 465–66
Slobin, Mark, 44–45, 459
Sloboda, John, 349–51
Slonimsky, Nicolas, 129, 169, 459
Smash Hits, 220
Smijers, Albert, 415, 434, 436
Smith, Bessie, 179

Smith, Bill, 88–90
Smith, Carleton Sprague, 169
Smith, Catherine P., 445
Smith, Cecil, 269, 271, 328
Smith, Charles J., 162–63
Smith, F. Joseph, 200–202
Smith, G. Jean, 31
Smith, Johnny, 153
Smith, Julius O., 96
Smith, Patrick J., 328–29, 332–33
Smith, Patti, 105
Smith, Stuart, 337, 339
Snarrenberg, Robert, 163
Snell, John, 95–96, 98
Snyder, Ellsworth, 403
Snyder, John L., 164
Snyder, Laura Mattern, 164
Sociedad Española de Musicología, 364, 366
Società Italiana di Musicologia, 377–78
Société Belge de Musicologies, 368, 370
Société de Musique d'Autrefois, 33–36
Société Française de Musicologie, 370, 372
Society for Asian Music, 43–44
Society for Ethnomusicology, 44, 126–28, 445
Society for Music in the Liberal Arts College, 90
Society for Music Theory, 196, 259, 261
Society for Private Performances in Vienna, 111
Society for Research in Psychology of Music and Music Education, 349, 351
Society Newsletter, 21–22
Soler, Antonio, 365
Solomon, Dave, 232
Solow, Linda I., 319
Solti, Georg, 331
Somma, Robert, 103
Sommer, Susan T., 322
Sonneck, Oscar G., 274–75, 277
Sonneck Society, 459–60
Sonorum speculum, xiv, 211–12
Sørensen, Søren, 114
Sounds, 220
Source: Music of the Avant Garde, 401–3
Souster, Tim, 428
Southeast Asia, 43
Southern, Eileen, 57–59, 459
Southern, Joseph, 58
Sovetskaia muzyka, 403–6
Spaeth, Sigmund, 136, 275
Spanke, Hans, 37
Spanuth, August, 398

Spearitt, Gordon, 286
Spectrum, 28
Sperry, Gale, 190
Spies, Claudio, 340
Spitta, Philipp, 9, 40, 440–42
Spivacke, Harold, 23
Spottiswoode & Co., 384
Spottswood, Richard K., 459
Squire, William Barclay, 275
Staatliches Institut für deutsche Musikfor-
   schung, 38
Stackhouse, Houston, 216
Stafford, Peter, 103, 105
Stainer, John, 382
Stambler, Bernard, 108
Stampfel, Peter, 103
Standley, Jayne M., 102
Stanford, Sir Charles Villiers, 275
Starer, Robert, 343
Starks, George, 58
Steege, Jobter, 229
Steel, Matthew, 27, 160, 271, 412, 425
Stefan, Paul, 33
Stefani, G., 377
Steglich, Rudolph, 40
Steiger, Renate, 295
Stein, Erwin, 328, 428
Steiner, Max, 136
Steingräber-Verlag, 315
Steinhardt, Milton, 415
Stenkvist, Lennart, 422
Stephen F. Austin State University, 469
Stereo Review, 158, 219, 314, 406–8
Stern, David, 431
Sternfeld, Frederick W., 136–37, 172, 385
Stevens, Denis, 26, 159
Stevens, Jane R., 198
Stevens, Thomas, 62
Stevenson, Gordon, 46
Stevenson, Robert Murrel, 37, 168–70,
   367
Steward, Jack, 176
Stewart, Madeau, 124–25
Stewart-Baxter, Derrick, 182
Stiftung, Ernst Hohner, 41
Still, William Grant, 130
Stillings, Frank S., 20
Stitt, Margaret McClure, 92
Stochmann, Erich, 451
Stockhausen, Karlheinz, 171, 314, 323, 362–
   64, 401, 453
Stockman, Doris, 50

Stockmann, Bernhard, 289
Stoker, Richard, 95
Stokowski, Olga Samaroff, 331
Stollberg, Oskar, 292, 294
Stolzer, Thomas, 413
Stone, Christopher, 147
Stone, Faith, 145
Stooges, The, 105
Strad, 174, 408–9
Straeten, Edmond Vander, 150
Straight Arrow Publishers, Inc., 382
Strange, Richard, 390
Strangways, A. H. Fox, 244–46
Strauss, Richard, 46, 159, 164, 429
Stravinsky, Igor, 112, 158, 164, 201, 226,
   236, 317, 323, 341, 362–63, 373–74, 428–
   29, 437
Strawn, John, 96–97
Streisand, Barbra, 380
Strobel, Heinrich, 222–25
Strunk, Oliver, 21, 23–24, 34, 410
Stuart, Melanie, 115
Stuckenschmidt, H. H., 32, 222–23, 362
Studi musicali, 410–12
*Studia musicologica academia scientiarum
   hungaricae*, 303, 412–14, 450
Studien zur Musikwissenschaft, 414–17
Studies in Jazz Discography, 193
Studies in Music, 232, 285, 417–20
Stump, Carl, 440
Stumpf, Douglas A., 110
Stunzl, Jürg, 394
Suber, Charles, 118–19
Subirá, José, 36
Suchoff, Benjamin, 428
Süddeutscher Musik-Kurier, 12
Sugarman, Elias E., 55
Sullivan, Arthur, 91
Summy-Birchard, 272, 274
Sumsion, Calvin, 402
Sundström, Einar, 422
Superstar Productions, 104
Supičić, Ivo, 172–74, 393
Supplementary Research Memorandum Series,
   14–15
Surian, Elvidio, 468
Suskin Sylvan, 301
Süssmayer, Franz Xaver, 69, 413
Sutcliffe, Tom, 249
Sutton, Alan, 80
Suzuki, Shinicki, 166
Svensk Tidskrift för Musikforskning, 420–22

Svenska Samfundet för Musikforskning, 420–22

Svoboda, August, 311

Swan, John, 46

Swedish Music Information Center, 420, 422

Sweelinck, Jan Pieterszoon, 433, 440

Swenson, John, 104

Swets Publishing Service, 172

Swift, Frederic Fay, 444–46

Swift, Richard, 31

Swift-Dorr Publications, 444, 446

Syer, Warren, 159

Symons, David, 420

Symphony, 423, 445

Symphony Magazine, 422–25, 445

Symposium on the Ethnomusicology of Cultural Change in Asia, 43

Szabolcsi, Bence, 412–14

Szepesi, Zsuzsanna, 414

Szigeti, Joseph, 428

Szymanowski, Karol, 302

Tageblatt, Berliner, 456

Tagore, Surindro Mohun, 208

Talbot, James, 143

Tank, Ulrich, 297

Tapes in Review, 158

Tapper, Thomas, 284

Tappert, Wilhelm, 11, 14

Tarkelar, 208

Tarr, Edward, 62

Tausig, Carl, 242

Taylor, Bernard Underhill, 309

Taylor, Deems, 269, 271

Taylor, Jack A., 205

Taylor, Raynor, 132

Taylor, Rebecca Grier, 253

Tchaikovsky, Peter Illich, 242, 317

Tedesco, Tommy, 152

Tello, Francisco José Léon, 365

Tempelaars, Stan, 172

Temperley, Nicholas, 21–22, 24, 156, 280, 316

Temple University, 15

Tempo, xiv, 94, 427–30

Tepperman, Barry, 88

Tepping, Susan, 164–65

Terry, R. R., 244

Tessier, André, 372, 373

Thayer, Alexander Wheelock, 120, 275

Theory and Practice, 161, 430–32

Thibault, Genevieve, 34–36, 371

Thierstappen, Hans Joachim, 40

This Little Light of Mine Project, 56

Thomas, A. F. Leighton, 256

Thomas, Ambroise, 226

Thomas, Ernst, 225, 316

Thomas, Kurt, 15, 295

Thomas, T. Donley, 64

Thomas, Theodore, 60

Thompson, Donald, 170

Thompson, Helen M., 423, 425

Thompson, Hunter, 381

Thompson, Oscar, 269, 271

Thompson, Randall, 14

Thoms, Paul E., 390

Thomson, J. T., 359

Thomson, John, 93

Thomson, John M., 123, 125

Thomson, Virgil, 26, 235, 331, 374, 459

Thooft, W. F., 74

Thym, Jurgen, 431

Tibet, 43

Tiersot, Julien, 150, 226, 371–72

Tijdschrift van de Vereniging voor Nederlandse Muziekgeschiedenis, xiii, 433–36

Tijdschrift voor Muziekwetenschap, 434

Tilmouth, Michael, 385–86

Tin Pan Alley, 220

Tiomkin, Dimitri, 136

Tippett, Michael, 94, 429

Tirro, Frank, 22

Titelouze, Jean, 357

Tobin, J. Raymond, 259

Tokumaru, Yoshihiko, 451

Tollefsen, Randall H., 433

Toloza, Dom Leon, 367

Tolson, Margaret, 344

Tomek, Otto, 225

Toncitch, Voya, 37

Tonger, P. J., 311

Tonic Sol-Fa Reporter, 278

Tonietti, Tito, 376

Tonwille, Der, 436–38

Torme, Mel, 390

Torrejón y Velasco, Tomás de, 169

Tosches, Nick, 191, 380

Tovey, Donald, 254

Towe, Teri Noel, 28

Tracey, Andrew, 7

Tracey, Hugh, 5, 7

Tracy, Jack, 119

Trade Publications Corporation, 269, 271

Traill, Sinclair, 181, 183–84

Traum, Happy, 400
Trautwein, T., 241
Travis, Roy, 162
Travis, Stephen, 98
Treitler, Leo, 108
Tretbar, Helen D., 131
Triebels, Hans, 229
Trompeter, Lisa Roma, 274
Troop, H. Judson, 85
Troy State University Press, 190
Truax, Barry, 96
True and Greene, 132
Truscott, Harold, 428
Tudor, David, 401
Tunley, David, 233, 359, 418, 420
Tynan, William, 159–60

Uitgeversmaatschappij Caecilia, 74
Ujfalussy, József, 412, 414
Ulanov, Barry, 232
Ulrich, Homer, 19–21
UNESCO, 173, 448
Unger, Max, 288, 315
Union of Composers of the USSR, 406
Union of Soviet Composers, 403
United Nations Education, Scientific and Cul-
    tural Organization (UNESCO), 451
Universal Edition, 32–33, 222, 364, 437
University of Adelaide, South Australia,
    234
University of British Columbia, 468
University of California at Los Angeles
    (UCLA), 185–86
University of California Press, 318, 465
University of Illinois Press, 459–60
University of Maryland, College Park, 468
University of Michigan School of Music Grad-
    uate Theory Association, 163
University of Missouri Press, 16
University of North Carolina, Chapel Hill,
    186
University of North Carolina Press, 466
University of Reading Conferences on Re-
    search in Music Education, 348
University of South Carolina, 470
University of Texas Press, 462
University of Utrecht, 171
University of Washington Press, 342
University of Western Australia Press, 419
University of Wisconsin, Madison, 116
Unterredungen, Monatliche, x
USSR Ministry of Culture, 406

Valentin, Erich, 315–16
Vallas, Léon, 372
van de Stichting Donemus, Mededelingen,
    211, 213
van den Borren, Charles, 368–69, 374
van der Linden, Albert, 5, 10, 370
van der Pot, C. W., 228
Van Eps, George, 153
van Hasselt, Luc, 229
van Holkema & Warendorf, 74
Van Hoorickx, Reinhard, 369
Van Horn, James, 424
van Milligen, Simon, 74
van Nassouwe, Wilhelmus, 434
Van Sickle, Howard, 31
van Wachten, Ernest, 74
VanCleve, John S., 131
Vander Weg, John D., 162–63
Vanguard, 179
Vanhulst, Henri, 370
Varèse, Edgard, 46, 341, 374
Varney, Mike, 152
Vaughan Williams, Ralph, 247, 328, 449
Vega, Aurelio de la, 367
Vega, Carlos, 367
Vega, Daniel, 365
Veldkamp, K., 75
Velvet Underground, The, 106
Vennard, William, 309
Verband der Komponisten und Musikwissen-
    schaftler der DDR1, 290
Verband deutscher Komponisten und Musik-
    wissenschaftler, 49
Verchaly, André, 373
Vercoe, Barry, 97
Verdi, Giuseppe, 81, 174, 316–17, 328,
    463
Vereniging voor Nederlandse Muziekgeschie-
    denis (VNM), 433–35
Verhey, Toon, 75
Verlag Archiv für Musikwissenshaft, 43
Verlag Franz Steiner, 43
Verlag Gustav V. Döring, 455
Verlag Icythys, 455
Verlag Max Hesses, 289
Verlag Melos, 224
Verlag Neue Musik for the Verband deutscher
    Komponisten und Musikwissenschaftler,
    51
Verlagsbuchhandlung, Georg Ohms, 40
Vermeulen, Ernst, 229
Vermeulen, G., 172

Via, David, 338
Vian, Boris, 179–80
Victoria, Tomás Luis de, 36, 365
Vicuña, Magdalena, 368
Videro, Finn, 113
Vierteljahrschrift für Musikgeschichte, xiii
Vierteljahrschrift für Musikwissenschaft, 439–42
Vigolo, Giorgia, 411–12
Vila, Cirilo, 368
Vink, Frans, 75
Vinquist, Mary, 109
Viotta, Henri, 72, 74
Virdung, Sebastian, 239
Viret, Jacques, 359
Viu, Vicente Sales, 366, 368
Vivaldi, Antonio, 81, 324
Voce, Steve, 182
Vogel, Emil, 320, 440
Vogl, Heinrich, 287
Vogler, Rudolf, 397–98
Voigt, F. A., 440
Vore, Nicholas de, 283–84
Vorwaert Press, 32
Vötterle, Karl, 261, 263, 292
Vox, 146
Vratislavia Cantans (festival), 386
Vroon, Donald R., 29
Vuillermoz, Emil, 235

W. Heffer & Sons, Ltd., 254, 256
Waardt, Piet de, 74
Wagner, Richard, 11, 72, 120, 150, 159, 164, 233, 242, 262, 272, 289, 313, 317, 322, 324, 395, 420, 466
Waldrop, Gid W., 274
Walker, D. P., 255
Walker, Malcolm, 147
Walker, Robert, 349
Walker, Thomas, 379
Wallace, Paul, 306–7
Wallaschek, Richard, 440
Wallbaum, Christel, 66
Waller, Fats, 88, 182
Walsh, Stephen, 428
Walter, Bruno, 287, 331
Walts, Anthony, 198
Wangermée, Robert, 370
Wannenmacker, Johannes, 395
Ward, Ed, 105
Warren, Fred Anthony, 205
Warsaw Autumn festival, 386–87
Washington, George, 169

Washington Post, 381
Watanabe, Ruth, 85, 87, 320, 322
Waterman, Richard A., 32
Waters, Edward, 119, 121
Waters, Edward N., 273, 322
Watson, Doc, 153
Watts, Cecil, 360
Weaver, Paul J., 250–53
Webb, Roy, 136
Weber, Carl Maria von, xi, 287
Weber, Jacob Gottfried, 69, 71
Weber, Johann R., 394
Weber, Karl G., 394
Weber, R., 394
Webern, Anton, 164, 362–63
Webster, Peter R., 100
Weekblad voor Muziek, 72
Weerts, Richard K., 306–7
Wegelin, Emil, 74
Weidensaul, Jane, 17
Weil, Alfred R., 344
Weil, Milton, 271
Weiland, Frits C., 172
Weill, Kurt, 32
Weingartner, Felix, 12
Weiser, Norman, 119
Weissman, Adoph, 235
Weissmann, John S., 428
Welch, Chris, 221
Welding, Pete, 399
Wellesz, Egon, 32, 41, 242, 254–55, 275, 373, 456
Wells, Graham, 124
Wells, Patricia Atkinson, 186
Welt der Musik, Die, 448
Wen, Eric, 281, 408–9
Wenner, Jann, 379–82
Wennerstrom, Mary, 164, 259
Wenzel, Eberhard, 295
Wenzeslaus, Clemens, 205
Werker, Gerard, 228
Werner, Svend Erik, 114
Wessely, Othmar, 415–17
West, Robert, 350
Westergaard, Peter, 340
Western Musical World/A Journal of Music, Art, and Literature, 59
Westrup, Jack A., 24, 143, 145, 243–44, 246, 254
Wheeler, Tom, 153
Whenham, John, 246
Whitall, Susan, 107

White, Adam, 55
White, Chappell, 93
White, Christopher, 58
White, Eric Walter, 328, 428
White, J. D., 201
Whitehead and Miller, 384
Whiteman, Paul, 361
Whitney, John, 362
Whitney, Maurice, 445
Whittall, Arnold, 385, 463
Whitten, Lynn, 85
Whitwell, David, 14
Widor, Charles, 226
Wieck, Friedrich, xi
Wiener Musikwissenschaftliches Institut, 416
Wieniawski, Joseph, 386
Wilber, Bob, 182
Wild, Stephen, 286
Wile, Ray, 46
Wilhelm, András, 414
Wilhem, Guillaume, 278
Willett, William C., 306
Williams, David Brian, 468–69
Williams, Hank, 191
Williams, Martin, 194
Williams, Michael D., 402–3
Williams, Ned, 119
Williams, Paul, 103–5
Williams, Richard, 221–22
Williams, William Carlos, 92
Willink, Bastiaan, 229
Willner, Channan, 432
Wilson, Teddy, 179
Wimbush, Roger, 147
Windham, Donald, 375–76
Windisch, Fritz, 225
Winkler, Martin, 344
Winold, Allen, 164
Winter, Johnny, 153
Winter, Robert, 23, 318
Winternitz, Emmanuel, 410
Wisconsin Delta Blues Festival, 216
Witten, Laurence C., II, 206
Wittke, Paul, 276–77
Wittlich, Gary, 164, 390
Wöchentliche Nachrichten und Anmerkungen die Musik betreffend, xi
Woitach, Richard, 465
Woldike, Mogens, 113
Wolf, Grace, 29
Wolf, Johannes, 40–41, 455

Wolfe, David E., 200
Wolfe, Robert, 400
Wolfe, Tom, 381
Wolff, Christian, 362
Wolff, Christoph, 108
Wolff, Konrad, 344
Wolgast, Johannes, 295
Wolpe, Stefan, 341
Women's Band Directors National Association, 391
Wood, Gerry, 55
Wood, Ross, 227
Wood, Ruzena, 66–67
Woodbury, Arthur, 402–3
Woodhouse, Violet Gordon, 244
Woodward, Henry, 91–93
Woodwind World, 443–46
Woodwind/Brass & Percussion, 444
Woodworth, G. Wallace, 90
World of Music, The, 446–48
Wörmer, Karl H., 315
Wortsman, Peter, 401
Wouters, Jos, 211–13
Wright, Josephine, 58
Wu, Olivia, 87
Wuorinen, Charles, 97, 340
Wustmann, G., 315
Wyeth Press, 158

Xenakis, Iannis, 96, 148, 171, 374

Yale University, 195, 198
Yasser, Joseph, 236
Yates, Frances, 34
Yates, Peter, 344
Yearbook for Inter-American Musical Research, 461
Yearbook for Traditional Music, 449–51
Yes, 220
Yost, Lee Prater, 87
Young, Israel, 399
Young, Kyle D., 192
Young, Lester, 88
Young, Percy M., 15
Young, Rusty, 153

Zafred, Mario, 411–12
Zagreb Music Academy, 172, 174
Zaimont, Judith Lang, 345
Zaslaw, Neal, 24, 109–110
Zeffirelli, Franco, 328
Zeitschrift der Internationalen Musik-Gesellschaft, xii

Zeitschrift für evangelische Kirchenmusik, 292
Zeitschrift für Hausmusik, 263
Zeitschrift für Musik, 13, 223
Zeitschrift für Musiktheorie, xiv, 453–55
Zeitschrift für Musikwissenschaft, xiii, 38, 41–42, 295–96, 455–57
Zeller, Hans Rudolf, 363
Zentral Institut für Musikforschung, 50

Zhito, Lee, 55
Zibits, Paul, 176
Ziff-Davis Publishing Company, 408
Ziino, Agostino, 411–12
Zimmerman, Franklin, 26
Zumaya, Manuel de, 169
Zurfluh, John, 31

Contributors

J. HEYWOOD ALEXANDER is Professor of Music at Cleveland State University and Director of Music at The Church of the Covenant, Cleveland. His specialities include sacred music and music in Cleveland.

ALFONS ANNEGARN was librarian at the Music Department of the Gemeentemuseum in The Hague from 1955–59 and librarian at the University of Utrecht's Institute of Musicology from 1959 until his retirement in 1986. A student of fifteenth- through seventeenth-century Dutch music, he edited music by Sweelinck and Cornelis Schuyt. Dr. Annegarn passed away in 1987.

DAVID R. BEVERIDGE, a specialist in the orchestral and chamber literature of the nineteenth century, is currently on the faculty of the University of New Orleans.

PAUL W. BORG teaches at Illinois State University and is an expert on polyphonic music found in Guatemalan manuscripts.

PATRICIA J. BUCKWELL, a former music education faculty member at Bowling Green State University, has research and teaching interests in the area of teaching music in the special education setting.

ROBERT BYLER, after extensive and varied experience in television, radio, trade and corporate journalism, teaches journalism at Bowling Green State University. He is also a freelance writer and photographer, one of whose specialities is jazz and jazz musicians. He has published more than fifty articles on jazz topics in such publications as *The Mississippi Rag, TJ Today,* and *The Jazzologist.*

JEAN CHRISTENSEN is on the musicology faculty at the University of Louisville. Her particular interests include the music and thought of composers Arnold Schoenberg and Dane Per Norgaard.

MICHAEL COLBY is Music and Art Cataloger at San Francisco Public Library. He holds degrees from the University of Portland and the University of California at Berkeley. Active in the Music Library Association, Colby has recently served as the chair of the MLA Nothern California chapter.

CARMELO P. COMBERIATI teaches at Manhattanville College and is book review editor for the *Journal of Musicological Research*. He has published on a variety of Renaissance music topics, including a monograph entitled *Late Renaissance Music at the Hapsburg Court: Polyphonic Settings of the Mass Ordinary at the Court of Rudolph VI, 1576–1612* (1987). He also served as co-editor with Matthew Steel for *Music from the Middle Ages Through the Twentieth Century: Essays in Honor of Gwynn S. McPeek* (1988).

SUSAN C. COOK, a musicologist on the faculty at Middlebury College, specializes in German opera during the Weimar Republic, American music, and the role of women in music. Her publications include *Virtuose in Italy 1600–1640: A Reference Guide* (1984) and *Opera for A New Republic: The Zeitopern of Krenek, Weill and Hindemith* (1988).

VINCENT J. CORRIGAN teaches musicology and harpsichord at Bowling Green State University and maintains research interests in early medieval polyphony, harpsichord performance, and seventeenth- and eighteenth-century vocal literature. He is also an active solo harpsichordist and accompanist.

PEGGY E. DAUB is head of the music library and a library science faculty member at the University of Michigan. She worked as a sub-editor for *The New Grove*, was Chair of the Research Libraries Group's Music Program Committee, and has had articles published in *Notes, Reference Services Review, The New Grove Dictionary of Music and Musicians*, and *The New Grove Dictionary of American Music*.

MARILYN DEKKER is the choir director at St. James Episcopal Church in Washington, D.C. and works for the Music Division of the Library of Congress. Dekker holds degrees from Denison College and the University of Michigan. Her areas of research include Renaissance choral music.

JOHN E. DRUESEDOW is head of the music library at Duke University, a member of the MLA Board, and past-Chair of the Midwest MLA. His areas of special interest include the organ, music of the Spanish baroque, and American music before 1900. He is also the author of *Library Research Guide to Music* (1982).

TERRY E. EDER conducts several university and community choirs and teaches choral music education courses and choral conducting at Bowling Green State University, where he is co-director of Choral Activities. His choirs have toured Europe and been invited to perform at numerous state and regional conventions.

STEFAN M. EHRENKREUTZ studied music theory at the University of Michigan and in Poland. He currently resides in Melbourne, Australia.

VICTOR ELLSWORTH has been active as an orchestral and studio double bassist, has taught all levels of public school, and served as a guest clinician and conductor in Florida, Ohio, and Wisconsin. He currently teaches string techniques, and string and orchestral methods at Bowling Green State University.

BÉLA FOLTIN, JR. is Assistant Director for Public Services and Collection Development at Virginia Polytechnic Institute and State University. He has co-authored publications on Persian music and the folk music of Georgia.

DAVID D. GINSBURG, a librarian at Central Michigan University, is especially interested in fanzines and has published in *Reference Services Review, Serials Review, Goldmine,* and *R.P.M.: Record Profile Magazine.*

JANE MORLET HARDIE is Senior Lecturer in Musicology at New South Wales State Conservatorium of Music in Sydney, Australia, and Chairperson for RISM-Australia. Her research has focused on liturgy and liturgical music, particularly that of Spain.

FRANK W. HOFFMAN, professor of library science at Sam Houston State University, has published *The Development of Library Collections of Sound Recordings* (1979), *The Literature of Rock, 1954–1978* (1981), *Popular Culture and Libraries* (1984) and *The Cash Box Album Charts, 1955–1974* (1988).

LYN HUBLER studied organ and musicology at Stanford University and has concertized, as an organist, in the United States, Europe and Japan. She is presently writing a book on seventeenth-century French organ playing.

PAUL B. HUNT is professor of trombone at Bowling Green State University and Literature Reviews Editor for the *International Trombone Society Journal.* He specializes in twentieth-century literature for the trombone and in the alto trombone repertoire. He has performed with the Denver, Toledo, Youngstown, Binghamton (NY), and Midland (MI) symphony orchestras and recorded with the Chicago-based Music of the Baroque Ensemble and the Eastman Wind Ensemble.

RUTH K. INGLEFIELD teaches harp and musicology at Bowling Green State University, has recorded on the Orion and Access labels and performs throughout the world. She has contributed to *The New Grove* and *Musical Quarterly*, and co-authored *Essays on Music in American Education and Society* (1982) and a monograph on Marcel Grandjany (1977). Recently, she has completed the editing of a book on the history of conducting. Additional research interests include musical style, aesthetics, and French music.

L. JAFRAN JONES, ethnomusicologist on the Bowling Green State University faculty, specializes in the music of the Middle Eastern and Mediterranean countries. She has done extensive work on numerous grants and fellowships that include a National Endowment for the Humanities Fellowship and a Fulbright Senior Research Grant. Her "A Sociohistorical Perspective on Tunisian Women as Professional Musicians" has recently appeared in *Women and Music in Cross-Cultural Perspective* (1988).

VINCENT J. KANTORSKI teaches graduate core courses in music education at Bowling Green State University. He is an active scholar with contributions to *The American String Teacher* and *The Journal of Research in Music Education*.

RICHARD P. KENNELL is Assistant Dean at Bowling Green State University, a saxophonist with numerous performing credits, and a specialist in private studio teaching methods and concepts.

DAVID KNAPP is Conservatory Librarian for Technical Services at Oberlin College. He is past-Chair of the OCLC Users Group, a former Music Librarian at the Graz-Festival, and an active pianist.

ROSALIND KNOWLES teaches music education at Nazareth College and maintains research interests in Orff, Dalcroze, and Kodály.

JOHN K. KRATUS teaches at Case Western Reserve University. His professional interests include music education methods, music curricula, musical development, and aesthetics. He has published several articles on musical creativity in children.

PAUL B. MAST is professor and chairman of the Department of Music Theory at the Oberlin Conservatory of Music. He has published on Brahms and Schenker in *The Music Forum* and co-authored the third edition of *Music for Study* (1988).

DIANE McMULLEN is an expert in eighteenth-century German music, is a performing harpsichordist and organist, and teaches on the University of Michigan-Dearborn faculty. She studied at the Universität Hamburg under the auspices of the DAAD program and held a Fulbright award at the Universität Gottingen and the Universität Munchen.

J. SCOTT MESSING teaches at Alma College and specializes in Stravinsky, Debussy, Neoclassicism, and attendant cultural issues, while maintaining interests in Renaissance music and manuscripts studies. He is the author of *Neo-classicism in Music: From the Genesis of the Concept through the Schoenberg/Stravinsky Polemic* (1987).

DALE E. MONSON is a specialist in Italian Baroque music, particularly opera, and teaches at the University of Michigan. He served as the editor for *Adriano in Siria* (1984), the third volume of the Complete Works of Giovanni Pergolesi.

MARY SUE MORROW, a member of the musicology faculty at Loyola University of New Orleans, is a specialist in Viennese classical concert life, composers, and culture.

ROBERT W. OLDANI, a musicologist on the Arizona State University School of Music faculty, is an expert on Russian music, particularly the works of Modest Mussorgsky. He has published in *19th-Century Music*.

STEVEN PLANK, a member of the musicology faculty at Oberlin College, has contributed to *Music & Letters, The Consort, The Courant,* and *Franciscan Studies*.

RONNIE PUGH is the Head of Reference at the Country Music Foundation. He has written widely on the career of Ernest Tubb, and contributed numerous liner notes for historical country music record reissues.

KATHRYN REED-MAXFIELD is a student of American music, particularly the minstrel show, related popular song in America, and composer Dan Emmett. She has taught at the Interlochen National Music Camp and is a performing harpsichordist.

THOMAS L. RIIS, professor of music history and literature at the University of Georgia, has wide-ranging interests in nineteenth- and twentieth-century American music and has written for the *New Grove Dictionary of American Music, Black Perspectives in Music* and *American Music*. He has also written *Just Before Jazz: Black Musical Theater in New York, 1890–1915*.

ESTHER ROTHENBUSCH specializes in American hymnody, particularly of the nineteenth century, and is a member of the Adrian College faculty.

WILLIAM L. SCHURK is Sound Recordings Archivist at Bowling Green State University and an expert in many aspects of twentieth-century American popular music, particularly the sound recording industry.

MARILYN SHRUDE is a noted composer, particularly of orchestral music and music for the saxophone. She received the Kennedy Center Friedheim Award for Orchestral Music in 1984, teaches composition at Bowling Green State University, and is Director of the BGSU New Music Program. Recent commissions include the Fox Valley Symphony (1987) and St. Louis Orchestra "On-Stage" Series (1988). Her work is recorded on the Orion, Ohio Brassworks, and Access labels.

F. JOSEPH SMITH is editor of *The Journal of Musicological Research* and a noted medievalist and organist. He has taught at DePaul and Emory Universities and the University Conservatory in Bucharest, and both lectured and concertized in America and Europe, including at the University of Lund, Sweden, and the Royal Academy of Music in Stockholm.

MATTHEW STEEL has taught musicology and early music performance on the faculties of the University of Michigan-Dearborn and Western Michigan University. He publishes on topics in medieval music.

SYLVAN SUSKIN teaches music history at Oberlin Conservatory and is an expert in French music and opera.

RUTH WATANABE is emeritis librarian at the Eastman School of Music's Sibley Library, past-President of the MLA, and a noted authority on music libraries and music librarianship, with numerous articles in *Notes* and other publications, including her monograph *Introduction to Music Research*.

ROSS WOOD became Music Librarian at Wellesley College in 1984 after serving as a Reference Librarian at Eastman School of Music's Sibley Library. His published reviews appear in *Notes, Library Journal,* and *American Reference Books Annual*.

About the Editors

LINDA M. FIDLER is Head Music Librarian at Bowling Green State University and teaches the graduate research course for music students. She has contributed articles and reviews to *Notes, Critical Studies in Mass Communications,* and *Library Quarterly,* co-edited both the *Directory of Music Library Instruction Programs in the Midwest Chapter of Music Library Association* and *Historical Sets, Monuments of Music and Collected Editions in the Cleveland Area Music Libraries,* and presented papers at national and regional meetings of the Music Library Association and College Music Society. Her areas of research include bibliographic instruction, the origins of the operetta, and vocal chamber music. In addition to her teaching and research, Fidler, a clarinetist, is also a professional musician.

RICHARD S. JAMES teaches musicology, music appreciation, and early music performance at Bowling Green State University. As a twentieth-century music specialist, he has done extensive research on Edgard Varèse, Maurice Ravel, the origins of electronic music, and post–1950 multimedia trends, particularly the ONCE Group. He has contributed articles and reviews on a wide variety of topics in twentieth-century French and American music to *Musical Quarterly, The New Grove Dictionary of American Music, The New Grove Dictionary of Opera, American Music, Journal of Musicological Research,* a festschrift honoring Professor Gwynn McPeek, and has presented papers at the national meetings of the American Musicological Society, Sonneck Society, College Music Society, and the American Society of University Composers. As a recorder player, he is also an active chamber musician.